WHAT MAKES
A GREAT SHORT STORY?

The sudden unforgettable revelation of character; the vision of a world through another's eyes; the glimpse of truth; the capture of a moment in time.

All this the short story, at its best, is uniquely capable of conveying, for in its very shortness lies its greatest strength.

It can discover depths of meaning in the casual word or action; it can suggest in a page what could not be stated in a volume.

Such is the quality of experience offered you, in many and diverse ways, by the fifty short stories which make up this book.

MILTON CRANE, EDITOR

50
GREAT
SHORT STORIES

Edited by Milton Crane

BANTAM CLASSIC

To Tom and Peter

50 GREAT SHORT STORIES
A Bantam Book

PUBLISHING HISTORY
Original Bantam edition published August 1952
New Bantam edition / December 1954
Bantam Classic edition / May 1959
Bantam Literature edition / September 1971
Bantam Classic reissue / September 2005

Published by Bantam Dell
A Division of Random House, Inc.
New York, New York

Bantam Books and the rooster colophon are registered trademarks of Random House, Inc.

ISBN 978-0-553-27745-6

Printed in the United States of America
Published simultaneously in Canada

randomhousebooks.com

OPM 110 109 108 107 106 105

CONTENTS

A NOTE ON THE MAKING OF THIS BOOK

Milton Crane, The University of Chicago

EVERY EDITOR and compiler, whatever the nature of the book on which he is working, inevitably consults his friends and associates. I determined, in planning the preparation of FIFTY GREAT SHORT STORIES, to solicit the collective experience of as large a group of teachers of literature as I could reach. I therefore compiled a list of one hundred stories—twice as many as the projected volume was to contain. Copies of this list were sent to professors of English at colleges and universities throughout the country, who were asked to check the fifty stories of their preference and to add whatever other titles they held especially dear. Some five hundred responded. The finished book represents, at least in part, the experience and judgment of these men and women, whose profession is the teaching of literature, and I welcome this opportunity to thank them, my colleagues, for their friendly cooperation.

Needless to say, I have not always followed the suggestions of my five hundred collaborators, who frequently were in sharp disagreement with one another; but no anthologist can hope to satisfy all his readers. Moreover, I passed over in silence various proposals that I reprint certain familiar stories of known worth, which have already graced numerous anthologies, for fear that I might produce a mere anthology of anthologies. The present collection is intended to be a representation of the best short stories by English, American and Continental writers of the past hundred years, maintaining a balance between works by earlier and more recent writers. For the ultimate selection of stories, I, as editor, am of course entirely responsible.

THE GARDEN PARTY*

BY KATHERINE MANSFIELD

AND AFTER all the weather was ideal. They could not have had a more perfect day for a garden-party if they had ordered it. Windless, warm, the sky without a cloud. Only the blue was veiled with a haze of light gold, as it is sometimes in early summer. The gardener had been up since dawn, mowing the lawns and sweeping them, until the grass and the dark flat rosettes where the daisy plants had been seemed to shine. As for the roses, you could not help feeling they understood that roses are the only flowers that impress people at garden-parties; the only flowers that everybody is certain of knowing. Hundreds, yes, literally hundreds, had come out in a single night; the green bushes bowed down as though they had been visited by archangels.

Breakfast was not yet over before men came to put up the marquee.

"Where do you want the marquee put, mother?"

"My dear child, it's no use asking me. I'm determined to leave everything to you children this year. Forget I am your mother. Treat me as an honoured guest."

But Meg could not possibly go and supervise the men. She had washed her hair before breakfast, and she sat drinking her coffee in a green turban, with a dark wet curl stamped on each cheek. Jose, the butterfly, always came down in a silk petticoat and a kimono jacket.

"You'll have to go, Laura; you're the artistic one."

Away Laura flew, still holding her piece of bread-and-butter. It's so delicious to have an excuse for eating out of doors and

* from *The Short Stories of Katherine Mansfield*

besides, she loved to arrange things; she always felt she could do it so much better than anybody else.

Four men in their shirt-sleeves stood grouped together on the garden path. They carried staves covered with rolls of canvas, and they had big tool-bags slung on their backs. They looked impressive. Laura wished now that she had not got the bread-and-butter, but there was nowhere to put it, and she couldn't possibly throw it away. She blushed and tried to look severe and even a little bit short-sighted as she came up to them.

"Good morning," she said, copying her mother's voice. But that sounded so fearfully affected that she was ashamed, and stammered like a little girl, "Oh—er—have you come—is it about the marquee?"

"That's right, miss," said the tallest of the men, a lanky freckled fellow, and he shifted his tool-bag, knocked back his straw hat and smiled down at her.

"That's about it."

His smile was so easy, so friendly that Laura recovered. What nice eyes he had, small, but such a dark blue! And now she looked at the others, they were smiling too. "Cheer up, we won't bite," their smile seemed to say. How very nice workmen were! And what a beautiful morning! She mustn't mention the morning; she must be business-like. The marquee.

"Well, what about the lily-lawn? Would that do?"

And she pointed to the lily-lawn with the hand that didn't hold the bread-and-butter. They turned, they stared in the direction. A little fat chap thrust out his under-lip, and the tall fellow frowned.

"I don't fancy it," said he. "Not conspicuous enough. You see, with a thing like a marquee," and he turned to Laura in his easy way, "you want to put it somewhere where it'll give you a bang slap in the eye, if you follow me."

Laura's upbringing made her wonder for a moment whether it was quite respectful of a workman to talk to her of bangs slap in the eye. But she did quite follow him.

"A corner of the tennis-court," she suggested. "But the band's going to be in one corner."

"H'm, going to have a band, are you?" said another of the workmen. He was pale. He had a haggard look as his dark eyes scanned the tennis-court. What was he thinking?

"Only a very small band," said Laura gently. Perhaps he wouldn't mind so much if the band was quite small. But the tall fellow interrupted.

"Look here, miss, that's the place. Against those trees. Over there. That'll do fine."

Against the karakas. Then the karaka-trees would be hidden. And they were so lovely, with their broad, gleaming leaves, and their clusters of yellow fruit. They were like trees you imagined growing on a desert island, proud, solitary, lifting their leaves and fruits to the sun in a kind of silent splendour. Must they be hidden by a marquee?

They must. Already the men had shouldered their staves and were making for the place. Only the tall fellow was left. He bent down, pinched a sprig of lavender, put his thumb and forefinger to his nose and snuffed up the smell. When Laura saw that gesture she forgot all about the karakas in her wonder at him caring for things like that—caring for the smell of lavender. How many men that she knew would have done such a thing? Oh, how extraordinarily nice workmen were, she thought. Why couldn't she have workmen for friends rather than the silly boys she danced with and who came to Sunday night supper? She would get on much better with men like these.

It's all the fault, she decided, as the tall fellow drew something on the back of an envelope, something that was to be looped up or left to hang, of these absurd class distinctions. Well, for her part, she didn't feel them. Not a bit, not an atom. . . . And now there came the chock-chock of wooden hammers. Some one whistled, some one sang out, "Are you right there, matey?" "Matey!" The friendliness of it, the—the— Just to prove how happy she was, just to show the tall fellow how at home she felt, and how she despised stupid conventions, Laura took a big bite of her bread-and-butter as she stared at the little drawing. She felt just like a work-girl.

"Laura, Laura, where are you? Telephone, Laura!" a voice cried from the house.

"Coming!" Away she skimmed, over the lawn, up the path, up the steps, across the veranda, and into the porch. In the hall her father and Laurie were brushing their hats ready to go to the office.

"I say, Laura," said Laurie very fast, "you might just give a squiz at my coat before this afternoon. See if it wants pressing."

"I will," said she. Suddenly she couldn't stop herself. She ran at Laurie and gave him a small, quick squeeze. "Oh, I do love parties, don't you?" gasped Laura.

"Ra-ther," said Laurie's warm, boyish voice, and he squeezed his sister too, and gave her a gentle push. "Dash off to the telephone, old girl."

The telephone. "Yes, yes; oh yes. Kitty? Good morning, dear. Come to lunch? Do, dear. Delighted of course. It will only be a very scratch meal—just the sandwich crusts and broken meringue-shells and what's left over. Yes, isn't it a perfect morning? Your white? Oh, I certainly should. One moment—hold the line. Mother's calling." And Laura sat back. "What, mother? Can't hear."

Mrs. Sheridan's voice floated down the stairs. "Tell her to wear that sweet hat she had on last Sunday."

"Mother says you're to wear that *sweet* hat you had on last Sunday. Good. One o'clock. Bye-bye."

Laura put back the receiver, flung her arms over her head, took a deep breath, stretched and let them fall. "Huh," she sighed, and the moment after the sigh she sat up quickly. She was still, listening. All the doors in the house seemed to be open. The house was alive with soft, quick steps and running voices. The green baize door that led to the kitchen regions swung open and shut with a muffled thud. And now there came a long, chuckling absurd sound. It was the heavy piano being moved on its stiff castors. But the air! If you stopped to notice, was the air always like this? Little faint winds were playing chase, in at the tops of the windows, out at the doors. And there were two tiny spots of sun, one on the inkpot, one on a silver photograph frame, playing too. Darling little spots. Especially the one on the inkpot lid. It was quite warm. A warm little silver star. She could have kissed it.

The front door bell pealed, and there sounded the rustle of Sadie's print skirt on the stairs. A man's voice murmured; Sadie answered, careless, "I'm sure I don't know. Wait. I'll ask Mrs. Sheridan."

"What is it, Sadie?" Laura came into the hall.

"It's the florist, Miss Laura."

It was, indeed. There, just inside the door, stood a wide, shallow tray full of pots of pink lilies. No other kind. Nothing but lilies—canna lilies, big pink flowers, wide open, radiant, almost frighteningly alive on bright crimson stems.

"O-oh, Sadie!" said Laura, and the sound was like a little moan. She crouched down as if to warm herself at that blaze of lilies; she felt they were in her fingers, on her lips, growing in her breast.

"It's some mistake," she said faintly. "Nobody ever ordered so many. Sadie, go and find mother."

But at that moment Mrs. Sheridan joined them.

"It's quite right," she said calmly. "Yes, I ordered them. Aren't they lovely?" She pressed Laura's arm. "I was passing the shop yesterday, and I saw them in the window. And I suddenly thought for once in my life I shall have enough canna lilies. The garden-party will be a good excuse."

"But I thought you said you didn't mean to interfere," said Laura. Sadie had gone. The florist's man was still outside at his van. She put her arm round her mother's neck and gently, very gently, she bit her mother's ear.

"My darling child, you wouldn't like a logical mother, would you? Don't do that. Here's the man."

He carried more lilies still, another whole tray.

"Bank them up, just inside the door, on both sides of the porch, please," said Mrs. Sheridan. "Don't you agree, Laura?"

"Oh, I *do,* mother."

In the drawing-room Meg, Jose and good little Hans had at last succeeded in moving the piano.

"Now, if we put this chesterfield against the wall and move everything out of the room except the chairs, don't you think?"

"Quite."

"Hans, move these tables into the smoking-room, and bring

a sweeper to take these marks off the carpet and—one moment, Hans—" Jose loved giving orders to the servants, and they loved obeying her. She always made them feel they were taking part in some drama. "Tell mother and Miss Laura to come here at once."

"Very good, Miss Jose."

She turned to Meg. "I want to hear what the piano sounds like, just in case I'm asked to sing this afternoon. Let's try over 'This Life is Weary.'"

Pom! Ta-ta-ta *Tee*-ta! The piano burst out so passionately that Jose's face changed. She clasped her hands. She looked mournfully and enigmatically at her mother and Laura as they came in.

> *This Life is* Wee-*ary,*
> *A Tear—a Sigh.*
> *A Love that* Chan-*ges,*
> *This Life is* Wee-*ary,*
> *A Tear—a Sigh.*
> *A Love that* Chan-*ges,*
> *And then . . . Goodbye!*

But at the word "Good-bye," and although the piano sounded more desperate than ever, her face broke into a brilliant, dreadfully unsympathetic smile.

"Aren't I in good voice, mummy?" she beamed.

> *This Life is* Wee-*ary,*
> *Hope comes to Die.*
> *A Dream—a Wa-*kening.

But now Sadie interrupted them. "What is it, Sadie?"

"If you please, m'm, cook says have you got the flags for the sandwiches?"

"The flags for the sandwiches, Sadie?" echoed Mrs. Sheridan dreamily. And the children knew by her face that she hadn't got them. "Let me see." And she said to Sadie firmly, "Tell cook I'll let her have them in ten minutes."

Sadie went.

"Now, Laura," said her mother quickly. "Come with me into the smoking-room. I've got the names somewhere on the back of an envelope. You'll have to write them out for me. Meg, go upstairs this minute and take that wet thing off your head. Jose, run and finish dressing this instant. Do you hear me, children, or shall I have to tell your father when he comes home to-night? And—and, Jose, pacify cook if you do go into the kitchen, will you? I'm terrified of her this morning."

The envelope was found at last behind the dining-room clock, though how it had got there Mrs. Sheridan could not imagine.

"One of you children must have stolen it out of my bag, because I remember vividly—cream cheese and lemon-curd. Have you done that?"

"Yes."

"Egg and—" Mrs. Sheridan held the envelope away from her. "It looks like mice. It can't be mice, can it?"

"Olive, pet," said Laura, looking over her shoulder.

"Yes, of course, olive. What a horrible combination it sounds. Egg and olive."

They were finished at last, and Laura took them off to the kitchen. She found Jose there pacifying the cook, who did not look at all terrifying.

"I have never seen such exquisite sandwiches," said Jose's rapturous voice. "How many kinds did you say there were, cook? Fifteen?"

"Fifteen, Miss Jose."

"Well, cook, I congratulate you."

Cook swept up crusts with the long sandwich knife, and smiled broadly.

"Godber's has come," announced Sadie, issuing out of the pantry. She had seen the man pass the window.

That meant the cream puffs had come. Godber's were famous for their cream puffs. Nobody ever thought of making them at home.

"Bring them in and put them on the table, my girl," ordered cook.

Sadie brought them in and went back to the door. Of course Laura and Jose were far too grown-up to really care about such things. All the same, they couldn't help agreeing that the puffs looked very attractive. Very. Cook began arranging them, shaking off the extra icing sugar.

"Don't they carry one back to all one's parties?" said Laura.

"I suppose they do," said practical Jose, who never liked to be carried back. "They look beautifully light and feathery, I must say."

"Have one each, my dears," said cook in her comfortable voice. "Yer ma won't know."

Oh, impossible. Fancy cream puffs so soon after breakfast. The very idea made one shudder. All the same, two minutes later Jose and Laura were licking their fingers with that absorbed inward look that only comes from whipped cream.

"Let's go into the garden, out by the back way," suggested Laura. "I want to see how the men are getting on with the marquee. They're such awfully nice men."

But the back door was blocked by cook, Sadie, Godber's man and Hans.

Something had happened.

"Tuk-tuk-tuk," clucked cook like an agitated hen. Sadie had her hand clapped to her cheek as though she had toothache. Hans's face was screwed up in the effort to understand. Only Godber's man seemed to be enjoying himself; it was his story.

"What's the matter? What's happened?"

"There's been a horrible accident," said cook. "A man killed."

"A man killed! Where? How? When?"

But Godber's man wasn't going to have his story snatched from under his very nose.

"Know those little cottages just below here, miss?" Know them? Of course, she knew them. "Well, there's a young chap living there, name of Scott, a carter. His horse shied at a traction-engine, corner of Hawke Street this morning, and he was thrown out on the back of his head. Killed."

"Dead!" Laura stared at Godber's man.

"Dead when they picked him up," said Godber's man with

relish. "They were taking the body home as I come up here."
And he said to the cook, "He's left a wife and five little ones."

"Jose, come here." Laura caught hold of her sister's sleeve
and dragged her through the kitchen to the other side of the
green baize door. There she paused and leaned against it.
"Jose!" she said, horrified, "however are we going to stop
everything?"

"Stop everything, Laura!" cried Jose in astonishment.
"What do you mean?"

"Stop the garden-party, of course." Why did Jose pretend?

But Jose was still more amazed. "Stop the garden-party?
My dear Laura, don't be so absurd. Of course we can't do anything of the kind. Nobody expects us to. Don't be so extravagant."

"But we can't possibly have a garden-party with a man dead
just outside the front gate."

That really was extravagant, for the little cottages were in a
lane to themselves at the very bottom of a steep rise that led up
to the house. A broad road ran between. True, they were far too
near. They were the greatest possible eyesore, and they had no
right to be in that neighbourhood at all. They were little mean
dwellings painted a chocolate brown. In the garden patches
there was nothing but cabbage stalks, sick hens and tomato
cans. The very smoke coming out of their chimneys was
poverty-stricken. Little rags and shreds of smoke, so unlike the
great silvery plumes that uncurled from the Sheridans' chimneys. Washer-women lived in the lane and sweeps and a cob-
bler, and a man whose house-front was studded all over with
minute bird-cages. Children swarmed. When the Sheridans
were little they were forbidden to set foot there because of the
revolting language and of what they might catch. But since
they were grown up, Laura and Laurie on the prowls sometimes walked through. It was disgusting and sordid. They came
out with a shudder. But still one must go everywhere; one must
see everything. So through they went.

"And just think of what the band would sound like to that
poor woman," said Laura.

"Oh, Laura!" Jose began to be seriously annoyed. "If you're

going to stop a band playing every time some one has an accident, you'll lead a very strenuous life. I'm every bit as sorry about it as you. I feel just as sympathetic." Her eyes hardened. She looked at her sister just as she used to when they were little and fighting together. "You won't bring a drunken workman back to life by being sentimental," she said softly.

"Drunk! Who said he was drunk?" Laura turned furiously on Jose. She said, just as they had used to say on those occasions, "I'm going straight up to tell mother."

"Do, dear," cooed Jose.

"Mother, can I come into your room?" Laura turned the big glass doorknob.

"Of course, child. Why, what's the matter? What's given you such a colour?" And Mrs. Sheridan turned round from her dressing-table. She was trying on a new hat.

"Mother, a man's been killed," began Laura.

"Not in the garden?" interrupted her mother.

"No, no!"

"Oh, what a fright you gave me!" Mrs. Sheridan sighed with relief, and took off the big hat and held it on her knees.

"But listen, mother," said Laura. Breathless, half-choking, she told the dreadful story. "Of course, we can't have our party, can we?" she pleaded. "The band and everybody arriving. They'd hear us, mother; they're nearly neighbours!"

To Laura's astonishment her mother behaved just like Jose; it was harder to bear because she seemed amused. She refused to take Laura seriously.

"But, my dear child, use your common sense. It's only by accident we've heard of it. If some one had died there normally—and I can't understand how they keep alive in those poky little holes—we should still be having our party, shouldn't we?"

Laura had to say "yes" to that, but she felt it was all wrong. She sat down on her mother's sofa and pinched the cushion frill.

"Mother, isn't it really terribly heartless of us?" she asked.

"Darling!" Mrs. Sheridan got up and came over to her, carrying the hat. Before Laura could stop her she had popped it on. "My child!" said her mother, "the hat is yours. It's made for you. It's much too young for me. I have never seen you look such a picture. Look at yourself!" And she held up her hand-mirror.

"But, mother," Laura began again. She couldn't look at herself; she turned aside.

This time Mrs. Sheridan lost patience just as Jose had done.

"You are being very absurd, Laura," she said coldly. "People like that don't expect sacrifices from us. And it's not very sympathetic to spoil everybody's enjoyment as you're doing now."

"I don't understand," said Laura, and she walked quickly out of the room into her own bedroom. There, quite by chance, the first thing she saw was this charming girl in the mirror, in her black hat trimmed with gold daisies, and a long black velvet ribbon. Never had she imagined she could look like that. Is mother right? she thought. And now she hoped her mother was right. Am I being extravagant? Perhaps it was extravagant. Just for a moment she had another glimpse of that poor woman and those little children, and the body being carried into the house. But it all seemed blurred, unreal, like a picture in the newspaper. I'll remember it again after the party's over, she decided. And somehow that seemed quite the best plan. . . .

Lunch was over by half-past one. By half-past two they were all ready for the fray. The green-coated band had arrived and was established in a corner of the tennis-court.

"My dear!" trilled Kitty Maitland, "aren't they too like frogs for words? You ought to have arranged them round the pond with the conductor in the middle on a leaf."

Laurie arrived and hailed them on his way to dress. At the sight of him Laura remembered the accident again. She wanted to tell him. If Laurie agreed with the others, then it was bound to be all right. And she followed him into the hall.

"Laurie!"

"Hallo!" He was half-way upstairs, but when he turned round and saw Laura he suddenly puffed out his cheeks and goggled his eyes at her. "My word, Laura! You do look stunning," said Laurie. "What an absolutely topping hat!"

Laura said faintly "Is it?" and smiled up at Laurie, and didn't tell him after all.

Soon after that people began coming in streams. The band struck up; the hired waiters ran from the house to the marquee. Wherever you looked there were couples strolling, bending to the flowers, greeting, moving on over the lawn. They were like bright birds that had alighted in the Sheridans' garden for this one afternoon, on their way to where? Ah, what happiness it is to be with people who all are happy, to press hands, press cheeks, smile into eyes.

"Darling Laura, how well you look!"

"What a becoming hat, child!"

"Laura, you look quite Spanish. I've never seen you look so striking."

And Laura, glowing, answered softly, "Have you had tea? Won't you have an ice? The passion-fruit ices really are rather special." She ran to her father and begged him. "Daddy darling, can't the band have something to drink?"

And the perfect afternoon slowly ripened, slowly faded, slowly its petals closed.

"Never a more delightful garden party..." "The greatest success..." "Quite the most..."

Laura helped her mother with good-byes. They stood side by side in the porch till it was all over.

"All over, all over, thank heaven," said Mrs. Sheridan. "Round up the others, Laura. Let's go and have some fresh coffee. I'm exhausted. Yes, it's been very successful. But oh, these parties, these parties! Why will you children insist on giving parties!" And they all of them sat down in the deserted marquee.

"Have a sandwich, daddy dear. I wrote the flag."

"Thanks." Mr. Sheridan took a bite and the sandwich was gone. He took another. "I suppose you didn't hear of a beastly accident that happened to-day?" he said.

"My dear," said Mrs. Sheridan, holding up her hand, "we did. It nearly ruined the party. Laura insisted we should put it off."

"Oh, mother!" Laura didn't want to be teased about it.

"It was a horrible affair all the same," said Mr. Sheridan. "The chap was married too. Lived just below in the lane, and leaves a wife and half a dozen kiddies, so they say."

An awkward little silence fell. Mrs. Sheridan fidgeted with her cup. Really, it was very tactless of father...

Suddenly she looked up. There on the table were all those sandwiches, cakes, puffs, all uneaten, all going to be wasted. She had one of her brilliant ideas.

"I know," she said. "Let's make up a basket. Let's send that poor creature some of this perfectly good food. At any rate, it will be the greatest treat for the children. Don't you agree? And she's sure to have neighbours calling in and so on. What a point to have it all ready prepared. Laura!" She jumped up. "Get me the big basket out of the stairs cupboard."

"But, mother, do you really think it's a good idea?" said Laura.

Again, how curious, she seemed to be different from them all. To take scraps from their party. Would the poor woman really like that?

"Of course! What's the matter with you to-day? An hour or two ago you were insisting on us being sympathetic, and now—"

Oh, well! Laura ran for the basket. It was filled, it was heaped by her mother.

"Take it yourself, darling," said she. "Run down just as you are. No, wait, take the arum lilies too. People of that class are so impressed by arum lilies."

"The stems will ruin her lace frock," said practical Jose.

So they would. Just in time. "Only the basket, then. And, Laura!"—her mother followed her out of the marquee—"don't on any account—"

"What, mother?"

No, better not put such ideas into the child's head! "Nothing! Run along."

It was just growing dusky as Laura shut their garden gates. A big dog ran by like a shadow. The road gleamed white, and down below in the hollow the little cottages were in deep shade. How quiet it seemed after the afternoon. Here she was going down the hill to somewhere where a man lay dead, and she couldn't realize it. Why couldn't she? She stopped a minute. And it seemed to her that kisses, voices, tinkling spoons, laughter, the smell of crushed grass were somehow inside her. She had no room for anything else. How strange! She looked up at the pale sky, and all she thought was, "Yes, it was the most successful party."

Now the broad road was crossed. The lane began, smoky and dark. Women in shawls and men's tweed caps hurried by. Men hung over the palings; the children played in the doorways. A low hum came from the mean little cottages. In some of them there was a flicker of light, and a shadow, crab-like, moved across the window. Laura bent her head and hurried on. She wished now she had put on a coat. How her frock shone! And the big hat with the velvet streamer—if only it was another hat! Were the people looking at her? They must be. It was a mistake to have come; she knew all along it was a mistake. Should she go back even now?

No, too late. This was the house. It must be. A dark knot of people stood outside. Beside the gate an old, old woman with a crutch sat in a chair, watching. She had her feet on a newspaper. The voices stopped as Laura drew near. The group parted. It was as though she was expected, as though they had known she was coming here.

Laura was terribly nervous. Tossing the velvet ribbon over her shoulder, she said to a woman standing by, "Is this Mrs. Scott's house?" and the woman, smiling queerly, said, "It is, my lass."

Oh, to be away from this! She actually said, "Help me, God," as she walked up the tiny path and knocked. To be away from those staring eyes, or to be covered up in anything, one of those women's shawls even. I'll just leave the basket and go, she decided. I shan't even wait for it to be emptied.

Then the door opened. A little woman in black showed in the gloom.

Laura said, "Are you Mrs. Scott?" But to her horror the woman answered, "Walk in please, miss," and she was shut in the passage.

"No," said Laura, "I don't want to come in. I only want to leave this basket. Mother sent—"

The little woman in the gloomy passage seemed not to have

heard her. "Step this way, please, miss," she said in an oily voice, and Laura followed her.

She found herself in a wretched little low kitchen, lighted by a smoky lamp. There was a woman sitting before the fire.

"Em," said the little creature who had led her in. "Em! It's young lady." She turned to Laura. She said meaningly, "I'm 'er sister, miss. You'll excuse 'er, won't you?"

"Oh, but of course!" said Laura. "Please, please don't disturb her. I—I only want to leave—"

But at that moment the woman at the fire turned round. Her face, puffed up, red, with swollen eyes and swollen lips, looked terrible. She seemed as though she couldn't understand why Laura was there. What did it mean? Why was this stranger standing in the kitchen with a basket? What was it all about? And the poor face puckered up again.

"All right, my dear," said the other. "I'll thenk the young lady."

And again she began. "You'll excuse her, miss, I'm sure," and her face, swollen too, tried an oily smile.

Laura only wanted to get out, to get away. She was back in the passage. The door opened. She walked straight through into the bedroom, where the dead man was lying.

"You'd like a look at 'im, wouldn't you?" said Em's sister, and she brushed past Laura over to the bed. "Don't be afraid, my lass,—" and now her voice sounded fond and sly, and fondly she drew down the sheet—" 'e looks a picture. There's nothing to show. Come along, my dear."

Laura came.

There lay a young man, fast asleep—sleeping so soundly, so deeply, that he was far, far away from them both. Oh, so remote, so peaceful. He was dreaming. Never wake him up again. His head was sunk in the pillow, his eyes were closed; they were blind under the closed eyelids. He was given up to his dream. What did garden-parties and baskets and lace frocks matter to him? He was far from all those things. He was wonderful, beautiful. While they were laughing and while the band was playing, this marvel had come to the lane. Happy...

happy.... All is well, said that sleeping face. This is just as it should be. I am content.

But all the same you had to cry, and she couldn't go out of the room without saying something to him. Laura gave a loud childish sob.

"Forgive my hat," she said.

And this time she didn't wait for Em's sister. She found her way out of the door, down the path, past all those dark people. At the corner of the lane she met Laurie.

He stepped out of the shadow. "Is that you, Laura?"

"Yes."

"Mother was getting anxious. Was it all right?"

"Yes, quite. Oh, Laurie!" She took his arm, she pressed up against him.

"I say, you're not crying, are you?" asked her brother.

Laura shook her head. She was.

Laurie put his arm round her shoulder. "Don't cry," he said in his warm, loving voice. "Was it awful?"

"No," sobbed Laura. "It was simply marvellous. But, Laurie—" She stopped, she looked at her brother. "Isn't life," she stammered, "isn't life—" But what life was she couldn't explain. No matter. He quite understood.

"*Isn't* it, darling?" said Laurie.

THE THREE-DAY BLOW*

BY ERNEST HEMINGWAY

T HE RAIN stopped as Nick turned into the road that went up through the orchard. The fruit had been picked and the fall wind blew through the bare trees. Nick stopped and picked up a Wagner apple from beside the road, shiny in the brown

---

* from *In Our Time*

grass from the rain. He put the apple in the pocket of his Mackinaw coat.

The road came out of the orchard on to the top of the hill. There was the cottage, the porch bare, smoke coming from the chimney. In back was the garage, the chicken coop and the second-growth timber like a hedge against the woods behind. The big trees swayed far over in the wind as he watched. It was the first of the autumn storms.

As Nick crossed the open field above the orchard the door of the cottage opened and Bill came out. He stood on the porch looking out.

"Well, Wemedge," he said.

"Hey, Bill," Nick said, coming up the steps.

They stood together, looking out across the country, down over the orchard, beyond the road, across the lower fields and the woods of the point to the lake. The wind was blowing straight down the lake. They could see the surf along Ten Mile point.

"She's blowing," Nick said.

"She'll blow like that for three days," Bill said.

"Is your dad in?" Nick said.

"No. He's out with the gun. Come on in."

Nick went inside the cottage. There was a big fire in the fireplace. The wind made it roar. Bill shut the door.

"Have a drink?" he said.

He went out to the kitchen and came back with two glasses and a pitcher of water. Nick reached the whisky bottle from the shelf above the fireplace.

"All right?" he said.

"Good," said Bill.

They sat in front of the fire and drank the Irish whisky and water.

"It's got a swell, smoky taste," Nick said, and looked at the fire through the glass.

"That's the peat," Bill said.

"You can't get peat into liquor," Nick said.

"That doesn't make any difference," Bill said.

"You ever seen any peat?" Nick asked.

"No," said Bill.

"Neither have I," Nick said.

His shoes, stretched out on the hearth, began to steam in front of the fire.

"Better take your shoes off," Bill said.

"I haven't got any socks on."

"Take them off and dry them and I'll get you some," Bill said. He went upstairs into the loft and Nick heard him walking about overhead. Upstairs was open under the roof and was where Bill and his father and he, Nick, sometimes slept. In back was a dressing room. They moved the cots back out of the rain and covered them with rubber blankets.

Bill came down with a pair of heavy wool socks.

"It's getting too late to go around without socks," he said.

"I hate to start them again," Nick said. He pulled the socks on and slumped back in the chair, putting his feet up on the screen in front of the fire.

"You'll dent in the screen," Bill said. Nick swung his feet over to the side of the fireplace.

"Got anything to read?" he asked.

"Only the paper."

"What did the Cards do?"

"Dropped a double header to the Giants."

"That ought to cinch it for them."

"It's a gift," Bill said. "As long as McGraw can buy every good ball player in the league there's nothing to it."

"He can't buy them all," Nick said.

"He buys all the ones he wants," Bill said. "Or he makes them discontented so they have to trade them to him."

"Like Heinie Zim," Nick agreed.

"That bonehead will do him a lot of good."

Bill stood up.

"He can hit," Nick offered. The heat from the fire was baking his legs.

"He's a sweet fielder, too," Bill said. "But he loses ball games."

"Maybe that's what McGraw wants him for," Nick suggested.

"Maybe," Bill agreed.

"There's always more to it than we know about," Nick said.

"Of course. But we've got pretty good dope for being so far away."

"Like how much better you can pick them if you don't see the horses."

"That's it."

Bill reached down the whisky bottle. His big hand went all the way around it. He poured the whisky into the glass Nick held out.

"How much water?"

"Just the same."

He sat down on the floor beside Nick's chair.

"It's good when the fall storms come, isn't it?" Nick said.

"It's swell."

"It's the best time of year," Nick said.

"Wouldn't it be hell to be in town?" Bill said.

"I'd like to see the World Series," Nick said.

"Well, they're always in New York or Philadelphia now," Bill said. "That doesn't do us any good."

"I wonder if the Cards will ever win a pennant?"

"Not in our lifetime," Bill said.

"Gee, they'd go crazy," Nick said.

"Do you remember when they got going that once before they had the train wreck?"

"Boy!" Nick said, remembering.

Bill reached over to the table under the window for the book that lay there, face down, where he had put it when he went to the door. He held his glass in one hand and the book in the other, leaning back against Nick's chair.

"What are you reading?"

"Richard Feverel."

"I couldn't get into it."

"It's all right," Bill said. "It ain't a bad book, Wemedge."

"What else have you got I haven't read?" Nick asked.

"Did you read the *Forest Lovers?*"

"Yup. That's the one where they go to bed every night with the naked sword between them."

"That's a good book, Wemedge."

"It's a swell book. What I couldn't ever understand was what good the sword would do. It would have to stay edge up all the time because if it went over flat you could roll right over it and it wouldn't make any trouble."

"It's a symbol," Bill said.

"Sure," said Nick, "but it isn't practical."

"Did you ever read *Fortitude?*"

"It's fine," Nick said. "That's a real book. That's where his old man is after him all the time. Have you got any more by Walpole?"

"*The Dark Forest,*" Bill said. "It's about Russia."

"What does he know about Russia?" Nick asked.

"I don't know. You can't ever tell about those guys. Maybe he was there when he was a boy. He's got a lot of dope on it."

"I'd like to meet him," Nick said.

"I'd like to meet Chesterton," Bill said.

"I wish he was here now," Nick said. "We'd take him fishing to the 'Voix tomorrow."

"I wonder if he'd like to go fishing," Bill said.

"Sure," said Nick. "He must be about the best guy there is. Do you remember the *Flying Inn?*"

> " 'If an angel out of heaven
> Gives you something else to drink,
> Thank him for his kind intentions;
> Go and pour them down the sink.' "

"That's right," said Nick. "I guess he's a better guy than Walpole."

"Oh, he's a better guy, all right," Bill said. "But Walpole's a better writer."

"I don't know," Nick said. "Chesterton's a classic."

"Walpole's a classic, too," Bill insisted.

"I wish we had them both here," Nick said. "We'd take them both fishing to the 'Voix tomorrow."

"Let's get drunk," Bill said.

"All right," Nick agreed.

"My old man won't care," Bill said.

"Are you sure?" said Nick.

"I know it," Bill said.

"I'm a little drunk now," Nick said.

"You aren't drunk," Bill said.

He got up from the floor and reached for the whisky bottle. Nick held out his glass. His eyes fixed on it while Bill poured.

Bill poured the glass half full of whisky.

"Put in your own water," he said. "There's just one more shot."

"Got any more?" Nick asked.

"There's plenty more but dad only likes me to drink what's open."

"Sure," said Nick.

"He says opening bottles is what makes drunkards," Bill explained.

"That's right," said Nick. He was impressed. He had never thought of that before. He had always thought it was solitary drinking that made drunkards.

"How is your dad?" he asked respectfully.

"He's all right," Bill said. "He gets a little wild sometimes."

"He's a swell guy," Nick said. He poured water into his glass out of the pitcher. It mixed slowly with the whisky. There was more whisky than water.

"You bet your life he is," Bill said.

"My old man's all right," Nick said.

"You're damn right he is," said Bill.

"He claims he's never taken a drink in his life," Nick said, as though announcing a scientific fact.

"Well, he's a doctor. My old man's a painter. That's different."

"He's missed a lot," Nick said sadly.

"You can't tell," Bill said. "Everything's got its compensations."

"He says he's missed a lot himself," Nick confessed.

"Well, dad's had a tough time," Bill said.

"It all evens up," Nick said.

They sat looking into the fire and thinking of this profound truth.

"I'll get a chunk from the back porch," Nick said. He had noticed while looking into the fire that the fire was dying down. Also he wished to show he could hold his liquor and be practical. Even if his father had never touched a drop Bill was not going to get him drunk before he himself was drunk.

"Bring one of the big beech chunks," Bill said. He was also being consciously practical.

Nick came in with the log through the kitchen and in passing knocked a pan off the kitchen table. He laid the log down and picked up the pan. It had contained dried apricots, soaking in water. He carefully picked up all the apricots off the floor, some of them had gone under the stove, and put them back in the pan. He dipped some more water onto them from the pail by the table. He felt quite proud of himself. He had been thoroughly practical.

He came in carrying the log and Bill got up from the chair and helped him put it on the fire.

"That's a swell log," Nick said.

"I'd been saving it for the bad weather," Bill said. "A log like that will burn all night."

"There'll be coals left to start the fire in the morning," Nick said.

"That's right," Bill agreed. They were conducting the conversation on a high plane.

"Let's have another drink," Nick said.

"I think there's another bottle open in the locker," Bill said.

He kneeled down in the corner in front of the locker and brought out a square-faced bottle.

"It's Scotch," he said.

"I'll get some more water," Nick said. He went out into the kitchen again. He filled the pitcher with the dipper dipping cold spring water from the pail. On his way back to the living room he passed a mirror in the dining room and looked in it. His face looked strange. He smiled at the face in the mirror and it grinned back at him. He winked at it and went on. It was not his face but it didn't make any difference.

Bill had poured out the drinks.

"That's an awfully big shot," Nick said.

"Not for us, Wemedge," Bill said.

"What'll we drink to?" Nick asked, holding up the glass.

"Let's drink to fishing," Bill said.

"All right," Nick said. "Gentlemen, I give you fishing."

"All fishing," Bill said. "Everywhere."

"Fishing," Nick said. "That's what we drink to."

"It's better than baseball," Bill said.

"There isn't any comparison," said Nick. "How did we ever get talking about baseball?"

"It was a mistake," Bill said. "Baseball is a game for louts."

They drank all that was in their glasses.

"Now let's drink to Chesterton."

"And Walpole," Nick interposed.

Nick poured out the liquor. Bill poured in the water. They looked at each other. They felt very fine.

"Gentlemen," Bill said, "I give you Chesterton and Walpole."

"Exactly, gentlemen," Nick said.

They drank. Bill filled up the glasses. They sat down in the big chairs in front of the fire.

"You were very wise, Wemedge," Bill said.

"What do you mean?" asked Nick.

"To bust off that Marge business," Bill said.

"I guess so," said Nick.

"It was the only thing to do. If you hadn't, by now you'd be back home working trying to get enough money to get married."

Nick said nothing.

"Once a man's married he's absolutely bitched," Bill went on. "He hasn't got anything more. Nothing. Not a damn thing. He's done for. You've seen the guys that get married."

Nick said nothing.

"You can tell them," Bill said. "They get this sort of fat married look. They're done for."

"Sure," said Nick.

"It was probably bad busting it off," Bill said. "But you

always fall for somebody else and then it's all right. Fall for them but don't let them ruin you."

"Yes," said Nick.

"If you'd have married her you would have had to marry the whole family. Remember her mother and that guy she married."

Nick nodded.

"Imagine having them around the house all the time and going to Sunday dinners at their house, and having them over to dinner and her telling Marge all the time what to do and how to act."

Nick sat quiet.

"You came out of it damned well," Bill said. "Now she can marry somebody of her own sort and settle down and be happy. You can't mix oil and water and you can't mix that sort of thing any more than if I'd marry Ida that works for Strattons. She'd probably like it, too."

Nick said nothing. The liquor had all died out of him and left him alone. Bill wasn't there. He wasn't sitting in front of the fire or going fishing tomorrow with Bill and his dad or anything. He wasn't drunk. It was all gone. All he knew was that he had once had Marjorie and that he had lost her. She was gone and he had sent her away. That was all that mattered. He might never see her again. Probably he never would. It was all gone, finished.

"Let's have another drink," Nick said.

Bill poured it out. Nick splashed in a little water.

"If you'd gone on that way we wouldn't be here now," Bill said.

That was true. His original plan had been to go down home and get a job. Then he had planned to stay in Charlevoix all winter so he could be near Marge. Now he did not know what he was going to do.

"Probably we wouldn't even be going fishing tomorrow," Bill said. "You had the right dope, all right."

"I couldn't help it," Nick said.

"I know. That's the way it works out," Bill said.

"All of a sudden everything was over," Nick said. "I don't

know why it was. I couldn't help it. Just like when the three-day blows come now and rip all the leaves off the trees."

"Well, it's over. That's the point," Bill said.

"It was my fault," Nick said.

"It doesn't make any difference whose fault it was," Bill said.

"No, I suppose not," Nick said.

The big thing was that Marjorie was gone and that probably he would never see her again. He had talked to her about how they would go to Italy together and the fun they would have. Places they would be together. It was all gone now.

"So long as it's over that's all that matters," Bill said. "I tell you, Wemedge, I was worried while it was going on. You played it right. I understand her mother is sore as hell. She told a lot of people you were engaged."

"We weren't engaged," Nick said.

"It was all around that you were."

"I can't help it," Nick said. "We weren't."

"Weren't you going to get married?" Bill asked.

"Yes. But we weren't engaged," Nick said.

"What's the difference?" Bill asked judicially.

"I don't know. There's a difference."

"I don't see it," said Bill.

"All right," said Nick. "Let's get drunk."

"All right," Bill said. "Let's get really drunk."

"Let's get drunk and then go swimming," Nick said.

He drank off his glass.

"I'm sorry as hell about her but what could I do?" he said. "You know what her mother was like!"

"She was terrible," Bill said.

"All of a sudden it was over," Nick said. "I oughtn't to talk about it."

"You aren't," Bill said. "I talked about it and now I'm through. We won't ever speak of it again. You don't want to think about it. You might get back into it again."

Nick had not thought about that. It had seemed so absolute. That was a thought. That made him feel better.

"Sure," he said. "There's always that danger."

He felt happy now. There was not anything that was irrevocable. He might go into town Saturday night. Today was Thursday.

"There's always a chance," he said.

"You'll have to watch yourself," Bill said.

"I'll watch myself," he said.

He felt happy. Nothing was finished. Nothing was ever lost. He would go into town on Saturday. He felt lighter, as he had felt before Bill started to talk about it. There was always a way out.

"Let's take the guns and go down to the point and look for your dad," Nick said.

"All right."

Bill took down the two shotguns from the rack on the wall. He opened a box of shells. Nick put on his Mackinaw coat and his shoes. His shoes were stiff from the drying. He was still quite drunk but his head was clear.

"How do you feel?" Nick asked.

"Swell. I've just got a good edge on." Bill was buttoning up his sweater.

"There's no use getting drunk."

"No. We ought to get outdoors."

They stepped out the door. The wind was blowing a gale.

"The birds will lie right down in the grass with this," Nick said.

They struck down toward the orchard.

"I saw a woodcock this morning," Bill said.

"Maybe we'll jump him," Nick said.

"You can't shoot in this wind," Bill said.

Outside now the Marge business was no longer so tragic. It was not even very important. The wind blew everything like that away.

"It's coming right off the big lake," Nick said.

Against the wind they heard the thud of a shotgun.

"That's dad," Bill said. "He's down in the swamp."

"Let's cut down that way," Nick said.

"Let's cut across the lower meadow and see if we jump anything," Bill said.

"All right," Nick said.

None of it was important now. The wind blew it out of his head. Still he could always go into town Saturday night. It was a good thing to have in reserve.

THE STANDARD OF LIVING*

BY DOROTHY PARKER

ANNABEL AND Midge came out of the tea room with the arrogant slow gait of the leisured, for their Saturday afternoon stretched ahead of them. They had lunched, as was their wont, on sugar, starches, oils, and butter-fats. Usually they ate sandwiches of spongy new white bread greased with butter and mayonnaise; they ate thick wedges of cake lying wet beneath ice cream and whipped cream and melted chocolate gritty with nuts. As alternates, they ate patties, sweating beads of inferior oil, containing bits of bland meat bogged in pale, stiffening sauce; they ate pastries, limber under rigid icing, filled with an indeterminate yellow sweet stuff, not still solid, not yet liquid, like salve that has been left in the sun. They chose no other sort of food, nor did they consider it. And their skin was like the petals of wood anemones, and their bellies were as flat and their flanks as lean as those of young Indian braves.

Annabel and Midge had been best friends almost from the day that Midge had found a job as stenographer with the firm that employed Annabel. By now, Annabel, two years longer in the stenographic department, had worked up to the wages of eighteen dollars and fifty cents a week; Midge was still at sixteen dollars. Each girl lived at home with her family and paid half her salary to its support.

The girls sat side by side at their desks, they lunched to-

* from *The New Yorker* and *The Portable Dorothy Parker*

gether every noon, together they set out for home at the end of
the day's work. Many of their evenings and most of their Sundays were passed in each other's company. Often they were
joined by two young men, but there was no steadiness to any
such quartet; the two young men would give place, unlamented,
to two other young men, and lament would have been inappro-
priate, really, since the newcomers were scarcely distinguish-
able from their predecessors. Invariably the girls spent the fine
idle hours of their hot-weather Saturday afternoons together.
Constant use had not worn ragged the fabric of their friendship.

They looked alike, though the resemblance did not lie in
their features. It was in the shape of their bodies, their movements, their style, and their adornments. Annabel and Midge
did, and completely, all that young office workers are besought
not to do. They painted their lips and their nails, they darkened
their lashes and lightened their hair, and scent seemed to shim-
mer from them. They wore thin, bright dresses, tight over their
breasts and high on their legs, and tilted slippers, fancifully
strapped. They looked conspicuous and cheap and charming.

Now, as they walked across to Fifth Avenue with their skirts
swirled by the hot wind, they received audible admiration.
Young men grouped lethargically about newsstands awarded
them murmurs, exclamations, even—the ultimate tribute—
whistles. Annabel and Midge passed without the condescen-
sion of hurrying their pace; they held their heads higher and set
their feet with exquisite precision, as if they stepped over the
necks of peasants.

Always the girls went to walk on Fifth Avenue on their free
afternoons, for it was the ideal ground for their favorite game.
The game could be played anywhere, and indeed, was, but the
great shop windows stimulated the two players to their best
form.

Annabel had invented the game; or rather she had evolved it
from an old one. Basically, it was no more than the ancient
sport of what-would-you-do-if-you-had-a-million-dollars? But
Annabel had drawn a new set of rules for it, had narrowed it,
pointed it, made it stricter. Like all games, it was the more ab-
sorbing for being more difficult.

Annabel's version went like this: You must suppose that somebody dies and leaves you a million dollars, cool. But there is a condition to the bequest. It is stated in the will that you must spend every nickel of the money on yourself.

There lay the hazard of the game. If, when playing it, you forgot and listed among your expenditures the rental of a new apartment for your family, for example, you lost your turn to the other player. It was astonishing how many—and some of them among the experts, too—would forfeit all their winnings by such slips.

It was essential, of course, that it be played in passionate seriousness. Each purchase must be carefully considered and, if necessary, supported by argument. There was no zest to playing it wildly. Once Annabel had introduced the game to Sylvia, another girl who worked in the office. She explained the rules to Sylvia and then offered her the gambit "What would be the first thing you'd do?" Sylvia had not shown the decency of even a second of hesitation. "Well," she said, "the first thing I'd do, I'd go out and hire somebody to shoot Mrs. Gary Cooper, and then . . ." So it is to be seen that she was no fun.

But Annabel and Midge were surely born to be comrades, for Midge played the game like a master from the moment she learned it. It was she who added the touches that made the whole thing cozier. According to Midge's innovations, the eccentric who died and left you the money was not anybody you loved, or, for the matter of that, anybody you even knew. It was somebody who had seen you somewhere and had thought, "That girl ought to have lots of nice things. I'm going to leave her a million dollars when I die." And the death was to be neither untimely nor painful. Your benefactor, full of years and comfortably ready to depart, was to slip softly away during sleep and go right to heaven. These embroideries permitted Annabel and Midge to play their game in the luxury of peaceful consciences.

Midge played with a seriousness that was not only proper but extreme. The single strain on the girls' friendship had followed an announcement once made by Annabel that the first thing she would buy with her million dollars would be a silver-fox coat. It was as if she had struck Midge across the mouth. When Midge recovered her breath, she cried that she couldn't imagine how Annabel could do such a thing—silver-fox coats were so common! Annabel defended her taste with the retort that they were not common, either. Midge then said that they were so. She added that everybody had a silver-fox coat. She went on, with perhaps a slight toss of head, to declare that she herself wouldn't be caught dead in silver fox.

For the next few days, though the girls saw each other as constantly, their conversation was careful and infrequent, and they did not once play their game. Then one morning, as soon as Annabel entered the office, she came to Midge and said she had changed her mind. She would not buy a silver-fox coat with any part of her million dollars. Immediately on receiving the legacy, she would select a coat of mink.

Midge smiled and her eyes shone. "I think," she said, "you're doing absolutely the right thing."

Now, as they walked along Fifth Avenue, they played the game anew. It was one of those days with which September is repeatedly cursed; hot and glaring, with slivers of dust in the wind. People drooped and shambled, but the girls carried themselves tall and walked a straight line, as befitted young heiresses on their afternoon promenade. There was no longer need for them to start the game at its formal opening. Annabel went direct to the heart of it.

"All right," she said. "So you've got this million dollars. So what would be the first thing you'd do?"

"Well, the first thing I'd do," Midge said, "I'd get a mink coat." But she said it mechanically, as if she were giving the memorized answer to an expected question.

"Yes," Annabel said. "I think you ought to. The terribly dark kind of mink." But she, too, spoke as if by rote. It was too hot; fur, no matter how dark and sleek and supple, was horrid to the thoughts.

They stepped along in silence for a while. Then Midge's eye was caught by a shop window. Cool, lovely gleamings were there set off by chaste and elegant darkness.

"No," Midge said, "I take it back. I wouldn't get a mink coat the first thing. Know what I'd do? I'd get a string of pearls. Real pearls."

Annabel's eyes turned to follow Midge's.

"Yes," she said, slowly. "I think that's a kind of a good idea. And it would make sense, too. Because you can wear pearls with anything."

Together they went over to the shop window and stood pressed against it. It contained but one object—a double row of great, even pearls clasped by a deep emerald around a little pink velvet throat.

"What do you suppose they cost?" Annabel said.

"Gee, I don't know," Midge said. "Plenty, I guess."

"Like a thousand dollars?" Annabel said.

"Oh, I guess like more," Midge said. "On account of the emerald."

"Well, like ten thousand dollars?" Annabel said.

"Gee, I wouldn't even know," Midge said.

The devil nudged Annabel in the ribs. "Dare you to go in and price them," she said.

"Like fun!" Midge said.

"Dare you," Annabel said.

"Why, a store like this wouldn't even be open this afternoon," Midge said.

"Yes, it is so, too," Annabel said. "People just came out. And there's a doorman on. Dare you."

"Well," Midge said. "But you've got to come too."

They tendered thanks, icily, to the doorman for ushering them into the shop. It was cool and quiet, a broad, gracious room with paneled walls and soft carpet. But the girls wore expressions of bitter disdain, as if they stood in a sty.

A slim, immaculate clerk came to them and bowed. His neat face showed no astonishment at their appearance.

"Good afternoon," he said. He implied that he would never forget it if they would grant him the favor of accepting his soft-spoken greeting.

"Good afternoon," Annabel and Midge said together, and in like freezing accents.

"Is there something—?" the clerk said.

"Oh, we're just looking," Annabel said. It was as if she flung the words down from a dais.

The clerk bowed.

"My friend and myself merely happened to be passing," Midge said, and stopped, seeming to listen to the phrase. "My friend here and myself," she went on, "merely happened to be wondering how much are those pearls you've got in your window."

"Ah, yes," the clerk said. "The double rope. That is two hundred and fifty thousand dollars, Madam."

"I see," Midge said.

The clerk bowed. "An exceptionally beautiful necklace," he said. "Would you care to look at it?"

"No, thank you," Annabel said.

"My friend and myself merely happened to be passing," Midge said.

They turned to go; to go, from their manner, where the tumbrel awaited them. The clerk sprang ahead and opened the door. He bowed as they swept by him.

The girls went on along the Avenue and disdain was still on their faces.

"Honestly!" Annabel said. "Can you imagine a thing like that?"

"Two hundred and fifty thousand dollars!" Midge said. "That's a quarter of a million dollars right there!"

"He's got his nerve!" Annabel said.

They walked on. Slowly the disdain went, slowly and completely as if drained from them, and with it went the regal carriage and tread. Their shoulders dropped and they dragged their feet; they bumped against each other, without notice or apology, and caromed away again. They were silent and their eyes were cloudy.

Suddenly Midge straightened her back, flung her head high, and spoke, clear and strong.

"Listen, Annabel," she said. "Look. Suppose there was this terribly rich person, see? You don't know this person, but this person has seen you somewhere and wants to do something for you. Well, it's a terribly old person, see? And so this person dies, just like going to sleep, and leaves you ten million dollars. Now, what would be the first thing you'd do?"

THE SAINT*

BY V. S. PRITCHETT

WHEN I was seventeen years old I lost my religious faith. It had been unsteady for some time and then, very suddenly, it went as the result of an incident in a punt on the river outside the town where we lived. My uncle, with whom I was obliged to stay for long periods of my life, had started a small furniture-making business in the town. He was always in difficulties about money, but he was convinced that in some way God would help him. And this happened. An investor arrived who belonged to a sect called the Church of the Last Purification, of Toronto, Canada. Could we imagine, this man asked, a good and omnipotent God allowing his children to be short of money? We had to admit we could not imagine this. The man paid some capital into my uncle's business and we were converted. Our family were the first Purifiers—as they were called—in the town. Soon a congregation of fifty or more were meeting every Sunday in a room at the Corn Exchange.

At once we found ourselves isolated and hated people. Everyone made jokes about us. We had to stand together because we were sometimes dragged into the courts. What the unconverted could not forgive in us was first that we believed in successful prayer and, secondly, that our revelation came from Toronto. The success of our prayers had a simple foundation. We regarded it as "Error"—our name for Evil—to believe the evidence of our senses and if we had influenza or consumption,

* from *Harper's Magazine*

or had lost our money or were unemployed, we denied the reality of these things, saying that since God could not have made them they therefore did not exist. It was exhilarating to look at our congregation and to know that what the vulgar would call miracles were performed among us, almost as a matter of routine, every day. Not very big miracles, perhaps; but up in London and out in Toronto, we knew that deafness and blindness, cancer and insanity, the great scourges, were constantly vanishing before the prayers of the more advanced Purifiers.

"What!" said my schoolmaster, an Irishman with eyes like broken glass and a sniff of irritability in the bristles of his nose. "What! Do you have the impudence to tell me that if you fell off the top floor of this building and smashed your head in, you would say you hadn't fallen and were not injured?"

I was a small boy and very afraid of everybody, but not when it was a question of my religion. I was used to the kind of conundrum the Irishman had set. It was useless to argue, though our religion had already developed an interesting casuistry.

"I *would* say so," I replied with coldness and some vanity. "And my head would not be smashed."

"You would not say so," answered the Irishman. "You would not say so." His eyes sparkled with pure pleasure. "You'd be dead."

The boys laughed, but they looked at me with admiration.

Then I do not know how or why, I began to see a difficulty. Without warning and as if I had gone into my bedroom at night and had found a gross ape seated in my bed and thereafter following me about with his grunts and his fleas and a look, relentless and ancient, scored on his brown face, I was faced with the problem which prowls at the centre of all religious faith. I was faced by the difficulty of the origin of evil. Evil was an illusion, we were taught. But even illusions have an origin. The Purifiers denied this.

I consulted my uncle. Trade was bad at the time and this made his faith abrupt. He frowned as I spoke.

"When did you brush your coat last?" he said. "You're getting slovenly about your appearance. If you spent more time

studying books"—that is to say, the Purification literature—
"and less with your hands in your pockets and playing about
with boats on the river, you wouldn't be letting Error in."

. All dogmas have their jargon; my uncle as a business man
loved the trade terms of the Purification. "Don't let Error in,"
was a favorite one. The whole point about the Purification, he
said, was that it was scientific and therefore exact; in consequence it was sheer weakness to admit discussion. Indeed, be-
trayal. He unpinched his pince-nez, stirred his tea and
indicated I must submit or change the subject. Preferably the
latter. I saw, to my alarm, that my arguments had defeated my
uncle. Faith and doubt pulled like strings round my throat.

"You don't mean to say you don't believe that what our Lord
said was true?" my aunt asked nervously, following me out of
the room. "Your uncle does, dear."

I could not answer. I went out of the house and down the
main street to the river where the punts were stuck like insects
in the summery flash of the reach. Life was a dream, I thought;
no, a nightmare, for the ape was beside me.

I was still in this state, half sulking and half exalted, when
Mr. Hubert Timberlake came to the town. He was one of the
important people from the headquarters of our Church and he
had come to give an address on the Purification at the Corn
Exchange. Posters announcing this were everywhere. Mr.
Timberlake was to spend Sunday afternoon with us. It was unbelievable that a man so eminent would actually sit in our
dining-room, use our knives and forks, and eat our food. Every
imperfection in our home and our characters would jump out at
him. The Truth had been revealed to man with scientific accuracy—an accuracy we could all test by experiment—and the
future course of human development on earth was laid down,
finally. And here in Mr. Timberlake was a man who had not
merely performed many miracles—even, it was said with
proper reserve, having twice raised the dead—but who had actually been to Toronto, our headquarters, where this great and
revolutionary revelation had first been given.

"This is my nephew," my uncle said, introducing me. "He
lives with us. He thinks he thinks, Mr. Timberlake, but I tell

him he only thinks he does. Ha, ha." My uncle was a humorous man when he was with the great. "He's always on the river," my uncle continued. "I tell him he's got water on the brain. I've been telling Mr. Timberlake about you, my boy."

A hand as soft as the best quality chamois leather took mine. I saw a wide upright man in a double-breasted navy blue suit. He had a pink square head with very small ears and one of those torpid, enamelled smiles which were said by our enemies to be too common in our sect.

"Why, isn't that just fine?" said Mr. Timberlake who, owing to his contacts with Toronto, spoke with an American accent. "What say we tell your uncle it's funny he thinks he's funny."

The eyes of Mr. Timberlake were direct and colourless. He had the look of a retired merchant captain who had become de-contaminated from the sea and had reformed and made money. His defence of me had made me his at once. My doubts vanished. Whatever Mr. Timberlake believed must be true and as I listened to him at lunch, I thought there could be no finer life than his.

"I expect Mr. Timberlake's tired after his address," said my aunt.

"Tired?" exclaimed my uncle, brilliant with indignation. "How can Mr. Timberlake be tired? Don't let Error in!"

For in our faith the merely inconvenient was just as illusory as a great catastrophe would have been, if you wished to be strict, and Mr. Timberlake's presence made us very strict.

I noticed then that, after their broad smiles, Mr. Timberlake's lips had the habit of setting into a long depressed sarcastic curve.

"I guess," he drawled, "I guess the Almighty must have been tired sometimes, for it says He relaxed on the seventh day. Say, do you know what I'd like to do this afternoon," he said, turning to me. "While your uncle and aunt are sleeping off this meal let's you and me go on the river and get water on the brain. I'll show you how to punt."

Mr. Timberlake, I saw to my disappointment, was out to show he understood the young. I saw he was planning a "quiet talk" with me about my problems.

"There are too many people on the river on Sundays," said my uncle uneasily.

"Oh, I like a crowd," said Mr. Timberlake, giving my uncle a tough look. "This is the day of rest, you know." He had had my uncle gobbling up every bit of gossip from the sacred city of Toronto all the morning.

My uncle and aunt were incredulous that a man like Mr. Timberlake should go out among the blazers and gramophones of the river on a Sunday afternoon. In any other member of our Church they would have thought this sinful.

"Waal, what say?" said Mr. Timberlake. I could only murmur.

"That's fixed," said Mr. Timberlake. And on came the smile as simple, vivid and unanswerable as the smile on an advertisement. "Isn't that just fine!"

Mr. Timberlake went upstairs to wash his hands. My uncle was deeply offended and shocked, but he could say nothing. He unpinched his glasses.

"A very wonderful man," he said. "So human," he apologized.

"My boy," my uncle said. "This is going to be an experience for you. Hubert Timberlake was making a thousand a year in the insurance business ten years ago. Then he heard of the Purification. He threw everything up, just like that. He gave up his job and took up the work. It was a struggle, he told me so himself this morning. 'Many's the time,' he said to me this morning, 'when I wondered where my next meal was coming from.' But the way was shown. He came down from Worcester to London and in two years he was making fifteen hundred a year out of his practice."

To heal the sick by prayer according to the tenets of the Church of the Last Purification was Mr. Timberlake's profession.

My uncle lowered his eyes. With his glasses off the lids were small and uneasy. He lowered his voice too.

"I have told him about your little trouble," my uncle said quietly, with emotion. I was burned with shame. My uncle looked up and stuck out his chin confidently.

"He just smiled," my uncle said. "That's all."

Then we waited for Mr. Timberlake to come down.

I put on white flannels and soon I was walking down to the river with Mr. Timberlake. I felt that I was going with him under false pretences; for he would begin explaining to me the origin of evil and I would have to pretend politely that he was converting me when, already, at the first sight of him, I had believed. A stone bridge, whose two arches were like an owlish pair of eyes gazing up the reach, was close to the landing-stage. I thought what a pity it was the flannelled men and the sunburned girls there did not know I was getting a ticket for *the* Mr. Timberlake who had been speaking in the town that very morning. I looked round for him and when I saw him I was a little startled. He was standing at the edge of the water looking at it with an expression of empty incomprehension. Among the white crowds his air of brisk efficiency had dulled. He looked middle-aged, out of place and insignificant. But the smile switched on when he saw me.

"Ready?" he called. "Fine!"

I had the feeling that inside him there must be a gramophone record going round and round, stopping at that word.

He stepped into the punt and took charge.

"Now I just want you to paddle us over to the far bank," he said, "and then I'll show you how to punt."

Everything Mr. Timberlake said still seemed unreal to me. The fact that he was sitting in a punt, of all commonplace material things, was incredible. That he should propose to pole us up the river was terrifying. Suppose he fell into the river? At once I checked the thought. A leader of our Church under the direct guidance of God could not possibly fall into a river.

The stream is wide and deep in this reach, but on the southern bank there is a manageable depth and a hard bottom. Over the clay banks the willows hang, making their basket-work print of sun and shadow on the water, while under the gliding boats lie cloudy, chloride caverns. The hoop-like branches of the trees bend down until their tips touch the water like fingers making musical sounds. Ahead in midstream, on a day sunny as this one was, there is a path of strong light which is hard to look at unless you half close your eyes and down this path on the crowded Sundays, go the launches with their parasols and their pennants; and also the rowing boats with their beetle-leg oars, which seem to dig the sunlight out of the water as they rise. Upstream one goes, on and on between the gardens and then between fields kept for grazing. On the afternoon when Mr. Timberlake and I went out to settle the question of the origin of evil, the meadows were packed densely with buttercups.

"Now," said Mr. Timberlake decisively when I had paddled to the other side. "Now I'll take her."

He got over the seat into the well at the stern.

"I'll just get you clear of the trees," I said.

"Give me the pole," said Mr. Timberlake, standing up on the little platform and making a squeak with his boots as he did so. "Thank you, sir. I haven't done this for eighteen years but I can tell you, brother, in those days I was considered some poler."

He looked around and let the pole slide down through his hands. Then he gave the first difficult push. The punt rocked pleasantly and we moved forward. I sat facing him, paddle in hand, to check any inward drift of the punt.

"How's that, you guys?" said Mr. Timberlake, looking round at our eddies and drawing in the pole. The delightful water swished down it.

"Fine," I said. Deferentially I had caught the word.

He went on to his second and his third strokes, taking too much water on his sleeve, perhaps, and uncertain in his steering, which I corrected, but he was doing well.

"It comes back to me," he said. "How am I doing?"

"Just keep her out from the trees," I said.

"The trees?" he said.

"The willows," I said.

"I'll do it now," he said. "How's that? Not quite enough? Well, how's this?"

"Another one," I said. "The current runs strong this side."

"What? More trees?" he said. He was getting hot.

"We can shoot out past them," I said. "I'll ease over with the paddle."

Mr. Timberlake did not like this suggestion.

"No, don't do that. I can manage it," he said. I did not want to offend one of the leaders of our Church, so I put the paddle down; but I felt I ought to have taken him farther along away from the irritation of the trees.

"Of course," I said. "We could go under them. It might be nice."

"I think," said Mr. Timberlake, "that would be a very good idea."

He lunged hard on the pole and took us towards the next archway of willow branches.

"We may have to duck a bit, that's all," I said.

"Oh, I can push the branches up," said Mr. Timberlake.

"It is better to duck," I said.

We were gliding now quickly towards the arch, in fact I was already under it.

"I think I should duck," I said. "Just bend down for this one."

"What makes the trees lean over the water like this?" asked Mr. Timberlake. "Weeping willows—I'll give you a thought there. Now Error likes to make us dwell on sorrow. Why not call them *laughing* willows?" discoursed Mr. Timberlake as the branch passed over my head.

"Duck," I said.

"Where? I don't see them," said Mr. Timberlake turning round.

"No, your head," I said. "The branch," I called.

"Oh, the branch. This one?" said Mr. Timberlake, finding a branch just against his chest, and he put out a hand to lift it. It is not easy to lift a willow branch and Mr. Timberlake was surprised. He stepped back as it gently and firmly leaned against him. He leaned back and pushed from his feet. And he pushed too far. The boat went on, I saw Mr. Timberlake's boots leave the stern as he took an unthoughtful step backwards. He made a last-minute grasp at a stronger and higher branch, and then, there he hung a yard above the water, round as a blue damson that is ripe and ready, waiting only for a touch to make it fall. Too late with the paddle and shot ahead by the force of his thrust, I could not save him.

For a full minute I did not believe what I saw; indeed our religion taught us never to believe what we saw. Unbelieving I could not move. I gaped. The impossible had happened. Only a miracle, I found myself saying, could save him.

What was the most striking was the silence of Mr. Timberlake as he hung from the tree. I was lost between gazing at him and trying to get the punt out of the small branches of the tree. By the time I had got the punt out there were several yards of water between us and the soles of his boots were very near the water as the branch bent under his weight. Boats were passing at the time but no one seemed to notice us. I was glad about this. This was a private agony. A double chin had appeared on the face of Mr. Timberlake and his head was squeezed between his shoulders and his hanging arms. I saw him blink and look up at the sky. His eyelids were pale like a chicken's. He was tidy and dignified as he hung there, the hat was not displaced and the top button of his coat was done up. He had a blue silk handkerchief in his breast pocket. So unperturbed and genteel he seemed that as the tips of his shoes came nearer and nearer to the water, I became alarmed. He could perform what are called miracles. He would be thinking at this moment that only in an erroneous and illusory sense was he hanging from the branch of the tree over six feet of water. He was probably praying one of the closely reasoned prayers of our faith which were more like conversations with Euclid than appeals to God. The calm of his face suggested this. Was he, I asked myself, within sight of the main road, the town Recreation Ground and the landing-stage crowded with people, was he about to re-enact a well-known miracle? I hoped that he was not. I prayed that he was not. I prayed with all my will that Mr. Timberlake would not walk upon the water. It was my prayer and not his that was answered.

I saw the shoes dip, water rise above his ankles and up his socks. He tried to move his grip now to a yet higher branch— he did not succeed—and in making this effort his coat and waist-coat rose and parted from his trousers. One seam of shirt with its pant-loops and brace-tabs broke like a crack across the middle of Mr. Timberlake. It was like a fatal flaw in a statue, an earthquake crack which made the monumental mortal. The last Greeks must have felt as I felt then, when they saw a crack across the middle of some statue of Apollo. It was at this moment I realized that the final revelation about man and society on earth had come to nobody and that Mr. Timberlake knew nothing at all about the origin of evil.

All this takes long to describe, but it happened in a few seconds as I paddled towards him. I was too late to get his feet on the boat and the only thing to do was to let him sink until his hands were nearer the level of the punt and then to get him to change hand-holds. Then I would paddle him ashore. I did this. Amputated by the water, first a torso, then a bust, then a mere head and shoulders, Mr. Timberlake, I noticed, looked sad and lonely as he sank. He was a declining dogma. As the water lapped his collar—for he hesitated to let go of the branch to hold the punt—I saw a small triangle of deprecation and pathos between his nose and the corners of his mouth. The head resting on the platter of water had the sneer of calamity on it, such as one sees in the pictures of a beheaded saint.

"Hold on to the punt, Mr. Timberlake," I said urgently. "Hold on to the punt."

He did so.

"Push from behind," he directed in a dry businesslike voice. They were his first words. I obeyed him. Carefully I paddled him towards the bank. He turned and, with a splash, climbed ashore. There he stood, raising his arms and looking at the water running down his swollen suit and making a puddle at his feet.

"Say," said Mr. Timberlake coldly, "we let some Error in that time."

How much he must have hated our family.

"I am sorry, Mr. Timberlake," I said. "I am most awfully sorry. I should have paddled. It was my fault. I'll get you home at once. Let me wring out your coat and waist-coat. You'll catch your death . . ."

I stopped. I had nearly blasphemed. I had nearly suggested that Mr. Timberlake had fallen into the water and that to a man of his age that might be dangerous.

Mr. Timberlake corrected me. His voice was impersonal, addressing the laws of human existence, rather than myself.

"If God made water it would be ridiculous to suggest He made it capable of harming His creatures. Wouldn't it?"

"Yes," I murmured hypocritically.

"O.K.," said Mr. Timberlake. "Let's go."

"I'll soon get you across," I said.

"No," he said. "I mean let's go on. We're not going to let a little thing like this spoil a beautiful afternoon. Where were we going? You spoke of a pretty landing-place farther on. Let's go there."

"But I must take you home. You can't sit there soaked to the skin. It will spoil your clothes."

"Now, now," said Mr. Timberlake. "Do as I say. Go on."

There was nothing to be done with him. I held the punt into the bank and he stepped in. He sat like a bursting and sodden bolster in front of me while I paddled. We had lost the pole of course.

For a long time I could hardly look at Mr. Timberlake. He was taking the line that nothing had happened and this put me at a disadvantage. I knew something considerable had happened. That glaze, which so many of the members of our sect had on their faces and persons, their minds and manners, had been washed off. There was no gleam for me from Mr. Timberlake.

"What's the house over there?" he asked. He was making conversation. I had steered into the middle of the river to get him into the strong sun. I saw steam rise from him.

I took courage and studied him. He was a man, I realized, in poor physical condition, unexercised and sedentary. Now the gleam had left him one saw the veined empurpled skin of the stoutish man with a poor heart. I remember he had said at lunch:

"A young woman I know said, 'Isn't it wonderful. I can walk thirty miles in a day without being in the least tired.' I said, 'I don't see that bodily indulgence is anything a member of the Church of the Last Purification should boast about.'"

Yes, there was something flaccid, passive and slack about

Mr. Timberlake. Bunched in swollen clothes, he refused to take them off. It occurred to me, as he looked with boredom at the water, the passing boats and the country, that he had not been in the country before. That it was something he had agreed to do but wanted to get over quickly. He was totally uninterested. By his questions—what is that church? Are there any fish in this river? Is that a wireless or a gramophone?—I understood that Mr. Timberlake was formally acknowledging a world he did not live in. It was too interesting, too eventful a world. His spirit, inert and preoccupied, was elsewhere in an eventless and immaterial habitation. He was a dull man, duller than any man I have ever known; but his dullness was a sort of earthly deposit left by a being whose diluted mind was far away in the effervescence of metaphysical matters. There was a slightly pettish look on his face as (to himself, of course) he declared he was not wet and that he would not have a heart attack or catch pneumonia.

Mr. Timberlake spoke little. Sometimes he squeezed water out of his sleeve. He shivered a little. He watched his steam. I had planned when we set out to go up as far as the lock but now the thought of another two miles of this responsibility was too much. I pretended I wanted to go only as far as the bend which we were approaching, where one of the richest buttercup meadows was. I mentioned this to him. He turned and looked with boredom at the field. Slowly we came to the bank.

We tied up the punt and we landed.

"Fine," said Mr. Timberlake. He stood at the edge of the meadow, just as he had stood at the landing-stage—lost, stupefied, uncomprehending.

"Nice to stretch our legs," I said. I led the way into the deep flowers. So dense were the buttercups there was hardly any green. Presently I sat down. Mr. Timberlake looked at me and sat down also. Then I turned to him with a last try at persuasion. Respectability, I was sure, was his trouble.

"No one will see us," I said. "This is out of sight of the river. Take off your coat and trousers and wring them out."

Mr. Timberlake replied firmly:

"I am satisfied to remain as I am.

"What is this flower?" he asked to change the subject.

"Buttercup," I said.

"Of course," he replied.

I could do nothing with him. I lay down full length in the sun; and, observing this and thinking to please me, Mr. Timberlake did the same. He must have supposed that this was what I had come out in the boat to do. It was only human. He had come out with me, I saw, to show me that he was only human.

But as we lay there I saw the steam still rising. I had had enough.

"A bit hot," I said getting up.

He got up at once.

"Do you want to sit in the shade?" he asked politely.

"No," I said. "Would you like to?"

"No," he said. "I was thinking of you."

"Let's go back," I said. We both stood up and I let him pass in front of me. When I looked at him again I stopped dead. Mr. Timberlake was no longer a man in a navy blue suit. He was blue no longer. He was transfigured. He was yellow. He was covered with buttercup pollen, a fine yellow paste of it made by the damp, from head to foot.

"Your suit," I said.

He looked at it. He raised his thin eyebrows a little, but he did not smile or make any comment.

The man is a saint, I thought. As saintly as any of those gold-leaf figures in the churches of Sicily. Golden he sat in the punt; golden he sat for the next hour as I paddled him down the river. Golden and bored. Golden, as we landed at the town and as we walked up the street back to my uncle's house. There he refused to change his clothes or to sit by a fire. He kept an eye on the time for his train back to London. By no word did he acknowledge the disasters or the beauties of the world. If they were printed upon him, they were printed upon a husk.

Sixteen years have passed since I dropped Mr. Timberlake in the river and since the sight of his pant-loops destroyed my faith. I have not seen him since, and today I heard that he was dead. He was fifty-seven. His mother, a very old lady with whom he had lived all his life, went into his bedroom when he was getting ready for church and found him lying on the floor in his shirt-sleeves. A stiff collar with the tie half inserted was in one hand. Five minutes before, she told the doctor, she had been speaking to him.

The doctor who looked at the heavy body lying on the single bed saw a middle-aged man, wide rather than stout and with an extraordinary box-like thick-jawed face. He had got fat, my uncle told me, in later years. The heavy liver-coloured cheeks were like the chaps of a hound. Heart disease, it was plain, was the cause of the death of Mr. Timberlake. In death the face was lax, even coarse and degenerate. It was a miracle, the doctor said, that he had lived so long. Any time during the last twenty years the smallest shock might have killed him.

I thought of our afternoon on the river. I thought of him hanging from the tree. I thought of him, indifferent and golden in the meadow. I understood why he had made for himself a protective, sedentary blandness, an automatic smile a collection of phrases. He kept them on like the coat after his ducking. And I understood why—though I had feared it all the time we were on the river—I understood why he did not talk to me about the origin of evil. He was honest. The ape was with us. The ape that merely followed me was already inside Mr. Timberlake eating out his heart.

THE OTHER SIDE OF
THE HEDGE*

BY E. M. FORSTER

M Y PEDOMETER told me that I was twenty-five; and, though it is a shocking thing to stop walking, I was so tired that I sat down on a milestone to rest. People outstripped me, jeering as they did so, but I was too apathetic to feel resentful, and even when Miss Eliza Dimbleby, the great educationist, swept past, exhorting me to persevere, I only smiled and raised my hat.

At first I thought I was going to be like my brother, whom I had had to leave by the roadside a year or two round the corner. He had wasted his breath on singing, and his strength on helping others. But I had travelled more wisely, and now it was only the monotony of the highway that oppressed me—dust under foot and brown crackling hedges on either side, ever since I could remember.

And I had already dropped several things—indeed, the road behind was strewn with the things we all had dropped; and the white dust was settling down on them, so that already they looked no better than stones. My muscles were so weary that I could not even bear the weight of those things I still carried. I slid off the milestone into the road, and lay there prostrate, with my face to the great parched hedge, praying that I might give up.

A little puff of air revived me. It seemed to come from the hedge; and, when I opened my eyes, there was a glint of light through the tangle of boughs and dead leaves. The hedge could not be as thick as usual. In my weak, morbid state, I longed to

* from The Collected Tales of E. M. Forster

force my way in, and see what was on the other side. No one was in sight, or I should not have dared to try. For we of the road do not admit in conversation that there is another side at all.

I yielded to the temptation, saying to myself that I would come back in a minute. The thorns scratched my face, and I had to use my arms as a shield, depending on my feet alone to push me forward. Halfway through I would have gone back, for in the passage all the things I was carrying were scraped off me, and my clothes were torn. But I was so wedged that return was impossible, and I had to wriggle blindly forward, expecting every moment that my strength would fail me, and that I should perish in the undergrowth.

Suddenly cold water closed round my head, and I seemed sinking down for ever. I had fallen out of the hedge into a deep pool. I rose to the surface at last, crying for help, and I heard someone on the opposite bank laugh and say: "Another!" And then I was twitched out and laid panting on the dry ground.

Even when the water was out of my eyes, I was still dazed, for I had never been in so large a space, nor seen such grass and sunshine. The blue sky was no longer a strip, and beneath it the earth had risen gradually into hills—clean, bare buttresses, with beech trees in their folds, and meadows and clear pools at their feet. But the hills were not high, and there was in the landscape a sense of human occupation—so that one might have called it a park, or garden, if the words did not imply a certain triviality and constraint.

As soon as I got my breath, I turned to my rescuer and said: "Where does this place lead to?"

"Nowhere, thank the Lord!" said he, and laughed. He was a man of fifty or sixty—just the kind of age we mistrust on the road—but there was no anxiety in his manner, and his voice was that of a boy of eighteen.

"But it must lead somewhere!" I cried, too much surprised at his answer to thank him for saving my life.

"He wants to know where it leads!" he shouted to some men on the hill side, and they laughed back, and waved their caps.

I noticed then that the pool into which I had fallen was really a moat which bent round to the left and to the right, and that the hedge followed it continually. The hedge was green on this side—its roots showed through the clear water, and fish swam about in them—and it was wreathed over with dog-roses and Traveller's Joy. But it was a barrier, and in a moment I lost all pleasure in the grass, the sky, the trees, the happy men and women, and realized that the place was but a prison, for all its beauty and extent.

We moved away from the boundary, and then followed a path almost parallel to it, across the meadows. I found it difficult walking, for I was always trying to out-distance my companion, and there was no advantage in doing this if the place led nowhere. I had never kept step with anyone since I left my brother.

I amused him by stopping suddenly and saying disconsolately, "This is perfectly terrible. One cannot advance: one cannot progress. Now we of the road——"

"Yes. I know."

"I was going to say, we advance continually."

"I know."

"We are always learning, expanding, developing. Why, even in my short life I have seen a great deal of advance—the Transvaal War, the Fiscal Question, Christian Science, Radium. Here for example—"

I took out my pedometer, but it still marked twenty-five, not a degree more.

"Oh, it's stopped! I meant to show you. It should have registered all the time I was walking with you. But it makes me only twenty-five."

"Many things don't work in here," he said. "One day a man brought in a Lee-Metford, and that wouldn't work."

"The laws of science are universal in their application. It must be the water in the moat that has injured the machinery. In normal conditions everything works. Science and the spirit of emulation—those are the forces that have made us what we are."

I had to break off and acknowledge the pleasant greetings of people whom we passed. Some of them were singing, some talking, some engaged in gardening, hay-making, or other rudimentary industries. They all seemed happy; and I might have been happy too, if I could have forgotten that the place led nowhere.

I was startled by a young man who came sprinting across our path, took a little fence in fine style, and went tearing over a ploughed field till he plunged into a lake, across which he began to swim. Here was true energy, and I exclaimed: "A cross-country race! Where are the others?"

"There are no others," my companion replied; and, later on, when we passed some long grass from which came the voice of a girl singing exquisitely to herself, he said again: "There are no others." I was bewildered at the waste in production, and murmured to myself, "What does it all mean?"

He said: "It means nothing but itself"—and he repeated the words slowly, as if I were a child.

"I understand," I said quietly, "but I do not agree. Every achievement is worthless unless it is a link in the chain of development. And I must not trespass on your kindness any longer. I must get back somehow to the road, and have my pedometer mended."

"First, you must see the gates," he replied, "for we have gates, though we never use them."

I yielded politely, and before long we reached the moat again, at a point where it was spanned by a bridge. Over the bridge was a big gate, as white as ivory, which was fitted into a gap in the boundary hedge. The gate opened outwards, and I exclaimed in amazement, for from it ran a road—just such a road as I had left—dusty under foot, with brown crackling hedges on either side as far as the eye could reach.

"That's my road!" I cried.

He shut the gate and said: "But not your part of the road. It is through this gate that humanity went out countless ages ago, when it was first seized with the desire to walk."

I denied this, observing that the part of the road I myself had left was not more than two miles off. But with the obstinacy of his years he repeated: "It is the same road. This is the beginning, and though it seems to run straight away from us, it doubles so often, that it is never far from our boundary and sometimes touches it." He stooped down by the moat, and traced on its moist margin an absurd figure like a maze. As we walked back through the meadows, I tried to convince him of his mistake.

"The road sometimes doubles, to be sure, but that is part of our discipline. Who can doubt that its general tendency is onward? To what goal we know not—it may be to some mountain where we shall touch the sky, it may be over precipices into the sea. But that it goes forward—who can doubt that? It is the thought of that that makes us strive to excel, each in his own way, and gives us an impetus which is lacking with you. Now that man who passed us—it's true that he ran well, and jumped well, and swam well; but we have men who can run better, and men who can jump better, and who can swim better. Specialization has produced results which would surprise you. Similarly, that girl——"

Here I interrupted myself to exclaim: "Good gracious me! I could have sworn it was Miss Eliza Dimbleby over there, with her feet in the fountain!"

He believed that it was.

"Impossible! I left her on the road, and she is due to lecture this evening at Tunbridge Wells. Why, her train leaves Cannon Street in—of course my watch has stopped like everything else. She is the last person to be here."

"People always are astonished at meeting each other. All kinds come through the hedge, and come at all times—when they are drawing ahead in the race, when they are lagging behind, when they are left for dead. I often stand near the boundary listening to the sounds of the road—you know what they are—and wonder if anyone will turn aside. It is my great happiness to help someone out of the moat, as I helped you. For our country fills up slowly, though it was meant for all mankind."

"Mankind have other aims," I said gently, for I thought him well-meaning; "and I must join them." I bade him good evening, for the sun was declining, and I wished to be on the road by nightfall. To my alarm, he caught hold of me, crying: "You are not to go yet!" I tried to shake him off, for we had no interests in common, and his civility was becoming irksome to me. But for all my struggles the tiresome old man would not let go; and, as wrestling is not my specialty, I was obliged to follow him.

It was true that I could have never found alone the place where I came in, and I hoped that, when I had seen the other sights about which he was worrying, he would take me back to it. But I was determined not to sleep in the country, for I mistrusted it, and the people too, for all their friendliness. Hungry though I was, I would not join them in their evening meals of milk and fruit, and, when they gave me flowers, I flung them away as soon as I could do so unobserved. Already they were lying down for the night like cattle—some out on the bare hillside, others in groups under the beeches. In the light of an orange sunset I hurried on with my unwelcome guide, dead tired, faint for want of food, but murmuring indomitably: "Give me life, with its struggles and victories, with its failures and hatreds, with its deep moral meaning and its unknown goal!"

At last we came to a place where the encircling moat was spanned by another bridge, and where another gate interrupted the line of the boundary hedge. It was different from the first gate; for it was half transparent like horn, and opened inwards. But through it, in the waning light, I saw again just such a road as I had left—monotonous, dusty, with brown crackling hedges on either side, as far as the eye could reach.

I was strangely disquieted at the sight, which seemed to deprive me of all self-control. A man was passing us, returning for the night to the hills, with a scythe over his shoulder and a can of some liquid in his hand. I forgot the destiny of our race. I forgot the road that lay before my eyes, and I sprang at him, wrenched the can out of his hand, and began to drink.

It was nothing stronger than beer, but in my exhausted state it overcame me in a moment. As in a dream, I saw the old man shut the gate, and heard him say: "This is where your road ends, and through this gate humanity—all that is left of it— will come in to us."

Though my senses were sinking into oblivion, they seemed to expand ere they reached it. They perceived the magic song of

nightingales, and the odour of invisible hay, and stars piercing
the fading sky. The man whose beer I had stolen lowered me
down gently to sleep off its effects, and, as he did so, I saw that
he was my brother.

BROOKSMITH[*]

BY HENRY JAMES

W E ARE scattered now, the friends of the late Mr. Oliver
Offord; but whenever we chance to meet I think we are
conscious of a certain esoteric respect for each other. "Yes, you
too have been in Arcadia," we seem not too grumpily to allow.
When I pass the house in Mansfield Street I remember that
Arcadia was there. I don't know who has it now, and don't want
to know; it's enough to be so sure that if I should ring the bell
there would be no such luck for me as that Brooksmith should
open the door. Mr. Offord, the most agreeable, the most attach-
ing of bachelors, was a retired diplomatist, living on his pension and on something of his own over and above; a good deal
confined, by his infirmities, to his fireside and delighted to be
found there any afternoon in the year, from five o'clock on, by
such visitors as Brooksmith allowed to come up. Brooksmith
was his butler and his most intimate friend, to whom we all
stood, or I should say sat, in the same relation in which the subject of the sovereign finds himself to the prime minister. By
having been for years, in foreign lands, the most delightful
Englishman any one had ever known, Mr. Offord had in my
opinion rendered signal service to his country. But I suppose he
had been too much liked—liked even by those who didn't like
it—so that as people of that sort never get titles or dotations for

[*] from *The Lesson of the Master*

the horrid things they've *not* done, his principal reward was simply that we went to see him.

Oh we went perpetually, and it was not our fault if he was not overwhelmed with this particular honour. Any visitor who came once came again; to come merely once was a slight nobody, I'm sure, had ever put upon him. His circle therefore was essentially composed of habitués, who were habitués for each other as well as for him, as those of a happy salon should be. I remember vividly every element of the place, down to the intensely Londonish look of the grey opposite houses, in the gap of the white curtains of the high windows, and the exact spot where, on a particular afternoon, I put down my tea-cup for Brooksmith, lingering an instant, to gather it up as if he were plucking a flower. Mr. Offord's drawing-room was indeed Brooksmith's garden, his pruned and tended human parterre, and if we all flourished there and grew well in our places it was largely owing to his supervision.

Many persons have heard much, though most have doubtless seen little, of the famous institution of the salon, and many are born to the depression of knowing that this finest flower of social life refuses to bloom where the English tongue is spoken. The explanation is usually that our women have not the skill to cultivate it—the art to direct through a smiling land, between suggestive shores, a sinuous stream of talk. My affectionate, my pious memory of Mr. Offord contradicts this induction only, I fear, more insidiously to confirm it. The sallow and slightly smoked drawing-room in which he spent so large a portion of the last years of his life certainly deserved the distinguished name; but on the other hand it couldn't be said at all to owe its stamp to any intervention throwing into relief the fact that there was no Mrs. Offord. The dear man had indeed, at the most, been capable of one of those sacrifices to which women are deemed peculiarly apt: he had recognised—under the influence, in some degree, it is true, of physical infirmity— that if you wish people to find you at home you must manage not to be out. He had in short accepted the truth which many dabblers in the social art are slow to learn, that you must really, as they say, take a line, and that the only way as yet discovered of being at home is to stay at home. Finally his own fireside had become a summary of his habits. Why should he ever have left it?—since this would have been leaving what was notoriously pleasantest in London, the compact charmed cluster (thinning away indeed into casual couples) round the fine old last-century chimney-piece which, with the exception of the remarkable collection of miniatures, was the best thing the place contained. Mr. Offord wasn't rich; he had nothing but his pension and the use for life of the somewhat superannuated house.

When I'm reminded by some opposed discomfort of the present hour how perfectly we were all handled there, I ask myself once more what had been the secret of such perfection. One had taken it for granted at the time, for anything that is supremely good produces more acceptance than surprise. I felt we were all happy, but I didn't consider how our happiness was managed. And yet there were questions to be asked, questions that strike me as singularly obvious now that there's nobody to answer them. Mr. Offord had solved the insoluble; he had, without feminine help—save in the sense that ladies were dying to come to him and that he saved the lives of several—established a salon; but I might have guessed that there was a method in his madness, a law in his success. He hadn't hit it off by a mere fluke. There was an art in it all, and how was the art so hidden? Who indeed if it came to that was the occult artist? Launching this enquiry the other day I had already got hold of the tail of my reply. I was helped by the very wonder of some of the conditions that came back to me—those that used to seem as natural as sunshine in a fine climate.

How was it for instance that we never were a crowd, never either too many or too few, always the right people *with* the right people—there must really have been no wrong people at all—always coming and going, never sticking fast nor over-staying, yet never popping in or out with an indecorous familiarity? How was it that we all sat where we wanted and moved when we wanted and met whom we wanted and escaped whom we wanted; joining, according to the accident of inclination, the general circle or falling in with a single talker on a convenient sofa? Why were all the sofas so convenient, the accidents so happy, the talkers so ready, the listeners so willing, the subjects presented to you in a rotation as quickly foreordained as the courses at dinner? A dearth of topics would have been as unheard of as a lapse in the service. These speculations couldn't fail to lead me to the fundamental truth that Brooksmith had been somehow at the bottom of the mystery. If he hadn't established the salon at least he had carried it on. Brooksmith in short was the artist!

We felt this covertly at the time, without formulating it, and were conscious, as an ordered and prosperous community, of his evenhanded justice, all untainted with flunkeyism. He had none of that vulgarity—his touch was infinitely fine. The delicacy of it was clear to me on the first occasion my eyes rested, as they were so often to rest again, on the domestic revealed, in the turbid light of the street, by the opening of the housedoor. I saw on the spot that though he had plenty of school he carried it without arrogance—he had remained articulate and human. *L'Ecole Anglaise* Mr. Offord used laughingly to call him when, later on, it happened more than once that we had some conversation about him. But I remember accusing Mr. Offord of not doing him quite ideal justice. That he wasn't one of the giants of the school, however, was admitted by my old friend, who really understood him perfectly and was devoted to him, as I shall show; which doubtless poor Brooksmith had himself felt, to his cost, when his value in the market was originally determined. The utility of his class in general is estimated by the foot and the inch, and poor Brooksmith had only about five feet three to put into circulation. He acknowledged the inadequacy of this provision, and I'm sure was penetrated with the everlasting fitness of the relation between service and stature. If *he* had been Mr. Offord he certainly would have found Brooksmith wanting, and indeed the laxity of his employer on this score was one of many things he had had to condone and to which he had at last indulgently adapted himself.

I remember the old man's saying to me: "Oh my servants, if they can live with me a fortnight they can live with me for ever. But it's the first fortnight that tries 'em." It was in that first fortnight for instance that Brooksmith had had to learn that he was exposed to being addressed as "my dear fellow" and "my poor child." Strange and deep must such a probation have been to him, and he doubtless emerged from it tempered and purified. This was written to a certain extent in his appearance; in his spare brisk little person, in his cloistered white face and extraordinarily polished hair, which told of responsibility, looked as if it were kept up to the same high standard as the plate; in his small clear anxious eyes, even in the permitted, though not exactly encouraged, tuft on his chin. "He thinks me rather mad, but I've broken him in, and now he likes the place, he likes the company," said the old man. I embraced this fully after I had become aware that Brooksmith's main characteristic was a deep and shy refinement, though I remember I was rather puzzled when, on another occasion, Mr. Offord remarked: "What he likes is the talk—mingling in the conversation." I was conscious I had never seen Brooksmith permit himself this freedom, but I guessed in a moment that what Mr. Offord alluded to was a participation more intense than any speech could have represented—that of being perpetually present on a hundred legitimate pretexts, errands, necessities, and breathing the very atmosphere of criticism, the famous criticism of life. "Quite an education, sir, isn't it, sir?" he said to me one day at the foot of the stairs when he was letting me out; and I've always remembered the words and the tone as the first sign of the quickening drama of poor Brooksmith's fate. It was indeed an education, but to what was this sensitive young man of thirty-five, of the servile class, being educated?

Practically and inevitably, for the time, to companionship, to the perpetual, the even exaggerated reference and appeal of a person brought to dependence by his time of life and his infirmities and always addicted moreover—this was the exaggeration—to the art of giving you pleasure by letting you do things for him. There were certain things Mr. Offord was capable of pretending he liked you to do even when he didn't—this, I mean, if he thought you liked them. If it happened that you didn't either—which was rare, yet might be—of course there were cross-purposes; but Brooksmith was there to prevent their

going very far. This was precisely the way he acted as modera-
tor; he averted misunderstandings or cleared them up. He had
been capable, strange as it may appear, of acquiring for this
purpose an insight into the French tongue, which was often
used at Mr. Offord's; for besides being habitual to most of the
foreigners, and they were many, who haunted the place or arrived with letters—letters often requiring a little worried con-
sideration, of which Brooksmith always had cognisance—it
had really become the primary language of the master of the
house. I don't know if all the *malentendus* were in French, but
almost all the explanations were, and this didn't a bit prevent
Brooksmith's following them. I know Mr. Offord used to read
passages to him from Montaigne and Saint-Simon, for he read
perpetually when alone—when *they* were alone, that is—and
Brooksmith was always about. Perhaps you'll say no wonder
Mr. Offord's butler regarded him as "rather mad." However, if
I'm not sure what he thought about Montaigne I'm convinced
he admired Saint-Simon. A certain feeling for letters must have
rubbed off on him from the mere handling of his master's
books, which he was always carrying to and fro and putting
back in their places.

I often noticed that if an anecdote or a quotation, much
more a lively discussion, was going forward, he would, if busy
with the fire or the curtains, the lamp or the tea, find a pretext
for remaining in the room till the point should be reached. If his
purpose was to catch it you weren't discreet, you were in fact
scarce human, to call him off, and I shall never forget a look, a
hard stony stare—I caught it in its passage—which, one day
when there were a good many people in the room, he fastened
upon the footman who was helping him in the service and who,
in an undertone, had asked him some irrelevant question. It
was the only manifestation of harshness I ever observed on
Brooksmith's part, and I at first wondered what was the matter.
Then I became conscious that Mr. Offord was relating a very
curious anecdote, never before perhaps made so public, and
imparted to the narrator by an eye-witness of the fact, bearing
on Lord Byron's life in Italy. Nothing would induce me to reproduce it here, but Brooksmith had been in danger of losing it.

If I ever should venture to reproduce it I shall feel how much I lose in not having my fellow auditor to refer to.

The first day Mr. Offord's door was closed was therefore a dark date in contemporary history. It was raining hard and my umbrella was wet, but Brooksmith received it from me exactly as if this were a preliminary for going upstairs. I observed however that instead of putting it away he held it poised and trickling over the rug, and I then became aware that he was looking at me with deep acknowledging eyes—his air of universal responsibility. I immediately understood—there was scarce need of question and answer as they passed between us. When I took in that our good friend had given up as never before, though only for the occasion, I exclaimed dolefully: "What a difference it will make—and to how many people!"

"I shall be one of them, sir!" said Brooksmith; and that was the beginning of the end.

Mr. Offord came down again, but the spell was broken, the great sign being that the conversation was for the first time not directed. It wandered and stumbled, a little frightened, like a lost child—it had let go the nurse's hand. "The worst of it is that now we shall talk about my health—*c'est la fin de tout,*" Mr. Offord said when he reappeared; and then I recognised what a note of change that would be—for he had never tolerated anything so provincial. We "ran" to each other's health as little as to the daily weather. The talk became ours, in a word—not his; and as ours, even when *he* talked, it could only be inferior. In this form it was a distress to Brooksmith, whose attention now wandered from it altogether: he had so much closer a vision of his master's intimate conditions than our superficialities represented. There were better hours, and he was more in and out of the room, but I could see he was conscious of the decline, almost of the collapse, of our great institution. He seemed to wish to take counsel with me about it, to feel responsible for its going on in some form or other. When for the second period—the first had lasted several days—he had to tell me that his employer didn't receive, I half-expected to hear him say after a moment "Do you think I ought to, sir, in his place?"—as he

might have asked me, with the return of autumn, if I thought he
had better light the drawing-room fire.

He had a resigned philosophic sense of what his guests—
our guests, as I came to regard them in our colloquies—would
expect. His feeling was that he wouldn't absolutely have approved of himself as a substitute for Mr. Offord; but he was so
saturated with the religion of habit that he would have made,
for our friends, the necessary sacrifice to the divinity. He would
take them on a little further and till they could look about them.
I think I saw him also mentally confronted with the opportunity
to deal—for once in his life—with some of his own dumb pref-
erences, his limitations of sympathy, *weeding* a little in
prospect and returning to a purer tradition. It was not unknown
to me that he considered that toward the end of our host's career
a certain laxity of selection had crept in.

At last it came to be the case that we all found the closed
door more often than the open one; but even when it was closed
Brooksmith managed a crack for me to squeeze through; so
that practically I never turned away without having paid a visit.
The difference simply came to be that the visit was to
Brooksmith. It took place in the hall, at the familiar foot of the
stairs, and we didn't sit down, at least Brooksmith didn't;
moreover it was devoted wholly to one topic and always had the
air of being already over—beginning, so to say, at the end. But
it was always interesting—it always gave me something to
think about. It's true that the subject of my meditation was ever
the same—ever "It's all very well, but what *will* become of
Brooksmith?" Even my private answer to this question left me
still unsatisfied. No doubt Mr. Offord would provide for him,
but *what* would he provide?—that was the great point. He
couldn't provide society; and society had become a necessity
of Brooksmith's nature. I must add that he never showed a
symptom of what I may call sordid solicitude—anxiety on his
own account. He was rather livid and intensely grave, as befitted a man before whose eyes the "shade of that which once was
great" was passing away. He had the solemnity of a person
winding up, under depressing circumstances, a long-established
and celebrated business; he was a kind of social executor or

liquidator. But his manner seemed to testify exclusively to the uncertainty of *our* future. I couldn't in those days have afforded it—I lived in two rooms in Jermyn Street and didn't "keep a man"; but even if my income had permitted I shouldn't have ventured to say to Brooksmith (emulating Mr. Offord) "My dear fellow, I'll take you on." The whole tone of our intercourse was so much more an implication that it was *I* who should now want a lift. Indeed there was a tacit assurance in Brooksmith's whole attitude that he should have me on his mind.

One of the most assiduous members of our circle had been Lady Kenyon, and I remember his telling me one day that her ladyship had in spite of her own infirmities, lately much aggravated, been in person to inquire. In answer to this I remarked that she would feel it more than any one. Brooksmith had a pause before saying in a certain tone—there's no reproducing some of his tones—"I'll go and see her." I went to see her myself and learned he had waited on her; but when I said to her, in the form of a joke but with a core of earnest, that when all was over some of us ought to combine, to club together, and set Brooksmith up on his own account, she replied a trifle disappointingly: "Do you mean in a public-house?" I looked at her in a way that I think Brooksmith himself would have approved, and then I answered: "Yes, the Offord Arms." What I had meant of course was that for the love of art itself we ought to look to it that such a peculiar faculty and so much acquired experience shouldn't be wasted. I really think that if we had caused a few black-edged cards to be struck off and circulated—"Mr. Brooksmith will continue to receive on the old premises from four to seven; business carried on as usual during the alterations"—the greater number of us would have rallied.

Several times he took me upstairs—always by his own proposal—and our dear old friend, in bed (in a curious flowered and brocaded casaque which made him, especially as his head was tied up in a handkerchief to match, look, to my imagination, like the dying Voltaire) held for ten minutes a sadly shrunken little salon. I felt indeed each time as if I were attending the last *coucher* of some social sovereign. He was royally

whimsical about his sufferings and not at all concerned—quite
as if the Constitution provided for the case—about his successor. He glided over *our* sufferings charmingly, and none of his
jokes—it was a gallant abstention, some of them would have
been so easy—were at our expense. Now and again, I confess,
there was one at Brooksmith's, but so pathetically sociable as
to make the excellent man look at me in a way that seemed to
say: "Do exchange a glance with me, or I shan't be able to stand
it." What he wasn't able to stand was not what Mr. Offord said
about him, but what he wasn't able to say in return. His idea of
conversation for himself was giving you the convenience of
speaking to him; and when he went to "see" Lady Kenyon for
instance it was to carry her the tribute of his receptive silence.
Where would the speech of his betters have been if proper service had been a manifestation of sound? In that case the fundamental difference would have had to be shown by *their*
dumbness, and many of them, poor things, were dumb enough
without that provision. Brooksmith took an unfailing interest
in the preservation of the fundamental difference; it was the
thing he had most on his conscience.

What had become of it however when Mr. Offord passed
away like any inferior person—was relegated to eternal stillness after the manner of a butler above-stairs? His aspect on the
event—for the several successive days—may be imagined, and
the multiplication by funereal observance of the things he
didn't say. When everything was over—it was late the same
day—I knocked at the door of the house of mourning as I so often had done before. I could never call on Mr. Offord again, but
I had come literally to call on Brooksmith. I wanted to ask him
if there was anything I could do for him, tainted with vagueness
as this enquiry could only be. My presumptuous dream of taking him into my own service had died away; my service wasn't
worth his being taken into. My offer could only be to help him
to find another place, and yet there was an indelicacy, as it
were, in taking for granted that his thoughts would immediately be fixed on another. I had a hope that he would be able to
give his life a different form—though certainly not the form,
the frequent result of such bereavements, of his setting up a lit-

tle shop. That would have been dreadful; for I should have wished to forward any enterprise he might embark in, yet how could I have brought myself to go and pay him shillings and take back coppers over a counter? My visit then was simply an intended compliment. He took it as such, gratefully and with all the tact in the world. He knew I really couldn't help him and that I knew he knew I couldn't; but we discussed the situation—with a good deal of elegant generality—at the foot of the stairs, in the hall already dismantled, where I had so often discussed other situations with him. The executors were in possession, as was still more apparent when he made me pass for a few minutes into the dining-room, where various objects were muffled up for removal.

Two definite facts, however, he had to communicate; one being that he was to leave the house for ever that night (servants, for some mysterious reason, seem always to depart by night), and the other—he mentioned it only at the last and with hesitation—that he was already aware his late master had left him a legacy of eighty pounds. "I'm very glad," I said, and Brooksmith was of the same mind: "It was so like him to think of me." This was all that passed between us on the subject, and I know nothing of his judgement of Mr. Offord's memento. Eighty pounds are always eighty pounds, and no one has ever left *me* an equal sum; but, all the same, for Brooksmith, I was disappointed. I don't know what I had expected, but it was almost a shock. Eighty pounds might stock a small shop—a *very* small shop; but, I repeat, I couldn't bear to think of that. I asked my friend if he had been able to save a little, and he replied: "No, sir; I've had to do things." I didn't enquire what things they might have been; they were his own affair, and I took his word for them as assentingly as if he had had the greatness of an ancient house to keep up; especially as there was something in his manner that seemed to convey a prospect of further sacrifice.

"I shall have to turn round a bit, sir—I shall have to look about me," he said; and then he added indulgently, magnanimously: "If you should happen to hear of anything for me—"

I couldn't let him finish; this was, in its essence, too much in

the really grand manner. It would be a help to my getting him
off my mind to be able to pretend I *could* find the right place,
and that help he wished to give me, for it was doubtless painful
to him to see me in so false a position. I interposed with a few
words to the effect of how well aware I was that wherever he
should go, whatever he should do, he would miss our old friend
terribly—miss him even more than I should, having been with
him so much more. This led him to make the speech that has remained with me as the very text of the whole episode.

"Oh sir, it's sad for *you,* very sad indeed, and for a great
many gentlemen and ladies; that it is, sir. But for me, sir, it is,
if I may say so, still graver even than that: it's just the loss of
something that was everything. For me, sir," he went on with
rising tears, "he was just *all,* if you know what I mean, sir. You
have others, sir, I dare say—not that I would have you understand me to speak of them as in any way tantamount. But you
have the pleasures of society, sir; if it's only in talking about
him, sir, as I dare say you do freely—for all his blest memory
has to fear from it—with gentlemen and ladies who have had
the same honour. That's not for me, sir, and I've to keep my associations to myself. Mr. Offord was *my* society, and now, you
see, I just haven't any. You go back to conversation, sir, after all,
and I go back to my place," Brooksmith stammered, without
exaggerated irony or dramatic bitterness, but with a flat un-
studied veracity and his hand on the knob of the street-door. He
turned it to let me out and then he added: "I just go downstairs,
sir, again, and I stay there."

"My poor child," I replied in my emotion, quite as Mr.
Offord used to speak, "my dear fellow, leave it to me: *we'll* look
after you, we'll all do something for you."

"Ah if you could give me some one *like* him! But there ain't
two such in the world," Brooksmith said as we parted.

He had given me his address—the place where he would be
to be heard of. For a long time I had no occasion to make use of
the information: he proved on trial so very difficult a case. The
people who knew him and had known Mr. Offord didn't want
to take him, and yet I couldn't bear to try to thrust him among
strangers—strangers to his past when not to his present. I

spoke to many of our old friends about him and found them all governed by the odd mixture of feelings of which I myself was conscious—as well as disposed, further, to entertain a suspicion that he was "spoiled," with which I then would have nothing to do. In plain terms a certain embarrassment, a sensible awkwardness when they thought of it, attached to the idea of using him as a menial; they had met him so often in society. Many of them would have asked him, and did ask him, or rather did ask me to ask him, to come and see them; but a mere visiting-list was not what I wanted for him. He was too short for people who were very particular; nevertheless I heard of an opening in a diplomatic household which led me to write him a note, though I was looking much less for something grand than for something human. Five days later I heard from him. The secretary's wife had decided, after keeping him waiting till then, that she couldn't take a servant out of a house in which there hadn't been a lady. The note had a P.S.: "It's a good job there wasn't, sir, such a lady as some."

A week later he came to see me and told me he was "suited," committed to some highly respectable people—they were something quite immense in the City—who lived on the Bayswater side of the Park. "I dare say it will be rather poor, sir," he admitted; "but I've seen the fireworks, haven't I, sir?— it can't be fireworks every night. After Mansfield Street there ain't much choice." There was a certain amount, however, it seemed; for the following year, calling one day on a country cousin, a lady of a certain age who was spending a fortnight in town with some friends of her own, a family unknown to me and resident in Chester Square, the door of the house was opened, to my surprise and gratification, by Brooksmith in person. When I came out I had some conversation with him from which I gathered that he had found the large City people too dull for endurance, and I guessed, though he didn't say it, that he had found them vulgar as well. I don't know what judgement he would have passed on his actual patrons if my relative hadn't been their friend; but in view of that connexion he abstained from comment.

None was necessary, however, for before the lady in question brought her visit to a close they honoured me with an invitation to dinner, which I accepted. There was a largeish party on the occasion, but I confess I thought of Brooksmith rather more than of the seated company. They required no depth of attention—they were all referable to usual irredeemable inevitable types. It was the world of cheerful commonplace and conscious gentility and prosperous density, a full-fed material insular world, a world of hideous florid plate and ponderous order and thin conversation. There wasn't a word said about Byron, or even about a minor bard then much in view. Nothing would have induced me to look at Brooksmith in the course of the repast, and I felt sure that not even my overturning the wine would have induced him to meet my eye. We were in intellectual sympathy—we felt, as regards each other, a degree of social responsibility. In short we had been in Arcadia together, and we had both come to *this*! No wonder we were ashamed to be confronted. When he had helped on my overcoat, as I was going away, we parted, for the first time since the earliest days of Mansfield Street, in silence. I thought he looked lean and wasted, and I guessed that his new place wasn't more "human" than his previous one. There was plenty of beef and beer, but there was no reciprocity. The question for him to have asked before accepting the position wouldn't have been "How many footmen are kept?" but "How much imagination?"

The next time I went to the house—I confess it wasn't very soon—I encountered his successor, a personage who evidently enjoyed the good fortune of never having quitted his natural level. Could any be higher? he seemed to ask—over the heads of three footmen and even of some visitors. He made me feel as if Brooksmith were dead; but I didn't dare to enquire—I couldn't have borne his "I haven't the least idea, sir." I dispatched a note to the address that worthy had given me after Mr. Offord's death, but I received no answer. Six months later however I was favoured with a visit from an elderly dreary dingy person who introduced herself to me as Mr. Brooksmith's aunt and from whom I learned that he was out of place and out of health and had allowed her to come and say to me that if I could spare half an hour to look in at him he would take it as a rare honour.

I went the next day—his messenger had given me a new address—and found my friend lodged in a short sordid street in
Marylebone, one of those corners of London that wear the last
expression of sickly meanness. The room into which I was
shown was above the small establishment of a dyer and cleaner
who had inflated kid gloves and discoloured shawls in his
shop-front. There was a great deal of grimy infant life up and
down the place, and there was a hot moist smell within, as of
the "boiling" of dirty linen. Brooksmith sat with a blanket over
his legs at a clean little window where, from behind stiff bluish-
white curtains, he could look across at a huckster's and a tin-
smith's and a small greasy public-house. He had passed
through an illness and was convalescent, and his mother, as
well as his aunt, was in attendance on him. I liked the nearest
relative, who was bland and intensely humble, but I had my
doubts of the remoter, whom I connected perhaps unjustly with
the opposite public-house—she seemed somehow greasy with
the same grease—and whose furtive eye followed every movement of my hand as if to see if it weren't going into my pocket.
It didn't take this direction—I couldn't, unsolicited, put myself
at that sort of ease with Brooksmith. Several times the door
of the room opened and mysterious old women peeped in
and shuffled back again. I don't know who they were; poor
Brooksmith seemed encompassed with vague prying beery fe-
males.

He was vague himself, and evidently weak, and much embarrassed, and not an allusion was made between us to Mansfield Street. The vision of the salon of which he had been an
ornament hovered before me however, by contrast, sufficiently.
He assured me he was really getting better, and his mother remarked that he would come round if he could only get his spirits up. The aunt echoed this opinion, and I became more sure
that in her own case she knew where to go for such a purpose.
I'm afraid I was rather weak with my old friend, for I neglected
the opportunity, so exceptionally good, to rebuke the levity
which had led him to throw up honourable positions—fine stiff
steady berths in Bayswater and Belgravia, with morning
prayers, as I knew, attached to one of them. Very likely his

reasons had been profane and sentimental; he didn't want
morning prayers, he wanted to be somebody's dear fellow; but
I couldn't be the person to rebuke him. He shuffled these
episodes out of sight—I saw he had no wish to discuss them. I
noted further, strangely enough, that it would probably be a
questionable pleasure for him to see me again: he doubted now
even of my power to condone his aberrations. He didn't wish to
have to explain; and his behaviour was likely in future to need
explanation. When I bade him farewell he looked at me a moment with eyes that said everything: "How can I talk about
those exquisite years in this place, before these people, with the
old women poking their heads in? It was very good of you to
come to see me; it wasn't my idea—*she* brought you. We've
said everything; it's over; you'll lose all patience with me, and
I'd rather you shouldn't see the rest." I sent him some money in
a letter the next day, but I saw the rest only in the light of a barren sequel.

A whole year after my visit to him I became aware once, in
dining out, that Brooksmith was one of the several servants
who hovered behind our chairs. He hadn't opened the door of
the house to me, nor had I recognised him in the array of retain-
ers in the hall. This time I tried to catch his eye, but he never
gave me a chance, and when he handed me a dish I could only
be careful to thank him audibly. Indeed I partook of two *entrées*
of which I had my doubts, subsequently converted into certain-
ties, in order not to snub him. He looked well enough in health,
but much older, and wore in an exceptionally marked degree
the glazed and expressionless mask of the British domestic *de
race*. I saw with dismay that if I hadn't known him I should
have taken him, on the showing of his countenance, for an extravagant illustration of irresponsive servile gloom. I said to
myself that he had become a reactionary, gone over to the
Philistines, thrown himself into religion, the religion of his
"place," like a foreign lady *sur le retour*. I divined moreover
that he was only engaged for the evening—he had become a
mere waiter, had joined the band of the white-waistcoated who
"go out." There was something pathetic in this fact—it was a
terrible vulgarisation of Brooksmith. It was the mercenary

prose of butlerhood; he had given up the struggle for the poetry. If reciprocity was what he had missed where was the reciprocity now? Only in the bottoms of the wine-glasses and the
five shillings—or whatever they get—clapped into his hand by
the permanent man. However, I supposed he had taken up a
precarious branch of his profession because it after all sent him
less downstairs. His relations with London society were more
superficial, but they were of course more various. As I went
away on this occasion I looked out for him eagerly among the
four or five attendants whose perpendicular persons, fluting
the walls of London passages, are supposed to lubricate the
process of departure; but he was not on duty. I asked one of
the others if he were not in the house, and received the prompt
answer: "Just left, sir. Anything I can do for you, sir?" I wanted
to say "Please give him my kind regards"; but I abstained—I
didn't want to compromise him; and I never came across him
again.

Often and often, in dining out, I looked for him, sometimes
accepting invitations on purpose to multiply the chances of my
meeting him. But always in vain; so that as I met many other
members of the casual class over and over again I at last
adopted the theory that he always procured a list of expected
guests beforehand and kept away from the banquets which he
thus learned I was to grace. At last I gave up hope, and one day
at the end of three years I received another visit from his aunt.
She was drearier and dingier, almost squalid, and she was in
great tribulation and want. Her sister, Mrs. Brooksmith, had
been dead a year, and three months later her nephew had disappeared. He had always looked after her a bit—since her troubles; I never knew what her troubles had been—and now she
hadn't so much as a petticoat to pawn. She had also a niece, to
whom she had been everything before her troubles, but the
niece had treated her most shameful. These were details; the
great and romantic fact was Brooksmith's final evasion of his
fate. He had gone out to wait one evening as usual, in a white
waistcoat she had done up for him with her own hands—being
due at a large party up Kensington way. But he had never come
home again and had never arrived at the large party, nor at any

party that any one could make out. No trace of him had come to light—no gleam of the white waistcoat had pierced the obscurity of his doom. This news was a sharp shock to me, for I had my ideas about his real destination. His aged relative had promptly, as she said, guessed the worst. Somehow and somewhere he had got out of the way altogether, and now I trust that, with characteristic deliberation, he is changing the plates of the immortal gods. As my depressing visitant also said, he never *had* got his spirits up. I was fortunately able to dismiss her with her own somewhat improved. But the dim ghost of poor Brooksmith is one of those that I see. He had indeed been spoiled.

THE JOCKEY*

BY CARSON McCULLERS

THE JOCKEY came to the doorway of the dining room, then after a moment stepped to one side and stood motionless, with his back to the wall. The room was crowded, as this was the third day of the season and all the hotels in the town were full. In the dining room bouquets of August roses scattered their petals on the white table linen and from the adjoining bar came a warm, drunken wash of voices. The jockey waited with his back to the wall and scrutinized the room with pinched, crêpy eyes. He examined the room until at last his eyes reached a table in a corner diagonally across from him, at which three men were sitting. As he watched, the jockey raised his chin and tilted his head back to one side, his dwarfed body grew rigid, and his hands stiffened so that the fingers curled inward like gray claws. Tense against the wall of the dining room, he watched and waited in this way.

* from *The New Yorker* and *The Ballad of the Sad Cafe*

He was wearing a suit of green Chinese silk that evening, tailored precisely and the size of a costume outfit for a child. The shirt was yellow, the tie striped with pastel colors. He had no hat with him and wore his hair brushed down in a stiff, wet bang on his forehead. His face was drawn, ageless, and gray. There were shadowed hollows at his temples and his mouth was set in a wiry smile. After a time he was aware that he had been seen by one of the three men he had been watching. But the jockey did not nod; he only raised his chin still higher and hooked the thumb of his tense hand in the pocket of his coat.

The three men at the corner table were a trainer, a bookie, and a rich man. The trainer was Sylvester—a large, loosely built fellow with a flushed nose and slow blue eyes. The bookie was Simmons. The rich man was the owner of a horse named Seltzer, which the jockey had ridden that afternoon. The three of them drank whiskey with soda, and a white-coated waiter had just brought on the main course of the dinner.

It was Sylvester who first saw the jockey. He looked away quickly, put down his whiskey glass, and nervously mashed the tip of his red nose with his thumb. "It's Bitsy Barlow," he said. "Standing over there across the room. Just watching us."

"Oh, the jockey," said the rich man. He was facing the wall and he half turned his head to look behind him. "Ask him over."

"God no," Sylvester said.

"He's crazy," Simmons said. The bookie's voice was flat and without inflection. He had the face of a born gambler, carefully adjusted, the expression a permanent deadlock between fear and greed.

"Well, I wouldn't call him that exactly," said Sylvester. "I've known him a long time. He was O.K. until about six months ago. But if he goes on like this, I can't see him lasting out another year. I just can't."

"It was what happened in Miami," said Simmons.

"What?" asked the rich man.

Sylvester glanced across the room at the jockey and wet the corner of his mouth with his red, fleshy tongue. "A accident. A kid got hurt on the track. Broke a leg and a hip. He was a particular pal of Bitsy's. A Irish kid. Not a bad rider, either."

"That's a pity," said the rich man.

"Yeah. They were particular friends," Sylvester said. "You would always find him up in Bitsy's hotel room. They would be playing rummy or else lying on the floor reading the sports page together."

"Well, those things happen," said the rich man.

Simmons cut into his beefsteak. He held his fork prongs downward on the plate and carefully piled on mushrooms with the blade of his knife. "He's crazy," he repeated. "He gives me the creeps."

All the tables in the dining room were occupied. There was a party at the banquet table in the center, and green-white August moths had found their way in from the night and fluttered about the clear candle flames. Two girls wearing flannel slacks and blazers walked arm in arm across the room into the bar. From the main street outside came the echoes of holiday hysteria.

"They claim that in August Saratoga is the wealthiest town per capita in the world." Sylvester turned to the rich man. "What do you think?"

"I wouldn't know," said the rich man. "It may very well be so."

Daintily, Simmons wiped his greasy mouth with the tip of his forefinger. "How about Hollywood? And Wall Street—"

"Wait," said Sylvester. "He's decided to come over here."

The jockey had left the wall and was approaching the table in the corner. He walked with a prim strut, swinging out his legs in a half-circle with each step, his heels biting smartly into the red velvet carpet on the floor. On the way over he brushed against the elbow of a fat woman in white satin at the banquet table; he stepped back and bowed with dandified courtesy, his eyes quite closed. When he had crossed the room he drew up a chair and sat at a corner of the table, between Sylvester and the rich man, without a nod of greeting or a change in his set, gray face.

"Had dinner?" Sylvester asked.

"Some people might call it that." The jockey's voice was high, bitter, clear.

Sylvester put his knife and fork down carefully on his plate.

The rich man shifted his position, turning sidewise in his chair and crossing his legs. He was dressed in twill riding pants, unpolished boots, and a shabby brown jacket—this was his outfit day and night in the racing season, although he was never seen on a horse. Simmons went on with his dinner.

"Like a spot of seltzer water?" asked Sylvester. "Or something like that?"

The jockey didn't answer. He drew a gold cigarette case from his pocket and snapped it open. Inside were a few cigarettes and a tiny gold penknife. He used the knife to cut a cigarette in half. When he had lighted his smoke he held up his hand to a waiter passing by the table. "Kentucky bourbon, please."

"Now, listen, Kid," said Sylvester.

"Don't Kid me."

"Be reasonable. You know you got to behave reasonable."

The jockey drew up the left corner of his mouth in a stiff jeer. His eyes lowered to the food spread out on the table, but instantly he looked up again. Before the rich man was a fish casserole, baked in a cream sauce and garnished with parsley. Sylvester had ordered eggs Benedict. There was asparagus, fresh buttered corn, and a side dish of wet black olives. A plate of French-fried potatoes was in the corner of the table before the jockey. He didn't look at the food again, but kept his pinched eyes on the centerpiece of full-blown lavender roses. "I don't suppose you remember a certain person by the name of McGuire," he said.

"Now, listen," said Sylvester.

The waiter brought the whiskey, and the jockey sat fondling the glass with his small, strong, callused hands. On his wrist was a gold link bracelet that clinked against the table edge. After turning the glass between his palms, the jockey suddenly drank the whiskey neat in two swallows. He set down the glass sharply. "No, I don't suppose your memory is that long and extensive," he said.

"Sure enough, Bitsy," said Sylvester. "What makes you act like this? You hear from the kid today?"

"I received a letter," the jockey said. "The certain person

we were speaking about was taken out from the cast on
Wednesday. One leg is two inches shorter than the other one.
That's all."

Sylvester clucked his tongue and shook his head. "I realize
how you feel."

"Do you?" The jockey was looking at the dishes on the
table. His gaze passed from the fish casserole to the corn, and
finally fixed on the plate of fried potatoes. His face tightened
and quickly he looked up again. A rose shattered and he picked
up one of the petals, bruised it between his thumb and forefinger, and put it in his mouth.

"Well, those things happen," said the rich man.

The trainer and bookie had finished eating, but there was
food left on the serving dishes before their plates. The rich man
dipped his buttery fingers in his water glass and wiped them
with his napkin.

"Well," said the jockey. "Doesn't somebody want me to pass
them something? Or maybe perhaps you desire to re-order.
Another hunk of beefsteak, gentlemen, or—"

"Please," said Sylvester. "Be reasonable. Why don't you go
on upstairs?"

"Yes, why don't I?" the jockey said.

His prim voice had risen higher and there was about it the
sharp whine of hysteria.

"Why don't I go up to my god-damn room and walk around
and write some letters and go to bed like a good boy? Why
don't I just—" He pushed his chair back and got up. "Oh, foo,"
he said. "Foo to you. I want a drink."

"All I can say is it's your funeral," said Sylvester. "You know
what it does to you. You know well enough."

The jockey crossed the dining room and went into the bar.
He ordered a Manhattan, and Sylvester watched him stand with
his heels pressed tight together, his body hard as a lead soldier's, holding his little finger out from the cocktail glass and
sipping the drink slowly.

"He's crazy," said Simmons. "Like I said."

Sylvester turned to the rich man. "If he eats a lamb chop,
you can see the shape of it in his stomach a hour afterward. He

can't sweat things out of him any more. He's a hundred and twelve and a half. He's gained three pounds since we left Miami."

"A jockey shouldn't drink," said the rich man.

"The food don't satisfy him like it used to and he can't sweat it out. If he eats a lamb chop, you can watch it tooching out in his stomach and it don't go down."

The jockey finished his Manhattan. He swallowed, crushed the cherry in the bottom of the glass with his thumb, then pushed the glass away from him. The two girls in blazers were standing at his left, their faces turned toward each other, and at the other end of the bar two touts had started an argument about which was the highest mountain in the world. Everyone was with somebody else; there was no other person drinking alone that night. The jockey paid with a brand-new fifty-dollar bill and didn't count the change.

He walked back to the dining room and to the table at which the three men were sitting, but he did not sit down. "No, I wouldn't presume to think your memory is that extensive," he said. He was so small that the edge of the table top reached almost to his belt, and when he gripped the corner with his wiry hands he didn't have to stoop. "No, you're too busy gobbling up dinners in dining rooms. You're too—"

"Honestly," begged Sylvester. "You got to behave reasonable."

"Reasonable! Reasonable!" The jockey's gray face quivered, then set in a mean, frozen grin. He shook the table so that the plates rattled, and for a moment it seemed that he would push it over. But suddenly he stopped. His hand reached out toward the plate nearest to him and deliberately he put a few French-fried potatoes in his mouth. He chewed slowly, his upper lip raised, then he turned and spat out the pulpy mouthful on the smooth red carpet which covered the floor. "Libertines," he said, and his voice was thin and broken. He rolled the word in his mouth, as though it had a flavor and a substance that gratified him. "You libertines," he said again, and turned and walked with his rigid swagger out of the dining room.

Sylvester shrugged one of his loose, heavy shoulders. The

rich man sopped up some water that had been spilled on the tablecloth, and they didn't speak until the waiter came to clear away.

THE COURTING OF
DINAH SHADD*

BY RUDYARD KIPLING

What did the colonel's lady think?
  Nobody never knew.
Somebody asked the sergeant's wife
  An' she told 'em true.
When you git to a man in the case
  They're like as a row o' pins,
For the colonel's lady an' Judy O'Grady
  Are sisters under their skins.

— BARRACK-ROOM BALLAD

ALL DAY I had followed at the heels of a pursuing army, engaged on one of the finest battles that ever camp of exercise beheld. Thirty thousand troops had by the wisdom of the government of India been turned loose over a few thousand square miles of country to practise in peace what they would never attempt in war. The Army of the South had finally pierced the centre of the Army of the North, and was pouring through the gap, hot foot, to capture a city of strategic importance. Its front extended fan-wise, the sticks being represented by regiments strung out along the line of the route backward to the divisional transport columns, and all the lumber that trails behind an army on the move. On its right the broken left of the Army

* from *Life's Handicap*

of the North was flying in mass, chased by the Southern horse and hammered by the Southern guns, till these had been pushed far beyond the limits of their last support. Then the flying Army of the North sat down to rest, while the commandant of the pursuing force telegraphed that he held it in check and observation.

Unluckily he did not observe that three miles to his right flank a flying column of Northern horse, with a detachment of Ghoorkhas and British troops, had been pushed round, as fast as the falling light allowed, to cut across the entire rear of the Southern Army, to break, as it were, all the ribs of the fan where they converged, by striking at the transport reserve, ammunition, and artillery supplies. Their instructions were to go in, avoiding the few scouts who might not have been drawn off by the pursuit, and create sufficient excitement to impress the Southern Army with the wisdom of guarding their own flank and rear before they captured cities. It was a pretty manœuvre, neatly carried out.

Speaking for the second division of the Southern Army, our first intimation of it was at twilight, when the artillery were laboring in deep sand, most of the escort were trying to help them out, and the main body of the infantry had gone on. A Noah's ark of elephants, camels, and the mixed menagerie of an Indian transport train bubbled and squealed behind the guns, when there rose up from nowhere in particular British infantry to the extent of three companies, who sprang to the heads of the gun horses, and brought all to a stand-still amid oaths and cheers.

"How's that, umpire?" said the major commanding the attack, and with one voice the drivers and limber gunners answered, "Hout!" while the colonel of artillery sputtered.

"All your scouts are charging our main body," said the major. "Your flanks are unprotected for two miles. I think we've broken the back of this division. And listen! there go the Ghoorkhas!"

A weak fire broke from the rear-guard more than a mile away, and was answered by cheerful howlings. The Ghoorkhas, who should have swung clear of the second division, had stepped on its tail in the dark, but, drawing off, hastened to reach the next line, which lay almost parallel to us, five or six miles away.

Our column swayed and surged irresolutely—three batteries, the divisional ammunition reserve, the baggage, and a section of hospital and bearer corps. The commandant ruefully promised to report himself "cut up" to the nearest umpire, and commending his cavalry and all other cavalry to the care of Eblis, toiled on to resume touch with the rest of the division.

"We'll bivouac here to-night," said the major. "I have a notion that the Ghoorkhas will get caught. They may want us to reform on. Stand easy till the transport gets away."

A hand caught my beast's bridle and led him out of the choking dust; a large hand deftly canted me out of the saddle, and two of the hugest hands in the world received me sliding. Pleasant is the lot of the special correspondent who falls into such hands as those of Privates Mulvaney, Ortheris, and Learoyd.

"An' that's all right," said the Irishman calmly. "We thought we'd find you somewheres here by. Is there anything of yours in the transport? Orth'ris'll fetch ut out."

Ortheris did "fetch ut out" from under the trunk of an elephant, in the shape of a servant and an animal, both laden with medical comforts. The little man's eyes sparkled.

"If the brutil an' licentious soldiery av these parts gets sight av the thruck," said Mulvaney, making practised investigation, "they'll loot ev'rything. They're bein' fed on iron-filin's an' dog biscuit these days, but glory's no compensation for a bellyache. Praise be, we're here to protect you, sorr. Beer, sausage, bread (soft, an' that's a cur'osity), soup in a tin; whiskey by the smell av ut, an' fowls. Mother av Moses, but ye take the field like a confectioner! 'Tis scand'lus."

"'Ere's a orficer," said Ortheris significantly. "When the sergent's done lushin', the privit may clean the pot."

I bundled several things into Mulvaney's haversack before the major's hand fell on my shoulder, and he said, tenderly, "Requisitioned for the queen's service. Wolseley was quite wrong about special correspondents. They are the best friends of the soldier. Come an' take pot-luck with us to-night."

And so it happened amid laughter and shoutings that my well-considered commissariat melted away to reappear on the mess-table, which was a waterproof sheet spread on the ground. The flying column had taken three days' rations with it, and there be few things nastier than government rations—especially when government is experimenting with German toys. Erbswurst, tinned beef, of surpassing tinniness, compressed vegetables, and meat biscuits may be nourishing, but what Thomas Atkins wants is bulk in his inside. The major, assisted by his brother officers, purchased goats for the camp, and so made the experiment of no effect. Long before the fatigue-party sent to collect brushwood had returned, the men were settled down by their valises; kettles and pots had appeared from the surrounding country, and were dangling over fires as the kid and the compressed vegetables bubbled together; there rose a cheerful clinking of mess tins, outrageous demands for a "little more stuffin' with that there liver wing," and gust on gust of chaff as pointed as a bayonet and as delicate as a gun butt.

"The boys are in a good temper," said the major. "They'll be singing presently. Well, a night like this is enough to keep them happy."

Over our heads burned the wonderful Indian stars, which are not all pricked in on one plane, but preserving an orderly perspective, draw the eye through the velvet darkness of the void up to the barred doors of heaven itself. The earth was a gray shadow more unreal than the sky. We could hear her breathing lightly in the pauses between the howling of the jackals, the movement of the wind in the tamarisks and the fitful mutter of musketry fire leagues away to the left. A native woman in some unseen hut began to sing, the mail train thundered past on its way to Delhi, and a roosting crow cawed drowsily. Then there was a belt-loosening silence about the fires, and the even breathing of the crowded earth took up the story.

The men, full fed, turned to tobacco and song—their officers with them. Happy is the subaltern who can win the approval of the musical critics in his regiment, and is honored among the more intricate step dancers. By him, as by him who plays cricket craftily, will Thomas Atkins stand in time of need when he will let a better officer go on alone. The ruined tombs of forgotten Mussulman saints heard the ballad of "Agra Town," "The Buffalo Battery," "Marching to Kabul," "The long, long, Indian Day," "The Place where the Punka Coolie Died," and that crushing chorus which announces

> *"Youth's daring spirit, manhood's fire,*
> *Firm hand, and eagle eye*
> *Must he acquire who would aspire*
> *To see the gray boar die."*

To-day, of all those jovial thieves who appropriated my commissariat, and lay and laughed round that water-proof sheet, not one remains. They went to camps that were not of exercise and battles without umpires. Burmah, the Soudan, and the frontier fever and fight took them in their time.

I drifted across to the men's fires in search of Mulvaney, whom I found greasing his feet by the blaze. There is nothing particularly lovely in the sight of a private thus engaged after a long day's march, but when you reflect on the exact proportion of the "might, majesty, dominion, and power" of the British Empire that stands on those feet, you take an interest in the proceedings.

"There's a blister—bad luck to ut!—on the heel," said Mulvaney. "I can't touch ut. Prick ut out, little man."

Ortheris produced his housewife, eased the trouble with a needle, stabbed Mulvaney in the calf with the same weapon, and was incontinently kicked into the fire.

"I've bruk the best av my toes over you, ye grinnin' child av disruption!" said Mulvaney, sitting cross-legged and nursing his feet; then, seeing me: "Oh, ut's you, sorr! Be welkim, an' take that maraudin' scutt's place. Jock, hold him down on the cindhers for a bit."

But Ortheris escaped and went elsewhere as I took possession of the hollow he had scraped for himself and lined with his great-coat. Learoyd, on the other side of the fire, grinned affably, and in a minute fell fast asleep.

"There's the height av politeness for you," said Mulvaney, lighting his pipe with a flaming branch. "But Jock's eaten half a box av your sardines at wan gulp, an' I think the tin too. What's the best wid you, sorr; an' how did you happen to be on the losin' side this day when we captured you?"

"The Army of the South is winning all along the line," I said.

"Thin that line's the hangman's rope, savin' your presence. You'll learn to-morrow how we retreated to dhraw thim on before we made thim trouble, an' that's what a woman does. By the same token, we'll be attacked before the dawnin', an' ut would be betther not to slip your boots. How do I know that? By the light av pure reason. Here are three companies av us ever so far inside av the enemy's flank, an' a crowd av roarin', t'arin', an' squealin' cavalry gone on just to turn out the whole av thim. Av course the enemy will pursue by brigades like as not, an' then we'll have to run for ut. Mark my words. I am av the opinion av Polonius whin he said, 'Don't fight wid ivry scutt for the pure joy av fightin'; but if you do, knock the nose av him first an' frequint!' We ought to ha' gone on an' helped the Ghoorkhas."

"But what do you know about Polonius?" I demanded. This was a new side of Mulvaney's character.

"All that Shakespeare ever wrote, an' a dale more that the gallery shouted," said the man of war, carefully lacing his boots. "Did I tell you av Silver's Theatre in Dublin whin I was younger than I am now an' a patron av the drama? Ould Silver wud never pay actor, man or woman, their just dues, an' by consequence his comp'nies was collapsible at the last minut'. Then the bhoys would clamor to take a part, an' oft as not ould Silver made thim pay for the fun. Faith, I've seen Hamlut played wid a new black eye, an' the Queen as full as a cornucopia. I remember wanst Hogin, that 'listed in the Black Tyrone an' was shot in South Africa, he sejuced ould Silver into givin' him Hamlut's part instid av me, that had a fine fancy for rhetoric in those days. Av course I wint into the gallery an' began to fill the pit wid other people's hats, an' I passed the time av day to Hogin walkin' through Denmark like a hamstrung mule wid a

pall on his back. 'Hamlut,' sez I, 'there's a hole in your heel.
Pull up your shtockin's, Hamlut,' sez I. 'Hamlut, Hamlut, for
the love av decincy dhrop that skull, an' pull up your
shtockin's.' The whole house begun to tell him that. He stopped
his soliloquishms mid between. 'My shtockin's may be comin'
down or they may not,' sez he, screwin' his eye into the gallery,
for well he knew who I was; 'but afther the performance is
over, me an' the Ghost'll trample the guts out av you, Terence,
wid your ass' bray.' An' that's how I come to know about
Hamlut. Eyah! Those days, those days! Did you iver have
onendin' develmint an' nothin' to pay for it in your life, sorr?"

"Never without having to pay," I said.

"That's thrue. 'Tis mane, whin you considher on ut: but ut's
the same wid horse or fut. A headache if you dhrink, an' a
bellyache if you eat too much, an' a heartache to kape all down.
Faith, the beast only gets the colic, an' he's the lucky man."

He dropped his head and stared into the fire, fingering his
mustache the while. From the far side of the bivouac the voice
of Corbet-Nolan, senior subaltern of B Company, uplifted itself in an ancient and much-appreciated song of sentiment, the
men moaning melodiously behind him:

> *"The north wind blew coldly, she drooped from that*
> *   hour,*
> *My own little Kathleen, my sweet little Kathleen,*
> *Kathleen, my Kathleen, Kathleen O'Moore!"*

with forty-five o's in the last word. Even at that distance you
might have cut the soft South Irish accent with a shovel.

"For all we take we must pay; but the price is cruel high,"
murmured Mulvaney when the chorus had ceased.

"What's the trouble?" I said gently, for I knew that he was a
man of an inextinguishable sorrow.

"Hear now," said he. "Ye know what I am now. I know what
I mint to be at the beginnin' av my service. I've tould you time
an' again, an' what I have not, Dinah Shadd has. An' what am
I? Oh, Mary Mother av Hiven! an ould dhrunken, untrustable
baste av a privit that has seen the regiment change out from

colonel to drummer-boy, not wanst or twicet, but scores av times! Ay, scores! An' me not so near gettin' promotion as in the furst. An' me livin' on an' kapin' clear o' clink not by my own good conduck, but the kindness av some orf'cer—bhoy young enough to be son to me! Do I not know ut? Can I not tell whin I'm passed over at p'rade, tho' I'm rockin' full av liquor an' ready to fall all in wan piece, such as even a suckin' child might see, bekaze, 'Oh, 'tis only ould Mulvaney!' An' whin I'm let off in the ord'ly room, though some thrick av the tongue an' a ready answer an' the ould man's mercy, is ut smilin' I feel whin I fall away an' go back to Dinah Shadd, thryin' to carry ut all off as a joke? Not I. 'Tis hell to me—dumb hell through ut all; an' next time whin the fit comes I will be as bad again. Good cause the reg'ment has to know me for the best soldier in ut. Better cause have I to know mesilf for the worst man. I'm only fit to tache the new drafts what I'll never learn myself; an' I am sure as tho' I heard ut, that the minut wan av these pink-eyed recruities gets away from my 'Mind ye, now,' an' 'Listen to this, Jim, bhoy,' sure I am that the sergint houlds me up to him for a warnin'. So I tache, as they say at musketry instruc-tion, by direct an' ricochet fire. Lord be good to me! for I have stud some trouble."

"Lie down and go to sleep," said I, not being able to comfort or advise. "You're the best man in the regiment, and, next to Ortheris, the biggest fool. Lie down, and wait till we're at-tacked. What force will they turn out? Guns, think you?"

"Thry that wid your lorrds an' ladies, twistin' an' turnin' the talk, tho' you mint ut well. Ye cud say nothin' to help me; an' yet ye never knew what cause I had to be what I am."

"Begin at the beginning and go on to the end," I said royally. "But rake up the fire a bit first." I passed Ortheris' bayonet for a poker.

"That shows how little you know what to do," said Mulvaney, putting it aside. "Fire takes all the heat out av the steel, an' the next time, maybe, that our little man is fightin' for his life his brad-awl'll break, an' so you'll 'ave killed him, manin' no more than to kape yourself warm. 'Tis a recruitie's thrick that. Pass the cl'anin'-rod, sorr."

I snuggled down, abashed, and after an interval the low, even voice of Mulvaney began.

II

"Did I ever tell you how Dinah Shadd came to be wife av mine?"

I dissembled a burning anxiety that I had felt for some months—ever since Dinah Shadd, the strong, the patient, and the infinitely tender, had, of her own good love and free-will, washed a shirt for me, moving in a barren land where washing was not.

"I can't remember," I said casually. "Was it before or after you made love to Annie Bragin, and got no satisfaction?"

The story of Annie Bragin is written in another place. It is one of the many episodes in Mulvaney's checkered career.

"Before—before—long before was that business av Annie Bragin an' the corp'ril's ghost. Never woman was the worse for me whin I had married Dinah. There's a time for all things, an' I know how to kape all things in place—barrin' the dhrink, that kapes me in my place, wid no hope av comin' to be aught else."

"Begin at the beginning," I insisted. "Mrs. Mulvaney told me that you married her when you were quartered in Krab Bokhar barracks."

"An' the same is a cess-pit," said Mulvaney, piously. "She spoke thrue, did Dinah. 'Twas this way. Talkin' av that, have ye iver fallen in love, sorr?"

I preserved the silence of the damned. Mulvaney continued:

"Thin I will assume that ye have not. *I* did. In the days av my youth, as I have more than wanst told you, I was a man that filled the eye an' delighted the sowl av women. Niver man was hated as I have been. Niver man was loved as I—no, not within half a day's march av ut. For the first five years av my service, whin I was what I wud give my sowl to be now, I tuk whatever was widin my reach an' digested ut, an' that's more than most men can say. Dhrink, I tuk, an' ut did me no harm. By the hollow av hiven, I could play wid four women at wanst, an' kape thim from findin' out anything about the other three, and smile like a full-blown marigold through ut all. Dick Coulhan, of the battery we'll have down on us to-night, could dhrive his team no better than I mine; an' I hild the worser cattle. An' so I lived an' so I was happy, till afther that business wid Annie Bragin— she that turned me off as cool as a meat-safe, an' taught me where I stud in the mind av an honest woman. 'Twas no sweet dose to take.

"Afther that I sickened awhile, an' tuk thought to my reg'-mental work, conceiting mesilf I wud study an' be a sergint, an' a major-gineral twinty minutes afther that. But on top o' my ambitiousness there was an empty place in my sowl, an' me own opinion av mesilf cud not fill ut. Sez I to mesilf: 'Terence, you're a great man an' the best set up in the reg'ment. Go on an' get promotion.' Sez mesilf to me, 'What for?' Sez I to mesilf, 'For the glory av ut.' Sez mesilf to me, 'Will that fill these two strong arrums av yours, Terence?' 'Go to the divil,' sez I to mesilf. 'Go to the married lines,' sez mesilf to me. ' 'Tis the same thing,' sez I to mesilf. 'Av you're the same man, ut is,' said mesilf to me. An' wid that I considhered on ut a long while. Did you iver feel that way, sorr?"

I snored gently, knowing that if Mulvaney were uninter-rupted he would go on. The clamor from the bivouac fires beat up to the stars as the rival singers of the companies were pitted against each other.

"So I felt that way, an' a bad time ut was. Wanst, bein' a fool, I went into the married lines, more for the sake av spakin' to our ould color-sergint Shadd than for any thruck wid wimmen-folk. I was a corp'ril then—rejuced afthwards; but a corp'ril then. I've got a photograft av mesilf to prove ut. 'You'll take a cup av tay wid us?' sez he. 'I will that,' I sez; 'tho' tay is not my divarsion.' ' 'Twud be better for you if ut were,' sez ould Mother Shadd. An' she had ought to know, for Shadd, in the ind av his service, dhrank bung-full each night.

"Wid that I tuk off my gloves—there was pipe-clay in thim so that they stud alone—an' pulled up my chair, lookin' round at the china ornamints an' bits av things in the Shadds' quar-ters. They were things that belonged to a woman, an' no camp kit, here to-day an' dishipated next. 'You're comfortable in this place, sergint,' sez I. ' 'Tis the wife that did ut, boy,' sez he, pointin' the stem av his pipe to ould Mother Shadd, an' she smacked the top av his bald head apon the compliment. 'That manes you want money,' sez she.

"An thin—an' thin whin the kettle was to be filled, Dinah came in—my Dinah—her sleeves rowled up to the elbow, an' her hair in a gowlden glory over her forehead, the big blue eyes beneath twinklin' like stars on a frosty night, an' the tread of her two feet lighter than waste paper from the colonel's basket in ord'ly room when ut's emptied. Bein' but a shlip av a girl, she went pink at seein' me, an' I twisted me mustache an' looked at a picture forninst the wall. Never show a woman that ye care the snap av a finger for her, an' begad she'll come bleatin' to your boot heels."

"I suppose that's why you followed Annie Bragin till everybody in the married quarters laughed at you," said I, remembering that unhallowed wooing, and casting off the disguise of drowsiness.

"I'm layin' down the gineral theory av the attack," said Mulvaney, driving his foot into the dying fire. "If you read the 'Soldier's Pocket-Book,' which never any soldier reads, you'll see that there are exceptions. When Dinah was out av the door (an' 'twas as tho' the sunlight had gone too), 'Mother av Hiven, sergint!' sez I, 'but is that your daughter?' 'I've believed that way these eighteen years,' sez ould Shadd, his eyes twinklin'. 'But Mrs. Shadd has her own opinion, like ivry other woman.' ' 'Tis wid yours this time, for a mericle,' sez Mother Shadd. 'Then why, in the name av fortune, did I never see her before?' sez I. 'Bekaze, you've been thraipsin' round wid the married women these three years past. She was a bit av a child till last year, an' she shot up wid the spring,' sez ould Mother Shadd. 'I'll thraipse no more,' sez I. 'D'you mane that?' sez ould Mother Shadd, lookin' at me sideways, like a hen looks at a hawk whin the chickens are runnin' free. 'Try me, an' tell,' sez I. Wid that I pulled on my gloves, dhrank off the tea, an' wint out av the house as stiff as at gineral p'rade, for well I knew that Dinah Shadd's eyes were in the small av my back out av the scullery window. Faith, that was the only time I mourned I was not a cav'lryman, for the sake av the spurs to jingle.

"I wint out to think, an' I did a powerful lot av thinkin', but ut all came round to that shlip av a girl in the dotted blue dhress, wid the blue eyes an' the sparkil in them. Thin I kept off canteen, an' I kept to the married quarthers or near by on the chanst av meetin' Dinah. Did I meet her? Oh, my time past, did I not, wid a lump in my throat as big as my valise, an' my heart goin' like a farrier's forge on a Saturday mornin'! 'Twas 'Good-day to ye, Miss Dinah,' an' 'Good-day t'you, corp'ril,' for a week or two, an' divil a bit further could I get, bekase av the respict I had to that girl that I cud ha' broken betune finger an' thumb."

Here I giggled as I recalled the gigantic figure of Dinah Shadd when she handed me my shirt.

"Ye may laugh," grunted Mulvaney. "But I'm speakin' the trut' an' 'tis you that are in fault. Dinah was a girl that wud ha' taken the imperiousness out av the Duchess av Clonmel in those days. Flower hand, foot av shod air, an' the eyes av the mornin' she had. That is my wife to-day—ould Dinah, an' never aught else than Dinah Shadd to me.

" 'Twas after three weeks standin' off an' on, an' niver makin' headway excipt through the eyes, that a little drummer-boy grinned in me face whin I had admonished him wid the buckle av my belt for riotin' all over the place. 'An' I'm not the only wan that doesn't kape to barricks,' sez he. I tuk him by the scruff av his neck—my heart was hung on a hair-trigger those days, you will understand—an' 'Out wid ut,' sez I, 'or I'll lave no bone av you unbruk.' 'Speak to Dempsey,' sez he, howlin'. 'Dempsey which?' sez I, 'ye unwashed limb av Satan.' 'Of the Bobtailed Dhragoons,' sez he. 'He's seen her home from her aunt's house in the civil lines four times this fortnight.' 'Child,' sez I, dhroppin' him, 'your tongue's stronger than your body. Go to your quarters. I'm sorry I dhressed you down.'

"At that I went four ways to wanst huntin' Dempsey. I was mad to think that wid all my airs among women I shud ha' been ch'ated by a basin-faced fool av a cav'lryman not fit to trust on a mule thrunk. Presently I found him in our lines—the Bobtails was quartered next us—an' a tallowy, top-heavy son av a she-mule he was, wid his big brass spurs an' his plastrons on his epigastons an' all. But he never flinched a hair.

"'A word wid you, Dempsey,' sez I. 'You've walked wid Dinah Shadd four times this fortnight gone.'

"'What's that to you?' sez he. 'I'll walk forty times more, an' forty on top av that, ye shovel-futted, clod-breakin' infantry lance-corp'ril.'

"Before I cud gyard he had his gloved fist home on me cheek, an' down I went full sprawl. 'Will that content you?' sez he, blowin' on his knuckles for all the world like a Scots Grays orf'cer. 'Content?' sez I. 'For your own sake, man, take off your spurs, peel your jackut, and onglove. 'Tis the beginnin' av the overture. Stand up!'

"He stud all he knew, but he niver peeled his jackut, an' his shoulders had no fair play. I was fightin' for Dinah Shadd an' that cut on me cheek. What hope had he forninst me? 'Stand up!' sez I, time an' again, when he was beginnin' to quarter the ground an' gyard high an' go large. 'This isn't ridin'-school,' sez I. 'Oh, man, stand up, an' let me get at ye!' But whin I saw he wud be runnin' about, I grup his shtock in me left an' his waist-belt in me right an' swung him clear to me right front, head undher, he hammerin' me nose till the wind was knocked out av him on the bare ground. 'Stand up,' sez I, 'or I'll kick your head into your chest.' An' I wud ha' done ut, too, so ragin' mad I was.

"'Me collar-bone's bruk,' sez he. 'Help me back to lines. I'll walk wid her no more.' So I helped him back."

"And was his collar-bone broken?" I asked, for I fancied that only Learoyd could neatly accomplish that terrible throw.

"He pitched on his left shoulder-point. It was. Next day the news was in both barracks; an' whin I met Dinah Shadd wid a cheek like all the reg'mintal tailors' samples, there was no 'Good-mornin', corp'ril,' or aught else. 'An' what have I done, Miss Shadd,' sez I, very bould, plantin' mesilf forninst her, 'that ye should not pass the time of day?'

"'Ye've half killed rough-rider Dempsey,' sez she, her dear blue eyes fillin' up.

" 'Maybe,' sez I. 'Was he a friend av yours that saw ye home four times in a fortnight?'

" 'Yes,' sez she, very bould; but her mouth was down at the corners. 'An'—an' what's that to you?'

" 'Ask Dempsey,' sez I, purtendin' to go away.

" 'Did you fight for me then, ye silly man?' she sez, tho' she knew ut all along.

" 'Who else?' sez I; an' I tuk wan pace to the front.

" 'I wasn't worth ut,' sez she, fingerin' her apron.

" 'That's for me to say,' sez I. 'Shall I say ut?'

" 'Yes,' sez she, in a saint's whisper; an' at that I explained mesilf; an' she tould me what ivry man that is a man, an' many that is a woman, hears wanst in his life.

" 'But what made ye cry at startin', Dinah darlin'?' sez I.

" 'Your—your bloody cheek,' sez she, duckin' her little head down on my sash (I was duty for the day), an' whimperin' like a sorrowful angel.

"Now a man cud take that two ways. I tuk ut as pleased me best, an' my first kiss wid ut. Mother av Innocence! but I kissed her on the tip av the nose an' undher the eye, an' a girl that lets a kiss come tumbleways like that has never been kissed before. Take note av that, sorr. Thin we wint, hand in hand, to ould Mother Shadd like two little childher, an' she said it was no bad thing; an' ould Shadd nodded behind his pipe, an' Dinah ran away to her own room. That day I throd on rollin' clouds. All earth was too small to hould me. Begad, I cud ha' picked the sun out av the sky for a live coal to me pipe, so magnificent I was. But I tuk recruities at squad drill, an' began with general battalion advance whin I shud ha' been balance-steppin' 'em. Eyah! that day! that day!"

A very long pause. "Well?" said I.

"It was all wrong," said Mulvaney, with an enormous sigh. "An' sure I know that ev'ry bit av ut was me own foolishness. That night I tuk maybe the half av three pints—not enough to turn the hair of a man in his natural sinses. But I was more than half dhrunk wid pure joy, an' that canteen beer was so much whiskey to me. I can't tell how ut came about, but *bekase* I had no thought for any wan except Dinah, *bekase* I hadn't slipped her little white arms from me neck five minutes, *bekase* the breath av her kiss was not gone from my mouth, I must go through the married lines on me way to quarthers, an' I must stay talkin' to a red-headed Mullengar heifer av a girl, Judy Sheehy, that was daughter to Mother Sheehy, the wife av Nick Sheehy, the canteen sergint—the black curse av Shielygh be on the whole brood that are above groun' this day!

"'An' what are ye houldin' your head that high for, corp'ril?' sez Judy. 'Come in an' thry a cup av tay,' she sez, standin' in the doorway.

"Bein' an onbustable fool, an' thinkin' av anythin' but tay, I wint.

"'Mother's at canteen,' sez Judy, smoothin' the hair av hers that was like red snakes, an' lookin' at me cornerways out av her green cat's eyes. 'Ye will not mind, corp'ril?'

"'I can endure,' sez I. 'Ould Mother Sheehy bein' no divarsion av mine, nor her daughter too.' Judy fetched the tea-things an' put thim on the table, leanin' over me very close to get them square. I dhrew back, thinkin' of Dinah.

"'Is ut afraid you are av a girl alone?' sez Judy.

"'No,' sez I. 'Why should I be?'

"'That rests wid the girl,' sez Judy, dhrawin' her chair next to mine.

"'Thin there let ut rest,' sez I; an' thinkin' I'd been a trifle onpolite, I sez, 'The tay's not quite sweet enough for me taste. Put your little finger in the cup, Judy; 'twill make ut necthar.'

"'What's necthar?' sez she.

"'Somethin' very sweet,' sez I; an' for the sinful life av me I cud not help lookin' at her out av the corner av my eye, as I used to look at a woman.

"'Go on wid ye, corp'ril,' sez she. 'You're a flirrt.'

"'On me sowl I'm not,' sez I.

"'Then you're a cruel handsome man, an' that's worse,' sez she, heavin' big sighs an' lookin' crossways.

"'You know your own mind,' sez I.

"''Twud be better for me if I did not,' she sez.

"'There's a dale to be said on both sides av that,' sez I, nu-thinkin.'

" 'Say your own part av ut, then, Terence darlin',' sez she; 'for begad I'm thinkin' I've said too much or too little for an honest girl'; an' wid that she put her arms round me neck an' kissed me.

" 'There's no more to be said afther that,' sez I, kissin' her back again. Oh, the mane scutt that I was, my head ringin' wid Dinah Shadd! How does ut come about, sorr, that whin a man had put the comether on wan woman he's sure bound to put ut on another? 'Tis the same thing at musketry. Wan day ev'ry shot goes wide or into the bank, an' the next—lay high, lay low, sight or snap—ye can't get off the bull's-eye for ten shots runnin'."

"That only happens to a man who has had a good deal of experience; he does it without thinking," I replied.

"Thankin' you for the complimint, sorr, ut may be so; but I'm doubtin' whether you mint ut for a complimint. Hear, now. I sat there wid Judy on my knee, tellin' me all manner av nonsinse, an' only sayin' 'yes' an' 'no,' when I'd much better ha' kept tongue betune teeth. An' that was not an hour afther I had left Dinah. What I was thinkin' av I cannot say.

"Presently, quiet as a cat, ould Mother Sheehy came in velvet-dhrunk. She had her daughter's red hair, but 'twas bald in patches, an' I cud see in her wicked ould face, clear as lightnin', what Judy wud be twenty year to come. I was for jumpin' up, but Judy niver moved.

" 'Terence has promust, mother,' sez she, an' the cowld sweat bruk out all over me.

"Ould Mother Sheehy sat down of a heap, an' began playin' wid the cups. 'Thin you're a well-matched pair,' she sez, very thick; 'for he's the biggest rogue that iver spoiled the queen's shoe-leather, an——"

" 'I'm off, Judy,' sez I. 'Ye should not talk nonsinse to your mother. Get her to bed, girl.'

" 'Nonsinse?' sez the ould woman, prickin' up her ears like a cat, an' grippin' the table-edge. ' 'Twill be the most nonsinsical nonsinse for you, ye grinnin' badger, if nonsinse 'tis. Git clear, you. I'm goin' to bed.'

"I ran out into the dhark, me head in a stew an' me heart

sick, but I had sinse enough to see that I'd brought ut all on mesilf. 'It's this to pass the time av day to a panjandhrum of hell-cats,' sez I. 'What I've said an' what I've not said do not matther. Judy an' her dam will hould me for a promust man, an' Dinah will give me the go, an' I desarve ut. I will go an' get dhrunk,' sez I, 'an' forgit about ut, for 'tis plain I'm not a marryin' man.'

"On me way to canteen I ran against Lascelles, color-sergint that was, av E Comp'ny—a hard, hard man, wid a tormint av a wife. 'You've the head av a drowned man on your shoulders,' sez he, 'an' you're goin' where you'll get a worse wan. Come back,' sez he. 'Let me go,' sez I. 'I've thrown me luck over the wall wid me own hand.' 'Then that's not the way to get ut back,' sez he. 'Have out wid your trouble, ye fool-bhoy.' An' I tould him how the matther was.

"He sucked in his lower lip. 'You've been thrapped,' sez he. 'Ju Sheehy wud be the betther for a man's name to hers as soon as she can. An' ye thought ye'd put the comether on her. That's the naturil vanity av the baste. Terence, you're a big born fool, but you're not bad enough to marry into that comp'ny. If you said anythin', an' for all your protestations I'm sure you did— or did not, which is worse—eat ut all. Lie like the father av all lies, but come out av ut free av Judy. Do I not know what ut is to marry a woman that was the very spit av Judy when she was young? I'm gettin' ould, an' I've larnt patience; but you, Terence, you'd raise hand on Judy an' kill her in a year. Never mind if Dinah gives you the go; you've desarved ut. Never mind if the whole reg'mint laughs at you all day. Get shut av Judy an' her mother. They can't dhrag you to church, but if they do, they'll dhrag you to hell. Go back to your quarthers an' lie down,' sez he. Thin, over his shoulder, 'You *must* ha' done with thim.'

"Nixt day I wint to see Dinah; but there was no tucker in me as I walked. I knew the throuble wud come soon enough widout any handlin' av mine, an' I dreaded ut sore.

"I heard Judy callin' me, but I hild straight on to the Shadd's quarthers, an' Dinah wud ha' kissed me, but I hild her back.

"'Whin all's said, darlin',' sez I, 'you can give ut me if you will, tho' I misdoubt 'twill be so easy to come by thin.'

"I had scarce begun to put the explanation into shape before Judy an' her mother came to the door. I think there was a veranda, but I'm forgettin'.

"'Will ye not step in?' sez Dinah, pretty and polite, though the Shadds had no dealin's with the Sheehys. Ould Mother Shadd looked up quick, an' she was the fust to see the throuble, for Dinah was her daughter.

"'I'm pressed for time to-day,' sez Judy, as bould as brass; 'an' I've only come for Terence—my promust man. 'Tis strange to find him here the day afther the day.'

"Dinah looked at me as though I had hit her, an' I answered straight.

"'There was some nonsinse last night at the Sheehys' quarthers, an' Judy's carryin' on the joke, darlin',' sez I.

"'At the Sheehys' quarthers?' sez Dinah, very slow; an' Judy cut in wid,

"'He was there from nine till tin, Dinah Shadd, an' the betther half av that time I was sittin' on his knee, Dinah Shadd. Ye may look an' ye may look an' ye may look me up an' down, but ye won't look away that Terence is my promust man. Terence, darlin', 'tis time for us to be comin' home.'

"Dinah Shadd never said word to Judy. 'Ye left me at half-past eight,' she sez to me, 'an' I never thought that ye'd leave me for Judy, promises or no promises. Go back wid her, you that have to be fetched by a girl! I'm done with you,' sez she; and she ran into her own room, her mother followin'. So I was alone with those two women, and at liberty to spake me sintiments.

"'Judy Sheehy,' sez I, 'if you made a fool av me betune the lights, you shall not do ut in the day. I never promised you words or lines.'

"'You lie,' sez ould Mother Sheehy; 'an' may ut choke you where you stand!' She was far gone in dhrink.

"'An' tho' ut choked me where I stud I'd not change,' sez I. 'Go home, Judy. I take shame for a decent girl like you dhraggin' your mother out bare-headed on this errand. Hear, now, and have ut for an answer. I gave me word to Dinah Shadd yesterday, an' more blame to me I was with you last night talkin' nonsinse, but nothin' more. You've chosen to thry to hould me on ut. I will not be held thereby for anythin' in the world. Is that enough?'

"Judy wint pink all over. 'An' I wish you joy av the perjury,' sez she. 'You've lost a woman that would ha' wore her hand to the bone for your pleasure; an' 'deed, Terence, ye were not thrapped,' ... Lascelles must ha' spoken plain to her. 'I am such as Dinah is—'deed I am! Ye've lost a fool av a girl that'll never look at you again, an' ye've lost what ye niver had—your common honesty. If you manage your men as you manage your love-makin', small wondher they call you the worst corp'ril in the comp'ny. Come away, mother,' sez she.

"But divil a fut would the ould woman budge! 'D'you hould by that?' sez she, peerin' up under her thick gray eyebrows.

" 'Ay, an' wud,' said I, 'tho' Dinah gave me the go twinty times. I'll have no thruck with you or yours,' sez I. 'Take your child away, ye shameless woman.'

" 'An' am I shameless?' sez she, bringin' her hands up above her head. "Thin what are you, ye lyin', schamin', weak-kneed, dhirty-souled son of a sutler? Am _I_ shameless? Who put the open shame on me an' my child that we shud go beggin' through the lines in daylight for the broken word of a man? Double portion of my shame be on you, Terence Mulvaney, that think yourself so strong! By Mary and the saints, by blood and water, an' by ivry sorrow that came into the world since the beginnin', the black blight fall on you and yours, so that you may niver be free from pain for another when ut's not your own! May your heart bleed in your breast drop by drop wid all your friends laughin' at the bleedin'! Strong you think yourself? May your strength be a curse to you to dhrive you into the divil's hands against your own will! Clear-eyed you are? May your eyes see clear ivry step av the dark path you take till the hot cinders av hell put thim out! May the ragin' dry thirst in my own ould bones go to you that you shall never pass bottle full nor glass empty! God preserve the light av your understandin' to you, my jewel av a bhoy, that ye may niver forget what you mint to be an' do, when you're wallowin' in the muck! May ye see the betther and follow the worse as long as there's breath in your body! an' may ye die quick in a strange land watchin' your death before ut takes you an' onable to stir hand or fut!'

"I heard a scufflin' in the room behind, and thin Dinah Shadd's hand dhropped into mine like a roseleaf into a muddy road.

" 'The half av that I'll take,' sez she, 'an' more too, if I can. Go home, ye silly-talkin' woman—go home an' confess.'

" 'Come away! Come away!' sez Judy, pullin' her mother by the shawl. " 'Twas none av Terence's fault. For the love av Mary stop the talkin'!'

" 'An' you!' said ould Mother Sheehy, spinnin' round forninst Dinah. 'Will ye take the half av that man's load? Stand off from him, Dinah Shadd, before he takes you down too—you that look to be a quarthermaster-sergint's wife in five years. Ye look too high, child. Ye shall wash for the quarthermaster-sergint, whin he pl'ases to give you the job out av charity; but a privit's wife ye shall be to the end, an' ivry sorrow of a privit's wife ye shall know, an' niver a job but wan, that shall go from you like the tide from a rock. The pain of bearin' ye shall know, but niver the pleasure of givin' the breast; an' you shall put away a man-child into the common ground wid niver a priest to say a prayer over him, an' on that man-child ye shall think ivry day av your life. Think long, Dinah Shadd, for you'll niver have another tho' you pray till your knees are bleedin'. The mothers av children shall mock you behind your back whin you're wringin' over the wash-tub. You shall know what it is to take a dhrunken husband home an' see him go to the gyard-room. Will that pl'ase you, Dinah Shadd, that won't be seen talkin' to my daughter? You shall talk to worse than Judy before all's over. The sergints' wives shall look down on you, contemptu-ous daughter av a sergint, an' you shall cover ut all up wid a smilin' face whin your heart's burstin'. Stand off him, Dinah Shadd, for I've put the Black Curse of Shielygh upon him, an' his own mouth shall make ut good.'

"She pitched forward on her head an' began foamin' at the

mouth. Dinah Shadd ran out with water, an' Judy dhragged the
ould woman into the veranda till she sat up.

"'I'm old an' forlore,' she sez, tremblin' an' cryin', 'an' 'tis
like I say a dale more than I mane.'

"'When you're able to walk—go,' says ould Mother Shadd.
'This house has no place for the likes av you, that have cursed
my daughter.'

"'Eyah!' said the ould woman. 'Hard words break no
bones, an' Dinah Shadd'll kape the love av her husband till
my bones are green corn. Judy, darlin', I misremember what I
came here for. Can you lend us the bottom av a taycup av tay,
Mrs. Shadd?'

"But Judy dhragged her off, cryin' as tho' her heart wud
break. An' Dinah Shadd an' I, in ten minutes we had forgot
ut all."

"Then why do you remember it now?" said I.

"Is ut like I'd forgit? Ivry word that wicked ould woman
spoke fell thrue in my life afterward; an' I cud ha' stud ut all—
stud ut all, except fwhen little Shadd was born. That was on the
line av march three months afther the regiment was taken wid
cholera. We were betune Umballa an' Kalka thin, an' I was on
picket. When I came off, the women showed me the child, an'
ut turned on ut's side an' died as I looked. We buried him by the
road, an' Father Victor was a day's march behind wid the heavy
baggage, so the comp'ny captain read prayer. An' since then
I've been a childless man, an' all else that ould Mother Sheehy
put upon me an' Dinah Shadd. What do you think, sorr?"

I thought a good deal, but it seemed better then to reach out
for Mulvaney's hand. This demonstration nearly cost me the
use of three fingers. Whatever he knows of his weaknesses,
Mulvaney is entirely ignorant of his strength.

"But what do you think?" he insisted, as I was straightening
out the crushed members.

My reply was drowned in yells and outcries from the next
fire, where ten men were shouting for "Orth'ris!" "Privit Orth'ris!" "Mistah Or-ther-ris!" "Deah boy!" "Cap'n Orth-ris!"
"Field-Marshal Orth'ris!" "Stanley, you penn'orth o'pop, come

'ere to your own comp'ny!" And the cockney, who had been delighting another audience with recondite and Rabelaisian yarns, was shot down among his admirers by the major force.

"You've crumpled my dress-shirt 'orrid," said he; "an' I shan't sing no more to this 'ere bloomin' drawin'-room."

Learoyd, roused by the confusion, uncoiled himself, crept behind Ortheris, and raised him aloft on his shoulders.

"Sing, ye bloomin' hummin'-bird!" said he; and Ortheris, beating time on Learoyd's skull, delivered himself, in the raucous voice of the Ratcliff Highway, of the following chaste and touching ditty:

> "My girl she give me the go oncet,
>   When I was a London lad,
> An' I went on the drink for a fortnight,
>   An' then I went to the bad.
> The queen she gave me a shillin',
>   To fight for 'er over the seas;
> But guv'ment built me a fever-trap,
>   An' Injia gave me disease.
>
> "Chorus—Ho! don't you 'eed what a girl says,
>   An' don't you go for the beer;
> But I was an ass when I was at grass,
>   An' that is why I'm 'ere.
>
> "I fired a shot at an Afghan;
>   The beggar 'e fired again;
> An' I lay on my bed with a 'ole in my 'ead,
>   An' missed the next campaign
> I up with my gun at a Burman
>   Who carried a bloomin' dah,
> But the cartridge stuck an' the bay'nit bruk,
>   An' all I got was the scar.
>
> "Chorus—Ho! don't you aim at a Afghan
>   When you stand on the sky-line clear;
> An' don't you go for a Burman
>   If none o' your friends is near.

"I served my time for a corp'ral,
  An' wetted my stripes with pop,
For I went on the bend with a intimate friend,
  An' finished the night in the Shop.
I served my time for a sergeant;
  The colonel 'e sez 'No!
The most you'll be is a full C. B.;'*
  An'—very next night 'twas so.

"Chorus—*Ho! don't you go for a corp'ral,*
  Unless your 'ead is clear;
But I was an ass when I was at grass,
  An' that is why I'm 'ere.

"I've tasted the luck o' the army
  In barrack an' camp an' clink,
An' I lost my tip through the bloomin' trip
  Along o' the women an' drink.
I'm down at the heel o' my service,
  An' when I am laid on the shelf,
My very wust friend from beginning to end,
  By the blood of a mouse, was myself.

"Chorus—*Ho! don't you 'eed what a girl says,*
  An' don't you go for the beer;
But I was an ass when I was at grass,
  An' that is why I'm 'ere."

"Ay, listen to our little man now, singin' an' shoutin' as tho' trouble had never touched him! D'you remember when he went mad with the homesickness?" said Mulvaney, recalling a never-to-be-forgotten season when Ortheris waded through the deep waters of affliction and behaved abominably. "But he's talkin' the bitter truth, tho'. Eyah!

  " 'My very worst friend from beginning to end
    By the blood of a mouse, was mesilf.'

---

* Confined to barracks.

Hark out!" he continued, jumping to his feet. "What did I tell you, sorr?"

Fttl! spttl! whttl! went the rifles of the picket in the darkness, and we heard their feet rushing toward us as Ortheris tumbled past me and into his great-coat. It is an impressive thing, even in peace, to see an armed camp spring to life with clatter of accoutrements, click of Martini levers, and blood-curdling speculations as to the fate of missing boots. "Pickets dhriven in," said Mulvaney, staring like a buck at bay into the soft, clinging gloom. "Stand by an' kape close to us. If 'tis cav'lry they may blundher into the fires."

Tr—ra ra!—ta—ra—la! sang the thrice-blessed bugle, and the rush to form square began. There is much rest and peace in the heart of a square if you arrive in time and are not trodden upon too frequently. The smell of leather belts, fatigue uniform, and packed humanity is comforting.

A dull grumble, that seemed to come from every point of the compass at once, struck our listening ears, and little thrills of excitement ran down the faces of the square. Those who write so learnedly about judging distance by sound should hear cavalry on the move at night. A high-pitched yell on the left told us that the disturbers were friends—the cavalry of the attack, who had missed their direction in the darkness, and were feeling blindly for some sort of support and camping-ground. The difficulty explained, they jingled on.

"Double pickets out there; by your arms lie down and sleep the rest," said the major, and the square melted away as the men scrambled for their places by the fires.

When I woke I saw Mulvaney, the night-dew gemming his moustache, leaning on his rifle at picket, lonely as Prometheus on his rock, with I know not what vultures tearing his liver.

THE SHOT *

BY ALEXANDER POUSHKIN

(Translated by T. Keane)

I

WE WERE stationed in the town of N——. The life of an officer in the army is well known. In the morning, drill and the riding-school; dinner with the Colonel or at a Jewish restaurant; in the evening, punch and cards. In N——there was not one open house, nor a single marriageable girl. We used to meet in each other's rooms, where all we saw was men in uniform.

One civilian only was admitted into our society. He was about thirty-five years of age, and therefore we looked upon him as an old fellow. His experience gave him great advantage over us, and his habitual sullenness, stern disposition and caustic tongue produced a deep impression upon our young minds. Some mystery surrounded his existence; he had the appearance of a Russian, although his name was a foreign one. He had formerly served in the Hussars, and with distinction. Nobody knew the cause that had induced him to retire from the service and settle in a wretched town, where he lived poorly and, at the same time, extravagantly. He always went on foot, and constantly wore a shabby black overcoat, but the officers of our regiment were ever welcome at his table. His dinners, it is true, never consisted of more than two or three dishes, prepared by a retired soldier, but the champagne flowed like water. Nobody

* from *Poushkin's Prose Tales* (Bohn Library)

knew what his circumstances were, or what his income was, and nobody dared to question him about them. He had a collection of books, chiefly works on military matters and novels. He willingly lent them to us to read, and never asked for their return; on the other hand, he never returned to the owner the books that were lent to him. His principal amusement was shooting with a pistol. The walls of his room were riddled with bullets, and were as full of holes as a honey-comb. A rich collection of pistols was the only luxury in the humble cottage where he lived. The skill which he had acquired with his favorite weapon was simply incredible; and if he had offered to shoot a pear off somebody's forage-cap, not a man in our regiment would have hesitated to expose his head to the bullet.

Our conversation often turned upon duels. Silvio—so I will call him—never joined in it. When asked if he had ever fought, he drily replied that he had; but he entered into no particulars, and it was evident that such questions were not to his liking. We imagined that he had upon his conscience the memory of some unhappy victim of his terrible skill. It never entered into the head of any of us to suspect him of anything like cowardice. There are persons whose mere look is sufficient to repel such suspicions. But an unexpected incident occurred which astounded us all.

One day, about ten of our officers dined with Silvio. They drank as usual, that is to say, a great deal. After dinner we asked our host to hold the bank for a game at faro. For a long time he refused, as he hardly ever played, but at last he ordered cards to be brought, placed half a hundred gold coins upon the table, and sat down to deal. We took our places around him, and the game began. It was Silvio's custom to preserve complete silence when playing. He never argued, and never entered into explanations. If the punter made a mistake in calculating, he immediately paid him the difference or noted down the surplus. We were acquainted with this habit of his, and we always allowed him to have his own way; but among us on this occasion was an officer who had only recently been transferred to our regiment. During the course of the game, this officer absently scored one point too many. Silvio took the chalk and

noted down the correct account according to his usual custom.
The officer, thinking that he had made a mistake, began to
enter into explanations. Silvio continued dealing in silence.
The officer, losing patience, took the brush and rubbed out
what he considered an error. Silvio took the chalk and corrected the score again. The officer, heated with wine, play, and
the laughter of his comrades, considered himself grossly insulted, and in his rage he seized a brass candle-stick from the
table, and hurled it at Silvio, who barely succeeded in avoiding
the missile. We were filled with consternation. Silvio rose,
white with rage, and with gleaming eyes, said:

"My dear sir, have the goodness to withdraw, and thank God
that this has happened in my house."

None of us entertained the slightest doubt as to what the result would be, and we already looked upon our new comrade as
a dead man. The officer withdrew, saying that he was ready to
answer for his offense in whatever way the banker liked. The
play went on for a few minutes longer, but feeling that our host
was too overwrought to care for the game, we withdrew one after the other, and repaired to our respective quarters, after having exchanged a few words upon the probability of there soon
being a vacancy in the regiment.

The next day, at the riding-school, we were already asking
each other if the poor lieutenant was still alive, when he himself appeared among us. We put the same question to him, and
he replied that he had not yet heard from Silvio. This astonished us. We went to Silvio's house and found him in the courtyard shooting bullet after bullet into an ace pasted upon the
gate. He received us as usual, but did not utter a word about the
event of the previous evening. Three days passed, and the lieutenant was still alive. We asked each other in astonishment:
"Can it be possible that Silvio is not going to fight?"

Silvio did not fight. He was satisfied with a very lame explanation, and made peace with his assailant.

This lowered him very much in the opinion of all our young
fellows. Want of courage is the last thing to be pardoned by
young men, who usually look upon bravery as the chief of all
human virtues, and the excuse for every possible fault. But, by

degrees, everything was forgotten, and Silvio regained his former influence.

I alone could not approach him on the old footing. Being endowed by nature with a romantic imagination, I had become attached more than all the others to the man whose life was an enigma, and who seemed to me the hero of some mysterious tale. He was fond of me; at least, with me alone did he drop his customary sarcastic tone, and converse on different subjects in a simple and unusually agreeable manner. But after this unlucky evening, the thought that his honor had been tarnished, and that the stain had been allowed to remain upon it through his own fault, was ever present in my mind, and prevented me from treating him as before. I was ashamed to look at him. Silvio was too intelligent and experienced not to observe this and guess the cause of it. This seemed to vex him; at least I observed once or twice a desire on his part to enter into an explanation with me, but I avoided such opportunities, and Silvio gave up the attempt. From that time forward I saw him only in the presence of my comrades, and our former confidential conversations came to an end.

Those who live amidst the excitements of the capital have no idea of the many experiences familiar to the inhabitants of the villages and small towns, as, for instance, waiting for the arrival of the post. On Tuesdays and Fridays our regimental bureau used to be filled with officers: some expecting money, some letters, and others newspapers. The packets were usually opened on the spot, items of news were communicated from one to another, and the bureau used to present a very animated picture. Silvio used to have his letters addressed to our regiment, and he was generally there to receive them.

One day he received a letter, the seal of which he broke with a look of the greatest impatience. As he read the contents, his eyes sparkled. The officers, each occupied with his own mail, did not observe anything.

"Gentlemen," said Silvio, "circumstances demand my immediate departure; I leave tonight. I hope that you will not refuse to dine with me for the last time. I shall expect you, too," he added, turning toward me. "I shall expect you without fail."

With these words he hastily departed, and we, after agreeing to meet at Silvio's, dispersed to our various quarters.

I arrived at Silvio's house at the appointed time, and found nearly the whole regiment there. All his belongings were already packed; nothing remained but the bare, bullet-riddled walls. We sat down to table. Our host was in an excellent humor, and his gaiety was quickly communicated to the rest. Corks popped every moment, glasses foamed incessantly, and, with the utmost warmth, we wished our departing friend a pleasant journey and every happiness. When we rose from the table it was already late in the evening. After having wished everybody good-bye, Silvio took me by the hand and detained me just at the moment when I was preparing to depart.

"I want to speak to you," he said in a low voice.

I stopped behind.

The guests had departed, and we two were left alone. Sitting down opposite each other, we silently lit our pipes. Silvio seemed greatly troubled; not a trace remained of his former feverish gaiety. The intense pallor of his face, his sparkling eyes, and the thick smoke issuing from his mouth, gave him a truly diabolical appearance. Several minutes elapsed, and then Silvio broke the silence.

"Perhaps we shall never see each other again," said he; "before we part, I should like to have an explanation with you. You may have observed that I care very little for the opinion of other people, but I like you, and I feel that it would be painful to me to leave you with a wrong impression upon your mind."

He paused, and began to refill his pipe. I sat gazing silently at the floor.

"You thought it strange," he continued, "that I did not demand satisfaction from that drunken idiot R——. You will admit, however, that since I had the choice of weapons, his life was in my hands, while my own was in no great danger. I could ascribe my forbearance to generosity alone, but I will not tell a lie. If I could have chastised R—— without the least risk to my own life, I should never have pardoned him."

I looked at Silvio with astonishment. Such a confession completely astounded me. Silvio continued:

"Exactly so: I have no right to expose myself to death. Six years ago I received a slap in the face, and my enemy still lives."

My curiosity was greatly excited.

"Did you not fight with him?" I asked. "Circumstances probably separated you."

"I did fight with him," replied Silvio: "and here is a souvenir of our duel."

Silvio rose and took from a cardboard box a red cap with a gold tassel and galloon (what the French call a *bonnet de police*); he put it on—a bullet had passed through it about an inch above the forehead.

"You know," continued Silvio, "that I served in one of the Hussar regiments. My character is well known to you: I am accustomed to taking the lead. From my youth this has been my passion. In our time dissoluteness was the fashion, and I was the wildest man in the army. We used to boast of our drunkenness: I outdrank the famous B——,[1] of whom D. D—[2] has sung. In our regiment duels were constantly taking place, and in all of them I was either second or principal. My comrades adored me, while the regimental commanders, who were constantly being changed, looked upon me as a necessary evil.

"I was calmly, or rather boisterously enjoying my reputation, when a young man belonging to a wealthy and distinguished family—I will not mention his name—joined our regiment. Never in my life have I met with such a fortunate fellow! Imagine to yourself youth, wit, beauty, unbounded gaiety, the most reckless bravery, a famous name, untold wealth—imagine all these, and you can form some idea of the effect that he would be sure to produce among us. My supremacy was shaken. Dazzled by my reputation, he began to seek my friendship, but I received him coldly, and without the least regret he held aloof from me. I began to hate him. His success in the regiment and in the society of ladies brought me to the verge of

---

[1] Burtzov, an officer of the Hussars, notorious for his drinking powers and escapades.

[2] Denis Davydov, author (1781–1839).   TRANSLATOR'S NOTE

despair. I began to seek a quarrel with him; to my epigrams he replied with epigrams which always seemed to me more spontaneous and more cutting than mine, and which were decidedly more amusing, for he joked while I fumed. At last, at a ball given by a Polish landed proprietor, seeing him the object of the attention of all the ladies, and especially of the mistress of the house, with whom I was having a liaison, I whispered some grossly insulting remark in his ear. He flamed up and gave me a slap in the face. We grasped our swords; the ladies fainted; we were separated; and that same night we set out to fight.

"The dawn was just breaking. I was standing at the appointed place with my three seconds. With indescribable impatience I awaited my opponent. The spring sun rose, and it was already growing hot. I saw him coming in the distance. He was on foot, in uniform, wearing his sword, and was accompanied by one second. We advanced to meet him. He approached, holding his cap filled with black cherries. The seconds measured twelve paces for us. I had to fire first, but my agitation was so great, that I could not depend upon the steadiness of my hand; and in order to give myself time to become calm, I ceded to him the first shot. My adversary would not agree to this. It was decided that we should cast lots. The first number fell to him, the constant favorite of fortune. He took aim, and his bullet went through my cap. It was now my turn. His life at last was in my hands; I looked at him eagerly, endeavoring to detect if only the faintest shadow of uneasiness. But he stood in front of my pistol, picking out the ripest cherries from his cap and spitting out the stones, which flew almost as far as my feet. His indifference enraged me beyond measure. 'What is the use,' thought I, 'of depriving him of life, when he attaches no value whatever to it?' A malicious thought flashed through my mind. I lowered my pistol.

" 'You don't seem to be ready for death just at present,' I said to him; 'you wish to have your breakfast; I do not wish to hinder you.'

" 'You are not hindering me in the least,' he replied. 'Have the goodness to fire, or just as you please—you owe me a shot; I shall always be at your service.'

"I turned to the seconds, informing them that I had no intention of firing that day, and with that the duel came to an end.

"I resigned my commission and retired to this little place. Since then, not a day has passed that I have not thought of revenge. And now my hour has arrived."

Silvio took from his pocket the letter that he had received that morning, and gave it to me to read. Someone (it seemed to be his business agent) wrote to him from Moscow, that a *certain person* was going to be married to a young and beautiful girl.

"You can guess," said Silvio, "who the certain person is. I am going to Moscow. We shall see if he will look death in the face with as much indifference now, when he is on the eve of being married, as he did once when he was eating cherries!"

With these words, Silvio rose, threw his cap upon the floor, and began pacing up and down the room like a tiger in his cage. I had listened to him in silence; strange conflicting feelings agitated me.

The servant entered and announced that the horses were ready. Silvio grasped my hand tightly, and we embraced each other. He seated himself in the carriage, in which there were two suitcases, one containing his pistols, the other his effects. We said good-bye once more, and the horses galloped off.

II

Several years passed, and family circumstances compelled me to settle in a poor little village of the N—— district. Occupied with farming, I continued to sigh in secret for my former active and carefree life. The most difficult thing of all was having to accustom myself to passing the spring and winter evenings in perfect solitude. Until the hour for dinner I managed to pass away the time somehow or other, talking with the bailiff, riding about to inspect the work, or going round to look at the new buildings; but as soon as it began to get dark, I positively did not know what to do with myself. The few books that I had found in the cupboards and store-rooms, I already knew by heart. All the stories that my housekeeper Kirilovna could remember, I had heard over and over again. The songs of the peasant woman made me feel depressed. I tried drinking spirits, but it made my head ache; and moreover, I confess I was afraid of becoming a drunkard from mere chagrin, that is to say, the saddest kind of drunkard, of which I had seen many examples in our district. I had no near neighbors, except two or three topers, whose conversation consisted for the most part of hiccups and sighs. Solitude was preferable to their society.

Four versts from my house there was a rich estate belonging to the Countess B——; but nobody lived there except the steward. The Countess had only visited her estate once, during the first year of her married life, and then she had remained there only a month. But in the second spring of my secluded life, a report was circulated that the Countess, with her husband, was coming to spend the summer on her estate. Indeed, they arrived at the beginning of June.

The arrival of a rich neighbor is an important event in the lives of country people. The landed proprietors and the people of their household talk about it for two months beforehand, and for three years afterward. As for me, I must confess that the news of the arrival of a young and beautiful neighbor affected me strongly. I burned with impatience to see her, and the first Sunday after her arrival I set out after dinner for the village of A——, to pay my respects to the Countess and her husband, as their nearest neighbor and most humble servant.

A lackey conducted me into the Count's study, and then went to announce me. The spacious room was furnished with every possible luxury. The walls were lined with bookcases, each surmounted by a bronze bust; over the marble mantelpiece was a large mirror; on the floor was a green cloth covered with carpets. Unaccustomed to luxury in my own poor corner, and not having seen the wealth of other people for a long time, I awaited the appearance of the Count with some little trepidation, as a suppliant from the provinces awaits the entrance of the minister. The door opened, and a handsome-looking man, of about thirty-two, entered the room. The Count approached me with a frank and friendly air: I tried to be self-possessed and began to introduce myself, but he anticipated me. We sat down. His conversation, which was easy and agreeable, soon dissipated my awkward bashfulness; and I was already beginning to recover my usual composure, when the Countess suddenly entered, and I became more confused than ever. She was indeed beautiful. The Count presented me. I wished to appear at ease, but the more I tried to assume an air of unconstraint, the more awkward I felt. In order to give me time to recover myself and to become accustomed to my new acquaintances, they began to talk to each other, treating me as a good neighbor, and without ceremony. Meanwhile, I walked about the room, examining the books and pictures. I am no judge of pictures, but one of them attracted my attention. It represented some view in Switzerland, but it was not the painting that struck me, but the circumstance that the canvas was shot through by two bullets, one planted just above the other.

"A good shot, that!" said I, turning to the Count.

"Yes," replied he, "a very remarkable shot.... Do you shoot well?" he continued.

"Tolerably," I replied, rejoicing that the conversation had turned at last upon a subject that was familiar to me. "At thirty paces I can manage to hit a card without fail—I mean, of course, with a pistol that I am used to."

"Really?" said the Countess, with a look of the greatest interest. "And you, my dear, could you hit a card at thirty paces?"

"Some day," replied the Count, "we will try. In my time I did not shoot badly, but it is now four years since I touched a pistol."

"Oh!" I observed, "in that case, I don't mind laying a wager that Your Excellency will not hit the card at twenty paces; the pistol demands daily practice. I know that from experience. In our regiment I was reckoned one of the best shots. It once happened that I did not touch a pistol for a whole month, as I had sent mine to be mended; and would you believe it, Your Excellency, the first time I began to shoot again, I missed a bottle four times in succession at twenty paces! Our captain, a witty and amusing fellow, happened to be standing by, and he said to me: 'It is evident, my friend, that you will not lift your hand against the bottle.' No, Your Excellency, you must not neglect to practice, or your hand will soon lose its cunning. The best shot that I ever met used to shoot at least three times every day before dinner. It was as much his custom to do this, as it was to drink his daily glass of brandy."

The Count and Countess seemed pleased that I had begun to talk.

"And what sort of a shot was he?" asked the Count.

"Well, it was this way with him, Your Excellency: if he saw a fly settle on the wall—you smile, Countess, but, before Heaven, it is the truth—if he saw a fly, he would call out: 'Kuzka, my pistol!' Kuzka would bring him a loaded pistol—bang! and the fly would be crushed against the wall."

"Wonderful!" said the Count. "And what was his name?"

"Silvio, Your Excellency."

"Silvio!" exclaimed the Count, starting up. "Did you know Silvio?"

"How could I help knowing him, Your Excellency: we were intimate friends; he was received in our regiment like a brother officer, but it is now five years since I had any news of him. Then Your Excellency also knew him?"

"Oh, yes, I knew him very well. Did he ever tell you of one very strange incident in his life?"

"Does Your Excellency refer to the slap in the face that he received from some scamp at a ball?"

"Did he tell you the name of this scamp?"

"No, Your Excellency, he never mentioned his name.... Ah! Your Excellency!" I continued, guessing the truth: "pardon me ... I did not know ... could it have been you?"

"Yes, I myself," replied the Count, with a look of extraordinary distress; "and that picture with a bullet through it is a memento of our last meeting."

"Ah, my dear," said the Countess, "for Heaven's sake, do not speak about that; it would be too terrible for me to listen to."

"No," replied the Count; "I will relate everything. He knows how I insulted his friend, and it is only right that he should know how Silvio revenged himself."

The Count pushed a chair towards me, and with the liveliest interest I listened to the following story:

"Five years ago I got married. The first month—the honeymoon—I spent here, in this village. To this house I am indebted for the happiest moments of my life, as well as for one of its most painful recollections.

"One evening we went out together for a ride on horseback. My wife's horse became restive; she grew frightened, gave the reins to me, and returned home on foot. I rode on before. In the courtyard I saw a traveling carriage, and I was told that in my study sat waiting for me a man who would not give his name, but who merely said that he had business with me. I entered the room and saw in the darkness a man, covered with dust and wearing a beard of several days' growth. He was standing there, near the fireplace. I approached him trying to remember his features.

" 'You do not recognize me, Count?' said he, in a quivering voice.

" 'Silvio!' I cried, and I confess that I felt as if my hair had suddenly stood on end.

" 'Exactly,' continued he. 'There is a shot due me, and I have come to discharge my pistol. Are you ready?'

"His pistol protruded from a side pocket. I measured twelve paces and took my stand there in that corner, begging him to fire quickly, before my wife arrived. He hesitated, and asked for a light. Candles were brought in. I closed the doors, gave orders that nobody was to enter, and again begged him to fire. He drew out his pistol and took aim. . . . I counted the seconds . . . I thought of her . . . A terrible minute passed! Silvio lowered his hand.

" 'I regret,' said he, 'that the pistol is not loaded with cherry-stones . . . the bullet is heavy. It seems to me that this is not a duel, but a murder. I am not accustomed to taking aim at unarmed men. Let us begin all over again; we will cast lots as to who shall fire first.'

"My head went round . . . I think I raised some objection. . . . At last we loaded another pistol, and rolled up two pieces of paper. He placed these latter in his cap—the same through which I had once sent a bullet—and again I drew the first number.

" 'You are devilishly lucky, Count,' said he, with a smile that I shall never forget.

"I don't know what was the matter with me, or how it was that he managed to make me do it ... but I fired and hit that picture."

The Count pointed with his finger to the perforated picture; his face burned like fire; the Countess was whiter than her own handkerchief; and I could not restrain an exclamation.

"I fired," continued the Count, "and, thank Heaven, missed my aim. Then Silvio ... at that moment he was really terrible.... Silvio raised his hand to take aim at me. Suddenly the door opens, Masha rushes into the room, and with a shriek throws herself upon my neck. Her presence restored to me all my courage.

" 'My dear,' said I to her, 'don't you see that we are joking? How frightened you are! Go and drink a glass of water and then come back to us; I will introduce you to an old friend and comrade.'

"Masha still doubted.

" 'Tell me, is my husband speaking the truth?' said she, turning to the terrible Silvio; 'is it true that you are only joking?'

" 'He is always joking, Countess,' replied Silvio: 'once he gave me a slap in the face in jest; on another occasion he sent a bullet through my cap in jest; and just now, when he fired at me and missed me, it was all in jest. And now I feel inclined to have a joke.'

"With these words he raised his pistol to take aim at me— right before her! Masha threw herself at his feet.

" 'Rise, Masha; are you not ashamed!' I cried in a rage: 'and you, sir, will you stop making fun of a poor woman? Will you fire or not?' "

" 'I will not,' replied Silvio: 'I am satisfied. I have seen your confusion, your alarm. I forced you to fire at me. That is sufficient. You will remember me. I leave you to your conscience.'

"Then he turned to go, but pausing in the doorway, and looking at the picture that my shot had passed through, he fired at it almost without taking aim, and disappeared. My wife had fainted away; the servants did not venture to stop him, the mere look of him filled them with terror. He went out upon the steps, called his coachman, and drove off before I could recover myself."

The Count fell silent. In this way I learned the end of the story, whose beginning had once made such a deep impression upon me. The hero of it I never saw again. It is said that Silvio commanded a detachment of hetaerists during the revolt under Alexander Ypsilanti, and that he was killed in the battle of Skulyani.

GRAVEN IMAGE*

BY JOHN O'HARA

T HE CAR turned in at the brief, crescent-shaped drive and waited until the two cabs ahead had pulled away. The car pulled up, the doorman opened the rear door, a little man got out. The little man nodded pleasantly enough to the doorman and said "Wait" to the chauffeur. "Will the Under Secretary be here long?" asked the doorman.

"Why?" said the little man.

"Because if you were going to be here, sir, only a short while, I'd let your man leave the car here, at the head of the rank."

"Leave it there *anyway*," said the Under Secretary.

"Very good, sir," said the doorman. He saluted and frowned only a little as he watched the Under Secretary enter the hotel. "Well," the doorman said to himself, "it was a long time coming. It took him longer than most, but sooner or later all of them—" He opened the door of the next car, addressed a

* from *The New Yorker* and *Pipe Night*

colonel and a major by their titles, and never did anything about the Under Secretary's car, which pulled ahead and parked in the drive.

The Under Secretary was spoken to many times in his progress to the main dining room. One man said, "What's your hurry, Joe?," to which the Under Secretary smiled and nodded. He was called Mr. Secretary most often, in some cases easily, by the old Washington hands, but more frequently with that embarrassment which Americans feel in using titles. As he passed through the lobby, the Under Secretary himself addressed by their White House nicknames two gentlemen whom he had to acknowledge to be closer to The Boss. And, bustling all the while, he made his way to the dining room, which was already packed. At the entrance he stopped short and frowned. The man he was to meet, Charles Browning, was chatting, in French, very amiably with the maître d'hôtel. Browning and the Under Secretary had been at Harvard at the same time.

The Under Secretary went up to him. "Sorry if I'm a little late," he said, and held out his hand, at the same time looking at his pocket watch. "Not so very, though. How are you, Charles? Fred, you got my message?"

"Yes, sir," said the maître d'hôtel. "I put you at a nice table all the way back to the right." He meanwhile had wig-wagged a captain, who stood by to lead the Under Secretary and his guest to Table 12. "Nice to have seen you again, Mr. Browning. Hope you come see us again while you are in Washington. Always a pleasure, sir."

"Always a pleasure, Fred," said Browning. He turned to the Under Secretary. "Well, shall we?"

"Yeah, let's sit down," said the Under Secretary.

The captain led the way, followed by the Under Secretary, walking slightly sideways. Browning, making one step to two of the Under Secretary's, brought up the rear. When they were seated, the Under Secretary took the menu out of the captain's hands. "Let's order right away so I don't have to look up and talk to those two son of a bitches. I guess you know which two I mean." Browning looked from right to left, as anyone does on just sitting down in a restaurant. He nodded and said, "Yes, I think I know. You mean the senators."

"That's right," said the Under Secretary. "I'm not gonna have a cocktail, but you can.... I'll have the lobster. Peas. Shoestring potatoes.... You want a cocktail?"

"I don't think so. I'll take whatever you're having."

"O.K., waiter?" said the Under Secretary.

"Yes, sir," said the captain, and went away.

"Well, Charles, I was pretty surprised to hear from you."

"Yes," Browning said, "I should imagine so, and by the way, I want to thank you for answering my letter so promptly. I know how rushed you fellows must be, and I thought, as I said in my letter, at your convenience."

"Mm. Well, frankly, there wasn't any use in putting you off. I mean till next week or two weeks from now or anything like that. I could just as easily see you today as a month from now. Maybe easier. I don't know where I'll be likely to be a month from now. In more ways than one. I may be taking the Clipper to London, and then of course I may be out on my can! Coming to New York and asking *you* for a job. I take it that's what you wanted to see me about."

"Yes, and with hat in hand."

"Oh, no. I can't see you waiting with hat in hand, not for anybody. Not even for The Boss."

Browning laughed.

"What are you laughing at?" asked the Under Secretary.

"Well, you know how I feel about him, so I'd say least of all The Boss."

"Well, you've got plenty of company in this goddam town. But why'd you come to me, then? Why didn't you go to one of your Union League or Junior League or what-ever-the-hell-it-is pals? There, that big jerk over there with the blue suit and the striped tie, for instance?"

Browning looked over at the big jerk with the blue suit and striped tie, and at that moment their eyes met and the two men nodded.

"You *know* him?" said the Under Secretary.

"Sure, I know him, but that doesn't say I *approve* of him."

"Well, at least that's something. And I notice he knows you."

"I've been to his house. I think he's been to our house when my father was alive, and naturally I've seen him around New York all my life."

"Naturally. Naturally. Then why didn't you go to *him?*"

"That's easy. I wouldn't like to ask him for anything. I don't approve of the man, at least as a politician, so I couldn't go to him and ask him a favor."

"But, on the other hand, you're not one of our team, but yet you'd ask me a favor. I don't get it."

"Oh, yes you do, Joe. You didn't get where you are by not being able to understand a simple thing like that."

Reluctantly—and quite obviously it was reluctantly—the Under Secretary grinned. "All right. I was baiting you."

"I know you were, but I expected it. I have it coming to me. I've always been against you fellows. I wasn't even for you in 1932, and that's a hell of an admission, but it's the truth. But that's water under the bridge—or isn't it?" The waiter interrupted with the food, and they did not speak until he had gone away.

"You were asking me if it isn't water under the bridge. Why should it be?"

"The obvious reason," said Browning.

" 'My country, 'tis of thee'?"

"Exactly. Isn't that enough?"

"It isn't for your Racquet Club pal over there."

"You keep track of things like that?"

"Certainly," said the Under Secretary. "I know every goddam club in this country, beginning back about twenty-three years ago. I had ample time to study them all then, you recall, objectively, from the outside. By the way, I notice you wear a wristwatch. What happens to the little animal?"

Browning put his hand in his pocket and brought out a small bunch of keys. He held the chain so that the Under Secretary could see, suspended from it, a small golden pig. "I still carry it," he said.

"They tell me a lot of you fellows put them back in your pockets about five years ago, when one of the illustrious brethren closed his downtown office and moved up to Ossining."

"Oh, probably," Browning said, "but quite a few fellows, I believe, that hadn't been wearing them took to wearing them again out of simple loyalty. Listen, Joe, are we talking like grown men? Are you sore at the Pork? Do you think you'd have enjoyed being a member of it? If being sore at it was even partly responsible for getting you where you are, then I think you ought to be a little grateful to it. You'd show the bastards. O.K. You showed them. Us. If you hadn't been so sore at the Porcellian so-and-so's, you might have turned into just another lawyer."

"My wife gives me that sometimes."

"There, do you see?" Browning said. "Now then, how about the job?"

The Under Secretary smiled. "There's no getting away from it, you guys have got something. O.K., what are you interested in? Of course, I make no promises, and I don't even know if what you're interested in is something I can help you with."

"That's a chance I'll take. That's why I came to Washington, on just that chance, but it's my guess you can help me." Browning went on to tell the Under Secretary about the job he wanted. He told him why he thought he was qualified for it, and the Under Secretary nodded. Browning told him everything he knew about the job, and the Under Secretary continued to nod silently. By the end of Browning's recital the Under Secretary had become thoughtful. He told Browning that he thought there might be some little trouble with a certain character but that that character could be handled, because the real say so, the green light, was controlled by a man who was a friend of the Under Secretary's, and the Under Secretary could almost say at this moment that the matter could be arranged.

At this, Browning grinned. "By God, Joe, we've got to have a drink on this. This is the best news since—" He summoned the waiter. The Under Secretary yielded and ordered a cordial. Browning ordered a Scotch. The drinks were brought. Browning said, "About the job. I'm not going to say another word but just keep my fingers crossed. But as to you, Joe, you're the best.

I drink to you." The two men drank, the Under Secretary sipping at his, Browning taking half of his. Browning looked at the drink in his hand. "You know, I was a little afraid. That other stuff, the club stuff."

"Yes," said the Under Secretary.

"I don't know why fellows like you—you never would have made it in a thousand years, but"—then, without looking up, he knew everything had collapsed—"but I've said exactly the wrong thing, haven't I?"

"That's right, Browning," said the Under Secretary. "You've said exactly the wrong thing. I've got to be going." He stood up and turned and went out, all dignity.

PUTOIS[*]

BY ANATOLE FRANCE

(Translated by Frederic Chapman)

I

"WHEN WE were children, our tiny garden, which you could go from end to end of in twenty strides, seemed to us a vast universe, made up of joys and terrors," said Monsieur Bergeret.

"Do you remember Putois, Lucien?" asked Zoé, smiling as was her wont, with lips compressed and her nose over her needlework.

"Do I remember Putois! . . . Why, of all the figures which pass before my childhood's eyes, that of Putois remains the clearest in my memory. Not a single feature of his face or his character have I forgotten. He had a long head. . . ."

---

[*] from *Crainquebille*

"A low forehead," added Mademoiselle Zoé.

Then, antiphonally, in a monotonous voice, with mock gravity, the brother and sister recited the following points of a kind of police description:

"A low forehead."

"Wall-eyed."

"Furtive looking."

"A crow's foot on his temple."

"High cheek-bones, red and shiny."

"His ears were ragged."

"His face was blank and expressionless."

"It was only by his hands, which were constantly moving, that you divined his thoughts."

"Thin, rather bent, weak in appearance."

"In reality of unusual strength."

"He could easily bend a five-franc piece between his thumb and forefinger."

"His thumb was huge."

"He spoke with a drawl."

"His tone was unctuous."

Suddenly Monsieur Bergeret cried eagerly:

"Zoé! We have forgotten his yellow hair and his scant beard. We must begin again."

Pauline had been listening with astonishment to this strange recital. She asked her father and her aunt how they had come to learn this prose passage by heart, and why they recited it like a Litany.

Monsieur Bergeret replied gravely:

"Pauline, what you have just heard is the sacred text, I may say the liturgy of the Bergeret family. It is right that it should be transmitted to you in order that it may not perish with your aunt and me. Your grandfather, my child, your grandfather, Eloi Bergeret, who was not one to be amused with trifles, set a high value on this passage, principally on account of its origin. He entitled it 'The Anatomy of Putois.' And he was accustomed to say that in certain respects he set the anatomy of Putois above the anatomy of Quaresmeprenant. 'If the description written by Zenomanes,' he said, 'is more learned and richer in rare and precious terms, the description of Putois greatly excels it in the lucidity of its ideas and the clearness of its style.' Such was his opinion, for in those days Doctor Ledouble, of Tours, had not yet expounded chapters thirty, thirty-one and thirty-two of the fourth book of Rabelais."

"I can't understand you," said Pauline.

"It is because you don't know Putois, my daughter. You must learn that, in the childhood of your father and your Aunt Zoé, there was no more familiar figure than Putois. In the home of your grandfather Bergeret, Putois was a household word. We all, in turn, believed that we had seen him."

"But who was Putois?" asked Pauline.

Instead of replying her father began to laugh, and Mademoiselle Bergeret also laughed, though her lips were closed.

Pauline looked first at one and then at the other. It seemed to her odd that her aunt should laugh so heartily, and odder still that she should laugh at the same thing as her brother; for strange to say the minds of the brother and sister moved in different grooves.

"Tell me who Putois was, papa. Since you want me to know, tell me."

"Putois, my child, was a gardener. The son of honest farmers of Artois, he had set up as a nursery-man at Saint-Omer. But he was unable to please his customers and failed in business. He gave up his nursery and went out to work by the day. His employers were not always satisfied."

At these words, Mademoiselle Bergeret, still laughing, remarked:

"You remember, Lucien, when father couldn't find his inkpot, his pens, his sealing-wax or his scissors on his desk, how he used to say: 'I think Putois must have been here.'"

"Ah!" said Monsieur Bergeret, "Putois had not a good reputation."

"Is that all?" asked Pauline.

"No, my child it is not all. There was something odd about Putois; we knew him, he was familiar to us and yet..."

..."He did not exist," said Zoé.

Monsieur Bergeret looked reproachfully at her.

"What a thing to say, Zoé! Why thus break the charm? Putois did not exist! Dare you say so, Zoé? Can you maintain it? Before affirming that Putois did not exist, that Putois never was, you should consider the condition of being and the modes of existence. Putois existed, sister. But it is true that his was a peculiar existence."

"I understand less and less," said Pauline, growing discouraged.

"The truth will dawn upon you directly, child. Know that Putois was born in the fullness of age. I was still a child; your aunt was a little girl. We lived in a small house, in a suburb of Saint-Omer. Our parents led a quiet retired life, until they were discovered by an old lady of Saint-Omer, Madame Cornouiller, who lived in her manor of Monplaisir, some twelve miles from the town, and who turned out to be my mother's great-aunt. She took advantage of the privilege of friendship to insist on our father and mother coming to dine with her at Monplaisir every Sunday. There they were bored to death. But the old lady said it was right for relatives to dine together on Sundays, and that only ill-bred persons neglected the observance of this ancient custom. Our father was miserable. His sufferings were pitiful to behold. But Madame Cornouiller did not see them. She saw nothing. My mother bore it better. She suffered as much as my father, and perhaps more, but she contrived to smile."

"Women are made to suffer," said Zoé.

"Every living creature in the world is born to suffer, Zoé. It was in vain that our parents refused these terrible invitations; Madame Cornouiller's carriage came to fetch them every Sunday afternoon. They were bound to go to Monplaisir; it was an obligation which they could not possibly avoid. It was an established order which only open rebellion could disturb. At length my father revolted, and swore he would not accept another of Madame Cornouiller's invitations. To my mother he left the task of finding decent pretexts and varying reasons for their repeated refusals; it was a task for which she was ill fitted; for she was incapable of dissimulation."

"Say, rather, Lucien, that she was not willing to dissimulate. Had she wished she could have fibbed like anyone else."

"It is true that when she had good reasons she preferred giving them to inventing bad ones. You remember, sister, that one day she said at table: 'Fortunately Zoé has whooping-cough: so we shall not have to go to Monplaisir for a long time.'"

"Yes, that did happen," said Zoé.

"You recovered, Zoé. And one day Madame Cornouiller came and said to our mother: 'My dear, I am counting on you and your husband to dine at Monplaisir on Sunday.' Our mother had been expressly enjoined by her husband to give Madame Cornouiller some plausible pretext for refusing. In her extremity the only excuse she could think of was absolutely devoid of probability: 'I am extremely sorry, madame, but it will be impossible. On Sunday I expect the gardener.'

"At these words Madame Cornouiller looked through the glazed door of the drawing-room at the wilderness of a little garden, where the spindle-trees and the lilacs looked as if they never had and never would make the acquaintance of a pruning-hook. 'You are expecting the gardener! What for? To work in your garden?'

"Then, our mother, having involuntarily cast eyes on the patch of rough grass and half-wild plants, which she had just called a garden, realized with alarm that her excuse must appear a mere invention. 'Why couldn't this man come on Monday or Tuesday to work in your...garden? Either of these days would be better. It is wrong to work on Sunday. Is he occupied during the week?'

"I have often noticed that the most impudent and the most absurd reasons meet with the least resistance; they disconcert the opponent. Madame Cornouiller insisted less than might have been expected of a person so disinclined to give in. Rising from her chair she asked: 'What is your gardener's name, dear?'

"'Putois,' replied our mother promptly.

"Putois had a name. Henceforth he existed. Madame Cornouiller went off mumbling: 'Putois! I seem to know that name, Putois? Putois? Why, yes, I know him well enough. But I can't recall him. Where does he live? He goes out to work by the day. When people want him, they send for him to some house where he is working. Ah! Just as I thought; he is a loafer, a vagabond... a good-for-nothing. You should beware of him, my dear.'

"Henceforth Putois had a character."

II

Monsieur Goubin and Monsieur Jean Marteau came in. Monsieur Bergeret told them the subject of the conversation:

"We were talking of the man whom my mother one day caused to exist, and created gardener at Saint-Omer. She gave him a name. Henceforth he acted."

"I beg your pardon, sir?" said Monsieur Goubin, wiping his eye-glasses. "Do you mind saying that over again?"

"Willingly," replied Monsieur Bergeret. "There was no gardener. The gardener did not exist. My mother said: 'I expect the gardener!' Straightway the gardener existed—and acted."

"But, Professor," inquired Monsieur Goubin, "how can he have acted if he did not exist?"

"In a manner, he did exist," replied Monsieur Bergeret.

"You mean he existed in imagination," scornfully retorted Monsieur Goubin.

"And is not imaginary existence, existence?" exclaimed the Professor. "Are not mythical personages capable of influencing men? Think of mythology, Monsieur Goubin, and you will perceive that it is not the real characters, but rather the imaginary ones that exercise the profoundest and the most durable influence over our minds. In all times and in all lands, beings who were no more real than Putois have inspired nations with love and hatred, with terror and hope, they have counselled crimes, they have received offerings, they have moulded manners and laws. Monsieur Goubin, think on the mythology of the ages. Putois is a mythological personage, obscure, I admit, and of the humblest order. The rude satyr, who used to sit at a table with our northern peasants, was deemed worthy to figure in one of Jordaëns' pictures, and in a fable of La Fontaine. The hairy son of Sycorax was introduced into the sublime world of Shakespeare.

Putois, less fortunate, will be forever scorned by poets and artists. He is lacking in grandeur and mystery; he has no distinction, no character. He is the offspring of too rational a mind; he was conceived by persons who knew how to read and write, who lacked the enchanting imagination which gives birth to fables. Gentlemen, I think what I have said is enough to reveal to you the true nature of Putois."

"I understand it," said Monsieur Goubin.

Then Monsieur Bergeret continued:

"Putois existed. I maintain it. He was. Consider, gentlemen, and you will conclude that the condition of being in no way implies matter; it signifies only the connection between attribute and subject, it expresses merely a relation."

"Doubtless," said Jean Marteau, "but to be without attributes is to be practically nothing. Someone said long ago: 'I am what I am.' Pardon my bad memory; but one can't recollect everything. Whoever it was who spoke thus committed a great imprudence. By those thoughtless words he implied that he was devoid of attributes and without relation, wherefore he asserted his own non-existence and rashly suppressed himself. I wager that he has never been heard of since."

"Then your wager is lost," replied Monsieur Bergeret. "He corrected the bad effect of those egotistical words by applying to himself a whole string of adjectives. He has been greatly talked of, but generally without much sense."

"I don't understand," said Monsieur Goubin.

"That does not matter," replied Jean Marteau.

And he requested Monsieur Bergeret to tell them about Putois.

"It is very kind of you to ask me," said the Professor. "Putois was born in the second half of the nineteenth century, at Saint-Omer. It would have been better for him had he been born some centuries earlier, in the Forest of Arden or in the Wood of Broceliande. He would then have been an evil spirit of extraordinary cleverness."

"A cup of tea, Monsieur Goubin," said Pauline.

"Was Putois an evil spirit then?" inquired Jean Marteau.

"He was evil," replied Monsieur Bergeret, "in a certain way,

and yet not absolutely evil. He was like those devils who are
said to be very wicked, but in whom, when one comes to know
them, one discovers good qualities. I am disposed to think that
justice has not been done to Putois. Madame Cornouiller was
prejudiced against him; she immediately suspected him of being a loafer, a drunkard, a thief. Then, reflecting that since he
was employed by my mother, who was not rich, he could not
ask for high pay, she wondered whether it might not be to her
advantage to engage him in the place of her own gardener, who
had a better reputation, but also, alas! more requirements. It
would soon be the season for trimming the yew trees. She
thought that if Madame Eloi Bergeret, who was poor, paid
Putois little, she who was rich might give him still less, since it
is the custom for the rich to pay less than the poor. And already
in her mind's eye she beheld her yew trees cut into walls,
spheres and pyramids, all for but a trifling outlay. 'I should
look after Putois,' she said to herself, 'and see that he did not
loaf and thieve. I risk nothing and save a good deal. These casual laborers sometimes do better than skilled workmen.' She
resolved to make the experiment; she said to my mother: 'Send
Putois to me, my dear. I will give him work at Monplaisir.' My
mother promised. She would willingly have done it. But really
it was impossible. Madame Cornouiller expected Putois at
Monplaisir and expected him in vain. She was a persistent person, and, once having made a resolve, she was determined to
carry it out. When she saw my mother, she complained of having heard nothing of Putois. 'Did you not tell him, my dear, that
I was expecting him?' 'Yes, but he is so strange, so erratic...'
'Oh! I know that sort of person. I know your Putois through
and through. But no workman can be so mad as to refuse to
come to work at Monplaisir. My house is well known, I should
think. Putois will come for my instructions, and quickly, my
dear. Only tell me where he lives; and I will go and find him
myself.' My mother replied that she did not know where Putois
lived, he was not known to have a home, he was without an address. 'I have not seen him again, Madame. He seems to have
gone into hiding.' She could not have come nearer the truth.
And yet Madame Cornouiller listened to her with mistrust. She

suspected her of beguiling Putois and keeping him out of sight for fear of losing him or rendering him more exacting. And she mentally pronounced her overselfish. Many a judgment ratified by history has no better foundation."

"That is quite true," said Pauline.

"What is true?" asked Zoé, who was half asleep.

"That the judgments of history are often false. I remember, papa, that you said one day: 'It was very naive of Madame Roland to appeal to an impartial posterity, and not to see that if her contemporaries were malevolent, those who came after them would be equally so.'"

"Pauline," inquired Mademoiselle Zoé, sternly, "what has that to do with the story of Putois?"

"A great deal, aunt."

"I don't see it."

Monsieur Bergeret, who did not object to digressions, replied to his daughter:

"If every injustice were ultimately repaired in this world, it would never have been necessary to invent another for the purpose. How can posterity judge the dead justly? Into the shades whither they pass can they be pursued, can they there be questioned? As soon as it is possible to regard them justly, they are forgotten. But is it possible ever to be just? What is justice? At any rate, in the end, Madame Cornouiller was obliged to admit that my mother was not deceiving her, and that Putois was not to be found.

"Nevertheless, she did not give up looking for him. Of all her relations, friends, neighbors, servants and tradesmen she inquired whether they knew Putois. Only two or three replied that they had never heard of him. The majority thought they had seen him. 'I have heard the name,' said the cook, 'but I can't put a face to it.' 'Putois! Why! I know him very well,' said the road surveyor, scratching his ear. 'But I couldn't exactly point him out to you.' The most precise information came from Monsieur Blaise, the registrar, who declared that he had employed Putois to chop wood in his yard, from the 19th until the 23rd of October, in the year of the comet.

"One morning, Madame Cornouiller rushed panting into

my father's study: 'I have just seen Putois,' she exclaimed. 'Ah! Yes. I've just seen him. Do I think so? But I am sure. He was creeping along by Monsieur Tenchant's wall. He turned into the Rue des Abbesses; he was walking quickly. Then I lost him. Was it really he? There's no doubt of it. A man about fifty, thin, bent, looking like a loafer, wearing a dirty blouse.' 'Such is indeed Putois' description,' said my father. 'Ah! I told you so! Besides, I called him. I cried: Putois! and he turned round. That is what detectives do when they want to make sure of the identity of a criminal they are in search of. Didn't I tell you it was he! ... I managed to get on his track, your Putois. Well! he is very evil looking. And it was extremely imprudent of you and your wife to employ him. I can read character; and though I only saw his back, I would swear that he is a thief, and perhaps a murderer. His ears are ragged; and that is an infallible sign.' 'Ah! you noticed that his ears were ragged?' 'Nothing escapes me. My dear Monsieur Bergeret, if you don't want to be murdered with your wife and children, don't let Putois come into your house again. Take my advice and have all your locks changed.'

"Now a few days later it happened that Madame Cornouiller had three melons stolen from her kitchen garden. As the thief was not discovered, she suspected Putois. The *gendarmes* were summoned to Monplaisir, and their statements confirmed Madame Cornouiller's suspicions. Just then gangs of thieves were prowling around the gardens of the countryside. But this time the theft seemed to have been committed by a single person, and with extraordinary skill. He had not damaged anything, and had left no footprint on the moist ground. The delinquent could be none other than Putois. Such was the opinion of the police sergeant who had long known all about Putois, and was making every effort to put his hand on the fellow.

"In the *Journal de Saint-Omer* appeared an article on the three melons of Madame Cornouiller. It contained a description of Putois, according to information obtained in the town. 'His forehead is low,' said the newspaper, 'he is wall-eyed, his look is shifty, he has a crow's foot on the temple, high cheekbones red and shiny. His ears are ragged. Thin, slightly bent, weak in appearance, in reality he is extraordinarily strong: he can easily bend a five-franc piece between his thumb and forefinger.

" 'There were good reasons,' said the newspaper, 'for attributing to him a long series of robberies perpetrated with marvelous skill.'

"Putois was the talk of the town. One day it was said that he had been arrested and committed to prison. But it was soon discovered that the man who had been taken for Putois was a peddler named Rigobert. As nothing could be proved against him, he was discharged after a fortnight's precautionary detention. And still Putois could not be found. Madame Cornouiller fell a victim to another robbery still more audacious than the first. Three silver teaspoons were stolen from her sideboard.

"She recognized the hand of Putois, had a chain put on her bedroom door, and lay awake at night."

III

About ten o'clock, when Pauline had gone to bed. Mademoiselle Bergeret said to her brother:

"Don't forget to tell how Putois seduced Madame Cornouiller's cook."

"I was just thinking of it, sister," replied her brother. "To omit that incident would be to omit the best part of the story. But we must come to it in its proper place. The police made a careful search for Putois but they did not find him. When it was known that he could not be found, everyone made it a point of honour to discover him; and the malicious succeeded. As there were not a few malicious folk at Saint-Omer and in the neighbourhood, Putois was observed at one and the same time in street, field and wood. Thus, another trait was added to his character. To him was attributed that gift of ubiquity which is possessed by so many popular heroes. A being capable of traveling long distances in a moment, and of appearing suddenly in the place where he is least expected, is naturally alarming. Putois was the terror of Saint-Omer. Madame Cornouiller, convinced that Putois had robbed her of three melons and three teaspoons, barricaded herself at Monplaisir and lived in perpetual fear. Bars, bolts and locks were powerless to reassure her. Putois was for her a terribly subtle creature, who could pass through closed doors. A domestic event redoubled her alarm. Her cook was seduced; and a time came when she could conceal her fault no longer. But she obstinately refused to indicate her betrayer."

"Her name was Gudule," said Mademoiselle Zoé.

"Her name was Gudule; and she was thought to be protected against the perils of love by a long and forked beard. A beard, which suddenly appeared on the chin of that saintly royal maiden venerated at Orague, protected her virginity. A beard, which was no longer young, sufficed not to protect the virtue of Gudule. Madame Cornouiller urged Gudule to utter the name of the man who betrayed her and then abandoned her to distress. Gudule burst into tears, but refused to speak. Threats and entreaties were alike useless. Madame Cornouiller made a long and minute inquiry. She diplomatically questioned her neighbours—both men and women—the tradesmen, the gardener, the road surveyor, the *gendarmes;* nothing put her on the track of the culprit. Again she endeavoured to extract a full confession from Gudule. 'In your own interest, Gudule, tell me who it is.' Gudule remained silent. Suddenly Madame Cornouiller had a flash of enlightenment: 'It is Putois!' The cook wept and said nothing. 'It is Putois! Why did I not guess it before? It is Putois! You unhappy girl! Oh, you poor, unhappy girl!'

"Henceforth Madame Cornouiller was persuaded that Putois was the father of her cook's child. Everyone at Saint-Omer, from the President of the Tribunal to the lamplighter's mongrel dog, knew Gudule and her basket. The news that Putois had seduced Gudule filled the town with laughter, astonishment and admiration. Putois was hailed as an irresistible lady-killer and the lover of the eleven thousand virgins. On these slight grounds there was ascribed to him the paternity of five or six other children born that year, who, considering the happiness that awaited them and the joy they brought to their mothers, would have done just as well not to put in an

appearance. Among others were included the servant of
Monsieur Maréchal, who kept the general shop with the sign of
'Le Rendezvous des Pecheurs,' a baker's errand girl, and the lit-
tle cripple of the Pont-Biquet, who had all fallen victims to
Putois' charms. 'The monster!' cried the gossips.

"Thus Putois, invisible satyr, threatened with woes irretriev-
able all the maidens of a town, wherein, according to the oldest
inhabitants, virgins had from time immemorial lived free from
danger.

"Though celebrated thus throughout the city and its neighbourhood, he continued in a subtle manner to be associated especially with our home. He passed by our door, and it was
believed that from time to time he climbed over our garden wall.
He was never seen face to face. But we were constantly recog-
nizing his shadow, his voice, his footprints. More than once, in
the twilight, we thought we saw his back at the bend of the road.
My sister and I were changing our opinions of him. He remained wicked and malevolent, but he was becoming child-like
and simple. He was growing less real, and, if I may say so, more
poetical. He was about to be included in the naive cycles of children's fairy tales. He was turning into Croquemitaine, into Père
Fouettard, into the dustman who shuts little children's eyes at
night. He was not that sprite who by night entangles the colt's
tail in the stable. Not so rustic or so charming, yet he was just as
frankly mischievous; he used to draw ink moustaches on my
sisters' dolls. In our beds we used to hear him before we went to
sleep; he was barking with the dogs; he was groaning in the
mill-hopper; he was mimicking the songs of belated drunkards
in the street.

"What rendered Putois present and familiar to us, what interested us in him was that his memory was associated with all
the objects that surrounded us. Zoé's dolls, my exercise-books,
the pages of which he had so often blotted and crumpled, the
garden wall over which we had seen his red eyes gleam in the
shadow, the blue flower-pot one winter's night cracked by him
if it were not by the frost; trees, streets, benches, everything reminded us of Putois, our Putois, the children's Putois, a being
local and mythical. In grace and in poetry he fell far short of

the most awkward wild man of the woods, of the uncouthest Sicilian or Thessalian faun. But he was a demi-god all the same.

"To our father Putois' character appeared very differently; it was symbolical and had a philosophical signification. Our father had a vast pity for humanity. He did not think men very reasonable. Their errors, when they were not cruel, entertained and amused him. The belief in Putois interested him as a compendium and abridgement of all the beliefs of humanity. Our father was ironical and sarcastic; he spoke of Putois as if he were an actual being. He was sometimes so persistent, and described each detail with such precision, that our mother was quite astonished. 'Anyone would say that you are serious, my love,' she would say frankly, 'and yet you know perfectly...' He replied gravely, 'The whole of Saint-Omer believes in the existence of Putois. Could I be a good citizen and deny it? One must think well before suppressing an article of universal belief.'

"Only very clear-headed persons are troubled by such scruples. At heart my father was a follower of Gassendi. He compromised between his individual views and those of the public: with the Saint-Omerites he believed in the existence of Putois, but he did not admit his direct intervention in the theft of the melons and the seduction of the cook. In short, like a good citizen he professed his faith in the existence of Putois, and he dispensed with Putois when explaining the events which happened in the town. Wherefore, in this case as in all others, he proved himself a good man and thoughtful.

"As for our mother, she felt herself in a way responsible for the birth of Putois, and she was right. For in reality Putois was born of our mother's taradiddle, as Caliban was born of a poet's invention. The two crimes, of course, differed greatly in magnitude, and my mother's guilt was not so great as Shakespeare's. Nevertheless, she was alarmed and dismayed at seeing so tiny a falsehood grow indefinitely, and so trifling a deception meet with a success so prodigious that it stopped nowhere, spread throughout the whole town, and threatened to spread throughout the whole world. One day she grew pale, believing that she was about to see her fib rise in person before her. On that day, her servant, who was new to the house and neighbourhood, came and told her that a man was asking for her. He wanted, he said, to speak to Madame. 'What kind of a man is he?' 'A man in a blouse. He looked like a country labourer.' 'Did he give his name?' 'Yes, Madame.' 'Well, what is it?' 'Putois.' 'Did he tell you that that was his name?' 'Putois, yes Madame.' 'And he is here?' 'Yes, Madame. He is waiting in the kitchen.' 'You have seen him?' 'Yes, Madame.' 'What does he want?' 'He did not say. He will only tell Madame.' 'Go and ask him.'

"When the servant returned to the kitchen, Putois was no longer there. This meeting between Putois and the new servant was never explained. But I think that from that day my mother began to believe that Putois might possibly exist, and that perhaps she had not invented."

ONLY THE DEAD KNOW BROOKLYN*

BY THOMAS WOLFE

DERE'S NO guy livin' dat knows Brooklyn t'roo an' t'roo, because it'd take a guy a lifetime just to find his way aroun' duh f—— town.

So like I say, I'm waitin' for my train t' come when I sees dis big guy standin' deh—dis is duh foist I eveh see of him. Well, he's lookin' wild, y'know, an' I can see dat he's had plenty, but still he's holdin' it; he talks good an' is walkin' straight enough. So den, dis big guy steps up to a little guy dat's standin' deh an' says, "How d'yuh get t' Eighteent' Avenoo an' Sixty-sevent' Street?" he says.

_____
* from *The New Yorker* and *From Death to Morning*

"Jesus! Yuh got me, chief," duh little guy says to him. "I ain't been heah long myself. Where is duh place?" he says. "Out in duh Flatbush sections somewhere?"

"Nah," duh big guy says. "It's out in Bensonhoist. But I was neveh deh befoeh. How d'yuh get deh?"

"Jesus," duh little guy says, scratchin' his head, y'know— yuh could see duh little guy didn't know his way about—"yuh got me, chief. I neveh hoid of it. Do any of youse guys know where it is?" he says to me.

"Sure," I says. "It's out in Bensonhoist. Yuh take duh Fourt' Avenoo express, get off at Fifty-nint' Street, change to a Sea Beach local deh, get off at Eighteent' Avenoo an' Sixty-toid, an' den walk down foeh blocks. Dat's all yuh got to do," I says.

"G'wan!" some wise guy dat I neveh seen befoeh pipes up. "Whatcha talkin' about?" he says—oh, he was wise, y'know. "Duh guy is crazy! I tell yuh what yuh do," he says to duh big guy. "Yuh change to duh West End line at Toity-sixt'," he tells him. "Get off at Noo Utrecht and Sixteent' Avenoo," he says. "Walk two blocks oveh, foeh blocks up," he says, "an' you'll be right deh." Oh, a *wise* guy, y'know.

"Oh, yeah?" I says. "Who told *you* so much?" He got me sore because he was so wise about it. "How long you been livin' heah?" I says.

"All my life," he says. "I was bawn in Williamsboig," he says. "An' I can tell you t'ings about dis town you neveh hoid of," he says.

"Yeah?" I says.

"Yeah," he says.

"Well, den, you can tell me t'ings about dis town dat nobody else has eveh hoid of, either. Maybe you make it all up yoehself at night," I says, "befoeh you go to sleep—like cuttin' out papeh dolls, or somp'n."

"Oh, yeah?" he says. "You're pretty wise, ain't yuh?"

"Oh, I don't know," I says. "Duh boids ain't usin' my hea' for Lincoln's statue yet," I says. "But I'm wise enough to know a phony when I see one."

"Yeah?" he says. "A wise guy, huh? Well, you're so wise dat

someone's goin' t'bust yuh one right on duh snoot some day," he says. "Dat's how wise *you* are."

Well, my train was comin', or I'da smacked him den and dere: but when I seen duh train was comin', all I said was, "All right, mug! I'm sorry I can't stay to take keh of you, but I'll be seein' yuh sometime, I hope, out in duh cemetery." So den I says to duh big guy, who'd been standin' deh all duh time, "You come wit me," I says. So when we gets on to duh train I says to him, "Where yuh goin' out in Bensonhoist?" I says. "What number are yuh lookin' for?" I says. *You* know—I t'ought if he told me duh address I might be able to help him out.

"Oh," he says, "I'm not lookin' for no one. I don't know no one out deh."

"Then whatcha goin' out deh for?" I says.

"Oh," duh guy says, "I'm just goin' out to see duh place," he says. "I like duh sound of duh name—Bensonhoist, y'know—so I t'ought I'd go out an' have a look at it."

"Whatcha tryin' t'hand me?" I says. "Whatcha tryin' t'do—kid me?" *You* know I t'ought duh guy was bein' wise wit me.

"No," he says, "I'm tellin' yuh duh troot. I like to go out an' take a look at places wit nice names like dat. I like to go out an' look at all kinds of places," he says.

"How'd yuh know deh was such a place," I says, "if yuh neveh been deh befoeh?"

"Oh," he says, "I got a map."

"A *map?*" I says.

"Sure," he says, "I got a map dat tells me about all dese places. I take it wit me every time I come out heah," he says.

And Jesus! Wit dat, he pulls it out of his pocket, an' so help me, but he's *got* it—he's tellin' duh troot—a big map of duh whole f—— place with all duh different pahts mahked out. You know Canarsie an' East Noo Yawk an' Flatbush, Bensonhoist, Sout' Brooklyn, duh Heights, Bay Ridge, Greenpernt—duh whole goddam layout, he's got it right deh on duh map.

"You been to any of dose places?" I says.

"Sure," he says, "I been to most of 'em. I was down in Red Hook just last night," he says.

"Jesus! Red Hook!" I says. "Whatcha do down deh?"

"Oh," he says, "nuttin' much. I just walked aroun'. I went into a coupla places an' had a drink," he says, "but most of the time I just walked aroun'."

"Just walked aroun'?" I says.

"Sure," he says, "just lookin' at t'ings, y'know."

"Where'd yuh go?" I asts him.

"Oh," he says, "I don't know duh name of duh place, but I could find it on my map," he says. "One time I was walkin' across some big fields where deh ain't no houses," he says, "but I could see ships oveh deh all lighted up. Dey was loadin'. So I walks across duh fields," he says, "to where duh ships are."

"Sure," I says, "I know where you was. You was down to duh Erie Basin."

"Yeah," he says, "I guess dat was it. Dey had some of dose big elevators an' cranes an' dey was loadin' ships, an' I could see some ships in dry dock all lighted up; so I walks across duh fields to where dey are," he says.

"Den what did yuh do?" I says.

"Oh," he says, "nuttin' much. I came on back across duh fields after a while an' went into a couple places an' had a drink."

"Didn't nuttin' happen while yuh was in dere?" I says.

"No," he says. "Nuttin' much. A coupla guys was drunk in one of duh places an' stahted a fight, but dey bounced 'em out," he says, "an' den one of duh guys stahted to come back again, but duh bartender gets his baseball bat out from under duh counteh; so duh guy goes on."

"Jesus!" I said. "Red Hook!"

"Sure," he says. "Dat's where it was, all right."

"Well, you keep outa deh," I says. "You stay away from deh."

"Why?" he says. "What's wrong wit it?"

"Oh," I says, "it's a good place to stay away from, dat's all. It's a good place to keep out of."

"Why?" he says. "Why is it?"

Jesus! Whatcha gonna do wit a guy as dumb as dat? I saw it wasn't no use to try to tell him nuttin'—he wouldn't know what I was talkin' about; so I just says to him, "Oh, nuttin'. Yuh might get lost down deh, dat's all."

"Lost?" he says. "No, I wouldn't get lost. I got a map," he says.

A map! Red Hook! Jesus!

So den duh guy begins to ast me all kinds of nutty questions: how big was Brooklyn, an' could I find my way aroun' in it, an' how long would it take a guy to know duh place.

"Listen!" I says. "You get dat idea outa yoeh head right now," I says. "You ain't neveh gonna get to know Brooklyn," I says. "Not in a hunderd yeahs. I been livin' heah all my life," I says, "an' I don't even know all deh is to know about it, so how do you expect to know duh town," I says, "when you don't even live heah?"

"Yes," he says, "but I got a map to help me find my way about."

"Map or no map," I says, "yuh ain't gonna get to know Brooklyn wit no map," I says.

"Can you swim?" he says, just like dat. Jesus! By dat time, y'know, I begun to see dat duh guy was some kind of nut. He'd had plenty to drink, of course, but he had dat crazy look in his eye I didn't like. "Can you swim?" he says.

"Sure," I says. "Can't you?"

"No," he says. "Not more'n a stroke or two. I neveh loined good."

"Well, it's easy," I says. "All yuh need is a little confidence. Duh way I loined, me older bruddeh pitched me off duh dock one day when I was eight yeahs old, cloes an' all. 'You'll swim,' he says. 'You'll swim all right—or drown.' An' believe me, I *swam!* When yuh know yuh got to, you'll do it. Duh only t'ing yuh need is confidence. An' once you've loined," I says, "you've got nuttin' else to worry about. You'll neveh forget it. It's somp'n dat stays wit yuh as long as yuh live."

"Can yuh swim good?" he says.

"Like a fish," I tells him. "I'm a regulah fish in duh wateh," I says. "I loined to swim right off duh docks with all duh oddeh kids," I says.

"What would you do if yuh saw a man drownin'?" duh guy says.

"Do? Why, I'd jump in an' pull him out," I says. "Dat's what I'd do."

"Did yuh eveh see a man drown?" he says.

"Sure," I says. "I see two guys—bot' times at Coney Island. Dey got out too far, an' neider one could swim. Dey drowned befoeh anyone could get to 'em."

"What becomes of people after dey've drowned out heah?" he says.

"Drowned out where?" I says.

"Out heah in Brooklyn."

"I don't know whatcha mean," I says. "Neveh hoid of no one drownin' heah in Brooklyn, unless you mean a swimmin' pool. Yuh can't drown in Brooklyn," I says. "Yuh gotta drown somewhere else—in duh ocean, where dere's wateh."

"Drownin'," duh guy says, lookin' at his map. "Drownin'."

Jesus! I could see by den he was some kind of nut; he had dat crazy expression in his eyes when he looked at you, an' I didn't know what he might do. So we was comin' to a station, an' it wasn't my stop, but I got off anyway, an' waited for duh next train.

"Well, so long, chief," I says. "Take it easy, now."

"Drownin'," duh guy says, lookin' at his map. "Drownin'."

Jesus! I've t'ought about dat guy a t'ousand times since den an' wondered what evah happened to 'm goin' out to look at Bensonhoist because he liked duh name! Walkin' aroun' t'roo Red Hook by himself at night an' lookin' at his map! How many people did I see get drowned out heah in Brooklyn! How long would it take a guy wit a good map to know all deh was to know about Brooklyn!

Jesus! What a nut *he* was! I wondeh what evah happened to 'im, anyway! I wondeh if someone knocked him on duh head or if he's still wanderin' aroun' in duh subway in duh middle of duh night wit his little map! Duh poor guy! Say, I've got to laugh at dat, when I t'ink about him! Maybe he's found out by now dat he'll neveh live long enough to know duh whole of Brooklyn. It'd take a guy a lifetime to know Brooklyn t'roo an' t'roo. An' even den, yuh wouldn't know it all.

A. V. LAIDER*

BY MAX BEERBOHM

I UNPACKED my things and went down to await luncheon.

It was good to be here again in this little old sleepy hostel by the sea. Hostel I say, though it spelt itself without an *s* and even placed a circumflex above the *o*. It made no other pretension. It was very cosy indeed.

I had been here just a year before, in mid-February, after an attack of influenza. And now I had returned, after an attack of influenza. Nothing was changed. It had been raining when I left, and the waiter—there was but a single, a very old waiter—had told me it was only a shower. That waiter was still here, not a day older. And the shower had not ceased.

Steadfastly it fell on to the sands, steadfastly into the iron-grey sea. I stood looking out at it from the windows of the hall, admiring it very much. There seemed to be little else to do. What little there was I did. I mastered the contents of a blue hand-bill which, pinned to the wall just beneath the framed engraving of Queen Victoria's Coronation, gave token of a concert that was to be held—or rather, was to have been held some weeks ago—in the Town Hall, for the benefit of the Life-Boat Fund. I looked at the barometer, tapped it, was not the wiser. I glanced at a pamphlet about Our Dying Industries (a theme on which Mr. Joseph Chamberlain was at that time trying to alarm us). I wandered to the letter-board.

These letter-boards always fascinate me. Usually some two or three of the envelopes stuck into the cross-garterings have a certain newness and freshness. They seem sure they will yet be

* from Seven Men

claimed. Why not? Why *shouldn't* John Doe, Esq., or Mrs. Richard Roe, turn up at any moment? I do not know. I can only say that nothing in the world seems to me more unlikely. Thus it is that these young bright envelopes touch my heart even more than do their dusty and sallow seniors. Sour resignation is less touching than impatience for what will not be, than the eagerness that has to wane and wither. Soured beyond measure these old envelopes are. They are not nearly so nice as they should be to the young ones. They lose no chance of sneering and discouraging. Such dialogues as this are only too frequent:

A VERY YOUNG ENVELOPE. Something in me whispers that he will come to-day!

A VERY OLD ENVELOPE. He? Well, that's good! Ha, ha, ha! Why didn't he come last week, when *you* came? What reason have you for supposing he'll ever come *now?* It isn't as if he were a frequenter of the place. He's never been here. His name is utterly unknown here. You don't suppose he's coming on the chance of finding *you?*

A. V. Y. E. It may seem silly, but—something in me whispers—

A. V. O. E. Something in *you?* One has only to look at you to see there's nothing in you but a note scribbled to him by a cousin. Look at *me!* There are three sheets, closely written, in *me.* The lady to whom I am addressed—

A. V. Y. E. Yes, sir, yes; you told me all about her yesterday.

A. V. O. E. And I shall do so to-day and to-morrow and every day and all day long. That young lady was a widow. She stayed here many times. She was delicate, and the air suited her. She was poor, and the tariff was just within her means. She was lonely, and had need of love. I have in me for her a passionate avowal and strictly honourable proposal, written to her, after many rough copies, by a gentleman who had made her acquaintance under this very roof. He was rich, he was charming, he was in the prime of life. He had asked if he might write to her. She had flutteringly granted his request. He posted me to her the day after his return to London. I looked forward to being torn open by her. I was very sure she would wear me and my contents next to her bosom. She was gone. She had left no

address. She never returned.... This I tell you, and shall continue to tell you, not because I want any of your callow sympathy,—no *thank* you!—but that you may judge how much less
than slight are the chances that you yourself——

But my reader has overheard these dialogues as often as I. He
wants to know what was odd about this particular letter-board
before which I was standing. At first glance I saw nothing odd
about it. But presently I distinguished a handwriting that was
vaguely familiar. It was mine. I stared, I wondered. There is always a slight shock in seeing an envelope of one's own after it
has gone through the post. It looks as if it had gone through so
much. But this was the first time I had ever seen an envelope of
mine eating its heart out in bondage on a letter-board. This was
outrageous. This was hardly to be believed. Sheer kindness had
impelled me to write to "A. V. Laider, Esq.," and this was the result! I hadn't minded receiving no answer. Only now, indeed,
did I remember that I hadn't received one. In multitudinous
London the memory of A. V. Laider and his trouble had soon
passed from my mind. But—well, what a lesson not to go out of
one's way to write to casual acquaintances!

My envelope seemed not to recognise me as its writer. Its
gaze was the more piteous for being blank. Even so had I once
been gazed at by a dog that I had lost and, after many days,
found in the Battersea Home. "I don't know who you are, but,
whoever you are, claim me, take me out of this!" That was my
dog's appeal. This was the appeal of my envelope.

I raised my hand to the letter-board, meaning to effect a
swift and lawless rescue, but paused at sound of a footstep behind me. The old waiter had come to tell me that my luncheon
was ready. I followed him out of the hall, not, however, without
a bright glance across my shoulder to reassure the little captive
that I should come back.

I had the sharp appetite of the convalescent, and this the sea-
air had whetted already to a finer edge. In touch with a dozen
oysters, and with stout, I soon shed away the unreasoning anger
I had felt against A. V. Laider. I became merely sorry for him
that he had not received a letter which might perhaps have
comforted him. In touch with cutlets, I felt how sorely he had

needed comfort. And anon, by the big bright fireside of that small dark smoking-room where, a year ago, on the last evening of my stay here, he and I had at length spoken to each other, I reviewed in detail the tragic experience he had told me; and I fairly revelled in reminiscent sympathy with him....

A. V. Laider—I had looked him up in the visitors' book on the night of his arrival. I myself had arrived the day before, and had been rather sorry there was no one else staying here. A convalescent by the sea likes to have some one to observe, to wonder about, at meal-time. I was glad when, on my second evening, I found seated at the table opposite to mine another guest. I was the gladder because he was just the right kind of guest. He was enigmatic. By this I mean that he did not look soldierly nor financial nor artistic nor anything definite at all. He offered a clean slate for speculation. And thank heaven! he evidently wasn't going to spoil the fun by engaging me in conversation later on. A decently unsociable man, anxious to be left alone.

The heartiness of his appetite, in contrast with his extreme fragility of aspect and limpness of demeanour, assured me that he, too, had just had influenza. I liked him for that. Now and again our eyes met and were instantly parted. We managed, as a rule, to observe each other indirectly. I was sure it was not merely because he had been ill that he looked interesting. Nor did it seem to me that a spiritual melancholy, though I imagined him sad at the best of times, was his sole asset. I conjectured that he was clever. I thought he might also be imaginative. At first glance I had mistrusted him. A shock of white hair, combined with a young face and dark eyebrows, does somehow make a man look like a charlatan. But it is foolish to be guided by an accident of colour. I had soon rejected my first impression of my fellow-diner. I found him very sympathetic.

Anywhere but in England it would be impossible for two solitary men, howsoever much reduced by influenza, to spend five or six days in the same hostel and not exchange a single word. That is one of the charms of England. Had Laider and I been born and bred in any other land we should have become acquainted before the end of our first evening in the small smoking-room, and have found ourselves irrevocably committed to go on talking to each other throughout the rest of our visit. We might, it is true, have happened to like each other more than any one we had ever met. This off-chance may have occurred to us both. But it counted for nothing as against the certain surrender of quietude and liberty. We slightly bowed to each other as we entered or left the dining-room or smoking-room, and as we met on the widespread sands or in the shop that had a small and faded circulating library. That was all. Our mutual aloofness was a positive bond between us.

Had he been much older than I, the responsibility for our silence would of course have been his alone. But he was not, I judged, more than five or six years ahead of me, and thus I might without impropriety have taken it on myself to perform that hard and perilous feat which English people call, with a shiver, "breaking the ice." He had reason, therefore, to be as grateful to me as I to him. Each of us, not the less frankly because silently, recognised his obligation to the other. And when, on the last evening of my stay, the ice actually was broken no ill-will rose between us: neither of us was to blame.

It was a Sunday evening. I had been out for a long last walk and had come in very late to dinner. Laider left his table almost immediately after I sat down to mine. When I entered the smoking-room I found him reading a weekly review which I had bought the day before. It was a crisis. He could not silently offer, nor could I have silently accepted, sixpence. It was a crisis. We faced it like men. He made, by word of mouth, a graceful apology. Verbally, not by signs, I besought him to go on reading. But this, of course, was a vain counsel of perfection. The social code forced us to talk now. We obeyed it like men. To reassure him that our position was not so desperate as it might seem, I took the earliest opportunity to mention that I was going away early next morning. In the tone of his "Oh, are you?" he tried bravely to imply that he was sorry, even now, to hear that. In a way, perhaps, he really was sorry. We had got on so well together, he and I. Nothing could efface the memory of that. Nay, we seemed to be hitting it off even now. Influenza was not our sole theme. We passed from that to the aforesaid weekly review, and to a correspondence that was raging therein on Faith and Reason.

This correspondence had now reached its fourth and penultimate stage—its Australian stage. It is hard to see why these correspondences spring up; one only knows that they do spring up, suddenly, like street crowds. There comes, it would seem, a moment when the whole English-speaking race is unconsciously bursting to have its say about some one thing—the split infinitive, or the habits of migratory birds, or faith and reason, or what-not. Whatever weekly review happens at such a moment to contain a reference, however remote, to the theme in question reaps the storm. Gusts of letters blow in from all corners of the British Isles. These are presently reinforced by Canada in full blast. A few weeks later the Anglo-Indians weigh in. In due course we have the help of our Australian cousins. By that time, however, we of the Mother Country have got our second wind, and so determined are we to make the most of it that at last even the Editor suddenly loses patience and says "This correspondence must now cease.—Ed." and wonders why on earth he ever allowed anything so tedious and idiotic to begin.

I pointed out to Laider one of the Australian letters that had especially pleased me in the current issue. It was from "A Melbourne Man," and was of the abrupt kind which declares that "all your correspondents have been groping in the dark" and then settles the whole matter in one short sharp flash. The flash in this instance was "Reason is faith, faith reason—that is all we know on earth and all we need to know." The writer then inclosed his card and was, etc., "A Melbourne Man." I said to Laider how very restful it was, after influenza, to read anything that meant nothing whatsoever. Laider was inclined to take the letter more seriously than I, and to be mildly metaphysical. I said that for me faith and reason were two separate things, and (as I am no good at metaphysics, however mild) I offered a definite example, to coax the talk on to ground where I should be safer. "Palmistry, for example," I said. "Deep down in my heart I believe in palmistry."

Laider turned in his chair. "You believe in palmistry?"

I hesitated. "Yes, somehow I do. Why? I haven't the slight-est notion. I can give myself all sorts of reasons for laughing it to scorn. My common sense utterly rejects it. Of course the shape of the hand means something—is more or less an index of character. But the idea that my past and future are neatly mapped out on my palms—" I shrugged my shoulders.

"You don't like that idea?" asked Laider in his gentle, rather academic voice.

"I only say it's a grotesque idea."

"Yet you do believe in it?"

"I've a grotesque belief in it, yes."

"Are you sure your reason for calling this idea 'grotesque' isn't merely that you dislike it?"

"Well," I said, with the thrilling hope that he was a compan-ion in absurdity, "doesn't it seem grotesque to *you*?"

"It seems strange."

"You believe in it?"

"Oh, absolutely."

"Hurrah!"

He smiled at my pleasure, and I, at the risk of reentangle-ment in metaphysics, claimed him as standing shoulder to shoulder with me against "A Melbourne Man." This claim he gently disputed. "You may think me very prosaic," he said, "but I can't believe without evidence."

"Well, I'm equally prosaic and equally at a disadvantage: I can't take my own belief as evidence, and I've no other evi-dence to go on."

He asked me if I had ever made a study of palmistry. I said I had read one of Desbarolles' books years ago, and one of Heron-Allen's. But, he asked, had I tried to test them by the lines on my own hands or on the hands of my friends? I con-fessed that my actual practice in palmistry had been a merely passive kind—the prompt extension of my palm to any one who would be so good as to "read" it and truckle for a few min-utes to my egoism. (I hoped Laider might do this.)

"Then I almost wonder," he said, with his sad smile, "that you haven't lost your belief, after all the nonsense you must have heard. There are so many young girls who go in for palmistry. I am sure all the five foolish virgins were 'awfully keen on it' and used to say 'You can be led, but not driven,' and 'You are likely to have a serious illness between the ages of forty and forty-five,' and 'You are by nature rather lazy, but can be very energetic by fits and starts.' And most of the professionals, I'm told, are as silly as the young girls."

For the honour of the profession, I named three practitioners whom I had found really good at reading character. He asked whether any of them had been right about past events. I confessed that, as a matter of fact, all three of them had been right in the main. This seemed to amuse him. He asked whether any of them had predicted anything which had since come true. I confessed that all three had predicted that I should do several things which I had since done rather unexpectedly. He asked if I didn't accept this as at any rate a scrap of evidence. I said I could only regard it as a fluke—a rather remarkable fluke.

The superiority of his sad smile was beginning to get on my nerves. I wanted him to see that he was as absurd as I. "Suppose," I said, "suppose for sake of argument that you and I are nothing but helpless automata created to do just this and that, and to have just that and this done to us. Suppose, in fact, we *haven't* any free will whatsoever. Is it likely or conceivable that the Power that fashioned us would take the trouble to jot down in cipher on our hands just what was in store for us?"

Laider did not answer this question, he did but annoyingly ask me another. "You believe in free will?"

"Yes, of course. I'll be hanged if I'm an automaton."

"And you believe in free will just as in palmistry—without any reason?"

"Oh, no. Everything points to our having free will."

"Everything? What, for instance?"

This rather cornered me. I dodged out, as lightly as I could, by saying "I suppose *you* would say it was written in my hand that I should be a believer in free will."

"Ah, I've no doubt it is."

I held out my palms. But, to my great disappointment, he looked quickly away from them. He had ceased to smile. There was agitation in his voice as he explained that he never looked at people's hands now. "Never now—never again." He shook his head as though to beat off some memory.

I was much embarrassed by my indiscretion. I hastened to tide over the awkward moment by saying that if *I* could read hands I wouldn't, for fear of the awful things I might see there.

"Awful things, yes," he whispered, nodding at the fire.

"Not," I said in self-defense, "that there's anything very awful, so far as I know, to be read in *my* hands."

He turned his gaze from the fire to me. "You aren't a murderer, for example?"

"Oh, no," I replied, with a nervous laugh.

"*I* am."

This was a more than awkward, it was a painful, moment for me; and I am afraid I must have started or winced, for he instantly begged my pardon. "I don't know," he exclaimed, "why I said it. I'm usually a very reticent man. But sometimes—" He pressed his brow. "What you must think of me!"

I begged him to dismiss the matter from his mind.

"It's very good of you to say that; but—I've placed myself as well as you in a false position. I ask you to believe that I'm not the sort of man who is 'wanted' or ever was 'wanted' by the police. I should be bowed out of any police-station at which I gave myself up. I'm not a murderer in any bald sense of the word. No."

My face must have perceptibly brightened, for "Ah," he said, "don't imagine I'm not a murderer at all. Morally, I am." He looked at the clock. I pointed out that the night was young. He assured me that his story was not a long one. I assured him that I hoped it was. He said I was very kind. I denied this. He warned me that what he had to tell might rather tend to stiffen my unwilling faith in palmistry, and to shake my opposite and cherished faith in free will. I said "Never mind." He stretched his hands pensively toward the fire. I settled myself back in my chair.

"My hands," he said, staring at the backs of them, "are the hands of a very weak man. I dare say you know enough of palmistry to see that for yourself. You notice the slightness of the thumbs and of the two 'little' fingers. They are the hands of a weak and over-sensitive man—a man without confidence, a man who would certainly waver in an emergency. Rather Hamlet-ish hands," he mused. "And I'm like Hamlet in other respects, too: I'm no fool, and I've rather a noble disposition, and I'm unlucky. But Hamlet was luckier than I in one thing: he was a murderer by accident, whereas the murders that I committed one day fourteen years ago—for I must tell you it wasn't one murder, but many murders that I committed—were all of them due to the wretched inherent weakness of my own wretched self.

"I was twenty-six—no, twenty-seven years old, and rather a nondescript person, as I am now. I was supposed to have been called to the Bar. In fact, I believe I *had* been called to the Bar. I hadn't listened to the call. I never intended to practise, and I never did practise. I only wanted an excuse in the eyes of the world for existing. I suppose the nearest I have ever come to practising is now at this moment: I am defending a murderer. My father had left me well enough provided with money. I was able to go my own desultory way, riding my hobbies where I would. I had a good stableful of hobbies. Palmistry was one of them. I was rather ashamed of this one. It seemed to me absurd, as it seems to you. Like you, though, I believed in it. Unlike you, I had done more than merely read a book or so about it. I had read innumerable books about it. I had taken casts of all my friends' hands. I had tested and tested again the points at which Desbarolles dissented from the gypsies, and—well, enough that I had gone into it all rather thoroughly, and was as sound a palmist as a man may be without giving his whole life to palmistry.

"One of the first things I had seen in my own hand, as soon as I had learned to read it, was that at about the age of twenty-six I should have a narrow escape from death—from a violent death. There was a clean break in the lifeline, and a square joining it—the protective square, you know. The markings were precisely the same in both hands. It was to be the narrowest escape possible. And I wasn't going to escape without injury, either. That is what bothered me. There was a faint line connecting the break in the life-line with a star on the line of

health. Against that star was another square. I was to recover
from the injury, whatever it might be. Still, I didn't exactly look
forward to it. Soon after I had reached the age of twenty-five, I
began to feel uncomfortable. The thing might be going to happen at any moment. In palmistry, you know, it is impossible to
pin an event down hard and fast to one year. This particular
event was to be when I was *about* twenty-six; it mightn't be till
I was twenty-seven; it might be while I was only twenty-five.

"And I used to tell myself that it mightn't be at all. My reason rebelled against the whole notion of palmistry, just as yours
does. I despised my faith in the thing, just as you despise yours.
I used to try not to be so ridiculously careful as I was whenever
I crossed a street. I lived in London at that time. Motor-cars had
not come in, but—what hours, all told, I must have spent
standing on curbs, very circumspect, very lamentable! It was a
pity, I suppose, that I had no definite occupation—something
to take me out of myself. I was one of the victims of private
means. There came a time when I drove in four-wheelers rather
than in hansoms, and was doubtful of four-wheelers. Oh, I assure you, I was very lamentable indeed.

"If a railway-journey could be avoided, I avoided it. My uncle had a place in Hampshire. I was very fond of him and his
wife. Theirs was the only house I ever went to stay in now. I was
there for a week in November, not long after my twenty-
seventh birthday. There were other people staying there, and at
the end of the week we all travelled back to London together.
There were six of us in the carriage: Colonel Elbourn and his
wife and their daughter, a girl of seventeen; and another married couple, the Blakes. I had been at Winchester with Blake,
but had hardly seen him since that time. He was in the Indian
Civil, and was home on leave. He was sailing for India next
week. His wife was to remain in England for some months, and
then join him out there. They had been married five years. She
was now just twenty-four years old. He told me that this was
her age.

"The Elbourns I had never met before. They were charming
people. We had all been very happy together. The only trouble
had been that on the last night, at dinner, my uncle asked me if

I still went in for 'the gypsy business,' as he always called it; and of course the three ladies were immensely excited, and implored me to 'do' their hands. I told them it was all nonsense, I said I had forgotten all I once knew. I made various excuses; and the matter dropped. It was quite true that I had given up reading hands. I avoided anything that might remind me of what was in my own hands. And so, next morning, it was a great bore to me when, soon after the train started, Mrs. Elbourn said it would be 'too cruel' of me if I refused to do their hands now. Her daughter and Mrs. Blake also said it would be 'brutal'; and they were all taking off their gloves, and—well, of course I had to give in.

"I went to work methodically on Mrs. Elbourn's hands, in the usual way, you know, first sketching the character from the backs of them; and there was the usual hush, broken by the usual little noises—grunts of assent from the husband, cooings of recognition from the daughter. Presently I asked to see the palms, and from them I filled in the details of Mrs. Elbourn's character before going on to the events in her life. But while I talked I was calculating how old Mrs. Elbourn might be. In my first glance at her palms I had seen that she could not have been less than twenty-five when she married. The daughter was seventeen. Suppose the daughter had been born a year later—how old would the mother be? Forty-three, yes. Not less than that, poor woman!"

Laider looked at me. "Why 'poor woman,' you wonder? Well, in that first glance I had seen other things than her marriage-line. I had seen a very complete break in the lines of life and of fate. I had seen violent death there. At what age? Not later, not possibly *later,* than forty-three. While I talked to her about the things that had happened in her girl-hood, the back of my brain was hard at work on those marks of catastrophe. I was horribly wondering that she was still alive. It was impossible that between her and that catastrophe there could be more than a few short months. And all the time I was talking; and I suppose I acquitted myself well, for I remember that when I ceased I had a sort of ovation from the Elbourns.

"It was a relief to turn to another pair of hands. Mrs. Blake

was an amusing young creature, and her hands were very
characteristic, and prettily odd in form. I allowed myself to be
rather whimsical about her nature, and, having begun in that
vein, I went on in it—somehow—even after she had turned her
palms. In those palms were reduplicated the signs I had seen in
Mrs. Elbourn's. It was as though they had been copied neatly
out. The only difference was in the placing of them; and it was
this difference that was the most horrible point. The fatal age
in Mrs. Blake's hands was—not past, no, for here *she* was. But
she might have died when she was twenty-one. Twenty-three
seemed to be the utmost span. She was twenty-four, you know.

"I have said that I am a weak man. And you will have good
proof of that directly. Yet I showed a certain amount of strength
that day—yes, even on that day which has humiliated and saddened the rest of my life. Neither my face nor my voice betrayed me when in the palms of Dorothy Elbourn I was again
confronted with those same signs. She was all for knowing the
future, poor child! I believe I told her all manner of things that
were to be. And she had no future—none, none in *this* world—
except——

"And then, while I talked, there came to me suddenly a suspicion. I wondered it hadn't come before. You guess what it
was? It made me feel very cold and strange. I went on talking.
But, also, I went on—quite separately—thinking. The suspicion wasn't a certainty. This mother and daughter were always
together. What was to befall the one might anywhere—anywhere—befall the other. But a like fate, in an equally near future, was in store for that other lady. The coincidence was
curious, very. Here we all were together—here, they and I—I
who was narrowly to escape, so soon now, what they, so soon
now, were to suffer. Oh, there was an inference to be drawn.
Not a *sure* inference, I told myself. And always I was talking,
talking, and the train was swinging and swaying noisily
along—to what? It was a fast train. Our carriage was near the
engine. I was talking loudly. Full well I had known what I
should see in the Colonel's hand. I told myself I had not known.
I told myself that even now the thing I dreaded was not sure
to be. Don't think I was dreading it for myself. I wasn't so

'lamentable' as all that—now. It was only of them that I thought—only for them. I hurried over the Colonel's character and career; I was perfunctory. It was Blake's hands that I wanted. *They* were the hands that mattered. If *they* had the marks— Remember, Blake was to start for India in the coming week, his wife was to remain in England. They would be apart. Therefore——

"And the marks were there. And I did nothing—nothing but hold forth on the subtleties of Blake's character. There was a thing for me to do. I wanted to do it. I wanted to spring to the window and pull the communication-cord. Quite a simple thing to do. Nothing easier than to stop a train. You just give a sharp pull, and the train slows down, comes to a standstill. And the Guard appears at your window. You explain to the Guard.

"Nothing easier than to tell him there is going to be a collision. Nothing easier than to insist that you and your friends and every other passenger in the train must get out at once.... There *are* easier things than this? Things that need less courage than this? Some of *them* I could have done, I daresay. This thing I was going to do. Oh, I was determined that I would do it—directly.

"I had said all I had to say about Blake's hands. I had brought my entertainment to an end. I had been thanked and complimented all around. I was quite at liberty. I was going to do what I had to do. I was determined, yes.

"We were near the outskirts of London. The air was grey, thickening; and Dorothy Elbourn had said, 'Oh, this horrible old London! I suppose there's the same old fog!' and presently I heard her father saying something about 'prevention' and 'a short act of Parliament' and 'anthracite.' And I sat and listened and agreed and——"

Laider closed his eyes. He passed his hand slowly through the air.

"I had a racking headache. And when I said so, I was told not to talk. I was in bed, and the nurses were always telling me not to talk. I was in a hospital. I knew that. But I didn't know why I was there. One day I thought I should like to know why, and so I asked. I was feeling much better now. They told me, by degrees, that I had had concussion of the brain. I had been brought there unconscious, and had remained unconscious for forty-eight hours. I had been in an accident—a railway accident. This seemed to me odd. I had arrived quite safely at my uncle's place, and I had no memory of any journey since that. In cases of concussion, you know, it's not uncommon for the patient to forget all that happened just before the accident; there may be a blank of several hours. So it was in my case. One day my uncle was allowed to come and see me. And somehow, suddenly, at sight of him, the blank was filled in. I remembered, in a flash, everything. I was quite calm, though. Or I made myself seem so, for I wanted to know how the collision had happened. My uncle told me that the engine-driver had failed to see a signal because of the fog, and our train crashed into a goods-train. I didn't ask him about the people who were with me. You see, there was no need to ask. Very gently my uncle began to tell me, but—I had begun to talk strangely, I suppose. I remember the frightened look of my uncle's face, and the nurse scolding him in whispers.

"After that, all a blur. It seems that I became very ill indeed, wasn't expected to live. However, I live."

There was a long silence. Laider did not look at me, nor I at him. The fire was burning low, and he watched it.

At length he spoke. "You despise me. Naturally. I despise myself."

"No, I don't despise you; but——"

"You blame me." I did not meet his gaze. "You blame me," he repeated.

"Yes."

"And there, if I may say so, you are a little unjust. It isn't my fault that I was born weak."

"But a man may conquer weakness."

"Yes, if he is endowed with the strength for that."

His fatalism drew from me a gesture of disgust. "Do you really mean," I asked, "that because you didn't pull that cord you *couldn't* have pulled it?"

"Yes."

"And it's written in your hands that you couldn't?"

He looked at the palms of his hands. "They are the hands of a very weak man," he said.

"A man so weak that he cannot believe in the possibility of free will for himself or for any one?"

"They are the hands of an intelligent man, who can weigh evidence and see things as they are."

"But answer me: Was it fore-ordained that you should not pull that cord?"

"It was fore-ordained."

"And was it actually marked in your hands that you were not going to pull it?"

"Ah, well, you see, it is rather the things one *is* going to do that are actually marked. The things one *isn't* going to do,—the innumerable negative things,—how could one expect *them* to be marked?"

"But the consequences of what one leaves undone may be positive?"

"Horribly positive," he winced. "My hand is the hand of a man who has suffered a great deal in later life."

"And was it the hand of a man *destined* to suffer?"

"Oh, yes. I thought I told you that."

There was a pause.

"Well," I said, with awkward sympathy, "I suppose all hands are the hands of people destined to suffer."

"Not of people destined to suffer so much as *I* have suffered—as I still suffer."

The insistence of his self-pity chilled me, and I harked back to a question he had not straightly answered. "Tell me: Was it marked in your hands that you were not going to pull that cord?"

Again he looked at his hands, and then, having pressed them for a moment to his face, "It was marked very clearly," he answered, "in *their* hands."

Two or three days after this colloquy there had occurred to me in London an idea—an ingenious and comfortable doubt. How was Laider to be sure that his brain, recovering from concussion, had *remembered* what happened in the course of that railway-journey? How was he to know that his brain hadn't simply, in its abeyance, *invented* all this for him? It might be that he had never seen those signs in those hands. Assuredly, here was a bright loophole. I had forthwith written to Laider, pointing it out.

This was the letter which now, at my second visit, I had found miserably pent on the letter-board. I remembered my promise to rescue it. I arose from the retaining fireside, stretched my arms, yawned, and went forth to fulfill my Christian purpose. There was no one in the hall. The "shower" had at length ceased. The sun had positively come out, and the front door had been thrown open in its honour. Everything along the sea-front was beautifully gleaming, drying, shimmering. But I was not to be diverted from my errand. I went to the letter-board. And—my letter was not there! Resourceful and plucky little thing—it had escaped! I did hope it would not be captured and brought back. Perhaps the alarm had already been raised by the tolling of that great bell which warns the inhabitants for miles around that a letter has broken loose from the letter-board. I had a vision of my envelope skimming wildly along the coast-line, pursued by the old but active waiter and a breathless pack of local worthies. I saw it outdistancing them all, dodging past coastguards, doubling on its tracks, leaping breakwaters, unluckily injuring itself, losing speed, and at last, in a splendour of desperation, taking to the open sea. But suddenly I had another idea. Perhaps Laider had returned?

He had. I espied afar on the sands a form that was recognisably, by the listless droop of it, his. I was glad and sorry—rather glad, because he completed the scene of last year; and very sorry, because this time we should be at each other's mercy: no restful silence and liberty, for either of us, this time. Perhaps he had been told I was here, and had gone out to avoid me while he yet could. Oh weak, weak! Why palter? I put on my hat and coat, and marched out to meet him.

"Influenza, of course?" we asked simultaneously.

There is a limit to the time which one man may spend in talking to another about his own influenza; and presently, as we paced the sands, I felt that Laider had passed this limit. I wondered that he didn't break off and thank me now for my letter. He must have read it. He ought to have thanked me for it at once. It was a very good letter, a remarkable letter. But surely he wasn't waiting to answer it by post? His silence about it gave me the absurd sense of having taken a liberty, confound him! He was evidently ill at ease while he talked. But it wasn't for me to help him out of his difficulty, whatever that might be. It was for him to remove the strain imposed on myself.

Abruptly, after a long pause, he did now manage to say, "It was—very good of you to—to write me that letter." He told me he had only just got to it, and he drifted away into otiose explanations of this fact. I thought he might at least say it was a remarkable letter; and you can imagine my annoyance when he said, after another interval, "I was very much touched indeed." I had wished to be convincing, not touching. I can't bear to be called touching.

"Don't you," I asked, "think it *is* quite possible that your brain invented all those memories of what—what happened before that accident?"

He drew a sharp sigh. "You make me feel very guilty."

"That's exactly what I tried to make you *not* feel!"

"I know, yes. That's why I feel so guilty."

We had paused in our walk. He stood nervously prodding the hard wet sand with his walking-stick. "In a way," he said, "your theory was quite right. But—it didn't go far enough. It's not only possible, it's a fact, that I didn't see those signs in those hands. I never examined those hands. They weren't there. *I* wasn't there. I haven't an uncle in Hampshire, even. I never had."

I too, prodded the sand. "Well," I said at length, "I do feel rather a fool."

"I've no right even to beg your pardon, but——"

"Oh, I'm not vexed. Only—I rather wish you hadn't told me this."

"I wish I hadn't had to. It was your kindness, you see, that forced me. By trying to take an imaginary load off my conscience, you laid a very real one on it."

"I'm sorry. But you, of your own free will, you know, exposed your conscience to me last year. I don't yet quite understand why you did that."

"No, of course not. I don't deserve that you should. But I think you will. May I explain? I'm afraid I've talked a great deal already about my influenza, and I shan't be able to keep it out of my explanation. Well, my weakest point—I told you this last year, but it happens to be perfectly true that my weakest point—is my will. Influenza, as you know, fastens unerringly on one's weakest point. It doesn't attempt to undermine my imagination. That would be a forlorn hope. I have, alas! a very strong imagination. At ordinary times my imagination allows itself to be governed by my will. My will keeps it in check by constant nagging. But when my will isn't strong enough even to nag, then my imagination stampedes. I become even as a little child. I tell myself the most preposterous fables, and—the trouble is—I can't help telling them to my friends. Until I've thoroughly shaken off influenza, I'm not fit company for any one. I perfectly realise this, and I have the good sense to go right away till I'm quite well again. I come here usually. It seems absurd, but I must confess I was sorry last year when we fell into conversation. I knew I should very soon be letting myself go, or rather, very soon be swept away. Perhaps I ought to have warned you; but—I'm a rather shy man. And then you mentioned the subject of palmistry. You said you believed in it. I wondered at that. I had once read Desbarolles' book about it, but I am bound to say I thought the whole thing very great nonsense indeed."

"Then," I gasped, "it isn't even true that you believe in palmistry?"

"Oh, no. But I wasn't able to tell you that. You had begun by saying that you believed in palmistry, and then you proceeded to scoff at it. While you scoffed I saw myself as a man with a terribly good reason for *not* scoffing; and in a flash I saw the terribly good reason; I had the whole story—at least I had the broad outlines of it—clear before me."

"You hadn't ever thought of it before?" He shook his head. My eyes beamed. "The whole thing was a sheer improvisation?"

"Yes," said Laider, humbly, "I am as bad as all that. I don't say that all the details of the story I told you that evening were filled in at the very instant of its conception. I was filling them in while we talked about palmistry in general, and while I was waiting for the moment when the story would come in most effectively. And I've no doubt I added some extra touches in the course of the actual telling. Don't imagine that I took the slightest pleasure in deceiving you. It's only my will, not my conscience, that is weakened after influenza. I simply can't help telling what I've made up, and telling it to the best of my ability. But I'm thoroughly ashamed all the time."

"Not of your ability, surely?"

"Yes, of that, too," he said with his sad smile. "I always feel that I'm not doing justice to my idea."

"You are too stern a critic, believe me."

"It is kind of you to say that. You are very kind altogether. Had I known that you were so essentially a man of the world—in the best sense of that term—I shouldn't have so much dreaded seeing you just now and having to confess to you. But I'm not going to take advantage of your urbanity and your easy-going ways. I hope that some day we may meet somewhere when I haven't had influenza and am a not wholly undesirable acquaintance. As it is, I refuse to let you associate with me. I am an older man than you, and so I may without impertinence warn you against having anything to do with me."

I deprecated this advice, of course; but, for a man of weakened will, he showed great firmness. "You," he said, "in your heart of hearts don't want to have to walk and talk continually with a person who might at any moment try to bamboozle you with some ridiculous tale. And I, for my part, don't want to degrade myself by trying to bamboozle any one—especially one whom I have taught to see through me. Let the two talks we have had be as though they had not been. Let us bow to each other, as last year, but let that be all. Let us follow in all things the precedent of last year."

With a smile that was almost gay he turned on his heel, and moved away with a step that was almost brisk. I was a little disconcerted. But I was also more than a little glad. The restfulness of silence, the charm of liberty—these things were not, after all, forfeit. My heart thanked Laider for that; and throughout the week I loyally seconded him in the system he had laid down for us. All was as it had been last year. We did not smile to each other, we merely bowed, when we entered or left the dining-room or smoking-room, and when we met on the widespread sands or in that shop which had a small and faded, but circulating, library.

Once or twice in the course of the week it did occur to me that perhaps Laider had told the simple truth at our first interview and an ingenious lie at our second. I frowned at this possibility. The idea of any one wishing to be quit of *me* was most distasteful. However, I was to find reassurance. On the last evening of my stay, I suggested, in the small smoking-room, that he and I should, as sticklers for precedent, converse. We did so, very pleasantly. And after a while I happened to say that I had seen this afternoon a great number of sea-gulls flying close to the shore.

"Sea-gulls?" said Laider, turning in his chair.

"Yes. And I don't think I had ever realised how extraordinarily beautiful they are when their wings catch the light."

"Beautiful?" Laider threw a quick glance at me and away from me. "You think them beautiful?"

"Surely."

"Well, perhaps they are, yes; I suppose they are. But—I don't like seeing them. They always remind me of something—rather an awful thing—that once happened to me."...

It was a very awful thing indeed.

THE LOTTERY*

BY SHIRLEY JACKSON

THE MORNING of June 27th was clear and sunny, with the fresh warmth of a full-summer day; the flowers were blossoming profusely and the grass was richly green. The people of the village began to gather in the square, between the post office and the bank, around ten o'clock; in some towns there were so many people that the lottery took two days and had to be started on June 26th, but in this village, where there were only about three hundred people, the whole lottery took less than two hours, so it could begin at ten o'clock in the morning and still be through in time to allow the villagers to get home for noon dinner.

The children assembled first, of course. School was recently over for the summer, and the feeling of liberty sat uneasily on most of them; they tended to gather together quietly for a while before they broke into boisterous play, and their talk was still of the classroom and the teacher, of books and reprimands. Bobby Martin had already stuffed his pockets full of stones, and the other boys soon followed his example, selecting the smoothest and roundest stones; Bobby and Harry Jones and Dickie Delacroix—the villagers pronounced this name "Dellacroy"—eventually made a great pile of stones in one corner of the square and guarded it against the raids of the other boys. The girls stood aside, talking among themselves, looking over their shoulders at the boys, and the very small children rolled in the dust or clung to the hands of their older brothers or sisters.

* from The New Yorker

Soon the men began to gather, surveying their own children, speaking of planting and rain, tractors and taxes. They stood together, away from the pile of stones in the corner, and their jokes were quiet and they smiled rather than laughed. The women, wearing faded house dresses and sweaters, came shortly after their menfolk. They greeted one another and exchanged bits of gossip as they went to join their husbands. Soon the women, standing by their husbands, began to call to their children, and the children came reluctantly, having to be called four or five times. Bobby Martin ducked under his mother's grasping hand and ran, laughing, back to the pile of stones. His father spoke up sharply, and Bobby came quickly and took his place between his father and his oldest brother.

The lottery was conducted—as were the square dances, the teen-age club, the Halloween program—by Mr. Summers, who had time and energy to devote to civic activities. He was a round-faced, jovial man and he ran the coal business, and people were sorry for him, because he had no children and his wife was a scold. When he arrived in the square, carrying the black wooden box, there was a murmur of conversation among the villagers, and he waved and called, "Little late today, folks." The postmaster, Mr. Graves, followed him, carrying a three-legged stool, and the stool was put in the center of the square and Mr. Summers set the black box down on it. The villagers kept their distance, leaving a space between themselves and the stool, and when Mr. Summers said, "Some of you fellows want to give me a hand?" there was a hesitation before two men, Mr. Martin and his oldest son, Baxter, came forward to hold the box steady on the stool while Mr. Summers stirred up the papers inside it.

The original paraphernalia for the lottery had been lost long ago, and the black box now resting on the stool had been put into use even before Old Man Warner, the oldest man in town, was born. Mr. Summers spoke frequently to the villagers about making a new box, but no one liked to upset even as much tradition as was represented by the black box. There was a story that the present box had been made with some pieces of the box that had preceded it, the one that had been constructed when the first people settled down to make a village here. Every year, after the lottery, Mr. Summers began talking again about a new box, but every year the subject was allowed to fade off without anything's being done. The black box grew shabbier each year; by now it was no longer completely black but splintered badly along one side to show the original wood color, and in some places faded or stained.

Mr. Martin and his oldest son, Baxter, held the black box securely on the stool until Mr. Summers had stirred the papers thoroughly with his hand. Because so much of the ritual had been forgotten or discarded, Mr. Summers had been successful in having slips of paper substituted for the chips of wood that had been used for generations. Chips of wood, Mr. Summers had argued, had been all very well when the village was tiny, but now that the population was more than three hundred and likely to keep on growing, it was necessary to use something that would fit more easily into the black box. The night before the lottery, Mr. Summers and Mr. Graves made up the slips of paper and put them in the box, and it was then taken to the safe of Mr. Summers' coal company and locked up until Mr. Summers was ready to take it to the square next morning. The rest of the year, the box was put away, sometimes one place, sometimes another; it had spent one year in Mr. Graves's barn and another year underfoot in the post office, and sometimes it was set on a shelf in the Martin grocery and left there.

There was a great deal of fussing to be done before Mr. Summers declared the lottery open. There were the lists to make up—of heads of families, heads of households in each family, members of each household in each family. There was the proper swearing-in of Mr. Summers by the postmaster, as the official of the lottery; at one time, some people remembered, there had been a recital of some sort, performed by the official of the lottery, a perfunctory, tuneless chant that had been rattled off duly each year; some people believed that the official of the lottery used to stand just so when he said or sang it, others believed that he was supposed to walk among the people, but years and years ago this part of the ritual had been allowed to lapse. There had been, also, a ritual salute, which the official of the lottery had had to use in addressing each person who came up to draw from the box, but this also had changed with time, until now it was felt necessary only for the official to speak to each person approaching. Mr. Summers was very good at all this; in his clean white shirt and blue jeans, with one hand resting carelessly on the black box, he seemed very proper and important as he talked interminably to Mr. Graves and the Martins.

Just as Mr. Summers finally left off talking and turned to the assembled villagers, Mrs. Hutchinson came hurriedly along the path to the square, her sweater thrown over her shoulders, and slid into place in the back of the crowd. "Clean forgot what day it was," she said to Mrs. Delacroix, who stood next to her, and they both laughed softly. "Thought my old man was out back stacking wood," Mrs. Hutchinson went on, "and then I looked out the window and the kids were gone, and then I remembered it was the twenty-seventh and came a-running." She dried her hands on her apron, and Mrs. Delacroix said, "You're in time, though. They're still talking away up there."

Mrs. Hutchinson craned her neck to see through the crowd and found her husband and children standing near the front. She tapped Mrs. Delacroix on the arm as a farewell and began to make her way through the crowd. The people separated good-humoredly to let her through; two or three people said, in voices just loud enough to be heard across the crowd, "Here comes your Missus, Hutchinson," and "Bill, she made it after all." Mrs. Hutchinson reached her husband, and Mr. Summers, who had been waiting, said cheerfully, "Thought we were going to have to get on without you, Tessie." Mrs. Hutchinson said, grinning, "Wouldn't have me leave m'dishes in the sink, now, would you, Joe?" and soft laughter ran through the crowd as the people stirred back into position after Mrs. Hutchinson's arrival.

"Well, now," Mr. Summers said soberly, "guess we better get started, get this over with, so's we can go back to work. Anybody ain't here?"

"Dunbar," several people said. "Dunbar, Dunbar."

Mr. Summers consulted his list. "Clyde Dunbar," he said.

"That's right. He's broke his leg, hasn't he? Who's drawing for him?"

"Me, I guess," a woman said, and Mr. Summers turned to look at her. "Wife draws for her husband," Mr. Summers said. "Don't you have a grown boy to do it for you, Janey?" Although Mr. Summers and everyone else in the village knew the answer perfectly well, it was the business of the official of the lottery to ask such questions formally. Mr. Summers waited with an expression of polite interest while Mrs. Dunbar answered.

"Horace's not but sixteen yet," Mrs. Dunbar said regretfully. "Guess I gotta fill in for the old man this year."

"Right," Mr. Summers said. He made a note on the list he was holding. Then he asked, "Watson boy drawing this year?"

A tall boy in the crowd raised his hand. "Here," he said. "I'm drawing for m'mother and me." He blinked his eyes nervously and ducked his head as several voices in the crowd said things like "Good fellow, Jack," and "Glad to see your mother's got a man to do it."

"Well," Mr. Summers said, "guess that's everyone. Old Man Warner make it?"

"Here," a voice said, and Mr. Summers nodded.

A sudden hush fell on the crowd as Mr. Summers cleared his throat and looked at the list. "All ready?" he called. "Now, I'll read the names—heads of families first—and the men come up and take a paper out of the box. Keep the paper folded in your hand without looking at it until everyone has had a turn. Everything clear?"

The people had done it so many times that they only half listened to the directions; most of them were quiet, wetting their lips, not looking around. Then Mr. Summers raised one hand high and said, "Adams." A man disengaged himself from the crowd and came forward. "Hi, Steve," Mr. Summers said, and Mr. Adams said, "Hi, Joe." They grinned at one another humorlessly and nervously. Then Mr. Adams reached into the black box and took out a folded paper. He held it firmly by one corner as he turned and went hastily back to his place in the crowd, where he stood a little apart from his family, not looking down at his hand.

"Allen," Mr. Summers said. "Andrews.... Bentham."

"Seems like there's no time at all between lotteries any more," Mrs. Delacroix said to Mrs. Graves in the back row. "Seems like we got through with the last one only last week."

"Time sure goes fast," Mrs. Graves said.

"Clark.... Delacroix."

"There goes my old man," Mrs. Delacroix said. She held her breath while her husband went forward.

"Dunbar," Mr. Summers said, and Mrs. Dunbar went steadily to the box while one of the women said, "Go on, Janey," and another said, "There she goes."

"We're next," Mrs. Graves said. She watched while Mr. Graves came around from the side of the box, greeted Mr. Summers gravely, and selected a slip of paper from the box. By now, all through the crowd there were men holding the small folded papers in their large hands, turning them over and over nervously. Mrs. Dunbar and her two sons stood together, Mrs. Dunbar holding the slip of paper.

"Harburt.... Hutchinson."

"Get up there, Bill," Mrs. Hutchinson said, and the people near her laughed.

"Jones."

"They do say," Mr. Adams said to Old Man Warner, who stood next to him, "that over in the north village they're talking of giving up the lottery."

Old Man Warner snorted. "Pack of crazy fools," he said. "Listening to the young folks, nothing's good enough for *them.* Next thing you know, they'll be wanting to go back to living in caves, nobody work any more, live *that* way for a while. Used to be a saying about 'Lottery in June, corn be heavy soon.' First thing you know, we'd all be eating stewed chickweed and acorns. There's *always* been a lottery," he added petulantly. "Bad enough to see young Joe Summers up there joking with everybody."

"Some places have already quit lotteries," Mrs. Adams said.

"Nothing but trouble in *that*," Old Man Warner said stoutly. "Pack of young fools."

"Martin." And Bobby Martin watched his father go forward. "Overdyke.... Percy."

"I wish they'd hurry," Mrs. Dunbar said to her older son. "I wish they'd hurry."

"They're almost through," her son said.

"You get ready to run tell Dad," Mrs. Dunbar said.

Mr. Summers called his own name and then stepped forward precisely and selected a slip from the box. Then he called, "Warner."

"Seventy-seventh year I been in the lottery," Old Man Warner said as he went through the crowd. "Seventy-seventh time."

"Watson." The tall boy came awkwardly through the crowd. Someone said, "Don't be nervous, Jack," and Mr. Summers said, "Take your time, son."

"Zanini."

After that, there was a long pause, a breathless pause, until Mr. Summers, holding his slip of paper in the air, said, "All right, fellows." For a minute, no one moved, and then all the slips of paper were opened. Suddenly, all women began to speak at once, saying, "Who is it?," "Who's got it?," "Is it the Dunbars?," "Is it the Watsons?" Then the voices began to say, "It's Hutchinson. It's Bill." "Bill Hutchinson got it."

"Go tell your father," Mrs. Dunbar said to her older son.

People began to look around to see the Hutchinsons. Bill Hutchinson was standing quiet, staring down at the paper in his hand. Suddenly, Tessie Hutchinson shouted to Mr. Summers, "You didn't give him time enough to take any paper he wanted. I saw you. It wasn't fair."

"Be a good sport, Tessie," Mrs. Delacroix called, and Mrs. Graves said, "All of us took the same chance."

"Shut up, Tessie," Bill Hutchinson said.

"Well, everyone," Mr. Summers said, "that was done pretty fast, and now we've got to be hurrying a little more to get done in time." He consulted his next list. "Bill," he said, "you draw for the Hutchinson family. You got any other households in the Hutchinsons?"

"There's Don and Eva," Mrs. Hutchinson yelled. "Make *them* take their chance!"

"Daughters draw with their husbands' families, Tessie," Mr. Summers said gently. "You know that as well as anyone else."

"It wasn't *fair*," Tessie said.

"I guess not, Joe," Bill Hutchinson said regretfully. "My daughter draws with her husband's family, that's only fair. And I've got no other family except the kids."

"Then, as far as drawing for families is concerned, it's you," Mr. Summers said in explanation, "and as far as drawing for households is concerned, that's you, too. Right?"

"Right," Bill Hutchinson said.

"How many kids, Bill?" Mr. Summers asked formally.

"Three," Bill Hutchinson said. "There's Bill, Jr., and Nancy, and little Dave. And Tessie and me."

"All right, then," Mr. Summers said. "Harry, you got their tickets back?"

Mr. Graves nodded and held up the slips of paper. "Put them in the box, then," Mr. Summers directed. "Take Bill's and put it in."

"I think we ought to start over," Mrs. Hutchinson said, as quietly as she could. "I tell you it wasn't *fair*. You didn't give him time enough to choose. *Every*body saw that."

Mr. Graves had selected the five slips and put them in the box, and he dropped all the papers but those onto the ground, where the breeze caught them and lifted them off.

"Listen, everybody," Mrs. Hutchinson was saying to the people around her.

"Ready, Bill?" Mr. Summers asked, and Bill Hutchinson, with one quick glance around at his wife and children, nodded.

"Remember," Mr. Summers said, "take the slips and keep them folded until each person has taken one. Harry, you help little Dave." Mr. Graves took the hand of the little boy, who came willingly with him up to the box. "Take a paper out of the box, Davy," Mr. Summers said. Davy put his hand into the box and laughed. "Take just *one* paper," Mr. Summers said. "Harry, you hold it for him." Mr. Graves took the child's hand and removed the folded paper from the tight fist and held it while little Dave stood next to him and looked up at him wonderingly.

"Nancy next," Mr. Summers said. Nancy was twelve, and

her school friends breathed heavily as she went forward, switching her skirt, and took a slip daintily from the box. "Bill, Jr.," Mr. Summers said, and Billy, his face red and his feet over-large, nearly knocked the box over as he got a paper out. "Tessie," Mr. Summers said. She hesitated for a minute, look-ing around defiantly, and then set her lips and went up to the box. She snatched a paper out and held it behind her.

"Bill," Mr. Summers said, and Bill Hutchinson reached into the box and felt around, bringing his hand out at last with the slip of paper in it.

The crowd was quiet. A girl whispered, "I hope it's not Nancy," and the sound of the whisper reached the edges of the crowd.

"It's not the way it used to be," Old Man Warner said clearly. "People ain't the way they used to be."

"All right," Mr. Summers said. "Open the papers. Harry, you open little Dave's."

Mr. Graves opened the slip of paper and there was a general sigh through the crowd as he held it up and everyone could see that it was blank. Nancy and Bill, Jr., opened theirs at the same time, and both beamed and laughed, turning around to the crowd and holding their slips of paper above their heads.

"Tessie," Mr. Summers said. There was a pause, and then Mr. Summers looked at Bill Hutchinson, and Bill unfolded his paper and showed it. It was blank.

"It's Tessie," Mr. Summers said, and his voice was hushed. "Show us her paper, Bill."

Bill Hutchinson went over to his wife and forced the slip of paper out of her hand. It had a black spot on it, the black spot Mr. Summers had made the night before with the heavy pencil in the coal-company office. Bill Hutchinson held it up, and there was a stir in the crowd.

"All right, folks," Mr. Summers said. "Let's finish quickly."

Although the villagers had forgotten the ritual and lost the original black box, they still remembered to use stones. The pile of stones the boys had made earlier was ready; there were stones on the ground with the blowing scraps of paper that had come out of the box. Mrs. Delacroix selected a stone so large she had to pick it up with both hands and turned to Mrs. Dunbar. "Come on," she said. "Hurry up."

Mrs. Dunbar had small stones in both hands, and she said, gasping for breath, "I can't run at all. You'll have to go ahead and I'll catch up with you."

The children had stones already, and someone gave little Davy Hutchinson a few pebbles.

Tessie Hutchinson was in the center of a cleared space by now, and she held her hands out desperately as the villagers moved in on her. "It isn't fair," she said. A stone hit her on the side of the head.

Old Man Warner was saying, "Come on, come on, everyone." Steve Adams was in the front of the crowd of villagers, with Mrs. Graves beside him.

"It isn't fair, it isn't right," Mrs. Hutchinson screamed, and then they were upon her.

THE MASQUE OF THE RED DEATH*

BY EDGAR ALLAN POE

T HE "RED DEATH" had long devastated the country. No pestilence had ever been so fatal, or so hideous. Blood was its Avatar and its seal—the redness and the horror of blood. There were sharp pains, and sudden dizziness, and then profuse bleeding at the pores, with dissolution. The scarlet stains upon the body and especially upon the face of the victim, were the pest ban which shut him out from the aid and from the sympathy of his fellowmen. And the whole seizure, progress and termination of the disease, were the incidents of half an hour.

* from *Graham's Magazine*

But the Prince Prospero was happy and dauntless and saga-cious. When his dominions were half depopulated, he sum-moned to his presence a thousand hale and lighthearted friends from among the knights and dames of his court, and with these retired to the deep seclusion of one of his castellated abbeys. This was an extensive and magnificent structure, the creation of the prince's own eccentric yet august taste. A strong and lofty wall girdled it in. This wall had gates of iron. The court-iers, having entered, brought furnaces and massy hammers and welded the bolts. They resolved to leave means neither of ingress or egress to the sudden impulses of despair or of frenzy from within. The abbey was amply provisioned. With such pre-cautions the courtiers might bid defiance to contagion. The ex-ternal world could take care of itself. In the meantime it was folly to grieve, or to think. The prince had provided all the ap-pliances of pleasure. There were buffoons, there were impro-visatori, there were ballet-dancers, there were musicians, there was Beauty, there was wine. All these and security were within. Without was the "Red Death."

It was toward the close of the fifth or sixth month of his seclusion, and while the pestilence raged most furiously abroad, that the Prince Prospero entertained his thousand friends at a masked ball of the most unusual magnificence.

It was a voluptuous scene, that masquerade. But first let me tell of the rooms in which it was held. There were seven—an imperial suite. In many palaces, however, such suites form a long and straight vista, while the folding doors slide back nearly to the walls on either hand, so that the view of the whole extent is scarcely impeded. Here the case was very different; as might have been expected from the duke's love of the *bizarre*. The apartments were so irregularly disposed that the vision em-braced but little more than one at a time. There was a sharp turn at every twenty or thirty yards, and at each turn a novel effect. To the right and left, in the middle of each wall, a tall and nar-row Gothic window looked out upon a closed corridor which pursued the windings of the suite. These windows were of stained glass whose color varied in accordance with the prevail-ing hue of the decorations of the chamber into which it opened.

That at the eastern extremity was hung, for example, in blue—
and vividly blue were its windows. The second chamber was
purple in its ornaments and tapestries, and here the panes were
purple. The third was green throughout, and so were the casements. The fourth was furnished and lighted with orange—the
fifth with white—the sixth with violet. The seventh apartment
was closely shrouded in black velvet tapestries that hung all
over the ceiling and down the walls, falling in heavy folds upon
a carpet of the same material and hue. But in this chamber only,
the color of the windows failed to correspond with the decorations. The panes here were scarlet—a deep blood color. Now in
no one of the seven apartments was there any lamp or cande-
labrum, amid the profusion of golden ornaments that lay scattered to and fro or depended from the roof. There was no light
of any kind emanating from lamp or candle within the suite of
chambers. But in the corridors that followed the suite, there
stood, opposite to each window, a heavy tripod, bearing a bra-
zier of fire that projected its rays through the tinted glass and so
glaringly illumined the room. And thus were produced a multitude of gaudy and fantastic appearances. But in the western or
black chamber the effect of the fire-light that streamed upon the
dark hangings through the blood-tinted panes, was ghastly in
the extreme, and produced so wild a look upon the counte-
nances of those who entered, that there were few of the company bold enough to set foot within its precincts at all.

It was in this apartment, also, that there stood against the
western wall, a gigantic clock of ebony. Its pendulum swung to
and fro with a dull, heavy, monotonous clang; and when the
minute-hand made the circuit of the face, and the hour was to
be stricken, there came from the brazen lungs of the clock a
sound which was clear and loud and deep and exceedingly musical, but of so peculiar a note and emphasis that, at each lapse
of an hour, the musicians of the orchestra were constrained to
pause, momentarily, in their performance, to hearken to the
sound; and thus the waltzers perforce ceased their evolutions;
and there was a brief disconcert of the whole gay company;
and, while the chimes of the clock yet rang, it was observed that
the giddiest grew pale, and the more aged and sedate passed

their hands over their brows as if in confused revery or meditation. But when the echoes had fully ceased, a light laughter at once pervaded the assembly; the musicians looked at each other and smiled as if at their own nervousness and folly, and made whispering vows, each to the other, that the next chiming of the clock should produce in them no similar emotion; and then, after the lapse of sixty minutes (which embrace three thousand and six hundred seconds of the Time that flies), there came yet another chiming of the clock, and then were the same disconcert and tremulousness and meditation as before.

But, in spite of these things, it was a gay and magnificent revel. The tastes of the duke were peculiar. He had a fine eye for colors and effects. He disregarded the *decora* of mere fashion. His plans were bold and fiery, and his conceptions glowed with barbaric lustre. There are some who would have thought him mad. His followers felt that he was not. It was necessary to hear and see and touch him to be *sure* that he was not.

He had directed, in great part, the movable embellishments of the seven chambers, upon occasion of this great *fête;* and it was his own guiding taste which had given character to the masqueraders. Be sure they were grotesque. There were much glare and glitter and piquancy and phantasm—much of what has been since seen in "Hernani." There were arabesque figures with unsuited limbs and appointments. There were delirious fancies such as the madman fashions. There was much of the beautiful, much of the wanton, much of the *bizarre,* something of the terrible, and not a little of that which might have excited disgust. To and fro in the seven chambers there stalked, in fact, a multitude of dreams. And these—the dreams—writhed in and about, taking hue from the rooms, and causing the wild music of the orchestra to seem as the echo of their steps. And, anon, there strikes the ebony clock which stands in the hall of the velvet. And then, for a moment, all is still, and all is silent save the voice of the clock. The dreams are stiff-frozen as they stand. But the echoes of the chime die away—they have endured but an instant—and a light, half-subdued laughter floats after them as they depart. And now again the music swells, and the dreams live, and writhe to and fro more merrily than ever, taking hue from the many tinted windows through which stream the rays from the tripods. But to the chamber which lies most westwardly of the seven, there are now none of the maskers who venture, for the night is waning away; and there flows a ruddier light through the blood-colored panes; and the blackness of the sable drapery appalls; and to him whose foot falls upon the sable carpet, there comes from the near clock of ebony a muffled peal more solemnly emphatic than any which reaches *their* ears who indulge in the more remote gayeties of the other apartments.

But these other apartments were densely crowded, and in them beat feverishly the heart of life. And the revel went whirlingly on, until at length there commenced the sounding of midnight upon the clock. And then the music ceased, as I have told; and the revolutions of the waltzers were quieted; and there was an uneasy cessation of all things as before. But now there were twelve strokes to be sounded by the bell of the clock; and thus it happened, perhaps, that before the last echoes of the last chime had utterly sunk into silence, there were many individuals in the crowd who had found leisure to become aware of the presence of a masked figure which had arrested the attention of no single individual before. And the rumor of this new presence having spread itself whisperingly around, there arose at length from the whole company, a buzz, or murmur, expressive of disapprobation and surprise—then, finally, of terror, of horror, and of disgust.

In an assembly of phantasms such as I have painted, it may well be supposed that no ordinary appearance could have excited such sensation. In truth the masquerade license of the night was nearly unlimited; but the figure in question had out-Heroded Herod, and gone beyond the bounds of even the prince's indefinite decorum. There are chords in the hearts of the most reckless which cannot be touched without emotion. Even with the utterly lost, to whom life and death are equally jests, there are matters of which no jest can be made. The whole company, indeed, seemed now deeply to feel that in the costume and bearing of the stranger neither wit nor propriety existed. The figure was tall and gaunt, and shrouded from head to foot in the habiliments of the grave. The mask which concealed the visage was made so nearly to resemble the countenance of a stiffened corpse that the closest scrutiny must have had difficulty in detecting the cheat. And yet all this might have been endured, if not approved, by the mad revellers around. But the mummer had gone so far as to assume the type of the Red Death. His vesture was dabbled in *blood*—and his broad brow, with all the features of the face, was besprinkled with the scarlet horror.

When the eyes of the Prince Prospero fell upon this spectral image (which with a slow and solemn movement, as if more fully to sustain its *rôle,* stalked to and fro among the waltzers) he was seen to be convulsed, in the first moment, with a strong shudder either of terror or distaste; but, in the next, his brow reddened with rage.

"Who dares?" he demanded hoarsely of the courtiers who stood near him—"who dares insult us with this blasphemous mockery? Seize him and unmask him—that we may know whom we have to hang at sunrise, from the battlements!"

It was in the eastern or blue chamber in which stood the Prince Prospero as he uttered these words. They rang throughout the seven rooms loudly and clearly—for the prince was a bold and robust man, and the music had become hushed at the waving of his hand.

It was in the blue room where stood the prince, with a group of pale courtiers by his side. At first, as he spoke, there was a slight rushing movement of this group in the direction of the intruder, who at the moment was also near at hand, and now, with deliberate and stately step, made closer approach to the speaker. But from a certain nameless awe with which the mad assumptions of the mummer had inspired the whole party, there were found none who put forth hand to seize him; so that, unimpeded, he passed within a yard of the prince's person; and, while the vast assembly, as if with one impulse, shrank from the centres of the room to the walls, he made his way uninterruptedly, but with the same solemn and measured step which had distinguished him from the first, through the blue chamber to the purple—through the purple to the green—through the green to the orange—through this again to the white—and even thence to the violet, ere a decided movement had been made to arrest him. It was then, however, that the Prince Prospero, maddening with rage and the shame of his own momentary cowardice, rushed hurriedly through the six chambers, while none followed him on account of a deadly terror that had seized upon all. He bore aloft a drawn dagger, and had approached, in rapid impetuosity, to within three or four feet of the retreating figure, when the latter, having attained the extremity of the velvet apartment, turned suddenly and confronted his pursuer. There was a sharp cry—and the dagger dropped gleaming upon the sable carpet, upon which, instantly afterwards, fell prostrate in death the Prince Prospero. Then, summoning the wild courage of despair, a throng of the revellers at once threw themselves into the black apartment, and, seizing the mummer, whose tall figure stood erect and motionless within the shadow of the ebony clock, gasped in unutterable horror at finding the grave-cerements and corpse-like mask which they handled with so violent a rudeness, untenanted by any tangible form.

And now was acknowledged the presence of the Red Death. He had come like a thief in the night. And one by one dropped the revellers in the blood-bedewed halls of their revel, and died each in the despairing posture of his fall. And the life of the ebony clock went out with that of the last of the gay. And the flames of the tripods expired. And Darkness and Decay and the Red Death held illimitable dominion over all.

LOOKING BACK*

BY GUY DE MAUPASSANT

(Translated by H. N. P. Sloman)

"NOW, darlings," said the Comtesse, "it's bed-time."

The three children, two girls and a boy, got up and went across to kiss their grandmother.

After that they went to say good-night to the Curé, who had been dining at the castle, as he always did on Thursdays.

The Abbé Mauduit took the two girls on his knee, put his long arms in the black-sleeved cassock round their necks and, drawing their heads towards him with a fatherly gesture; he pressed a long affectionate kiss on each forehead.

Then he put them down and the little things left the room, the boy in front and the girls behind.

"You are fond of children, M. le Curé?" said the Comtesse.

"Very fond, Madame."

The old lady raised her eyes to the priest's face:

"And don't you ever find it hard living alone?"

"Yes, sometimes."

He fell silent and after a pause he went on: "But I was never made for everyday life."

"What do you know about it?"

"Oh! I know well enough. I was made to be a priest. I have followed my vocation."

The Comtesse was still looking at him.

"Come, M. le Curé, tell me about it; tell me how you made up your mind to renounce all that makes the rest of us love life,

---

* from *Miss Harriet and Other Stories*

all that comforts and consoles us. What decided you not to follow the normal path of marriage and family life? You are neither a mystic nor a fanatic, neither a kill-joy nor a pessimist.
Was it something that happened, a great sorrow, that made you
take life vows?"

The Abbé Mauduit got up and went to the fire, holding
out the heavy shoes of a country priest to the flames. He still
seemed to hesitate about answering.

He was a tall, white-haired old man, who had been the
parish priest of Saint-Antoine-du-Rocher and the neighbourhood for twenty years. The peasants always said of him: "He's
a real good sort."

He was a good man, kindly, good-tempered, accessible and,
above all, generous. He would have divided his cloak like Saint
Martin. He was ready to laugh and equally ready to cry, like a
woman, which lowered his reputation a little in the eyes of the
dour peasants.

The old Comtesse de Saville, who had retired to her castle
at Rocher to bring up her grandchildren after the deaths in
close succession of her son and daughter-in-law, was very fond
of her curé and used to say of him: "He's got a good heart."

He came every Thursday and spent the evening at the castle,
and he and the Comtesse had become close friends with the
genuine, open-hearted friendship possible only to the old. They
were so much of a mind that they hardly needed to put their
thoughts into words, being both good souls with the simple
goodness of unsophisticated kindly folk.

She insisted: "Now, M. le Curé, it's time for *you* to make
your confession to *me*."

He repeated: "I was not born for ordinary life. Fortunately I
discovered it in time and I have very often had cause to know
how right I was.

"My parents, who were wholesale haberdashers at Verdiers
and quite well off, were very ambitious for me. They sent me to
a boarding-school very young. People do not realize how unhappy a boy can be at school simply from loneliness and being
away from home. The routine life without affection is good for
some but disastrous for others. Children are often more sensi-

tive than people think, and, if they are shut up in this way too early away from those they love, excessive sensitiveness, which plays havoc with their nerves, may develop and become pathological and dangerous.

"I hardly played any games; I made no friends and was violently home-sick all the time; I cried in bed at night and was always trying to recall memories of home, trivial memories of little insignificant things and happenings. I could not get out of my mind all I had left behind me. I gradually became a nervous wreck, for whom trifling difficulties assumed the proportions of acute misery.

"The result was that I remained morose and self-centred, inhibited and friendless. The process of increasing mental strain went on subconsciously but surely. Children's nerves are easily affected; great care ought to be taken to avoid any disturbance in their lives, until they are practically mature. But who realizes that for some boys at school an undeserved imposition may cause as much mental anguish as the death of a friend will later on? Who really appreciates that something quite trivial may cause in certain immature minds an emotional upset which may in a very short time inflict incurable damage?

"This is what happened in my case; home-sickness developed in me to such an extent that my whole life became one long agony.

"I told no one and said nothing about it. My natural sensitiveness gradually increased till it became pathological and my mind was one open wound. The slightest touch produced twinges of pain and agonizing repercussions which did me permanent harm. Happy indeed are those to whom nature has given a thick skin and the armour of stoicism!

"I reached the age of sixteen. The fact that everything hurt me made me abnormally shy. Knowing that I had no defence against the blows of chance or fate, I shrank from all contacts, all advances, all the activities of school life. I was continually on the defensive, as if constantly threatened by some unknown but always anticipated misfortune. I dared not speak or act in public. I was obsessed with the idea that life was a battle, a frightful struggle, in which one received terrible blows and wounds not only painful but mortal.

"Instead of hopes of happiness for the morrow, such as normal people have, I was conscious only of an undefined terror and I wanted to hide and avoid the struggle, in which I was bound to be defeated and killed.

"When I had finished my studies, I was given six months' holiday in which to choose my career. A very simple incident suddenly enabled me to understand myself and revealed to me my unhealthy psychological condition; I realized my danger and made up my mind to avoid it.

"Verdiers is a small town in flat country with woods all round it. My parents' house was in the main street. I now spent my time away from the home I had missed and longed for so much. I wandered over the countryside, day-dreaming, by myself, so that my dreams could develop without interruption.

"My father and mother, wrapped up in their business and anxious about my future, could talk of nothing but their sales and the careers open to me. They loved me like hard-headed practical people with their head rather than their heart. I lived in the prison of my own thoughts, never free from the terrors of anxiety.

"Well, one evening after a long day out, as I was walking fast in order not to be late home, I saw a dog running at full speed towards me. He was a sort of red spaniel, very thin, with long curly ears.

"He halted ten yards from me; I stopped too. He began to wag his tail and came slowly towards me with timid movements of his whole body, cowering down as if begging and moving his head gently from side to side. I spoke to him. Then he began to crawl towards me on his belly, looking so humble, so miserable, so appealing that tears came into my eyes. I went towards him but he ran away; he soon came back and I knelt down on one knee and spoke kindly to him, enticing him to come closer. At last he was within reach of my hand and I stroked him very gently, taking great care not to frighten him.

"He became bolder, gradually stood upright, put his paws on my shoulder and began to lick my face. He followed me home.

"This was the first living creature I had ever loved passionately, because he returned my affection. My love for the animal was, no doubt, exaggerated and ridiculous. I had a vague idea that in some way we were brothers, both lost in life, both lonely and defenceless. He never left me, slept at the foot of my bed, was fed in the dining-room in spite of my parents' protests and he came with me on my solitary walks.

"I often stopped on the edge of a ditch and sat down on the grass. Sam immediately ran to me and lay down by my side or on my knee, nosing at my hand to make me stroke him.

"One day towards the end of June, as we were on the road to Saint-Pierre-de-Chavrol, I saw the bus from Ravereau coming. It was travelling fast with the four horses at full gallop; it had a yellow body and a black leather tilt over the seats on the top like a cap. The driver was cracking his whip and a cloud of dust rose under the wheels of the heavy vehicle and drifted away behind.

"Suddenly, just as it reached me, Sam, perhaps frightened by the noise and wanting to get to me, dashed in front of it. The hoof of one of the horses knocked him over; I saw him roll, summersault, get up and fall again amid the forest of legs; the whole bus gave two great bumps and I saw behind it something writhing in the dust. He was almost severed in two; his belly was torn open and his entrails were hanging out, spouting blood. He tried to get up and walk, but he could only move his fore legs, which scrabbled at the ground; his hind quarters were already dead. And he was howling pitiably, mad with pain.

"In a minute or two he was dead. I cannot describe my feelings and how much I was affected. I could not leave my room for a month.

"One evening my father, who was furious with me for making such a fuss over such a little thing, cried: 'What will you do when you have a real sorrow, if you lose a wife or children?'

"In a flash I began to understand myself. I realized why little everyday troubles assumed catastrophic proportions in my eyes; I saw that I was so constituted that I felt everything over-keenly and was hyper-susceptible to painful impressions, which

were intensified by my abnormal sensitiveness; and a para-
lysing fear of life gripped me.

"I was without physical desires or ambition; so I decided to
sacrifice the possibility of happiness to the certainty of suffering. 'Life is short; I will devote myself to the service of others;
I will soothe their sorrows and rejoice in their happiness,' I said
to myself. 'As I shall not feel either myself directly, I shall experience these emotions only with diminished intensity.'

"And if you only knew how suffering still tortures me and
wrings my heart! But what would have been intolerable agony
in my own case has been sublimated into sympathy and pity.

"I could never have endured the sorrow with which I come
into contact every day had it been my own. I could not have
seen a child of my own die without dying myself. And, in spite
of everything I still have such an undefined, subconscious fear
of something happening, that the sight of the postman coming
to my door sends a shiver down my spine, though now I have
nothing to fear."

The Abbé Mauduit fell silent. He was looking into the fire in
the great fireplace, as if seeking to read there all the mysteries
and secrets of the life he might have lived, if he had faced suffering more bravely. He went on in a lower voice:

"I was right; I am not made to live in this world."

The Comtesse said nothing; at last, after a long silence, she
commented:

"As for me, if I had not got my grandchildren, I don't think
I should have the courage to go on living."

The Curé got up without another word.

As the servants in the kitchen were asleep, she took him herself to the door into the garden and watched his tall, slow-
moving shadow in the light of his lantern plunge into the
darkness.

Then she went back and sat down by the fire, and thought of
many things that do not occur to the young.

THE MAN HIGHER UP[*]

BY O. HENRY

ACROSS OUR two dishes of spaghetti, in a corner of Provenzano's restaurant, Jeff Peters was explaining to me the three kinds of graft.

Every winter Jeff comes to New York to eat spaghetti, to watch the shipping in East River from the depths of his chinchilla overcoat, and to lay in a supply of Chicago-made clothing at one of the Fulton street stores. During the other three seasons he may be found further west—his range is from Spokane to Tampa. In his profession he takes a pride which he supports and defends with a serious and unique philosophy of ethics. His profession is no new one. He is an incorporated, uncapitalized, unlimited asylum for the reception of the restless and unwise dollars of his fellowmen.

In the wilderness of stone in which Jeff seeks his annual lonely holiday he is glad to palaver of his many adventures, as a boy will whistle after sundown in a wood. Wherefore, I mark on my calendar the time of his coming, and open a question of privilege at Provenzano's concerning the little wine-stained table in the corner between the rakish rubber plant and the framed palazzo della something on the wall.

"There are two kinds of graft," said Jeff, "that ought to be wiped out by law. I mean Wall Street speculation and burglary."

"Nearly everybody will agree with you as to one of them," said I, with a laugh.

"Well, burglary ought to be wiped out, too," said Jeff; and I wondered if the laugh had been redundant.

[*] from *The Gentle Grafter*

"About three months ago," said Jeff, "it was my privilege to become familiar with a sample of each of the aforesaid branches of illegitimate art. I was *sine qua grata* with a member of the housebreakers' union and one of the John D. Napoleons of finance at the same time."

"Interesting combination," said I, with a yawn. "Did I tell you I bagged a duck and a ground-squirrel at one shot last week over in the Ramapos?" I knew well how to draw Jeff's stories.

"Let me tell you first about these barnacles that clog the wheels of society by poisoning the springs of rectitude with their upas-like eye," said Jeff, with the pure gleam of the muckraker in his own.

"As I said, three months ago I got into bad company. There are two times in a man's life when he does this—when he's dead broke, and when he's rich.

"Now and then the most legitimate business runs out of luck. It was out in Arkansas I made the wrong turn at a crossroad, and drive into this town of Peavine by mistake. It seems I had already assaulted and disfigured Peavine the spring of the year before I had sold $600 worth of young fruit trees there—plums, cherries, peaches and pears. The Peaviners were keeping an eye on the country road and hoping I might pass that way again. I drove down Main Street as far as the Crystal Palace drugstore before I realized I had committed ambush upon myself and my white horse Bill.

"The Peaviners took me by surprise and Bill by the bridle and began a conversation that wasn't entirely disassociated with the subject of fruit trees. A committee of 'em ran some trace-chains through the armholes of my vest, and escorted me through their gardens and orchards.

"Their fruit trees hadn't lived up to their labels. Most of 'em had turned out to be persimmons and dogwoods, with a grove or two of blackjacks and poplars. The only one that showed any signs of bearing anything was a fine young cottonwood that had put forth a hornet's nest and half of an old corset-cover.

"The Peaviners protracted our fruitless stroll to the edge of town. They took my watch and money on account; and they kept Bill and the wagon as hostages. They said the first time one of them dogwood trees put forth an Amsden's June peach I might come back and get my things. Then they took off the trace-chains and jerked their thumbs in the direction of the Rocky Mountains; and I struck a Lewis and Clark lope for the swollen rivers and impenetrable forests.

"When I regained intellectualness I found myself walking into an unidentified town on the A., T. & S. F. railroad. The Peaviners hadn't left anything in my pockets except a plug of chewing—they wasn't after my life—and that saved it. I bit off a chunk and sits down on a pile of ties by the track to recogitate my sensations of thought and perspicacity.

"And then along comes a fast freight which slows up a little at the town; and off of it drops a black bundle that rolls for twenty yards in a cloud of dust and then gets up and begins to spit soft coal and interjections. I see it is a young man broad across the face, dressed more for Pullmans than freights, and with a cheerful kind of smile in spite of it all that made Phœbe Snow's job look like a chimney-sweep's.

" 'Fall off?' says I.

" 'Nunk,' says he. 'Got off. Arrived at my destination. What town is this?'

" 'Haven't looked it up on the map yet,' says I. 'I got in about five minutes before you did. How does it strike you?'

" 'Hard,' says he, twisting one of his arms around. 'I believe that shoulder—no, it's all right.'

"He stoops over to brush the dust off his clothes, when out of his pocket drops a fine, nine-inch burglar's steel jimmy. He picks it up and looks at me sharp, and then grins and holds out his hand.

" 'Brother,' says he, 'greetings. Didn't I see you in Southern Missouri last summer selling colored sand at half-a-dollar a teaspoonful to put into lamps to keep the oil from exploding?'

" 'Oil,' says I, 'never explodes. It's the gas that forms that explodes.' But I shakes hands with him, anyway.

" 'My name's Bill Bassett,' says he to me, 'and if you'll call it professional pride instead of conceit, I'll inform you that you have the pleasure of meeting the best burglar that ever set a gum-shoe on ground drained by the Mississippi River.'

"Well, me and this Bill Bassett sits on the ties and ex-changes brags as artists in kindred lines will do. It seems he didn't have a cent, either, and we went into close caucus. He ex-plained why an able burglar sometimes had to travel on freights by telling me that a servant girl had played him false in Little Rock, and he was making a quick get away.

" 'It's part of my business,' says Bill Bassett, 'to play up to the ruffles when I want to make a riffle as Raffles. 'Tis loves that make the bit go 'round. Show me a house with the swag in it and a pretty parlor-maid and you might as well call the silver melted down and sold, and me spilling truffles and that Château stuff on the napkin under my chin, while the police are calling it an inside job because the old lady's nephew teaches a Bible class. I first make an impression on the girl,' says Bill, 'and when she lets me inside I make an impression on the locks. But this one in Little Rock done me,' says he. 'She saw me taking a trolley ride with another girl, and when I came 'round on the night she was to leave the door open for me it was fast. And I had keys made for the doors upstairs. But, no sir. She had sure cut off my locks. She was a Delilah,' says Bill Bassett.

"It seems that Bill tried to break in anyhow with his jimmy, but the girl emitted a succession of bravura noises like the top-riders of a tally-ho, and Bill had to take all hurdles between there and the depot. As he had no baggage they tried hard to check his departure, but he made a train that was just pulling out.

" 'Well,' says Bassett, when we had exchanged memoirs of our dead lives, 'I could eat. This town don't look like it was kept under a Yale lock. Suppose we commit some mild atrocity that will bring in temporary expense money. I don't suppose you've brought along any hair tonic or rolled gold watch-chains, or similar law-defying swindles that you could sell on the plaza to the pikers of the paretic populace, have you?'

" 'No,' says I, 'I left an elegant line of Patagonian diamond earrings and rainy-day sunbursts in my valise at Peavine. But they're to stay there till some of them black-gum trees begin to glut the market with yellow clings and Japanese plums. I reckon we can't count on them unless we take Luther Burbank in for a partner.'

"'Very well,' says Bassett, 'we'll do the best we can. Maybe after dark I'll borrow a hairpin from some lady, and open the Farmers and Drovers Marine Bank with it.'

"While we were talking, up pulls a passenger train to the depot near by. A person in a high hat gets off on the wrong side of the train and comes tripping down the track towards us. He was a little, fat man with a big nose and rat's eyes, but dressed expensive, and carrying a hand-satchel careful, as if it had eggs or railroad bonds in it. He passes by us and keeps on down the track, not appearing to notice the town.

"'Come on,' says Bill Bassett to me, starting after him.

"'Where?' I asks.

"'Lordy!' says Bill, 'had you forgot you was in the desert? Didn't you see Colonel Manna drop down right before your eyes? Don't you hear the rustling of General Raven's wings? I'm surprised at you, Elijah.'

"We overtook the stranger in the edge of some woods, and, as it was after sun-down and in a quiet place, nobody saw us stop him. Bill takes the silk hat off the man's head and brushes it with his sleeve and puts it back.

"'What does this mean, sir?' says the man.

"'When I wore one of these,' says Bill, 'and felt embarrassed, I always done that. Not having one now I had to use yours. I hardly know how to begin, sir, in explaining our business with you, but I guess we'll try your pockets first.'

"Bill Bassett felt in all of them, and looked disgusted.

"'Not even a watch,' he says. 'Ain't you ashamed of yourself, you whited sculpture? Going about dressed like a head-waiter, and financed like a Count! You haven't even got carfare. What did you do with your transfer?'

"The man speaks up and says he has no assets or valuables of any sort. But Bassett takes his hand-satchel and opens it. Out comes some collars and socks and a half a page of a newspaper clipped out. Bill reads the clipping careful, and holds out his hand to the help-up party.

"'Brother,' says he, 'greetings! Accept the apologies of friends. I am Bill Bassett, the burglar. Mr. Peters, you must make the acquaintance of Mr. Alfred E. Ricks. Shake hands.

Mr. Peters,' says Bill, 'stands about halfway between me and you, Mr. Ricks, in the line of havoc and corruption. He always gives something for the money he gets. I'm glad to meet you, Mr. Ricks—you and Mr. Peters. This is the first time I ever attended a full gathering of the National Synod of Sharks—housebreaking, swindling, and financiering all represented. Please examine Mr. Ricks's credentials, Mr. Peters.'

"The piece of newspaper that Bill Bassett handed me had a good picture of this Ricks on it. It was a Chicago paper, and it had obloquies of Ricks in every paragraph. By reading it over I harvested the intelligence that said alleged Ricks had laid off all that portion of the State of Florida that lies under water into town lots and sold 'em to alleged innocent investors from his magnificently furnished offices in Chicago. After he had taken in a hundred thousand or so dollars one of these fussy purchasers that are always making trouble (I've had 'em actually try gold watches I've sold 'em with acid) took a cheap excursion down to the land where it is always just before supper to look at his lot and see if it didn't need a new paling or two on the fence, and market a few lemons in time for the Christmas present trade. He hires a surveyor to find his lot for him. They run the line out and find the flourishing town of Paradise Hollow, so advertised, to be about 40 rods and 16 poles S., 27° E. of the middle of Lake Okeechobee. This man's lot was under thirty-six feet of water, and, besides, had been preëmpted so long by the alligators and gars that his title looked fishy.

"Naturally, the man goes back to Chicago and makes it as hot for Alfred E. Ricks as the morning after a prediction of snow by the weather bureau. Ricks defied the allegation, but he couldn't deny the alligators. One morning the papers came out with a column about it, and Ricks come out by the fire-escape. It seems the alleged authorities had beat him to the safe-deposit box where he kept his winnings, and Ricks has to westward ho! with only feetwear and a dozen 15½ English pokes in his shopping bag. He happened to have some mileage left in his book, and that took him as far as the town in the wilderness where he was spilled out on me and Bill Bassett as Elijah III with not a raven in sight for any of us.

"Then this Alfred E. Ricks lets out a squeak that he is hungry, too, and denies the hypothesis that he is good for the value, let alone the price of a meal. And so, there was the three of us, representing, if we had a mind to draw syllogisms and parabolas, labor and trade and capital. Now, when trade has no capital there isn't a dicker to be made. And when capital has no money there's a stagnation in steak and onions. That put it up to the man with the jimmy.

" 'Brother bushrangers,' says Bill Bassett, 'never yet, in trouble, did I desert a pal. Hard-by, in yon wood, I seem to see unfurnished lodgings. Let us go there and wait till dark.'

"There was an old, deserted cabin in the grove, and we three took possession of it. After dark Bill Bassett tells us to wait, and goes out for half an hour. He comes back with an armful of bread and spareribs and pies.

" 'Panhandled 'em at a farmhouse on Washita Avenue,' says he. 'Eat, drink and be leary.'

"The full moon was coming up bright, so we sat on the floor of the cabin and ate in the light of it. And this Bill Bassett begins to brag.

" 'Sometimes,' says he, with his mouth full of country produce, 'I lose all patience with you people that think you are higher up in the profession than I am. Now, what could either of you have done in the present emergency to set us on our feet again? Could you do it, Ricksy?'

" 'I must confess, Mr. Bassett,' says Ricks, speaking nearly inaudible out of a slice of pie, 'that at this immediate juncture I could not, perhaps, promote an enterprise to relieve the situation. Large operations, such as I direct, naturally require careful preparation in advance. I—'

" 'I know, Ricksy,' breaks in Bill Bassett. 'You needn't finish. You need $500 to make the first payment on a blond typewriter, and four roomsful of quartered oak furniture. And you need $500 more for advertising contracts. And you need two weeks' time for the fish to begin to bite. Your line of relief would be about as useful in an emergency as advocating municipal ownership to cure a man suffocated by eighty-cent gas. And your graft ain't much swifter, Brother Peters,' he winds up.

" 'Oh,' says I, 'I haven't seen you turn anything into gold with your wand yet, Mr. Good Fairy. 'Most anybody could rub the magic ring for a little leftover victuals.'

" 'That was only getting the pumpkin ready,' says Bassett, braggy and cheerful. 'The coach and six'll drive up to the door before you know it, Miss Cinderella. Maybe you've got some scheme under your sleeve-holders that will give us a start.'

" 'Son,' says I, 'I'm fifteen years older than you are, and young enough yet to take out an endowment policy. I've been broke before. We can see the lights of that town not half a mile away. I learned under Montague Silver, the greatest street man that ever spoke from a wagon. There are hundreds of men walking the streets this moment with grease spots on their clothes. Give me a gasoline lamp, a dry-goods box, and a two-dollar bar of white castile soap, cut into little—'

" 'Where's your two dollars?' snickered Bill Bassett into my discourse. There was no use arguing with that burglar.

" 'No,' he goes on; 'you're both babes-in-the-wood. Finance has closed the mahogany desk, and trade has put the shutters up. Both of you look to labor to start the wheels going. All right. You admit it. To-night I'll show you what Bill Bassett can do.'

"Bassett tells me and Ricks not to leave the cabin till he comes back, even if it's daylight, and then he struts off toward town, whistling gay.

"This Alfred E. Ricks pulls off his shoes and his coat, lays a silk handkerchief over his hat, and lays down on the floor.

" 'I think I will endeavour to secure a little slumber,' he squeaks. 'The day has been fatiguing. Goodnight, my dear Mr. Peters.'

" 'My regards to Morpheus,' says I. 'I think I'll sit up a while.'

"About two o'clock, as near as I could guess by my watch in Peavine, home comes our laboring man and kicks up Ricks, and calls us to the streak of bright moonlight shining in the cabin door. Then he spreads out five packages of one thousand dollars each on the floor, and begins to cackle over the nest egg like a hen.

" 'I'll tell you a few things about that town,' says he. 'It's named Rocky Springs, and they're building a Masonic Temple, and it looks like the Democratic candidate for mayor is going to get soaked by a Pop, and Judge Tucker's wife, who has been down with pleurisy, is some better. I had a talk with these lilliputian thesises before I got a siphon in the fountain of knowledge that I was after. And there's a bank there called the Lumberman's Fidelity and Plowman's Savings Institution. It closed for business yesterday with $23,000 cash on hand. It will open this morning with $18,000—all silver—that's the reason I didn't bring more. There you are, trade and capital. Now, will you be bad?'

"'My young friend,' says Alfred E. Ricks, holding up his hands, 'have you robbed this bank? Dear me, dear me!'

"'You couldn't call it that,' says Bassett. '"Robbing" sounds harsh. All I had to do was to find out what street it was on. That town is so quiet that I could stand on the corner and hear the tumblers clicking in that safe lock—"right to 45; left twice to 80; right to 60; left to 15"—as plain as the Yale captain giving orders in the football dialect. Now, boys,' says Bassett, 'this is an early rising town. They tell me the citizens are all up and stirring before daylight. I asked what for, and they said because breakfast was ready at that time. And what of merry Robin Hood? It must be Yoicks! and away with the tinkers' chorus. I'll stake you. How much do you want? Speak up. Capital.'

"'My dear young friend,' says this ground squirrel of a Ricks, standing on his hind legs and juggling nuts in his paws, 'I have friends in Denver who would assist me. If I had a hundred dollars I—'

"Bassett unpins a package of the currency and throws five twenties to Ricks.

"'Trade, how much?' he says to me.

"'Put your money up, Labor,' says I. 'I never yet drew upon honest toil for its hard-earned pittance. The dollars I get are surplus ones that are burning the pockets of damfools and greenhorns. When I stand on a street corner and sell a solid gold diamond ring to a yap for $3.00, I make just $2.60. And I know he's going to give it to a girl in return for all the benefits accruing from a $125.00 ring. His profits are $122.00. Which of us is the biggest fakir?'

" 'And when you sell a poor woman a pinch of sand for fifty cents to keep her lamp from exploding,' says Bassett, 'what do you figure her gross earnings to be, with sand at forty cents a ton?'

" 'Listen,' says I, 'I instruct her to keep her lamp clean and well filled. If she does that it can't burst. And with the sand in it she knows it can't, and she don't worry. It's a kind of Industrial Christian Science. She pays fifty cents, and gets both Rockefeller and Mrs. Eddy on the job. It ain't everybody that can let the gold-dust twins do their work.'

"Alfred E. Ricks all but licks the dust off of Bill Bassett's shoes.

" 'My dear young friend,' says he, 'I will never forget your generosity. Heaven will reward you. But let me implore you to turn from your ways of violence and crime.'

" 'Mousie,' says Bill, 'the hole in the wainscoting for yours. Your dogmas and inculcations sound to me like the last words of a bicycle pump. What has your high moral, elevator-service system of pillage brought you to? Penuriousness and want. Even Brother Peters, who insists upon contaminating the art of robbery with theories of commerce and trade, admitted he was on the lift. Both of you live by the gilded rule. Brother Peters,' says Bill, 'you'd better choose a slice of his embalmed currency. You're welcome.'

"I told Bill Bassett once more to put his money in his pocket. I never had the respect for burglary that some people have. I always gave something for the money I took, even if it's only some little trifle for a souvenir to remind 'em not to get caught again.

"And then Alfred E. Ricks grovels at Bill's feet again, and bids us adieu. He says he will have a team at a farmhouse, and drive to the station below, and take the train for Denver. It salubrified the atmosphere when that lamentable boll-worm took his departure. He was a disgrace to every non-industrial profession in the country. With all his big schemes and fine offices he had wound up unable even to get an honest meal except by the kindness of a strange and maybe unscrupulous burglar. I was glad to see him go, though I felt a little sorry for him, now that he was ruined forever. What could such a man do without a big capital to work with? Why, Alfred E. Ricks, as we left him, was as helpless as a turtle on its back. He couldn't have worked a scheme to beat a little girl out of a penny slate-pencil.

"When me and Bill Bassett was left alone I did a little sleight-of-mind turn in my head with a trade secret at the end of it. Thinks I, I'll show this Mr. Burglar Man the difference between business and labor. He had hurt some of my professional self-adulation by casting his Persians upon commerce and trade.

" 'I won't take any of your money as a gift, Mr. Bassett,' says I to him, 'but if you'll pay my expenses as a traveling companion until we get out of the danger zone of the immoral deficit you have caused in this town's finances to-night, I'll be obliged.'

"Bill Bassett agreed to that, and we hiked westward as soon as we could catch a safe train.

"When we got to a town in Arizona called Los Perros I suggested that we once more try our luck on terra-cotta. That was the home of Montague Silver, my old instructor, now retired from business. I knew Monty would stake me to web money if I could show him a fly buzzing 'round in the locality. Bill Bassett said all towns looked alike to him as he worked mainly in the dark. So we got off the train in Los Perros, a fine little town in the silver region.

"I had an elegant little sure thing in the way of a commercial slungshot that I intended to hit Bassett behind the ear with. I wasn't going to take his money while he was asleep, but I was going to leave him with a lottery ticket that would represent in experience to him $4,755—I think that was the amount he had when he got off the train. But the first time I hinted to him about an investment, he turns on me and disencumbers himself of the following terms and expressions.

" 'Brother Peters,' says he, 'it ain't a bad idea to go into an enterprise of some kind, as you suggest. I think I will. But if I do it will be such a cold proposition that nobody but Robert E. Peary and Charlie Fairbanks will be able to sit on the board of directors.'

" 'I thought you might want to turn your money over,' says I.

" 'I do,' says he, 'frequently. I can't sleep on one side all night. I'll tell you, Brother Peters,' says he, 'I'm going to start a poker room. I don't seem to care for the humdrum in swindling, such as peddling egg-beaters and working off breakfast food on Barnum and Bailey for sawdust to strew in their circus rings. But the gambling business,' says he, 'from the profitable side of the table is a good compromise between swiping silver spoons and selling penwipers at a Waldorf-Astoria charity bazaar.'

" 'Then,' says I, 'Mr. Bassett, you don't care to talk over my business proposition?'

" 'Why,' says he, 'do you know, you can't get a Pasteur institute to start up within fifty miles of where I live. I bite so seldom.'

"So, Bassett rents a room over a saloon and looks around for some furniture and chromos. The same night I went to Monty Silver's house, and he let me have $200 on my prospects. Then I went to the only store in Los Perros that sold playing cards and bought every deck in the house. The next morning when the store opened I was there bringing all the cards back with me. I said that my partner that was going to back me in the game had changed his mind; and I wanted to sell the cards back again. The storekeeper took 'em at half price.

"Yes, I was seventy-five dollars loser up to that time. But while I had the cards that night I marked every one in every deck. That was labor. And then trade and commerce had their innings, and the bread I had cast upon the waters began to come back in the form of cottage pudding with wine sauce.

"Of course I was among the first to buy chips at Bill Bassett's game. He had bought the only cards there was to be had in town; and I knew the back of every one of them better than I know the back of my head when the barber shows me my haircut in the two mirrors.

"When the game closed I had the five thousand and a few odd dollars, and all Bill Bassett had was the wanderlust and a black cat he had bought for a mascot. Bill shook hands with me when I left.

" 'Brother Peters,' says he, 'I have no business being in busi-

ness. I was preordained to labor. When a No. 1 burglar tries to
make a James out of his jimmy he perpetrates an improfundity.
You have a well-oiled and efficacious system of luck at cards,'
says he. 'Peace go with you.' And I never afterward sees Bill
Bassett again."

"Well, Jeff," said I, when the Autolycan adventure seemed
to have divulged the gist of his life, "I hope you took care of the
money. That would be a respecta—that is a considerable working capital if you should choose some day to settle down to
some sort of regular business."

"Me?" said Jeff, virtuously. "You can bet I've taken care of
that five thousand."

He tapped his coat over the region of his chest exultantly.

"Gold mining stock," he explained, "every cent of it. Shares
par value one dollar. Bound to go up 500 per cent within a year.
Non-assessable. The Blue Gopher Mine. Just discovered a
month ago. Better get in yourself if you've any spare dollars on
hand."

"Sometimes," said I, "these mines are not—"

"Oh, this one's solid as an old goose," said Jeff. "Fifty thousand dollars worth of ore in sight, and 10 per cent monthly
earnings guaranteed."

He drew a long envelope from his pocket and cast it on the
table.

"Always carry it with me," said he. "So the burglar can't
corrupt or the capitalist break in and water it."

I looked at the beautifully engraved certificate of stock.

"In Colorado, I see," said I. "And, by the way, Jeff, what was
the name of the little man who went to Denver—the one you
and Bill met at the station?"

"Alfred E. Ricks," said Jeff, "was the toad's designation."

"I see," said I, "the president of this mining company signs
himself A. L. Fredericks. I was wondering—"

"Let me see that stock," said Jeff quickly, almost snatching
it from me.

To mitigate, even though slightly, the embarrassment I summoned the waiter and ordered another bottle of the Barbera. I
thought it was the least I could do.

THE SUMMER OF THE
BEAUTIFUL WHITE HORSE*

BY WILLIAM SAROYAN

ONE DAY back there in the good old days when I was nine and the world was full of every imaginable kind of magnificence, and life was still a delightful and mysterious dream, my cousin Mourad, who was considered crazy by everybody who knew him except me, came to my house at four in the morning and woke me up by tapping on the window of my room.

Aram, he said.

I jumped out of bed and looked out the window.

I couldn't believe what I saw.

It wasn't morning yet, but it was summer and with daybreak not many minutes around the corner of the world it was light enough for me to know I wasn't dreaming.

My cousin Mourad was sitting on a beautiful white horse.

I stuck my head out of the window and rubbed my eyes.

Yes, he said in Armenian. It's a horse. You're not dreaming. Make it quick if you want a ride.

I knew my cousin Mourad enjoyed being alive more than anybody else who had ever fallen into the world by mistake, but this was more than even I could believe.

In the first place, my earliest memories had been memories of horses and my first longings had been longings to ride.

This was the wonderful part.

In the second place, we were poor.

This was the part that wouldn't permit me to believe what I saw.

* from *My Name Is Aram*

We were poor. We had no money. Our whole tribe was poverty-stricken. Every branch of the Garoghlanian family was living in the most amazing and comical poverty in the world. Nobody could understand where we ever got money enough to keep us with food in our bellies, not even the old men of the family. Most important of all, though, we were famous for our honesty. We had been famous for our honesty for something like eleven centuries, even when we had been the wealthiest family in what we liked to think was the world. We were proud first, honest next, and after that we believed in right and wrong. None of us would take advantage of anybody in the world, let alone steal.

Consequently, even though I could see the horse, so magnificent; even though I could *smell* it, so lovely; even though I could *hear* it breathing, so exciting; I couldn't *believe* the horse had anything to do with my cousin Mourad or with me or with any of the other members of our family, asleep or awake, because I *knew* my cousin Mourad couldn't have *bought* the horse, and if he couldn't have bought it he must have *stolen* it, and I refused to believe he had stolen it.

No member of the Garoghlanian family could be a thief.

I stared first at my cousin and then at the horse. There was a pious stillness and humor in each of them which on the one hand delighted me and on the other frightened me.

Mourad, I said, where did you steal this horse?

Leap out of the window, he said, if you want a ride.

It was true, then. He *had* stolen the horse. There was no question about it. He had come to invite me to ride or not, as I chose.

Well, it seemed to me stealing a horse for a ride was not the same thing as stealing something else, such as money. For all I knew, maybe it wasn't stealing at all. If you were crazy about horses the way my cousin Mourad and I were, it wasn't stealing. It wouldn't become stealing until we offered to sell the horse, which of course I knew we would never do.

Let me put on some clothes, I said.

All right, he said, but hurry.

I leaped into my clothes.

I jumped down to the yard from the window and leaped up onto the horse behind my cousin Mourad.

That year we lived at the edge of town, on Walnut Avenue. Behind our house was the country: vineyards, orchards, irrigation ditches, and country roads. In less than three minutes we were on Olive Avenue, and then the horse began to trot. The air was new and lovely to breathe. The feel of the horse running was wonderful. My cousin Mourad who was considered one of the craziest members of our family began to sing. I mean, he began to roar.

Every family has a crazy streak in it somewhere, and my cousin Mourad was considered the natural descendant of the crazy streak in our tribe. Before him was our uncle Khosrove, an enormous man with a powerful head of black hair and the largest mustache in the San Joaquin Valley, a man so furious in temper, so irritable, so impatient that he stopped anyone from talking by roaring, *It is no harm; pay no attention to it.*

That was all, no matter what anybody happened to be talking about. Once it was his own son Arak running eight blocks to the barber shop where his father was having his mustache trimmed to tell him their house was on fire. The man Khosrove sat up in the chair and roared, It is no harm; pay no attention to it. The barber said, But the boy says your house is on fire. So Khosrove roared, Enough, it is no harm, I say.

My cousin Mourad was considered the natural descendant of this man, although Mourad's father was Zorab, who was practical and nothing else. That's how it was in our tribe. A man could be the father of his son's flesh, but that did not mean that he was also the father of his spirit. The distribution of the various kinds of spirit of our tribe had been from the beginning capricious and vagrant.

We rode and my cousin Mourad sang. For all anybody knew we were still in the old country where, at least according to our neighbors, we belonged. We let the horse run as long as it felt like running.

At last my cousin Mourad said, Get down. I want to ride alone.

Will you let me ride alone? I said.

That is up to the horse, my cousin said. Get down.

The *horse* will let me ride, I said.

We shall see, he said. Don't forget that I have a way with a horse.

Well, I said, any way you have with a horse, I have also.

For the sake of your safety, he said, let us hope so. Get down.

All right, I said, but remember you've got to let me try to ride alone.

I got down and my cousin Mourad kicked his heels into the horse and shouted, *Vazire,* run. The horse stood on its hind legs, snorted, and burst into a fury of speed that was the loveliest thing I had ever seen. My cousin Mourad raced the horse across a field of dry grass to an irrigation ditch, crossed the ditch on the horse, and five minutes later returned, dripping wet.

The sun was coming up.

Now it's my turn to ride, I said.

My cousin Mourad got off the horse.

Ride, he said.

I leaped to the back of the horse and for a moment knew the awfulest fear imaginable. The horse did not move.

Kick into his muscles, my cousin Mourad said. What are you waiting for? We've got to take him back before everybody in the world is up and about.

I kicked into the muscles of the horse. Once again it reared and snorted. Then it began to run. I didn't know what to do. Instead of running across the field to the irrigation ditch the horse ran down the road to the vineyard of Dikran Halabian where it began to leap over vines. The horse leaped over seven vines before I fell. Then it continued running.

My cousin Mourad came running down the road.

I'm not worried about you, he shouted. We've got to get that horse. You go this way and I'll go this way. If you come upon him, be kindly. I'll be near.

I continued down the road and my cousin Mourad went across the field toward the irrigation ditch.

It took him half an hour to find the horse and bring him back.

All right, he said, jump on. The whole world is awake now.

What will we do? I said.

Well, he said, we'll either take him back or hide him until to-morrow morning.

He didn't sound worried and I knew he'd hide him and not take him back. Not for a while, at any rate.

Where will you hide him? I said.

I know a place, he said.

How long ago did you steal this horse? I said.

It suddenly dawned on me that he had been taking these early morning rides for some time and had come for me this morning only because he knew how much I longed to ride.

Who said anything about stealing a horse? he said.

Anyhow, I said, how long ago did you begin riding every morning?

Not until this morning, he said.

Are you telling the truth? I said.

Of course not, he said, but if we are found out, that's what you're to say. I don't want both of us to be liars. All you know is that we started riding this morning.

All right, I said.

He walked the horse quietly to the barn of a deserted vine-yard which at one time had been the pride of a farmer named Fetvajian. There were some oats and dry alfalfa in the barn.

We began walking home.

It wasn't easy, he said, to get the horse to behave so nicely. At first it wanted to run wild, but as I've told you, I have a way with a horse. I can get it to want to do anything *I* want it to do. Horses understand me.

How do you do it? I said.

I have an understanding with a horse, he said.

Yes, but what sort of an understanding? I said.

A simple and honest one, he said.

Well, I said, I wish I knew how to reach an understanding like that with a horse.

You're still a small boy, he said. When you get to be thirteen you'll know how to do it.

I went home and ate a hearty breakfast.

That afternoon my uncle Khosrove came to our house for

coffee and cigarettes. He sat in the parlor, sipping and smoking and remembering the old country. Then another visitor arrived, a farmer named John Byro, an Assyrian who, out of loneliness, had learned to speak Armenian. My mother brought the lonely visitor coffee and tobacco and he rolled a cigarette and sipped and smoked, and then at last, sighing sadly, he said, My white horse which was stolen last month is still gone. I cannot understand it.

My uncle Khosrove became very irritated and shouted, It's no harm. What is the loss of a horse? Haven't we all lost the homeland? What is this crying over a horse?

That may be all right for you, a city dweller, to say, John Byro said, but what of my surrey? What good is a surrey without a horse?

Pay no attention to it, my uncle Khosrove roared.

I walked ten miles to get here, John Byro said.

You have legs, my uncle Khosrove shouted.

My left leg pains me, the farmer said.

Pay no attention to it, my uncle Khosrove roared.

That horse cost me sixty dollars, the farmer said.

I spit on money, my uncle Khosrove said.

He got up and stalked out of the house, slamming the screen door.

My mother explained.

He has a gentle heart, she said. It is simply that he is homesick and such a large man.

The farmer went away and I ran over to my cousin Mourad's house.

He was sitting under a peach tree, trying to repair the hurt wing of a young robin which could not fly. He was talking to the bird.

What is it? he said.

The farmer, John Byro, I said. He visited our house. He wants his horse. You've had it a month. I want you to promise not to take it back until I learn to ride.

It will take you a *year* to learn to ride, my cousin Mourad said.

We could keep the horse a year, I said.

My cousin Mourad leaped to his feet.

What? he roared. Are you inviting a member of the Garoghlanian family to steal? The horse must go back to its true owner.

When? I said.

In six months at the latest, he said.

He threw the bird into the air. The bird tried hard, almost fell twice, but at last flew away, high and straight.

Early every morning for two weeks my cousin Mourad and I took the horse out of the barn of the deserted vineyard where we were hiding it and rode it, and every morning the horse, when it was my turn to ride alone, leaped over grape vines and small trees and threw me and ran away. Nevertheless, I hoped in time to learn to ride the way my cousin Mourad rode.

One morning on the way to Fetvajian's deserted vineyard we ran into the farmer John Byro who was on his way to town.

Let me do the talking, my cousin Mourad said. I have a way with farmers.

Good morning, John Byro, my cousin Mourad said to the farmer.

The farmer studied the horse eagerly.

Good morning, sons of my friends, he said. What is the name of your horse?

My Heart, my cousin Mourad said in Armenian.

A lovely name, John Byro said, for a lovely horse. I could swear it is the horse that was stolen from me many weeks ago. May I look into its mouth?

Of course, Mourad said.

The farmer looked into the mouth of the horse.

Tooth for tooth, he said. I would swear it *is* my horse if I didn't know your parents. The fame of your family for honesty is well known to me. Yet the horse is the twin of my horse. A suspicious man would believe his eyes instead of his heart. Good day, my young friends.

Good day, John Byro, my cousin Mourad said.

Early the following morning we took the horse to John Byro's vineyard and put it in the barn. The dogs followed us around without making a sound.

The dogs, I whispered to my cousin Mourad. I thought they would bark.

They would at somebody else, he said. I have a way with dogs.

My cousin Mourad put his arms around the horse, pressed his nose into the horse's nose, patted it, and then we went away.

That afternoon John Byro came to our house in his surrey and showed my mother the horse that had been stolen and returned.

I do not know what to think, he said. The horse is stronger than ever. Better-tempered, too. I thank God.

My uncle Khosrove, who was in the parlor, became irritated and shouted, Quiet, man, quiet. Your horse has been returned. Pay no attention to it.

THE OTHER TWO*

BY EDITH WHARTON

WAYTHORN, ON the drawing-room hearth, waited for his wife to come down to dinner.

It was their first night under his own roof, and he was surprised at his thrill of boyish agitation. He was not so old, to be sure—his glass gave him little more than the five-and-thirty years to which his wife confessed—but he had fancied himself already in the temperate zone; yet here he was listening for her step with a tender sense of all it symbolized, with some old trail of verse about the garlanded nuptial door-posts floating through his enjoyment of the pleasant room and the good dinner just beyond it.

They had been hastily recalled from their honeymoon by the illness of Lily Haskett, the child of Mrs. Waythorn's first mar-

* from *The Descent of Man*

riage. The little girl, at Waythorn's desire, had been transferred to his house on the day of her mother's wedding, and the doctor, on their arrival, broke the news that she was ill with typhoid, but declared that all the symptoms were favorable. Lily could show twelve years of unblemished health, and the case promised to be a light one. The nurse spoke as reassuringly, and after a moment of alarm Mrs. Waythorn had adjusted herself to the situation. She was very fond of Lily—her affection for the child had perhaps been her decisive charm in Waythorn's eyes—but she had the perfectly balanced nerves which her little girl had inherited, and no woman ever wasted less tissue in unproductive worry. Waythorn was therefore quite prepared to see her come in presently, a little late because of a last look at Lily, but as serene and well-appointed as if her good-night kiss had been laid on the brow of health. Her composure was restful to him; it acted as ballast to his somewhat unstable sensibilities. As he pictured her bending over the child's bed he thought how soothing her presence must be in illness: her very step would prognosticate recovery.

His own life had been a gray one, from temperament rather than circumstance, and he had been drawn to her by the unperturbed gaiety which kept her fresh and elastic at an age when most women's activities are growing either slack or febrile. He knew what was said about her; for, popular as she was, there had always been a faint undercurrent of detraction. When she had appeared in New York, nine or ten years earlier, as the pretty Mrs. Haskett whom Gus Varick had unearthed somewhere— was it in Pittsburgh or Utica?—society, while promptly accepting her, had reserved the right to cast a doubt on its own indiscrimination. Inquiry, however, established her undoubted connection with a socially reigning family, and explained her recent divorce as the natural result of a runaway match at seventeen; and as nothing was known of Mr. Haskett it was easy to believe the worst of him.

Alice Haskett's remarriage with Gus Varick was a passport to the set whose recognition she coveted, and for a few years the Varicks were the most popular couple in town. Unfortunately the alliance was brief and stormy, and this time the husband had his champions. Still, even Varick's staunchest supporters admitted that he was not meant for matrimony, and Mrs. Varick's grievances were of a nature to bear the inspection of the New York courts. A New York divorce is in itself a diploma of virtue, and in the semi-widowhood of this second separation Mrs. Varick took on an air of sancity, and was allowed to confide her wrongs to some of the most scrupulous ears in town. But when it was known that she was to marry Waythorn there was a momentary reaction. Her best friends would have preferred to see her remain in the rôle of the injured wife, which was as becoming to her as crape to a rosy complexion. True, a decent time had elapsed, and it was not even suggested that Waythorn had supplanted his predecessor. People shook their heads over him, however, and one grudging friend, to whom he affirmed that he took the step with his eyes open, replied oracularly: "Yes—and with your ears shut."

Waythorn could afford to smile at these innuendoes. In the Wall Street phrase, he had "discounted" them. He knew that society has not yet adapted itself to the consequences of divorce, and that till the adaptation takes place every woman who uses the freedom the law accords her must be her own social justification. Waythorn had an amused confidence in his wife's ability to justify herself. His expectations were fulfilled, and before the wedding took place Alice Varick's group had rallied openly to her support. She took it all imperturbably; she had a way of surmounting obstacles without seeming to be aware of them, and Waythorn looked back with wonder at the trivialities over which he had worn his nerves thin. He had the sense of having found refuge in a richer, warmer nature than his own, and his satisfaction, at the moment, was humorously summed up in the thought that his wife, when she had done all she could for Lily, would not be ashamed to come down and enjoy a good dinner.

The anticipation of such enjoyment was not, however, the sentiment expressed by Mrs. Waythorn's charming face when she presently joined him. Though she had put on her most engaging teagown she had neglected to assume the smile that went with it, and Waythorn thought he had never seen her look so nearly worried.

"What is it?" he asked. "Is anything wrong with Lily?"

"No; I've just been in and she's still sleeping." Mrs. Waythorn hesitated. "But something tiresome has happened."

He had taken her two hands, and now perceived that he was crushing a paper between them.

"This letter?"

"Yes—Mr. Haskett has written—I mean his lawyer has written."

Waythorn felt himself flush uncomfortably. He dropped his wife's hands.

"What about?"

"About seeing Lily. You know the courts—"

"Yes, yes," he interrupted nervously.

Nothing was known about Haskett in New York. He was vaguely supposed to have remained in the outer darkness from which his wife had been rescued, and Waythorn was one of the few who were aware that he had given up his business in Utica and followed her to New York in order to be near his little girl. In the days of his wooing, Waythorn had often met Lily on the doorstep, rosy and smiling, on her way "to see papa."

"I am so sorry," Mrs. Waythorn murmured.

He roused himself. "What does he want?"

"He wants to see her. You know she goes to him once a week."

"Well—he doesn't expect her to go to him now, does he?"

"No—he has heard of her illness; but he expects to come here."

"*Here?*"

Mrs. Waythorn reddened under his gaze. They looked away from each other.

"I'm afraid he has the right.... You'll see...." She made a proffer of the letter.

Waythorn moved away with a gesture of refusal. He stood staring about the softly lighted room, which a moment before had seemed so full of bridal intimacy.

"I'm so sorry," she repeated. "If Lily could have been moved—"

"That's out of the question," he returned impatiently.

"I suppose so."

Her lip was beginning to tremble, and he felt himself a brute.

"He must come, of course," he said. "When is—his day?"

"I'm afraid—tomorrow."

"Very well. Send a note in the morning."

The butler entered to announce dinner.

Waythorn turned to his wife. "Come—you must be tired. It's beastly, but try to forget about it," he said, drawing her hand through his arm.

"You're so good, dear. I'll try," she whispered back.

Her face cleared at once, and as she looked at him across the flowers, between the rosy candle-shades, he saw her lips waver back into a smile.

"How pretty everything is!" she sighed luxuriously.

He turned to the butler. "The champagne at once, please. Mrs. Waythorn is tired."

In a moment or two their eyes met above the sparkling glasses. Her own were quite clear and untroubled: he saw that she had obeyed his injunction and forgotten.

II

Waythorn, the next morning, went down town earlier than usual. Haskett was not likely to come till the afternoon, but the instinct of flight drove him forth. He meant to stay away all day—he had thoughts of dining at his club. As his door closed behind him he reflected that before he opened it again it would have admitted another man who had as much right to enter it as himself, and the thought filled him with a physical repugnance.

He caught the "elevated" at the employees' hour, and found himself crushed between two layers of pendulous humanity. At Eighth Street the man facing him wriggled out, and another took his place. Waythorn glanced up and saw that it was Gus Varick. The men were so close together that it was impossible to ignore the smile of recognition on Varick's handsome over-blown face. And after all—why not? They had always been on good terms, and Varick had been divorced before Waythorn's attentions to his wife began. The two exchanged a word on the perennial grievance of the congested trains, and when a seat at their side was miraculously left empty the instinct of self-preservation made Waythorn slip into it after Varick.

The latter drew the stout man's breath of relief. "Lord—I was beginning to feel like a pressed flower." He leaned back, looking unconcernedly at Waythorn. "Sorry to hear that Sellers is knocked out again."

"Sellers?" echoed Waythorn, starting at his partner's name.

Varick looked surprised. "You didn't know he was laid up with the gout?"

"No, I've been away—I only got back last night." Waythorn felt himself reddening in anticipation of the other's smile.

"Ah—yes; to be sure. And Sellers' attack came on two days ago. I'm afraid he's pretty bad. Very awkward for me, as it happens, because he was just putting through a rather important thing for me."

"Ah?" Waythorn wondered vaguely since when Varick had been dealing in "important things." Hitherto he had dabbled only in the shallow pools of speculation, with which Waythorn's office did not usually concern itself.

It occurred to him that Varick might be talking at random, to relieve the strain of their propinquity. That strain was becoming momentarily more apparent to Waythorn, and when, at Cortlandt Street, he caught sight of an acquaintance and had a sudden vision of the picture he and Varick must present to an initiated eye, he jumped up with a muttered excuse.

"I hope you'll find Sellers better," said Varick civilly, and he stammered back: "If I can be of any use to you—" and let the departing crowd sweep him to the platform.

At his office he heard that Sellers was in fact ill with the gout, and would probably not be able to leave the house for some weeks.

"I'm sorry it should have happened so, Mr. Waythorn," the senior clerk said with affable significance. "Mr. Sellers was very much upset at the idea of giving you such a lot of extra work just now."

"Oh, that's no matter," said Waythorn hastily. He secretly

welcomed the pressure of additional business, and was glad to think that, when the day's work was over, he would have to call at his partner's on the way home.

He was late for luncheon, and turned in at the nearest restaurant instead of going to his club. The place was full and the waiter hurried him to the back of the room to capture the only vacant table. In the cloud of cigar-smoke Waythorn did not at once distinguish his neighbors; but presently, looking about him, he saw Varick seated a few feet off. This time, luckily, they were too far apart for conversation, and Varick who faced another way, had probably not even seen him; but there was an irony in their renewed nearness.

Varick was said to be fond of good living, and as Waythorn sat dispatching his hurried luncheon he looked across half enviously at the other's leisurely degustation of his meal. When Waythorn first saw him he had been helping himself with critical deliberation to a bit of Camembert at the ideal point of liquefaction, and now, the cheese removed, he was just pouring his *café double* from its little two-storied earthern pot. He poured slowly, his ruddy profile bent above the task, and one beringed white hand steadying the lid of the coffee-pot; then he stretched his other hand to the decanter of cognac at his elbow, filled a liqueur-glass, took a tentative sip, and poured the brandy into his coffee-cup.

Waythorn watched him in a kind of fascination. What was he thinking of—only the flavor of the coffee and the liqueur? Had the morning's meeting left no more trace in his thoughts than on his face? Had his wife so completely passed out of his life that even this odd encounter with her present husband, within a week after her remarriage, was no more than an incident in his day? And as Waythorn mused, another idea struck him: had Haskett ever met Varick as Varick and he had just met? The recollection of Hasket perturbed him, and he rose and left the restaurant, taking a circuitous way out to escape the placid irony of Varick's nod.

It was after seven when Waythorn reached home. He thought the footman who opened the door looked at him oddly.

"How is Miss Lily?" he asked in haste.

"Doing very well, sir. A gentleman—"

"Tell Barlow to put off dinner for half an hour," Waythorn cut him off, hurrying upstairs.

He went straight to his room and dressed without seeing his wife. When he reached the drawing-room she was there, fresh and radiant. Lily's day had been good; the doctor was not coming back that evening.

At dinner Waythorn told her of Sellers' illness and of the resulting complications. She listened sympathetically, adjuring him not to let himself be overworked, and asking vague feminine questions about the routine of the office. Then she gave him the chronicle of Lily's day; quoted the nurse and doctor, and told him who had called to inquire. He had never seen her more serene and unruffled. It struck him, with a curious pang, that she was very happy in being with him, so happy that she found a childish pleasure in rehearsing the trivial incidents of her day.

After dinner they went to the library, and the servant put the coffee and liqueurs on a low table before her and left the room. She looked singularly soft and girlish in her rosy pale dress, against the dark leather of one of his bachelor armchairs. A day earlier the contrast would have charmed him.

He turned away now, choosing a cigar with affected deliberation.

"Did Haskett come?" he asked, with his back to her.

"Oh, yes—he came."

"You didn't see him, of course?"

She hesitated a moment. "I let the nurse see him."

That was all. There was nothing more to ask. He swung round toward her, applying a match to his cigar. Well, the thing was over for a week, at any rate. He would try not to think of it. She looked up at him, a trifle rosier than usual, with a smile in her eyes.

"Ready for your coffee, dear?"

He leaned against the mantelpiece, watching her as she lifted the coffee-pot. The lamplight struck a gleam from her bracelets and tipped her soft hair with brightness. How light and slender she was, and how each gesture flowed into the next! She seemed a creature all compact of harmonies. As the thought of Haskett receded, Waythorn felt himself yielding again to the joy of possessorship. They were his, those white hands with their flitting motions, his the light haze of hair, the lips and eyes. . . .

She set down the coffee-pot, and reached for the decanter of cognac, measured off a liqueur-glass and poured it into his cup.

Waythorn uttered a sudden exclamation.

"What is the matter?" she said, startled.

"Nothing; only—I don't take cognac in my coffee."

"Oh, how stupid of me," she cried.

Their eyes met, and she blushed a sudden agonized red.

III

Ten days later, Mr. Sellers, still house-bound, asked Waythorn to call on his way down town.

The senior partner, with his swaddled foot propped up by the fire, greeted his associate with an air of embarrassment.

"I'm sorry, my dear fellow; I've got to ask you to do an awkward thing for me."

Waythorn waited, and the other went on, after a pause apparently given to the arrangement of his phrases: "The fact is, when I was knocked out I had just gone into a rather complicated piece of business for—Gus Varick."

"Well?" said Waythorn, with an attempt to put him at his ease.

"Well—it's this way: Varick came to me the day before my attack. He had evidently had an inside tip from somebody, and had made about a hundred thousand. He came to me for advice, and I suggested his going in with Vanderlyn."

"Oh, the deuce!" Waythorn exclaimed. He saw in a flash what had happened. The investment was an alluring one, but required negotiation. He listened quietly while Sellers put the case before him, and, the statement ended, he said: "You think I ought to see Varick?"

"I'm afraid I can't as yet. The doctor is obdurate. And this thing can't wait. I hate to ask you, but no one else in the office knows the ins and outs of it."

Waythorn stood silent. He did not care a farthing for the success of Varick's venture, but the honor of the office was to be considered, and he could hardly refuse to oblige his partner.

"Very well," he said, "I'll do it."

That afternoon, apprised by telephone, Varick called at the office. Waythorn, waiting in his private room, wondered what the others thought of it. The newspapers, at the time of Mrs. Waythorn's marriage, had acquainted their readers with every detail of her previous matrimonial ventures, and Waythorn could fancy the clerks smiling behind Varick's back as he was ushered in.

Varick bore himself admirably. He was easy without being undignified, and Waythorn was conscious of cutting a much less impressive figure. Varick had no experience of business, and the talk prolonged itself for nearly an hour while Waythorn set forth with scrupulous precision the details of the proposed transaction.

"I'm awfully obliged to you," Varick said as he rose. "The fact is I'm not used to having much money to look after, and I don't want to make an ass of myself—" He smiled, and Waythorn could not help noticing that there was something pleasant about his smile. "It feels uncommonly queer to have enough cash to pay one's bills. I'd have sold my soul for it a few years ago!"

Waythorn winced at the allusion. He had heard it rumored that a lack of funds had been one of the determining causes of the Varick separation, but it did not occur to him that Varick's words were intentional. It seemed more likely that the desire to keep clear of embarrassing topics had fatally drawn him into one. Waythorn did not wish to be outdone in civility.

"We'll do the best we can for you," he said. "I think this is a good thing you're in."

"Oh, I'm sure it's immense. It's awfully good of you—" Varick broke off, embarrassed. "I suppose the thing's settled now—but if—"

"If anything happens before Sellers is about, I'll see you again," said Waythorn quietly. He was glad, in the end, to appear the more self-possessed of the two.

The course of Lily's illness ran smooth, and as the days passed Waythorn grew used to the idea of Haskett's weekly visit. The first time the day came round, he stayed out late, and questioned his wife as to the visit on his return. She replied at once that Haskett had merely seen the nurse downstairs, as the doctor did not wish anyone in the child's sickroom till after the crisis.

The following week, Waythorn was again conscious of the recurrence of the day, but had forgotten it by the time he came home to dinner. The crisis of the disease came a few days later, with a rapid decline of fever, and the little girl was pronounced out of danger. In the rejoicing which ensued the thought of Haskett passed out of Waythorn's mind, and one afternoon, letting himself into the house with a latch-key, he went straight to his library without noticing a shabby hat and umbrella in the hall.

In the library he found a small effaced-looking man with a thinnish gray beard sitting on the edge of a chair. The stranger might have been a piano-tuner, or one of those mysteriously efficient persons who are summoned in emergencies to adjust some detail of the domestic machinery. He blinked at Waythorn through a pair of gold-rimmed spectacles and said mildly: "Mr. Waythorn, I presume? I am Lily's father."

Waythorn flushed. "Oh—" he stammered uncomfortably. He broke off, disliking to appear rude. Inwardly he was trying to adjust the actual Haskett to the image of him projected by his wife's reminiscences. Waythorn had been allowed to infer that Alice's first husband was a brute.

"I am sorry to intrude," said Haskett, with his over-the-counter politeness.

"Don't mention it," returned Waythorn, collecting himself. "I suppose the nurse has been told?"

"I presume so. I can wait," said Haskett. He had a resigned way of speaking, as though life had worn down his natural powers of resistance.

Waythorn stood on the threshold, nervously pulling off his gloves.

"I'm sorry you've been detained. I will send for the nurse," he said; and as he opened the door he added with an effort: "I'm glad we can give you a good report of Lily." He winced as the *we* slipped out, but Haskett seemed not to notice it.

"Thank you, Mr. Waythorn. It's been an anxious time for me."

"Ah, well, that's past. Soon she'll be able to go to you." Waythorn nodded and passed out.

In his own room he flung himself down with a groan. He hated the womanish sensibility which made him suffer so acutely for the grotesque chances of life. He had known when he married that his wife's former husbands were both living, and that amid the multiplied contacts of modern existence there were a thousand chances to one that he would run against one or the other, yet he found himself as much disturbed by his brief encounter with Haskett as though the law had not obligingly removed all difficulties in the way of their meeting.

Waythorn sprang up and began to pace the room nervously. He had not suffered half as much from his two meetings with Varick. It was Haskett's presence in his own house that made the situation so intolerable. He stood still, hearing steps in the passage.

"This way, please," he heard the nurse say. Haskett was being taken upstairs, then: not a corner of the house but was open to him. Waythorn dropped into another chair, staring vaguely ahead of him. On his dressing-table stood a photograph of Alice, taken when he had first known her. She was Alice Varick then—how fine and exquisite he had thought her! Those were Varick's pearls about her neck. At Waythorn's insistence they had been returned before her marriage. Had Haskett ever given her any trinkets—and what had become of them, Waythorn wondered? He realized suddenly that he knew very little of Haskett's past or present situation; but from the man's appearance and manner of speech he could reconstruct with curious precision the surroundings of Alice's first marriage. And it startled him to think that she had, in the background of her life, a phase of existence so different from anything with which he had connected her. Varick, whatever his faults, was a gentleman, in the conventional, traditional sense of the term: the sense which at that moment seemed, oddly enough, to have most meaning to Waythorn. He and Varick had the same social habits, spoke the same language, understood the same allusions. But this other man... it was grotesquely uppermost in Waythorn's mind that Haskett had worn a made-up tie attached with an elastic. Why should that ridiculous detail symbolize the whole man? Waythorn was exasperated by his own paltriness, but the fact of the tie expanded, forced itself on him, became as it were the key to Alice's past. He could see her, as Mrs. Haskett, sitting in a "front parlor" furnished in plush, with a pianola, and a copy of *Ben Hur* on the center-table. He could see her going to the theater with Haskett—or perhaps even to a "Church Sociable"—she in a "picture hat" and Haskett in a black frock-coat, a little creased, with the made-up tie on an elastic. On the way home they would stop and look at the illuminated shop windows, lingering over the photographs of New York actresses. On Sunday afternoons Haskett would take her for a walk, pushing Lily ahead of them in a white enameled perambulator, and Waythorn had a vision of the people they would stop and talk to. He could fancy how pretty Alice must have looked, in a dress adroitly constructed from the hints of a New York fashion-paper, and how she must have looked down on the other women, chafing at her life, and secretly feeling that she belonged in a bigger place.

For the moment his foremost thought was one of wonder at the way in which she had shed the phase of existence which her marriage with Haskett implied. It was as if her whole aspect, every gesture, every inflection, every allusion, were a studied negation of that period of her life. If she had denied being married to Haskett she could hardly have stood more convicted of duplicity than in this obliteration of the self which had been his wife.

Waythorn started up, checking himself in the analysis of her motives. What right had he to create a fantastic effigy of her and then pass judgment on it? She had spoken vaguely of her first marriage as unhappy, had hinted, with becoming reticence, that Haskett had brought havoc among her young illusions.... It was a pity for Waythorn's peace of mind that Haskett's very inoffensiveness shed a new light on the nature of those illusions. A man would rather think that his wife has been brutalized by her first husband than that the process has been reversed.

IV

"Mr. Waythorn, I don't like that French governess of Lily's."

Haskett, subdued and apologetic, stood before Waythorn in the library, revolving his shabby hat in his hand.

Waythorn, surprised in his armchair over the evening paper, stared back perplexedly at his visitor.

"You'll excuse my asking to see you," Haskett continued. "But this is my last visit, and I thought if I could have a word with you it would be a better way than writing to Mrs. Waythorn's lawyer."

Waythorn rose uneasily. He did not like the French governess either; but that was irrelevant.

"I am not so sure of that," he returned stiffly; "but since you wish it I will give your message to—my wife." He always hesitated over the possessive pronoun in addressing Haskett.

The latter sighed. "I don't know as that will help much. She didn't like it when I spoke to her."

Waythorn turned red. "When did you see her?" he asked.

"Not since the first day I came to see Lily—right after she was taken sick. I remarked to her then that I didn't like the governess."

Waythorn made no answer. He remembered distinctly that, after that first visit, he had asked his wife if she had seen Haskett. She had lied to him then, but she had respected his wishes since; and the incident cast a curious light on her character. He was sure she would not have seen Haskett that first day if she had divined that Waythorn would object, and the fact that she did not divine it was almost as disagreeable to the latter as the discovery that she had lied to him.

"I don't like the woman," Haskett was repeating with mild persistency. "She ain't straight, Mr. Waythorn—she'll teach the child to be underhand. I've noticed a change in Lily—she's too anxious to please—and she don't always tell the truth. She used to be the straightest child, Mr. Waythorn—" He broke off, his voice a little thick. "Not but what I want her to have a stylish education," he ended.

Waythorn was touched. "I'm sorry, Mr. Haskett; but frankly, I don't quite see what I can do."

Haskett hesitated. Then he laid his hat on the table, and advanced to the hearth-rug, on which Waythorn was standing. There was nothing aggressive in his manner, but he had the solemnity of a timid man resolved on a decisive measure.

"There's just one thing you can do, Mr. Waythorn," he said. "You can remind Mrs. Waythorn that, by the decree of the courts, I am entitled to have a voice in Lily's bringing up." He paused, and went on more deprecatingly: "I'm not the kind to talk about enforcing my rights, Mr. Waythorn. I don't know as I think a man is entitled to rights he hasn't known how to hold on to; but this business of the child is different. I've never let go there—and I never mean to."

The scene left Waythorn deeply shaken. Shamefacedly, in indirect ways, he had been finding out about Haskett; and all that he had learned was favorable. The little man, in order to be near his daughter, had sold out his share in a profitable business in Utica, and accepted a modest clerkship in a New York manufacturing house. He boarded in a shabby street and had few acquaintances. His passion for Lily filled his life. Waythorn felt that this exploration of Haskett was like groping about with a dark-lantern in his wife's past; but he saw now that there were recesses his lantern had not explored. He had never inquired into the exact circumstances of his wife's first matrimonial rupture. On the surface all had been fair. It was she who had obtained the divorce, and the court had given her the child. But Waythorn knew how many ambiguities such a verdict might cover. The mere fact that Haskett retained a right over his daughter implied an unsuspected compromise. Waythorn was an idealist. He always refused to recognize unpleasant contingencies till he found himself confronted with them, and then he saw them followed by a spectral train of consequences. His next days were thus haunted, and he determined to try to lay the ghosts by conjuring them up in his wife's presence.

When he repeated Haskett's request a flame of anger passed over her face; but she subdued it instantly and spoke with a slight quiver of outraged motherhood.

"It is very ungentlemanly of him," she said.

The word grated on Waythorn. "That is neither here nor there. It's a bare question of rights."

She murmured: "It's not as if he could ever be a help to Lily—"

Waythorn flushed. This was even less to his taste. "The question is," he repeated, "what authority has he over her?"

She looked downward, twisting herself a little in her seat. "I am willing to see him—I thought you objected," she faltered.

In a flash he understood that she knew the extent of Haskett's claims. Perhaps it was not the first time she had resisted them.

"My objecting has nothing to do with it," he said coldly; "if Haskett has a right to be consulted you must consult him."

She burst into tears, and he saw that she expected him to regard her as a victim.

Haskett did not abuse his rights. Waythorn had felt miserably sure that he would not. But the governess was dismissed, and from time to time the little man demanded an interview with Alice. After the first outburst she accepted the situation with her usual adaptability. Haskett had once reminded Waythorn of the piano-tuner, and Mrs. Waythorn, after a month or two, appeared to class him with that domestic familiar. Waythorn could not but respect the father's tenacity. At first he had tried to cultivate the suspicion that Haskett might be "up to" something, that he had an object in securing a foothold in the house. But in his heart Waythorn was sure of Haskett's single-mindedness; he even guessed in the latter a mild contempt for such advantages as his relation with the Waythorns might offer. Haskett's sincerity of purpose made him invulnerable, and his successor had to accept him as a lien on the property.

Mr. Sellers was sent to Europe to recover from his gout, and

Varick's affairs hung on Waythorn's hands. The negotiations were prolonged and complicated; they necessitated frequent conferences between the two men, and the interests of the firm forbade Waythorn's suggesting that his client should transfer his business to another office.

Varick appeared well in the transaction. In moments of relaxation his coarse streak appeared, and Waythorn dreaded his geniality; but in the office he was concise and clear-headed, with a flattering deference to Waythorn's judgment. Their business relations being so affably established, it would have been absurd for the two men to ignore each other in society. The first time they met in a drawing-room, Varick took up their intercourse in the same easy key, and his hostess's grateful glance obliged Waythorn to respond to it. After that they ran across each other frequently, and one evening at a ball Waythorn, wandering through the remoter rooms, came upon Varick seated beside his wife. She colored a little, and faltered in what she was saying; but Varick nodded to Waythorn without rising, and the latter strolled on.

In the carriage, on the way home, he broke out nervously; "I didn't know you spoke to Varick."

Her voice trembled a little. "It's the first time—he happened to be standing near me; I didn't know what to do. It's so awkward, meeting everywhere—and he said you had been very kind about some business."

"That's different," said Waythorn.

She paused a moment. "I'll do just as you wish," she returned pliantly. "I thought it would be less awkward to speak to him when we meet."

Her pliancy was beginning to sicken him. Had she really no will of her own—no theory about her relation to these men? She had accepted Haskett—did she mean to accept Varick? It was "less awkward," as she had said, and her instinct was to evade difficulties or to circumvent them. With sudden vividness Waythorn saw how the instinct had developed. She was "as easy as an old shoe"—a shoe that too many feet had worn. Her elasticity was the result of tension in too many different directions. Alice Haskett—Alice Varick—Alice Waythorn—she

had been each in turn, and had left hanging to each name a little of her privacy, a little of her personality, a little of the inmost
self where the unknown god abides.

"Yes—it's better to speak to Varick," said Waythorn wearily.

V

The winter wore on, and society took advantage of the
Waythorns' acceptance of Varick. Harassed hostesses were
grateful to them for bridging over a social difficulty, and Mrs.
Waythorn was held up as a miracle of good taste. Some exper-
imental spirits could not resist the diversion of throwing Varick
and his former wife together, and there were those who thought
he found a zest in the propinquity. But Mrs. Waythorn's conduct remained irreproachable. She neither avoided Varick nor
sought him out. Even Waythorn could not but admit that she
had discovered the solution of the newest social problem.

He had married her without giving much thought to that
problem. He had fancied that a woman can shed her past like a
man. But now he saw Alice was bound to hers both by the circumstances which forced her into continued relation with it,
and by the traces it had left on her nature. With grim irony
Waythorn compared himself to a member of a syndicate. He
held so many shares in his wife's personality and his predecessors were his partners in the business. If there had been any element of passion in the transaction he would have felt less
deteriorated by it. The fact that Alice took her change of husbands like a change of weather reduced the situation to medi-
ocrity. He could have forgiven her for blunders, for excesses;
for resisting Haskett, for yielding to Varick; for anything but
her acquiescence and her tact. She reminded him of a juggler
tossing knives; but the knives were blunt and she knew they
would never cut her.

And then, gradually, habit formed a protecting surface for
his sensibilities. If he paid for each day's comfort with the
small change of his illusions, he grew daily to value the comfort more and set less store upon the coin. He had drifted into a

dulling propinquity with Haskett and Varick and he took refuge in the cheap revenge of satirizing the situation. He even began to reckon up the advantages which accrued from it, to ask himself if it were not better to own a third of a wife who knew how to make a man happy than a whole one who had lacked opportunity to acquire the art. For it *was* an art, and made up, like all others, of concessions, eliminations and embellishments; of lights judiciously thrown and shadows skillfully softened. His wife knew exactly how to manage the lights, and he knew exactly to what training she owed her skill. He even tried to trace the source of his obligations, to discriminate between the influences which had combined to produce his domestic happiness: he perceived that Haskett's commonness had made Alice worship good breeding, while Varick's liberal construction of the marriage bond had taught her to value the conjugal virtues; so that he was directly indebted to his predecessors for the devotion which made his life easy if not inspiring.

From this phase he passed into that of complete acceptance. He ceased to satirize himself because time dulled the irony of the situation and the joke lost its humor with its sting. Even the sight of Haskett's hat on the hall table had ceased to touch the springs of epigram. The hat was often seen there now, for it had been decided that it was better for Lily's father to visit her than for the little girl to go to his boarding-house. Waythorn, having acquiesced in this arrangement, had been surprised to find how little difference it made. Haskett was never obtrusive, and the few visitors who met him on the stairs were unaware of his identity. Waythorn did not know how often he saw Alice, but with himself Haskett was seldom in contact.

One afternoon, however, he learned on entering that Lily's father was waiting to see him. In the library he found Haskett occupying a chair in his usual provisional way. Waythorn always felt grateful to him for not leaning back.

"I hope you'll excuse me, Mr. Waythorn," he said rising. "I wanted to see Mrs. Waythorn about Lily, and your man asked me to wait here till she came in."

"Of course," said Waythorn, remembering that a sudden

leak had that morning given over the drawing-room to the plumbers.

He opened his cigar-case and held it out to his visitor, and Haskett's acceptance seemed to mark a fresh stage in their intercourse. The spring evening was chilly, and Waythorn invited his guest to draw up his chair to the fire. He meant to find an excuse to leave Haskett in a moment; but he was tired and cold, and after all the little man no longer jarred on him.

The two were enclosed in the intimacy of their blended cigar-smoke when the door opened and Varick walked into the room. Waythorn rose abruptly. It was the first time that Varick had come to the house, and the surprise of seeing him, combined with the singular inopportuneness of his arrival, gave a new edge to Waythorn's blunted sensibilities. He stared at his visitor without speaking.

Varick seemed too preoccupied to notice his host's embarrassment.

"My dear fellow," he exclaimed in his most expansive tone, "I must apologize for tumbling in on you in this way, but I was too late to catch you down town, and so I thought—"

He stopped short, catching sight of Haskett, and his sanguine color deepened to a flush which spread vividly under his scant blond hair. But in a moment he recovered himself and nodded slightly. Haskett returned the bow in silence, and Waythorn was still groping for speech when the footman came in carrying a tea-table.

The intrusion offered a welcome vent to Waythorn's nerves. "What the deuce are you bringing this here for?" he said sharply.

"I beg your pardon, sir, but the plumbers are still in the drawing-room, and Mrs. Waythorn said she would have tea in the library." The footman's perfectly respectful tone implied a reflection on Waythorn's reasonableness.

"Oh, very well," said the latter resignedly, and the footman proceeded to open the folding tea-table and set out its complicated appointments. While this interminable process continued the three men stood motionless, watching it with a fascinated stare, till Waythorn, to break the silence, said to Varick: "Won't you have a cigar?"

He held out the case he had just tendered to Haskett, and Varick helped himself with a smile. Waythorn looked about for a match, and finding none, proffered a light from his own cigar. Haskett, in the background, held his ground mildly, examining his cigar-tip now and then, and stepping forward at the right moment to knock its ashes into the fire.

The footman at last withdrew, and Varick immediately began: "If I could just say half a word to you about this business—"

"Certainly," stammered Waythorn; "in the dining-room—"

But as he placed his hand on the door it opened from without, and his wife appeared on the threshold.

She came in fresh and smiling, in her street dress and hat, shedding a fragrance from the boa which she loosened in advancing.

"Shall we have tea in here, dear?" she began; and then she caught sight of Varick. Her smile deepened, veiling a slight tremor of surprise.

"Why, how do you do?" she said with a distinct note of pleasure.

As she shook hands with Varick she saw Haskett standing behind him. Her smile faded for a moment, but she recalled it quickly, with a scarcely perceptible side-glance at Waythorn.

"How do you do, Mr. Haskett?" she said, and shook hands with him a shade less cordially.

The three men stood awkwardly before her, till Varick, always the most self-possessed, dashed into an explanatory phrase.

"We—I had to see Waythorn a moment on business," he stammered, brick-red from chin to nape.

Haskett stepped forward with his air of mild obstinacy. "I am sorry to intrude; but you appointed five o'clock—" he directed his resigned glance to the time-piece on the mantel.

She swept aside their embarrassment with a charming gesture of hospitality.

"I'm sorry—I'm always late; but the afternoon was so lovely." She stood drawing off her gloves, propitiatory and graceful, diffusing about her a sense of ease and familiarity in which the situation lost its grotesqueness. "But before talking business," she added brightly, "I'm sure everyone wants a cup of tea."

She dropped into her low chair by the tea-table, and the two visitors, as if drawn by her smile, advanced to receive the cups she held out.

She glanced about for Waythorn, and he took the third cup with a laugh.

THEFT*

BY KATHERINE ANNE PORTER

S HE HAD the purse in her hand when she came in. Standing in the middle of the floor, holding her bathrobe around her and trailing a damp towel in one hand, she surveyed the immediate past and remembered everything clearly. Yes, she had opened the flap and spread it out on the bench after she had dried the purse with her handkerchief.

She had intended to take the Elevated, and naturally she looked in her purse to make certain she had the fare, and was pleased to find forty cents in the coin envelope. She was going to pay her own fare, too, even if Camilo did have the habit of seeing her up the steps and dropping a nickel in the machine before he gave the turnstile a little push and sent her through it with a bow. Camilo by a series of compromises had managed to make effective a fairly complete set of smaller courtesies, ignoring the larger and more troublesome ones. She had walked with him to the station in a pouring rain, because she knew he was almost as poor as she was, and when he insisted on a taxi, she was firm and said, "You know it simply will not do." He was wearing a new hat of a pretty biscuit shade, for it never occurred to him to buy

* from *Flowering Judas and Other Stories*

anything of a practical color; he had put it on for the first time and the rain was spoiling it. She kept thinking, "But this is dreadful, where will he get another?" She compared it with Eddie's hats that always seemed to be precisely seven years old and as if they had been quite purposely left out in the rain, and yet they sat with a careless and incidental rightness on Eddie. But Camilo was far different; if he wore a shabby hat it would be merely shabby on him, and he would lose his spirits over it. If she had not feared Camilo would take it badly, for he insisted on the practice of his little ceremonies up to the point he had fixed for them, she would have said to him as they left Thora's house, "Do go home. I can surely reach the station by myself."

"It is written that we must be rained upon tonight," said Camilo, "so let it be together."

At the foot of the platform stairway she staggered slightly— they were both nicely set up on Thora's cocktails—and said: "At least, Camilo, do me the favor not to climb these stairs in your present state, since for you it is only a matter of coming down again at once, and you'll certainly break your neck."

He made three quick bows, he was Spanish, and leaped off through the rainy darkness. She stood watching him, for he was a very graceful young man, thinking that tomorrow morning he would gaze soberly at his spoiled hat and soggy shoes and pos- sibly associate her with his misery. As she watched, he stopped at the far corner and took off his hat and hid it under his over- coat. She felt she had betrayed him by seeing, because he would have been humiliated if he thought she even suspected him of trying to save his hat.

Roger's voice sounded over her shoulder above the clang of the rain falling on the stairway shed, wanting to know what she was doing out in the rain at this time of night, and did she take herself for a duck? His long, imperturbable face was streaming with water, and he tapped a bulging spot on the breast of his buttoned-up overcoat: "Hat," he said. "Come on, let's take a taxi."

She settled back against Roger's arm which he laid around her shoulders, and with the gesture they exchanged a glance full of long amiable associations, then she looked through the window at the rain changing the shapes of everything, and the colors. The taxi dodged in and out between the pillars of the Elevated, skidding slightly on every curve, and she said: "The more it skids the calmer I feel, so I really must be drunk."

"You must be," said Roger. "This bird is a homicidal maniac, and I could do with a cocktail myself this minute."

They waited on the traffic at Fortieth Street and Sixth Avenue, and three boys walked before the nose of the taxi. Under the globes of light they were cheerful scarecrows, all very thin and all wearing very seedy snappy-cut suits and gay neckties. They were not very sober either, and they stood for a moment wobbling in front of the car, and there was an argument going on among them. They leaned toward each other as if they were getting ready to sing, and the first one said: "When I get married it won't be jus' for getting married, I'm gonna marry for *love,* see?" and the second one said, "Aw, gwan and tell that stuff to *her,* why n't yuh?" and the third one gave a kind of hoot, and said, "Hell, dis guy? Wot the hell's he got?" and the first one said: "Aaah, shurrup yuh mush, I got plenty." Then they all squealed and scrambled across the street beating the first one on the back and pushing him around.

"Nuts," commented Roger, "pure nuts."

Two girls went skittering by in short transparent raincoats, one green, one red, their heads tucked against the drive of the rain. One of them was saying to the other, "Yes, I know all about *that.* But what about me?" You're always so sorry for *him . . .*" and they ran on with their little pelican legs flashing back and forth.

The taxi backed up suddenly and leaped forward again, and after a while Roger said: "I had a letter from Stella today, and she'll be home on the twenty-sixth, so I suppose she's made up her mind and it's all settled."

"I had a sort of letter today too," she said, "making up my mind for me. I think it is time for you and Stella to do something definite."

When the taxi stopped on the corner of West Fifty-third Street, Roger said, "I've just enough if you'll add ten cents," so she opened her purse and gave him a dime, and he said, "That's beautiful, that purse."

"It's a birthday present," she told him, "and I like it. How's your show coming?"

"Oh, still hanging on, I guess. I don't go near the place. Nothing sold yet. I mean to keep right on the way I'm going and they can take it or leave it. I'm through with the argument."

"It's absolutely a matter of holding out, isn't it?"

"Holding out's the tough part."

"Good night, Roger."

"Good night, you should take aspirin and push yourself into a tub of hot water, you look as though you're catching cold."

"I will."

With the purse under her arm she went upstairs, and on the first landing Bill heard her step and poked his head out with his hair tumbled and his eyes red, and he said: "For Christ's sake, come in and have a drink with me. I've had some bad news."

"You're perfectly sopping," said Bill, looking at her drenched feet. They had two drinks, while Bill told how the director had thrown his play out after the cast had been picked over twice, and had gone through three rehearsals. "I said to him, 'I didn't say it was a masterpiece, I said it would make a good show.' And he said, 'It just doesn't *play,* do you see? It needs a doctor.' So I'm stuck, absolutely stuck," said Bill, on the edge of weeping again. "I've been crying," he told her, "in my cups." And he went on to ask her if she realized his wife was ruining him with her extravagance. "I send her ten dollars every week of my unhappy life, and I don't really have to. She threatens to jail me if I don't, but she can't do it. God, let her try it after the way she treated me! She's no right to alimony and she knows it. She keeps on saying she's got to have it for the baby and I keep on sending it because I can't bear to see anybody suffer. So I'm way behind on the piano and the victrola, both—"

"Well, this is a pretty rug, anyhow," she said.

Bill stared at it and blew his nose. "I got it at Ricci's for ninety-five dollars," he said. "Ricci told me it once belonged to Marie Dressler, and cost fifteen hundred dollars, but there's a burnt place on it, under the divan. Can you beat that?"

"No," she said. She was thinking about her empty purse and

that she could not possibly expect a check for her latest review for another three days, and her arrangement with the basement restaurant could not last much longer if she did not pay something on account. "It's no time to speak of it," she said, "but I've been hoping you would have by now that fifty dollars you promised for my scene in the third act. Even if it doesn't play. You were to pay me for the work anyhow out of your advance."

"Weeping Jesus," said Bill, "you, too?" He gave a loud sob, or hiccough, in his moist handkerchief. "Your stuff was no better than mine, after all. Think of that."

"But you got something for it," she said. "Seven hundred dollars."

Bill said, "Do me a favor, will you? Have another drink and forget about it. I can't, you know I can't, I would if I could, but you know the fix I'm in."

"Let it go, then," she found herself saying almost in spite of herself. She had meant to be quite firm about it. They drank again without speaking, and she went to her apartment on the floor above.

There, she now remembered distinctly, she had taken the letter out of the purse before she spread the purse out to dry.

She had sat down and read the letter over again: but there were phrases that insisted on being read many times, they had a life of their own separate from the others, and when she tried to read past and around them, they moved with the movement of her eyes, and she could not escape them . . . "thinking about you more than I mean to . . . yes, I even talk about you . . . why were you so anxious to destroy . . . even if I could see you now I would not . . . not worth all this abominable . . . the end . . ."

Carefully she tore the letter into narrow strips and touched a lighted match to them in the coal grate.

Early the next morning she was in the bathtub when the janitress knocked and then came in, calling out that she wished to examine the radiators before she started the furnace going for the winter. After moving about the room for a few minutes, the janitress went out, closing the door very sharply.

She came out of the bathroom to get a cigarette from the package in the purse. The purse was gone. She dressed and made coffee, and sat by the window while she drank it. Certainly the janitress had taken the purse, and certainly it would be impossible to get it back without a great deal of ridiculous excitement. Then let it go. With this decision of her mind, there rose coincidentally in her blood a deep almost murderous anger. She set the cup carefully in the center of the table, and walked steadily downstairs, three long flights and a short hall and a steep short flight into the basement, where the janitress, her face streaked with coal dust, was shaking up the furnace. "Will you please give me back my purse? There isn't any money in it. It was a present, and I don't want to lose it."

The janitress turned without straightening up and peered at her with hot flickering eyes, a red light from the furnace reflected in them. "What do you mean, your purse?"

"The gold cloth purse you took from the wooden bench in my room," she said. "I must have it back."

"Before God I never laid eyes on your purse, and that's the holy truth," said the janitress.

"Oh, well then, keep it," she said, but in a very bitter voice; "keep it if you want it so much." And she walked away.

She remembered how she had never locked a door in her life, on some principle of rejection in her that made her uncomfortable in the ownership of things, and her paradoxical boast before the warnings of her friends, that she had never lost a penny by theft; and she had been pleased with the bleak humility of this concrete example designed to illustrate and justify a certain fixed, otherwise baseless and general faith which ordered the movements of her life without regard to her will in the matter.

In this moment she felt that she had been robbed of an enormous number of valuable things, whether material or intangible: things lost or broken by her own fault, things she had forgotten and left in houses when she moved: books borrowed from her and not returned, journeys she had planned and had not made, words she had waited to hear spoken to her and had not heard, and the words she had meant to answer with; bitter alternatives and intolerable substitutes worse than nothing, and yet inescapable: the long patient suffering of dying friendships and the dark inexplicable death of love—all that she had had, and all that she had missed, were lost together, and were twice lost in this landslide of remembered losses.

The janitress was following her upstairs with the purse in her hand and the same deep red fire flickering in her eyes. The janitress thrust the purse towards her while they were still a half dozen steps apart, and said: "Don't never tell on me. I musta been crazy. I get crazy in the head sometimes, I swear I do. My son can tell you."

She took the purse after a moment, and the janitress went on: "I got a niece who is going on seventeen, and she's a nice girl and I thought I'd give it to her. She needs a pretty purse. I musta been crazy; I thought maybe you wouldn't mind, you leave things around and don't seem to notice much."

She said: "I missed this because it was a present to me from someone..."

The janitress said: "He'd get you another if you lost this one. My niece is young and needs pretty things, we oughta give the young ones a chance. She's got young men after her maybe will want to marry her. She ought have nice things. She needs them bad right now. You're a grown woman, you've had your chance, you ought to know how it is!"

She held the purse out to the janitress saying: "You don't know what you're talking about. Here, take it, I've changed my mind. I really don't want it."

The janitress looked up at her with hatred and said: "I don't want it either now. My niece is young and pretty, she don't need fixin' up to be pretty, she's young and pretty anyhow! I guess you need it worse than she does!"

"It wasn't really yours in the first place," she said, turning away. "You mustn't talk as if I had stolen it from you."

"It's not from me, it's from her you're stealing it," said the janitress, and went back downstairs.

She laid the purse on the table and sat down with the cup of chilled coffee, and thought: I was right not to be afraid of any thief but myself, who will end by leaving me nothing.

A GOOD MAN
IS HARD TO FIND

BY FLANNERY O'CONNOR

THE GRANDMOTHER didn't want to go to Florida. She wanted to visit some of her connections in east Tennessee and she was seizing at every chance to change Bailey's mind. Bailey was the son she lived with, her only boy. He was sitting on the edge of his chair at the table, bent over the orange sports section of the *Journal*. "Now look here, Bailey," she said, "see here, read this," and she stood with one hand on her thin hip and the other rattling the newspaper at his bald head. "Here this fellow that calls himself The Misfit is aloose from the Federal Pen and headed toward Florida and you read here what it says he did to these people. Just you read it. I wouldn't take my children in any direction with a criminal like that aloose in it. I couldn't answer to my conscience if I did."

Bailey didn't look up from his reading so she wheeled around then and faced the children's mother, a young woman in slacks, whose face was as broad and innocent as a cabbage and was tied around with a green head-kerchief that had two points on the top like a rabbit's ears. She was sitting on the sofa, feeding the baby his apricots out of a jar. "The children have been to Florida before," the old lady said. "You all ought to take them somewhere else for a change so they would see different parts of the world and be broad. They never have been to east Tennessee."

The children's mother didn't seem to hear her but the eight-year-old boy, John Wesley, a stocky child with glasses, said, "If you don't want to go to Florida, why dontcha stay at home?" He and the little girl, June Star, were reading the funny papers on the floor.

"She wouldn't stay at home to be queen for a day," June Star said without raising her yellow head.

"Yes and what would you do if this fellow, The Misfit, caught you?" the grandmother asked.

"I'd smack his face," John Wesley said.

"She wouldn't stay at home for a million bucks," June Star said. "Afraid she'd miss something. She has to go everywhere we go."

"All right, Miss," the grandmother said. "Just remember that the next time you want me to curl your hair."

June Star said her hair was naturally curly.

The next morning the grandmother was the first one in the car, ready to go. She had her big black valise that looked like the head of a hippopotamus in one corner, and underneath it she was hiding a basket with Pitty Sing, the cat, in it. She didn't intend for the cat to be left alone in the house for three days because he would miss her too much and she was afraid he might brush against one of the gas burners and accidentally asphyxiate himself. Her son, Bailey, didn't like to arrive at a motel with a cat.

She sat in the middle of the back seat with John Wesley and June Star on either side of her. Bailey and the children's mother and the baby sat in front and they left Atlanta at eight forty-five with the mileage on the car at 55890. The grandmother wrote this down because she thought it would be interesting to say how many miles they had been when they got back. It took them twenty minutes to reach the outskirts of the city.

The old lady settled herself comfortably, removing her white cotton gloves and putting them up with her purse on the shelf in front of the back window. The children's mother still had on slacks and still had her head tied up in a green kerchief, but the grandmother had on a navy blue straw sailor hat with a bunch of white violets on the brim and a navy blue dress with a small white dot in the print. Her collars and cuffs were white organdy trimmed with lace and at her neckline she had pinned a purple spray of cloth violets containing a sachet. In case of an accident, anyone seeing her dead on the highway would know at once that she was a lady.

She said she thought it was going to be a good day for driving, neither too hot nor too cold, and she cautioned Bailey that the speed limit was fifty-five miles an hour and that the patrolmen hid themselves behind billboards and small clumps of trees and sped out after you before you had a chance to slow down. She pointed out interesting details of the scenery: Stone Mountain; the blue granite that in some places came up to both sides of the highway; the brilliant red clay banks slightly streaked with purple; and the various crops that made rows of green lacework on the ground. The trees were full of silver-white sunlight and the meanest of them sparkled. The children were reading comic magazines and their mother had gone back to sleep.

"Let's go through Georgia fast so we won't have to look at it much," John Wesley said.

"If I were a little boy," said the grandmother, "I wouldn't talk about my native state that way. Tennessee has the mountains and Georgia has the hills."

"Tennessee is just a hillbilly dumping ground," John Wesley said, "and Georgia is a lousy state too."

"You said it," June Star said.

"In my time," said the grandmother, folding her thin veined fingers, "children were more respectful of their native states and their parents and everything else. People did right then. Oh look at the cute little pickaninny!" she said and pointed to a Negro child standing in the door of a shack. "Wouldn't that make a picture, now?" she asked and they all turned and looked at the little Negro out of the back window. He waved.

"He didn't have any britches on," June Star said.

"He probably didn't have any," the grandmother explained. "Little niggers in the country don't have things like we do. If I could paint, I'd paint that picture," she said.

The children exchanged comic books.

The grandmother offered to hold the baby and the children's mother passed him over the front seat to her. She set him on her knee and bounced him and told him about the things they were passing. She rolled her eyes and screwed up her mouth and stuck her leathery thin face into his smooth bland one. Occasionally he gave her a faraway smile. They passed a large cotton field with five or six graves fenced in the middle of it, like a small island. "Look at the graveyard!" the grandmother said, pointing it out. "That was the old family burying ground. That belonged to the plantation."

"Where's the plantation?" John Wesley asked.

"Gone With the Wind," said the grandmother. "Ha. Ha."

When the children finished all the comic books they had brought, they opened the lunch and ate it. The grandmother ate a peanut butter sandwich and an olive and would not let the children throw the box and the paper napkins out the window. When there was nothing else to do they played a game by choosing a cloud and making the other two guess what shape it suggested. John Wesley took one the shape of a cow and June Star guessed a cow and John Wesley said, no, an automobile, and June Star said he didn't play fair, and they began to slap each other over the grandmother.

The grandmother said she would tell them a story if they would keep quiet. When she told a story, she rolled her eyes and waved her head and was very dramatic. She said once when she was a maiden lady she had been courted by a Mr. Edgar Atkins Teagarden from Jasper, Georgia. She said he was a very good-looking man and a gentleman and that he brought her a watermelon every Saturday afternoon with his initials cut in it, E. A. T. Well, one Saturday, she said, Mr. Teagarden brought the watermelon and there was nobody at home and he left it on the front porch and returned in his buggy to Jasper, but she never got the watermelon, she said, because a nigger boy ate it when he saw the initials, E. A. T.! This story tickled John Wesley's funny bone and he giggled and giggled but June Star didn't think it was any good. She said she wouldn't marry a man that just brought her a watermelon on Saturday. The grandmother said she would have done well to marry Mr. Teagarden because he was a gentleman and had bought Coca-Cola stock when it first came out and that he had died only a few years ago, a very wealthy man.

They stopped at The Tower for barbecued sandwiches. The Tower was a part stucco and part wood filling station and dance hall set in a clearing outside of Timothy. A fat man named Red Sammy Butts ran it and there were signs stuck here and there on the building and for miles up and down the highway saying, TRY RED SAMMY'S FAMOUS BARBECUE. NONE LIKE FAMOUS RED SAMMY'S! RED SAM! THE FAT BOY WITH THE HAPPY LAUGH! A VETERAN! RED SAMMY'S YOUR MAN!

Red Sammy was lying on the bare ground outside The Tower with his head under a truck while a gray monkey about a foot high, chained to a small chinaberry tree, chattered nearby. The monkey sprang back into the tree and got on the highest limb as soon as he saw the children jump out of the car and run toward him.

Inside, The Tower was a long dark room with a counter at one end and tables at the other and dancing space in the middle. They all sat down at a board table next to the nickelodeon and Red Sam's wife, a tall burnt-brown woman with hair and eyes lighter than her skin, came and took their order. The children's mother put a dime in the machine and played "The Tennessee Waltz," and the grandmother said that tune always made her want to dance. She asked Bailey if he would like to dance but he only glared at her. He didn't have a naturally sunny disposition like she did and trips made him nervous. The grandmother's brown eyes were very bright. She swayed her head from side to side and pretended she was dancing in her chair. June Star said play something she could tap to so the children's mother put in another dime and played a fast number and June Star stepped out onto the dance floor and did her tap routine.

"Ain't she cute?" Red Sam's wife said, leaning over the counter. "Would you like to come be my little girl?"

"No I certainly wouldn't," June Star said. "I wouldn't live in a broken-down place like this for a million bucks!" and she ran back to the table.

"Ain't she cute?" the woman repeated, stretching her mouth politely.

"Aren't you ashamed?" hissed the grandmother.

Red Sam came in and told his wife to quit lounging on the counter and hurry up with these people's order. His khaki trousers reached just to his hip bones and his stomach hung over them like a sack of meal swaying under his shirt. He came over and sat down at a table nearby and let out a combination sigh and yodel. "You can't win," he said. "You can't win," and he wiped his sweating red face off with a gray handkerchief. "These days you don't know who to trust," he said. "Ain't that the truth?"

"People are certainly not nice like they used to be," said the grandmother.

"Two fellers come in here last week," Red Sammy said, "driving a Chrysler. It was an old beat-up car but it was a good one and these boys looked all right to me. Said they worked at the mill and you know I let them fellers charge the gas they bought? Now why did I do that?"

"Because you're a good man!" the grandmother said at once.

"Yes'm, I suppose so," Red Sam said as if he were struck with this answer.

His wife brought the orders, carrying the five plates all at once without a tray, two in each hand and one balanced on her arm. "It isn't a soul in this green world of God's that you can trust," she said. "And I don't count nobody out of that, not nobody," she repeated, looking at Red Sammy.

"Did you read about that criminal, The Misfit, that's escaped?" asked the grandmother.

"I wouldn't be a bit surprised if he didn't attack this place right here," said the woman. "If he hears about it being here, I wouldn't be none surprised to see him. If he hears it's two cent in the cash register, I wouldn't be a tall surprised if he ..."

"That'll do," Red Sam said. "Go bring these people their Co'Colas," and the woman went off to get the rest of the order.

"A good man is hard to find," Red Sammy said. "Everything is getting terrible. I remember the day you could go off and leave your screen door unlatched. Not no more."

He and the grandmother discussed better times. The old lady said that in her opinion Europe was entirely to blame for the way things were now. She said the way Europe acted you would think we were made of money and Red Sam said it was no use talking about it, she was exactly right. The children ran outside into the white sunlight and looked at the monkey in the lacy chinaberry tree. He was busy catching fleas on himself and biting each one carefully between his teeth as if it were a delicacy.

They drove off again into the hot afternoon. The grandmother took cat naps and woke up every few minutes with her own snoring. Outside of Toombsboro she woke up and recalled an old plantation that she had visited in this neighborhood once when she was a young lady. She said the house had six white columns across the front and that there was an avenue of oaks leading up to it and two little wooden trellis arbors on either side in front where you sat down with your suitor after a stroll in the garden. She recalled exactly which road to turn off to get to it. She knew that Bailey would not be willing to lose any time looking at an old house, but the more she talked about it, the more she wanted to see it once again and find out if the little twin arbors were still standing. "There was a secret panel in this house," she said craftily, not telling the truth but wishing that she were, "and the story went that all the family silver was hidden in it when Sherman came through but it was never found..."

"Hey!" John Wesley said. "Let's go see it! We'll find it! We'll poke all the woodwork and find it! Who lives there? Where do you turn off at? Hey Pop, can't we turn off there?"

"We never have seen a house with a secret panel!" June Star shrieked. "Let's go to the house with the secret panel! Hey Pop, can't we go see the house with the secret panel!"

"It's not far from here, I know," the grandmother said. "It wouldn't take over twenty minutes."

Bailey was looking straight ahead. His jaw was as rigid as a horseshoe. "No," he said.

The children began to yell and scream that they wanted to see the house with the secret panel. John Wesley kicked the back of the front seat and June Star hung over her mother's shoulder and whined desperately into her ear that they never had any fun even on their vacation, that they could never do what THEY wanted to do. The baby began to scream and John Wesley kicked the back of the seat so hard that his father could feel the blows in the kidney.

"All right!" he shouted and drew the car to a stop at the side of the road. "Will you all shut up? Will you all just shut up for one second? If you don't shut up, we won't go anywhere."

"It would be very educational for them," the grandmother murmured.

"All right," Bailey said, "but get this: this is the only time we're going to stop for anything like this. This is the one and only time."

"The dirt road that you have to turn down is about a mile back," the grandmother directed. "I marked it when we passed."

"A dirt road," Bailey groaned.

After they had turned around and were headed toward the dirt road, the grandmother recalled other points about the house, the beautiful glass over the front doorway and the candle-lamp in the hall. John Wesley said that the secret panel was probably in the fireplace.

"You can't go inside this house," Bailey said. "You don't know who lives there."

"While you all talk to the people in front, I'll run around behind and get in a window," John Wesley suggested.

"We'll all stay in the car," his mother said.

They turned onto the dirt road and the car raced roughly along in a swirl of pink dust. The grandmother recalled the times when there were no paved roads and thirty miles was a day's journey. The dirt road was hilly and there were sudden washes in it and sharp curves on dangerous embankments. All at once they would be on a hill, looking down over the blue tops of trees for miles around, then the next minute, they would be in a red depression with the dust-coated trees looking down on them.

"This place had better turn up in a minute," Bailey said, "or I'm going to turn around."

The road looked as if no one had traveled on it in months.

"It's not much farther," the grandmother said and just as she said it, a horrible thought came to her. The thought was so embarrassing that she turned red in the face and her eyes dilated and her feet jumped up, upsetting her valise in the corner. The instant the valise moved, the newspaper top she had over the basket under it rose with a snarl and Pitty Sing, the cat, sprang onto Bailey's shoulder.

The children were thrown to the floor and their mother, clutching the baby, was thrown out the door onto the ground; the old lady was thrown into the front seat. The car turned over once and landed right-side-up in a gulch off the side of the road. Bailey remained in the driver's seat with the cat—gray-striped with a broad white face and an orange nose—clinging to his neck like a caterpillar.

As soon as the children saw they could move their arms and legs, they scrambled out of the car, shouting, "We've had an ACCIDENT!" The grandmother was curled up under the dashboard, hoping she was injured so that Bailey's wrath would not come down on her all at once. The horrible thought she had had before the accident was that the house she had remembered so vividly was not in Georgia but in Tennessee.

Bailey removed the cat from his neck with both hands and flung it out the window against the side of a pine tree. Then he got out of the car and started looking for the children's mother. She was sitting against the side of the red gutted ditch, holding the screaming baby, but she only had a cut down her face and a broken shoulder. "We've had an ACCIDENT!" the children screamed in a frenzy of delight.

"But nobody's killed," June Star said with disappointment as the grandmother limped out of the car, her hat still pinned to her head but the broken front brim standing up at a jaunty angle and the violet spray hanging off the side. They all sat down in the ditch, except the children, to recover from the shock. They were all shaking.

"Maybe a car will come along," said the children's mother hoarsely.

"I believe I have injured an organ," said the grandmother, pressing her side, but no one answered her. Bailey's teeth were clattering. He had on a yellow sport shirt with bright blue parrots designed in it and his face was as yellow as the shirt. The grandmother decided that she would not mention that the house was in Tennessee.

The road was about ten feet above and they could see only

the tops of the trees on the other side of it. Behind the ditch they were sitting in there were more woods, tall and dark and deep. In a few minutes they saw a car some distance away on top of a hill, coming slowly as if the occupants were watching them. The grandmother stood up and waved both arms dramatically to attract their attention. The car continued to come on slowly, disappeared around a bend and appeared again, moving even slower, on top of the hill they had gone over. It was a big black battered hearselike automobile. There were three men in it.

It came to a stop just over them and for some minutes, the driver looked down with a steady expressionless gaze to where they were sitting, and didn't speak. Then he turned his head and muttered something to the other two and they got out. One was a fat boy in black trousers and a red sweatshirt with a silver stallion embossed on the front of it. He moved around on the right side of them and stood staring, his mouth partly open in a kind of loose grin. The other had on khaki pants and a blue striped coat and a gray hat pulled down very low, hiding most of his face. He came around slowly on the left side. Neither spoke.

The driver got out of the car and stood by the side of it, looking down at them. He was an older man than the other two. His hair was just beginning to gray and he wore silver-rimmed spectacles that gave him a scholarly look. He had a long creased face and didn't have on any shirt or undershirt. He had on blue jeans that were too tight for him and was holding a black hat and a gun. The two boys also had guns.

"We've had an ACCIDENT!" the children screamed.

The grandmother had the peculiar feeling that the bespectacled man was someone she knew. His face was as familiar to her as if she had known him all her life but she could not recall who he was. He moved away from the car and began to come down the embankment, placing his feet carefully so that he wouldn't slip. He had on tan and white shoes and no socks, and his ankles were red and thin. "Good afternoon," he said. "I see you all had you a little spill."

"We turned over twice!" said the grandmother.

"Oncet," he corrected. "We seen it happen. Try their car and see will it run, Hiram," he said quietly to the boy with the gray hat.

"What you got that gun for?" John Wesley asked. "Whatcha gonna do with that gun?"

"Lady," the man said to the children's mother, "would you mind calling them children to sit down by you? Children make me nervous. I want all you to sit down right together there where you're at."

"What are you telling US what to do for?" June Star asked.

Behind them the line of woods gaped like a dark open mouth. "Come here," said their mother.

"Look here now," Bailey began suddenly, "we're in a predicament! We're in . . ."

The grandmother shrieked. She scrambled to her feet and stood staring. "You're The Misfit!" she said. "I recognized you at once!"

"Yes'm," the man said, smiling slightly as if he were pleased in spite of himself to be known, "but it would have been better for all of you, lady, if you hadn't of reckernized me."

Bailey turned his head sharply and said something to his mother that shocked even the children. The old lady began to cry and The Misfit reddened.

"Lady," he said, "don't you get upset. Sometimes a man says things he don't mean. I don't reckon he meant to talk to you thataway."

"You wouldn't shoot a lady, would you?" the grandmother said and removed a clean handkerchief from her cuff and began to slap at her eyes with it.

The Misfit pointed the toe of his shoe into the ground and made a little hole and then covered it up again. "I would hate to have to," he said.

"Listen," the grandmother almost screamed. "I know you're a good man. You don't look a bit like you have common blood. I know you must come from nice people!"

"Yes mam," he said, "finest people in the world." When he smiled he showed a row of strong white teeth. "God never made a finer woman than my mother and my daddy's heart was pure gold," he said. The boy with the red sweatshirt had come around behind them and was standing with his gun at his hip. The Misfit squatted down on the ground. "Watch them children,

Bobby Lee," he said. "You know they make me nervous." He looked at the six of them huddled together in front of him and he seemed to be embarrassed as if he couldn't think of anything to say. "Ain't a cloud in the sky," he remarked, looking up at it. "Don't see no sun but don't see no cloud neither."

"Yes, it's a beautiful day," said the grandmother. "Listen," she said, "you shouldn't call yourself The Misfit because I know you're a good man at heart. I can just look at you and tell."

"Hush!" Bailey yelled. "Hush! Everybody shut up and let me handle this!" He was squatting in the position of a runner about to sprint forward but he didn't move.

"I pre-chate that, lady," The Misfit said and drew a little circle in the ground with the butt of his gun.

"It'll take a half a hour to fix this here car," Hiram called, looking over the raised hood of it.

"Well, first you and Bobby Lee get him and that little boy to step over yonder with you," The Misfit said, pointing to Bailey and John Wesley. "The boys want to ast you something," he said to Bailey. "Would you mind stepping back in them woods there with them?"

"Listen," Bailey began, "we're in a terrible predicament! Nobody realizes what this is," and his voice cracked. His eyes were as blue and intense as the parrots in his shirt and he remained perfectly still.

The grandmother reached up to adjust her hat brim as if she were going to the woods with him but it came off in her hand. She stood staring at it and after a second she let it fall on the ground. Hiram pulled Bailey up by the arm as if he were assisting an old man. John Wesley caught hold of his father's hand and Bobby Lee followed. They went off toward the woods and just as they reached the dark edge, Bailey turned and supporting himself against a gray naked pine trunk, he shouted, "I'll be back in a minute, Mamma, wait on me!"

"Come back this instant!" his mother shrilled but they all disappeared into the woods.

"Bailey Boy!" the grandmother called in a tragic voice but she found she was looking at The Misfit squatting on the ground in front of her. "I just know you're a good man," she said desperately. "You're not a bit common!"

"Nome, I ain't a good man," The Misfit said after a second as if he had considered her statement carefully, "but I ain't the worst in the world neither. My daddy said I was a different breed of dog from my brothers and sisters. 'You know,' Daddy said, 'it's some that can live their whole life out without asking about it and it's others has to know why it is, and this boy is one of the latters. He's going to be into everything!'" He put on his black hat and looked up suddenly and then away deep into the woods as if he were embarrassed again. "I'm sorry I don't have on a shirt before you ladies," he said, hunching his shoulders slightly. "We buried our clothes that we had on when we escaped and we're just making do until we can get better. We borrowed these from some folks we met," he explained.

"That's perfectly all right," the grandmother said. "Maybe Bailey has an extra shirt in his suitcase."

"I'll look and see terrectly," The Misfit said.

"Where are they taking him?" the children's mother screamed.

"Daddy was a card himself," The Misfit said. "You couldn't put anything over on him. He never got in trouble with the Authorities though. Just had the knack of handling them."

"You could be honest too if you'd only try," said the grandmother. "Think how wonderful it would be to settle down and live a comfortable life and not have to think about somebody chasing you all the time."

The Misfit kept scratching in the ground with the butt of his gun as if he were thinking about it. "Yes'm, somebody is always after you," he murmured.

The grandmother noticed how thin his shoulder blades were just behind his hat because she was standing up looking down on him. "Do you ever pray?" she asked.

He shook his head. All she saw was the black hat wiggle between his shoulder blades. "Nome," he said.

There was a pistol shot from the woods, followed closely by another. Then silence. The old lady's head jerked around. She could hear the wind move through the tree tops like a long satisfied insuck of breath. "Bailey Boy!" she called.

"I was a gospel singer for a while," The Misfit said. "I been most everything. Been in the arm service, both land and sea, at home and abroad, been twict married, been an undertaker, been with the railroads, plowed Mother Earth, been in a tornado, seen a man burnt alive oncet," and looked up at the children's mother and the little girl who were sitting close together, their faces white and their eyes glassy; "I even seen a woman flogged," he said.

"Pray, pray," the grandmother began, "pray, pray . . ."

"I never was a bad boy that I remember of," The Misfit said in an almost dreamy voice, "but somewheres along the line I done something wrong and got sent to the penitentiary. I was buried alive," and he looked up and held her attention to him by a steady stare.

"That's when you should have started to pray," she said. "What did you do to get sent to the penitentiary that first time?"

"Turn to the right, it was a wall," The Misfit said, looking up again at the cloudless sky. "Turn to the left, it was a wall. Look up it was a ceiling, look down it was a floor. I forget what I done, lady. I set there and set there trying to remember what it was I done and I ain't recalled it to this day. Oncet in a while, I would think it was coming to me, but it never come."

"Maybe they put you in by mistake," the old lady said vaguely.

"Nome," he said. "It wasn't no mistake. They had the papers on me."

"You must have stolen something," she said.

The Misfit sneered slightly. "Nobody had nothing I wanted," he said. "It was a head-doctor at the penitentiary said what I had done was kill my daddy but I known that for a lie. My daddy died in nineteen ought nineteen of the epidemic flu and I never had a thing to do with it. He was buried in the Mount Hopewell Baptist churchyard and you can go there and see for yourself."

"If you would pray," the old lady said, "Jesus would help you."

"That's right," The Misfit said.

"Well then, why don't you pray?" she asked trembling with delight suddenly.

"I don't want no hep," he said. "I'm doing all right by my-self."

Bobby Lee and Hiram came ambling back from the woods. Bobby Lee was dragging a yellow shirt with bright blue parrots in it.

"Thow me that shirt, Bobby Lee," The Misfit said. The shirt came flying at him and landed on his shoulder and he put it on. The grandmother couldn't name what the shirt reminded her of. "No, lady," The Misfit said while he was buttoning it up, "I found out the crime don't matter. You can do one thing or you can do another, kill a man or take a tire off his car, because sooner or later you're going to forget what it was you done and just be punished for it."

The children's mother had begun to make heaving noises as if she couldn't get her breath. "Lady," he asked, "would you and that little girl like to step off yonder with Bobby Lee and Hiram and join your husband?"

"Yes, thank you," the mother said faintly. Her left arm dangled helplessly and she was holding the baby, who had gone to sleep, in the other. "Hep that lady up, Hiram," The Misfit said as she struggled to climb out of the ditch, "and Bobby Lee, you hold onto that little girl's hand."

"I don't want to hold hands with him," June Star said. "He reminds me of a pig."

The fat boy blushed and laughed and caught her by the arm and pulled her off into the woods after Hiram and her mother.

Alone with The Misfit, the grandmother found that she had lost her voice. There was not a cloud in the sky nor any sun. There was nothing around her but woods. She wanted to tell him that he must pray. She opened and closed her mouth several times before anything came out. Finally she found herself saying, "Jesus, Jesus," meaning, Jesus will help you, but the way she was saying it, it sounded as if she might be cursing.

"Yes'm," The Misfit said as if he agreed. "Jesus thrown everything off balance. It was the same case with Him as with me except He hadn't committed any crime and they could prove I had committed one because they had the papers on me. Of course," he said, "they never shown me my papers. That's why I sign myself now. I said long ago, you get you a signature and sign everything you do and keep a copy of it. Then you'll know what you done and you can hold up the crime to the punishment and see do they match and in the end you'll have something to prove you ain't been treated right. I call myself The Misfit," he said, "because I can't make what all I done wrong fit what all I gone through in punishment."

There was a piercing scream from the woods, followed closely by a pistol report. "Does it seem right to you, lady, that one is punished a heap and another ain't punished at all?"

"Jesus!" the old lady cried. "You've got good blood! I know you wouldn't shoot a lady! I know you come from nice people! Pray! Jesus, you ought not to shoot a lady. I'll give you all the money I've got!"

"Lady," The Misfit said, looking beyond her far into the woods, "there never was a body that give the undertaker a tip."

There were two more pistol reports and the grandmother raised her head like a parched old turkey hen crying for water and called, "Bailey Boy, Bailey Boy!" as if her heart would break.

"Jesus was the only One that ever raised the dead," The Misfit continued, "and He shouldn't have done it. He thown everything off balance. If He did what He said, then it's nothing for you to do but thow away everything and follow Him, and if He didn't, then it's nothing for you to do but enjoy the few minutes you got left the best way you can—by killing somebody or burning down his house or doing some other meanness to him. No pleasure but meanness," he said and his voice had become almost a snarl.

"Maybe He didn't raise the dead," the old lady mumbled, not knowing what she was saying and feeling so dizzy that she sank down in the ditch with her legs twisted under her.

"I wasn't there so I can't say He didn't," The Misfit said. "I wisht I had of been there," he said, hitting the ground with his fist. "It ain't right I wasn't there because if I had of been there I would of known. Listen lady," he said in a high voice, "if I had of been there I would of known and I wouldn't be like I am now." His voice seemed about to crack and the grandmother's head cleared for an instant. She saw the man's face twisted close to her own as if he were going to cry and she murmured, "Why you're one of my babies. You're one of my own children!" She reached out and touched him on the shoulder. The Misfit sprang back as if a snake had bitten him and shot her three times through the chest. Then he put his gun down on the ground and took off his glasses and began to clean them.

Hiram and Bobby Lee returned from the woods and stood over the ditch, looking down at the grandmother who half sat and half lay in a puddle of blood with her legs crossed under her like a child's and her face smiling up at the cloudless sky.

Without his glasses, The Misfit's eyes were red-rimmed and pale and defenseless-looking. "Take her off and thow her where you thown the others," he said, picking up the cat that was rubbing itself against his leg.

"She was a talker, wasn't she?" Bobby Lee said, sliding down the ditch with a yodel.

"She would of been a good woman," The Misfit said, "if it had been somebody there to shoot her every minute of her life."

"Some fun!" Bobby Lee said.

"Shut up, Bobby Lee," The Misfit said. "It's no real pleasure in life."

THE MAN OF THE HOUSE*

BY FRANK O'CONNOR

WHEN I woke, I heard my mother coughing, below in the kitchen. She had been coughing for days, but I had paid no attention. We were living on the Old Youghal Road at the time, the old hilly coaching road into East Cork. The coughing sounded terrible. I dressed and went downstairs in my stocking feet, and in the clear morning light I saw her, unaware that she

* from The New Yorker

was being watched, collapsed into a little wickerwork armchair, holding her side. She had made an attempt to light the fire, but it had gone against her. She looked so tired and helpless that my heart turned over with compassion. I ran to her.

"Are you all right, Mum?" I asked.

"I'll be all right in a second," she replied, trying to smile. "The old sticks were wet, and the smoke started me coughing."

"Go back to bed and I'll light the fire," I said.

"Ah, how can I, child?" she said anxiously. "Sure, I have to go to work."

"You couldn't work like that," I said. "I'll stop at home from school and look after you."

It's a funny thing about women, the way they'll take orders from anything in trousers, even if it's only ten.

"If you could make yourself a cup of tea, I might be all right later on," she said guiltily, and she rose, very shakily, and climbed back up the stairs. I knew then she must be feeling really bad.

I got more sticks out of the coalhole, under the stairs. My mother was so economical that she never used enough, and that was why the fire sometimes went against her. I used a whole bundle, and I soon had the fire roaring and the kettle on. I made her toast while I was about it. I was a great believer in hot buttered toast at all hours of the day. Then I made the tea and brought her up a cup on the tray. "Is that all right?" I asked.

"Would you have a sup of boiling water left?" she asked doubtfully.

" 'Tis too strong," I agreed cheerfully, remembering the patience of the saints in their many afflictions. "I'll pour half of it out."

"I'm an old nuisance," she sighed.

" 'Tis my fault," I said, taking the cup. "I can never remember about tea. Put the shawl round you while you're sitting up. Will I shut the skylight?"

"Would you be able?" she asked doubtfully.

" 'Tis no trouble," I said, getting the chair to it. "I'll do the messages after."

I had my own breakfast alone by the window, and then I

went out and stood by the front door to watch the kids from the road on their way to school.

"You'd better hurry or you'll be killed, Sullivan," they shouted.

"I'm not going," I said. "My mother is sick, and I have to mind the house."

I wasn't a malicious child, by any means, but I liked to be able to take out my comforts and study them by the light of others' misfortunes. Then I heated another kettle of water and cleared up the breakfast things before I washed my face and came up to the attic with my shopping basket, a piece of paper, and a lead pencil.

"I'll do the messages now if you'll write them down," I said. "Would you like me to get the doctor?"

"Ah," said my mother impatiently, "he'd only want to send me to hospital, and how would I go to hospital? You could call in at the chemist's and ask him to give you a good, strong cough bottle."

"Write it down," I said. "If I haven't it written down, I might forget it. And put 'strong' in big letters. What will I get for the dinner? Eggs?"

As boiled eggs were the only dish I could manage, I more or less knew it would be eggs, but she told me to get sausages as well, in case she could get up.

I passed the school on my way. Opposite it was a hill, and I went up a short distance and stood there for ten minutes in quiet contemplation. The schoolhouse and yard and gate were revealed as in a painted picture, detached and peaceful except for the chorus of voices through the opened windows and the glimpse of Danny Delaney, the teacher, passing the front door with his cane behind his back, stealing a glance at the world outside. I could have stood there all day. Of all the profound and simple pleasures of those days, that was the richest.

When I got home, I rushed upstairs and found Minnie Ryan sitting with my mother. She was a middle-aged woman, very knowledgeable, gossipy, and pious.

"How are you, Mum?" I asked.

"Grand," said my mother, with a smile.

"You can't get up today, though," said Minnie Ryan.

"I'll put the kettle on and make a cup of tea for you," I said.

"Sure, I'll do that," said Minnie.

"Ah, don't worry, Miss Ryan," I said lightly. "I can manage it all right."

"Wisha, isn't he very good?" I heard her say in a low voice to my mother.

"As good as gold," said my mother.

"There's not many like that, then," said Minnie. "The most of them that's going now are more like savages than Christians."

In the afternoon, my mother wanted me to run out and play, but I didn't go far. I knew if once I went a certain distance from the house, I was liable to stray into temptation. Below our house, there was a glen, the drill field of the barracks perched high above it on a chalky cliff, and below, in a deep hollow, the millpond and millstream running between wooded hills—the Rockies, the Himalayas, or the Highlands, according to your mood. Once down there, I tended to forget the real world, so I sat on a wall outside the house, running in every half hour to see how the mother was and if there was anything she wanted.

Evening fell; the street lamps were lit, and the paper boy went crying up the road. I bought a paper, lit the lamp in the kitchen and the candle in my mother's attic, and tried to read to her, not very successfully, because I was only at words of one syllable, but I had a great wish to please, and she to be pleased, so we got on quite well, considering.

Later, Minnie Ryan came again, and as she was going, I saw her to the door.

"If she's not better in the morning, I think I'd get the doctor, Flurry," she said, over her shoulder.

"Why?" I asked, in alarm. "Do you think is she worse, Miss Ryan."

"Ah, I wouldn't say so," she replied with affected nonchalance, "but I'd be frightened she might get pneumonia."

"But wouldn't he send her to hospital, Miss Ryan?"

"Wisha, he mightn't," she said with a shrug, pulling her old shawl about her. "But even if he did, wouldn't it be better than neglecting it? Ye wouldn't have a drop of whiskey in the house?"

"I'll get it," I said at once. I knew what might happen to people who got pneumonia, and what was bound to happen afterward to their children.

"If you could give it to her hot, with a squeeze of lemon in it, it might help her to shake it off," said Minnie.

My mother said she didn't want the whiskey, dreading the expense, but I had got such a fright that I wouldn't be put off. When I went to the public house, it was full of men, who drew aside to let me reach the bar. I had never been in a public house before, and I was frightened.

"Hullo, my old flower," said one man, grinning diabolically at me. "It must be ten years since I seen you last. What are you having?"

My pal, Bob Connell, had told me how he once asked a drunk man for a half crown and the man gave it to him. I always wished I could bring myself to do the same, but I didn't feel like it just then.

"I want a half glass of whiskey for my mother," I said.

"Oh, the thundering ruffian!" said the man. "Pretending 'tis for his mother, and the last time I seen him he had to be carried home."

"I had not," I shouted indignantly. "And 'tis for my mother. She's sick."

"Ah, let the child alone, Johnnie," said the barmaid. She gave me the whiskey, and then, still frightened of the men in the public house, I went off to a shop for a lemon.

When my mother had drunk the hot whiskey, she fell asleep, and I quenched the lights and went to bed, but I couldn't sleep very well. I was regretting I hadn't asked the man in the pub for a half crown. I was wakened several times by the coughing, and when I went into my mother's room her head felt very hot, and she was rambling in her talk. It frightened me more than anything else when she didn't know me, and I lay awake, thinking of what would happen to me if it were really pneumonia.

The depression was terrible when, next morning, my mother seemed not to be any better. I had done all I could do, and I felt helpless. I lit the fire and got her breakfast, but this time I didn't stand at the front door to see the other fellows on their way to school. I should have been too inclined to envy them. Instead, I went over to Minnie Ryan and reported.

"I'd go for the doctor," she said firmly. "Better be sure than sorry."

I had first to go to the house of a Poor Law Guardian, for a ticket to show we couldn't pay. Then I went down to the dispensary, which was in a deep hollow beyond the school. After that I had to go back to ready the house for the doctor. I had to have a basin of water and soap and a clean towel laid out for him, and I had to get the dinner, too.

It was after dinner when he called. He was a fat, loud-voiced man and, like all the drunks of the medical profession, supposed to be "the cleverest doctor in Cork, if only he'd mind himself." He hadn't been minding himself much that morning, it seemed.

"How are you going to get this now?" he grumbled, sitting on the bed with the prescription pad on his knee. "The only place open is the North Dispensary."

"I'll go, Doctor," I said at once, relieved that he had said nothing about hospital.

" 'Tis a long way," he said, doubtfully. "Do you know where it is?"

"I'll find it," I said.

"Isn't he a great little fellow?" he said to my mother.

"Oh, the best in the world, Doctor!" she said. "A daughter couldn't be better to me."

"That's right," said the doctor. "Look after your mother; she'll be the best for you in the long run. We don't mind them when we have them," he added, to my mother, "and then we spend the rest of our lives regretting it."

I wished he hadn't said that; it tuned in altogether too well with my mood. To make it worse, he didn't even use the soap and water I had laid ready for him.

My mother gave me directions how to reach the dispensary, and I set off with a bottle wrapped in brown paper under my arm. The road led uphill, through a thickly populated poor locality, as far as the barracks, which was perched on the very top of the hill, over the city, and then descended, between high walls, till it suddenly almost disappeared in a stony path, with red brick corporation houses to one side of it, that dropped steeply, steeply, to the valley of the little river, where a brewery stood, and the opposite hillside, a murmuring honeycomb of houses, rose to the gently rounded top, on which stood the purple sandstone tower of the cathedral and the limestone spire of Shandon church, on a level with your eye.

It was so wide a view that it was never all lit up together, and the sunlight wandered across it as across a prairie, picking out first a line of roofs with a brightness like snow, and then delving into the depth of some dark street and outlining in shadow figures of climbing carts and straining horses. I leaned on the low wall and thought how happy a fellow could be, looking at that, if he had nothing to trouble him. I tore myself from it with a sigh, slithered without stopping to the bottom of the hill, and climbed up a series of shadowy and stepped lanes around the back of the cathedral, which now seemed enormous. I had a penny, which my mother had given me by way of encouragement, and I made up my mind that when I had done my business, I should go into the cathedral and spend it on a candle to the Blessed Virgin, to make my mother better quick. I felt sure it would be more effective in a really big church like that, so very close to Heaven.

The dispensary was a sordid little hallway with a bench to one side and a window like the one in a railway ticket office at the far end. There was a little girl with a green plaid shawl about her shoulders sitting on the bench. I knocked at the window, and a seedy, angry-looking man opened it. Without waiting for me to finish what I was saying, he grabbed bottle and prescription from me and banged the shutter down again without a word. I waited for a moment and then lifted my hand to knock again.

"You'll have to wait, little boy," said the girl quickly.

"What will I have to wait for?" I asked.

"He have to make it up," she explained. "You might as well sit down."

I did, glad of anyone to keep me company.

"Where are you from?" she asked. "I live in Blarney Lane," she added when I had told her. "Who's the bottle for?"

"My mother," I said.

"What's wrong with her?"

"She have a bad cough."

"She might have consumption," she said thoughtfully. "That's what my sister that died last year had. This is a tonic for my other sister. She have to have tonics all the time. Is it nice where you live?"

I told her about the glen, and then she told me about the river near their place. It seemed to be a nicer place than ours, as she described it. She was a pleasant, talkative little girl, and I didn't notice the time until the window opened again and a red bottle was thrust out.

"Dooley!" shouted the seedy man, and closed the window again.

"That's me," said the little girl. "Yours won't be ready for a good while yet. I'll wait for you."

"I have a penny," I said boastfully.

She waited until my bottle was thrust out, and then she accompanied me as far as the steps leading down to the brewery. On the way, I bought a pennyworth of sweets, and we sat on the other steps, beside the infirmary, to eat them. It was nice there, with the spire of Shandon in shadow behind us, the young trees overhanging the high walls, and the sun, when it came out in great golden blasts, throwing our linked shadows onto the road.

"Give us a taste of your bottle, little boy," she said.

"Why?" I asked. "Can't you taste your own?"

"Mine is awful," she said. "Tonics is awful to taste. You can try it if you like."

I took a taste of it and hastily spat out. She was right; it was awful. After that, I couldn't do less than let her taste mine.

"That's grand," she said enthusiastically, after taking a swig from it. "Cough bottles are nearly always grand. Try it, can't you?"

I did, and saw she was right about that, too. It was very sweet and sticky.

"Give us another," she said excitedly, grabbing at it.

" 'Twill be all gone," I said.

"Erra, 'twon't," she replied with a laugh. "You have gallons of it."

Somehow, I couldn't refuse her. I was swept from my anchorage into an unfamiliar world of spires and towers, trees, steps, shadowy laneways, and little girls with red hair and green eyes.

I took a drink myself and gave her another. Then I began to panic. " 'Tis nearly gone," I said. "What am I going to do now?"

"Finish it and say the cork fell out," she replied, and again, as she said it, it sounded plausible enough. We finished the bottle between us, and then, slowly, as I looked at it in my hand, empty as I had brought it, and remembered that I had not kept my word to the Blessed Virgin and had spent her penny on sweets, a terrible despondency swept over me. I had sacrificed everything for the little girl and she didn't even care for me. It was my cough bottle she had coveted all the time. I saw her guile too late. I put my head in my hands and began to cry.

"What are you crying for?" the little girl asked in astonishment.

"My mother is sick, and we're after drinking her medicine," I said.

"Ah, don't be an old crybaby!" she said contemptuously. "You have only to say the cork fell out. Sure, that's a thing could happen to anybody."

"And I promised the Blessed Virgin a candle, and I spent the money on you!" I screamed, and, suddenly grabbing the empty bottle, I ran up the road from her, wailing. Now I had only one refuge and one hope—a miracle. I went back to the cathedral, and, kneeling before the shrine of the Blessed Virgin, I begged her pardon for having spent her penny, and promised her a candle from the next penny I got, if only she would work a miracle and make my mother better before I got back. After that, I crawled miserably homeward, back up the great hill, but now all the light had gone out of the day, and the murmuring hillside had become a vast, alien, cruel world. Besides, I felt very sick. I thought I might be going to die. In one way it would be better.

When I got back into the house, the silence of the kitchen and then the sight of the fire gone out in the grate smote me with the cruel realization that the Blessed Virgin had let me down. There was no miracle, and my mother was still in bed. At once, I began to howl.

"What is it at all, child?" she call in alarm from upstairs.

"I lost the medicine," I bellowed, and rushed up the stairs to throw myself on the bed and bury my face in the clothes.

"Oh, wisha, if that's all that's a trouble to you!" she exclaimed with relief, running her hand through my hair. "Is anything the matter?" she added, after a moment. "You're very hot."

"I drank the medicine," I bawled.

"Ah, what harm?" she murmured soothingly. "You poor, unfortunate child! 'Twas my own fault for letting you go all that way by yourself. And then to have your journey for nothing. Undress yourself now, and you can lie down here."

She got up, put on her slippers and coat, and unlaced my boots while I sat on the bed. But even before she had finished I was fast asleep. I didn't see her dress herself or hear her go out, but some time later I felt a hand on my forehead and saw Minnie Ryan peering down at me, laughing.

"Ah, 'twill be nothing," she said, giving her shawl a pull about her. "He'll sleep it off by morning. The dear knows, Mrs. Sullivan, 'tis you should be in bed."

I knew that was a judgment on me, but I could do nothing about it. Later I saw my mother come in with the candle and her paper, and I smiled up at her. She smiled back. Minnie Ryan might despise me as much as she liked, but there were others who didn't. The miracle had happened, after all.

THE MAN WHO SHOT SNAPPING TURTLES*

BY EDMUND WILSON

IN THE days when I lived in Hecate County, I had an uncomfortable neighbor, a man named Asa M. Stryker. He had at one time, he told me, taught chemistry in some sorry-sounding

---

* from *Memoirs of Hecate County*

college in Pennsylvania, but he now lived on a little money which he had been "lucky enough to inherit." I had the feeling about him that somewhere in the background was defeat or frustration or disgrace. He was a bachelor and kept house with two servants—a cook and a man around the place. I never knew anyone to visit him, though he would occasionally go away for short periods—when, he would tell me, he was visiting his relatives.

Mr. Stryker had a small pond on his place, and from the very first time I met him, his chief topic of conversation was the wild ducks that used to come to this pond. In his insensitive-sounding way he admired them, minutely observing their markings, and he cherished and protected them like pets. Several pairs, in fact, which he fed all the year round, settled permanently on the pond. He would call my attention in his hard accent to the richness of their chestnut browns; the ruddiness of their backs or breasts; their sharp contrasts of light with dark, and their white neck-rings and purple wing-bars, like the decorative liveries and insignia of some exalted order; the cupreous greens and blues that gave them the look of being expensively dressed.

Mr. Stryker was particularly struck by the idea that there was something princely about them—something which, as he used to say, Frick or Charlie Schwab couldn't buy; and he would point out to me their majesty as they swam, cocking their heads with such dignity and nonchalantly wagging their tails. He was much troubled by the depredations of snapping turtles, which made terrible ravages on the ducklings. He would sit on his porch, he said, and see the little ducks disappear, as the turtles grabbed their feet and dragged them under, and feel sore at his helplessness to prevent it.

As he lost brood after brood in this way, the subject came, in fact, to obsess him. He had apparently hoped that his pond might be made a sort of paradise for ducks, in which they could breed without danger: he never shot them even in season and did not approve of their being shot at all. But sometimes not one survived the age when it was little enough to fall victim to the turtles.

These turtles he fought in a curious fashion. He would stand on the bank with a rifle and pot them when they stuck up their heads, sometimes hitting a duck by mistake. Only the ducks that were thus killed accidentally did he think it right to eat. One night when he had invited me to dine with him on one of them, I asked him why he did not protect the ducklings by shutting them up in a wire pen and providing them with a small pool to swim in. He told me that he had already decided to try this, and the next time I saw him he reported that the ducklings were doing finely.

Yet the pen, as it turned out later, did not permanently solve the problem, for the wild ducks, when they got old enough, flew out of it, and they were still young enough to be caught by the turtles. Mr. Stryker could not, as he said, keep them captive all their lives. The thing was rather, he finally concluded, to try to get rid of the turtles, against which he was coming, I noted, to display a slightly morbid animosity, and, after a good deal of serious thought, he fixed upon an heroic method.

He had just come into a new inheritance, which, he told me, made him pretty well off; and he decided to drain the pond. The operation took the whole of one summer: it horribly disfigured his place, and it afflicted the neighborhood with the stench of the slime that was now laid bare. One family whose place adjoined Stryker's were obliged to go away for weeks during the heaviest days of August, when the draining had become complete. Stryker, however, stayed and personally attended to the turtles, cutting off their heads himself; and he had men posted day and night at the places where they went to lay their eggs. At last someone complained to the Board of Health, and they made him fill up his pond. He was indignant with the town authorities, and declared that he had not yet got all the turtles, some of which were still hiding in the mud; and he and his crew put in a mad last day combing the bottom with giant rakes.

The next spring the turtles reappeared, though at first there were only a few. Stryker came over to see me and told me a harrowing story. He described how he had been sitting on his porch watching "my finest pair of mallards; out with their new brood of young ones. They were still just little fluffy balls, but they sailed along with that air they have of knowing that they're somebody special. From the moment that they can catch a water bug for themselves, they know that they're the lords of the pond. And I was just thinking how damn glad I was that no goblins were going to git them any more. Well, the phone rang and I went in to answer it, and when I came out again I distinctly had the impression that there were fewer ducks on the pond. So I counted them, and, sure enough, there was one duckling shy!" The next day another had vanished, and he had hired a man to watch the pond. Several snapping turtles were seen, but he had not succeeded in catching them. By the middle of the summer the casualties seemed almost as bad as before.

This time Mr. Stryker decided to do a better job. He came to see me again and startled me by holding forth in a vein that recalled the pulpit. "If God has created the mallard," he said, "a thing of beauty and grace, how can He allow these dirty filthy mud-turtles to prey upon His handiwork and destroy it?" "He created the mud-turtles first," I said. "The reptiles came before the birds. And they survive with the strength God gave them. There is no instance on record of God's intervention in the affairs of any animal species lower in the scale than man." "But if Evil triumphs there," said Stryker, "it may triumph everywhere, and we must fight it with every weapon in our power!" "That's the Manichaean heresy," I replied. "It is an error to assume that the Devil is contending on equal terms with God and that the fate of the world is in doubt." "I'm not sure of that sometimes," said Stryker, and I noticed that his bright little eyes seemed to dim in a curious way as if he were drawing into himself to commune with some private fear. "How do we know that God isn't getting old? How do we know that some of His lowest creatures aren't beginning to get out of hand and clean up on the higher ones?"

He decided to poison the turtles, and he brushed up, as he told me, on his chemistry. The result, however, was all too devastating. The chemicals he put into the water wiped out not only the turtles, but also all the other animals and most of the vegetation in the pond. When his chemical analysis showed that the water was no longer tainted, he put back the ducks again, but they found so little to eat that they presently flew away and ceased to frequent the place. In the meantime, some new ones that had come there had died from the poisoned water. One day, as Asa M. Stryker was walking around his estate, he encountered a female snapping turtle unashamedly crawling in the direction of the pond. She had obviously just been laying her eggs. He had had the whole of his place closed in with a fence of thick-meshed wire which went down a foot into the ground (I had asked him why he didn't have the pond rather than the estate thus enclosed, and he had explained that this would have made it impossible for him to look at the ducks from the porch); but turtles must have got in through the gate when it was open or they must have been in hiding all the time. Stryker was, as the English say, livid, and people became a little afraid of him because they thought he was getting cracked.

II

That afternoon he paid a visit to a man named Clarence Latouche, whose place was just behind Stryker's. Latouche was a native of New Orleans, and he worked in the advertising business. When Asa Stryker arrived, he was consuming a tall Scotch highball, unquestionably not his first, and he tried to make Stryker have a drink in the hope it would relieve his tension. But "I don't use it, thanks," said Stryker, and he started his theological line about the ducks and the snapping turtles. Clarence Latouche, while Stryker was talking, dropped his eyes for a moment to the wing collar and the large satin cravat which his neighbor always wore in the country and which were evidently associated in his mind with some idea, acquired in a provincial past, of the way for a "man of means" to dress. It seemed to him almost indecent that this desperate moral anxiety should agitate a being like Stryker.

"Well," he commented in his easy way when he had listened for a few minutes, "if the good God can't run the universe where He's supposed to be the supreme authority so as to eliminate the forces of Evil, I don't see how we poor humans in our weakness can expect to do any better with a few acres of Hecate County, where we're at the mercy of all the rest of creation." "It *ought* to be possible," said Stryker. "And I say it damn well *shall* be possible!" "As I see it," said Clarence Latouche—again, and again unsuccessfully, offering Stryker a drink—"you're faced with a double problem. On the one hand, you've got to get rid of the snappers; and, on the other hand, you've got to keep the ducks. So far you haven't been able to do either. Whatever measures you take, you lose the ducks and you can't kill the snappers. Now it seems to me, if you'll pardon my saying so, that you've overlooked the real solution—the only and, if you don't mind my saying so, the obvious way to deal with the matter." "I've been over the whole ground," said Stryker, growing more tense and turning slightly hostile under pressure of his pent-up passion, "and I doubt whether there's any method that I haven't considered with the utmost care." "It seems to me," said Clarence Latouche in his gentle Louisiana voice, "that, going about the thing as you have been, you've arrived at a virtual *impasse* and that you ought to approach the problem from a totally different angle. If you do that, you'll find it perfectly simple"—Stryker seemed about to protest fiercely, but Clarence continued in a vein of mellow alcoholic explaining: "The trouble is, as I see it, that up to now you've been going on the assumption that you ought to preserve the birds at the expense of getting rid of the turtles. Why not go on the opposite assumption: that you ought to work at cultivating the snappers? Shoot the ducks when they come around, and eat them—that is, when the law permits it,"—Mr. Stryker raised a clenched fist and started up in articulate anger,—"or if you don't want to do that, shoo them off. Then feed up the snappers on raw meat. Snappers are right good eating, too. We make soup out of 'em down in my part of the country."

Mr. Stryker stood speechless for such a long moment that Clarence was afraid, he said afterwards, that his neighbor would fall down in a fit; and he got up and patted him on the shoulder and exerted all his tact and charm. "All I can say," said Stryker, as he was going out the door, "is that I can't understand your attitude. Right is Right and Wrong is Wrong, and you have to choose between them!"

"I've never been much of a moralist," said Clarence, "and I dare say my whole point of view is a low and pragmatical one."

III

Stryker spent a troubled and restless night—so he afterwards told Clarence Latouche; but he got up very early, as he always did, to go hunting for breakfasting turtles, which he baited with pieces of steak. He now scooped them up with a net, and he paused for a moment over the first one he caught before he cut off its head. He scrutinized it with a new curiosity, and its appearance enraged him afresh: he detested its blunt sullen visage, its thick legs with their outspread claws, and its thick and thorny-toothed tail that it could not even pull into its shell as other turtles could. It was not even a genuine turtle: *Chelydra serpentina* they called it, because it resembled a snake, and it crawled around like a lizard. He baited it with a stick, and it snapped with a sharp popping sound; and as he held the beast up in his net, in the limpid morning air which was brimming the day like a tide, it looked, with its feet dripping slime, its dull shell that resembled a sunken log, as fetid, as cold and as dark as the bottom of the pond itself; and he was almost surprised at the gush of blood when he sawed away the head. What good purpose, he asked himself in horror, could such a creature serve? Subterranean, ugly and brutal—with only one idea in its head, or rather one instinct in its nature: to seize and hold down its prey. The turtle had snapped at the hoop of the net, and even now that its head was severed, its jaws were still holding on.

Stryker pried the head off the net and tossed it into the water; another turtle rose to snatch it. Then why not even the tables on Nature? Why not prey on what preyed on us? Why not exploit the hideous mud-turtle, as his friend from the South had suggested? Why not devour him daily in the form of turtle soup? And if one could not eat soup every day, why not turn him into an object of commerce? Why not make the public eat him? Let the turtles create economic, instead of killing aesthetic, value! He snickered at what seemed to him a fantasy; but he returned to Clarence Latouche's that day in one of his expansive moods that rather gave Clarence the creeps.

"Nothing easier!" cried Latouche, much amused—his advertising copy irked him, and he enjoyed an opportunity to burlesque it. "You know, the truth is that a great big proportion of the canned turtle soup that's sold is made of snapping turtles, but that isn't the way they advertise it. If you advertise it frankly as snapper, it will look like something brand-new, and all you'll need is the snob appeal to put it over on the can-opening public. There's a man canning rattlesnakes in Florida, and it ought to be a lot easier to sell snappers. All you've got to do up here in the North to persuade people to buy a product is to convince them that there's some kind of social prestige attached to it—and all you'd have to do with your snappers would be to give the customers the idea that a good ole white-haired darky with a beaming smile used to serve turtle soup to Old Massa. All you need is a little smart advertising and you can have as many people eating snapper as are eating [he named a popular canned salmon], which isn't even nutritious like snapper is—they make it out of the sweepings from a tire factory. I tell you what I'll do," he said, carried away by eloquence and whisky, "you organize a turtle farm and I'll write you some copy free. You can pay me when and if you make money."

Asa M. Stryker went away, scooped out two of the largest snappers, and that evening tried some snapping-turtle soup, which seemed to him surprisingly savory. Then he looked up the breeding of turtles, about which, in the course of his war with them, he had already come to know a good deal. He replenished his depleted pond with turtles brought from other ponds, for which he paid the country boys a dime apiece, and at the end of a couple of years he had such a population of snappers that he had to stock the pond with more frogs. He was afraid they wouldn't snap at raw meat because it didn't move.

Clarence Latouche helped him launch his campaign, and, as he had promised, wrote the copy for it. At that time there had already appeared in advertising a new angle on animal food, of which Clarence had been one of the originators. This was the device of representing the animals as gratified and even gleeful at the idea of being eaten. You saw pictures of manicured and beribboned porkers capering and smirking at the prospect of being put up in glass jars as sausages, and of steers in white aprons and chefs' hats that offered you their own sizzling beefsteaks. Clarence Latouche converted the snapping turtle into a genial and lovable creature, which became a familiar character to the readers of magazines and the passengers on subway trains. He was pictured as always smiling, with a twinkle in his wise old eye, and he had always had some pungent saying which smacked of the Southern backwoods, and which Clarence had great fun writing. As for the plantation angle, that was handled in a novel fashion. By this time the public had been oversold on Old Massa with the white mustaches, so Clarence Latouche invented a listless Southern lady, rather like Mrs. St. Clare in *Uncle Tom's Cabin,* who had to be revived by turtle soup. "Social historians tell us," one of the advertisements ran, "that more than 70 per cent of the women of the Old South suffered from anemia of phthisis [here there was an asterisk referring to a note, which said 'Tuberculosis']. Turtle soup saved the sweethearts and mothers of a proud and gallant race. The rich juices of the Alabama snapping turtle, fed on a special diet handed down from the time of Jefferson and raised on immaculate turtle farms famous for a century in the Deep South, supply the vital calories that are lacking in the modern meal." The feminine public were thus led to identify themselves with the lady in the advertisement, who was distinguished by a slim and supercilious chic, and to feel that they could enjoy a rich soup and yet remain slender and snooty. The advertisement went on to explain that a great many women still suffered, without knowing it, from anemia and t.b., and that a regular consumption of turtle soup could cure or ward off these diseases.

Deep South Snapper Soup became an immense success; and they presently stimulated the demand by putting on the market three kinds: Deep South Snapper Consommé, Deep South Snapper Tureen (Extra Thick), and Deep South Snapper Medium Thick, with Alabama Whole-Flour Noodles.

Stryker had to employ more helpers, and he eventually built a small cannery, out of sight of the house, on his place. The turtles were raised in shallow tanks, where they were easier to catch and control.

IV

Mr. Stryker, who had not worked for years at anything but his struggle with the turtles, turned out to be startlingly able as a businessman and industrial organizer. He kept down his working crew, handled his correspondence himself, browbeat a small corps of salesmen, and managed to make a very large profit. He went himself to the city relief bureaus and unerringly picked out men who were capable and willing to work but not too independent or intelligent, and he put over them his gardener as foreman. He would begin by lending these employees money, and he boarded and fed them on the place—so that they found themselves perpetually in debt to him. For secretary, he found a former school-teacher, who had lost her job in the local school. A plain woman of middle age, she had suddenly had a baby by an irresponsible Italian who worked in a crossroads garage. Asa Stryker boarded the mother and agreed to pay board for the baby at a place he selected himself. As the business began to prosper, this secretary came to handle an immense amount of correspondence and other matters, but Stryker always criticized her severely and never let her feel she was important.

He had managed to accomplish all this without ever giving people the impression that he was particularly interested in the business; yet he had always followed everything done with a keen and remorseless attention that masked itself under an appearance of impassivity. Every break for a market was seized at once; every laxity of his working staff was pounced upon. And his attitude toward the turtles themselves had now changed in a fundamental fashion. He had come to admire their alertness and toughness; and when he would take me on a tour of his tanks, he would prod them and make them grip his stick, and then laugh proudly at their refusal to let go when he would bang them against the concrete.

Clarence Latouche himself, who had invented Snapper Tureen, presently began to believe that he was a victim of Stryker's sharp dealing. At the time that the business had begun to make money, they had signed an agreement which provided that Clarence should get 10 per cent; and he now felt that he ought to have a bigger share—all the more since his casual habits were proving fatal to his job at the agency. He had been kept on for the brilliant ideas which he had sometimes been able to contribute, but he had lately been drinking more heavily and it had been hinted that he might be fired. He was the kind of New Orleans man who, extraordinarily charming in youth, becomes rather overripe in his twenties and goes to pieces with an astonishing rapidity. In New Orleans this would not have been noticed; but in the North he had never been quite in key and he was now feeling more ill at ease and more hostile to his adopted environment. He had been carrying on an affair with a married woman, whom he had expected to divorce her husband and marry him; but he had become rather peevish with waiting, and she had decided that it was too much trouble, and that it was perhaps not really true that his drinking was due entirely to her failure to marry him. Lately Clarence had taken to brooding on Stryker, whom he had been finding it rather difficult to see, and he had come to the conclusion that the latter was devious as well as sordid, and that he had been misrepresenting to Clarence the amount of profit he made.

One Sunday afternoon, at last, when Clarence had been sitting alone with a succession of tall gin fizzes, he jumped up suddenly, strode out the door, cut straight through his grounds to the fence which divided his property from Stryker's, climbed over it with inspired agility, and made a beeline for Stryker's house, purposely failing to follow the drive and stepping through the flower-beds. Stryker came himself to the door with a look that, if Clarence had been sober, he would have realized was apprehensive; but when he saw who the visitor was, he greeted him with a special cordiality, and ushered him into his study. With his highly developed awareness, he had known at once what was coming.

This study, which Clarence had never seen, as he went rarely to Stryker's house, was a disorderly and darkish place. It was characteristic of Stryker that his desk should seem littered and neglected, as if he were not really in touch with his affairs; and there was dust on the books in his bookcase, drably bound and unappetizing volumes on zoölogical and chemical subjects. Though it was daytime, the yellow-brown shades were pulled three-quarters down. On the desk and on top of the bookcase stood a number of handsome stuffed ducks that Stryker had wished to preserve.

Stryker sat down at the desk and offered Clarence a cigarette. Instead of protesting at once that Clarence's demands were impossible, as he had done on previous occasions, he listened with amiable patience. "I'm going to go into the whole problem and put things on a different basis as soon as business slackens up in the spring. So I'd rather you'd wait till then, if you don't mind. We had a hard time filling the orders even before this strike began, and now I can hardly get the work done at all. They beat up two of my men yesterday, and they're threatening to make a raid on the factory. I've had to have the whole place guarded." (The breeding ponds and the factory, which were situated half a mile away, had been enclosed by a wire fence.) Clarence had forgotten the strike, and he realized that he *had* perhaps come at a rather inopportune time. "I can't attend to a reorganization," Stryker went on to explain—"which is what we've got to have at this point—till our labor troubles are settled and things have slowed up a bit. There ought to be more in this business for both of us," he concluded, with a businessman's smile, "and I won't forget your co-operative attitude when we make a new arrangement in the spring."

The tension was thus relaxed, and Stryker went on to address Clarence with something like friendly concern. "Why don't you have yourself a vacation?" he suggested. "I've noticed you were looking run-down. Why don't you go South for the winter? Go to Florida or someplace like that. It must be tough for a Southerner like you to spend this nasty part of the

year in the North. I'll advance you the money, if you need it."
Clarence was half tempted, and he began to talk to Stryker
rather freely about the idiocies of the advertising agency and
about the two aunts and a sister whom he had to support in
Baton Rouge. But in the course of the conversation, as his eye
escaped from Stryker's gaze, which he felt as uncomfortably
intent in the gaps between sympathetic smiles, it lit on some
old chemical apparatus, a row of glass test-tubes and jars,
which had presumably been carried along from Stryker's early
career as a teacher; and he remembered—though the steps of
his reasoning may have been guided, as he afterwards sometimes thought, by a delusion of persecution that had been growing on him in recent months—he remembered the deaths, at
intervals, of Stryker's well-to-do relatives. His eye moved on to
the mounted ducks, with their rich but rather lusterless colors.
He had always been half-conscious with the other of his own
superior grace of appearance and manner and speech, and had
sometimes felt that Stryker admired it; and now as he contem-
plated Stryker, at ease in his turbid room, upended, as it were,
behind his desk, with a broad expanse of plastron and a rub-
bery craning neck, regarding him with small bright eyes set
back in the brownish skin beyond a prominent snout-like for-
mation of which the nostrils were sharply in evidence—as
Clarence confronted Stryker, he felt first a fantastic suspicion,
then a sudden unnerving conviction.

Unhurriedly he got up to go and brushed away Stryker's regret that—since it was Sunday and the cook's day out—he was
unable to ask him to dinner. But his nonchalance now disguised
panic: it was hideously clear to him why Stryker had suggested
his taking a trip. He wouldn't take it, of course, but what then?
Stryker would surely try to get him in some other way. In his
emotion, he forgot his hat and did not discover it till they had
reached the porch. He stepped back into the study alone, and
on an impulse took down from its rack on the wall the rifle with
which Stryker, in the earlier days, had gone gunning for snapping turtles. He went to the open front door and shot Stryker.

The cook was out; only the gates were guarded; and
Clarence had arrived at Stryker's by taking the back cut through

the grounds. Nobody heard the shot. The suspicion all fell on the foreman, who had his own long-standing grudges against Stryker and had organized the current strike. He had already had to go into hiding to escape from his boss's thugs, and after the murder he disappeared.

Clarence Latouche decided very soon that he would sell his Hecate County place and travel for a year in Europe, which he had always wanted to see. But just after he had bought his passage the war with Hitler started, and prevented him from getting off—an ironic misadventure, as he said, for a smart advertising man who had believed in the exploitation of snapping turtles.

He had disassociated himself from the soup business, and he went to live in southern California, where, on his very much dwindled income, he is said to be drinking himself to death. He lives under the constant apprehension that the foreman may be found by the police, and that he will then have to confess his own guilt in order to save an innocent man—because Clarence is the soul of honor—so that Stryker may get him yet.

THE GIOCONDA SMILE[*]

BY ALDOUS HUXLEY

"MISS SPENCE will be down directly, sir."

"Thank you," said Mr. Hutton, without turning round. Janet Spence's parlormaid was so ugly, ugly on purpose, it always seemed to him, malignantly, criminally ugly, that he could not bear to look at her more than was necessary. The door closed. Left to himself, Mr. Hutton got up and began to wander round the room, looking with meditative eyes at the familiar objects it contained.

[*] from *Mortal Coils*

Photographs of Greek statuary, photographs of the Roman Forum, colored prints of Italian masterpieces, all very safe and well known. Poor, dear Janet, what a prig—what an intellectual snob! Her real taste was illustrated in that water color by the pavement artist, the one she had paid half a crown for (and thirty-five shillings for the frame). How often he had heard her tell the story, how often expatiated on the beauties of that skillful imitation of an oleograph! "A real Artist in the streets," and you could hear the capital A in Artist as she spoke the words. She made you feel that part of his glory had entered into Janet Spence when she tendered him that half-crown for the copy of the oleograph. She was implying a compliment to her own taste and penetration. A genuine Old Master for half a crown. Poor, dear Janet!

Mr. Hutton came to a pause in front of a small oblong mirror. Stooping a little to get a full view of his face, he passed a white, well-manicured finger over his mustache. It was as curly, as freshly auburn as it had been twenty years ago. His hair still retained its color, and there was no sign of baldness yet—only a certain elevation of the brow. "Shakespearean," thought Mr. Hutton, with a smile, as he surveyed the smooth and polished expanse of his forehead.

Others abide our question, thou art free.... Footsteps in the sea... Majesty... Shakespeare, thou shouldst be living at this hour. No, that was Milton, wasn't it? Milton, the Lady of Christ's. There was no lady about him. He was what the women would call a manly man. That was why they liked him—for the curly auburn mustache and the discreet redolence of tobacco. Mr. Hutton smiled again; he enjoyed making fun of himself. Lady of Christ's? No, no. He was the Christ of Ladies. Very pretty, very pretty. The Christ of Ladies. Mr. Hutton wished there were somebody he could tell the joke to. Poor, dear Janet wouldn't appreciate it, alas!

He straightened himself up, parted his hair, and resumed his peregrination. Damn the Roman Forum; he hated those dreary photographs.

Suddenly he became aware that Janet Spence was in the room, standing near the door. Mr. Hutton started, as though he had been taken in some felonious act. To make these silent and spectral appearances was one of Janet Spence's peculiar talents. Perhaps she had been there all the time, and seen him looking at himself in the mirror. Impossible! But, still, it was disquieting.

"Oh, you gave me such a surprise," said Mr. Hutton, recovering his smile and advancing with outstretched hand to meet her. .

Miss Spence was smiling too: her Gioconda smile, he had once called it in a moment of half-ironical flattery. Miss Spence had taken the compliment seriously, and always tried to live up to the Leonardo standard. She smiled on in silence while Mr. Hutton shook hands; that was part of the Gioconda business.

"I hope you're well," said Mr. Hutton. "You look it."

What a queer face she had! That small mouth pursed forward by the Gioconda expression into a little snout with a round hole in the middle, as though for whistling, was like a penholder seen from the front. Above the mouth a well-shaped nose, finely aquiline. Eyes large, lustrous, and dark, with the largeness, luster, and darkness that seem to invite sties and an occasional bloodshot suffusion. They were fine eyes, but unchangingly grave. The penholder might do its Gioconda trick, but the eyes never altered in their earnestness. Above them, a pair of boldly arched, heavily penciled black eyebrows lent a surprising air of power, as of a Roman matron, to the upper portion of the face. Her hair was dark and equally Roman; Agrippina from the brows upward.

"I thought I'd just look in on my way home," Mr. Hutton went on. "Ah, it's good to be back here—" he indicated with a wave of his hand the flowers in the vases, the sunshine and greenery beyond the windows—"it's good to be back in the country after a stuffy day of business in town."

Miss Spence, who had sat down, pointed to a chair at her side.

"No, really, I can't sit down," Mr. Hutton protested. "I must get back to see how poor Emily is. She was rather seedy this morning." He sat down, nevertheless. "It's these wretched liver chills. She's always getting them. Women—" He broke off and coughed, so as to hide the fact that he had uttered. He was about to say that women with weak digestions ought not to marry; but the remark was too cruel, and he didn't really believe it. Janet Spence, moreover, was a believer in eternal flames and spiritual attachments. "She hopes to be well enough," he added, "to see you at luncheon tomorrow. Can you come? Do?" He smiled persuasively. "It's my invitation too, you know."

She dropped her eyes, and Mr. Hutton almost thought that he detected a certain reddening of the cheek. It was a tribute; he stroked his mustache.

"I should like to come if you think Emily's really well enough to have a visitor."

"Of course. You'll do her good. You'll do us both good. In married life three is often better company than two."

"Oh, you're cynical."

Mr. Hutton always had a desire to say "Bow-wow-wow" whenever that last word was spoken. It irritated him more than any other word in the language. But instead of barking he made haste to protest.

"No, no. I'm only speaking a melancholy truth. Reality doesn't always come up to the ideal, you know. But that doesn't make me believe any the less in the ideal. Indeed, I believe in it passionately: the ideal of a matrimony between two people in perfect accord. I think it's realizable. I'm sure it is."

He paused significantly and looked at her with an arch expression. A virgin of thirty-six, but still unwithered; she had her charms. And there was something really rather enigmatic about her. Miss Spence made no reply, but continued to smile. There were times when Mr. Hutton got rather bored with the Gioconda. He stood up.

"I must really be going now. Farewell, mysterious Gioconda." The smile grew intenser, focused itself, as it were, in a narrower snout. Mr. Hutton made a Cinquecento gesture, and kissed her extended hand. It was the first time he had done such a thing; the action seemed not to be resented. "I look forward to tomorrow."

"Do you?"

For answer Mr. Hutton once more kissed her hand, then turned to go. Miss Spence accompanied him to the porch.

"Where's your car?" she asked.

"I left it at the gate of the drive."

"I'll come and see you off."

"No, no." Mr. Hutton was playful, but determined. "You must do no such thing. I simply forbid you."

"But I should like to come," Miss Spence protested, throwing a rapid Gioconda at him.

Mr. Hutton held up his hand. "No," he repeated, and then, with a gesture that was almost the blowing of a kiss, he started to run down the drive, lightly, on his toes, with long, bounding strides like a boy's. He was proud of that run; it was quite marvelously youthful. Still, he was glad the drive was no longer. At the last bend, before passing out of sight of the house, he halted and turned round. Miss Spence was still standing on the steps, smiling her smile. He waved his hand, and this time quite definitely and overtly wafted a kiss in her direction. Then, breaking once more into his magnificent canter, he rounded the last dark promontory of trees. Once out of sight of the house he let his high paces decline to a trot, and finally to a walk. He took out his handkerchief and began wiping his neck inside his collar. What fools, what fools! Had there ever been such an ass as poor, dear Janet Spence? Never, unless it was himself. Decidedly he was the more malignant fool, since he, at least, was aware of his folly and still persisted in it. Why did he persist? Ah, the problem that was himself, the problem that was other people...

He had reached the gate. A large, prosperous-looking motor was standing at the side of the road.

"Home, M'Nab." The chauffeur touched his cap. "And stop at the crossroads on the way, as usual," Mr. Hutton added, as he opened the door of the car. "Well?" he said, speaking into the obscurity that lurked within.

"Oh, Teddy Bear, what an age you've been!" It was a fresh and childish voice that spoke the words. There was the faintest hint of Cockney impurity about the vowel sounds.

Mr. Hutton bent his large form and darted into the car with the agility of an animal regaining his burrow.

"Have I?" he said, as he shut the door. The machine began to move. "You must have missed me a lot if you found the time so long." He sat back in the low seat; a cherishing warmth enveloped him.

"Teddy Bear..." and with a sigh of contentment a charming little head declined onto Mr. Hutton's shoulder. Ravished, he looked down sideways at the round, babyish face.

"Do you know, Doris, you look like the pictures of Louise de Kerouaille." He passed his fingers through a mass of curly hair.

"Who's Louise de Kera-whatever-it-is?" Doris spoke from remote distances.

"She was, alas! *Fuit.* We shall all be 'was' one of these days. Meanwhile..."

Mr. Hutton covered the babyish face with kisses. The car rushed smoothly along. M'Nab's back through the front window was stonily impassive, the back of a statue.

"Your hands," Doris whispered. "Oh, you mustn't touch me. They give me electric shocks."

Mr. Hutton adored her for the virgin imbecility of the words. How late in one's existence one makes the discovery of one's body!

"The electricity isn't in me, it's in you." He kissed her again, whispering her name several times: Doris, Doris, Doris. The scientific appellation of the sea mouse, he was thinking as he kissed the throat she offered him, white and extended like the throat of a victim awaiting the sacrificial knife. The sea mouse was a sausage with iridescent fur: very peculiar. Or was Doris the sea cucumber, which turns itself inside out in moments of alarm? He would really have to go to Naples again, just to see the aquarium. These sea creatures were fabulous, unbelievably fantastic.

"Oh, Teddy Bear!" (More zoology; but he was only a land animal. His poor little jokes!) "Teddy Bear, I'm so happy."

"So am I," said Mr. Hutton. Was it true?

"But I wish I knew if it were right. Tell me, Teddy Bear, is it right or wrong?"

"Ah, my dear, that's just what I've been wondering for the last thirty years."

"Be serious, Teddy Bear. I want to know if this is right; if it's right that I should be here with you and that we should love one another, and that it should give me electric shocks when you touch me."

"Right? Well, it's certainly good that you should have electric shocks rather than sexual repressions. Real Freud; repressions are the devil."

"Oh, you don't help me. Why aren't you ever serious? If only you knew how miserable I am sometimes, thinking it's not right. Perhaps, you know, there is a hell, and all that. I don't know what to do. Sometimes I think I ought to stop loving you."

"But could you?" asked Mr. Hutton, confident in the powers of his seduction and his mustache.

"No, Teddy Bear, you know I couldn't. But I could run away, I could hide from you, I could lock myself up and force myself not to come to you."

"Silly little thing!" He tightened his embrace.

"Oh, dear. I hope it isn't wrong. And there are times when I don't care if it is."

Mr. Hutton was touched. He had a certain protective affection for this little creature. He laid his cheek against her hair and so, interlaced, they sat in silence, while the car, swaying and pitching a little as it hastened along, seemed to draw in the white road and the dusty hedges toward it devouringly.

"Good-by, good-by."

The car moved on, gathered speed, vanished round a curve, and Doris was left standing by the signpost at the crossroads, still dizzy and weak with the languor born of those kisses and the electrical touch of those gentle hands. She had to take a deep breath, to draw herself up deliberately, before she was strong enough to start her homeward walk. She had half a mile in which to invent the necessary lies.

Alone, Mr. Hutton suddenly found himself the prey of an appalling boredom.

Mrs. Hutton was lying on the sofa in her boudoir, playing patience. In spite of the warmth of the July evening a wood fire was burning on the hearth. A black Pomeranian, extenuated by the heat and the fatigues of digestion, slept before the blaze.

"Phew! Isn't it rather hot in here?" Mr. Hutton asked as he entered the room.

"You know I have to keep warm, dear." The voice seemed breaking on the verge of tears. "I get so shivery."

"I hope you're better this evening."

"Not much, I'm afraid."

The conversation stagnated. Mr. Hutton stood leaning his back against the mantelpiece. He looked down at the Pomeranian lying at his feet, and with the toe of his right boot he rolled the little dog over and rubbed its white-flecked chest and belly. The creature lay in an inert ecstasy. Mrs. Hutton continued to play patience. Arrived at an *impasse,* she altered the position of one card, took back another, and went on playing. Her patiences always came out.

"Dr. Libbard thinks I ought to go to Llandrindod Wells this summer."

"Well, go, my dear, go, most certainly."

Mr. Hutton was thinking of the events of the afternoon: how they had driven, Doris and he, up to the hanging wood, had left the car to wait for them under the shade of the trees, and walked together out into the windless sunshine of the chalk down.

"I'm to drink the waters for my liver, and he thinks I ought to have massage and electric treatment, too."

Hat in hand, Doris had stalked four blue butterflies that were dancing together round a scabious flower with a motion that was like the flickering of blue fire. The blue fire burst and scattered into whirling sparks; she had given chase, laughing and shouting like a child.

"I'm sure it will do you good, my dear."

"I was wondering if you'd come with me, dear."

"But you know I'm going to Scotland at the end of the month."

Mrs. Hutton looked at him entreatingly. "It's the journey," she said. "The thought of it is such a nightmare. I don't know if I can manage it. And you know I can't sleep in hotels. And then there's the luggage and all the worries. I can't go alone."

"But you won't be alone. You'll have your maid with you." He spoke impatiently. The sick woman was usurping the place of the healthy one. He was being dragged back from the memory of the sunlit down and the quick, laughing girl, back to this unhealthy, overheated room and its complaining occupant.

"I don't think I shall be able to go."

"But you must, my dear, if the doctor tells you to. And, besides, a change will do you good."

"I don't think so."

"But Libbard thinks so, and he knows what he's talking about."

"No, I can't face it. I'm too weak. I can't go alone." Mrs. Hutton pulled a handkerchief out of her black-silk bag and put it to her eyes.

"Nonsense, my dear, you must make the effort."

"I had rather be left in peace to die here." She was crying in earnest now.

"O Lord! Now do be reasonable. Listen now, please." Mrs. Hutton only sobbed more violently. "Oh, what is one to do?" He shrugged his shoulders and walked out of the room.

Mr. Hutton was aware that he had not behaved with proper patience; but he could not help it. Very early in his manhood he had discovered that not only did he not feel sympathy for the poor, the weak, the diseased, and deformed; he actually hated them. Once, as an undergraduate, he spent three days at a mission in the East End. He had returned, filled with a profound and ineradicable disgust. Instead of pitying, he loathed the unfortunate. It was not, he knew, a very comely emotion, and he had been ashamed of it at first. In the end he had decided that it was temperamental, inevitable, and had felt no further qualms. Emily had been healthy and beautiful when he married her. He had loved her then. But now—was it his fault that she was like this?

Mr. Hutton dined alone. Food and drink left him more benevolent than he had been before dinner. To make amends for his show of exasperation he went up to his wife's room and offered to read to her. She was touched, gratefully accepted the offer, and Mr. Hutton, who was particularly proud of his accent, suggested a little light reading in French.

"French? I am so fond of French." Mrs. Hutton spoke of the language of Racine as though it were a dish of green peas.

Mr. Hutton ran down to the library and returned with a yellow volume. He began reading. The effort of pronouncing perfectly absorbed his whole attention. But how good his accent was! The fact of its goodness seemed to improve the quality of the novel he was reading.

At the end of fifteen pages an unmistakable sound aroused him. He looked up; Mrs. Hutton had gone to sleep. He sat still for a little while, looking with a dispassionate curiosity at the sleeping face. Once it had been beautiful; once, long ago, the sight of it, the recollection of it, had moved him with an emotion profounder, perhaps, than any he had felt before or since. Now it was lined and cadaverous. The skin was stretched tightly over the cheekbones, across the bridge of the sharp, birdlike nose. The closed eyes were set in profound bone-rimmed sockets. The lamplight striking on the face from the side emphasized with light and shade its cavities and projections. It was the face of a dead Christ by Morales.

> Le squelette était invisible
> Au temps heureux de l'art païen.

He shivered a little, and tiptoed out of the room.

On the following day Mrs. Hutton came down to luncheon. She had had some unpleasant palpitations during the night, but she was feeling better now. Besides, she wanted to do honor to her guest. Miss Spence listened to her complaints about Llandrindod Wells, and was loud in sympathy, lavish with advice. Whatever she said was always said with intensity. She leaned forward, aimed, so to speak, like a gun, and fired her words. Bang! the charge in her soul was ignited, the words whizzed forth at the narrow barrel of her mouth. She was a machine gun riddling her hostess with sympathy. Mr. Hutton had undergone similar bombardments, mostly of a literary or philosophic character, bombardments of Maeterlinck, of Mrs. Besant, of Bergson, of William James. Today the missiles were medical. She talked about insomnia, she expatiated on the virtues of harmless drugs and beneficient specialists. Under the bombardment Mrs. Hutton opened out, like a flower in the sun.

Mr. Hutton looked on in silence. The spectacle of Janet Spence evoked in him an unfailing curiosity. He was not romantic enough to imagine that every face masked an interior physiognomy of beauty or strangeness, that every woman's small talk was like a vapor hanging over mysterious gulfs. His wife, for example, and Doris; they were nothing more than what they seemed to be. But with Janet Spence it was somehow different. Here one could be sure that there was some kind of a queer face behind the Gioconda smile and the Roman eyebrows. The only question was: What exactly was there? Mr. Hutton could never quite make out.

"But perhaps you won't have to go to Llandrindod after all," Miss Spence was saying. "If you get well quickly Dr. Libbard will let you off."

"I only hope so. Indeed, I do really feel rather better today."

Mr. Hutton felt ashamed. How much was it his own lack of sympathy that prevented her from feeling well every day? But he comforted himself by reflecting that it was only a case of feeling, not of being better. Sympathy does not mend a diseased liver or a weak heart.

"My dear, I wouldn't eat those red currants if I were you," he said, suddenly solicitous. "You know that Libbard has banned everything with skins and pips."

"But I am so fond of them," Mrs. Hutton protested, "and I feel so well today."

"Don't be a tyrant," said Miss Spence, looking first at him and then at his wife. "Let the poor invalid have what she fancies; it will do her good." She laid her hand on Mrs. Hutton's arm and patted it affectionately two or three times.

"Thank you, my dear." Mrs. Hutton helped herself to the stewed currants.

"Well, don't blame me if they make you ill again."

"Do I ever blame you, dear?"

"You have nothing to blame me for," Mr. Hutton answered playfully. "I am the perfect husband."

They sat in the garden after luncheon. From the island of shade under the old cypress tree they looked out across a flat expanse of lawn, in which the parterres of flowers shone with a metallic brilliance.

Mr. Hutton took a deep breath of the warm and fragrant air. "It's good to be alive," he said.

"Just to be alive," his wife echoed, stretching one pale, knot-jointed hand into the sunlight.

A maid brought the coffee; the silver pots and the little blue cups were set on a folding table near the group of chairs.

"Oh, my medicine!" exclaimed Mrs. Hutton. "Run in and fetch it, Clara, will you? The white bottle on the sideboard."

"I'll go," said Mr. Hutton. "I've got to go and fetch a cigar in any case."

He ran in toward the house. On the threshold he turned round for an instant. The maid was walking back across the lawn. His wife was sitting up in her deck chair, engaged in opening her white parasol. Miss Spence was bending over the table, pouring out the coffee. He passed into the cool obscurity of the house.

"Do you like sugar in your coffee?" Miss Spence inquired.

"Yes, please. Give me rather a lot. I'll drink it after my medicine to take the taste away."

Mrs. Hutton leaned back in her chair, lowering the sunshade over her eyes so as to shut out from her vision the burning sky.

Behind her, Miss Spence was making a delicate clinking among the coffee cups.

"I've given you three large spoonfuls. That ought to take the taste away. And here comes the medicine."

Mr. Hutton had reappeared, carrying a wineglass, half full of a pale liquid.

"It smells delicious," he said, as he handed it to his wife.

"That's only the flavoring." She drank it off at a gulp, shuddered, and made a grimace. "Ugh, it's so nasty. Give me my coffee."

Miss Spence gave her the cup; she sipped at it. "You've made it like syrup. But it's very nice, after that atrocious medicine."

At half-past three Mrs. Hutton complained that she did not feel as well as she had done, and went indoors to lie down. Her husband would have said something about the red currants, but checked himself; the triumph of an "I told you so" was too cheaply won. Instead, he was sympathetic and gave her his arm to the house.

"A rest will do you good," he said. "By the way, I shan't be back till after dinner."

"But why? Where are you going?"

"I promised to go to Johnson's this evening. We have to discuss the war memorial, you know."

"Oh, I wish you weren't going." Mrs. Hutton was almost in tears. "Can't you stay? I don't like being alone in the house."

"But, my dear, I promised, weeks ago." It was a bother having to lie like this. "And now I must get back and look after Miss Spence."

He kissed her on the forehead and went out again into the garden. Miss Spence received him aimed and intense.

"Your wife is dreadfully ill," she fired off at him.

"I thought she cheered up so much when you came."

"That was purely nervous, purely nervous. I was watching her closely. With a heart in that condition and her digestion wrecked—yes, wrecked—anything might happen."

"Libbard doesn't take so gloomy a view of poor Emily's health." Mr. Hutton held open the gate that led from the garden into the drive; Miss Spence's car was standing by the front door.

"Libbard is only a country doctor. You ought to see a specialist."

He could not refrain from laughing. "You have a macabre passion for specialists."

Miss Spence held up her hand in protest. "I am serious. I think poor Emily is in a very bad state. Anything might happen—at any moment."

He handed her into the car and shut the door. The chauffeur started the engine and climbed into his place, ready to drive off.

"Shall I tell him to start?" He had no desire to continue the conversation.

Miss Spence leaned forward and shot a Gioconda in his

direction. "Remember, I expect you to come and see me again soon."

Mechanically he grinned, made a polite noise, and, as the car moved forward, waved his hand. He was happy to be alone.

A few minutes afterward Mr. Hutton himself drove away. Doris was waiting at the crossroads. They dined together twenty miles from home, at a roadside hotel. It was one of those bad, expensive meals which are only cooked in country hotels frequented by motorists. It revolted Mr. Hutton, but Doris enjoyed it. She always enjoyed things. Mr. Hutton ordered a not very good brand of champagne. He was wishing he had spent the evening in his library.

When they started homeward Doris was a little tipsy and extremely affectionate. It was very dark inside the car, but looking forward, past the motionless form of M'Nab, they could see a bright and a narrow universe of forms and colors scooped out of the night by the electric head lamps.

It was after eleven when Mr. Hutton reached home. Dr. Libbard met him in the hall. He was a small man with delicate hands and well-formed features that were almost feminine. His brown eyes were large and melancholy. He used to waste a great deal of time sitting at the bedside of his patients, looking sadness through those eyes and talking in a sad, low voice about nothing in particular. His person exhaled a pleasing odor, decidedly antiseptic but at the same time suave and discreetly delicious.

"Libbard?" said Mr. Hutton in surprise. "You here? Is my wife ill?"

"We tried to fetch you earlier," the soft, melancholy voice replied. "It was thought you were at Mr. Johnson's, but they had no news of you there."

"No, I was detained. I had a breakdown," Mr. Hutton answered irritably. It was tiresome to be caught out in a lie.

"Your wife wanted to see you urgently."

"Well, I can go now." Mr. Hutton moved toward the stairs.

Dr. Libbard laid a hand on his arm. "I am afraid it's too late."

"Too late?" He began fumbling with his watch; it wouldn't come out of his pocket.

"Mrs. Hutton passed away half an hour ago."

The voice remained even in its softness, the melancholy of the eyes did not deepen. Dr. Libbard spoke of death as he would speak of a local cricket match. All things were equally vain and equally deplorable.

Mr. Hutton found himself thinking of Janet Spence's words. At any moment, at any moment. She had been extraordinarily right.

"What happened?" he asked. "What was the cause?"

Dr. Libbard explained. It was heart failure brought on by a violent attack of nausea, caused in its turn by the eating of something of an irritant nature. Red currants? Mr. Hutton suggested. Very likely. It had been too much for the heart. There was chronic valvular disease: something had collapsed under the strain. It was all over; she could not have suffered much.

"It's a pity they should have chosen the day of the Eton and Harrow match for the funeral," old General Grego was saying as he stood up, his top hat in his hand, under the shadow of the lich gate, wiping his face with his handkerchief.

Mr. Hutton overheard the remark and with difficulty restrained a desire to inflict grievous bodily pain on the General. He would have liked to hit the old brute in the middle of his big red face. Monstrous great mulberry, spotted with meal! Was there no respect for the dead? Did nobody care? In theory he didn't much care; let the dead bury their dead. But here, at the graveside, he had found himself actually sobbing. Poor Emily, they had been pretty happy once. Now she was lying at the bottom of a seven-foot hole. And here was Grego complaining that he couldn't go to the Eton and Harrow match.

Mr. Hutton looked round at the group of black figures that were drifting slowly out of the churchyard toward the fleet of cabs and motors assembled in the road outside. Against the brilliant background of the July grass and flowers and foliage, they had a horribly alien and unnatural appearance. It pleased him to think that all these people would soon be dead too.

That evening Mr. Hutton sat up late in his library reading

the life of Milton. There was no particular reason why he should have chosen Milton; it was the book that first came to hand, that was all. It was after midnight when he had finished. He got up from his armchair, unbolted the French windows, and stepped out onto the little paved terrace. The night was quiet and clear. Mr. Hutton looked at the stars and at the holes between them, dropped his eyes to the dim lawns and hueless flowers of the garden, and let them wander over the farther landscape, black and gray under the moon.

He began to think with a kind of confused violence. There were the stars, there was Milton. A man can be somehow the peer of stars and night. Greatness, nobility. But is there seriously a difference between the noble and the ignoble? Milton, the stars, death, and himself, himself. The soul, the body; the higher and the lower nature. Perhaps there was something in it, after all. Milton had a god on his side and righteousness. What had he? Nothing, nothing whatever. There were only Doris's little breasts. What was the point of it all? Milton, the stars, death, and Emily in her grave. Doris and himself—always himself...

Oh, he was a futile and disgusting being. Everything convinced him of it. It was a solemn moment. He spoke aloud: "I will, I will." The sound of his own voice in the darkness was appalling; it seemed to him that he had sworn that infernal oath which binds even the gods: "I will, I will." There had been New Year's Days and solemn anniversaries in the past, when he had felt the same contritions and recorded similar resolutions. They had all thinned away, these resolutions, like smoke, into nothingness. But this was a greater moment and he had pronounced a more fearful oath. In the future it was to be different. Yes, he would live by reason, he would be industrious, he would curb his appetites, he would devote his life to some good purpose. It was resolved and it would be so.

In practice he saw himself spending his mornings in agricultural pursuit, riding round with the bailiff, seeing that his land was farmed in the best modern way, silos and artificial manures and continuous cropping, and all that. The remainder of the day should be devoted to serious study. There was that book he had been intending to write for so long: *The Effect of Diseases on Civilization*.

Mr. Hutton went to bed humble and contrite, but with a sense that grace had entered into him. He slept for seven and a half hours, and woke to find the sun brilliantly shining. The emotions of the evening before had been transformed by a good night's rest into his customary cheerfulness. It was not until a good many seconds after his return to conscious life that he remembered his resolution, his Stygian oath. Milton and death seemed somehow different in the sunlight. As for the stars, they were not there. But the resolutions were good; even in the daytime he could see that. He had his horse saddled after breakfast, and rode round the farm with the bailiff. After luncheon he read Thucydides on the plague at Athens. In the evening he made a few notes on malaria in Southern Italy. While he was undressing he remembered that there was a good anecdote in Skelton's jestbook about the Sweating Sickness. He would have made a note of it if only he could have found a pencil.

On the sixth morning of his new life Mr. Hutton found among his correspondence an envelope addressed in that peculiarly vulgar handwriting which he knew to be Doris's. He opened it, and began to read. She didn't know what to say, words were so inadequate. His wife dying like that, and so suddenly—it was too terrible. Mr. Hutton sighed, but his interest revived somewhat as he read on:

"Death is so frightening, I never think of it when I can help it. But when something like this happens, or when I am feeling ill or depressed, then I can't help remembering it is there so close, and I think about all the wicked things I have done and about you and me, and I wonder what will happen, and I am so frightened. I am so lonely, Teddy Bear, and so unhappy, and I don't know what to do. I can't get rid of the idea of dying, I am so wretched and helpless without you. I didn't mean to write to you; I meant to wait till you were out of mourning and could come and see me again, but I was so lonely and miserable, Teddy Bear, I had to write. I couldn't help it. Forgive me, I want you so much; I have nobody in the world but you. You are so good and gentle and understanding; there is nobody like you. I shall never forget how good and kind you have been to me, and you are so clever and know so much. I can't understand how you ever came to pay any attention to me, I am so dull and stupid, much less like me and love me, because you do love me a little, don't you, Teddy Bear?"

Mr. Hutton was touched with shame and remorse. To be thanked like this, worshiped for having seduced the girl, it was too much. It had just been a piece of imbecile wantonness. Imbecile, idiotic: there was no other way to describe it. For, when all was said, he had derived very little pleasure from it. Taking all things together, he had probably been more bored than amused. Once upon a time he had believed himself to be a hedonist. But to be a hedonist implies a certain process of reasoning, a deliberate choice of known pleasures, a rejection of known pains. This had been done without reason, against it. For he knew beforehand—so well, so well—that there was no interest or pleasure to be derived from these wretched affairs. And yet each time the vague itch came upon him he succumbed, involving himself once more in the old stupidity. There had been Maggie, his wife's maid, and Edith, the girl on the farm, and Mrs. Pringle, and the waitress in London, and others—there seemed to be dozens of them. It had all been so stale and boring. He knew it would be; he always knew. And yet, and yet . . . Experience doesn't teach.

Poor little Doris! He would write to her kindly, comfortingly, but he wouldn't see her again. A servant came to tell him that his horse was saddled and waiting. He mounted and rode off. That morning the old bailiff was more irritating than usual.

Five days later Doris and Mr. Hutton were sitting together on the pier at Southend; Doris, in white muslin with pink garnishings, radiated happiness; Mr. Hutton, legs outstretched and chair tilted, had pushed the panama back from his forehead and was trying to feel like a tripper. That night, when Doris was asleep, breathing and warm by his side, he recaptured, in this moment of darkness and physical fatigue, the rather cosmic emotion which had possessed him that evening, not a fortnight ago, when he had made his great resolution. And so his solemn oath had already gone the way of so many other resolutions. Unreason had triumphed; at the first itch of desire he had given way. He was hopeless, hopeless.

For a long time he lay with closed eyes, ruminating his humiliation. The girl stirred in her sleep. Mr. Hutton turned over and looked in her direction. Enough faint light crept in between the half-drawn curtains to show her bare arm and shoulder, her neck, and the dark tangle of hair on the pillow. She was beautiful, desirable. Why did he lie there moaning over his sins? What did it matter? If he were hopeless, then so be it; he would make the best of his hopelessness. A glorious sense of irresponsibility suddenly filled him. He was free, magnificently free. In a kind of exaltation he drew the girl toward him. She woke, bewildered, almost frightened under his rough kisses.

The storm of his desire subsided into a kind of serene merriment. The whole atmosphere seemed to be quivering with enormous silent laughter.

"Could anyone love you as much as I do, Teddy Bear?" The question came faintly from distant worlds of love.

"I think I know somebody who does," Mr. Hutton replied. The submarine laughter was swelling, rising, ready to break the surface of silence and resound.

"Who? Tell me. What do you mean?" The voice had come very close. Charged with suspicion, anguish, indignation, it belonged to this immediate world.

"Ah!"

"Who?"

"You'll never guess." Mr. Hutton kept up the joke until it began to grow tedious, and then pronounced the name: "Janet Spence."

Doris was incredulous. "Miss Spence of the Manor? That old woman?" It was too ridiculous. Mr. Hutton laughed too.

"But it's quite true," he said. "She adores me." Oh, the vast joke! He would go and see her as soon as he returned, see and conquer. "I believe she wants to marry me," he added.

"But you wouldn't... you don't intend..."

The air was fairly crepitating with humor. Mr. Hutton laughed aloud. "I intend to marry you," he said. It seemed to him the best joke he had ever made in his life.

When Mr. Hutton left Southend he was once more a married man. It was agreed that, for the time being, the fact should be kept secret. In the autumn they would go abroad together, and the world should be informed. Meanwhile he was to go back to his own house and Doris to hers.

The day after his return he walked over in the afternoon to see Miss Spence. She received him with the old Gioconda.

"I was expecting you to come."

"I couldn't keep away," Mr. Hutton gallantly replied.

They sat in the summerhouse. It was a pleasant place—a little old stucco temple bowered among dense bushes of evergreen. Miss Spence had left her mark on it by hanging up over the seat a blue-and-white Della Robbia plaque.

"I am thinking of going to Italy this autumn," said Mr. Hutton. He felt like a ginger-beer bottle, ready to pop with bubbling humorous excitement.

"Italy. . . ." Miss Spence closed her eyes ecstatically. "I feel drawn there too."

"Why not let yourself be drawn?"

"I don't know. One somehow hasn't the energy and initiative to set out alone."

"Alone. . . ." Ah, sounds of guitars and throaty singing! "Yes, traveling alone isn't much fun."

Miss Spence lay back in her chair without speaking. Her eyes were still closed. Mr. Hutton stroked his mustache. The silence prolonged itself for what seemed a very long time.

Pressed to stay to dinner, Mr. Hutton did not refuse. The fun had hardly started. The table was laid in the loggia. Through its arches they looked out onto the sloping garden, to the valley below and the farther hills. Light ebbed away; the heat and silence were oppressive. A huge cloud was mounting up the sky, and there were distant breathings of thunder. The thunder grew nearer, a wind began to blow, and the first drops of rain fell. The table was cleared. Miss Spence and Mr. Hutton sat on in the growing darkness.

Miss Spence broke a long silence by saying meditatively: "I think everyone has a right to a certain amount of happiness, don't you?"

"Most certainly." But what was she leading up to? Nobody makes generalizations about life unless they mean to talk about themselves. Happiness: he looked back on his own life, and saw a cheerful, placid existence disturbed by no great griefs or discomforts or alarms. He had always had money and freedom; he had been able to do very much as he wanted. Yes, he supposed he had been happy, happier than most men. And now he was not merely happy; he had discovered in irresponsibility the secret of gaiety. He was about to say something about his happiness when Miss Spence went on speaking.

"People like you and me have a right to be happy some time in our lives."

"Me?" said Mr. Hutton, surprised.

"Poor Henry! Fate hasn't treated either of us very well."

"Oh, well, it might have treated me worse."

"You're being cheerful. That's brave of you. But don't think I can't see behind the mask."

Miss Spence spoke louder and louder as the rain came down more and more heavily. Periodically the thunder cut across her utterances. She talked on, shouting against the noise.

"I have understood you so well and for so long."

A flash revealed her, aimed and intent, leaning toward him. Her eyes were two profound and menacing gun barrels. The darkness re-engulfed her.

"You were a lonely soul seeking a companion soul. I could sympathize with you in your solitude. Your marriage . . ."

The thunder cut short the sentence. Miss Spence's voice became audible once more with the words:

". . . could offer no companionship to a man of your stamp. You needed a soul mate."

A soul mate—he! A soul mate! It was incredibly fantastic. "Georgette Leblanc, the ex-soul mate of Maurice Maeterlinck." He had seen that in a paper a few days ago. So it was thus that Janet Spence had painted him in her imagination—as a soul-mater. And for Doris he was a picture of goodness and the cleverest man in the world. And actually, really, he was what? Who knows?

"My heart went out to you. I could understand; I was lonely, too." Miss Spence laid her hand on his knee. "You were so patient." Another flash. She was still aimed, dangerously. "You never complained. But I could guess, I could guess."

"How wonderful of you!" So he was an *âme incomprise.* "Only a woman's intuition..."

The thunder crashed and rumbled, died away, and only the sound of the rain was left. The thunder was his laughter, magnified, externalized. Flash and crash, there it was again, right on top of them.

"Don't you feel that you have within you something that is akin to this storm?" He could imagine her leaning forward as she uttered the word. "Passion makes one the equal of the elements."

What was his gambit now? Why, obviously, he should have said, "Yes," and ventured on some unequivocal gesture. But Mr. Hutton suddenly took fright. The ginger beer in him had gone flat. The woman was serious—terribly serious. He was appalled.

Passion? "No," he desperately answered. "I am without passion."

But his remark was either unheard or unheeded, for Miss Spence went on with a growing exaltation, speaking so rapidly, however, and in such a burningly intimate whisper that Mr. Hutton found it very difficult to distinguish what she was saying. She was telling him, as far as he could make out, the story of her life. The lightning was less frequent now, and there were long intervals of darkness. But at each flash he saw her still aiming toward him, still yearning forward with a terrifying intensity. Darkness, the rain, and then flash! her face was there, close at hand. A pale mask, greenish white; the large eyes, the narrow barrel of the mouth, the heavy eyebrows. Agrippina, or wasn't it rather—yes, wasn't it rather George Robey?

He began devising absurd plans for escaping. He might suddenly jump up, pretending he had seen a burglar—Stop thief! stop thief!—and dash off into the night in pursuit. Or should he say that he felt faint, a heart attack, or that he had seen a ghost—Emily's ghost—in the garden? Absorbed in his childish plotting, he had ceased to pay any attention to Miss Spence's words. The spasmodic clutching of her hand recalled his thoughts.

"I honored you for that, Henry," she was saying.

Honored him for what?

"Marriage is a sacred tie, and your respect for it, even when the marriage was, as it was in your case, an unhappy one, made me respect you and admire you, and—shall I dare say the word?—"

Oh, the burglar, the ghost in the garden! But it was too late.

". . . yes, love you, Henry, all the more. But we're free now, Henry."

Free? There was a movement in the dark, and she was kneeling on the floor by his chair.

"Oh, Henry, Henry, I have been unhappy too."

Her arms embraced him, and by the shaking of her body he could feel that she was sobbing. She might have been a suppliant crying for mercy.

"You mustn't, Janet," he protested. Those tears were terrible, terrible. "Not now, not now! You must be calm; you must go to bed." He patted her shoulder, then got up, disengaging himself from her embrace. He left her still crouching on the floor beside the chair on which he had been sitting.

Groping his way into the hall, and without waiting to look for his hat, he went out of the house, taking infinite pains to close the front door noiselessly behind him. The clouds had blown over, and the moon was shining from a clear sky. There were puddles all along the road, and a noise of running water rose from the gutters and ditches. Mr. Hutton splashed along, not caring if he got wet.

How heart-rendingly she had sobbed! With the emotions of pity and remorse that the recollection evoked in him there was a certain resentment: why couldn't she have played the game that he was playing, the heartless, amusing game? Yes, but he had known all the time that she wouldn't, she couldn't play that game; he had known and persisted.

What had she said about passion and the elements? Something absurdly stale, but true, true. There she was, a cloud black-bosomed and charged with thunder, and he, like some absurd little Benjamin Franklin, had sent up a kite into the heart of the menace. Now he was complaining that his toy had drawn the lightning.

She was probably still kneeling by that chair in the loggia, crying.

But why hadn't he been able to keep up the game? Why had his irresponsibility deserted him, leaving him suddenly sober in a cold world? There were no answers to any of his questions. One idea burned steady and luminous in his mind, the idea of flight. He must get away at once.

"What are you thinking about, Teddy Bear?"

"Nothing."

There was a silence. Mr. Hutton remained motionless, his elbows on the parapet of the terrace, his chin in his hands, looking down over Florence. He had taken a villa on one of the hilltops to the south of the city. From a little raised terrace at the end of the garden one looked down a long fertile valley on to the town and beyond it to the bleak mass of Monte Morello and, eastward of it, to the peopled hill of Fiesole, dotted with white houses. Everything was clear and luminous in the September sunshine.

"Are you worried about anything?"

"No, thank you."

"Tell me, Teddy Bear."

"But, my dear, there's nothing to tell." Mr. Hutton turned round, smiled, and patted the girl's hand. "I think you'd better go in and have your siesta. It's too hot for you here."

"Very well, Teddy Bear. Are you coming too?"

"When I've finished my cigar."

"All right. But do hurry up and finish it, Teddy Bear." Slowly, reluctantly, she descended the steps of the terrace and walked toward the house.

Mr. Hutton continued his contemplation of Florence. He

had need to be alone. It was good sometimes to escape from Doris and the restless solicitude of her passion. He had never known the pains of loving hopelessly, but he was experienced now in the pains of being loved. These last weeks had been a period of growing discomfort. Doris was always with him, like an obsession, like a guilty conscience. Yes, it was good to be alone.

He pulled an envelope out of his pocket and opened it, not without reluctance. He hated letters; they always contained something unpleasant, nowadays, since his second marriage. This was from his sister. He began skimming through the insulting home-truths of which it was composed. The words "indecent haste," "social suicide," "scarcely cold in her grave," "person of the lower classes," all occurred. They were inevitable now in any communication from a well-meaning and right-thinking relative. Impatient, he was about to tear the stupid letter to pieces when his eye fell on a sentence at the bottom of the third page. His heart beat with uncomfortable violence as he read it. It was too monstrous! Janet Spence was going about telling everyone that he had poisoned his wife in order to marry Doris. What damnable malice! Ordinarily a man of the suavest temper, Mr. Hutton found himself trembling with rage. He took the childish satisfaction of calling names—he cursed the woman.

Then suddenly he saw the ridiculous side of the situation. The notion that he should have murdered anyone in order to marry Doris! If they only knew how miserably bored he was. Poor, dear Janet! She had tried to be malicious, she had only succeeded in being stupid.

A sound of footsteps aroused him; he looked round. In the garden below the little terrace the servant girl of the house was picking fruit. A Neopolitan, strayed somehow as far north as Florence, she was a specimen of the classical type a little debased. Her profile might have been taken from a Sicilian coin of a bad period. Her features, carved floridly in the grand tradition, expressed an almost perfect stupidity. Her mouth was the most beautiful thing about her; the calligraphic hand of nature had richly curved it into an expression of mulish bad temper.

Under her hideous black clothes, Mr. Hutton divined a powerful body, firm and massive. He had looked at her before with a vague interest and curiosity. Today the curiosity defined and focused itself into a desire. An idyll of Theocritus. Here was the woman; he, alas, was not precisely like a goatherd on the volcanic hills. He called to her.

"Armida!"

The smile with which she answered him was so provocative, attested so easy a virtue, that Mr. Hutton took fright. He was on the brink once more—on the brink. He must draw back, oh! quickly, quickly, before it was too late. The girl continued to look up at him.

"Ha chiamato?" she asked at last.

Stupidity or reason? Oh, there was no choice now. It was imbecility every time.

"Scendo," he called back to her. Twelve steps led from the garden to the terrace. Mr. Hutton counted them. Down, down, down, down. . . . He saw a vision of himself descending from one circle of the inferno to the next, from a darkness full of wind and hail to an abyss of stinking mud.

For a good many days the Hutton case had a place on the front page of every newspaper. There had been no more popular murder trial since George Smith had temporarily eclipsed the European War by drowning in a warm bath his seventh bride. The public imagination was stirred by this tale of a murder brought to light months after the date of the crime. Here, it was felt, was one of those incidents in human life, so notable because they are so rare, which do definitely justify the ways of God to man. A wicked man had been moved by an illicit passion to kill his wife. For months he had lived in sin and fancied security, only to be dashed at last more horribly into the pit he had prepared for himself. "Murder will out," and here was a case of it. The readers of the newspapers were in a position to follow every movement of the hand of God. There had been vague, but persistent rumors in the neighborhood; the police had taken action at last. Then came the exhumation order, the post mortem examination, the inquest, the evidence of the experts, the verdict of the coroner's jury, the trial, the condemnation. For once Providence had done its duty, obviously, grossly, didactically, as in a melodrama. The newspapers were right in making of the case the staple intellectual food of a whole season.

Mr. Hutton's first emotion when he was summoned from Italy to give evidence at the inquest was one of indignation. It was a monstrous, a scandalous thing that the police should take such idle, malicious gossip seriously. When the inquest was over he would bring an action for malicious prosecution against the Chief Constable; he would sue the Spence woman for slander.

The inquest was opened; the astonishing evidence unrolled itself. The experts had examined the body, and had found traces of arsenic; they were of opinion that the late Mrs. Hutton had died of arsenic poisoning.

Arsenic poisoning... Emily had died of arsenic poisoning? After that, Mr. Hutton learned with surprise that there was enough arsenicated insecticide in his greenhouses to poison an army.

It was now, quite suddenly, that he saw it: there was a case against him. Fascinated, he watched it growing, growing, like some monstrous tropical plant. It was enveloping him, surrounding him; he was lost in a tangled forest.

When was the poison administered? The experts agreed that it must have been swallowed eight or nine hours before death. About lunchtime? Yes, about lunchtime. Clara, the parlormaid, was called. Mrs. Hutton, she remembered, had asked her to go and fetch her medicine, Mr. Hutton had volunteered to go instead; he had gone alone. Miss Spence—ah, the memory of the storm, the white face, the horror of it all!—Miss Spence confirmed Clara's statement, and added that Mr. Hutton had come back with the medicine already poured out in a wineglass, not in the bottle.

Mr. Hutton's indignation evaporated. He was dismayed, frightened. It was all too fantastic to be taken seriously, and yet this nightmare was a fact, it was actually happening.

M'Nab had seen them kissing, often. He had taken them for a drive on the day of Mrs. Hutton's death. He could see them reflected in the wind screen, sometimes out of the tail of his eye.

The inquest was adjourned. That evening Doris went to bed with a headache. When he went to her room after dinner, Mr. Hutton found her crying.

"What's the matter?" He sat down on the edge of her bed and began to stroke her hair. For a long time she did not answer, and he went on stroking her hair mechanically, almost unconsciously; sometimes, even, he bent down and kissed her bare shoulder. He had his own affairs, however, to think about. What had happened? How was it that the stupid gossip had actually come true? Emily had died of arsenic poisoning. It was absurd, impossible. The order of things had been broken, and he was at the mercy of an irresponsibility. What had happened, what was going to happen? He was interrupted in the midst of his thoughts.

"It's my fault, it's my fault!" Doris suddenly sobbed out. "I shouldn't have loved you; I oughtn't to have let you love me. Why was I ever born?"

Mr. Hutton didn't say anything, but looked down in silence at the abject figure of misery lying on the bed.

"If they do anything to you I shall kill myself."

She sat up, held him for a moment at arm's length, and looked at him with a kind of violence, as though she were never to see him again.

"I love you, I love you, I love you." She drew him, inert and passive, toward her, clasped him, pressed herself against him. "I didn't know you loved me as much as that, Teddy Bear. But why did you do it, why did you do it?"

Mr. Hutton undid her clasping arms and got up. His face became very red. "You seem to take it for granted that I murdered my wife," he said. "It's really too grotesque. What do you all take me for? A cinema hero?" He had begun to lose his temper. All the exasperation, all the fear and bewilderment of the day, was transformed into a violent anger against her. "It's all such damned stupidity. Haven't you any conception of a civilized man's mentality? Do I look the sort of man who'd go about slaughtering people? I suppose you imagined I was so insanely in love with you that I could commit any folly. When will you women understand that one isn't insanely in love? All one asks for is a quiet life, which you won't allow one to have. I don't know what the devil ever induced me to marry you. It was all a damned stupid, practical joke. And now you go about saying I'm a murderer. I won't stand it."

Mr. Hutton stamped toward the door. He had said horrible things, he knew, odious things that he ought speedily to unsay. But he wouldn't. He closed the door behind him.

"Teddy Bear!" He turned the handle; the latch clicked into place. "Teddy Bear!" The voice that came to him through the closed door was agonized. Should he go back? He ought to go back. He touched the handle, then withdrew his fingers and quickly walked away. When he was halfway down the stairs he halted. She might try to do something silly—throw herself out of the window or God knows what! He listened attentively; there was no sound. But he pictured her very clearly, tiptoeing across the room, lifting the sash as high as it would go, leaning out into the cold night air. It was raining a little. Under the window lay the paved terrace. How far below? Twenty-five or thirty feet? Once, when he was walking along Piccadilly, a dog had jumped out of a third-story window of the Ritz. He had seen it fall; he had heard it strike the pavement. Should he go back? He was damned if he would; he hated her.

He sat for a long time in the library. What had happened? What was happening? He turned the question over and over in his mind and could find no answer. Suppose the nightmare dreamed itself out to its horrible conclusion. Death was waiting for him. His eyes filled with tears; he wanted so passionately to live. "Just to be alive." Poor Emily had wished it too, he remembered: "Just to be alive." There were still so many places in this astonishing world unvisited, so many queer delightful people still unknown, so many lovely women never so much as seen. The huge white oxen would still be dragging their wains along the Tuscan roads, the cypresses would still go up, straight as pillars, to the blue heaven; but he would not be there to see them. And the sweet southern wines—Tears of Christ and Blood of

Judas—others would drink them, not he. Others would walk down the obscure and narrow lanes between the bookshelves in the London Library, sniffing the dusty perfume of good literature, peering at strange titles, discovering unknown names, exploring the fringes of vast domains of knowledge. He would be lying in a hole in the ground. And why, why? Confusedly he felt that some extraordinary kind of justice was being done. In the past he had been wanton and imbecile and irresponsible. Now Fate was playing as wantonly, as irresponsibly, with him. It was tit for tat, and God existed after all.

He felt that he would like to pray. Forty years ago he used to kneel by his bed every evening. The nightly formula of his childhood came to him almost unsought from some long-unopened chamber of the memory. "God bless Father and Mother, Tom and Cissie and the Baby, Mademoiselle and Nurse, and everyone that I love, and make me a good boy. Amen." They were all dead now, all except Cissie.

His mind seemed to soften and dissolve; a great calm descended upon his spirit. He went upstairs to ask Doris's forgiveness. He found her lying on the couch at the foot of the bed. On the floor beside her stood a blue bottle of liniment, marked NOT TO BE TAKEN; she seemed to have drunk about half of it.

"You didn't love me," was all she said when she opened her eyes to find him bending over her.

Dr. Libbard arrived in time to prevent any very serious consequences. "You mustn't do this again," he said while Mr. Hutton was out of the room.

"What's to prevent me?" she asked defiantly.

Dr. Libbard looked at her with his large, sad eyes. "There's nothing to prevent you," he said. "Only yourself and your baby. Isn't it rather bad luck on your baby, not allowing it to come into the world because you want to go out of it?"

Doris was silent for a time. "All right," she whispered, "I won't."

Mr. Hutton sat by her bedside for the rest of the night. He felt himself now to be indeed a murderer. For a time he persuaded himself that he loved this pitiable child. Dozing in his chair, he woke up, stiff and cold, to find himself drained dry, as it were, of every emotion. He had become nothing but a tired and suffering carcass. At six o'clock he undressed and went to bed for a couple of hour's sleep. In the course of the same afternoon the coroner's jury brought in a verdict of "Willful Murder," and Mr. Hutton was committed for trial.

Miss Spence was not at all well. She had found her public appearances in the witness box very trying, and when it was all over she had something that was very nearly a breakdown. She slept badly, and suffered from nervous indigestion. Dr. Libbard used to call every other day. She talked to him a great deal, mostly about the Hutton case. Her moral indignation was always on the boil. Wasn't it appalling to think that one had had a murderer in one's house? Wasn't it extraordinary that one could have been for so long mistaken about the man's character? (But she had had an inkling from the first.) And then the girl he had gone off with—so low class, so little better than a prostitute. The news that the second Mrs. Hutton was expecting a baby, the posthumous child of a condemned and executed criminal, revolted her; the thing was shocking, an obscenity. Dr. Libbard answered her gently and vaguely, and prescribed bromide.

One morning he interrupted her in the midst of her customary tirade. "By the way," he said in his soft, melancholy voice, "I suppose it was really you who poisoned Mrs. Hutton."

Miss Spence stared at him for two or three seconds with enormous eyes, and then quietly said, "Yes." After that she started to cry.

"In the coffee, I suppose."

She seemed to nod assent. Dr. Libbard took out his fountain pen, and in his neat, meticulous calligraphy wrote out a prescription for a sleeping draught.

THE CURFEW TOLLS[*]

BY STEPHEN VINCENT BENÉT

"It is not enough to be the possessor of genius—the time and the man must conjoin. An Alexander the Great, born into an age of profound peace, might scarce have troubled the world—a Newton, grown up in a thieves' den, might have devised little but a new and ingenious picklock...."

DIVERSIONS OF HISTORICAL THOUGHT BY
JOHN CLEVELAND COTTON.

(The following extracts have been made from the letters of General Sir Charles William Geoffrey Estcourt, C.B., to his sister, Harriet, Countess of Stokely, by permission of the Stokely family. Omissions are indicated by triple dots, thus . . .)

St. Philippe-des-Bains, September 3d, 1788.
My Dear Sister: . . . I could wish that my excellent Paris physician had selected some other spot for my convalescence. But he swears by the waters of St. Philip and I swear by him, so I must resign myself to a couple of yawning months ere my constitution mends. Nevertheless, you will get long letters from me, though I fear they may be dull ones. I cannot bring you the gossip of Baden or Aix—except for its baths, St. Philip is but one of a dozen small white towns on this agreeable coast. It has its good inn and its bad inn, its dusty, little square with its dusty, fleabitten beggar, its posting-station and its promenade of scrubby lindens and palms. From the heights one may see Corsica on a clear day, and the Mediterranean is of an unexam-

---

[*] from *Selected Works of Stephen Vincent Benét*

pled blue. To tell the truth, it is all agreeable enough, and an old Indian campaigner, like myself, should not complain. I am well treated at the Cheval Blanc—am I not an English milord?—and my excellent Gaston looks after me devotedly. But there is a blue-bottle drowsiness about small watering places out of season, and our gallant enemies, the French, know how to bore themselves more exquisitely in their provinces than any nation on earth. Would you think that the daily arrival of the diligence from Toulon would be an excitement? Yet it is to me, I assure you, and to all St. Philip. I walk, I take the waters, I read Ossian, I play piquet with Gaston, and yet I seem to myself but half-alive. . . .

. . . You will smile and say to me, "Dear brother, you have always plumed yourself on being a student of human nature. Is there no society, no character for you to study, even in St. Philippe-des-Bains?" My dear sister, I bend myself earnestly to that end, yet so far with little result. I have talked to my doctor—a good man but unpolished; I have talked to the curé—a good man but dull. I have even attempted the society of the baths, beginning with Monsieur le Marquis de la Percedragon, who has ninety-six quarterings, soiled wristbands, and a gloomy interest in my liver, and ending with Mrs. Macgregor Jenkins, a worthy and red-faced lady whose conversation positively cannonades with dukes and duchesses. But, frankly, I prefer my chair in the garden and my Ossian to any of them, even at the risk of being considered a bear. A witty scoundrel would be the veriest godsend to me, but do such exist in St. Philip? I trow not. As it is, in my weakened condition, I am positively agog when Gaston comes in every morning, with his budget of village scandal. A pretty pass to come to, you will say, for a man who has served with Eyre Coote and but for the mutabilities of fortune, not to speak of a most damnable cabal . . . (A long passage dealing with General Estcourt's East Indian services and his personal and unfavorable opinion of Warren Hastings is here omitted from the manuscript.) . . . But, at fifty, a man is either a fool or a philosopher. Nevertheless, unless Gaston provides me with a character to try my

wits on, shortly, I shall begin to believe that they too have deteriorated with Indian suns....

September 21st, 1788.
My Dear Sister: . . . Believe me, there is little soundness in the
views of your friend, Lord Martindale. The French monarchy is
not to be compared with our own, but King Louis is an excellent and well-beloved prince, and the proposed summoning of
the States-General cannot but have the most salutary effect....
(Three pages upon French politics and the possibility of cultivating sugar-cane in Southern France are here omitted.)... As
for news of myself, I continue my yawning course, and feel a
decided improvement from the waters.... So I shall continue
them though the process is slow....

You ask me, I fear a trifle mockingly, how my studies in human nature proceed?

Not so ill, my dear sister—I have, at least scraped acquaintance with one odd fish, and that, in St. Philip, is a triumph. For
some time, from my chair in the promenade, I have observed a
pursy little fellow, of my age or thereabouts, stalking up and
down between the lindens. His company seems avoided by
such notables of the place as Mrs. Macgregor Jenkins and at
first I put him down as a retired actor, for there is something a
little theatrical in his dress and walk. He wears a wide-
brimmed hat of straw, loose nankeen trousers and a quasi-
military coat, and takes his waters with as much ceremony as
Monsieur le Marquis, though not quite with the same *ton*. I
should put him down as a Meridional, for he has the quick,
dark eye, the sallow skin, the corpulence and the rodomontish
airs that mark your true son of the Midi, once he has passed his
lean and hungry youth.

And yet, there is some sort of unsuccessful oddity about
him, which sets him off from your successful bourgeois. I cannot put my finger on it yet, but it interests me.

At any rate, I was sitting in my accustomed chair, reading Ossian, this morning, as he made his solitary rounds of the promenade. Doubtless I was more than usually absorbed in my author,
for I must have pronounced some lines aloud as he passed. He

gave me a quick glance at the time, but nothing more. But on his next round, as he was about to pass me, he hesitated for a moment, stopped, and then, removing his straw hat, saluted me very civilly.

"Monsieur will pardon me," he said, with a dumpy hauteur, "but surely monsieur is English? And surely the lines that monsieur just repeated are from the great poet, Ossian?"

I admitted both charges, with a smile, and he bowed again.

"Monsieur will excuse the interruption," he said, "but I myself have long admired the poetry of Ossian"—and with that he continued my quotation to the end of the passage, in very fair English, too, though with a strong accent. I complimented him, of course, effusively—after all, it is not every day that one runs across a fellow-admirer of Ossian on the promenade of a small French watering place—and after that, he sat down in the chair beside me and we fell into talk. He seems, astonishingly for a Frenchman, to have an excellent acquaintance with our English poets—perhaps he has been a tutor in some English family. I did not press him with questions on this first encounter, though I noted that he spoke French with a slight accent also, which seems odd.

There is something a little rascally about him, to tell you the truth, though his conversation with me was both forceful and elevated. An ill man, too, and a disappointed one, or I miss my mark, yet his eyes, when he talks, are strangely animating. I fancy I would not care to meet him in a *guetapens,* and yet, he may be the most harmless of broken pedagogues. We took a glass of waters together, to the great disgust of Mrs. Macgregor Jenkins, who ostentatiously drew her skirts aside. She let me know, afterward, in so many words, that my acquaintance was a noted bandit, though when pressed, she could give no better reason than that he lives a little removed from the town, that "nobody knows where he comes from" and that his wife is "no better than she should be," whatever that portentous phrase entails. Well, one would hardly call him a gentleman, even by Mrs. Macgregor's somewhat easy standards, but he has given me better conversation than I have had in a month—and if he is a bandit, we might discuss thuggee together. But I hope for nothing so stimulating, though I must question Gaston about him....

October 11th.

... But Gaston could tell me little, except that my acquaintance comes from Sardinia or some such island originally, has served in the French army and is popularly supposed to possess the evil eye. About Madame he hinted that he could tell me a great deal, but I did not labor the point. After all, if my friend has been c-ck-ld-d—do not blush, my dear sister!—that, too, is the portion of a philosopher, and I find his wide range of conversation much more palatable than Mrs. Macgregor Jenkins' rewarmed London gossip. Nor has he tried to borrow money from me yet, something which, I am frank to say, I expected and was prepared to refuse....

November 20th.

... Triumph! My character is found—and a character of the first water, I assure you! I have dined with him in his house, and a very bad dinner it was. Madame is not a good housekeeper, whatever else she may be. And what she has been, one can see at a glance—she has all the little faded coquetries of the garrison coquette. Good-tempered, of course, as such women often are, and must have been pretty in her best days, though with shocking bad teeth. I suspect her of a touch of the tarbrush, though there I may be wrong. No doubt she caught my friend young—I have seen the same thing happen in India often enough—the experienced woman and the youngster fresh from England. Well, 'tis an old story—an old one with him, too—and no doubt Madame has her charms, though she is obviously one reason why he has not risen.

After dinner, Madame departed, not very willingly, and he took me into his study for a chat. He had even procured a bottle of port, saying he knew the Englishman's taste for it, and while it was hardly the right Cockburn, I felt touched by the attention. The man is desperately lonely—one reads that in his big eyes. He is also desperately proud, with the quick, touchy sensitiveness of the failure, and I quite exerted myself to draw him out.

And indeed, the effort repaid me. His own story is simple enough. He is neither bandit nor pedagogue, but, like myself, a broken soldier—a major of the French Royal Artillery, retired on half pay for some years. I think it creditable of him to have reached so respectable a rank, for he is of foreign birth—Sardinian, I think I told you—and the French service is by no means as partial to foreigners as they were in the days of the first Irish Brigade. Moreover, one simply does not rise in that service, unless one is a gentleman of quarterings, and that he could hardly claim. But the passion of his life has been India, and that is what interests me. And, 'pon my honor, he was rather astonishing about it.

As soon as, by a lucky chance, I hit upon the subject, his eyes lit up and his sickness dropped away. Pretty soon he began to take maps from a cabinet in the wall and ply me with questions about my own small experiences. And very soon indeed, I am abashed to state, I found myself stumbling in my answers. It was all book knowledge on his part, of course, but where the devil he could have got some of it, I do not know. Indeed, he would even correct me, now and then, as cool as you please. "Eight twelve pounders, I think, on the north wall of the old fortifications of Madras—" and the deuce of it is, he would be right. Finally, I could contain myself no longer.

"But, major, this is incredible," I said. "I have served twenty years with John Company and thought that I had some knowledge. But one would say you had fought over every inch of Bengal!"

He gave me a quick look, almost of anger, and began to roll up his maps. "So, I have, in my mind," he said, shortly, "but as my superiors have often informed me, my hobby is a tedious one."

"It is not tedious to me," I said boldly. "Indeed, I have often marveled at your government's neglect of their opportunities in India. True, the issue is settled now——"

"It is by no means settled," he said, interrupting me rudely. I stared at him.

"It was settled, I believe, by Baron Clive, at a spot named Plassey," I said frigidly. "And afterward, by my own old general, Eyre Coote, at another spot named Wandewash."

"Oh, yes—yes—yes," he said impatiently, "I grant you Clive—Clive was a genius and met the fate of geniuses. He steals an empire for you, and your virtuous English Parliament holds up its hands in horror because he steals a few lakhs of rupees for himself as well. So he blows out his brains in disgrace—you inexplicable English!—and you lose your genius. A great pity. I would not have treated Clive so. But then, if I had been Milord Clive, I would not have blown out my brains."

"And what would you have done, had you been Clive?" I said, for the man's calm, staring conceit amused me.

His eyes were dangerous for a moment and I saw why the worthy Mrs. Macgregor Jenkins had called him a bandit.

"Oh," he said coolly, "I would have sent a file of grenadiers to your English Parliament and told it to hold its tongue. As Cromwell did. Now there was a man. But your Clive— faugh!—he had the ball at his feet and he refused to kick it. I withdraw the word genius. He was a nincompoop. At the least, he might have made himself a rajah."

This was a little too much, as you may imagine. "General Clive had his faults," I said icily, "but he was a true Briton and a patriot."

"He was a fool," said my puffy little major, flatly, his lower lip struck out. "As big a fool as Dupleix, and that is saying much. Oh, some military skill, some talent for organization, yes. But a genius would have brushed him into the sea! It was possible to hold Arcot, it was possible to win Plassey—look!" and, with that, he ripped another map from his cabinet and began to expound to me eagerly exactly what he would have done in command of the French forces in India, in 1757, when he must have been but a lad in his twenties. He thumped the paper, he strewed corks along the table for his troops—corks taken from a supply in a tin box, so it must be an old game with him. And, as I listened, my irritation faded, for the man's monomania was obvious. Nor was it, to tell the truth, an ill-designed

plan of campaign, for corks on a map. Of course these things
are different, in the field.

I could say, with honesty, that his plan had features of nov-
elty, and he gulped the words down hungrily—he has a great
appetite for flattery.

"Yes, yes," he said. "That is how it should be done—the
thickest skull can see it. And, ill as I am, with a fleet and ten
thousand picked men——" He dreamed, obviously, the sweat
of his exertions on his waxy face—it was absurd and yet touching to see him dream.

"You would find a certain amount of opposition," I said, in
an amused voice.

"Oh, yes, yes," he said quickly, "I do not underrate the
English. Excellent horse, solid foot. But no true knowledge of
cannon, and I am a gunner——"

I hated to bring him down to earth and yet I felt that I must.

"Of course, major," I said, "you have had great experience
in the field."

He looked at me for a moment, his arrogance quite un-
shaken.

"I have had very little," he said, quietly, "but one knows how
the thing should be done or one does not know. And that is
enough."

He stared at me for an instant with his big eyes. A little mad,
of course. And yet I found myself saying, "But surely, major—
what happened?"

"Why," he said, still quietly, "what happens to folk who have
naught but their brains to sell? I staked my all on India when I
was young—I thought that my star shone over it. I ate dirty
puddings—*corpo di Baccho!*—to get there—I was no De
Rohan or Soubise to win the king's favor! And I reached there
indeed, in my youth, just in time to be included in the surrender
of Pondicherry." He laughed, rather terribly, and sipped at his
glass.

You English were very courteous captors," he said. "But I
was not released till the Seven Years War had ended—that was
in '63. Who asks for the special exchange of an unknown artillery lieutenant? And then ten years odd of garrison duty at

Mauritius. It was there that I met Madame—she is a Creole. A pleasant spot, Mauritius. We used to fire the cannon at the sea birds when we had enough ammunition for target practice," and he chuckled drearily. "By then I was thirty-seven. They had to make me a captain—they even brought me back to France to garrison duty. I have been on garrison duty, at Toulon, at Brest, at——" He ticked off the names on his fingers but I did not like his voice.

"But surely," I said, "the American war, though a small affair—there were opportunities——"

"And who did they send?" he said quickly. "Lafayette— Rochambeau—De Grasse—the springs of the nobility. Oh, at Lafayette's age, I would have volunteered like Lafayette. But one should be successful in youth—after that, the spring is broken. And when one is over forty, one has responsibilities. I have a large family, you see, though not of my own begetting," and he chuckled as if at a secret joke. "Oh, I wrote the Continental Congress," he said reflectively, "but they preferred a dolt like Von Steuben. A good dolt, an honest dolt, but there you have it. I also wrote your British War Office," he said in an even voice. "I must show you that plan of campaign—sometime—they could have crushed General Washington with it in three weeks."

I stared at him, a little appalled.

"For an officer who has taken his king's shilling to send to an enemy nation a plan for crushing his own country's ally," I said stiffly—"well, in England, we would call that treason."

"And what is treason?" he said lightly. "If we call it unsuccessful ambition we shall be nearer the truth." He looked at me, keenly. "You are shocked, General Estcourt," he said. "I am sorry for that. But have you never known the curse"—and his voice vibrated—"the curse of not being employed when you should be employed? The curse of being a hammer with no nail to drive? The curse—the curse of sitting in a dusty garrison town with dreams that would split the brain of a Caesar and no room on earth for those dreams?"

"Yes," I said, unwillingly, for there was something in him that demanded the truth, "I have known that."

"Then you know hells undreamed of by the Christian," he

said, with a sigh, "and if I committed treason—well, I have been punished for it. I might have been a brigadier, otherwise—I had Choiseul's ear for a few weeks, after great labor. As it is, I am here on half pay, and there will not be another war in my time. Moreover, M. de Ségur has proclaimed that all officers now must show sixteen quarterings. Well, I wish them joy of those officers, in the next conflict. Meanwhile, I have my corks, my maps and my family ailment." He smiled and tapped his side. "It killed my father at thirty-nine—it has not treated me quite so ill, but it will come for me soon enough."

And indeed, when I looked at him, I could well believe it, for the light had gone from his eyes and his cheeks were flabby. We chatted a little on indifferent subjects after that, then I left him, wondering whether to pursue the acquaintance. He is indubitably a character, but some of his speeches leave a taste in my mouth. Yet he can be greatly attractive—even now, with his mountainous failure like a cloak upon him. And yet why should I call it mountainous? His conceit is mountainous enough, but what else could he have expected of his career? Yet I wish I could forget his eyes.... To tell the truth, he puzzles me and I mean to get to the bottom of him....

February 12th, 1789.
...I have another sidelight on the character of my friend, the major. As I told you, I was half of a mind to break off the acquaintance entirely, but he came up to me so civilly, the following day, that I could find no excuse. And since then, he has made me no embarrassingly treasonable confidences, though whenever we discuss the art of war, his arrogance is unbelievable. He even informed me, the other day, that while Frederick of Prussia was a fair general, his tactics might have been improved upon. I merely laughed and turned the question. Now and then I play a war game with him, with his corks and maps, and when I let him win, he is as pleased as a child...His illness increases visibly, despite the waters, and he shows an eagerness for my company which I cannot but find touching.... After all, he is a man of intelligence, and the company he has had to keep must have galled him at times....

Now and then I amuse myself by speculating what might have happened to him, had he chosen some other profession than that of arms. He has, as I have told you, certain gifts of the actor, yet his stature and figure must have debarred him from tragic parts, while he certainly does not possess the humors of the comedian. Perhaps his best choice would have been the Romish church, for there, the veriest fisherman may hope, at least, to succeed to the keys of St. Peter. . . . And yet, Heaven knows, he would have made a very bad priest! . . .

But, to my tale. I had missed him from our accustomed walks for some days and went to his house—St. Helen's it is called, we live in a pother of saints' names hereabouts—one evening to inquire. I did not hear the quarreling voices till the tousle-haired servant had admitted me and then it was too late to retreat. Then my friend bounced down the corridor, his sallow face bored and angry.

"Ah, General Estcourt!" he said, with a complete change of expression as soon as he saw me. "What fortune! I was hoping you would pay us a call—I wish to introduce you to my family!"

He had told me previously of his pair of stepchildren by Madame's first marriage, and I must confess I felt curious to see them. But it was not of them he spoke, as I soon gathered.

"Yes," he said, "My brothers and sisters, or most of them, are here for a family council. You come in the nick of time!" He pinched my arm and his face glowed with the malicious näiveté of a child. "They do not believe that I really know an English general—it will be a great blow to them!" he whispered as we passed down the corridor. "Ah, if you had only worn your uniform and your Garters! But one cannot have everything in life!"

Well, my dear sister, what a group, when we entered the salon! It is a small room, tawdrily furnished in the worst French taste, with a jumble of Madame's feminities and souvenirs from the Island of Mauritius, and they were all sitting about in the French after-dinner fashion, drinking tisane and quarreling. And, indeed, had the room been as long as the nave of St. Peter's, it would yet have seemed too small for such a crew! An old mother, straight as a ramrod and as forbidding, with the burning eyes and the bitter dignity one sees on the faces of certain Italian peasants—you could see that they were all a little afraid of her except my friend, and he, I must say, treated her with a filial courtesy that was greatly to his credit. Two sisters, one fattish, swarthy and spiteful, the other with the wreck of great beauty and the evident marks of a certain profession on her shabby-fine *toilette* and her pinkened cheeks. An innkeeper brother-in-law called Buras or Durat, with a jowlish, heavily handsome face and the manners of a cavalry sergeant—he is married to the spiteful sister. And two brothers, one sheep-like, one fox-like, yet both bearing a certain resemblance to my friend.

The sheep-like brother is at least respectable, I gathered—a provincial lawyer in a small way of business whose great pride is that he has actually appeared before the Court of Appeals at Marseilles. The other, the fox-like one, makes his living more dubiously—he seems the sort of fellow who orates windily in taprooms about the Rights of Man, and other nonsense of M. Rousseau's. I would certainly not trust him with my watch, though he is trying to get himself elected to the States-General. And, as regards family concord, it was obvious at first glance that not one of them trusted the others. And yet, that is not all of the tribe. There are, if you will believe me, two other brothers living, and this family council was called to deal with the affairs of the next-to-youngest, who seems, even in this mélange, to be a black sheep.

I can assure you, my head swam, and when my friend introduced me, proudly, as a Knight of the Garter, I did not even bother to contradict him. For they admitted me to their intimate circle at once—there was no doubt about that. Only the old lady remained aloof, saying little and sipping her camomile tea as if it were the blood of her enemies. But, one by one, the others related to me, with an unasked-for frankness, the most intimate and scandalous details of their brothers' and sisters' lives. They seemed united only on two points, jealousy of my friend, the major, because he is his mother's favorite, and dislike of Madame Josephine because she gives herself airs. Except for the haggard beauty—I must say, that, while her remarks anent her sister-in-law were not such as I would care to repeat, she seemed

genuinely fond of her brother, the major, and expounded his
virtues to me through an overpowering cloud of scent.

It was like being in a nest of Italian smugglers, or a den of
quarrelsome foxes, for they all talked, or rather barked at once,
even the brother-in-law, and only Madame Mère could bring silence among them. And yet, my friend enjoyed it. It was obvious he showed them off before me as he might have displayed
the tricks of a set of performing animals. And yet with a certain
fondness, too—that is the inexplicable part of it. I do not know
which sentiment was upmost in my mind—respect for this
family feeling or pity for his being burdened with such a clan.

For though not the eldest, he is the strongest among them,
and they know it. They rebel, but he rules their family con-
claves like a petty despot. I could have laughed at the farce of
it, and yet, it was nearer tears. For here, at least, my friend was
a personage.

I got away as soon as I could, despite some pressing looks
from the haggard beauty. My friend accompanied me to the
door.

"Well, well," he said, chuckling and rubbing his hands, "I
am infinitely obliged to you, general. They will not forget this
in a hurry. Before you entered, Joseph"—Joseph is the sheep-
like one—"was boasting about his acquaintance with a *sousin-
tendant,* but an English general, bah! Joseph will have green
eyes for a fortnight!" And he rubbed his hands again in a perfect paroxysm of delight.

It was too childlike to make me angry. "I am glad, of course,
to have been of any service," I said.

"Oh, you have been a great service," he said. "They will not
plague my poor Josie for at least half an hour. Ah, this is a bad
business of Louis'—a bad business!"—Louis is the black
sheep—"but we will patch it up somehow. Hortense is worth
three of him—he must go back to Hortense!"

"You have a numerous family, major," I said for want of
something better to say.

"Oh, yes," he said, cheerfully. "Pretty numerous—I am
sorry you could not meet the others. Though Louis is a fool—I
pampered him in his youth. Well! He was a baby—and Jerome

a mule. Still, we haven't done so badly for ourselves; not badly. Joseph makes a go of his law practice—there are fools enough in the world to be impressed by Joseph—and if Lucien gets to the States-General, you may trust Lucien to feather his nest! And there are the grandchildren, and a little money—not much," he said, quickly. "They mustn't expect that from me. But it's a step up from where we started—if papa had lived, he wouldn't have been so ill-pleased. Poor Elisa's gone, but the rest of us have stuck together, and, while we may seem a little rough, to strangers, our hearts are in the right place. When I was a boy," and he chuckled again, "I had other ambitions for them. I thought, with luck on my side, I could make them all kings and queens. Funny, isn't it, to think of a numskull like Joseph as a king! Well, that was the boy of it. But, even so, they'd all be eating chestnuts back on the island without me, and that's something."

He said it rather defiantly, and I did not know which to marvel at most—his preposterous pride in the group or his cool contempt of them—So I said nothing but shook his hand instead. I could not help doing the latter. For surely, if anyone started in life with a millstone about his neck . . . and yet they are none of them ordinary people. . . .

March 13th, 1789.
. . . My friend's complaint has taken a turn for the worse and it is I who pay him visits now. It is the act of a Christian to do so and to tell the truth, I have become oddly attached to him, though I can give no just reason for the attachment. He makes a bad patient, by the way, and is often abominably rude to both myself and Madame, who nurses him devotedly though unskillfully. I told him yesterday that I could have no more of it and he looked at me with his strangely luminous eyes. "So," he said, "even the English desert the dying." . . . Well, I stayed; after that, what else might a gentleman do? . . . Yet I cannot feel that he bears me any real affection—he exerts himself to charm, on occasion, but one feels he is playing a game . . . yes, even upon his deathbed, he plays a game . . . a complex character. . . .

April 28th, 1789.

... My friend the major's malady approaches its term—the last few days find him fearfully enfeebled. He knows that the end draws nigh; indeed he speaks of it often, with remarkable calmness. I had thought it might turn his mind toward religion, but while he has accepted the ministrations of his Church, I fear it is without the sincere repentance of a Christian. When the priest had left him, yesterday, he summoned me, remarking, "Well, all that is over with," rather more in the tone of a man who has just reserved a place in a coach than one who will shortly stand before his Maker.

"It does no harm," he said, reflectively. "And, after all, it might be true. Why not?" and he chuckled in a way that repelled me. Then he asked me to read to him—not the Bible, as I had expected, but some verses of the poet Gray. He listened attentively, and when I came to the passage, "Hands, that the rod of empire might have swayed," and its successor, "Some mute inglorious Milton here may rest," he asked me to repeat them. When I had done so, he said, "Yes, yes. That is true. I did not think so in boyhood—I thought genius must force its own way. But your poet is right about it."

I found this painful, for I had hoped that his illness had brought him to a juster, if less arrogant, estimate of his own abilities. "Come, major," I said, soothingly, "we cannot all be great men, you know. And you have no need to repine. After all, as you say, you have risen in the world——"

"Risen?" he said, and his eyes flashed. "Risen? Oh, God, that I should die alone with my one companion an Englishman with a soul of suet! Fool, if I had had Alexander's chance, I would have bettered Alexander! And it will come, too, that is the worst of it. Already Europe is shaking with a new birth. If I had been born under the Sun-King, I would be a Marshal of France; if I had been born twenty years ago, I would mold a new Europe with my fists in the next half-dozen years. Why did they put my soul in my body at this infernal time? Do you not understand, imbecile? Is there no one who understands?"

I called Madame at this, as he was obviously delirious, and after some trouble, we got him quieted.

May 8th, 1789.

... My poor friend is gone, and peacefully enough at the last. His death, oddly enough, coincided with the date of the opening of the States-General at Versailles. The last moments of life are always painful for the observer, but his end was as relatively serene as might be hoped for, considering his character. I was watching at one side of the bed and a thunderstorm was raging at the time. No doubt, to his expiring consciousness, the cracks of the thunder sounded like artillery for, while we were awaiting the death-struggle, he suddenly raised himself in the bed and listened intently. His eyes glowed, a beatific expression passed over his features. "The army! Head of the army!" he whispered ecstatically, and, when we caught Him, he was lifeless ... I must say that, while it may not be very Christian, I am glad that death brought him what life could not, and that, in the very article of it, he saw himself at the head of victorious troops. Ah, Fame—delusive spectre ... (A page of disquisition by General Estcourt on the vanities of human ambition is here omitted.) ... The face, after death, was composed, with a certain majesty, even ... one could see that he might have been handsome as a youth. ...

May 26th, 1789.

... I shall return to Paris by easy stages and reach Stokely sometime in June. My health is quite restored and all that has kept me here this long has been the difficulty I have met with in attempting to settle my poor friend, the major's affairs. For one thing, he appears to have been originally a native of Corsica, not of Sardinia as I had thought, and while that explains much in his character, it has also given occupation to the lawyers. I have met his rapacious family, individually and in conclave, and, if there are further gray hairs on my head, you may put it down to them. ... However, I have finally assured the major's relict of her legitimate rights in his estate, and that is something—my one ray of comfort in the matter being the behavior of her son by the former marriage, who seems an excellent and virtuous young man. ...

... You will think me a very soft fellow, no doubt, for wasting so much time upon a chance acquaintance who was neither, in our English sense, a gentleman nor a man whose Christian virtues counterbalanced his lack of true breeding. Yet there was a tragedy about him beyond his station, and that verse of Gray's rings in my head. I wish I could forget the expression on his face when he spoke of it. Suppose a genius born in circumstances that made the development of that genius impossible— well, all this is the merest moonshine....

...To revert to more practical matters, I discover that the major has left me his military memoirs, papers and commentaries, including his maps. Heaven knows what I shall do with them! I cannot, in courtesy, burn them *sur-le-champ,* and yet they fill two huge packing cases and the cost of transporting them to Stokely will be considerable. Perhaps I will take them to Paris and quietly dispose of them there to some wastepaper merchant.... In return for this unsought legacy, Madame has consulted me in regard to a stone and epitaph for her late husband, and, knowing that otherwise the family would squabble over the affair for weeks, I have drawn up a design which I hope meets with their approval. It appears that he particularly desired that the epitaph should be writ in English, saying that France had had enough of him, living—a freak of dying vanity for which one must pardon him. However, I have produced the following, which I hope will answer.

HERE LIES

NAPOLEONE BUONAPARTE

MAJOR OF THE ROYAL ARTILLERY

OF FRANCE

BORN AUGUST 15TH, 1737

AT AJACCIO, CORSICA.

DIED MAY 5TH, 1789

AT ST. PHILIPPE-DES-BAINS

"REST, PERTURBED SPIRIT . . ."

...I had thought, for some hours, of excerpting the lines of Gray's—the ones that still ring in my head. But, on reflection, though they suit well enough, they yet seem too cruel to the dust.

FATHER WAKES UP
THE VILLAGE*

BY CLARENCE DAY

ONE OF the most disgraceful features of life in the country, Father often declared, was the general inefficiency and slackness of small village tradesmen. He said he had originally supposed that such men were interested in business, and that that was why they had opened their shops and sunk capital in them, but no, they never used them for anything but gossip and sleep. They took no interest in civilized ways. Hadn't heard of them, probably. He said that of course if he were camping out on the veldt or the tundra, he would expect few conveniences in the neighborhood and would do his best to forego them, but why should he be confronted with the wilds twenty miles from New York?

Usually, when Father talked this way, he was thinking of ice. He strongly objected to spending even one day of his life without a glass of cold water beside his plate at every meal. There was never any difficulty about this in our home in the city. A great silver ice-water pitcher stood on the sideboard all day, and when Father was home its outer surface was frosted with cold. When he had gone to the office, the ice was allowed to melt sometimes, and the water got warmish, but never in the evening, or on Sundays, when Father might want some. He said he liked water, he told us it was one of Nature's best gifts, but he said that like all her gifts it was unfit for human consumption unless served in a suitable manner. And the only right way to serve water was icy cold.

* from *The New Yorker* and *Life with Father*

It was still more important that each kind of wine should be served at whatever the right temperature was for it. And kept at it, too. No civilized man would take dinner without wine, Father said, and no man who knew the first thing about it would keep his wine in hot cellars. Mother thought this was a mere whim of Father's. She said he was fussy. How about people who lived in apartments, she asked him, who didn't have cellars? Father replied that civilized persons didn't live in apartments.

One of the first summers that Father ever spent in the country, he rented a furnished house in Irvington on the Hudson, not far from New York. It had a garden, a stable, and one or two acres of woods, and Father arranged to camp out there with many misgivings. He took a train for New York every morning at eight-ten, after breakfast, and he got back between five and six, bringing anything special we might need along with him, such as a basket of peaches from the city, or a fresh package of his own private coffee.

Things went well until one day in August the ice-man didn't come. It was hot, he and his horses were tired, and he hated to come to us anyhow because the house we had rented was perched up on top of a hill. He said afterward that on this particular day he had not liked the idea of making his horses drag the big ice-wagon up that sharp and steep road to sell fifty cents' worth of ice. Besides, all his ice was gone anyhow—the heat had melted it on him. He had four or five other good reasons. So he didn't come.

Father was in town. The rest of us waited in astonishment, wondering what could be the matter. We were so used to the regularity and punctilio of life in the city that it seemed unbelievable to us that the ice-man would fail to appear. We discussed it at lunch. Mother said that the minute he arrived she would have to give him a talking to. After lunch had been over an hour and he still hadn't come, she got so worried about what Father would say that she decided to send to the village.

There was no telephone, of course. There were no motors. She would have liked to spare the horse if she could, for he had been worked hard that week. But as this was a crisis, she sent for Morgan, the coachman, and told him to bring up the dog-cart.

The big English dog-cart arrived. Two of us boys and the coachman drove off. The sun beat down on our heads. Where the heavy harness was rubbing on Brownie's coat, he broke out into a thick, whitish lather. Morgan was sullen. When we boys were along he couldn't take off his stiff black hat or unbutton his thick, padded coat. Worse still, from his point of view, he couldn't stop at a bar for a drink. That was why Mother had sent us along with him, of course, and he knew it.

We arrived at the little town after a while and I went into the Coal & Ice Office. A wiry-looking old clerk was dozing in a corner, his chair tilted back and his chin resting on his dingy shirt-front. I woke this clerk up. I told him about the crisis at our house.

He listened unwillingly, and when I had finished he said it was a very hot day.

I waited. He spat. He said he didn't see what he could do, because the ice-house was locked.

I explained earnestly that this was the Day family and that something must be done right away.

He hunted around his desk a few minutes, found his chewing tobacco, and said, "Well, sonny, I'll see what I can do about it."

I thanked him very much, as that seemed to me to settle the matter. I went back to the dog-cart. Brownie's check-rein had been unhooked, and he stood with his head hanging down. He looked sloppy. It wouldn't have been so bad with a buggy, but a slumpy horse in a dog-cart can look pretty awful. Also, Morgan was gone. He reappeared soon, coming out of a side door down the street, buttoning up his coat, but with his hat tilted back. He looked worse than the horse.

We checked up the weary animal's head again and drove slowly home. A hot little breeze in our rear moved our dust along with us. At the foot of the hill, we boys got out, to spare Brownie our extra weight. We unhooked his check-rein again. He dragged the heavy cart up.

Mother was sitting out on the piazza. I said the ice would come soon now. We waited.

It was a long afternoon.

At five o'clock, Brownie was hitched up again. The coachman

and I drove back to the village. We had to meet Father's train. We also had to break the bad news to him that he would have no ice-water for dinner, and that there didn't seem to be any way to chill his Rhine wine.

The village was as sleepy as ever, but when Father arrived and learned what the situation was, he said it would have to wake up. He told me that he had had a long, trying day at the office, the city was hotter than the Desert of Sahara, and he was completely worn out, but that if any ice-man imagined for a moment he could behave in that manner, he, Father, would take his damned head off. He strode into the Coal & Ice Office.

When he came out, he had the clerk with him, and the clerk had put on his hat and was vainly trying to calm Father down. He was promising that he himself would come with the ice-wagon if the driver had left, and deliver all the ice we could use, and he'd be there inside an hour.

Father said, "Inside of an hour be hanged, you'll have to come quicker than that."

The clerk got rebellious. He pointed out that he'd have to go to the stables and hitch up the horses himself, and then get someone to help him hoist a block of ice out of the ice-house. He said it was 'most time for his supper and he wasn't used to such work. He was only doing it as a favor to Father. He was just being neighborly.

Father said he'd have to be neighborly in a hurry, because he wouldn't stand it, and he didn't know what the devil the ice company meant by such actions.

The clerk said it wasn't his fault, was it? It was the driver's.

This was poor tactics, of course, because it wound Father up again. He wasn't interested in whose fault it was, he said. It was everybody's. What he wanted was ice and plenty of it, and he wanted it in time for his dinner. A small crowd which had collected by this time listened admiringly as Father shook his finger at the clerk and said he dined at six-thirty.

The clerk went loping off toward the stables to hitch up the big horses. Father waited till he'd turned the corner.

Followed by the crowd, Father marched to the butcher's.

After nearly a quarter of an hour, the butcher and his assistant came out, unwillingly carrying what seemed to be a coffin, wrapped in a black mackintosh. It was a huge cake of ice.

Father got in, in front, sat on the box seat beside me, and took up the reins. We drove off. The coachman was on the rear seat, sitting back-to-back to us, keeping the ice from sliding out with the calves of his legs. Father went a few doors up the street to a little house-furnishings shop and got out again.

I went in the shop with him this time. I didn't want to miss any further scenes of this performance. Father began proceedings by demanding to see all the man's ice-boxes. There were only a few. Father selected the largest he had. Then, when the sale seemed arranged, and when the proprietor was smiling broadly with pleasure at this sudden windfall, Father said he was buying that refrigerator only on two conditions.

The first was that it had to be delivered at his home before dinner. Yes, now. Right away. The shopkeeper explained over and over that this was impossible, but that he'd have it up the next morning, sure. Father said no, he didn't want it the next morning, he had to have it at once. He added that he dined at six-thirty, and that there was no time to waste.

The shopkeeper gave in.

The second condition, which was then put to him firmly, was staggering. Father announced that that ice-box must be delivered to him full of ice.

The man said he was not in the ice business.

Father said, "Very well then. I don't want it."

The man said obstinately that it was an excellent ice-box.

Father made a short speech. It was the one we had heard so often at home about the slackness of village tradesmen, and he put such strong emotion and scorn into it that his voice rang through the shop. He closed it by saying, "An ice-box is of no use to a man without ice, and if you haven't the enterprise, the gumption, to sell your damned goods to a customer who wants them delivered in condition to use, you had better shut up your shop and be done with it. Not in the ice business, eh? You aren't in business at all!" He strode out.

The dealer came to the door just as Father was getting into

the dog-cart and called out anxiously, "All right, Mr. Day, I'll get that refrigerator filled for you and send it up right away."

Father drove quickly home. A thunderstorm seemed to be brewing and this had waked Brownie up, or else Father was putting some of his own supply of energy into him. The poor old boy probably needed it as again he climbed the steep hill. I got out at the foot, and as I walked along behind I saw that Morgan was looking kind of desperate trying to sit in the correct position with his arms folded while he held in the ice with his legs. The big cake was continually slipping and sliding around under the seat and doing its best to plunge out. It had bumped against his calves all the way home. They must have got good and cold.

When the dog-cart drew up at our door, Father remained seated a moment while Morgan, the waitress, and I pulled and pushed at the ice. The mackintosh had come off it by this time. We dumped it out on the grass. A little later, after Morgan had unharnessed and hurriedly rubbed down the horse, he ran back to help us boys break the cake up, push the chunks around to the back door, and cram them into the ice-box while Father was dressing for dinner.

Mother had calmed down by this time. The Rhine wine was cooling. "Don't get it too cold," Father called.

Then the ice-man arrived.

The old clerk was with him, like a warden in charge of a prisoner. Mother stepped out to meet them, and at once gave the ice-man the scolding that had been waiting for him all day.

The clerk asked how much ice we wanted. Mother said we didn't want any now. Mr. Day had brought home some, and we had no room for more in the ice-box.

The ice-man looked at the clerk. The clerk tried to speak, but no words came.

Father put his head out of the window. "Take a hundred pounds, Vinnie," he said. "There's another box coming."

A hundred-pound block was brought into the house and heaved into the washtub. The waitress put the mackintosh over it. The ice-wagon left.

Just as we all sat down to dinner, the new ice-box arrived, full.

Mother was provoked. She said "Really, Clare!" crossly. "Now what am I to do with that piece that's waiting out in the washtub?"

Father chuckled.

She told him he didn't know the first thing about keeping house, and went out to the laundry with the waitress to tackle the problem. The thunderstorm broke and crashed. We boys ran around shutting the windows upstairs.

Father's soul was at peace. He dined well, and he had his coffee and cognac served to him on the piazza. The storm was over by then. Father snuffed a deep breath of the sweet-smelling air and smoked his evening cigar.

"Clarence," he said, "King Solomon had the right idea about these things. 'Whatsoever thy hand findeth to do,' Solomon said, 'do thy damnedest.'"

Mother called me inside. "Whose mackintosh is that?" she asked anxiously. "Katie's torn a hole in the back."

I heard Father saying contentedly on the piazza, "I like plenty of ice."

IVY DAY IN THE COMMITTEE ROOM*

BY JAMES JOYCE

OLD JACK raked the cinders together with a piece of cardboard and spread them judiciously over the whitening dome of coals. When the dome was thinly covered his face lapsed into darkness but, as he set himself to fan the fire again, his crouching shadow ascended the opposite wall and his face slowly re-emerged into light. It was an old man's face, very bony and hairy. The moist blue eyes blinked at the fire and the

* from *The Portable James Joyce*

moist mouth fell open at times, munching once or twice mechanically when it closed. When the cinders had caught he laid the piece of cardboard against the wall, sighed and said:

"That's better now, Mr. O'Connor."

Mr. O'Connor, a grey-haired young man, whose face was disfigured by many blotches and pimples, had just brought the tobacco for a cigarette into a shapely cylinder but when spoken to he undid his handiwork meditatively. Then he began to roll the tobacco again meditatively and after a moment's thought decided to lick the paper.

"Did Mr. Tierney say when he'd be back?" he asked in a husky falsetto.

"He didn't say."

Mr. O'Connor put his cigarette into his mouth and began to search his pockets. He took out a pack of thin pasteboard cards.

"I'll get you a match," said the old man.

"Never mind, this'll do," said Mr. O'Connor.

He selected one of the cards and read what was printed on it:

MUNICIPAL ELECTIONS

ROYAL EXCHANGE WARD

Mr. Richard J. Tierney, P.L.G., respectfully solicits the
favour of your vote and influence at the coming election
in the Royal Exchange Ward.

Mr. O'Connor had been engaged by Tierney's agent to canvass one part of the ward but, as the weather was inclement and his boots let in the wet, he spent a great part of the day sitting by the fire in the Committee Room in Wicklow Street with Jack, the old caretaker. They had been sitting thus since the short day had grown dark. It was the sixth of October, dismal and cold out of doors.

Mr. O'Connor tore a strip off the card and, lighting it, lit his cigarette. As he did so the flame lit up a leaf of dark glossy ivy in the lapel of his coat. The old man watched him attentively and then, taking up the piece of cardboard again, began to fan the fire slowly while his companion smoked.

"Ah, yes," he said, continuing, "it's hard to know what way to bring up children. Now who'd think he'd turn out like that! I sent him to the Christian Brothers and I done what I could for him, and there he goes boozing about. I tried to make him someway decent."

He replaced the cardboard wearily.

"Only I'm an old man now I'd change his tune for him. I'd take the stick to his back and beat him while I could stand over him as I done many a time before. The mother, you know, she cocks him up with this and that. . . ."

"That's what ruins children," said Mr. O'Connor.

"To be sure it is," said the old man. "And little thanks you get for it, only impudence. He takes th' upper hand of me whenever he sees I've a sup taken. What's the world coming to when sons speaks that way to their fathers?"

"What age is he?" said Mr. O'Connor.

"Nineteen," said the old man.

"Why don't you put him to something?"

"Sure, amn't I never done at the drunken bowsy ever since he left school? 'I won't keep you,' I says. 'You must get a job for yourself.' But, sure, it's worse whenever he gets a job, he drinks it all."

Mr. O'Connor shook his head in sympathy, and the old man fell silent, gazing into the fire. Someone opened the door of the room and called out:

"Hello! Is this a Freemason's meeting?"

"Who's that?" said the old man.

"What are you doing in the dark?" asked a voice.

"Is that you, Hynes?" asked Mr. O'Connor.

"Yes. What are you doing in the dark?" said Mr. Hynes, advancing into the light of the fire.

He was a tall, slender young man with a light brown moustache. Imminent little drops of rain hung at the brim of his hat and the collar of his jacket-coat was turned up.

"Well, Mat," he said to Mr. O'Connor, "how goes it?"

Mr. O'Connor shook his head. The old man left the hearth, and after stumbling about the room returned with two candlesticks which he thrust one after the other into the fire and carried

to the table. A denuded room came into view and the fire lost all
its cheerful colour. The walls of the room were bare except for a
copy of an election address. In the middle of the room was a
small table on which papers were heaped.

Mr. Hynes leaned against the mantelpiece and asked:

"Has he paid you yet?"

"Not yet," said Mr. O'Connor. "I hope to God he'll not leave
us in the lurch to-night."

Mr. Hynes laughed.

"O, he'll pay you. Never fear," he said.

"I hope he'll look smart about it if he means business," said
Mr. O'Connor.

"What do you think, Jack?" said Mr. Hynes satirically to the
old man.

The old man returned to his seat by the fire, saying:

"It isn't but he has it, anyway. Not like the other tinker."

"What other tinker?" said Mr. Hynes.

"Colgan," said the old man scornfully.

"It is because Colgan's a working-man you say that? What's
the difference between a good honest bricklayer and a publi-
can—eh? Hasn't the working-man as good a right to be in the
Corporation as anyone else—ay, and a better right than those
shoneens that are always hat in hand before any fellow with a
handle to his name? Isn't that so, Mat?" said Mr. Hynes, addressing Mr. O'Connor.

"I think you're right," said Mr. O'Connor.

"One man is a plain honest man with no hunker-sliding
about him. He goes in to represent the labour classes. This fellow you're working for only wants to get some job or other."

"Of course, the working-classes should be represented,"
said the old man.

"The working-man," said Mr. Hynes, "gets all kicks and no
halfpence. But it's labour produces everything. The working-
man is not looking for fat jobs for his sons and nephews and
cousins. The working-man is not going to drag the honour of
Dublin in the mud to please a German monarch."

"How's that?" said the old man.

"Don't you know they want to present an address of welcome to Edward Rex if he comes here next year? What do we want kowtowing to a foreign king?"

"Our man won't vote for the address," said Mr. O'Connor. "He goes in on the Nationalist ticket."

"Won't he?" said Mr. Hynes. "Wait till you see whether he will or not. I know him. Is it Tricky Dicky Tierney?"

"By God! perhaps you're right, Joe," said Mr. O'Connor. "Anyway, I wish he'd turn up with the spondulics."

The three men fell silent. The old man began to rake more cinders together. Mr. Hynes took off his hat, shook it and then turned down the collar of his coat, displaying, as he did so, an ivy leaf in the lapel.

"If this man was alive," he said, pointing to the leaf, "we'd have no talk of an address of welcome."

"That's true," said Mr. O'Connor.

"Musha, God be with them times!" said the old man. "There was some life in it then."

The room was silent again. Then a bustling little man with a snuffling nose and very cold ears pushed in the door. He walked over quickly to the fire, rubbing his hands as if he intended to produce a spark from them.

"No money, boys," he said.

"Sit down here, Mr. Henchy," said the old man, offering him his chair.

"O, don't stir, Jack, don't stir," said Mr. Henchy.

He nodded curtly to Mr. Hynes and sat down on the chair which the old man vacated.

"Did you serve Aungier Street?" he asked Mr. O'Connor.

"Yes," said Mr. O'Connor, beginning to search his pockets for memoranda.

"Did you call on Grimes?"

"I did."

"Well? How does he stand?"

"He wouldn't promise. He said: 'I won't tell anyone what way I'm going to vote.' But I think he'll be all right."

"Why so?"

"He asked me who the nominators were; and I told him. I mentioned Father Burke's name. I think it'll be all right."

Mr. Henchy began to snuffle and to rub his hands over the fire at a terrific speed. Then he said:

"For the love of God, Jack, bring us a bit of coal. There must be some left."

The old man went out of the room.

"It's no go," said Mr. Henchy, shaking his head. "I asked the little shoeboy, but he said: 'O, now, Mr. Henchy, when I see the work going on properly I won't forget you, you may be sure.' Mean little tinker! 'Usha, how could he be anything else?"

"What did I tell you, Mat?" said Mr. Hynes. "Tricky Dicky Tierney."

"O, he's as tricky as they make 'em," said Mr. Henchy. "He hasn't got those little pigs' eyes for nothing. Blast his soul! Couldn't he pay up like a man instead of: 'O, now, Mr. Henchy, I must speak to Mr. Fanning.... I've spent a lot of money'? Mean little schoolboy of hell! I suppose he forgets the time his little old father kept the hand-me-down shop in Mary's Lane."

"But is that a fact?" asked Mr. O'Connor.

"God, yes," said Mr. Henchy. "Did you never hear that? And the men used to go in on Sunday morning before the houses were open to buy a waistcoat or a trousers—moya! But Tricky Dicky's little old father always had a tricky little black bottle up in a corner. Do you mind now? That's that. That's where he first saw the light."

The old man returned with a few lumps of coal which he placed here and there on the fire.

"That's a nice how-do-you-do," said Mr. O'Connor. "How does he expect us to work for him if he won't stump up?"

"I can't help it," said Mr. Henchy. "I expect to find the bailiffs in the hall when I go home."

Mr. Hynes laughed and, shoving himself away from the mantelpiece with the aid of his shoulders, made ready to leave.

"It'll be all right when King Eddie comes," he said. "Well, boys, I'm off for the present. See you later. 'Bye, 'bye."

He went out of the room slowly. Neither Mr. Henchy nor the old man said anything, but, just as the door was closing, Mr. O'Connor, who had been staring moodily into the fire, called out suddenly:

" 'Bye, Joe."

Mr. Henchy waited a few moments and then nodded in the direction of the door.

"Tell me," he said across the fire, "what brings our friend in here? What does he want?"

" 'Usha, poor Joe!" said Mr. O'Connor, throwing the end of his cigarette into the fire, "he's hard up, like the rest of us."

Mr. Henchy snuffled vigorously and spat so copiously that he nearly put out the fire, which uttered a hissing protest.

"To tell you my private and candid opinion," he said, "I think he's a man from the other camp. He's a spy of Colgan's, if you ask me. Just go round and try and find out how they're getting on. They won't suspect you. Do you twig?"

"Ah, poor Joe is a decent skin," said Mr. O'Connor.

"His father was a decent, respectable man," Mr. Henchy admitted. "Poor old Larry Hynes! Many a good turn he did in his day! But I'm greatly afraid our friend is not nineteen carat. Damn it, I can understand a fellow being hard up, but what I can't understand is a fellow sponging. Couldn't he have some spark of manhood about him?"

"He doesn't get a warm welcome from me when he comes," said the old man. "Let him work for his own side and not come spying around here."

"I don't know," said Mr. O'Connor dubiously, as he took out cigarette-papers and tobacco. "I think Joe Hynes is a straight man. He's a clever chap, too, with the pen. Do you remember that thing he wrote . . . ?"

"Some of these hillsiders and fenians are a bit too clever if you ask me," said Mr. Henchy. "Do you know what my private and candid opinion is about some of those little jokers? I believe half of them are in the pay of the Castle."

"There's no knowing," said the old man.

"O, but I know it for a fact," said Mr. Henchy. "They're Castle hacks. . . . I don't say Hynes. . . . No, damn it, I think he's a stroke above that . . . But there's a certain little nobleman with a cock-eye—you know the patriot I'm alluding to?"

Mr. O'Connor nodded.

"There's a lineal descendant of Major Sirr for you if you like!

O, the heart's blood of a patriot! That's a fellow now that'd sell his country for fourpence—ay—and go down on his bended knees and thank the Almighty Christ he had a country to sell."

There was a knock at the door.

"Come in!" said Mr. Henchy.

A person resembling a poor clergyman or a poor actor appeared in the doorway. His black clothes were tightly buttoned on his short body and it was impossible to say whether he wore a clergyman's collar or a layman's, because the collar of his shabby frock-coat, the uncovered buttons of which reflected the candlelight, was turned up about his neck. He wore a round hat of hard black felt. His face, shining with raindrops, had the appearance of damp yellow cheese save where two rosy spots indicated the cheekbones. He opened his very long mouth suddenly to express disappointment and at the same time opened wide his very bright blue eyes to express pleasure and surprise.

"O Father Keon!" said Mr. Henchy, jumping up from his chair. "Is that you? Come in!"

"Oh, no, no, no!" said Father Keon quickly, pursing his lips as if he were addressing a child.

"Won't you come in and sit down?"

"No, no, no!" said Father Keon, speaking in a discreet, indulgent, velvety voice. "Don't let me disturb you now! I'm just looking for Mr. Fanning...."

"He's round at the *Black Eagle*," said Mr. Henchy. "But won't you come in and sit down a minute?"

"No, no, thank you. It was just a little business matter," said Father Keon. "Thank you, indeed."

He retreated from the doorway and Mr. Henchy, seizing one of the candlesticks, went to the door to light him downstairs.

"O, don't trouble, I beg!"

"No, but the stairs is so dark."

"No, no, I can see.... Thank you, indeed."

"Are you right now?"

"All right, thanks.... Thanks."

Mr. Henchy returned with the candlestick and put it on the table. He sat down again at the fire. There was silence for a few moments.

"Tell me, John," said Mr. O'Connor, lighting his cigarette with another pasteboard card.

"Hm?"

"What he is exactly?"

"Ask me an easier one," said Mr. Henchy.

"Fanning and himself seem to me very thick. They're often in Kavanagh's together. Is he a priest at all?"

"'Mmmyes, I believe so.... I think he's what you call a black sheep. We haven't many of them, thank God! but we have a few.... He's an unfortunate man of some kind...."

"And how does he knock it out?" asked Mr. O'Connor.

"That's another mystery."

"Is he attached to any chapel or church or institution or——"

"No," said Mr. Henchy, "I think he's travelling on his own account.... God forgive me," he added, "I thought he was the dozen of stout."

"Is there any chance of a drink itself?" asked Mr. O'Connor.

"I'm dry too," said the old man.

"I asked that little shoeboy three times," said Mr. Henchy, "would he send up a dozen of stout. I asked him again now, but he was leaning on the counter in his shirt-sleeves having a deep goster with Alderman Cowley."

"Why didn't you remind him?" said Mr. O'Connor.

"Well, I couldn't go over while he was talking to Alderman Cowley. I just waited till I caught his eye, and said: 'About that little matter I was speaking to you about....' 'That'll be all right, Mr. H.,' he said. Yerra, sure the little hop-o'-my-thumb has forgotten all about it."

"There's some deal on in that quarter," said Mr. O'Connor thoughtfully. "I saw the three of them hard at it yesterday at Suffolk Street corner."

"I think I know the little game they're at," said Mr. Henchy. "You must owe the City Fathers money nowadays if you want to be made Lord Mayor. Then they'll make you Lord Mayor. By God! I'm thinking seriously of becoming a City Father my-self. What do you think? Would I do for the job?"

Mr. O'Connor laughed.

"So far as owing money goes...."

"Driving out of the Mansion House," said Mr. Henchy, "in all my vermin, with Jack here standing up behind me in a powdered wig—eh?"

"And make me your private secretary, John."

"Yes. And I'll make Father Keon my private chaplain. We'll have a family party."

"Faith, Mr. Henchy," said the old man, "you'd keep up better style than some of them. I was talking one day to old Keegan, the porter. 'And how do you like your new master, Pat?' says I to him. 'You haven't much entertaining now,' says I. 'Entertaining!' says he. 'He'd live on the smell of an oil-rag.' And do you know what he told me? Now, I declare to God, I didn't believe him."

"What?" said Mr. Henchy and Mr. O'Connor.

"He told me: 'What do you think of a Lord Mayor of Dublin sending out for a pound of chops for his dinner? How's that for high living?' says he. 'Wisha! wisha!,' says I. 'A pound of chops,' says he, 'coming into the Mansion House.' 'Wisha!' says I, 'what kind of people is going at all now?'"

At this point there was a knock at the door, and a boy put in his head.

"What is it?" said the old man.

"From the *Black Eagle,*" said the boy, walking in sideways and depositing a basket on the floor with a noise of shaken bottles.

The old man helped the boy to transfer the bottles from the basket to the table and counted the full tally. After the transfer the boy put his basket on his arm and asked:

"Any bottles?"

"What bottles?" said the old man.

"Won't you let us drink them first?" said Mr. Henchy.

"I was told to ask for bottles."

"Come back to-morrow," said the old man.

"Here, boy!" said Mr. Henchy, "will you run over to O'Farrell's and ask him to lend us a corkscrew—for Mr. Henchy, say. Tell him we won't keep it a minute. Leave the basket there."

The boy went out and Mr. Henchy began to rub his hands cheerfully, saying:

"Ah, well, he's not so bad after all. He's as good as his word, anyhow."

"There's no tumblers," said the old man.

"O, don't let that trouble you, Jack," said Mr. Henchy. "Many's the good man before now drank out of the bottle."

"Anyway, it's better than nothing," said Mr. O'Connor.

"He's not a bad sort," said Mr. Henchy, "only Fanning has such a loan of him. He means well, you know, in his own tinpot way."

The boy came back with the corkscrew. The old man opened three bottles and was handing back the corkscrew when Mr. Henchy said to the boy.

"Would you like a drink, boy?"

"If you please, sir," said the boy.

The old man opened another bottle grudgingly, and handed it to the boy.

"What age are you?" he asked.

"Seventeen," said the boy.

As the old man said nothing further, the boy took the bottle, said: "Here's my best respects, sir, to Mr. Henchy," drank the contents, put the bottle back on the table and wiped his mouth with his sleeve. Then he took up the cork-screw and went out of the door sideways, muttering some form of salutation.

"That's the way it begins," said the old man.

"The thin edge of the wedge," said Mr. Henchy.

The old man distributed the three bottles which he had opened and the men drank from them simultaneously. After having drank each placed his bottle on the mantelpiece within hand's reach and drew in a long breath of satisfaction.

"Well, I did a good day's work to-day," said Mr. Henchy, after a pause.

"That so, John?"

"Yes. I got him one or two sure things in Dawson Street, Crofton and myself. Between ourselves, you know, Crofton (he's a decent chap, of course), but he's not worth a damn as a canvasser. He hasn't a word to throw to a dog. He stands and looks at the people while I do the talking."

Here two men entered the room. One of them was a very fat

man, whose blue serge clothes seemed to be in danger of falling from his sloping figure. He had a big face which resembled a young ox's face in expression, staring blue eyes and a grizzled moustache. The other man, who was much younger and frailer, had a thin, clean-shaven face. He wore a very high double collar and a wide-brimmed bowler hat.

"Hello, Crofton!" said Mr. Henchy to the fat man. "Talk of the devil..."

"Where did the booze come from?" asked the young man. "Did the cow calve?"

"O, of course, Lyons spots the drink first thing!" said Mr. O'Connor, laughing.

"Is that the way you chaps canvass," said Mr. Lyons, "and Crofton and I out in the cold and rain looking for votes?"

"Why, blast your soul," said Mr. Henchy, "I'd get more votes in five minutes than you two'd get in a week."

"Open two bottles of stout, Jack," said Mr. O'Connor.

"How can I?" said the old man, "when there's no corkscrew?"

"Wait now, wait now!" said Mr. Henchy, getting up quickly. "Did you ever see this little trick?"

He took two bottles from the table and, carrying them to the fire, put them on the hob. Then he sat down again by the fire and took another drink from his bottle. Mr. Lyons sat on the edge of the table, pushed his hat towards the nape of his neck and began to swing his legs.

"Which is my bottle?" he asked.

"This lad," said Mr. Henchy.

Mr. Crofton sat down on a box and looked fixedly at the other bottle on the hob. He was silent for two reasons. The first reason, sufficient in itself, was that he had nothing to say; the second reason was that he considered his companions beneath him. He had been a canvasser for Wilkins, the Conservative, but when the Conservatives had withdrawn their man and, choosing the lesser of two evils, given their support to the Nationalist candidate, he had been engaged to work for Mr. Tierney.

In a few minutes an apologetic "Pok!" was heard as the cork flew out of Mr. Lyons' bottle. Mr. Lyons jumped off the table, went to the fire, took his bottle and carried it back to the table.

"I was just telling them, Crofton," said Mr. Henchy, "that we got a good few votes to-day."

"Who did you get?" asked Mr. Lyons.

"Well, I got Parkes for one, and I got Atkinson for two, and I got Ward of Dawson Street. Fine old chap he is, too—regular old toff, old Conservative! 'But isn't your candidate a Nationalist?' said he. 'He's a respectable man,' said I. 'He's in favour of whatever will benefit this country. He's a big ratepayer,' I said. 'He has extensive house property in the city and three places of business and isn't it to his own advantage to keep down the rates? He's a prominent and respected citizen,' said I, 'and a Poor Law Guardian, and he doesn't belong to any party, good, bad, or indifferent.' That's the way to talk to 'em."

"And what about the address to the King?" said Mr. Lyons, after drinking and smacking his lips.

"Listen to me," said Mr. Henchy. "What we want in this country, as I said to old Ward, is capital. The King's coming here will mean an influx of money into this country. The citizens of Dublin will benefit by it. Look at all the factories down by the quays there, idle! Look at all the money there is in the country if we only worked the old industries, the mills, the shipbuilding yards and factories. It's capital we want."

"But look here, John," said Mr. O'Connor. "Why should we welcome the King of England? Didn't Parnell himself . . ."

"Parnell," said Mr. Henchy, "is dead. Now, here's the way I look at it. Here's this chap come to the throne after his old mother keeping him out of it till the man was grey. He's a man of the world, and he means well by us. He's a jolly fine decent fellow, if you ask me, and no damn nonsense about him. He just says to himself: 'The old one never went to see these wild Irish. By Christ, I'll go myself and see what they're like.' And are we going to insult the man when he comes over here on a friendly visit? Eh? Isn't that right, Crofton?"

"But after all now," said Mr. Lyons argumentatively, "King Edward's life, you know, is not the very . . ."

"Let bygones be bygones," said Mr. Henchy. "I admire the man personally. He's just an ordinary knockabout like you and me. He's fond of his glass of grog and he's a bit of a rake, perhaps, and he's a good sportsman. Damn it, can't we Irish play fair?"

"That's all very fine," said Mr. Lyons. "But look at the case of Parnell now."

"In the name of God," said Mr. Henchy, "where's the analogy between the two cases?"

"What I mean," said Mr. Lyons, "is we have our ideals. Why, now, would we welcome a man like that? Do you think now after what he did Parnell was a fit man to lead us? And why, then, would we do it for Edward the Seventh?"

"This is Parnell's anniversary," said Mr. O'Connor, "and don't let us stir up any bad blood. We all respect him now that he's dead and gone—even the Conservatives," he added, turning to Mr. Crofton.

Pok! The tardy cork flew out of Mr. Crofton's bottle. Mr. Crofton got up from his box and went to the fire. As he returned with his capture he said in a deep voice:

"Our side of the house respects him, because he was a gentleman."

"Right you are, Crofton!" said Mr. Henchy fiercely. "He was the only man that could keep that bag of cats in order. 'Down, ye dogs! Lie down, ye curs!' That's the way he treated them. Come in Joe! Come in!" he called out, catching sight of Mr. Hynes in the doorway.

Mr. Hynes came in slowly.

"Open another bottle of stout, Jack," said Mr. Henchy. "O, I forgot there's no corkscrew! Here, show me one here and I'll put it at the fire."

The old man handed him another bottle and he placed it on the hob.

"Sit down, Joe," said Mr. O'Conner, "we're just talking about the Chief."

"Ay, ay!" said Mr. Henchy.

Mr. Hynes sat on the side of the table near Mr. Lyons but said nothing.

"There's one of them, anyhow," said Mr. Henchy, "that didn't renege him. By God, I'll say for you, Joe! No, by God, you stuck to him like a man!"

"O, Joe," said Mr. O'Connor suddenly. "Give us that thing you wrote—do you remember? Have you got it on you?"

"O, ay!" said Mr. Henchy. "Give us that. Did you ever hear that, Crofton? Listen to this now: splendid thing."

"Go on," said Mr. O'Connor. "Fire away, Joe."

Mr. Hynes did not seem to remember at once the piece to which they were alluding, but, after reflecting a while, he said:

"O, that thing is it.... Sure, that's old now."

"Out with it, man!" said Mr. O'Connor.

"'Sh, 'sh," said Mr. Henchy. "Now, Joe!"

Mr. Hynes hesitated a little longer. Then amid the silence he took off his hat, laid it on the table and stood up. He seemed to be rehearsing the piece in his mind. After a rather long pause he announced:

THE DEATH OF PARNELL

6TH OCTOBER, 1891

He cleared his throat once or twice and then began to recite:

He is dead. Our Uncrowned King is dead.
Oh, Erin, mourn with grief and woe
For he lies dead whom the fell gang
Of modern hypocrites laid low.

He lies slain by the coward hounds
He raised to glory from the mire;
And Erin's hopes and Erin's dreams
Perish upon her monarch's pyre.

In palace, cabin or in cot
The Irish heart where'er it be
Is bowed with woe—for he is gone
Who would have wrought her destiny.

He would have had his Erin famed,
The green flag gloriously unfurled,
Her statesmen, bards and warriors raised
Before the nations of the World.

He dreamed (alas, 'twas but a dream!)
Of Liberty: but as he strove
To clutch that idol, treachery
Sundered him from the thing he loved.

Shame on the coward, caitiff hands
That smote their Lord or with a kiss
Betrayed him to the rabble-rout
Of fawning priests—no friends of his.

May everlasting shame consume
The memory of those who tried
To befoul and smear the exalted name
Of one who spurned them in his pride.

He fell as fall the mighty ones,
Nobly undaunted to the last,
And death has now united him
With Erin's heroes of the past.

No sound of strife disturb his sleep!
Calmly he rests: no human pain
Or high ambition spurs him now
The peaks of glory to attain.

They had their way: they laid him low.
But Erin, list, his spirit may
Rise, like the Phoenix from the flames,
When breaks the dawning of the day,

The day that brings us Freedom's reign.
And on that day may Erin well
Pledge in the cup she lifts to Joy
One grief—the memory of Parnell.

Mr. Hynes sat down again on the table. When he had finished his recitation there was a silence and then a burst of clapping: even Mr. Lyons clapped. The applause continued for a little time. When it had ceased all the auditors drank from their bottles in silence.

Pok! The cork flew out of Mr. Hynes' bottle, but Mr. Hynes

remained sitting flushed and bareheaded on the table. He did not seem to have heard the invitation.

"Good man, Joe!" said Mr. O'Connor, taking out his cigarette papers and pouch the better to hide his emotion.

"What do you think of that, Crofton?" cried Mr. Henchy. "Isn't that fine? What?"

Mr. Crofton said that it was a very fine piece of writing.

THE CHRYSANTHEMUMS*

BY JOHN STEINBECK

THE HIGH grey-flannel fog of winter closed off the Salinas Valley from the sky and from all the rest of the world. On every side it sat like a lid on the mountains and made of the great valley a closed pot. On the broad, level land floor the gang plows bit deep and left the black earth shining like metal where the shares had cut. On the foothill ranches across the Salinas River, the yellow stubble fields seemed to be bathed in pale cold sunshine, but there was no sunshine in the valley now in December. The thick willow scrub along the river flamed with sharp and positive yellow leaves.

It was a time of quiet and of waiting. The air was cold and tender. A light wind blew up from the southwest so that the farmers were mildly hopeful of a good rain before long; but fog and rain do not go together.

Across the river, on Henry Allen's foothill ranch there was little work to be done, for the hay was cut and stored and the orchards were plowed up to receive the rain deeply when it should come. The cattle on the higher slopes were becoming shaggy and rough-coated.

Elisa Allen, working in her flower garden, looked down

* from *The Portable John Steinbeck*

across the yard and saw Henry, her husband, talking to two men in business suits. The three of them stood by the tractor shed, each man with one foot on the side of the little Fordson. They smoked cigarettes and studied the machine as they talked.

Elisa watched them for a moment and then went back to her work. She was thirty-five. Her face was lean and strong and her eyes were as clear as water. Her figure looked blocked and heavy in her gardening costume, a man's black hat pulled low down over her eyes, clod-hopper shoes, a figured print dress almost completely covered by a big corduroy apron with four big pockets to hold the snips, the trowel and scratcher, the seeds and the knife she worked with. She wore heavy leather gloves to protect her hands while she worked.

She was cutting down the old year's chrysanthemum stalks with a pair of short and powerful scissors. She looked down toward the men by the tractor shed now and then. Her face was eager and mature and handsome; even her work with the scissors was over-eager, over-powerful. The chrysanthemum stems seemed too small and easy for her energy.

She brushed a cloud of hair out of her eyes with the back of her glove, and left a smudge of earth on the cheek in doing it. Behind her stood the neat white farm house with red geraniums close-banked around it as high as the windows. It was a hard-swept looking little house, with hard-polished windows, and a clean mud-mat on the front steps.

Elisa cast another glance toward the tractor shed. The strangers were getting into their Ford coupe. She took off a glove and put her strong fingers down into the forest of new green chrysanthemum sprouts that were growing around the old roots. She spread the leaves and looked down among the close-growing stems. No aphids were there, no sowbugs or snails or cutworms. Her terrier fingers destroyed such pests before they could get started.

Elisa started at the sound of her husband's voice. He had come near quietly, and he leaned over the wire fence that protected her flower garden from cattle and dogs and chickens.

"At it again," he said. "You've got a strong new crop coming."

Elisa straightened her back and pulled on the gardening

glove again. "Yes. They'll be strong this coming year." In her tone and on her face there was a little smugness.

"You've got a gift with things," Henry observed. "Some of those yellow chrysanthemums you had this year were ten inches across. I wish you'd work out in the orchard and raise some apples that big."

Her eyes sharpened. "Maybe I could do it, too. I've a gift with things, all right. My mother had it. She could stick anything in the ground and make it grow. She said it was having planters' hands that knew how to do it."

"Well, it sure works with flowers," he said.

"Henry, who were those men you were talking to?"

"Why, sure, that's what I came to tell you. They were from the Western Meat Company. I sold those thirty head of three-year-old steers. Got nearly my own price, too."

"Good," she said. "Good for you."

"And I thought," he continued, "I thought how it's Saturday afternoon, and we might go into Salinas for dinner at a restaurant, and then to a picture show—to celebrate, you see."

"Good," she repeated. "Oh, yes. That will be good."

Henry put on his joking tone. "There's fights tonight. How'd you like to go to the fights?"

"Oh, no," she said breathlessly. "No, I wouldn't like fights."

"Just fooling, Elisa. We'll go to a movie. Let's see. It's two now. I'm going to take Scotty and bring down those steers from the hill. It'll take us maybe two hours. We'll go in town about five and have dinner at the Cominos Hotel. Like that?"

"Of course I'll like it. It's good to eat away from home."

"All right, then. I'll go get up a couple of horses."

She said, "I'll have plenty of time to transplant some of these sets, I guess."

She heard her husband calling Scotty down by the barn. And a little later she saw the two men ride up the pale yellow hillside in search of the steers.

There was a little square sandy bed kept for rooting the chrysanthemums. With her trowel she turned the soil over and over, and smoothed it and patted it firm. Then she dug ten parallel trenches to receive the sets. Back at the chrysanthemum bed she pulled out the little crisp shoots, trimmed off the leaves of each one with her scissors and laid it on a small orderly pile.

A squeak of wheels and plod of hoofs came from the road. Elisa looked up. The country road ran along the dense bank of willows and cottonwoods that bordered the river, and up this road came a curious vehicle, curiously drawn. It was an old spring-wagon, with a round canvas top on it like the cover of a prairie schooner. It was drawn by an old bay horse and a little grey-and-white burro. A big stubble-bearded man sat between the cover flaps and drove the crawling team. Underneath the wagon, between the hind wheels, a lean and rangy mongrel dog walked sedately. Words were painted on the canvas in clumsy, crooked letters. "Pots, pans, knives, sisors, lawn mores. Fixed." Two rows of articles and the triumphantly definitive "Fixed" below. The black paint had run down in little sharp points beneath each letter.

Elisa, squatting on the ground, watched to see the crazy, loose-jointed wagon pass by. But it didn't pass. It turned into the farm road in front of her house, crooked old wheels skirling and squeaking. The rangy dog darted from between the wheels and ran ahead. Instantly the two ranch shepherds flew out at him. Then all three stopped, and with stiff and quivering tails, with taut straight legs, with ambassadorial dignity, they slowly circled, sniffing daintily. The caravan pulled up to Elisa's wire fence and stopped. Now the newcomer dog, feeling outnumbered, lowered his tail and retired under the wagon with raised hackles and bared teeth.

The man on the wagon seat called out. "That's a bad dog in a fight when he gets started."

Elisa laughed. "I see he is. How soon does he generally get started?"

The man caught up her laughter and echoed it heartily. "Sometimes not for weeks and weeks," he said. He climbed stiffly down, over the wheel. The horse and the donkey drooped like unwatered flowers.

Elisa saw that he was a very big man. Although his hair and beard were greying, he did not look old. His worn black suit was wrinkled and spotted with grease. The laughter had disappeared from his face and eyes the moment his laughing voice ceased. His eyes were dark, and they were full of the brooding that gets in the eyes of teamsters and of sailors. The calloused hands he rested on the wire fence were cracked, and every crack was a black line. He took off his battered hat.

"I'm off my general road, ma'am," he said. "Does this dirt road cut over across the river to the Los Angeles highway?"

Elisa stood up and shoved the thick scissors in her apron pocket. "Well, yes, it does, but it winds around and then fords the river. I don't think your team could pull through the sand."

He replied with some asperity, "It might surprise you what them beasts can pull through."

"When they get started?" she asked.

He smiled for a second. "Yes. When they get started."

"Well," said Elisa, "I think you'll save time if you go back to the Salinas road and pick up the highway there."

He drew a big finger down the chicken wire and made it sing. "I ain't in any hurry, ma'am. I go from Seattle to San Diego and back every year. Takes all my time. About six months each way. I aim to follow nice weather."

Elisa took off her gloves and stuffed them in the apron pocket with the scissors. She touched the under edge of her man's hat, searching for fugitive hairs. "That sounds like a nice kind of a way to live," she said.

He leaned confidentially over the fence. "Maybe you noticed the writing on my wagon. I mend pots and sharpen knives and scissors. You got any of them things to do?"

"Oh, no," she said quickly. "Nothing like that." Her eyes hardened with resistance.

"Scissors is the worst thing," he explained. "Most people just ruin scissors trying to sharpen 'em, but I know how. I got a special tool. It's a little bobbit kind of thing, and patented. But it sure does the trick."

"No. My scissors are all sharp."

"All right, then. Take a pot," he continued earnestly, "a bent pot, or a pot with a hole. I can make it like new so you don't have to buy no new ones. That's a saving for you."

"No," she said shortly. "I tell you I have nothing like that for you to do."

His face fell to an exaggerated sadness. His voice took on a whining undertone. "I ain't had a thing to do today. Maybe I won't have no supper tonight. You see I'm off my regular road. I know folks on the highway clear from Seattle to San Diego. They save their things for me to sharpen up because they know I do it so good and save them money."

"I'm sorry," Elisa said irritably. "I haven't anything for you to do."

His eyes left her face and fell to searching the ground. They roamed about until they came to the chrysanthemum bed where she had been working. "What's them plants, ma'am?"

The irritation and resistance melted from Elisa's face. "Oh, those are chrysanthemums, giant whites and yellows. I raise them every year, bigger than anybody around here."

"Kind of a long-stemmed flower? Looks like a quick puff of colored smoke?" he asked.

"That's it. What a nice way to describe them."

"They smell kind of nasty till you get used to them," he said.

"It's a good bitter smell," she retorted, "not nasty at all."

He changed his tone quickly. "I like the smell myself."

"I had ten-inch blooms this year," she said.

The man leaned farther over the fence. "Look. I know a lady down the road a piece, has got the nicest garden you ever seen. Got nearly every kind of flower but no chrysanthemums. Last time I was mending a copper-bottom washtub for her (that's a hard job but I do it good), she said to me, 'If you ever run acrost some nice chrysanthemums I wish you'd try to get me a few seeds.' That's what she told me."

Elisa's eyes grew alert and eager. "She couldn't have known much about chrysanthemums. You can raise them from seed, but it's much easier to root the little sprouts you see there."

"Oh," he said. "I s'pose I can't take none to her, then."

"Why yes you can," Elisa cried. "I can put some in damp sand, and you can carry them right along with you. They'll take root in the pot if you keep them damp. And then she can transplant them."

"She'd sure like to have some, ma'am. You say they're nice ones?"

"Beautiful," she said. "Oh, beautiful." Her eyes shone. She tore off the battered hat and shook out her dark pretty hair. "I'll put them in a flower pot, and you can take them right with you. Come into the yard."

While the man came through the picket gate Elisa ran excitedly along the geranium-bordered path to the back of the house. And she returned carrying a big red flower pot. The gloves were forgotten now. She kneeled on the ground by the starting bed and dug up the sandy soil with her fingers and scooped it into the bright new flower pot. Then she picked up the little pile of shoots she had prepared. With her strong fingers she pressed them into the sand and tamped around them with her knuckles. The man stood over her. "I'll tell you what to do," she said. "You remember so you can tell the lady."

"Yes, I'll try to remember."

"Well, look. These will take root in about a month. Then she must set them out, about a foot apart in good rich earth like this, see?" She lifted a handful of dark soil for him to look at. "They'll grow fast and tall. Now remember this. In July tell her to cut them down, about eight inches from the ground.'

"Before they bloom?" he asked.

"Yes, before they bloom." Her face was tight with eagerness. "They'll grow right up again. About the last of September the buds will start."

She stopped and seemed perplexed. "It's the budding that takes the most care," she said hesitantly. "I don't know how to tell you." She looked deep into his eyes, searchingly. Her mouth opened a little, and she seemed to be listening. "I'll try to tell you," she said. "Did you ever hear of planting hands?"

"Can't say I have, ma'am."

"Well, I can only tell you what it feels like. It's when you're picking off the buds you don't want. Everything goes right down into your finger-tips. You watch your fingers work. They do it themselves. You can feel how it is. They pick and pick the buds. They never make a mistake. They're with the plant. Do you see? Your fingers and the plant. You can feel that, right up your arm. They know. They never make a mistake. You can feel it. When you're like that you can't do anything wrong. Do you see that? Can you understand that?"

She was kneeling on the ground looking up at him. Her breast swelled passionately.

The man's eyes narrowed. He looked away self-consciously. "Maybe I know," he said. "Sometimes in the night in the wagon there——"

Elisa's voice grew husky. She broke in on him. "I've never lived as you do, but I know what you mean. When the night is dark—why, the stars are sharp-pointed, and there's quiet. Why, you rise up and up! Every pointed star gets driven into your body. It's like that. Hot and sharp and—lovely."

Kneeling there, her hand went out toward his legs in the greasy black trousers. Her hesitant fingers almost touched the cloth. Then her hand dropped to the ground. She crouched low like a fawning dog.

He said, "It's nice, just like you say. Only when you don't have no dinner, it ain't."

She stood up then, very straight, and her face was ashamed. She held the flower pot out to him and placed it gently in his arms. "Here. Put it in your wagon, on the seat, where you can watch it. Maybe I can find something for you to do."

At the back of the house she dug in the can pile and found two old and battered aluminum saucepans. She carried them back and gave them to him. "Here, maybe you can fix these."

His manner changed. He became professional. "Good as new I can fix them." At the back of his wagon he set a little anvil, and out of an oily tool box dug a small machine hammer. Elisa came through the gate to watch him while he pounded out the dents in the kettles. His mouth grew sure and knowing. At a difficult part of the work he sucked his under-lip.

"You sleep right in the wagon?" Elisa asked.

"Right in the wagon, ma'am. Rain or shine I'm dry as a cow in there."

"It must be nice," she said. "It must be very nice. I wish women could do such things."

"It ain't the right kind of a life for a woman."

Her upper lip raised a little, showing her teeth. "How do you know? How can you tell?" she said.

"I don't know, ma'am," he protested. "Of course I don't know. Now here's your kettles, done. You don't have to buy no new ones."

"How much?"

"Oh, fifty cents'll do. I keep my prices down and my work good. That's why I have all them satisfied customers up and down the highway."

Elisa brought him a fifty-cent piece from the house and dropped it in his hand. "You might be surprised to have a rival some time. I can sharpen scissors, too. And I can beat the dents out of little pots. I could show you what a woman might do."

He put his hammer back in the oily box and shoved the little anvil out of sight. "It would be a lonely life for a woman, ma'am, and a scarey life, too, with animals creeping under the wagon all night." He climbed over the single-tree, steadying himself with a hand on the burro's white rump. He settled himself in the seat, picked up the lines. "Thank you kindly, ma'am," he said. "I'll do like you told me; I'll go back and catch the Salinas road."

"Mind," she called, "if you're long in getting there, keep the sand damp."

"Sand, ma'am?... Sand? Oh, sure. You mean around the chrysanthemums. Sure I will." He clucked his tongue. The beasts leaned luxuriously into their collars. The mongrel dog took his place between the back wheels. The wagon turned and crawled out the entrance road and back the way it had come, along the river.

Elisa stood in front of her wire fence watching the slow progress of the caravan. Her shoulders were straight, her head thrown back, her eyes half-closed, so that the scene came vaguely into them. Her lips moved silently, forming the words "Good-bye—good-bye." Then she whispered, "That's a bright direction. There's a glowing there." The sound of her whisper startled her. She shook herself free and looked about to see whether anyone had been listening. Only the dogs had heard. They lifted their heads toward her from their sleeping in the dust, and then stretched out their chins and settled asleep again. Elisa turned and ran hurriedly into the house.

In the kitchen she reached behind the stove and felt the water tank. It was full of hot water from the noonday cooking. In the bathroom she tore off her soiled clothes and flung them into the corner. And then she scrubbed herself with a little block of pumice, legs and thighs, loins and chest and arms, until her skin was scratched and red. When she had dried herself she stood in front of a mirror in her bedroom and looked at her body. She tightened her stomach and threw out her chest. She turned and looked over her shoulder at her back.

After a while she began to dress, slowly. She put on her newest under-clothing and her nicest stockings and the dress which was the symbol of her prettiness. She worked carefully on her hair, pencilled her eyebrows and rouged her lips.

Before she was finished she heard the little thunder of hoofs and the shouts of Henry and his helper as they drove the red steers into the corral. She heard the gate bang shut and set herself for Henry's arrival.

His step sounded on the porch. He entered the house calling, "Elisa, where are you?"

"In my room, dressing. I'm not ready. There's hot water for your bath. Hurry up. It's getting late."

When she heard him splashing in the tub, Elisa laid his dark suit on the bed, and shirt and socks and tie beside it. She stood his polished shoes on the floor beside the bed. Then she went to the porch and sat primly and stiffly down. She looked toward the river road where the willow-line was still yellow with frosted leaves so that under the high grey fog they seemed a thin band of sunshine. This was the only color in the grey afternoon. She sat unmoving for a long time. Her eyes blinked rarely.

Henry came banging out of the door, shoving his tie inside his vest as he came. Elisa stiffened and her face grew tight. Henry stopped short and looked at her. "Why—why, Elisa. You look so nice!"

"Nice? You think I look nice? What do you mean by 'nice'?"

Henry blundered on. "I don't know. I mean you look different, strong and happy."

"I am strong? Yes, strong. What do you mean 'strong'?"

He looked bewildered. "You're playing some kind of a game," he said helplessly. "It's a kind of a play. You look strong enough to break a calf over your knee, happy enough to eat it like a watermelon."

For a second she lost her rigidity. "Henry! Don't talk like that. You didn't know what you said." She grew complete again. "I'm strong," she boasted. "I never knew before how strong."

Henry looked down toward the tractor shed, and when he brought his eyes back to her, they were his own again. "I'll get out the car. You can put on your coat while I'm starting."

Elisa went into the house. She heard him drive to the gate and idle down his motor, and then she took a long time to put on her hat. She pulled it here and pressed it there. When Henry turned the motor off she slipped into her coat and went out.

The little roadster bounced along on the dirt road by the river, raising the birds and driving the rabbits into the brush. Two cranes flapped heavily over the willow-line and dropped into the river-bed.

Far ahead on the road Elisa saw a dark speck. She knew.

She tried not to look as they passed it, but her eyes would not obey. She whispered to herself sadly, "He might have thrown them off the road. That wouldn't have been much trouble, not very much. But he kept the pot," she explained. "He had to keep the pot. That's why he couldn't get them off the road."

The roadster turned a bend and she saw the caravan ahead. She swung full around toward her husband so she could not see the little covered wagon and the mismatched team as the car passed them.

In a moment it was over. The thing was done. She did not look back. She said loudly, to be heard above the motor, "It will be good, tonight, a good dinner."

"Now you're changed again," Henry complained. He took one hand from the wheel and patted her knee. "I ought to take you in to dinner oftener. It would be good for both of us. We get so heavy out on the ranch."

"Henry," she asked, "could we have wine at dinner?"

"Sure we could. Say! That will be fine."

She was silent for a while; then she said, "Henry, at those prize fights, do the men hurt each other very much?"

"Sometimes a little, not often. Why?"

"Well, I've read how they break noses, and blood runs down their chests. I've read how the fighting gloves get heavy and soggy with blood."

He looked around at her. "What's the matter, Elisa? I didn't know you read things like that." He brought the car to a stop, then turned to the right over the Salinas River bridge.

"Do any women ever go to the fights?" she asked.

"Oh, sure, some. What's the matter, Elisa? Do you want to go? I don't think you'd like it, but I'll take you if you really want to go."

She relaxed limply in the seat. "Oh, no. No. I don't want to go. I'm sure I don't." Her face was turned away from him. "It will be enough if we can have wine. It will be plenty." She turned up her coat collar so he could not see that she was crying weakly—like an old woman.

THE DOOR *

BY E. B. WHITE

EVERYTHING (HE kept saying) is something it isn't. And everybody is always somewhere else. Maybe it was the city, being in the city, that made him feel how queer everything was and that it was something else. Maybe (he kept thinking) it was the names of the things. The names were tex and frequently koid. Or they were flex and oid, or they were duroid (sani) or flexsan (duro), but everything was glass (but not quite

* from The New Yorker

glass) and the thing that you touched (the surface, washable, crease-resistant) was rubber, only it wasn't quite rubber and you didn't quite touch it but almost. The wall, which was glass but thrutex, turned out on being approached not to be a wall, it was something else, it was an opening or doorway—and the doorway (through which he saw himself approaching) turned out to be something else, it was a wall. And what he had eaten not having agreed with him.

He was in a washable house, but he wasn't sure. Now about those rats, he kept saying to himself. He meant the rats that the Professor had driven crazy by forcing them to deal with problems which were beyond the scope of rats, the insoluble problems. He meant the rats that had been trained to jump at the square card with the circle in the middle, and the card (because it was something it wasn't) would give way and let the rat into a place where the food was, but then one day it would be a trick played on the rat, and the card would be changed, and the rat would jump but the card wouldn't give way, and it was an impossible situation (for a rat) and the rat would go insane and into its eyes would come the unspeakably bright imploring look of the frustrated, and after the convulsions were over and the frantic racing around, then the passive stage would set in and the willingness to let anything be done to it, even if it was something else.

He didn't know which door (or wall) or opening in the house to jump at, to get through, because one was an opening that wasn't a door (it was a void, or koid) and the other was a wall that wasn't an opening, it was a sanitary cupboard of the same color. He caught a glimpse of his eyes staring into his eyes, in the thrutex, and in them was the expression he had seen in the picture of the rats—weary after convulsions and the frantic racing around, when they were willing and did not mind having anything done to them. More and more (he kept saying) I am confronted by a problem which is incapable of solution (for this time even if he chose the right door, there would be no food behind it) and that is what madness is, and things seeming different from what they are. He heard, in the house where he was, in the city to which he had gone (as toward a door which might, or might not, give way), a noise—not a loud noise but

more of a low prefabricated humming. It came from a place in
the base of the wall (or stat) where the flue carrying the filter-
able air was, and not far from the Minipiano, which was made
of the same material nail-brushes are made of, and which was
under the stairs. "This, too, has been tested," she said, pointing,
but not at it, "and found viable." It wasn't a loud noise, he kept
thinking, sorry that he had seen his eyes, even though it was
through his own eyes that he had seen them.

First will come the convulsions (he said), then the exhaustion, then the willingness to let anything be done. "And you
better believe it *will* be."

All his life he had been confronted by situations which were
incapable of being solved, and there was a deliberateness behind all this, behind this changing of the card (or door), because they would always wait till you had learned to jump at the
certain card (or door)—the one with the circle—and then they
would change it on you. There have been so many doors
changed on me, he said, in the last twenty years, but it is now
becoming clear that it is an impossible situation, and the question is whether to jump again, even though they ruffle you in
the rump with a blast of air—to make you jump. He wished he
wasn't standing by the Minipiano. First they would teach you
the prayers and the Psalms, and that would be the right door
(the one with the circle), and the long sweet words with the
holy sound, and that would be the one to jump at to get where
the food was. Then one day you jumped and it didn't give way,
so that all you got was the bump on the nose, and the first bewilderment, the first young bewilderment.

I don't know whether to tell her about the door they substituted or not, he said, the one with the equation on it and the picture of the amoeba reproducing itself by division. Or the one
with the photostatic copy of the check for thirty-two dollars
and fifty cents. But the jumping was so long ago, although the
bump is...how those old wounds hurt! Being crazy this way
wouldn't be so bad if only, if only. If only when you put your
foot forward to take a step, the ground wouldn't come up to
meet your foot the way it does. And the same way in the street
(only I may never get back to the street unless I jump at the

right door), the curb coming up to meet your foot, anticipating ever so delicately the weight of the body, which is somewhere else. "We could take your name," she said, "and send it to you." And it wouldn't be so bad if only you could read a sentence all the way through without jumping (your eye) to something else on the same page; and then (he kept thinking) there was that man out in Jersey, the one who started to chop his trees down, one by one, the man who began talking about how he would take his house to pieces, brick by brick, because he faced a problem incapable of solution, probably, so he began to hack at the trees in the yard, began to pluck with trembling fingers at the bricks in the house. Even if a house is not washable, it is worth taking down. It is not till later that the exhaustion sets in.

But it is inevitable that they will keep changing the doors on you, he said, because that is what they are for; and the thing is to get used to it and not let it unsettle the mind. But that would mean not jumping, and you can't. Nobody can not jump. There will be no not-jumping. Among rats, perhaps, but among people never. Everybody has to keep jumping at a door (the one with the circle on it) because that is the way everybody is, specially some people. You wouldn't want me, standing here, to tell you, would you, about my friend the poet (deceased) who said, "My heart has followed all my days something I cannot name"? (It had the circle on it.) And like many poets, although few so beloved, he is gone. It killed him, the jumping. First, of course, there were the preliminary bouts, the convulsions, and the calm and the willingness.

I remember the door with the picture of the girl on it (only it was spring), her arms outstretched in loveliness, her dress (it was the one with the circle on it) uncaught, beginning the slow, clear, blinding cascade—and I guess we would all like to try that door again, for it seemed like the way and for a while it was the way, the door would open and you would go through winged and exalted (like any rat) and the food would be there, the way the Professor had it arranged, everything O.K., and you had chosen the right door for the world was young. The time they changed that door on me, my nose bled for a hundred hours— how do you like that, Madam? Or would you prefer to show me

further through this so strange house, or you could take my
name and send it to me, for although my heart has followed all
my days something I cannot name, I am tired of the jumping and
I do not know which way to go, Madam, and I am not even sure
that I am not tried beyond the endurance of man (rat, if you will)
and have taken leave of sanity. What are you following these
days, old friend, after your recovery from the last bump? What
is the name, or is it something you cannot name? The rats have
a name for it by this time, perhaps, but I don't know what they
call it. I call it plexikoid and it comes in sheets, something like
insulating board, unattainable and ugli-proof.

And there was the man out in Jersey, because I keep thinking about his terrible necessity and the passion and trouble he
had gone to all those years in the indescribable abundance of a
householder's detail, building the estate and the planting of the
trees and in spring the lawn-dressing and in fall the bulbs for
the spring burgeoning, and the watering of the grass on the
long light evenings in summer and the gravel for the driveway
(all had to be thought out, planned) and the decorative borders,
probably, the perennials and the bug spray, and the building of
the house from plans of the architect, first the sills, then the
studs, then the full corn in the ear, the floors laid on the floor
timbers, smoothed, and then the carpets upon the smooth floors
and the curtains and the rods therefor. And then, almost without warning, he would be jumping at the same old door and it
wouldn't give: they had changed it on him, making life no
longer supportable under the elms in the elm shade, under the
maples in the maple shade.

"Here you have the maximum of openness in a small room."

It was impossible to say (maybe it was the city) what made
him feel the way he did, and I am not the only one either, he
kept thinking—ask any doctor if I am. The doctors, they know
how many there are, they even know where the trouble is only
they don't like to tell you about the prefrontal lobe because that
means making a hole in your skull and removing the work of
centuries. It took so long coming, this lobe, so many, many
years. (Is it something you read in the paper, perhaps?) And
now, the strain being so great, the door having been changed by

the Professor once too often...but it only means a whiff of ether, a few deft strokes, and the higher animal becomes a little easier in his mind and more like the lower one. From now on, you see, that's the way it will be, the ones with the small prefrontal lobes will win because the other ones are hurt too much by this incessant bumping. They can stand just so much, eh, Doctor? (And what is that, pray, that you have in your hand?) Still, you never can tell, eh, Madam?

He crossed (carefully) the room, the thick carpet under him softly, and went toward the door carefully, which was glass and he could see himself in it, and which, at his approach, opened to allow him to pass through; and beyond he half expected to find one of the old doors that he had known, perhaps the one with the circle, the one with the girl her arms outstretched in loveliness and beauty before him. But he saw instead a moving stairway, and descended in light (he kept thinking) to the street below and to the other people. As he stepped off, the ground came up slightly, to meet his foot.

AN UPHEAVAL [*]

BY ANTON CHEKHOV

MASHENKA PAVLETSKY, a young girl who had only just finished her studies at a boarding school, returning from a walk to the house of the Kushkins, with whom she was living as a governess, found the household in a terrible turmoil. Mihailo, the porter who opened the door to her, was excited and red as a crab.

Loud voices were heard from upstairs.

"Madame Kushkin is in a fit, most likely, or else she has quarrelled with her husband," thought Mashenka.

[*] from *The Lady with the Dog*

In the hall and in the corridor she met maidservants. One of them was crying. Then Mashenka saw, running out of her room, the master of the house himself, Nikolay Sergeitch, a little man with a flabby face and a bald head, though he was not old. He was red in the face and twitching all over. He passed the governess without noticing her, and throwing up his arms, exclaimed:

"Oh, how horrible it is! How tactless! How stupid! How barbarous! Abominable!"

Mashenka went into her room, and then, for the first time in her life, it was her lot to experience in all its acuteness the feeling that is so familiar to persons in dependent positions, who eat the bread of the rich and powerful, and cannot speak their minds. There was a search going on in her room. The lady of the house, Fedosya Vassilyevna, a stout, broad-shouldered, uncouth woman with thick black eyebrows, a faintly perceptible moustache, and red hands, who was exactly like a plain, illiterate cook in face and manners, was standing, without her cap on, at the table, putting back into Mashenka's work-bag balls of wool, scraps of materials, and bits of papers.... Evidently the governess's arrival took her by surprise, since, on looking round and seeing the girl's pale and astonished face, she was a little taken aback, and muttered:

"Pardon. I... I upset it accidentally.... My sleeve caught in it..."

And saying something more, Madame Kushkin rustled her long skirts and went out. Mashenka looked round her room with wondering eyes, and, unable to understand it, not knowing what to think, shrugged her shoulders, and turned cold with dismay. What had Fedosya Vassilyevna been looking for in her workbag? If she really had, as she said, caught her sleeve in it and upset everything, why had Nikolay Sergeitch dashed out of her room so excited and red in the face? Why was one drawer of the table pulled out a little way? The moneybox, in which the governess put away ten kopeck pieces and old stamps, was open. They had opened it, but did not know how to shut it, though they had scratched the lock all over. The whatnot with her books on it, the things on the table, the bed—all bore fresh traces of a search.

Her linen-basket, too. The linen had been carefully folded, but it was not in the same order as Mashenka had left it when she went out. So the search had been thorough, most thorough. But what was it for? Why? What had happened? Mashenka remembered the excited porter, the general turmoil which was still going on, the weeping servant-girl; had it not all some connection with the search that had just been made in her room? Was she not mixed up in something dreadful? Mashenka turned pale, and feeling cold all over, sank on to her linen-basket.

A maidservant came into the room.

"Liza, you don't know why they have been rummaging in my room?" the governess asked her.

"Mistress has lost a brooch worth two thousand," said Liza.

"Yes, but why have they been rummaging in my room?"

"They've been searching every one, miss. They've searched all my things, too. They stripped us all naked and searched us.... God knows, miss, I never went near her toilet-table, let alone touching the brooch. I shall say the same at the police-station."

"But... why have they been rummaging here?" the governess still wondered.

"A brooch has been stolen, I tell you. The mistress has been rummaging in everything with her own hands. She even searched Mihailo, the porter, herself. It's a perfect disgrace! Nikolay Sergeitch simply looks on and cackles like a hen. But you've no need to tremble like that, miss. They found nothing here. You've nothing to be afraid of it you didn't take the brooch."

"But Liza, it's vile... it's insulting," said Mashenka, breathless with indignation. "It's so mean, so low! What right had she to suspect me and to rummage in my things?"

"You are living with strangers, miss," sighed Liza. "Though you are a young lady, still you are... as it were... a servant.... It's not like living with your papa and mamma."

Mashenka threw herself on the bed and sobbed bitterly. Never in her life had she been subjected to such an outrage, never had she been so deeply insulted.... She, well-educated, refined, the daughter of a teacher, was suspected of theft; she had been searched like a street-walker! She could not imagine a greater insult. And to this feeling of resentment was added an oppressive dread of what would come next. All sorts of absurd ideas came into her mind. If they could suspect her of theft, then they might arrest her, strip her naked, and search her, then lead her through the street with an escort of soldiers, cast her into a cold, dark cell with mice and wood-lice, exactly like the dungeon in which Princess Tarakanov was imprisoned. Who would stand up for her? Her parents lived far away in the Provinces; they had not the money to come to her. In the capital she was as solitary as in a desert, without friends or kindred. They could do what they liked with her.

"I will go to all the courts and all the lawyers," Mashenka thought, trembling. "I will explain to them, I will take an oath. . . . They will believe that I could not be a thief!"

Mashenka remembered that under the sheets in her basket she had some sweetmeats, which, following the habits of her schooldays, she had put in her pocket at dinner and carried off to her room. She felt hot all over, and was ashamed at the thought that her little secret was known to the lady of the house; all this terror, shame, resentment, brought on an attack of palpitation of the heart, which set up a throbbing in her temples, in her heart, and deep down in her stomach.

"Dinner is ready," the servant summoned Mashenka.

"Shall I go, or not?"

Mashenka brushed her hair, wiped her face with a wet towel, and went into the dining-room. There they had already begun dinner. At one end of the table sat Fedosya Vassilyevna with a stupid, solemn, serious face; at the other end Nikolay Sergeitch. At the sides there were the visitors and the children. The dishes were handed by two footmen in swallowtails and white gloves. Everyone knew that there was an upset in the house, that Madame Kushkin was in trouble, and everyone was silent. Nothing was heard but the sound of munching and the rattle of spoons on the plates.

The lady of the house, herself, was the first to speak.

"What is the third course?" she asked the footman in a weary, injured voice.

"*Esturgeon à la russe,*" answered the footman.

"I ordered that, Fenya," Nikolay Sergeitch hastened to observe. "I wanted some fish. If you don't like it, *ma chère,* don't let them serve it. I just ordered it. . . ."

Fedosya Vassilyevna did not like dishes that she had not ordered herself, and now her eyes filled with tears.

"Come, don't let us agitate ourselves," Mamikov, her household doctor, observed in a honeyed voice, just touching her arm, with a smile as honeyed. "We are nervous enough as it is. Let us forget the brooch! Health is worth more than two thousand roubles!"

"It's not the two thousand I regret," answered the lady, and a big tear rolled down her check. "It's the fact itself that revolts me! I cannot put up with thieves in my house. I don't regret it—I regret nothing; but to steal from me is such ingratitude! That's how they repay me for my kindness. . . ."

They all looked into their plates, but Mashenka fancied after the lady's words that every one was looking at her. A lump rose in her throat; she began crying and put her handkerchief to her lips.

"*Pardon,*" she muttered. "I can't help it. My head aches. I'll go away."

And she got up from the table, scraping her chair awkwardly, and went out quickly, still more overcome with confusion.

"It's beyond everything!" said Nikolay Sergeitch, frowning. "What need was there to search her room? How out of place it was!"

"I don't say she took the brooch," said Fedosya Vassilyevna, "but can you answer for her? To tell the truth, I haven't much confidence in these learned paupers."

"It really was unsuitable, Fenya. . . . Excuse me, Fenya, but you've no kind of legal right to make a search."

"I know nothing about your laws. All I know is that I've lost my brooch. And I will find the brooch!" She brought her fork down on the plate with a clatter, and her eyes flashed angrily. "And you eat your dinner, and don't interfere in what doesn't concern you!"

Nikolay Sergeitch dropped his eyes mildly and sighed.

Meanwhile Mashenka, reaching her room, flung herself on her bed. She felt now neither alarm nor shame, but she felt an intense longing to go and slap the cheeks of this hard, arrogant, dull-witted, prosperous woman.

Lying on her bed she breathed into her pillow and dreamed of how nice it would be to go and buy the most expensive brooch and fling it into the face of this bullying woman. If only it were God's will that Fedosya Vassilyevna should come to ruin and wander about begging, and should taste all the horrors of poverty and dependence, and that Mashenka, whom she had insulted, might give her alms! Oh, if only she could come in for a big fortune, could buy a carriage, and could drive noisily past the windows so as to be envied by that woman!

But all these were only dreams, in reality there was only one thing left to do—to get away as quickly as possible, not to stay another hour in this place. It was true it was terrible to lose her place, to go back to her parents, who had nothing; but what could she do? Mashenka could not bear the sight of the lady of the house nor of her little room; she felt stifled and wretched here. She was so disgusted with Fedosya Vassilyevna, who was so obsessed by her illnesses and her supposed aristocratic rank, that everything in the world seemed to have become coarse and unattractive because this woman was living in it. Mashenka jumped up from the bed and began packing.

"May I come in?" asked Nikolay Sergeitch at the door; he had come up noiselessly to the door, and spoke in a soft, subdued voice. "May I?"

"Come in."

He came in and stood still near the door. His eyes looked dim and his red little nose was shiny. After dinner he used to drink beer, and the fact was perceptible in his walk, in his feeble, flabby hands.

"What's this?" he asked, pointing to the basket.

"I am packing. Forgive me, Nikolay Sergeitch, but I cannot remain in your house. I feel deeply insulted by this search!"

"I understand. . . . Only you are wrong to go. . . . Why should you? They've searched your things, but you . . . what does it matter to you? You will be none the worse for it."

Mashenka was silent and went on packing. Nikolay Sergeitch pinched his moustache, as though wondering what he should say next, and went on in an ingratiating voice:

"I understand, of course, but you must make allowances. You know my wife is nervous, headstrong; you mustn't judge her too harshly."

Mashenka did not speak.

"If you are so offended," Nikolay Sergeitch went on, "well, if you like, I'm ready to apologize. I ask your pardon."

Mashenka made no answer, but only bent lower over her box. This exhausted, irresolute man was of absolutely no significance in the household. He stood in the pitiful position of a dependent and hanger-on, even with the servants, and his apology meant nothing either.

"H'm... You say nothing! That's not enough for you. In that case, I will apologize for my wife. In my wife's name.... She behaved tactlessly, I admit it as a gentleman...."

Nikolay Sergeitch walked about the room, heaved a sigh, and went on:

"Then you want me to have it rankling here, under my heart.... You want my conscience to torment me...."

"I know it's not your fault, Nikolay Sergeitch," said Mashenka, looking him full in the face with her big tear-stained eyes. "Why should you worry yourself?"

"Of course, no.... But still, don't you... go away. I entreat you."

Mashenka shook her head. Nikolay Sergeitch stopped at the window and drummed on a pane with his fingertips.

"Such misunderstandings are simply torture to me," he said. "Why, do you want me to go down on my knees to you, or what? Your pride is wounded, and here you've been crying and packing up to go; but I have pride, too, and you do not spare it! Or do you want me to tell you what I would not tell at Confession? Do you? Listen; you want me to tell you what I won't tell the priest on my deathbed?"

Mashenka made no answer.

"I took my wife's brooch," Nikolay Sergeitch said quickly. "Is that enough now? Are you satisfied? Yes, I...took it...."

But, of course, I count on your discretion. . . . For God's sake, not a word, not half a hint to any one!"

Mashenka, amazed and frightened, went on packing; she snatched her things, crumpled them up, and thrust them anyhow into the box and the basket. Now, after this candid avowal on the part of Nikolay Sergeitch, she could not remain another minute, and could not understand how she could have gone on living in the house before.

"And it's nothing to wonder at," Nikolay Sergeitch went on after a pause. "It's an everyday story! I need money, and she . . . won't give it to me. It was my father's money that bought this house and everything, you know! It's all mine, and the brooch belonged to my mother, and . . . it's all mine! And she took it, took possession of everything. . . . I can't go to law with her, you'll admit. . . . I beg you most earnestly, overlook it . . . stay on. *Tout comprendre, tout pardonner.* Will you stay?"

"No!" said Mashenka resolutely, beginning to tremble. "Let me alone, I entreat you!"

"Well, God bless you!" sighed Nikolay Sergeitch, sitting down on the stool near the box. "I must own I like people who still can feel resentment, contempt, and so on. I could sit here forever and look at your indignant face. . . . So you won't stay, then? I understand. . . . It's bound to be so. . . . Yes, of course. . . . It's all right for you, but for me—wo-o-o-o! . . . I can't stir a step out of this cellar. I'd go off to one of our estates, but in every one of them there are some of my wife's rascals . . . stewards, experts, damn them all! They mortgage and remortgage. . . . You mustn't catch fish, must keep off the grass, mustn't break the trees."

"Nikolay Sergeitch!" his wife's voice called from the drawing-room. "Agnia, call your master!"

"Then you won't stay?" asked Nikolay Sergeitch, getting up quickly and going toward the door. "You might as well stay, really. In the evenings I could come and have a talk with you. Eh? Stay! If you go, there won't be a human face left in the house. It's awful!"

Nikolay Sergeitch's pale, exhausted face besought her, but

Mashenka shook her head, and with a wave of his hand he went out.

Half an hour later she was on her way.

HOW BEAUTIFUL
WITH SHOES *

BY WILBUR DANIEL STEELE

B Y THE time the milking was finished, the sow, which had farrowed the past week, was making such a row that the girl spilled a pint of the warm milk down the trough-lead to quiet the animal before taking the pail to the well-house. Then in the quiet she heard a sound of hoofs on the bridge, where the road crossed the creek a hundred yards below the house, and she set the pail down on the ground beside her bare, barn-soiled feet. She picked it up again. She set it down. It was as if she calculated its weight.

That was what she was doing, as a matter of fact, setting off against its pull toward the well-house the pull of that wagon team in the road, with little more of personal will or wish in the matter than has a wooden weather-vane between two currents in the wind. And as with the vane, so with the wooden girl—the added behest of a whip-lash cracking in the distance was enough; leaving the pail at the barn door, she set off in a deliberate, docile beeline through the cow-yard, over the fence, and down in a diagonal across the farm's one tilled field toward the willow brake that walled the road at the dip. And once under way, though her mother came to the kitchen door and called in her high, flat voice, "Amarantha, where you goin', Amarantha?" the girl went on apparently unmoved, as though she had been as deaf as the woman in the doorway; indeed, if there was emotion

* from *Harper's Magazine*

in her it was the purely sensuous one of feeling the clods of the furrows breaking softly between her toes. It was spring time in the mountains.

"Amarantha, why don't you answer me, Amarantha?"

For moments after the girl had disappeared beyond the willows the widow continued to call, unaware through long habit of how absurd it sounded, the name which that strange man her husband had put upon their daughter in one of his moods. Mrs. Doggett had been deaf so long she did not realize that nobody else ever thought of it for the broad-fleshed, slow-minded girl, but called her Mary or, even more simply, Mare.

Ruby Herter had stopped his team this side of the bridge, the mules' heads turned into the lane to his father's farm beyond the road. A big-barreled, heavy-limbed fellow with a square, sallow, not unhandsome face, he took out youth in ponderous gestures of masterfulness; it was like him to have cracked his whip above his animals' ears the moment before he pulled them to a halt. When he saw the girl getting over the fence under the willows he tongued the wad of tobacco out of his mouth into his palm, threw it away beyond the road, and drew a sleeve of his jumper across his lips.

"Don't run yourself out o' breath, Mare; I got all night."

"I was comin'." It sounded sullen only because it was matter of fact.

"Well, keep a-comin' and give us a smack." Hunched on the wagon seat, he remained motionless for some time after she had arrived at the hub, and when he stirred it was but to cut a fresh bit of tobacco, as if already he had forgotten why he threw the old one away. Having satisfied his humor, he unbent, climbed down, kissed her passive mouth, and hugged her up to him, roughly and loosely, his hands careless of contours. It was not out of the way; they were used to handling animals, both of them; and it was spring. A slow warmth pervaded the girl, formless, nameless, almost impersonal.

Her betrothed pulled her head back by the braid of her yellow hair. He studied her face, his brows gathered and his chin out.

"Listen, Mare, you wouldn't leave nobody else hug and kiss you, dang you!"

She shook her head, without vehemence or anxiety.

"Who's that?" She hearkened up the road. "Pull your team out," she added, as a Ford came in sight around the bend above the house, driven at speed. "Geddap!" she said to the mules herself.

But the car came to a halt near them, and one of the five men crowded in it called, "Come on, Ruby, climb in. They's a loony loose out o' Dayville Asylum, and they got him trailed over somewheres on Split Ridge and Judge North phoned up to Slosson's store for ever'body come help circle him—come on, hop the runnin'-board!"

Ruby hesitated, an eye on his team.

"Scared, Ruby?" The driver raced his engine. "They say this boy's a killer."

"Mare, take the team in and tell pa." The car was already moving when Ruby jumped in. A moment after it had sounded on the bridge it was out of sight.

"Amarantha, Amarantha, why don't you come, Amarantha?"

Returning from her errand, fifteen minutes later, Mare heard the plaint lifted in the twilight. The sun had dipped behind the back ridge, and though the sky was still bright with day, the dusk began to smoke up out of the plowed field like a ground-fog. The girl had returned through it, got the milk, and started toward the well-house before the widow saw her.

"Daughter, seems to me you might!" she expostulated without change of key. "Here's some young man friend o' yourn stopped to say howdy, and I been rackin' my lungs out after you.... Put that milk in the cool and come!"

Some young man friend? But there was no good to be got from puzzling. Mare poured the milk in the pan in the dark of the low house over the well, and as she came out, stooping, she saw a figure waiting for her, black in silhouette against the yellowing sky.

"Who are you?" she asked, a native timidity making her sound sulky.

"Amarantha!" the fellow mused. "That's poetry." And she knew then that she did not know him.

She walked past, her arms straight down and her eyes front. Strangers always affected her with a kind of muscular terror simply by being strangers. So she gained the kitchen steps, aware by his tread that he followed. There, taking courage at sight of her mother in the doorway, she turned on him, her eyes down at the level of his knees.

"Who are you and what d' y' want?"

He still mused. "Amarantha! Amarantha in Carolina! That makes me happy!"

Mare hazarded one upward look. She saw that he had red hair, brown eyes, and hollows under his cheekbones, and though the green sweater he wore on top of a gray overall was plainly not meant for him, sizes too large as far as girth went, yet he was built so long of limb that his wrists came inches out of the sleeves and made his big hands look even bigger.

Mrs. Doggett complained. "Why don't you introduce us, daughter?"

The girl opened her mouth and closed it again. Her mother, unaware that no sound had come out of it, smiled and nodded, evidently taking to the tall, homely fellow and tickled by the way he could not seem to get his eyes off her daughter. But the daughter saw none of it, all her attention centered upon the stranger's hands.

Restless, hard-fleshed, and chap-bitten, they were like a countryman's hands; but the fingers were longer than the ordinary, and slightly spatulate at their ends, and these ends were slowly and continuously at play among themselves.

The girl could not have explained how it came to her to be frightened and at the same time to be calm, for she was inept with words. It was simply that in an animal way she knew animals, knew them in health and ailing, and when they were ailing she knew by instinct, as her father had known, how to move so as not to fret them.

Her mother had gone in to light up; from beside the lamp-shelf she called back, "If he's aimin' to stay to supper you should've told me, Amarantha, though I guess there's plenty of the side-meat to go 'round, if you'll bring me in a few more turnips and potatoes, though it is late."

At the words the man's cheeks moved in and out. "I'm very hungry," he said.

Mare nodded deliberately. Deliberately, as if her mother could hear her, she said over her shoulder, "I'll go get the potatoes and turnips, ma." While she spoke she was moving, slowly, softly, at first, toward the right of the yard, where the fence gave over into the field. Unluckily her mother spied her through the window.

"Amarantha, where *are* you goin'?"

"I'm goin' to get the potatoes and turnips." She neither raised her voice nor glanced back, but lengthened her stride. "He won't hurt her," she said to herself. "He won't hurt her; it's me, not her," she kept repeating, while she got over the fence and down into the shadow that lay more than ever like a fog on the field.

The desire to believe that it actually did hide her, the temptation to break from her rapid but orderly walk grew till she could no longer fight it. She saw the road willows only a dash ahead of her. She ran, her feet floundering among the furrows.

She neither heard nor saw him, but when she realized he was with her she knew he had been with her all the while. She stopped, and he stopped, and so they stood, with the dark open of the field all around. Glancing sidewise presently, she saw he was no longer looking at her with those strangely importunate brown eyes of his, but had raised them to the crest of the wooded ridge behind her.

By and by, "What does it make you think of?" he asked. And when she made no move to see, "Turn around and look!" he said, and though it was low and almost tender in its tone, she knew enough to turn.

A ray of the sunset hidden in the west struck through the tops of the topmost trees, far and small up there, a thin, bright hem.

"What does it make you think of, Amarantha? . . . Answer!"

"Fire," she made herself say.

"Or blood."

"Or blood, yeh. That's right, or blood." She had heard a Ford going up the road beyond the willows, and her attention was not on what she said.

The man soliloquized. "Fire and blood, both; spare one or the other, and where is beauty, the way the world is? It's an awful thing to have to carry, but Christ had it. Christ came with a sword. I love beauty, Amarantha.... I say, I love beauty!"

"Yeh, that's right, I hear." What she heard was the car stopping at the house.

"Not prettiness. Prettiness'll have to go with ugliness, because it's only ugliness trigged up. But beauty!" Now again he was looking at her. "Do you know how beautiful you are, Amarantha, 'Amarantha sweet and fair'?" Of a sudden, reaching behind her, he began to unravel the meshes of her hair-braid, the long, flat-tipped fingers at once impatient and infinitely gentle. " 'Braid no more that shining hair!' "

Flat-faced Mare Doggett tried to see around those glowing eyes so near to hers, but wise in her instinct, did not try too hard. "Yeh," she temporized. "I mean, no, I mean."

"Amarantha, I've come a long, long way for you. Will you come away with me now?"

"Yeh—that is—in a minute I will, mister—yeh..."

"Because you want to, Amarantha? Because you love me as I love you? Answer!"

"Yeh—sure uh...*Ruby!*"

The man tried to run, but there were six against him, coming up out of the dark that lay in the plowed ground. Mare stood where she was while they knocked him down and got a rope around him; after that she walked back toward the house with Ruby and Older Haskins, her father's cousin.

Ruby wiped his brow and felt of his muscles. "Gees, you're lucky we come, Mare. We're no more'n past the town, when they come hollerin' he'd broke over this way."

When they came to the fence the girl sat on the rail for a moment and rebraided her hair before she went into the house, where they were making her mother smell ammonia.

Lots of cars were coming. Judge North was coming, somebody said. When Mare heard this she went into her bedroom off the kitchen and got her shoes and put them on. They were brand new two-dollar shoes with cloth tops, and she had only begun to break them in last Sunday; she wished afterwards she had put her stockings on too, for they would have eased the seams. Or else that she had put on the old button pair, even though the soles were worn through.

Judge North arrived. He thought first of taking the loony straight through to Dayville that night, but then decided to keep him in the lock-up at the courthouse till morning and make the drive by day. Older Haskins stayed in, gentling Mrs. Doggett, while Ruby went out to help get the man into the Judge's sedan. Now that she had them on, Mare didn't like to take the shoes off till Older went; it might make him feel small, she thought.

Older Haskins had a lot of facts about the loony.

"His name's Humble Jewett," he told them. "They belong back in Breed County, all them Jewetts, and I don't reckon there's none on 'em that's not a mite unbalanced. He went to college though, worked his way, and he taught somethin' 'rother in some academy-school a spell, till he went off his head all of a sudden and took after folks with an axe. I remember it in the paper at the time. They give out one while how the Principal wasn't goin' to live, and there was others—there was a girl he tried to strangle. That was four-five year back."

Ruby came in guffawing. "Know the only thing they can get 'im to say, Mare? Only God thing he'll say is, 'Amarantha, she's goin' with me.' . . . Mare!"

"Yeh, I know."

The cover of the kettle the girl was handling slid off on the stove with a clatter. A sudden sick wave passed over her. She went out to the back, out into the air. It was not till now she knew how frightened she had been.

Ruby went home, but Older Haskins stayed to supper with them, and helped Mare do the dishes afterward; it was nearly nine when he left. The mother was already in bed, and Mare was about to sit down to get those shoes off her wretched feet at last, when she heard the cow carrying on up at the barn, low-ing and kicking, and next minute the sow was in it with a horn-ing note. It might be a fox passing by to get at the henhouse, or a weasel. Mare forgot her feet, took a broom-handle they used in boiling clothes, opened the back door, and stepped out. Blinking the lamplight from her eyes, she peered up toward the outbuildings, and saw the gable end of the barn standing like a red arrow in the dark, and the top of a butternut tree beyond it drawn in skeleton traceries, and just then a cock crowed.

She went to the right corner of the house and saw where the light came from, ruddy above the woods down the valley. Returning into the house, she bent close to her mother's ear and shouted, "Somethin's a-fire down to the town, looks like," then went out again and up to the barn. "Soh! Soh!" she called to the animals. She climbed up and stood on the top rail of the cow-pen fence, only to find she could not locate the flame even there.

Ten rods behind the buildings a mass of rock mounted higher than their ridgepoles, a chopped-off buttress of the back ridge, covered with oak scrub and wild grapes and blackberries, whose thorny ropes the girl beat away from her skirt with the broom-handle as she scrambled up in the wine-colored dark. Once at the top, and the brush held aside, she could see the tongue-tip of the conflagration half a mile away at the town. And she knew by the bearing of the two church steeples that it was the building where the lock-up was that was burning.

There is a horror in knowing animals trapped in a fire, no matter what the animals.

"Oh, my God!" Mare said.

A car went down the road. Then there was a horse galloping. That would be Older Haskins probably. People were out at Ruby's father's farm; she could hear their voices raised. There must have been another car up from the other way, for lights wheeled and shouts were exchanged in the neighborhood of the bridge. Next thing she knew, Ruby was at the house below, looking for her probably.

He was telling her mother. Mrs. Doggett was not used to him, so he had to shout even louder than Mare had to.

"What y' reckon he done, the hellion! he broke the door and killed Lew Fyke and set the courthouse afire! . . . Where's Mare?"

Her mother would not know. Mare called. "Here, up the rock here."

She had better go down. Ruby would likely break his bones if he tried to climb the rock in the dark, not knowing the way. But the sight of the fire fascinated her simple spirit, the fearful element, more fearful than ever now, with the news. "Yes, I'm comin'," she called sulkily, hearing feet in the brush. "You wait; I'm comin'."

When she turned and saw it was Humble Jewett, right behind her among the branches, she opened her mouth to screech. She was not quick enough. Before a sound came out he got one hand over her face and the other arm around her body.

Mare had always thought she was strong, and the loony looked gangling, yet she was so easy for him that he need not hurt her. He made no haste and little noise as he carried her deeper into the undergrowth. Where the hill began to mount it was harder though. Presently he set her on her feet. He let the hand that had been over her mouth slip down to her throat, where the broad-tipped fingers wound, tender as yearning, weightless as caress.

"I was afraid you'd scream before you knew who 'twas, Amarantha. But I didn't want to hurt your lips, dear heart, your lovely, quiet lips."

It was so dark under the trees she could hardly see him, but she felt his breath on her mouth, near to. But then, instead of kissing her, he said, "No! No!" took from her throat an instant the hand that had held her mouth, kissed its palm, and put it back softly against her skin.

She stood stock still. Her mother's voice was to be heard in the distance, strident and meaningless. More cars were on the road. Nearer, around the rock, there were sounds of tramping and thrashing. Ruby fussed and cursed. He shouted, "Mare, dang you, where are you, Mare?" his voice harsh with uneasy anger. Now, if she aimed to do anything, was the time to do it. But there was neither breath nor power in her windpipe. It was as if those yearning fingers had paralyzed the muscles.

"Come!" The arm he put around her shivered against her shoulder blades. It was anger. "I hate killing. It's a dirty, ugly thing. It makes me sick." He gagged, judging by the sound. But then he ground his teeth. "Come away, my love!"

She found herself moving. Once when she broke a branch underfoot with an instinctive awkwardness he chided her. "Quiet, my heart, else they'll hear!" She made herself heavy. He thought she grew tired and bore more of her weight till he was breathing hard.

Men came up the hill. There must have been a dozen spread
out, by the angle of their voices as they kept touch. Always
Humble Jewett kept caressing Mare's throat with one hand; all
she could do was hang back.

"You're tired and you're frightened," he said at last. "Get
down here."

There were twigs in the dark, the overhang of a thicket of
some sort. He thrust her in under this, and lay beside her on the
bed of groundpine. The hand that was not in love with her
throat reached across her; she felt the weight of its forearm on
her shoulder and its fingers among the strands of her hair, eagerly, but tenderly, busy. Not once did he stop speaking, no
louder than breathing, his lips to her ear.

" 'Amarantha sweet and fair—Ah, braid no more that shining hair...' "

Mare had never heard of Lovelace, the poet; she thought the
loony was just going on, hardly listened, got little sense. But
the cadence of it added to the lethargy of all her flesh.

" 'Like a clew of golden thread—Most excellently ravelled...' "

Voices loudened; feet came tramping; a pair went past not
two rods away. " '...Do not then wind up the light—In rib-
bands, and o'ercloud in night...' "

The search went on up the woods, men shouting to one another and beating the brush.

" '...But shake your head and scatter day!' I've never
loved, Amarantha. They've tried me with prettiness, but prettiness is too cheap, yes, it's too cheap."

Mare was cold, and the coldness made her lazy. All she
knew was that he talked on.

"But dogwood blowing in the spring isn't cheap. The earth
of a field isn't cheap. Lots of times I've laid down and kissed
the earth of a field, Amarantha. That's beauty, and a kiss for
beauty." His breath moved up her cheek. He trembled violently.
"No, no, not yet!" He got to his knees and pulled her by an arm.
"We can go now."

They went back down the slope, but at an angle, so that
when they came to the level they passed two hundred yards to

the north of the house, and crossed the road there. More and more, her walking was like sleepwalking, the feet numb in their shoes. Even where he had to let go of her, crossing the creek on stones, she stepped where he stepped with an obtuse docility. The voices of the searchers on the back ridge were small in distance when they began to climb the face of Coward Hill, on the opposite side of the valley.

There is an old farm on top of Coward Hill, big hayfields as flat as tables. It had been half-past nine when Mare stood on the rock above the barn; it was toward midnight when Humble Jewett put aside the last branches of the woods and led her out on the height, and half a moon had risen. And a wind blew there, tossing the withered tops of last year's grasses, and mists ran with the wind, and ragged shadows with the mists, and mares'-tails of clear moonlight among the shadows, so that now the boles of birches on the forest's edge beyond the fences were but opal blurs and now cut alabaster. It struck so cold against the girl's cold flesh, this wind, that another wind of shivers blew through her, and she put her hands over her face and eyes. But the madman stood with his eyes wide open and his mouth open, drinking the moonlight and the wet wind.

His voice, when he spoke at last, was thick in his throat.

"Get down on your knees." He got down on his and pulled her after. "And pray!"

Once in England a poet sang four lines. Four hundred years have forgotten his name, but they have remembered his lines. The daft man knelt upright, his face raised to the wild scud, his long wrists hanging to the dead grass. He began simply:

> " 'O western wind, when wilt thou blow
>   That the small rain down can rain?' "

The Adam's-apple was big in his bent throat. As simply as he finished.

> " 'Christ, that my love were in my arms
>   And I in my bed again!' "

Mare got up and ran. She ran without aim or feeling in the power of the wind. She told herself again that the mists would hide her from him, as she had done at dusk. And again, seeing that he ran at her shoulder, she knew he had been there all the while, making a race of it, flailing the air with his long arms for joy of play in the cloud of spring, throwing his knees high, leaping the moon-blue waves of the brown grass, shaking his bright hair; and her own hair was a weight behind her, lying level on the wind. Once a shape went bounding ahead of them for instants; she did not realize it was a fox till it was gone.

She never thought of stopping; she never thought anything, except once, "Oh, my God, I wish I had my shoes off!" And what would have been the good in stopping or in turning another way, when it was only play? The man's ecstasy magnified his strength. When a snake-fence came at them he took the top rail in flight, like a college hurdler, and, seeing the girl hesitate and half turn as if to flee, he would have releaped it without touching a hand. But then she got a loom of buildings, climbed over quickly, before he should jump, and ran along the lane that ran with the fence.

Mare had never been up there, but she knew that the farm and the house belonged to a man named Wyker, a kind of cousin of Rudy Herter's, a violent, bearded old fellow who lived by himself. She could not believe her luck. When she had run half the distance and Jewett had not grabbed her, doubt grabbed her instead. "Oh, my God, go careful!" she told herself. "Go slow!" she implored herself, and stopped running, to walk.

Here was a misgiving the deeper in that it touched her special knowledge. She had never known an animal so far gone that its instincts failed it; a starving rat will scent the trap sooner than a fed one. Yet, after one glance at the house they approached, Jewett paid it no further attention, but walked with his eyes to the right, where the cloud had blown away, and wooded ridges, like black waves rimmed with silver, ran down away toward the Valley of Virginia.

"I've never lived!" In his single cry there were two things, beatitude and pain.

Between the bigness of the falling world and his eyes the flag of her hair blew. He reached out and let it whip between his fingers. Mare was afraid it would break the spell then, and he would stop looking away and look at the house again. So she did something almost incredible; she spoke.

"It's a pretty—I mean a beautiful view down that-away."

"God Almighty beautiful, to take your breath away. I knew I'd never loved, Belovéd—" He caught a foot under the long end of one of the boards that covered the well and went down heavily on his hand and knees. It seemed to make no difference. "But I never knew I'd never lived," he finished in the same tone of strong rapture, quadruped in the grass, while Mare ran for the door and grabbed the latch.

When the latch would not give, she lost what little sense she had. She pounded with her fists. She cried with all her might: "Oh—hey—in there—hey—in there!" Then Jewett came and took her gently between his hands and drew her away, and then, though she was free, she stood in something like an awful embarrassment while he tried shouting.

"Hey! Friend! whoever you are, wake up and let my love and me come in!"

"No!" wailed the girl.

He grew peremptory. "Hey, wake up!" He tried the latch. He passed to full fury in a wink's time; he cursed, he kicked, he beat the door till Mare thought he would break his hands. Withdrawing, he ran at it with his shoulder; it burst at the latch, went slamming in, and left a black emptiness. His anger dissolved in a big laugh. Turning in time to catch her by a wrist, he cried joyously, "Come, my Sweet One!"

"No! No! Please—aw—listen. There ain't nobody there. He ain't to home. It wouldn't be right to go in anybody's house if they wasn't to home, you know that."

His laugh was blither than ever. He caught her high in his arms.

"I'd do the same by his love and him if 'twas my house, I would." At the threshold he paused and thought, "That is, if she was the true love of his heart forever."

The room was the parlor. Moonlight slanted in at the door, and another shaft came through a window and fell across a sofa, its covering dilapidated, showing its wadding in places. The air was sour, but both of them were farm-bred.

"Don't, Amarantha!" His words were pleading in her ear. "Don't be so frightened."

He set her down on the sofa. As his hands let go of her they were shaking.

"But look, I'm frightened too." He knelt on the floor before her, reached out his hands, withdrew them. "See, I'm afraid to touch you." He mused, his eyes rounded. "Of all the ugly things there are, fear is the ugliest. And yet, see, it can be the very beautifulest. That's a strange queer thing."

The wind blew in and out of the room, bringing the thin, little bitter sweetness of new April at night. The moonlight that came across Mare's shoulders fell full upon his face, but hers it left dark, ringed by the aureole of her disordered hair.

"Why do you wear a halo, Love?" He thought about it. "Because you're an angel, is that why?" The swift, untempered logic of the mad led him to dismay. His hands came flying to hers, to make sure they were earth; and he touched her breast, her shoulders, and her hair. Peace returned to his eyes as his fingers twined among the strands.

" '*Thy hair is a flock of goats that appear from Gilead...*' " He spoke like a man dreaming. " '*Thy temples are like a piece of pomegranate within thy locks.*' "

Mare never knew that he could not see her for the moonlight.

"Do you remember, Love?"

She dared not shake her head under his hand. "Yeh, I reckon," she temporized.

"You remember how I sat at your feet, long ago, like this, and made up a song? And all the poets in all the world have never made one to touch it, have they, Love?"

"Ugh-ugh—never."

" '*How beautiful are thy feet with shoes...*' Remember?"

"Oh, my God, what's he sayin' now?" she wailed to herself.

> " '*How beautiful are thy feet with shoes, O prince's daughter! the joints of thy thighs are like jewels, the work of the hands of a cunning workman.*

> *Thy navel is like a round goblet, which wanteth not*
>   *liquor; thy belly is like an heap of wheat set about*
>   *with lilies.*
> *Thy two breasts are like two young roes that are*
>   *twins.' "*

Mare had not been to church since she was a little girl, when her mother's black dress wore out. "No, no!" she wailed under her breath. "You're awful to say such awful things." She might have shouted it; nothing could have shaken the man now, rapt in the immortal, passionate periods of Solomon's song.

> " '... *now also thy breasts shall be as clusters of the*
>   *vine, and the smell of thy nose like apples.' "*

Hotness touched Mare's face for the first time. "Aw, no, don't talk so!"

> " '*And the roof of thy mouth like the best wine for my*
>   *belovéd ... causing the lips of them that are asleep to*
>   *speak.' "*

He had ended. His expression changed. Ecstasy gave place to anger, love to hate. And Mare felt the change in the weight of the fingers in her hair.

"What do you mean, I mustn't say it like that?" But it was not to her his fury spoke for he answered himself straightaway. "Like poetry, Mr. Jewett; I won't have blasphemy around my school."

"Poetry! My God! if that isn't poetry—if that isn't music—" ... "It's Bible, Jewett. What you're paid to teach here is *literature*."

"Doctor Ryeworth, you're the blasphemer and you're an ignorant man." ... "And your Principal. And I won't have you going around reading sacred allegory like earthly love."

"Ryeworth, you're an old man, a dull man, a dirty man, and you'd be better dead."

Jewett's hand had slid down from Mare's head. "Then I went

to put my fingers around his throat, so. But my stomach turned, and I didn't do it. I went to my room. I laughed all the way to my room. I sat in my room at my table and I laughed. I laughed all afternoon and long after dark came. And then, about ten, somebody came and stood beside me in my room."

" 'Wherefore dost thou laugh, son?'

"Then I knew who He was, He was Christ.

" 'I was laughing about that dirty, ignorant, crazy old fool, Lord.'

" 'Wherefore dost thou laugh?'

"I didn't laugh any more. He didn't say any more. I kneeled down, bowed my head.

" 'Thy will be done! Where is he, Lord?'

" 'Over at the girls' dormitory, waiting for Blossom Sinckley.'

"Brassy Blossom, dirty Blossom..."

It had come so suddenly it was nearly too late. Mare tore at his hands with hers, tried with all her strength to pull her neck away.

"Filthy Blossom! and him an old filthy man, Blossom! and you'll find him in Hell when you reach there, Blossom..."

It was more the nearness of his face than the hurt of his hands that gave her power of fright to choke out three words. words.

"I—ain't—Blossom!"

Light ran in crooked veins. Through the veins she saw his face bewildered. His hands loosened. One fell down and hung; the other he lifted and put over his eyes, took away again and looked at her.

"Amarantha!" His remorse was fearful to see. "What have I done!" His hands returned to hover over the hurts, ravening with pity, grief and tenderness. Tears fell down his cheeks. And with that, dammed desire broke its dam.

"Amarantha, my love, my dove, my beautiful love—"

"And I ain't Amarantha neither, I'm Mary! Mary, that's my name!"

She had no notion what she had done. He was like a crystal crucible that a chemist watches, changing hue in a wink with one adeptly added drop; but hers was not the chemist's eye. All she knew was that she felt light and free of him; all she could see of his face as he stood away above the moonlight were the whites of his eyes.

"Mary!" he muttered. A slight paroxysm shook his frame. So in the transparent crucible desire changed its hue. He retreated farther, stood in the dark by some tall piece of furniture. And still she could see the whites of his eyes.

"Mary! Mary Adorable!" A wonder was in him. "Mother of God!"

Mare held her breath. She eyed the door, but it was too far. And already he came back to go on his knees before her, his shoulders so bowed and his face so lifted that it must have cracked his neck, she thought; all she could see on the face was pain.

"Mary Mother, I'm sick to my death. I'm so tired."

She had seen a dog like that, one she had loosed from a trap after it had been there three days, its caught leg half gnawed free. Something about the eyes.

"Mary Mother, take me in your arms..."

Once again her muscles tightened. But he made no move.

"...and give me sleep."

No, they were worse than the dog's eyes.

"Sleep, sleep! why won't they let me sleep? Haven't I done it all yet, Mother? Haven't I washed them yet of all their sins? I've drunk the cup that was given me; is there another? They've mocked me and reviled me, broken my brow with thorns and my hands with nails, and I've forgiven them, for they knew not what they did. Can't I go to sleep now, Mother?"

Mare could not have said why, but now she was more frightened than she had ever been. Her hands lay heavy on her knees, side by side, and she could not take them away when he bowed his head and rested his face upon them.

After a moment he said one thing more. "Take me down gently when you take me from the Tree."

Gradually the weight of his body came against her shins, and he slept.

The moon streak that entered by the eastern window crept

north across the floor, thinner and thinner; the one that fell
through the southern doorway traveled east and grew fat. For a
while Mare's feet pained her terribly and her legs too. She
dared not move them, though, and by and by they did not hurt
so much.

A dozen times, moving her head slowly on her neck, she
canvassed the shadows of the room for a weapon. Each time
her eyes came back to a heavy earthenware pitcher on a stand
some feet to the left of the sofa. It would have had flowers in it
when Wyker's wife was alive; probably it had not been moved
from its dust-ring since she died. It would be a long grab, perhaps too long; still, it might be done if she had her hands.

To get her hands from under the sleeper's head was the task
she set herself. She pulled first one, then the other, infinitesi-
mally. She waited. Again she tugged a very, very little. The order of his breathing was not disturbed. But at the third trial he
stirred.

"Gently! gently!" His own muttering waked him more. With
some drowsy instinct of possession he threw one hand across
her wrists, pinning them together between thumb and fingers.
She kept dead quiet, shut her eyes, lengthened her breathing, as
if she too slept.

There came a time when what was pretense grew to be a
peril; strange as it was, she had to fight to keep her eyes open.
She never knew whether or not she really napped. But something changed in the air, and she was wide awake again. The
moonlight was fading on the doorsill, and the light that runs
before dawn waxed in the window behind her head.

And then she heard a voice in the distance, lifted in maun-
dering song. It was old man Wyker coming home after a night,
and it was plain he had had some whisky.

Now a new terror laid hold of Mare.

"Shut up, you fool you!" she wanted to shout. "Come quiet,
quiet!" She might have chanced it now to throw the sleeper
away from her and scramble and run, had his powers of
strength and quickness not taken her simple imagination utterly in thrall.

Happily the singing stopped. What had occurred was that

the farmer has espied the open door and, even befuddled as he was, wanted to know more about it quietly. He was so quiet that Mare began to fear he had gone away. He had the squirrel-hunter's foot, and the first she knew of him was when she looked and saw his head in the doorway, his hard, soiled, whiskery face half-up-side-down with craning.

He had been to the town. Between drinks he had wandered in and out of the night's excitement; had even gone a short distance with one search party himself. Now he took in the situation in the room. He used his forefinger. First he held it to his lips. Next he pointed it with a jabbing motion at the sleeper. Then he tapped his own forehead and described wheels. Lastly, with his whole hand, he made pushing gestures, for Mare to wait. Then he vanished as silently as he had appeared.

The minutes dragged. The light in the east strengthened and turned rosy. Once she thought she heard a board creaking in another part of the house, and looked down sharply to see if the loony stirred. All she could see of his face was a temple with freckles on it and the sharp ridge of a cheekbone, but even from so little she knew how deeply and peacefully he slept. The door darkened. Wyker was there again. In one hand he carried something heavy; with the other he beckoned.

"Come jumpin'!" he said out loud.

Mare went jumping, but her cramped legs threw her down half way to the sill; the rest of the distance she rolled and crawled. Just as she tumbled through the door it seemed as if the world had come to an end above her; two barrels of a shotgun discharged into a room make a noise. Afterwards all she could hear in there was something twisting and bumping on the floor-boards. She got up and ran.

Mare's mother had gone to pieces; neighbor women put her to bed when Mare came home. They wanted to put Mare to bed, but she would not let them. She sat on the edge of her bed in her lean-to bedroom off the kitchen, just as she was, her hair down all over her shoulders and her shoes on, and stared away from them, at a place in the wallpaper.

"Yeh, I'll go myself. Lea' me be!"

The women exchanged quick glances, thinned their lips, and left her be. "God knows," was all they would answer to the questionings of those that had not gone in, "but she's gettin' herself to bed."

When the doctor came though he found her sitting just as she had been, still dressed, her hair down on her shoulders and her shoes on.

"What d' y' want?" she muttered and stared at the place in the wallpaper.

How could Doc Paradise say, when he did not know himself?

"I didn't know if you might be—might be feeling very smart, Mary."

"I'm all right. Lea' me be."

It was a heavy responsibility. Doc shouldered it. "No, it's all right," he said to the men in the road. Ruby Herter stood a little apart, chewing sullenly and looking another way. Doc raised his voice to make certain it carried. "Nope, nothing."

Ruby's ears got red, and he clamped his jaws. He knew he ought to go in and see Mare, but he was not going to do it while everybody hung around waiting to see if he would. A mule tied near him reached out and mouthed his sleeve in idle innocence; he wheeled and banged a fist against the side of the animal's head.

"Well, what d' y' aim to do 'bout it?" he challenged its owner.

He looked at the sun then. It was ten in the morning. "Hell, I got work!" he flared, and set off down the road for home. Doc looked at Judge North, and the Judge started after Ruby. But Ruby shook his head angrily. "Lea' me be!" He went on, and the Judge came back.

It got to be eleven and then noon. People began to say, "Like enough she'd be as thankful if the whole neighborhood wasn't camped here." But none went away.

As a matter of fact they were no bother to the girl. She never saw them. The only move she made was to bend her ankles over and rest her feet on edge; her shoes hurt terribly and her feet knew it, though she did not. She sat all the while staring at that one figure in the wallpaper, and she never saw the figure.

Strange as the night had been, this day was stranger. Fright and physical pain are perishable things once they are gone. But while pain merely dulls and telescopes in memory and remains diluted pain, terror looked back upon has nothing of terror left. A gambling chance taken, at no matter what odds, and won was a sure thing since the world's beginning; perils come through safely were never perilous. But what fright does do in retrospect is this—it heightens each sensuous recollection, like a hard, clear lacquer laid on wood, bringing out the color and grain of it vividly.

Last night Mare had lain stupid with fear on groundpine beneath a bush, loud foot-falls and light whispers confused in her ear. Only now, in her room, did she smell the groundpine.

Only now did the conscious part of her brain begin to make words of the whispering.

"*Amarantha*," she remembered, "*Amarantha sweet and fair.*" That was as far as she could go for the moment, except that the rhyme with "fair" was "hair." But then a puzzle, held in abeyance, brought other words. She wondered what "ravel Ed" could mean. "*Most excellently ravelléd.*" It was left to her mother to bring the end.

They gave up trying to keep her mother out at last. The poor woman's prostration took the form of fussiness.

"Good gracious, daughter, you look a sight. Them new shoes, half ruined; ain't your feet *dead*? And look at your hair, all tangled like a wild one!"

She got a comb.

"Be quiet, daughter; what's ailin' you. Don't shake your head!"

" '*But shake your head and scatter day.*' "

"What you say, Amarantha?" Mrs. Doggett held an ear down.

"Go 'way! Lea' me be!"

Her mother was hurt and left. And Mare ran, as she stared at the wallpaper.

"*Christ, that my love were in my arms . . .*"

Mare ran. She ran through a wind white with moonlight and wet with "the small rain." And the wind she ran through, it ran through her, and made her shiver as she ran. And the man beside her leaped high over the waves of the dead grasses and gathered the wind in his arms, and her hair was heavy and his was tossing, and a little fox ran before them across the top of the world. And the world spread down around in waves of black and silver, more immense than she had ever known the world could be, and more beautiful.

"God Almighty beautiful, to take your breath away!"

Mare wondered, and she was not used to wondering. "Is it only crazy folks ever run like that and talk that way?"

She no longer ran; she walked; for her breath was gone. And there was some other reason; some other reason. Oh, yes, it was because her feet were hurting her. So, at last, and roundabout, her shoes had made contact with her brain.

Bending over the side of the bed, she loosened one of them mechanically. She pulled it half off. But then she looked down at it sharply, and she pulled it on again.

"How beautiful..."

Color overspread her face in a slow wave.

"How beautiful are thy feet with shoes..."

"Is it only crazy folks ever say such things?"

"O prince's daughter!"

"Or call you that?"

By and by there was a knock at the door. It opened, and Ruby Herter came in.

"Hello, Mare old girl!" His face was red. He scowled and kicked at the floor. "I'd 'a' been over sooner, except we got a mule down sick." He looked at his dumb betrothed. "Come on, cheer up, forget it! He won't scare you no more, not that boy, not what's left o' him. What you lookin' at, sourface? Ain't you glad to see me?"

Mare quit looking at the wallpaper and looked at the floor.

"Yeh," she said.

"That's more like it, babe." He came and sat beside her; reached down behind her and gave her a spank. "Come on, give us a kiss, babe!" He wiped his mouth on his jumper sleeve, a good farmer's sleeve, spotted with milking. He put his hands on her; he was used to handling animals. "Hey, you, warm up a little, reckon I'm goin' to do all the lovin'?"

"Ruby, lea' me be!"

"What!"

She was up, twisting. He was up, purple.

"What's ailin' you, Mare? What you bawlin' about?"

"Nothin'—only go 'way!"

She pushed him to the door and through it with all her strength, and closed it in his face, and stood with her weight against it, crying, "Go 'way! Go 'way! Lea' me be!"

A HAUNTED HOUSE*

BY VIRGINIA WOOLF

WHATEVER HOUR you woke there was a door shutting. From room to room they went, hand in hand, lifting here, opening there, making sure—a ghostly couple.

"Here we left it," she said. And he added, "Oh, but here too!" "It's upstairs," she murmured. "And in the garden," he whispered. "Quietly," they said, "or we shall wake them."

But it wasn't that you woke us. Oh, no. "They're looking for it; they're drawing the curtain," one might say, and so read on a page or two. "Now they've found it," one would be certain, stopping the pencil on the margin. And then, tired of reading, one might rise and see for oneself, the house all empty, the doors standing open, only the wood pigeons bubbling with content and the hum of the threshing machine sounding from the farm. "What did I come in here for? What did I want to find?" My hands were empty. "Perhaps it's upstairs then?" The

* from *A Haunted House and Other Stories*

apples were in the loft. And so down again, the garden still as ever, only the book had slipped into the grass.

But they had found it in the drawing room. Not that one could ever see them. The window panes reflected apples, reflected roses; all the leaves were green in the glass. If they moved in the drawing room, the apple only turned its yellow side. Yet, the moment after, if the door was opened, spread about the floor, hung upon the walls, pendant from the ceiling—what? My hands were empty. The shadow of a thrush crossed the carpet; from the deepest wells of silence the wood pigeon drew its bubble of sound. "Safe, safe, safe," the pulse of the house beat softly. "The treasure buried; the room..." the pulse stopped short. Oh, was that the buried treasure?

A moment later the light had faded. Out in the garden then? But the trees spread darkness for a wandering beam of sun. So fine, so rare, coolly sunk beneath the surface the beam I sought always burnt behind the glass. Death was the glass; death was between us; coming to the woman first, hundreds of years ago, leaving the house, sealing all the windows; the rooms were darkened. He left it, left her, went North, went East, saw the stars turned in the Southern sky; sought the house, found it dropped beneath the Downs. "Safe, safe, safe," the pulse of the house beat gladly. "The Treasure yours."

The wind roars up the avenue. Trees stoop and bend this way and that. Moonbeams splash and spill wildly in the rain. But the beam of the lamp falls straight from the window. The candle burns stiff and still. Wandering through the house, opening the windows, whispering not to wake us, the ghostly couple seek their joy.

"Here we slept," she says. And he adds, "Kisses without number." "Waking in the morning—" "Silver between the trees." "Upstairs—" "In the garden—" "When summer came—" "In winter snowtime—" The doors go shutting far in the distance, gently knocking like the pulse of a heart.

Nearer they come; cease at the doorway. The wind falls, the rain slides silver down the glass. Our eyes darken; we hear no steps beside us; we see no lady spread her ghostly cloak. His hands shield the lantern. "Look," he breathes. "Sound asleep. Love upon their lips."

Stooping, holding their silver lamp above us, long they look and deeply. Long they pause. The wind drives straightly; the flame stoops slightly. Wild beams of moonlight cross both floor and wall, and, meeting, stain the faces bent; the faces pondering; the faces that search the sleepers and seek their hidden joy.

"Safe, safe, safe," the heart of the house beats proudly. "Long years—" he sighs. "Again you found me." "Here," she murmurs, "sleeping; in the garden reading; laughing, rolling apples in the loft. Here we left our treasure—" Stooping, their light lifts the lids upon my eyes. "Safe! safe! safe!" the pulse of the house beats wildly. Waking, I cry "Oh, is this *your* buried treasure? The light in the heart."

THE CATBIRD SEAT[*]

BY JAMES THURBER

M R. MARTIN bought the pack of Camels on Monday night in the most crowded cigar store on Broadway. It was theatre time and seven or eight men were buying cigarettes. The clerk didn't even glance at Mr. Martin, who put the pack in his overcoat pocket and went out. If any of the staff at F & S had seen him buy the cigarettes, they would have been astonished, for it was generally known that Mr. Martin did not smoke, and never had. No one saw him.

It was just a week to the day since Mr. Martin had decided to rub out Mrs. Ulgine Barrows. The term "rub out" pleased him because it suggested nothing more than the correction of an error—in this case an error of Mr. Fitweiler. Mr. Martin had spent each night of the past week working out his plan and ex-

[*] from *The New Yorker*

amining it. As he walked home now he went over it again. For the hundredth time he resented the element of imprecision, the margin of guesswork that entered into the business. The project as he had worked it out was casual and bold, the risks were considerable. Something might go wrong anywhere along the line. And therein lay the cunning of his scheme. No one would ever see in it the cautious, painstaking hand of Erwin Martin, head of the filing department at F & S, of whom Mr. Fitweiler had once said, "Man is fallible but Martin isn't." No one would see his hand, that is, unless it were caught in the act.

Sitting in his apartment, drinking a glass of milk, Mr. Martin reviewed his case against Mrs. Ulgine Barrows, as he had every night for seven nights. He began at the beginning. Her quacking voice and braying laugh had first profaned the halls of F & S on March 7, 1941 (Mr. Martin had a head for dates). Old Roberts, the personnel chief, had introduced her as the newly appointed special adviser to the president of the firm, Mr. Fitweiler. The woman had appalled Mr. Martin instantly, but he hadn't shown it. He had given her his dry hand, a look of studious concentration, and a faint smile. "Well," she had said, looking at the papers on his desk, "are you lifting the oxcart out of the ditch?" As Mr. Martin recalled that moment, over his milk, he squirmed slightly. He must keep his mind on her crimes as a special adviser, not on her peccadillos as a personality. This he found difficult to do, in spite of entering an objection and sustaining it. The faults of the woman as a woman kept chattering on in his mind like an unruly witness. She had, for almost two years now, baited him. In the halls, in the elevator, even in his own office, into which she romped now and then like a circus horse, she was constantly shouting these silly questions at him. "Are you lifting the oxcart out of the ditch? Are you tearing up the pea patch? Are you hollering down the rain barrel? Are you scraping around the bottom of the pickle barrel? Are you sitting in the catbird seat?"

It was Joey Hart, one of Mr. Martin's two assistants, who had explained what the gibberish meant. "She must be a Dodger fan," he had said. "Red Barber announces the Dodger games over the radio and he uses those expressions—picked 'em up down South." Joey had gone on to explain one or two. "Tearing up the pea patch" meant going on a rampage; "sitting in the catbird seat" meant sitting pretty, like a batter with three balls and no strikes on him. Mr. Martin dismissed all this with an effort. It had been annoying, it had driven him near to distraction, but he was too solid a man to be moved to murder by anything so childish. It was fortunate, he reflected as he passed on to the important charges against Mrs. Barrows, that he had stood up under it so well. He had maintained always an outward appearance of polite tolerance. "Why, I even believe you like the woman," Miss Paird, his other assistant, had once said to him. He had simply smiled.

A gavel rapped in Mr. Martin's mind and the case proper was resumed. Mrs. Ulgine Barrows stood charged with willful, blatant, and persistent attempts to destroy the efficiency and system of F & S. It was competent, material, and relevant to review her advent and rise to power. Mr. Martin had got the story from Miss Paird, who seemed always able to find things out. According to her, Mrs. Barrows had met Mr. Fitweiler at a party, where she had rescued him from the embraces of a powerfully built drunken man who had mistaken the president of F & S for a famous retired Middle Western football coach. She had led him to a sofa and somehow worked upon him a monstrous magic. The aging gentleman had jumped to the conclusion there and then that this was a woman of singular attainments, equipped to bring out the best in him and in the firm. A week later he had introduced her into F & S as his special adviser. On that day confusion got its foot in the door. After Miss Tyson, Mr. Brundage, and Mr. Bartlett had been fired and Mr. Munson had taken his hat and stalked out, mailing in his resignation later, old Roberts had been emboldened to speak to Mr. Fitweiler. He mentioned that Mr. Munson's department had been "a little disrupted" and hadn't they perhaps better resume the old system there? Mr. Fitweiler had said certainly not. He had the greatest faith in Mrs. Barrows' ideas. "They require a little seasoning, a little seasoning, is all," he had added. Mr. Roberts had given it up. Mr. Martin reviewed in detail all the changes wrought by Mrs. Barrows. She had begun chipping at the cornices of the firm's edifice and now she was swinging at the foundation stones with a pickaxe.

Mr. Martin came now, in his summing up, to the afternoon of Monday, November 2, 1942—just one week ago. On that day, at 3 P.M., Mrs. Barrows had bounced into his office. "Boo!" she had yelled. "Are you scraping around the bottom of the pickle barrel?" Mr. Martin had looked at her from under his green eyeshade, saying nothing. She had begun to wander about the office, taking it in with her great, popping eyes. "Do you really need *all* these filing cabinets?" she had demanded suddenly. Mr. Martin's heart had jumped. "Each of these files," he had said, keeping his voice even, "plays an indispensable part in the system of F & S." She had brayed at him, "Well, don't tear up the pea patch!" and gone to the door. From there she had bawled, "But you sure have got a lot of fine scrap in here!" Mr. Martin could no longer doubt that the finger was on his beloved department. Her pickaxe was on the upswing, poised for the first blow. It had not come yet; he had received no blue memo from the enchanted Mr. Fitweiler bearing nonsensical instructions deriving from the obscene woman. But there was no doubt in Mr. Martin's mind that one would be forthcoming. He must act quickly. Already a precious week had gone by. Mr. Martin stood up in his living room, still holding his milk glass. "Gentlemen of the jury," he said to himself, "I demand the death penalty for this horrible person."

The next day Mr. Martin followed his routine, as usual. He polished his glasses more often and once sharpened an already sharp pencil, but not even Miss Paird noticed. Only once did he catch sight of his victim; she swept past him in the hall with a patronizing "Hi!" At five-thirty he walked home, as usual, and had a glass of milk, as usual. He had never drunk anything stronger in his life—unless you could count ginger ale. The late Sam Schlosser, the S of F & S, had praised Mr. Martin at a staff meeting several years before for his temperate habits. "Our most efficient worker neither drinks nor smokes," he had said. "The results speak for themselves." Mr. Fitweiler had sat by, nodding approval.

Mr. Martin was still thinking about that red-letter day as he walked over to the Schrafft's on Fifth Avenue near Forty-Sixth Street. He got there, as he always did, at eight o'clock. He finished his dinner and the financial page of the *Sun* at a quarter to nine, as he always did. It was his custom after dinner to take a walk. This time he walked down Fifth Avenue at a casual pace. His gloved hands felt moist and warm, his forehead cold. He transferred the Camels from his overcoat to a jacket pocket. He wondered, as he did so, if they did not represent an unnecessary note of strain. Mrs. Barrows smoked only Luckies. It was his idea to puff a few puffs on a Camel (after the rubbing-out), stub it out in the ashtray holding her lipstick-stained Luckies, and thus drag a small red herring across the trail. Perhaps it was not a good idea. It would take time. He might even choke, too loudly.

Mr. Martin had never seen the house on West Twelfth Street where Mrs. Barrows lived, but he had a clear enough picture of it. Fortunately, she had bragged to everybody about her ducky first-floor apartment in the perfectly darling three-story redbrick. There would be no doorman or other attendants; just the tenants of the second and third floors. As he walked along, Mr. Martin realized that he would get there before nine-thirty. He had considered walking north on Fifth Avenue from Schrafft's to a point from which it would take him until ten o'clock to reach the house. At that hour people were less likely to be coming in or going out. But the procedure would have made an awkward loop in the straight thread of his casualness, and he had abandoned it. It was impossible to figure when people would be entering or leaving the house, anyway. There was a great risk at any hour. If he ran into anybody, he would simply have to place the rubbing-out of Ulgine Barrows in the inactive file forever. The same thing would hold true if there were someone in her apartment. In that case he would just say that he had been passing by, recognized her charming house, and thought to drop in.

It was eighteen minutes after nine when Mr. Martin turned into Twelfth Street. A man passed him, and a man and a woman, talking. There was no one within fifty paces when he came to the house, halfway down the block. He was up the steps and in the small vestibule in no time, pressing the bell under the card that said "Mrs. Ulgine Barrows." When the clicking in the lock started, he jumped forward against the door. He got inside fast, closing the door behind him. A bulb in a lantern hung from the hall ceiling on a chain seemed to give a monstrously bright light. There was nobody on the stair, which went up ahead of him along the left wall. A door opened down the hall in the wall on the right. He went toward it swiftly, on tiptoe.

"Well, for God's sake, look who's here!" bawled Mrs. Barrows, and her braying laugh rang out like the report of a shotgun. He rushed past her like a football tackle, bumping her. "Hey, quit shoving!" she said, closing the door behind them. They were in her living room, which seemed to Mr. Martin to be lighted by a hundred lamps. "What's after you?" she said. "You're as jumpy as a goat." He found he was unable to speak. His heart was wheezing in his throat. "I—yes," he finally brought out. She was jabbering and laughing as she started to help him off with his coat. "No, no," he said. "I'll put it here." He took it off and put it on a chair near the door. "Your hat and gloves, too," she said. "You're in a lady's house." He put his hat on top of the coat. Mrs. Barrows seemed larger than he had thought. He kept his gloves on. "I was passing by," he said. "I recognized—is there anyone here?" She laughed louder than ever. "No," she said, "we're all alone. You're as white as a sheet, you funny man. Whatever *has* come over you? I'll mix you a toddy." She started toward a door across the room. "Scotch-and-soda be all right? But say, you don't drink, do you?" She turned and gave him her amused look. Mr. Martin pulled himself together. "Scotch-and-soda will be all right," he heard himself say. He could hear her laughing in the kitchen.

Mr. Martin looked quickly around the living room for the weapon. He had counted on finding one there. There were andirons and a poker and something in a corner that looked like an Indian club. None of them would do. It couldn't be that way. He began to pace around. He came to a desk. On it lay a metal paper knife with an ornate handle. Would it be sharp enough? He reached for it and knocked over a small brass jar. Stamps spilled out of it and it fell to the floor with a clatter. "Hey," Mrs. Barrows yelled from the kitchen, "are you tearing up the pea patch?" Mr. Martin gave a strange laugh. Picking up the knife, he tried its point against his left wrist. It was blunt. It wouldn't do.

When Mrs. Barrows reappeared, carrying two highballs, Mr. Martin, standing there with his gloves on, became acutely conscious of the fantasy he had wrought. Cigarettes in his pocket, a drink prepared for him—it was all too grossly improbable. It was more than that; it was impossible. Somewhere in the back of his mind a vague idea stirred, sprouted. "For heaven's sake, take off those gloves," said Mrs. Barrows. "I always wear them in the house," said Mr. Martin. The idea began to bloom, strange and wonderful. She put the glasses on a coffee table in front of a sofa and sat on the sofa. "Come over here, you odd little man," she said. Mr. Martin went over and sat beside her. It was difficult getting a cigarette out of the pack of Camels, but he managed it. She held a match for him, laughing. "Well," she said, handing him his drink, "this is perfectly marvelous. You with a drink and a cigarette."

Mr. Martin puffed, not too awkwardly, and took a gulp of the highball. "I drink and smoke all the time," he said. He clinked his glass against hers. "Here's nuts to that old windbag, Fitweiler," he said, and gulped again. The stuff tasted awful, but he made no grimace. "Really, Mr. Martin," she said, her voice and posture changing, "you are insulting our employer." Mrs. Barrows was now all special adviser to the president. "I am preparing a bomb," said Mr. Martin, "which will blow the old goat higher than hell." He had only a little of the drink, which was not strong. It couldn't be that. "Do you take dope or something?" Mrs. Barrows asked coldly. "Heroin," said Mr. Martin. "I'll be coked to the gills when I bump that old buzzard off." "Mr. Martin!" she shouted, getting to her feet. "That will be all of that. You must go at once." Mr. Martin took another swallow of his drink. He tapped his cigarette out in the ashtray and put the pack of Camels on the coffee table. Then he got up. She stood glaring at him. He walked over and put on his hat and coat. "Not a word about this," he said, and laid an index finger against his lips. All Mrs. Barrows could bring out was "Really!" Mr. Martin put his hand on the doorknob. "I'm sitting in the catbird seat," he said. He stuck his tongue out at her and left. Nobody saw him go.

Mr. Martin got to his apartment, walking, well before eleven. No one saw him go in. He had two glasses of milk after brushing his teeth, and he felt elated. It wasn't tipsiness, because he hadn't been tipsy. Anyway, the walk had worn off all effects of the whiskey. He got in bed and read a magazine for a while. He was asleep before midnight.

Mr. Martin got to the office at eight-thirty the next morning, as usual. At a quarter to nine, Ulgine Barrows, who had never before arrived at work before ten, swept into his office. "I'm reporting to Mr. Fitweiler now!" she shouted. "If he turns you over to the police, it's no more than you deserve!" Mr. Martin gave her a look of shocked surprise. "I beg your pardon?" he said. Mrs. Barrows snorted and bounced out of the room, leaving Miss Paird and Joey Hart staring after her. "What's the matter with that old devil now?" asked Miss Paird. "I have no idea," said Mr. Martin, resuming his work. The other two looked at him and then at each other. Miss Paird got up and went out. She walked slowly past the closed door of Mr. Fitweiler's office. Mrs. Barrows was yelling inside, but she was not braying. Miss Paird could not hear what the woman was saying. She went back to her desk.

Forty-five minutes later, Mrs. Barrows left the president's office and went into her own, shutting the door. It wasn't until half an hour later that Mr. Fitweiler sent for Mr. Martin. The head of the filing department, neat, quiet, attentive, stood in front of the old man's desk. Mr. Fitweiler was pale and nervous. He took his glasses off and twiddled them. He made a small, bruffing sound in his throat. "Martin," he said, "you have been with us more than twenty years." "Twenty-two, sir," said Mr. Martin. "In that time," pursued the president, "your work and your—uh—manner have been exemplary." "I trust so, sir," said Mr. Martin. "I have understood, Martin," said Mr. Fitweiler, "that you have never taken a drink or smoked." "That is correct, sir," said Mr. Martin. "Ah, yes." Mr. Fitweiler polished his glasses. "You may describe what you did after leaving the office yesterday, Martin," he said. Mr. Martin allowed less than a second for his bewildered pause. "Certainly, sir," he said. "I walked home. Then I went to Schrafft's for dinner. Afterward I walked home again. I went to bed early, sir, and read a magazine for a while. I was asleep before eleven." "Ah, yes," said Mr. Fitweiler again. He was silent for a moment, searching for the proper words to say to the head of the filing department. "Mrs. Barrows," he said finally, "Mrs. Barrows has worked hard, Martin, very hard. It grieves me to report that she has suffered a severe breakdown. It has taken the form of a persecution complex accompanied by distressing hallucinations." "I am very sorry, sir," said Mr. Martin. "Mrs. Barrows is under the delusion," continued Mr. Fitweiler, "that you visited her last evening and behaved yourself in an—uh—unseemly manner." He raised his hand to silence Mr. Martin's little pained outcry. "It is the nature of these psychological diseases," Mr. Fitweiler said, "to fix upon the least likely and most innocent party as the—uh—source of persecution. These matters are not for the lay mind to grasp, Martin. I've just had my psychiatrist, Doctor Fitch, on the phone. He would not, of course, commit himself, but he made enough generalizations to substantiate my suspicions. I suggested to Mrs. Barrows, when she had completed her—uh—story to me this morning, that she visit Doctor Fitch, for I suspected a condition at once. She flew, I regret to say, into a rage, and demanded—uh—requested that I call you on the carpet. You may not know, Martin, but Mrs. Barrows had planned a reorganization of your department—subject to my approval, of course, subject to my approval. This brought you, rather than anyone else, to her mind—but again that is a phenomenon for Doctor Fitch and not for us. So, Martin, I am afraid Mrs. Barrows' usefulness here is at an end." "I am dreadfully sorry, sir," said Mr. Martin.

It was at this point that the door to the office blew open with

the suddenness of a gas-main explosion and Mrs. Barrows cat-
apulted through it. "Is the little rat denying it?" she screamed.
"He can't get away with that!" Mr. Martin got up and moved
discreetly to a point beside Mr. Fitweiler's chair. "You drank
and smoked at my apartment," she bawled at Mr. Martin, "and
you know it! You called Mr. Fitweiler an old windbag and said
you were going to blow him up when you got coked to the gills
on your heroin!" She stopped yelling to catch her breath and a
new glint came into her popping eyes. "If you weren't such a
drab, ordinary little man," she said, "I'd think you'd planned it
all. Sticking your tongue out, saying you were sitting in the catbird seat, because you thought no one would believe me when
I told it! My God, it's really too perfect!" She brayed loudly and
hysterically, and the fury was on her again. She glared at Mr.
Fitweiler. "Can't you see how he has tricked up, you old fool?
Can't you see his little game?" But Mr. Fitweiler had been sur-
reptitiously pressing all the buttons under the top of his desk
and employees of F & S began pouring into the room.
"Stockton," said Mr. Fitweiler, "you and Fishbein will take
Mrs. Barrows to her home. Mrs. Powell, you will go with
them." Stockton, who had played a little football in high
school, blocked Mrs. Barrows as she made for Mr. Martin. It
took him and Fishbein together to force her out of the door into
the hall, crowded with stenographers and office boys. She was
still screaming imprecations at Mr. Martin, tangled and contra-
dictory imprecations. The hubbub finally died down the corridor.

"I regret that this has happened," said Mr. Fitweiler. "I shall
ask you to dismiss it from your mind, Martin." "Yes, sir," said
Mr. Martin, anticipating his chief's "That will be all" by moving to the door. "I will dismiss it." He went out and shut the
door, and his step was light and quick in the hall. When he entered his department he had slowed down to his customary gait,
and he walked quietly across the room to the W20 file, wearing
a look of studious concentration.

THE SCHARTZ-METTERKLUME METHOD*

BY "SAKI" (H. H. MUNRO)

LADY CARLOTTA stepped out on to the platform of the small wayside station and took a turn or two up and down its uninteresting length, to kill time till the train should be pleased to proceed on its way. Then, in the roadway beyond, she saw a horse struggling with a more than ample load, and a carter of the sort that seems to bear a sullen hatred against the animal that helps him to earn a living. Lady Carlotta promptly betook her to the roadway, and put rather a different complexion on the struggle. Certain of her acquaintances were wont to give her plentiful admonition as to the undesirability of interfering on behalf of a distressed animal, such interference being "none of her business." Only once had she put the doctrine of non-interference into practice, when one of its most eloquent exponents had been besieged for nearly three hours in a small and extremely uncomfortable maytree by an angry boar-pig, while Lady Carlotta, on the other side of the fence, had proceeded with the water-colour sketch she was engaged on, and refused to interfere between the boar and his prisoner. It is to be feared that she lost the friendship of the ultimately rescued lady. On this occasion she merely lost the train, which gave way to the first sign of impatience it had shown throughout the journey, and steamed off without her. She bore the desertion with philosophical indifference; her friends and relations were thoroughly well used to the fact of her luggage arriving without her. She wired a vague noncommittal message to her

* from *The Short Stories of Saki*

destination to say that she was coming on "by another train." Before she had time to think what her next move might be she was confronted by an imposingly attired lady, who seemed to be taking a prolonged mental inventory of her clothes and looks.

"You must be Miss Hope, the governess I've come to meet," said the apparition, in a tone that admitted of very little argument.

"Very well, if I must I must," said Lady Carlotta to herself with dangerous meekness.

"I am Mrs. Quabarl," continued the lady; "and where, pray, is your luggage?"

"It's gone astray," said the alleged governess, falling in with the excellent rule of life that the absent are always to blame; the luggage had, in point of fact, behaved with perfect correctitude. "I've just telegraphed about it," she added, with a nearer approach to truth.

"How provoking," said Mrs. Quabarl; "these railway companies are so careless. However, my maid can lend you things for the night," and she led the way to her car.

During the drive to the Quabarl mansion Lady Carlotta was impressively introduced to the nature of the charge that had been thrust upon her; she learned that Claude and Wilfred were delicate, sensitive young people, that Irene had the artistic temperament highly developed, and that Viola was something or other else of a mould equally commonplace among children of that class and type in the twentieth century.

"I wish them not only to be *taught*," said Mrs. Quabarl, "but *interested* in what they learn. In their history lessons, for instance, you must try to make them feel that they are being introduced to the life-stories of men and women who really lived, not merely committing a mass of names and dates to memory. French, of course, I shall expect you to talk at mealtimes several days in the week."

"I shall talk French four days of the week and Russian in the remaining three."

"Russian? My dear Miss Hope, no one in the house speaks or understands Russian."

"That will not embarrass me in the least," said Lady Carlotta coldly.

Mrs. Quabarl, to use a colloquial expression, was knocked off her perch. She was one of those imperfectly self-assured individuals who are magnificent and autocratic as long as they are not seriously opposed. The least show of unexpected resistance goes a long way towards rendering them cowed and apologetic. When the new governess failed to express wondering admiration of the large newly purchased and expensive car, and lightly alluded to the superior advantages of one or two makes which had just been put on the market, the discomfiture of her patroness became almost abject. Her feelings were those which might have animated a general of ancient warfaring days, on beholding his heaviest battle-elephant ignominiously driven off the field by slingers and javelin throwers.

At dinner that evening, although reinforced by her husband, who usually duplicated her opinions and lent her moral support generally, Mrs. Quabarl regained none of her lost ground. The governess not only helped herself well and truly to wine, but held forth with considerable show of critical knowledge on various vintage matters, concerning which the Quabarls were in no wise able to pose as authorities. Previous governesses had limited their conversation on the wine topic to a respectful and doubtless sincere expression of a preference for water. When this one went as far as to recommend a wine firm in whose hands you could not go very far wrong Mrs. Quabarl thought it time to turn the conversation into more usual channels.

"We got very satisfactory references about you from Canon Teep," she observed; "a very estimable man, I should think."

"Drinks like a fish and beats his wife, otherwise a very lovable character," said the governess imperturbably.

"My *dear* Miss Hope! I trust you are exaggerating," exclaimed the Quabarls in unison.

"One must in justice admit that there is some provocation," continued the romancer. "Mrs. Teep is quite the most irritating bridge-player that I have ever sat down with; her leads and declarations would condone a certain amount of brutality in her partner, but to souse her with the contents of the only soda-water syphon in the house on a Sunday afternoon, when one couldn't get another, argues an indifference to the comfort of others which I cannot altogether overlook. You may think me hasty in my judgments, but it was practically on account of the syphon incident that I left."

"We will talk of this some other time," said Mrs. Quabarl hastily.

"I shall never allude to it again," said the governess with decision.

Mr. Quabarl made a welcome diversion by asking what studies the new instructress proposed to inaugurate on the morrow.

"History to begin with," she informed him.

"Ah, history," he observed sagely; "now, in teaching them history you must take care to interest them in what they learn. You must make them feel that they are being introduced to the life-stories of men and women who really lived—"

"I've told her all that," interposed Mrs. Quabarl.

"I teach history on the Schartz-Metterklume method," said the governess loftily.

"Ah, yes," said her listeners, thinking it expedient to assume an acquaintance at least with the name.

"What are you children doing out here?" demanded Mrs. Quabarl the next morning, on finding Irene sitting rather glumly at the head of the stairs, while her sister was perched in an attitude of depressed discomfort on the window-seat behind her, with a wolf-skin rug almost covering her.

"We are having a history lesson," came the unexpected reply. "I am supposed to be Rome, and Viola up there is the she-wolf; not a real wolf, but the figure of one that the Romans used to set store by—I forget why. Claude and Wilfred have gone to fetch the shabby women."

"The shabby women?"

"Yes, they've got to carry them off. They didn't want to, but Miss Hope got one of father's fives-bats and said she'd give them a number nine spanking if they didn't, so they've gone to do it."

A loud, angry screaming from the direction of the lawn drew Mrs. Quabarl thither in hot haste, fearful lest the threatened castigation might even now be in process of infliction. The outcry, however, came principally from the two small daughters of the lodge-keeper, who were being hauled and pushed towards the house by the panting and dishevelled Claude and Wilfred, whose task was rendered even more arduous by the incessant, if not very effectual, attacks of the captured maidens' small brother. The governess, fives-bat in hand, sat negligently on the stone balustrade, presiding over the scene with the cold impartiality of a Goddess of Battles. A furious and repeated chorus of "I'll tell muvver" rose from the lodge children, but the lodge-mother, who was hard of hearing, was for the moment immersed in the preoccupation of her washtub. After an apprehensive glance in the direction of the lodge (the good woman was gifted with the highly militant temper which is sometimes the privilege of deafness) Mrs. Quabarl flew indignantly to the rescue of the struggling captives.

"Wilfred! Claude! Let those children go at once. Miss Hope, what on earth is the meaning of this scene?"

"Early Roman history; the Sabine women, don't you know? It's the Schartz-Metterklume method to make children understand history by acting it themselves; fixes it in their memory, you know. Of course, if, thanks to your interference, your boys go through life thinking that the Sabine women ultimately escaped, I really cannot be held responsible."

"You may be very clever and modern, Miss Hope," said Mrs. Quabarl firmly, "but I should like you to leave here by the next train. Your luggage will be sent after you as soon as it arrives."

"I'm not certain exactly where I shall be for the next few days," said the dismissed instructress of youth; "you might keep my luggage till I wire my address. There are only a couple of trunks and some golf-clubs and a leopard cub."

"A leopard cub!" gasped Mrs. Quabarl. Even in her departure this extraordinary person seemed destined to leave a trail of embarrassment behind her.

"Well, it's rather left off being a cub; it's more than half-grown, you know. A fowl every day and a rabbit on Sundays is what it usually gets. Raw beef makes it too excitable. Don't trouble about getting the car for me, I'm rather inclined for a walk."

And Lady Carlotta strode out of the Quabarl horizon.

The advent of the genuine Miss Hope, who had made a mistake as to the day on which she was due to arrive, caused a turmoil which that good lady was quite unused to inspiring. Obviously the Quabarl family had been woefully befooled, but a certain amount of relief came with the knowledge.

"How tiresome for you, dear Carlotta," said her hostess, when the overdue guest ultimately arrived; "how very tiresome losing your train and having to stop overnight in a strange place."

"Oh, dear, no," said Lady Carlotta; "not at all tiresome—for me."

THE DEATH OF A BACHELOR[*]

BY ARTHUR SCHNITZLER

SOMEONE HAD knocked at the door, quite gently, but the doctor awoke at once, turned on the light, and sat up in bed. He glanced at his wife who was sleeping quietly, picked up his dressing-gown, and went into the hall. He did not at once recognise the old woman who stood there, with the grey shawl over her head.

"The master is suddenly taken very bad," she said; "would the doctor be kind enough to come at once?"

Now he recognised the voice: it was the housekeeper of that old friend of his who had never married. The doctor's first

[*] from *Little Novels*

thought was, "My friend is fifty-five years old, his heart has been out of order for years—it might well be something serious," and he said, "I'll come at once—will you wait for me?"

"Excuse me, doctor, but I have to hurry round to two other gentlemen," and she mentioned the names of the merchant and the author.

"But what is your business with them?"

"My master wants to see them again."

"See them again?"

"Yes, sir."

"He is sending for his friends," thought the doctor, "because he feels very near to death," . . . and he asked, "Is anyone with your master?"

"Of course," the old woman answered. "Johann is with him all the time." And she departed.

The doctor went back into his bedroom, and while he was dressing quickly and as noiselessly as possible, a feeling of bitterness came over him. It was not so much grief at the possibility of losing a good old friend, but the painful consciousness that they were all so far on in years, though not so long ago they had been young.

The doctor drove in an open carriage through the soft, heavy air of that spring night, to the neighbouring suburb where his friend lived. He looked up at the bedroom window which stood wide open, and whence the pale lamplight glimmered into the night.

The doctor went up the stairs, the servant opened the door, greeted him gravely, and dropped his left arm in a gesture of grief.

"What?" asked the doctor, catching his breath. "Am I too late?"

"Yes, sir," answered the servant, "my master died a quarter of an hour ago."

The doctor heaved a deep sigh and went into the room. There lay his dead friend, with thin, bluish, half-open lips, his arms outstretched over the white coverlet; his meagre beard was in disorder, and a few grey wisps of hair had strayed over his pale damp forehead. The silk-shaded electric lamp that stood on the night table cast a reddish shadow over the pillows. The doctor looked at the dead man. "When was he last in our house?" he thought to himself. "I remember it was snowing that evening. It must have been last winter." They had not seen much of each other latterly.

From without came the sound of horses' hoofs pawing the road. The doctor turned away from the dead man and looked across at the slender branches of the trees swaying in the night air.

The servant came in and the doctor then enquired how it had all happened.

The servant told a familiar story of a sudden attack of vomiting and breathlessness. Then his master had leapt out of bed, paced up and down the room, rushed to his writing-table, tottered back to bed again, where he lay racked with thirst and groaning and after one last effort to raise himself he had sunk back upon the pillows. The doctor nodded and laid his hand on the dead man's forehead.

A carriage drew up. The doctor went over to the window. He saw the merchant get out and glance enquiringly up at the house. Unconsciously the doctor let his hand fall just as the servant had done, who opened the door to him. The merchant threw back his head as if refusing to believe it, and the doctor shrugged his shoulders, left the window, and sat down, in sudden weariness, on a chair at the feet of the dead man. The merchant came in wearing a yellow overcoat unbuttoned, put his hat on a small table near the door, and shook the doctor by the hand. "How dreadful!" he said; "how did it happen?" And he stared dubiously at the dead man.

The doctor told him what he knew, and added: "Even if I had been able to come at once, I could have done nothing."

"Fancy," said the merchant, "it is exactly a week to-day since I last spoke to him at the theatre. I wanted to have supper with him afterwards, but he had one of his secret appointments."

"What, still?" said the doctor, with a gloomy smile.

Outside another carriage stopped. The merchant went to the window. When he saw the author getting out, he drew back, not wanting to announce the sad news by his expression. The doctor had taken a cigarette out of his case and was twisting it about in an embarrassed sort of way. "It's a habit I've had since my hospital days," he remarked apologetically. "When I left a sick-room at night, the first thing I always did was to light a cigarette, whether I had been to give an injection of morphia or to certify a death."

"Do you know," said the merchant, "how long it is since I saw a corpse? Fourteen years—not since my father lay in his coffin."

"But—your wife?"

"I saw my wife in her last moments, but—not afterwards."

The author appeared, shook hands with the other two, and glanced doubtfully at the bed. Then he walked resolutely up to it and looked earnestly at the dead man, yet not without a contemptuous twitch of the lips. "So it was he," he said to himself. For he had played with the question which of his more intimate friends was to be the first to take the last journey.

The housekeeper came in. With tears in her eyes she sank down by the bed, sobbed, and wrung her hands. The author laid his hand gently and soothingly on her shoulder.

The merchant and the doctor stood at the window, and the dank air of the spring night played upon their foreheads.

"It is really very odd," began the merchant, "that he has sent for all of us. Did he want to see us all gathered round his death-bed? Had he something important to say to us?"

"As far as I'm concerned," said the doctor, with a sad smile, "it would not be odd, as I am a doctor. And you," he said, turning to the merchant, "you were at times his business adviser. So perhaps it was a matter of some last instructions that he wanted to give you personally."

"That is possible," said the merchant.

The housekeeper had left the room, and the friends could hear her talking to the other servant in the hall. The author was still standing by the bed carrying on a silent dialogue with the dead man.

"I think," whispered the merchant to the doctor, "that latterly he saw more of our friend. Perhaps he can throw some light on the question."

The author stood motionless, gazing steadily into the closed eyes of the dead man. His hands, which held his broad-brimmed grey hat, were crossed behind his back. The two others began to grow impatient, and the merchant went up to him and cleared his throat.

"Three days ago," observed the author, "I went for a two-hours' walk with him among the hills and vineyards. Would you like to know what he talked about? A trip to Sweden, that he had planned for the summer, a new Rembrandt portfolio just published by Watson's in London, and last of all about Santos Dumont. He went into all sorts of mathematical and scientific details about a dirigible airship, which, to be frank with you, I did not entirely grasp. He certainly was not thinking about death. It must indeed be true that at a certain age people again stop thinking about it."

The doctor had gone into the adjoining room. Here he might certainly venture to light his cigarette. The sight of white ashes in the bronze tray on the writing-table struck him as strange and almost uncanny. He wondered why he was still there at all, as he sat down on the chair by the writing-table. He had the right to go as soon as he liked, since he had obviously been sent for as a doctor. For their friendship had nearly come to an end. "At my time of life," he went on, pursuing his reflection, "it is quite impossible for a man like me to keep friends with someone who has no profession and never has had one. What would he have taken up if he had not been rich? He would probably have turned to literature: he was very clever." And he remembered many malicious but pointed remarks the dead man had made, more especially about the works of their common friend, the author.

The author and the merchant came in. The author assumed an expression of disapproval when he saw the doctor sitting at the deserted writing-table with a cigarette in his hand, which was, however, still unlit, and he closed the door behind him. Here, however, they were to some extent in another world.

"Have you any sort of idea? . . ." asked the merchant.

"About what?" asked the author absent-mindedly.

"What made him send for us, and just us?"

The author thought it unnecessary to look for any special reason. "Our friend," he explained, "felt death was upon him, and if he had lived a rather solitary life, at least latterly, at such an hour people who are by nature socially inclined probably feel the need of seeing their friends about them."

"He had a mistress, though," remarked the merchant.

"Oh, a mistress," repeated the author, and contemptuously raised his eyebrows.

At this moment the doctor noticed that the middle drawer of the writing-table was half open.

"I wonder if his will is here?" he said.

"That's no concern of ours," observed the merchant, "at least at this moment. And in any case there is a married sister living in London."

The servant came in. He respectfully asked what arrangements he should make about having the body laid out, the funeral, and the mourning cards. He knew that a will was in the possession of his master's lawyer, but he was doubtful whether it contained instructions in these matters. The author found the room stuffy and close, he drew aside the heavy red curtains over one of the windows and threw open both casements, and a great waft of the dark blue spring night poured into the room. The doctor asked the servant whether he had any idea why the dead man had sent for him, because, if he remembered rightly, it was years since he had been summoned to that house in his capacity as doctor. The servant, who obviously expected the question, pulled a swollen-looking wallet from his jacket-pocket, took out a sheet of paper, and explained that seven years ago his master had written down the names of the friends whom he wanted sent for when he was dying. So that, even if the dead man had been unconscious at the time, he would have ventured to send for the gentlemen on his own responsibility.

The doctor took the sheet of paper from the servant's hand and found five names written on it: in addition to those present was the name of a friend who had died two years ago, and another that he did not know. The servant explained that the latter

was a manufacturer whose house the dead man used to visit
nine or ten years ago, and whose address had been lost and forgotten. The three looked at each other with uneasy curiosity.
"What does that mean?" asked the merchant. "Did he intend to
make a speech in his last hours?"

"A funeral oration on himself, no doubt," added the author.

The doctor had turned his eyes on the open drawer of the
writing-table, and suddenly these words, in large Roman letters, stared at him from the cover of an envelope: "To my
friends."

"Hullo!" he cried, took the envelope, held it up, and showed
it to the others. "This is for us." He turned to the servant and,
with a movement of the head, indicated that he was not wanted.
The servant went.

"For us?" said the author, with wide-open eyes.

"There can be no doubt," said the doctor, "that we are justified in opening this."

"It's our duty," said the merchant, and buttoned up his overcoat.

The doctor had taken a paper-knife from a glass tray,
opened the envelope, laid the letter down, and put on his eye-
glasses. The author took advantage of the brief interval to pick
up the letter and unfold it. "As it is for all of us," he remarked
casually, and bent over the writing-table so that the light from
the shaded lamp should fall on the paper. Near him stood the
merchant. The author remained seated.

"You might read it aloud," said the merchant, and the author
began.

" 'To my friends,' "—he stopped with a smile—"yes, it's
written here also," and he went on reading in a tone of ad-
mirable detachment. " 'About a quarter of an hour ago I
breathed my last. You are assembled at my death-bed, and you
are preparing to read this letter together—if it still exists in the
hour of my death, I ought to add. For it might so happen that I
should come to a better frame of mind . . .' "

"What?" asked the doctor.

" 'A better frame of mind,' " repeated the author, and continued: " 'and decide to destroy this letter, for it can do not the

slightest good to me, and, at the very least, may cause you some unpleasant hours, even if it does not absolutely poison the life of one or other of you.' "

"Poison our lives?" repeated the doctor, in a wondering tone, as he polished his eyeglasses.

"Quicker," said the merchant in a husky voice.

The author continued. " 'And I ask myself what kind of evil humour it is that sends me to the writing-table to-day and induces me to write down words whose effect I shall never be able to read upon your faces. And even if I could the pleasure I should get would be too trifling to serve as an excuse for the incredible act I am now about to commit with feelings of the heartiest satisfaction.' "

"Ha!" cried the doctor in a voice he did not recognise as his own. The author threw a glance of irritation at him, and read on, quicker and with less expression than before. " 'Yes, it is an evil humour, and nothing else, for I have really nothing whatever against any of you. I like you all very well in my own way, just as you like me in your way. I never despised you, and if I often laughed at you, I never mocked you. No, not once—and least of all in those hours of which you are so soon to call to mind such vivid and such painful images. Why, then, this evil humour? Perhaps it arose from a deep and not essentially ignoble desire not to leave the world with so many lies upon my soul. I might imagine so, if I had even once had the slightest notion of what men call remorse.' "

"Oh, get on to the end of it," said the doctor in a new and abrupt tone.

The merchant, without more ado, took the letter from the author, who felt a sort of paralysis creeping over his fingers, glanced down it quickly and read the words: "It was fate, my dear friends, and I could not alter it. I have had the wives of all of you: yes, every one.' "

The merchant stopped suddenly and turned back to the first sheet.

"The letter was written nine years ago," said the merchant.

"Go on," said the author sharply.

And the merchant proceeded. " 'Of course the circumstances were different in each case. With one of them I lived almost as though we had been married, for many months. The second was more or less what the world is accustomed to call a mad adventure. With the third, the affair went so far that I wanted us to kill ourselves together. The fourth I threw downstairs because she betrayed me with another. And the last was my mistress on one occasion only. Do you all breathe again— my good friends? You should not. It was perhaps the loveliest hour of my life . . . and hers. Well, my friends, I have nothing more to tell you. Now I am going to fold up this letter, put it away in my writing-desk—and there may it lie until my humour changes and I destroy it, or until it is given into your hands in that hour when I lie upon my death-bed. Farewell.' "

The doctor took the letter from the merchant's hands and read it with apparent care from the beginning to the end. Then he looked up at the merchant who stood by with folded arms and gazed down at him with something like derision.

"Although your wife died last year," said the doctor calmly, "it is none the less true."

The author paced up and down the room, jerked his head convulsively from side to side a few times, and suddenly hissed out through his clenched teeth, "the swine," and then stared in front of him as though looking for something that had dissolved into air. He was trying to recall the image of the youthful creature that he had once held in his arms as wife. Other women's faces appeared, often recalled but long since, he had thought, forgotten, but he could not bring before his mind the one he wanted. For his wife's body was withered and held no attraction for him, and it was so long since she had been his beloved. But she had become something other than that to him, something more and something nobler: a friend and a comrade; full of pride at his successes, full of sympathy with his disappointments, full of insight into his deepest nature. It seemed to him not impossible that the dead man had, in his wickedness, secretly envied him his comrade and tried to take her away. For all those others—what had they really meant to him? He called to mind certain adventures, some of old days and some more recent; there had been enough and to spare of them in his varied literary life, and his wife had smiled or wept over them as they went their course. Where was all this now? As faded as that far-off hour when his wife had flung herself into the arms of a man of no account, without reflection, perhaps without thought: almost as extinct as the recollection of that same hour in the dead skull that lay within on that pitifully crumpled pillow. But perhaps this last will and testament was a bundle of lies—the last revenge of a poor commonplace fellow who knew himself condemned to eternal oblivion, upon a distinguished man over whose works death has been given no power. This was not at all improbable. But even if it were true—it was a petty revenge and unsuccessful in either case.

The doctor stared at the sheet of paper that lay before him, and thought of his gentle, ever kindly wife, now growing old, who lay asleep at home. He thought also of his three children: of his eldest who was now doing his one year's military service, of his tall daughter, who was engaged to a lawyer, and of the youngest, who was so graceful and charming that a famous artist, who had lately met her at a ball, had asked if he might paint her. He thought of his comfortable home, and all this that surged up at him from the dead man's letter seemed to him not so much untrue as, in some mysterious way, almost sublimely insignificant. He scarcely felt that at this moment he had experienced anything new. A strange epoch in his existence came into his mind, fourteen or fifteen years before, when he had met with certain troubles over his profession, and, worn out and nearly crazy, had planned to leave the city, his wife and family. At the same time he had entered upon a kind of wild, reckless existence, in which a strange hysterical woman had played a part, who had subsequently committed suicide over another lover. How his life had gradually returned to its original course he could not now remember in the least. But it must have been in those bad times, which had passed away as they had come, like an illness, that his wife had betrayed him. Yes, it must so have happened, and it was clear to him that he had really always known it. Was she not once on the point of confessing it? Had she not given him hints? Thirteen or fourteen years ago.... When could it have been...? Wasn't it one summer on a holiday trip—late in the evening on the terrace of some hotel? In vain he tried to recall those vanished words.

The merchant stood at the window and stared into the soft pale night. He was determined he would remember his dead wife. But however much he searched his inmost consciousness, at first he could only see himself in the light of a grey morning, standing in black clothes outside a curtained doorway, receiving and returning sympathetic handshakes, with a stale reek of carbolic and flowers in his nostrils. Slowly he succeeded in recalling to his mind the image of his dead wife. And yet at first it was but the image of an image for he could only see the large portrait in a gilt frame that hung over the piano in the drawing-room at home and displayed a haughty-looking lady of thirty in a ball dress. Then at last she herself appeared as a young girl, who, nearly twenty years before, pale and trembling, had accepted his proposal of marriage. Then there arose before him the appearance of a woman in all her splendour, enthroned beside him in a theatre-box, gazing at the stage, but inwardly far away. Then he remembered a passionate creature who welcomed him with unexpected warmth on his return from a long journey. Swiftly again his thoughts turned to a nervous tearful being, with greenish heavy eyes, who had poisoned his days with all manner of evil humours. Next he saw an alarmed, affectionate mother, in a light morning frock, watching by the bedside of a sick child who, none the less, died. Last of all, he saw a pale, outstretched creature in a room reeking of ether, her mouth so pitifully drawn down at the corners, and cold beads of sweat on her forehead, who had shaken his very soul with pity. He knew that all these pictures, and a hundred others, that flashed past his mind's eye with incredible speed, were of one and the same being who had been lowered into the grave two years ago, over whom he had wept, and after whose death he had felt freed from bondage. It seemed to him he must choose one out of all these pictures to reach some definite reaction; for at present he was tossed by shame and anger, groping in the void. He stood there irresolute, and gazed across at the houses in their gardens, shimmering faintly red and yellow in the moonlight and looking like pale painted walls with only air behind them.

"Good-night," said the doctor and got up.

The merchant turned towards him and said: "There's nothing more for me to do here either."

The author had picked up the letter, stuffed it unobtrusively into his coat pocket, and opened the door into the adjoining room. Slowly he walked up to the death-bed, and the others watched him looking down silently at the corpse, his hands behind his back. Then they turned away.

In the hall the merchant said to the servant: "As regards the funeral, it is possible that the will in possession of the lawyers may contain some further instructions."

"And don't forget," pursued the doctor, "to telegraph to your master's sister in London."

"To be sure, sir," replied the servant, as he opened the front door.

The author overtook them on the doorstep. "I can take you both with me," said the doctor, whose carriage was waiting.

"Thank you, no," said the merchant. "I shall walk."

He shook hands with both of them and walked down the road towards the city, glad to feel the soft night air upon his face.

The author got into the carriage with the doctor. The birds were beginning to sing in the garden. The carriage drove past the merchant, and the three men raised their hats, ironically polite, each with an identical expression on his face. "Shall we soon see another play of yours?" the doctor asked the author in his usual voice.

The latter launched into an account of the extraordinary difficulties involved in the production of his latest drama which, he had to confess, contained the most sweeping attacks on everything generally held to be sacred. The doctor nodded and did not listen. Nor did the author, for the familiar sentences fell from his lips as though he had learned them by heart.

Both men got out at the doctor's house, and the carriage drove away.

The doctor rang. They both stood and said nothing. As the

footsteps of the porter approached, the author said, Good-
night, my dear doctor"; and he added slowly, with a twitch of
his nostrils, "I shan't mention this to my wife, you know."

The doctor threw a sidelong glance at him and smiled his
charming smile.

The door opened, they shook each other by the hand, the
doctor disappeared into the passage, and the door slammed.
The author went.

He felt in his breast pocket. Yes, the letter was there. His
wife would find it sealed and secure among his papers. And
with that strange power of imagination that was peculiarly his
own, he could already hear her whispering over his grave, "Oh,
how splendid of you . . . how noble!"

THE APOSTATE*

BY GEORGE MILBURN

HARRY, YOU been jacking me up about how I been neglecting Rotary here lately, so I'm just going to break
down and tell you something. Now I don't want you to take this
personal, Harry, because it's not meant personal at all. No
siree! Not a-tall! But, just between you and I, Harry, I'm not
going to be coming out to Rotary lunches any more. I mean I'm
quitting Rotary! . . .

Now whoa there! Whoa! Whoa just a minute and let me get
in a word edgeways. Just let me finish my little say.

Don't you never take it into your head that I haven't been
wrestling with this thing plenty. I mean I've argued it all out
with myself. Now I'm going to tell you the whyfor and the
whereof and the howcome about this, Harry, but kindly don't
let what I say go no further. Please keep it strictly on the Q.T.

* from *The New Yorker* and *No More Trumpets*

Because I guess the rest of the boys would suspicion that I was turning highbrow on them. But you've always been a buddy to me, Harry, you mangy old son of a hoss thief, you, so what I'm telling you is the straight dope.

Harry, like you no doubt remember, up till a few months ago Rotary was about "the most fondest thing I is of," as the nigger says. There wasn't nothing that stood higher for me than Rotary.

Well, here, about a year ago last fall I took a trip down to the university to visit my son and go to a football game. You know Hubert Junior, my boy. Sure. Well, this is his second year down at the university. Yes, that boy is getting a college education. I mean, I'm all for youth having a college education.

Of course I think there is such a thing as too much education working a detriment. Take, for instance, some of these long-hairs running around knocking the country right now. But what I mean is, a good, sound, substantial college education. I don't mean a string of letters a yard long for a man to write after his John Henry. I just mean that I want my boy to have his sheep-skin, they call it, before he starts out in the world. Like the fellow says, I want him to get his A.B. degree, and then he can go out and get his J.O.B.

Now, Harry, I always felt like a father has got certain responsibilities to his son. That's just good Rotary. That's all that is. You know that that's just good Rotary yourself, Harry. Well, I always wanted Hubert to think about me just like I was a pal to him, or say an older brother, maybe. Hubert always knew that all he had to do was come to me, and I would act like a big buddy to him, irregardless.

Well, like I was telling you, Harry, I started Hubert in to the university two years ago, and after he had been there about two months, I thought I would run down and see how he was getting along and go to a football game. So I and Mrs. T. drove over one Friday. We didn't know the town very well, so we stopped at a filling station, and I give Hubert a ring, and he come right on down to where we was to show us the way. Just as soon as he come up, I could see right then that he had something on his mind bothering him.

He called me aside and took me into the filling-station rest-room, and says: "For the love of God, Dad, take that Rotary button out of your coat lapel," he says to me.

Harry, that come as a big surprise to me, and I don't mind telling you that it just about took the wind out of my sails. But I wasn't going to let on to him, so I rared back on my dignity, and says, "Why, what do you mean, take that Rotary button out of my lapel, young man?" I says to him.

"Dad," Hubert says to me, serious, "any frat house has always got a few cynics in it. If you was to wear that Rotary button in your lapel out to the frat house, just as soon as you got out of sight, some of those boys at the house would razz the life out of me," he says.

"Hubert," I says, "there's not a thing that this lapel badge represents that any decent, moral person could afford to make fun of. If that's the kind of Reds you got out at your fraternity, the kind that would razz a what you might call sacred thing—yes sir, a sacred thing—like Rotary, well I and your mamma can just so somewheres else and put up. I don't guess the hotels have quit running," I says to him.

By now I was on my high horse right, see?

"Now, Dad," Hubert says, "it's not that. I mean, person'ly I'm awful proud of you. It's just that I haven't been pledged to this fraternity long, see, and when some of those older members found out you was a Rotarian they would deal me a lot of misery, and I couldn't say nothing. Person'ly I think Rotary is all right," he says to me.

"Well, you better, son," I says, "or I'm going to begin to think that you're sick in the head."

The way he explained it, though, Harry, that made it a horse of a different tail, as the saying goes, so I give in and took off my Rotary button right there. Stuck it in my pocket, see? So we went on out and visited at Hubert's fraternity house, and do you know that those boys just got around there and treated we folks like we was princes of the blood. I mean you would of thought that I was an old ex-graduate of that university. And we saw the big pigskin tussle the next day, fourteen to aught, favor us, and we had such a scrumptious time all around I forgot all about what Hubert had said.

Ever'thing would of been all right, except for what happened later. I guess some of those older boys at the frat house begin using their form of psychology on Hubert. I mean they finely got his mind set against Rotary, because when he come home for the summer vacation that was about the size of things.

I mean all last summer, I thought Hubert never would let up. He just kept it up, making sarcastic remarks about Rotary, see? Even when we was on our vacation trip. You know we drove out to California and back last summer, Harry. Come back with the same air in the tires we started out with. Well, I thought it would be kind of nice to drop in and eat with the Hollywood Rotary—you know, just to be able to say I had. Well, do you know that that boy Hubert made so much fun of the idea I just had to give it up? That was the way it was the whole trip. He got his mother around on his side, too. Just to be frank with you, I never got so sick and tired of anything in all my born days.

Well, Harry, I had my dander up there for a while, and all the bickering in the world couldn't of shook me from my stand. But finely Hubert went back to college in September, and I thought I would have a little peace. Then I just got to thinking about it, and it all come over me. "Look here, Mister Man," I says to myself, "your faith and loyalty to Rotary may be a fine thing, and all that, but it's just costing you the fellowship of your own son." Now a man can't practice Rotary in the higher sense, and yet at the same time be letting his own son's fellowship get loose from him. So there it was. Blood's thicker than water, Harry. You'll have to admit that.

Right along in there, Harry, was the first time I begin to attending meetings irregular. I'll tell you—you might not think so—but it was a pretty tough struggle for me. I remember one Monday noon, Rotary-meeting day, I happened to walk past the Hotel Beckman just at lunchtime. The windows of the Venetian Room was open, and I could hear you boys singing a Rotary song. You know that one we sing set to the tune of "Last Night on the Back Porch." It goes:

I love the Lions in the morning,
The Exchange Club at night,
I love the Y's men in the evening,
And Kiwanis are all right . . .

Well, I couldn't carry a tune if I had it in a sack, but anyway that's the way it goes. So I just stopped in my tracks and stood there listening to that song coming out of the Hotel Beckman dining room. And when the boys come to the last verse,

I love the Optimists in the springtime,
The Ad Club in the fall,
But each day—and in every way—
I love Rotary best of all. . . .

I tell you, Harry, that just got me. I had a lump in my throat big enough to choke a cow. The tears begin coming up in my eyes, and it might sound ridiculous to hear me tell it now, but I could of broke down and bawled right there on the street. I got a grip on myself and walked on off, but right then I says to myself, "The hell with Hubert and his highbrow college-fraternity ideas; I'm going back to Rotary next week."

Well, I did go back the next week, and what happened decided me on taking the step I decided on. Here's what decided me. You know I never got very well acquainted with Gay Harrison, the new secretary. I mean, of course, I know him all right, but he hasn't been in Rotary only but about a year. Well, on that particular day, I just happened to let my tongue slip and called him Mister Harrison, instead of by his nickname. Well, of course, the boys slapped a dollar fine on me right then and there. I haven't got no kick to make about that, but the point is, I had a letter from Hubert in my pocket right then, telling me that he had run short of money. So I just couldn't help but be struck by the idea "I wish I was giving Hubert this dollar." So that's what decided me on devoting my time and finances to another kind of fellowship, Harry.

I get down to the university to see Hubert more frequent now. I make it a point to. And the boys come to me, and I been helping them a little on their frat building fund. There's a fine spirit of fellowship in an organization like that. Some boys from the best families of the State are members, too. You might think from what I said that they'd be uppish, but they're not. No siree. Not a bit of it. I been down there enough for them to know me, now, and they all pound me on the back and call me H.T., just like I was one of them. And I do them, too. And I notice that when they sit down to a meal, they have some songs they sing just as lively and jolly as any we had at Rotary. Of course, like Hubert said, a few of them might have some wild-haired ideas about Rotary, but they're young yet. And as far as I can see there's not a knocker nor a sourbelly among them. Absolutely democratic.

It puts me in mind of a little incidence that happened last month when the frat threw a big Dad's Day banquet for us down there. All the fathers of the boys from all over the State was there. Well, to promote the spirit of fellowship between dad and son, the fraternity boys all agreed to call their dads by their first name, just treating their dads like big buddies. So at the table Hubert happened to forget for a minute, and says to me "Dad" something. Well sir, the president of the frat flashed right out, "All right, Hubie, we heard you call H.T. 'Dad.' So that'll just cost you a dollar for the ice-cream fund." Ever'body had a good laugh at Hubert getting caught like that, but do you know, that boy of mine just forked right over without making a kick. That shows the stuff, don't it, Harry? Nothing wrong with a boy like that.

And the whole bunch is like that, ever' one of them. I'll tell you, Harry, the boys at that frat of Hubert's are the builders in the coming generation. Any man of vision can see that.

Well, that's that. Now what was you going to say?

THE PHOENIX*

BY SYLVIA TOWNSEND WARNER

LORD STRAWBERRY, a nobleman, collected birds. He had the finest aviary in Europe, so large that eagles did not find it uncomfortable, so well laid out that both humming-birds and snow-buntings had a climate that suited them perfectly. But for many years the finest set of apartments remained empty, with just a label saying: "PHŒNIX. *Habitat: Arabia.*"

Many authorities on bird life had assured Lord Strawberry that the phœnix is a fabulous bird, or that the breed was long extinct. Lord Strawberry was unconvinced: his family had always believed in phœnixes. At intervals he received from his agents (together with statements of their expenses) birds which they declared were the phœnix but which turned out to be orioles, macaws, turkey buzzards dyed orange, etc., or stuffed cross-breeds, ingeniously assembled from various plumages. Finally Lord Strawberry went himself to Arabia, where, after some months, he found a phœnix, won its confidence, caught it, and brought it home in perfect condition.

It was a remarkably fine phœnix, with a charming character—affable to the other birds in the aviary and much attached to Lord Strawberry. On its arrival in England it made a great stir among ornithologists, journalists, poets, and milliners, and was constantly visited. But it was not puffed by these attentions, and when it was no longer in the news, and the visits fell off, it showed no pique or rancour. It ate well, and seemed perfectly contented.

It costs a great deal of money to keep up an aviary. When

* from *The Cat's Cradle-Book*

Lord Strawberry died he died penniless. The aviary came on the market. In normal times the rarer birds, and certainly the phœnix, would have been bid for by the trustees of Europe's great zoological societies, or by private persons in the U.S.A.; but as it happened Lord Strawberry died just after a world war, when both money and bird-seed were hard to come by (indeed the cost of bird-seed was one of the things which had ruined Lord Strawberry). The London *Times* urged in a leader that the phœnix be bought for the London Zoo, saying that a nation of bird-lovers had a moral right to own such a rarity; and a fund, called the Strawberry Phœnix Fund, was opened. Students, naturalists, and schoolchildren contributed according to their means; but their means were small, and there were no large donations. So Lord Strawberry's executors (who had the death duties to consider) closed with the higher offer of Mr. Tancred Poldero, owner and proprietor of Poldero's Wizard Wonderworld.

For quite a while Mr. Poldero considered his phœnix a bargain. It was a civil and obliging bird, and adapted itself readily to its new surroundings. It did not cost much to feed, it did not mind children; and though it had no tricks, Mr. Poldero supposed it would soon pick up some. The publicity of the Strawberry Phœnix Fund was now most helpful. Almost every contributor now saved up another half-crown in order to see the phœnix. Others, who had not contributed to the fund, even paid double to look at it on the five-shilling days.

But then business slackened. The phœnix was as handsome as ever, and as amiable; but, as Mr. Poldero said, it hadn't got Udge. Even at popular prices the phœnix was not really popular. It was too quiet, too classical. So people went instead to watch the antics of the baboons, or to admire the crocodile who had eaten the woman.

One day Mr. Poldero said to his manager, Mr. Ramkin:

"How long since any fool paid to look at the phœnix?"

"Matter of three weeks," replied Mr. Ramkin.

"Eating his head off," said Mr. Poldero. "Let alone the insurance. Seven shillings a week it costs me to insure that bird, and I might as well insure the Archbishop of Canterbury."

"The public don't like him. He's too quiet for them, that's the trouble. Won't mate nor nothing. And I've tried him with no end of pretty pollies, ospreys, and Cochin-Chinas, and the Lord knows what. But he won't look at them."

"Wonder if we could swap him for a livelier one," said Mr. Poldero.

"Impossible. There's only one of him at a time."

"Go on!"

"I mean it. Haven't you ever read what it says on the label?"

They went to the phœnix's cage. It flapped its wings politely, but they paid no attention. They read:

"PANSY. *Phœnix phœnixissima formosissima arabiana*. This rare and fabulous bird is UNIQUE. The World's Old Bachelor. Has no mate and doesn't want one. When old, sets fire to itself and emerges miraculously reborn. Specially imported from the East."

"I've got an idea," said Mr. Poldero. "How old do you suppose that bird is?"

"Looks in its prime to me," said Mr. Ramkin.

"Suppose," continued Mr. Poldero, "we could somehow get him alight? We'd advertise it beforehand, of course, work up interest. Then we'd have a new bird, and a bird with some romance about it, a bird with a life-story. We could sell a bird like that."

Mr. Ramkin nodded.

"I've read about it in a book," he said. "You've got to give them scented woods and what not, and they build a nest and sit down on it and catch fire spontaneous. But they won't do it till they're old. That's the snag."

"Leave that to me," said Mr. Poldero. "You get those scented woods, and I'll do the ageing."

It was not easy to age the phœnix. Its allowance of food was halved, and halved again, but though it grew thinner its eyes were undimmed and its plumage glossy as ever. The heating was turned off; but it puffed out its feathers against the cold, and seemed none the worse. Other birds were put into its cage, birds of a peevish and quarrelsome nature. They pecked and chivied it; but the phœnix was so civil and amiable that after a day or two they lost their animosity. Then Mr. Poldero tried alley cats. These could not be won by manners, but the phœnix darted above their heads and flapped its golden wings in their faces, and daunted them.

Mr. Poldero turned to a book on Arabia, and read that the climate was dry. "Aha!" said he. The phœnix was moved to a small cage that had a sprinkler in the ceiling. Every night the sprinkler was turned on. The phœnix began to cough. Mr. Poldero had another good idea. Daily he stationed himself in front of the cage to jeer at the bird and abuse it.

When spring was come, Mr. Poldero felt justified in beginning a publicity campaign about the ageing phœnix. The old public favourite, he said, was nearing its end. Meanwhile he tested the bird's reactions every few days by putting a few tufts of foul-smelling straw and some strands of rusty barbed wire into the cage, to see if it were interested in nesting yet. One day the phœnix began turning over the straw. Mr. Poldero signed a contract for the film rights. At last the hour seemed ripe. It was a fine Saturday evening in May. For some weeks the public interest in the ageing phœnix had been working up, and the admission charge had risen to five shillings. The enclosure was thronged. The lights and the cameras were trained on the cage, and a loud-speaker proclaimed to the audience the rarity of what was about to take place.

"The phœnix," said the loud-speaker, "is the aristocrat of bird-life. Only the rarest and most expensive specimens of oriental wood, drenched in exotic perfumes, will tempt him to construct his strange love-nest."

Now a neat assortment of twigs and shavings, strongly scented, was shoved into the cage.

"The phœnix," the loud-speaker continued, "is as capricious as Cleopatra, as luxurious as la du Barry, as heady as a strain of wild gypsy music. All the fantastic pomp and passion of the ancient East, its languorous magic, its subtle cruelties . . ."

"Lawks!" cried a woman in the crowd. "He's at it!"

A quiver stirred the dulled plumage. The phœnix turned its head from side to side. It descended, staggering, from its perch. Then wearily it began to pull about the twigs and shavings.

The cameras clicked, the lights blazed full on the cage. Rushing to the loud-speaker Mr. Poldero exclaimed:

"Ladies and gentlemen, this is the thrilling moment the world has breathlessly awaited. The legend of centuries is materializing before our modern eyes. The phœnix ..."

The phœnix settled on its pyre and appeared to fall asleep.

The film director said:

"Well, if it doesn't evaluate more than this, mark it instructional."

At that moment the phœnix and the pyre burst into flames. The flames streamed upwards, leaped out on every side. In a minute or two everything was burned to ashes, and some thousand people, including Mr. Poldero, perished in the blaze.

THAT EVENING SUN[*]

BY WILLIAM FAULKNER

MONDAY IS no different from any other weekday in Jefferson now. The streets are paved now, and the telephone and electric companies are cutting down more and more of the shade trees—the water oaks, the maples and locusts and elms—to make room for iron poles bearing clusters of bloated and ghostly and bloodless grapes, and we have a city laundry which makes the rounds on Monday morning, gathering the bundles of clothes into bright-colored, specially made motorcars: the soiled wearing of a whole week now flees apparition-like behind alert and irritable electric horns, with a long diminishing noise of rubber and asphalt like tearing silk, and even the Negro women who still take in white people's washing after the old custom, fetch and deliver it in automobiles.

But fifteen years ago, on Monday morning the quiet, dusty,

[*] from *These Thirteen*

shady streets would be full of Negro women with, balanced on their steady, turbaned heads, bundles of clothes tied up in sheets, almost as large as cotton bales, carried so without touch of hand between the kitchen door of the white house and the blackened washpot beside a cabin door in Negro Hollow.

Nancy would set her bundle on the top of her head, then upon the bundle in turn she would set the black straw sailor hat which she wore winter and summer. She was tall, with a high, sad face sunken a little where her teeth were missing. Sometimes we would go a part of the way down the lane and across the pasture with her, to watch the balanced bundle and the hat that never bobbed nor wavered, even when she walked down into the ditch and up the other side and stooped through the fence. She would go down on her hands and knees and crawl through the gap, her head rigid, uptilted, the bundle steady as a rock or a balloon, and rise to her feet again and go on.

Sometimes the husbands of the washing women would fetch and deliver the clothes, but Jesus never did that for Nancy, even before Father told him to stay away from our house, even when Dilsey was sick and Nancy would come to cook for us.

And then about half the time we'd have to go down the lane to Nancy's cabin and tell her to come on and cook breakfast. We would stop at the ditch, because Father told us to not have anything to do with Jesus—he was a short black man, with a razor scar down his face—and we would throw rocks at Nancy's house until she came to the door, leaning her head around it without any clothes on.

"What yawl mean, chunking my house?" Nancy said. "What you little devils mean?"

"Father says for you to come on and get breakfast," Caddy said. "Father says it's over a half an hour now, and you've got to come this minute."

"I ain't studying no breakfast," Nancy said. "I going to get my sleep out."

"I bet you're drunk," Jason said. "Father says you're drunk. Are you drunk, Nancy?"

"Who says I is?" Nancy said. "I got to get my sleep out. I ain't studying no breakfast."

So after a while we quit chunking the cabin and went back home. When she finally came, it was too late for me to go to school. So we thought it was whiskey until that day they arrested her again and they were taking her to jail and they passed Mr. Stovall. He was the cashier in the bank and a deacon in the Baptist church, and Nancy began to say:

"When you going to pay me, white man? When you going to pay me, white man? It's been three times now since you paid me a cent—" Mr. Stovall knocked her down, but she kept on saying, "When you going to pay me, white man? It's been three times now since—" until Mr. Stovall kicked her in the mouth with his heel and the marshal caught Mr. Stovall back, and Nancy lying in the street, laughing. She turned her head and spat out some blood and teeth and said, "It's been three times now since he paid me a cent."

That was how she lost her teeth, and all that day they told about Nancy and Mr. Stovall, and all that night the ones that passed the jail could hear Nancy singing and yelling. They could see her hands holding to the window bars, and a lot of them stopped along the fence, listening to her and the jailer trying to make her stop. She didn't shut up until almost day-light, when the jailer began to hear a bumping and scraping upstairs and he went up there and found Nancy hanging from the window bar. He said that it was cocaine and not whiskey, because no nigger would try to commit suicide unless he was full of cocaine, because a nigger full of cocaine wasn't a nigger any longer.

The jailer cut her down and revived her; then he beat her, whipped her. She had hung herself with her dress. She had fixed it all right, but when they arrested her she didn't have on anything except a dress and so she didn't have anything to tie her hands with, and she couldn't make her hands let go of the window ledge. So the jailer heard the noise and ran up there and found Nancy hanging from the window, stark naked, her belly already swelling out a little, like a little balloon.

When Dilsey was sick in her cabin and Nancy was cooking

for us, we could see her apron swelling out; that was before
Father told Jesus to stay away from the house. Jesus was in the
kitchen, sitting behind the stove, with his razor scar on his
black face like a piece of dirty string. He said it was a watermelon that Nancy had under her dress.

"It never come off of your vine, though," Nancy said.

"Off of what vine?" Caddy said.

"I can cut down the vine it did come off of," Jesus said.

"What makes you want to talk like that before these
chillen?" Nancy said. "Whyn't you go on to work? You done et.
You want Mr. Jason to catch you hanging around his kitchen,
talking that way before these chillen?"

"Talking what way?" Caddy said. "What vine?"

"I can't hang around white man's kitchen," Jesus said. "But
white man can hang around mine. White man can come in my
house, but I can't stop him. When white man want to come in
my house, I ain't got no house. I can't stop him, but he can't
kick me outen it. He can't do that."

Dilsey was still sick in her cabin. Father told Jesus to stay
off our place. Dilsey was still sick. It was a long time. We were
in the library after supper.

"Isn't Nancy through in the kitchen yet?" Mother said. "It
seems to me that she has had plenty of time to have finished the
dishes."

"Let Quentin go and see," Father said. "Go and see if Nancy
is through, Quentin. Tell her she can go on home."

I went to the kitchen. Nancy was through. The dishes were
put away and the fire was out. Nancy was sitting in a chair,
close to the cold stove. She looked at me.

"Mother wants to know if you are through," I said.

"Yes," Nancy said. She looked at me. "I done finished." She
looked at me.

"What is it?" I said. "What is it?"

"I ain't nothing but a nigger," Nancy said. "It ain't none of it
my fault."

She looked at me, sitting in the chair before the cold stove,
the sailor hat on her head. I went back to the library. It was the
cold stove and all, when you think of a kitchen being warm and

busy and cheerful. And with a cold stove and the dishes all put away, and nobody wanting to eat at that hour.

"Is she through?" Mother said.

"Yessum," I said.

"What is she doing?" Mother said.

"She's not doing anything. She's through."

"I'll go and see," Father said.

"Maybe she's waiting for Jesus to come and take her home," Caddy said.

"Jesus is gone," I said. Nancy told us how one morning she woke up and Jesus was gone.

"He quit me," Nancy said. "Done gone to Memphis, I reckon. Dodging them city *po*-lice for a while, I reckon."

"And a good riddance," Father said. "I hope he stays there."

"Nancy's scaired of the dark," Jason said.

"So are you," Caddy said.

"I'm not," Jason said.

"Scairy cat," Caddy said.

"I'm not," Jason said.

"You, Candace!" Mother said. Father came back.

"I am going to walk down the lane with Nancy," he said. "She says that Jesus is back."

"Has she seen him?" Mother said.

"No. Some Negro sent her word that he was back in town. I won't be long."

"You'll leave me alone, to take Nancy home?" Mother said. "Is her safety more precious to you than mine?"

"I won't be long," Father said.

"You'll leave these children unprotected, with that Negro about?"

"I'm going too," Caddy said. "Let me go, Father."

"What would he do with them, if he were unfortunate enough to have them?" Father said.

"I want to go, too," Jason said.

"Jason!" Mother said. She was speaking to Father. You could tell that by the way she said the name. Like she believed that all day Father had been trying to think of doing the thing she wouldn't like the most, and that she knew all the time that after a while he would think of it. I stayed quiet, because Father and I both knew that Mother would want him to make me stay with her if she just thought of it in time. So Father didn't look at me. I was the oldest. I was nine and Caddy was seven and Jason was five.

"Nonsense," Father said. "We won't be long."

Nancy had her hat on. We came to the lane. "Jesus always been good to me," Nancy said. "Whenever he had two dollars, one of them was mine." We walked in the lane. "If I can just get through the lane," Nancy said, "I be all right then."

The lane was always dark. "This is where Jason got scaired on Hallowe'en," Caddy said.

"I didn't," Jason said.

"Can't Aunt Rachel do anything with him?" Father said. Aunt Rachel was old. She lived in a cabin beyond Nancy's by herself. She had white hair and she smoked a pipe in the door, all day long; she didn't work any more. They said she was Jesus' mother. Sometimes she said she was and sometimes she said she wasn't any kin to Jesus.

"Yes you did," Caddy said. "You were scairder than Frony. You were scairder than T.P. even. Scairder than niggers."

"Can't nobody do nothing with him," Nancy said. "He say I done woke up the devil in him and ain't but one thing going to lay it down again."

"Well, he's gone now," Father said. "There's nothing for you to be afraid of now. And if you'd just let white men alone."

"Let what white men alone?" Caddy said. "How let them alone?"

"He ain't gone nowhere," Nancy said. "I can feel him. I can feel him now, in this lane. He hearing us talk, every word, hid somewhere, waiting. I ain't seen him, and I ain't going to see him again but once more, with that razor in his mouth. That razor on that string down his back, inside his shirt. And then I ain't going to be even surprised."

"I wasn't scaired," Jason said.

"If you'd behave yourself, you'd have kept out of this," Father said. "But it's all right now. He's probably in Saint Louis now. Probably got another wife by now and forgot all about you."

"If he has, I better not find out about it," Nancy said. "I'd stand there right over them, and every time he wropped her, I'd cut that arm off. I'd cut his head off and I'd slit her belly and I'd shove—"

"Hush," Father said.

"Slit whose belly, Nancy?" Caddy said.

"I wasn't scaired," Jason said. "I'd walk right down this lane by myself."

"Yah," Caddy said. "You wouldn't dare to put your foot down in it if we were not here too."

II

Dilsey was still sick, so we took Nancy home every night until Mother said, "How much longer is this going on? I to be left alone in this big house while you take home a frightened Negro?"

We fixed a pallet in the kitchen for Nancy. One night we waked up, hearing the sound. It was not singing and it was not crying, coming up the dark stairs. There was a light in Mother's room and we heard Father going down the hall, down the back stairs, and Caddy and I went into the hall. The floor was cold. Our toes curled away from it while we listened to the sound. It was like singing and it wasn't like singing, like the sound that Negroes make.

Then it stopped and we heard Father going down the back stairs, and we went to the head of the stairs. Then the sound began again, in the stairway, not loud, and we could see Nancy's eyes halfway up the stairs, against the wall. They looked like cat's eyes do, like a big cat against the wall, watching us. When we came down the steps to where she was, she quit making the sound again, and we stood there until Father came back up from the kitchen, with his pistol in his hand. He went back down with Nancy and they came back with Nancy's pallet.

We spread the pallet in our room. After the light in Mother's room went off, we could see Nancy's eyes again. "Nancy," Caddy whispered, "are you asleep, Nancy?"

Nancy whispered something. It was oh or no, I don't know which. Like nobody had made it, like it came from nowhere and went nowhere, until it was like Nancy was not there at all; that I had looked so hard at her eyes on the stairs that they had got printed on my eyeballs, like the sun does when you have closed your eyes and there is no sun. "Jesus," Nancy whispered. "Jesus."

"Was it Jesus?" Caddy said. "Did he try to come into the kitchen?"

"Jesus," Nancy said. Like this: Jeeeeeeeeeeeeeeeesus, until the sound went out, like a match or a candle does.

"It's the other Jesus she means," I said.

"Can you see us, Nancy?" Caddy whispered. "Can you see our eyes too?"

"I ain't nothing but a nigger," Nancy said. "God knows. God knows."

"What did you see down there in the kitchen?" Caddy whispered. "What tried to get in?"

"God knows," Nancy said. We could see her eyes. "God knows."

Dilsey got well. She cooked dinner. "You'd better stay in bed a day or two longer," Father said.

"What for?" Dilsey said. "If I had been a day later, this place would be to rack and ruin. Get on out of here now, and let me get my kitchen straight again."

Dilsey cooked supper too. And that night, just before dark, Nancy came into the kitchen.

"How do you know he's back?" Dilsey said. "You ain't seen him."

"Jesus is a nigger," Jason said.

"I can feel him," Nancy said. "I can feel him laying yonder in the ditch."

"Tonight?" Dilsey said. "Is he there tonight?"

"Dilsey's a nigger too," Jason said.

"You try to eat something," Dilsey said.

"I don't want nothing," Nancy said.

"I ain't a nigger," Jason said.

"Drink some coffee," Dilsey said. She poured a cup of coffee for Nancy. "Do you know he's out there tonight? How come you know it's tonight?"

"I know," Nancy said. "He's there, waiting. I know. I done lived with him too long. I know what he is fixing to do fore he know it himself."

"Drink some coffee," Dilsey said. Nancy held the cup to her mouth and blew into the cup. Her mouth pursed out like a spreading adder's, like a rubber mouth, like she had blown all the color out of her lips with blowing the coffee.

"I ain't a nigger," Jason said. "Are you a nigger, Nancy?"

"I hellborn, child," Nancy said. "I won't be nothing soon. I going back where I come from soon."

III

She began to drink the coffee. While she was drinking, holding the cup in both hands, she began to make the sound again. She made the sound into the cup and the coffee sploshed out onto her hands and her dress. Her eyes looked at us and she sat there, her elbows on her knees, holding the cup in both hands, looking at us across the wet cup, making the sound.

"Look at Nancy," Jason said. "Nancy can't cook for us now. Dilsey's got well now."

"You hush up," Dilsey said. Nancy held the cup in both hands, looking at us, making the sound, like there were two of them: one looking at us and the other making the sound. "Whyn't you let Mr. Jason telefoam the marshal?" Dilsey said. Nancy stopped then, holding the cup in her long brown hands. She tried to drink some coffee again, but it sploshed out of the cup, onto her hands and her dress, and she put the cup down. Jason watched her.

"I can't swallow it," Nancy said. "I swallows but it won't go down me."

"You go down to the cabin," Dilsey said. "Frony will fix you a pallet and I'll be there soon."

"Won't no nigger stop him," Nancy said.

"I ain't a nigger," Jason said. "Am I, Dilsey?"

"I reckon not," Dilsey said. She looked at Nancy. "I don't reckon so. What you going to do, then?"

Nancy looked at us. Her eyes went fast, like she was afraid there wasn't time to look, without hardly moving at all. She looked at us, at all three of us at one time. "You member that night I stayed in yawls' room?" she said. She told about how we waked up early the next morning, and played. We had to play quiet, on her pallet, until Father woke up and it was time to get breakfast. "Go and ask your maw to let me stay here tonight," Nancy said. "I won't need no pallet. We can play some more."

Caddy asked Mother. Jason went too. "I can't have Negroes sleeping in the bedrooms," Mother said. Jason cried. He cried until Mother said he couldn't have any dessert for three days if he didn't stop. Then Jason said he would stop if Dilsey would make a chocolate cake. Father was there.

"Why don't you do something about it?" Mother said. "What do we have officers for?"

"Why is Nancy afraid of Jesus?" Caddy said. "Are you afraid of Father, Mother?"

"What could the officers do?" Father said. "If Nancy hasn't seen him, how could the officers find him?"

"Then why is she afraid?" Mother said.

"She says he is there. She says she knows he is there tonight."

"Yet we pay taxes," Mother said. "I must wait here alone in this big house while you take a Negro woman home."

"You know that I am not lying outside with a razor," Father said.

"I'll stop if Dilsey will make a chocolate cake," Jason said. Mother told us to go out and Father said he didn't know if Jason would get a chocolate cake or not, but he knew what Jason was going to get in about a minute. We went back to the kitchen and told Nancy.

"Father said for you to go home and lock the door, and you'll be all right," Caddy said. "All right from what, Nancy? Is Jesus mad at you?" Nancy was holding the coffee cup in her hands again, her elbows on her knees and her hands holding the cup between her knees. She was looking into the cup. "What have you done that made Jesus mad?" Caddy said. Nancy let the cup go. It didn't break on the floor, but the coffee spilled out, and Nancy sat there with her hands still making the shape of the cup. She began to make the sound again, not loud. Not singing and not unsinging. We watched her.

"Here," Dilsey said. "You quit that, now. You get aholt of yourself. You wait here. I going to get Versh to walk home with you." Dilsey went out.

We looked at Nancy. Her shoulders kept shaking, but she quit making the sound. We stood and watched her.

"What's Jesus going to do to you?" Caddy said. "He went away."

Nancy looked at us. "We had fun that night I stayed in yawls' room, didn't we?"

"I didn't," Jason said. "I didn't have any fun."

"You were asleep in Mother's room," Caddy said. "You were not there."

"Let's go down to my house and have some more fun," Nancy said.

"Mother won't let us," I said. "It's too late now."

"Don't bother her," Nancy said. "We can tell her in the morning. She won't mind."

"She wouldn't let us," I said.

"Don't ask her now," Nancy said. "Don't bother her now."

"She didn't say we couldn't go," Caddy said.

"We didn't ask," I said.

"If you go, I'll tell," Jason said.

"We'll have fun," Nancy said. "They won't mind, just to my house. I been working for yawl a long time. They won't mind."

"I'm not afraid to go," Caddy said. "Jason is the one that's afraid. He'll tell."

"I'm not," Jason said.

"Yes, you are," Caddy said. "You'll tell."

"I won't tell," Jason said. "I'm not afraid."

"Jason ain't afraid to go with me," Nancy said. "Is you, Jason?"

"Jason is going to tell," Caddy said. The lane was dark. We passed the pasture gate. "I bet if something was to jump out from behind that gate, Jason would holler."

"I wouldn't," Jason said. We walked down the lane. Nancy was talking loud.

"What are you talking so loud for, Nancy?" Caddy said.

"Who; me?" Nancy said. "Listen at Quentin and Caddy and Jason saying I'm talking loud."

"You talk like there was five of us here," Caddy said. "You talk like Father was here too."

"Who; me talking loud, Mr. Jason?" Nancy said.

"Nancy called Jason 'Mister,'" Caddy said.

"Listen how Caddy and Quentin and Jason talk," Nancy said.

"We're not talking loud," Caddy said. "You're the one that's talking like Father—"

"Hush," Nancy said; "hush, Mr. Jason."

"Nancy called Jason 'Mister' aguh—"

"Hush," Nancy said. She was talking loud when we crossed the ditch and stooped through the fence where she used to stoop through with the clothes on her head. Then we came to her house. We were going fast then. She opened the door. The smell of the house was like the lamp and the smell of Nancy was like the wick, like they were waiting for one another to begin to smell. She lit the lamp and closed the door and put the bar up. Then she quit talking loud, looking at us.

"What're we going to do?" Caddy said.

"What do yawl want to do?" Nancy said.

"You said we would have some fun," Caddy said.

There was something about Nancy's house; something you could smell besides Nancy and the house. Jason smelled it, even. "I don't want to stay here," he said. "I want to go home."

"Go home, then," Caddy said.

"I don't want to go by myself," Jason said.

"We're going to have some fun," Nancy said.

"How?" Caddy said.

Nancy stood by the door. She was looking at us, only it was

like she had emptied her eyes, like she had quit using them. "What do you want to do?" she said.

"Tell us a story," Caddy said. "Can you tell a story?"

"Yes," Nancy said.

"Tell it," Caddy said. We looked at Nancy. "You don't know any stories."

"Yes," Nancy said. "Yes I do."

She came and sat in a chair before the hearth. There was a little fire there. Nancy built it up, when it was already hot inside. She built a good blaze. She told a story. She talked like her eyes looked, like her eyes watching us and her voice talking to us did not belong to her. Like she was living somewhere else, waiting somewhere else. She was outside the cabin. Her voice was inside and the shape of her, that Nancy that could stoop under a barbed wire fence with a bundle of clothes balanced on her head as though without weight, like a balloon, was there. But that was all. "And so this here queen come walking up to the ditch, where that bad man was hiding. She was walking up to the ditch, and she say, 'If I can just get past this here ditch,' was what she say..."

"What ditch?" Caddy said. "A ditch like that one out there? Why did a queen want to go into a ditch?"

"To get to her house," Nancy said. She looked at us. "She had to cross the ditch to get into her house quick and bar the door."

"Why did she want to go home and bar the door?" Caddy said.

IV

Nancy looked at us. She quit talking. She looked at us. Jason's legs stuck straight out of his pants where he sat on Nancy's lap. "I don't think that's a good story," he said. "I want to go home."

"Maybe we had better," Caddy said. She got up from the floor. "I bet they are looking for us right now." She went toward the door.

"No," Nancy said. "Don't open it." She got up quick and passed Caddy. She didn't touch the door, the wooden bar.

"Why not?" Caddy said.

"Come back to the lamp," Nancy said. "Well have fun. You don't have to go."

"We ought to go," Caddy said. "Unless we have a lot of fun." She and Nancy came back to the fire, the lamp.

"I want to go home," Jason said. "I'm going to tell."

"I know another story," Nancy said. She stood close to the lamp. She looked at Caddy, like when your eyes look up at a stick balanced on your nose. She had to look down to see Caddy, but her eyes looked like that, like when you are balancing a stick.

"I won't listen to it," Jason said. "I'll bang on the floor."

"It's a good one," Nancy said. "It's better than the other one."

"What's it about?" Caddy said. Nancy was standing by the lamp. Her hand was on the lamp, against the light, long and brown.

"Your hand is on that hot globe," Caddy said. "Don't it feel hot to your hand?"

Nancy looked at her hand on the lamp chimney. She took her hand away, slow. She stood there, looking at Caddy, wringing her long hand as though it were tied to her wrist with a string.

"Let's do something else," Caddy said.

"I want to go home," Jason said.

"I got some popcorn," Nancy said. She looked at Caddy and then at Jason and then at me and then at Caddy again. "I got some popcorn."

"I don't like popcorn," Jason said. "I'd rather have candy."

Nancy looked at Jason. "You can hold the popper." She was still wringing her hand; it was long and limp and brown.

"All right," Jason said. "I'll stay a while if I can do that. Caddy can't hold it. I'll want to go home again if Caddy holds the popper."

Nancy built up the fire. "Look at Nancy putting her hands in the fire," Caddy said. "What's the matter with you, Nancy?"

"I got popcorn," Nancy said. "I got some." She took the popper from under the bed. It was broken. Jason began to cry.

"Now we can't have any popcorn," he said.

"We ought to go home anyway," Caddy said. "Come on, Quentin."

"Wait," Nancy said; "wait. I can fix it. Don't you want to help me fix it?"

"I don't think I want any," Caddy said. "It's too late now."

"You help me, Jason," Nancy said. "Don't you want to help me?"

"No," Jason said. "I want to go home."

"Hush," Nancy said; "hush. Watch. Watch me. I can fix it so Jason can hold it and pop the corn." She got a piece of wire and fixed the popper.

"It won't hold good," Caddy said.

"Yes it will," Nancy said. "Yawl watch. Yawl help me shell some corn."

The popcorn was under the bed too. We shelled it into the popper and Nancy helped Jason hold the popper over the fire.

"It's not popping," Jason said. "I want to go home."

"You wait," Nancy said. "It'll begin to pop. We'll have fun then."

She was sitting close to the fire. The lamp was turned up so high it was beginning to smoke. "Why don't you turn it down some?" I said.

"It's all right," Nancy said. "I'll clean it. Yawl wait. The popcorn will start in a minute."

"I don't believe it's going to start," Caddy said. "We ought to start home, anyway. They'll be worried."

"No," Nancy said. "It's going to pop. Dilsey will tell um yawl with me. I been working for yawl long time. They won't mind if yawl at my house. You wait, now. It'll start popping any minute now."

Then Jason got some smoke in his eyes and he began to cry. He dropped the popper into the fire. Nancy got a wet rag and wiped Jason's face, but he didn't stop crying.

"Hush," she said. "Hush." But he didn't hush. Caddy took the popper out of the fire.

"It's burned up," she said. "You'll have to get some more popcorn, Nancy."

"Did you put all of it in?" Nancy said.

"Yes," Caddy said. Nancy looked at Caddy. Then she took the popper and opened it and poured the cinders into her apron and began to sort the grains, her hands long and brown, and we watched her.

"Haven't you got any more?" Caddy said.

"Yes," Nancy said; "yes. Look. This here ain't burnt. All we need to do is—"

"I want to go home," Jason said. "I'm going to tell."

"Hush," Caddy said. We all listened. Nancy's head was already turned toward the barred door, her eyes filled with red lamplight. "Somebody is coming," Caddy said.

Then Nancy began to make that sound again, not loud, sitting there above the fire, her long hands dangling between her knees; all of a sudden water began to come out on her face in big drops, running down her face, carrying in each one a little turning ball of firelight like a spark until it dropped off her chin. "She's not crying," I said.

"I ain't crying," Nancy said. Her eyes were closed. "I ain't crying. Who is it?"

"I don't know," Caddy said. She went to the door and looked out. "We've got to go now," she said. "Here comes Father."

"I'm going to tell," Jason said. "Yawl made me come."

The water still ran down Nancy's face. She turned in her chair. "Listen. Tell him. Tell him we going to have fun. Tell him I take good care of yawl until in the morning. Tell him to let me come home with yawl and sleep on the floor. Tell him I won't need no pallet. We'll have fun. You member last time how we had so much fun?"

"I didn't have fun," Jason said. "You hurt me. You put smoke in my eyes. I'm going to tell."

V

Father came in. He looked at us. Nancy did not get up.

"Tell him," she said.

"Caddy made us come down here," Jason said. "I didn't want to."

Father came to the fire. Nancy looked up at him. "Can't you go to Aunt Rachel's and stay?" he said. Nancy looked up at Father, her hands between her knees. "He's not here," Father said. "I would have seen him. There's not a soul in sight."

"He in the ditch," Nancy said. "He waiting in the ditch yonder."

"Nonsense," Father said. He looked at Nancy. "Do you know he's there?"

"I got the sign," Nancy said.

"What sign?"

"I got it. It was on the table when I come in. It was a hogbone, with blood meat still on it, laying by the lamp. He's out there. When yawl walk out that door, I gone."

"Gone where, Nancy?" Caddy said.

"I'm not a tattletale," Jason said.

"Nonsense," Father said.

"He out there," Nancy said. "He looking through that window this minute, waiting for yawl to go. Then I gone."

"Nonsense," Father said. "Lock up your house and we'll take you on to Aunt Rachel's."

" 'Twon't do no good," Nancy said. She didn't look at Father now, but he looked down at her, at her long, limp, moving hands. "Putting it off won't do no good."

"Then what do you want to do?" Father said.

"I don't know," Nancy said. "I can't do nothing. Just put it off. And that don't do no good. I reckon it belong to me. I reckon what I going to get ain't no more than mine."

"Get what?" Caddy said. "What's yours?"

"Nothing," Father said. "You all must get to bed."

"Caddy made me come," Jason said.

"Go on to Aunt Rachel's," Father said.

"It won't do no good," Nancy said. She sat before the fire, her elbows on her knees, her long hands between her knees. "When even your own kitchen wouldn't do no good. When even if I was sleeping on the floor in the room with your chillen, and the next morning there I am, and blood—"

"Hush," Father said. "Lock the door and put out the lamp and go to bed."

"I scaired of the dark," Nancy said. "I scaired for it to happen in the dark."

"You mean you're going to sit right here with the lamp lighted?" Father said. Then Nancy began to make the sound again, sitting before the fire, her long hands between her knees. "Ah, damnation," Father said. "Come along, chillen. It's past bedtime."

"When yawl go home, I gone," Nancy said. She talked quieter now, and her face looked quiet, like her hands. "Anyway, I got my coffin money saved up with Mr. Lovelady." Mr. Lovelady was a short, dirty man who collected the Negro insurance, coming around to the cabins or the kitchens every Saturday morning, to collect fifteen cents. He and his wife lived at the hotel. One morning his wife committed suicide. They had a child, a little girl. He and the child went away. After a week or two he came back alone. We would see him going along the lanes and the back streets on Saturday mornings.

"Nonsense," Father said. "You'll be the first thing I'll see in the kitchen tomorrow morning."

"You'll see what you'll see, I reckon," Nancy said. "But it will take the Lord to say what that will be."

VI

We left her sitting before the fire.

"Come and put the bar up," Father said. But she didn't move. She didn't look at us again, sitting quietly there between the lamp and the fire. From some distance down the lane we could look back and see her through the open door.

"What, Father?" Caddy said. "What's going to happen?"

"Nothing," Father said. Jason was on Father's back, so Jason was the tallest of all of us. We went down into the ditch. I looked at it, quiet. I couldn't see much where the moonlight and the shadows tangled.

"If Jesus *is* hid here, he can see us, can't he?" Caddy said.

"He's not there," Father said. "He went away a long time ago."

"You made me come," Jason said, high; against the sky it looked like Father had two heads, a little one and a big one. "I didn't want to."

We went up out of the ditch. We could still see Nancy's house and the open door, but we couldn't see Nancy now, sitting before the fire with the door open, because she was tired. "I just done got tired," she said. "I just a nigger. It ain't no fault of mine."

But we could hear her, because she began just after we came up out of the ditch, the sound that was not singing and not unsinging. "Who will do our washing now, Father?" I said.

"I'm not a nigger," Jason said, high and close above Father's head.

"You're worse," Caddy said, "you are a tattletale. If something was to jump out, you'd be scairder than a nigger."

"I wouldn't," Jason said.

"You'd cry," Caddy said.

"Caddy," Father said.

"I wouldn't," Jason said.

"Scairy cat," Caddy said.

"Candace!" Father said.

THE LAW*

BY ROBERT M. COATES

THE FIRST intimation that things were getting out of hand came one early-fall evening in the late nineteen-forties. What happened, simply, was that between seven and nine

---

* from *The New Yorker*

o'clock on that evening the Triborough Bridge had the heaviest concentration of out-bound traffic in its entire history.

This was odd, for it was a weekday evening (to be precise, a Wednesday), and though the weather was agreeably mild and clear, with a moon that was close enough to being full to lure a certain number of motorists out of the city, these facts alone were not enough to explain the phenomenon. No other bridge or main highway was affected, and though the two preceding nights had been equally balmy and moonlit, on both of these the bridge traffic had run close to normal.

The bridge personnel, at any rate, was caught entirely unprepared. A main artery of traffic, like the Triborough, operates under fairly predictable conditions. Motor travel, like most other large-scale human activities, obeys the Law of Averages—that great, ancient rule that states that the actions of people in the mass will always follow consistent patterns—and on the basis of past experience it had always been possible to foretell, almost to the last digit, the number of cars that would cross the bridge at any given hour of the day or night. In this case, though, all rules were broken.

The hours from seven till nearly midnight are normally quiet ones on the bridge. But on that night it was as if all the motorists in the city, or at any rate, a staggering proportion of them, had conspired together to upset tradition. Beginning almost exactly at seven o'clock, cars poured onto the bridge in such numbers and with such rapidity that the staff at the toll booths was overwhelmed almost from the start. It was soon apparent that this was no momentary congestion, and as it became more and more obvious that the traffic jam promised to be one of truly monumental proportions, added details of police were rushed to the scene to help handle it.

Cars streamed in from all directions—from the Bronx approach and the Manhattan one, from 125th Street and the East River Drive. (At the peak of the crush, about eight-fifteen, observers on the bridge reported that the drive was a solid line of car headlights as far south as the bend at Eighty-ninth Street, while the congestion cross-town in Manhattan disrupted traffic as far west as Amsterdam Avenue.) And perhaps the most confusing thing about the whole manifestation was that there seemed to be no reason for it.

Now and then, as the harried toll-booth attendants made change for the seemingly endless stream of cars, they would question the occupants, and it soon became clear that the very participants in the monstrous tie-up were as ignorant of its cause as anyone else was. A report made by Sergeant Alfonse O'Toole, who commanded the detail in charge of the Bronx approach, is typical. "I kept askin' them," he said, " 'Is there night football somewhere that we don't know about? Is it the races you're goin' to?' But the funny thing was half the time they'd be askin' me. 'What's the crowd for, Mac?' they would say. And I'd just look at them. There was one guy I mind, in a Ford convertible with a girl in the seat beside him, and when he asked me, I said to him, 'Hell, you're *in* the crowd, ain't you?' I said. 'What brings *you* here?' And the dummy just looks at me. 'Me?' he says. 'I just come out for a drive in the moonlight. But if I'd known there'd be a crowd like this . . .' he says. And then he asks me, 'Is there any place I can turn around and get out of this?' " As the *Herald Tribune* summed things up in its story next morning, it "just looked as if everybody in Manhattan who owned a motorcar had decided to drive out on Long Island that evening."

The incident was unusual enough to make all the front pages next morning, and because of this, many similar events, which might otherwise have gone unnoticed, received attention. The proprietor of the Aramis Theatre, on Eighth Avenue, reported that on several nights in the recent past his auditorium had been practically empty, while on others it had been jammed to suffocation. Lunchroom owners noted that increasingly their patrons were developing a habit of making runs on specific items; one day it would be roast shoulder of veal with pan gravy that was ordered almost exclusively, while the next everyone would be taking the Vienna loaf, and the roast veal went begging. A man who ran a small notions store in Bayside revealed that over a period of four days two hundred and seventy-four successive customers had entered his shop and asked for a spool of pink thread.

These were news items that would ordinarily have gone into the papers as fillers or in the sections reserved for oddities. Now, however, they seemed to have a more serious significance. It was apparent at last that something decidedly strange was happening to people's habits, and it was as unsettling as those occasional moments on excursion boats when the passengers are moved, all at once, to rush to one side or the other of the vessel. It was not till one day in December when, almost incredibly, the Twentieth Century Limited left New York for Chicago with just three passengers aboard that business leaders discovered how disastrous the new trend could be, too.

Until then, the New York Central, for instance, could operate confidently on the assumption that although there might be several thousand men in New York who had business relations in Chicago, on any single day no more—and no less—than some hundreds of them would have occasion to go there. The play producer could be sure that his patronage would sort itself out and that roughly as many persons would want to see the performance on Thursday as there had been on Tuesday or Wednesday. Now they couldn't be sure of anything. The Law of Averages had gone by the board, and if the effect on business promised to be catastrophic, it was also singularly unnerving for the general customer.

The lady starting downtown for a day of shopping, for example, could never be sure whether she would find Macy's department store a seething mob of other shoppers or a wilderness of empty, echoing aisles and unoccupied salesgirls. And the uncertainty produced a strange sort of jitteriness in the individual when faced with any impulse to action. "Shall we do it or shan't we?" people kept asking themselves, knowing that if they did do it, it might turn out that thousands of other individuals had decided similarly; knowing, too, that if they *didn't,* they might miss the one glorious chance of all chances to have Jones Beach, say, practically to themselves. Business languished, and a sort of desperate uncertainty rode everyone.

At this juncture, it was inevitable that Congress should be called on for action. In fact, Congress called on itself, and it must be said that it rose nobly to the occasion. A committee was appointed, drawn from both Houses and headed by Senator J. Wing Slooper (R.), of Indiana, and though after considerable investigation the committee was forced reluctantly to conclude that there was no evidence of Communist instigation, the unconscious subversiveness of the people's present conduct was obvious at a glance. The problem was what to do about it. You can't indict a whole nation, particularly on such vague grounds as these were. But, as Senator Slooper boldly pointed out, "You can control it," and in the end a system of reëducation and reform was decided upon, designed to lead people back to—again we quote Senator Slooper—"the basic regularities, the homely averages of the American way of life."

In the course of the committee's investigations, it had been discovered, to everyone's dismay, that the Law of Averages had never been incorporated into the body of federal jurisprudence, and though the upholders of States' Rights rebelled violently, the oversight was at once corrected, both by Constitutional amendment and by a law—the Hills-Slooper Act—implementing it. According to the Act, people were *required* to be average, and, as the simplest way of assuring it, they were divided alphabetically and their permissible activities catalogued accordingly. Thus, by the plan, a person whose name began with "G," "N," or "U," for example, could attend the theatre only on Tuesdays, and he could go to baseball games only on Thursdays, whereas his visits to a haberdashery were confined to the hours between ten o'clock and noon on Mondays.

The law, of course, had its disadvantages. It had a crippling effect on theatre parties, among other social functions, and the cost of enforcing it was unbelievably heavy. In the end, too, so many amendments had to be added to it—such as the one permitting gentlemen to take their fiancées (if accredited) along with them to various events and functions no matter what letter the said fiancées' names began with—that the courts were frequently at a loss to interpret it when confronted with violations.

In its way, though, the law did serve its purpose, for it did induce—rather mechanically, it is true, but still adequately—a return to that average existence that Senator Slooper desired. All, indeed, would have been well if a year or so later disquieting reports had not begun to seep in from the backwoods. It seemed that there, in what had hitherto been considered to be marginal areas, a strange wave of prosperity was making itself felt. Tennessee mountaineers were buying Packard convertibles, and Sears, Roebuck reported that in the Ozarks their sales of luxury items had gone up nine hundred per cent. In the scrub sections of Vermont, men who formerly had barely been able to scratch a living from their rock-strewn acres were now sending their daughters to Europe and ordering expensive cigars from New York. It appeared that the Law of Diminishing Returns was going haywire, too.

THE TALE*

BY JOSEPH CONRAD

OUTSIDE THE large single window the crepuscular light was dying out slowly in a great square gleam without colour, framed rigidly in the gathering shades of the room.

It was a long room. The irresistible tide of the night ran into the most distant part of it, where the whispering of a man's voice, passionately interrupted and passionately renewed, seemed to plead against the answering murmurs of infinite sadness.

At last no answering murmur came. His movement when he rose slowly from his knees by the side of the deep, shadowy

* from *Tales of Hearsay*

couch holding the shadowy suggestion of a reclining woman revealed him tall under the low ceiling, and sombre all over except for the crude discord of the white collar under the shape of his head and the faint, minute spark of a brass button here and there on his uniform.

He stood over her a moment, masculine and mysterious in his immobility, before he sat down on a chair near by. He could see only the faint oval of her upturned face and, extended on her black dress, her pale hands, a moment before abandoned to his kisses and now as if too weary to move.

He dared not make a sound, shrinking as a man would do from the prosaic necessities of existence. As usual, it was the woman who had the courage. Her voice was heard first—almost conventional while her being vibrated yet with conflicting emotions.

"Tell me something," she said.

The darkness hid his surprise and then his smile. Had he not just said to her everything worth saying in the world—and that not for the first time!

"What am I to tell you?" he asked, in a voice creditably steady. He was beginning to feel grateful to her for that something final in her tone which had eased the strain.

"Why not tell me a tale?"

"A tale!" He was really amazed.

"Yes. Why not?"

These words came with a slight petulance, the hint of a loved woman's capricious will, which is capricious only because it feels itself to be a law, embarrassing sometimes and always difficult to elude.

"Why not?" he repeated, with a slightly mocking accent, as though he had been asked to give her the moon. But now he was feeling a little angry with her for that feminine mobility that slips out of an emotion as easily as out of a splendid gown.

He heard her say, a little unsteadily, with a sort of fluttering intonation which made him think suddenly of a butterfly's flight:

"You used to tell—your—your simple and—and professional tales—tales very well at one time. Or well enough to interest me. You had a—sort of art—in the days—the days before the war."

"Really?" he said, with involuntary gloom. "But now, you see, the war is going on," he continued in such a dead, equable tone that she felt a slight chill far over her shoulders. And yet she persisted. For there's nothing more unswerving in the world than a woman's caprice.

"It could be a tale not of this world," she explained.

"You want a tale of the other, the better world?" he asked, with a matter-of-fact surprise. "You must evoke for that task those who have already gone there."

"No. I don't mean that. I mean another—some other—world. In the universe—not in heaven."

"I am relieved. But you forget that I have only five days' leave."

"Yes. And I've also taken a five days' leave from—from my duties."

"I like that word."

"What word?"

"Duty."

"It is horrible—sometimes."

"Oh, that's because you think it's narrow. But it isn't. It contains infinities, and—and so——"

"What is this jargon?"

He disregarded the interjected scorn. "An infinity of absolution, for instance," he continued. "But as to this 'another world'—who's going to look for it and for the tale that is in it?"

"You," she said, with a strange, almost rough, sweetness of assertion.

He made a shadowy movement of assent in his chair, the irony of which not even the gathered darkness could render mysterious.

"As you will. In that world, then, there was once upon a time a Commanding Officer and a Northman. Put in the capitals, please, because they had no other names. It was a world of seas and continents and islands——"

"Like the earth," she murmured, bitterly.

"Yes. What else could you expect from sending a man made

of our common, tormented clay on a voyage of discovery? What else could he find? What else could you understand or care for, or feel the existence of even? There was comedy in it, and slaughter."

"Always like the earth," she murmured.

"Always. And since I could find in the universe only what was deeply rooted in the fibres of my being there was love in it, too. But we won't talk of that."

"No. We won't," she said, in a neutral tone which concealed perfectly her relief—or her disappointment. Then after a pause she added: "It's going to be a comic story."

"Well——" he paused, too. "Yes. In a way. In a very grim way. It will be human, and, as you know, comedy is but a matter of the visual angle. And it won't be a noisy story. All the long guns in it will be dumb—as dumb as so many telescopes."

"Ah, there are guns in it, then! And may I ask—where?"

"Afloat. You remember that the world of which we speak had its seas. A war was going on in it. It was a funny world and terribly in earnest. Its war was being carried on over the land, over the water, under the water, up in the air, and even under the ground. And many young men in it, mostly in wardrooms and mess-rooms, used to say to each other—pardon the unparliamentary word—they used to say, 'It's a damned bad war, but it's better than no war at all.' Sounds flippant, doesn't it?"

He heard a nervous, impatient sigh in the depths of the couch while he went on without a pause.

"And yet there is more in it than meets the eye. I mean more wisdom. Flippancy, like comedy, is but a matter of visual first-impression. That world was not very wise. But there was in it a certain amount of common working sagacity. That, however, was mostly worked by the neutrals in diverse ways, public and private, which had to be watched; watched by acute minds and also by actual sharp eyes. They had to be very sharp indeed, too, I assure you."

"I can imagine," she murmured, appreciatively.

"What is there that you can't imagine?" he pronounced, soberly. "You have the world in you. But let us go back to our commanding officer, who, of course, commanded a ship of a sort. My tales if often professional (as you remarked just now) have never been technical. So I'll just tell you that the ship was of a very ornamental sort once, with lots of grace and elegance and luxury about her. Yes, once! She was like a pretty woman who had suddenly put on a suit of sackcloth and stuck revolvers in her belt. But she floated lightly, she moved nimbly, she was quite good enough."

"That was the opinion of the commanding officer?" said the voice from the couch.

"It was. He used to be sent out with her along certain coasts to see—what he could see. Just that. And sometimes he had some preliminary information to help him, and sometimes he had not. And it was all one, really. It was about as useful as information trying to convey the locality and intentions of a cloud, of a phantom taking shape here and there and impossible to seize, would have been.

"It was in the early days of the war. What at first used to amaze the commanding officer was the unchanged face of the waters, with its familiar expression, neither more friendly nor more hostile. On fine days the sun strikes sparks upon the blue; here and there a peaceful smudge of smoke hangs in the distance, and it is impossible to believe that the familiar clear horizon traces the limit of one great circular ambush.

"Yes, it is impossible to believe, till some day you see a ship not your own ship (that isn't so impressive), but some ship in company, blow up all of a sudden and plop under almost before you know what has happened to her. Then you begin to believe. Henceforth you go out for the work to see—what you can see; and you keep on it with the conviction that some day you will die from something you have not seen. One envies the soldiers at the end of the day, wiping the sweat and blood from their faces, counting the dead fallen to their hands, looking at the devastated fields, the torn earth that seems to suffer and bleed with them. One does, really. The final brutality of it—the taste of primitive passion—the ferocious frankness of the blow struck with one's hand—the direct call and the straight response. Well, the sea gave you nothing of that, and seemed to pretend that there was nothing the matter with the world."

She interrupted, stirring a little.

"Oh, yes. Sincerity—frankness—passion—three words of your gospel. Don't I know them!"

"Think! Isn't it ours—believed in common?" he asked, anxiously, yet without expecting an answer, and went on at once: "Such were the feelings of the commanding officer. When the night came trailing over the sea, hiding what looked like the hypocrisy of an old friend, it was a relief. The night blinds you frankly—and there are circumstances when the sunlight may grow as odious to one as faleshood itself. Night is all right.

"At night the commanding officer could let his thoughts get away—I won't tell you where. Somewhere where there was no choice but between truth and death. But thick weather, though it blinded one, brought no such relief. Mist is deceitful, the dead luminosity of the fog is irritating. It seems that you *ought* to see.

"One gloomy, nasty day the ship was steaming along her beat in sight of a rocky, dangerous coast that stood out intensely black like an India-ink drawing on grey paper. Presently the second in command spoke to his chief. He thought he saw something on the water, to seaward. Small wreckage, perhaps.

" 'But there shouldn't be any wreckage here, sir,' he remarked.

" 'No,' said the commanding officer. 'The last reported submarined ships were sunk a long way to the westward. But one never knows. There may have been others since then not reported nor seen. Gone with all hands.'

"That was how it began. The ship's course was altered to pass the object close; for it was necessary to have a good look at what one could see. Close, but without touching it; for it was not advisable to come in contact with objects of any form whatever floating casually about. Close, but without stopping or even diminishing speed; for in those times it was not prudent to linger on any particular spot, even for a moment. I may tell you at once that the object was not dangerous in itself. No use in describing it. It may have been nothing more remarkable than, say, a barrel of a certain shape and colour. But it was significant.

"The smooth bow-wave hove it up as if for a closer inspection, and then the ship, brought again to her course, turned her back on it with indifference, while twenty pairs of eyes on her deck stared in all directions trying to see—what they could see.

"The commanding officer and his second in command discussed the object with understanding. It appeared to them to be not so much a proof of the sagacity as of the activity of certain neutrals. This activity had in many cases taken the form of replenishing the stores of certain submarines at sea. This was generally believed, if not absolutely known. But the very nature of things in those early days pointed that way. The object, looked at closely and turned away from with apparent indifference, put it beyond doubt that something of the sort had been done somewhere in the neighborhood.

"The object in itself was more than suspect. But the fact of its being left in evidence roused other suspicions. Was it the result of some deep and devilish purpose? As to that all speculation soon appeared to be a vain thing. Finally the two officers came to the conclusion that it was left there most likely by accident, complicated possibly by some unforeseen necessity; such, perhaps, as the sudden need to get away quickly from the spot, or something of that kind.

"Their discussion had been carried on in curt, weighty phrases, separated by long, thoughtful silences. And all the time their eyes roamed about the horizon in an everlasting, almost mechanical effort of vigilance. The younger man summed up grimly:

"'Well, it's evidence. That's what this is. Evidence of what we were pretty certain of before. And plain, too.'

"'And much good it will do to us,' retorted the commanding officer. 'The parties are miles away; the submarine, devil only knows where, ready to kill; and the noble neutral slipping away to the eastward, ready to lie!'

"The second in command laughed a little at the tone. But he guessed that the neutral wouldn't even have to lie very much. Fellows like that, unless caught in the very act, felt themselves pretty safe. They could afford to chuckle. That fellow was probably chuckling to himself. It's very possible he had been before at the game and didn't care a rap for the bit of evidence left behind. It was a game in which practice made one bold and successful, too.

"And again he laughed faintly. But his commanding officer was in revolt against the murderous stealthiness of methods and the atrocious callousness of complicities that seemed to taint the very source of men's deep emotions and noblest activities; to corrupt their imagination which builds up the final conceptions of life and death. He suffered——"

The voice from the sofa interupted the narrator.

"How well I can understand that in him!"

He bent forward slightly.

"Yes. I, too. Everything should be open in love and war. Open as the day, since both are the call of an ideal which it is so easy, so terribly easy, to degrade in the name of Victory."

He paused, then went on:

"I don't know that the commanding officer delved so deep as that into his feelings. But he did suffer from them—a sort of disenchanted sadness. It is possible, even, that he suspected himself of folly. Man is various. But he had no time for much introspection, because from the southwest a wall of fog had advanced upon his ship. Great convolutions of vapours flew over, swirling about masts and funnel, which looked as if they were beginning to melt. Then they vanished.

"The ship was stopped, all sounds ceased, and the very fog became motionless, growing denser and as if solid in its amazing dumb immobility. The men at their stations lost sight of each other. Footsteps sounded stealthy; rare voices, impersonal and remote, died out without resonance. A blind white stillness took possession of the world.

"It looked, too, as if it would last for days. I don't mean to say that the fog did not vary a little in its density. Now and then it would thin out mysteriously, revealing to the men a more or less ghostly presentment of their ship. Several times the shadow of the coast itself swam darkly before their eyes through the fluctuating opaque brightness of the great white cloud clinging to the water.

"Taking advantage of these moments, the ship had been moved cautiously nearer the shore. It was useless to remain out in such thick weather. Her officers knew every nook and cranny of the coast along their beat. They thought that she would be much better in a certain cove. It wasn't a large place, just ample room for a ship to swing at her anchor. She would have an easier time of it till the fog lifted up.

"Slowly, with infinite caution and patience, they crept closer and closer, seeing no more of the cliffs than an evanescent dark loom with a narrow border of angry foam at its foot. At the moment of anchoring the fog was so thick that for all they could see they might have been a thousand miles out in the open sea. Yet the shelter of the land could be felt. There was a peculiar quality in the stillness of the air. Very faint, very elusive, the wash of the ripple against the encircling land reached their ears, with mysterious sudden pauses.

"The anchor dropped, the leads were laid in. The commanding officer went below into his cabin. But he had not been there very long when a voice outside his door requested his presence on deck. He thought to himself: 'What is it now?' He felt some impatience at being called out again to face the wearisome fog.

"He found that it had thinned again a little and had taken on a gloomy hue from the dark cliffs which had no form, no outline, but asserted themselves as a curtain of shadows all round the ship, except in one bright spot, which was the entrance from the open sea. Several officers were looking that way from the bridge. The second in command met him with the breathlessly whispered information that there was another ship in the cove.

"She had been made out by several pairs of eyes only a couple of minutes before. She was lying at anchor very near the entrance—a mere vague blot on the fog's brightness. And the commanding officer by staring in the direction pointed out to him by eager hands ended by distinguishing it at last himself. Indubitably a vessel of some sort.

" 'It's a wonder we didn't run slap into her when coming in,' observed the second in command.

" 'Send a boat on board before she vanishes,' said the commanding officer. He surmised that this was a coaster. It could hardly be anything else. But another thought came into his head suddenly. 'It is a wonder,' he said to his second in command, who had rejoined him after sending the boat away.

"By that time both of them had been struck by the fact that the ship so suddenly discovered had not manifested her presence by ringing her bell.

" 'We came in very quietly, that's true,' concluded the younger officer. 'But they must have heard our leadsman at least. We couldn't have passed her more than fifty yards off. The closest shave! They may even have made us out, since they were aware of something coming in. And the strange thing is that we never heard a sound from her. The fellows on board must have been holding their breath.'

" 'Aye,' said the commanding officer, thoughtfully.

"In due course the boarding-boat returned, appearing suddenly alongside, as though she had burrowed her way under the fog. The officer in charge came up to make his report, but the commanding officer didn't give him time to begin. He cried from a distance:

" 'Coaster, isn't she?'

" 'No, sir. A stranger—a neutral,' was the answer.

" 'No. Really! Well, tell us all about it. What is she doing here?'

"The young man stated then that he had been told a long and complicated story of engine troubles. But it was plausible enough from a strictly professional point of view and it had the usual features; disablement, dangerous drifting along the shore, weather more or less thick for days, fear of a gale, ultimately a resolve to go in and anchor anywhere on the coast, and so on. Fairly plausible.

" 'Engines still disabled?' inquired the commanding officer.

" 'No, sir. She has steam on them.'

"The commanding officer took his second aside. 'By Jove!'

he said, 'you were right! They were holding their breaths as we passed them. They were.'

"But the second in command had his doubts now.

"'A fog like this does muffle small sounds, sir,' he remarked. 'And what could his object be, after all?'

"'To sneak out unnoticed,' answered the commanding officer.

"'Then why didn't he? He might have done it, you know. Not exactly unnoticed, perhaps. I don't suppose he could have slipped his cable without making some noise. Still, in a minute or so he would have been lost to view—clean gone before we had made him out fairly. Yet he didn't.'

"They looked at each other. The commanding officer shook his head. Such suspicions as the one which had entered his head are not defended easily. He did not even state it openly. The boarding officer finished his report. The cargo of the ship was of a harmless and useful character. She was bound to an English port. Papers and everything in perfect order. Nothing suspicious to be detected anywhere.

"Then passing to the men, he reported the crew on deck as the usual lot. Engineers of the well-known type, and very full of their achievement in repairing the engines. The mate surly. The master a rather fine specimen of Northman, civil enough, but appeared to have been drinking. Seemed to be recovering from a regular bout of it.

"'I told him I couldn't give him permission to proceed. He said he wouldn't dare to move his ship her own length out in such weather as this, permission or no permission. I left a man on board, though.'

"'Quite right.'

"The commanding officer, after communing with his suspicions for a time, called his second aside.

"'What if she were the very ship which had been feeding some infernal submarine or other?' he said in an undertone.

"The other started. Then, with conviction:

"'She would get off scot-free. You couldn't prove it, sir.'

"'I want to look into it myself.'

" 'From the report we've heard I am afraid you couldn't even make a case for reasonable suspicion, sir.'

" 'I'll go on board all the same.'

"He had made up his mind. Curiosity is the great motive power of hatred and love. What did he expect to find? He could not have told anybody—not even himself.

"What he really expected to find there was the atmosphere, the atmosphere of gratuitous treachery, which in his view nothing could excuse; for he thought that even a passion of unrighteousness for its own sake could not excuse that. But could he detect it? Sniff it? Taste it? Receive some mysterious communication which would turn his invincible suspicions into a certitude strong enough to provoke action with all its risks?

"The master met him on the after-deck, looming up in the fog amongst the blurred shapes of the usual ship's fittings. He was a robust Northman, bearded, and in the force of his age. A round leather cap fitted his head closely. His hands were rammed deep into the pockets of his short leather jacket. He kept them there while he explained that at sea he lived in the chart-room, and led the way there, striding carelessly. Just before reaching the door under the bridge he staggered a little, recovered himself, flung it open, and stood aside, leaning his shoulder as if involuntarily against the side of the house, and staring vaguely into the fog-filled space. But he followed the commanding officer at once, flung the door to, snapped on the electric light, and hastened to thrust his hands back into his pockets, as though afraid of being seized by them either in friendship or in hostility.

"The place was stuffy and hot. The usual chart-rack overhead was full, and the chart on the table was kept unrolled by an empty cup standing on a saucer half-full of some spilt dark liquid. A slightly nibbled biscuit reposed on the chronometer-case. There were two settees, and one of them had been made up into a bed with a pillow and some blankets, which were now very much tumbled. The Northman let himself fall on it, his hands still in his pockets.

" 'Well, here I am,' he said, with a curious air of being surprised at the sound of his own voice.

"The commanding officer from the other settee observed the handsome, flushed face. Drops of fog hung on the yellow beard and moustaches of the Northman. The much darker eyebrows ran together in a puzzled frown, and suddenly he jumped up.

"'What I mean is that I don't know where I am. I really don't,' he burst out, with extreme earnestness. 'Hang it all! I got turned around somehow. The fog has been after me for a week. More than a week. And then my engines broke down. I will tell you how it was.'

"He burst out into loquacity. It was not hurried, but it was insistent. It was not continuous for all that. It was broken by the most queer, thoughtful pauses. Each of these pauses lasted no more than a couple of seconds, and each had the profundity of an endless meditation. When he began again nothing betrayed in him the slightest consciousness of these intervals. There was the same fixed glance, the same unchanged earnestness of tone. He didn't know. Indeed, more than one of these pauses occurred in the middle of a sentence.

"The commanding officer listened to the tale. It struck him as more plausible than simple truth is in the habit of being. But that, perhaps, was prejudice. All the time the Northman was speaking the commanding officer had been aware of an inward voice, a grave murmur in the depths of his very own self, telling another tale, as if on purpose to keep alive in him his indignation and his anger with that baseness of greed or of mere outlook which lies often at the root of simple ideas.

"It was the story that had been already told to the boarding officer an hour or so before. The commanding officer nodded slightly at the Northman from time to time. The latter came to an end and turned his eyes away. He added, as an afterthought:

"'Wasn't it enough to drive a man out of his mind with worry? And it's my first voyage to this part, too. And the ship's my own. Your officer has seen the papers. She isn't much, as you can see for yourself. Just an old cargo-boat. Bare living for my family.'

"He raised a big arm to point at a row of photographs plastering the bulkhead. That movement was ponderous, as if the arm had been made of lead. The commanding officer said, carelessly:

" 'You will be making a fortune yet for your family with this old ship.'

" 'Yes, if I don't lose her,' said the Northman, gloomily.

" 'I mean—out of this war,' added the commanding officer.

"The Northman stared at him in a curiously unseeing and at the same time interested manner, as only eyes of a particular blue shade can stare.

" 'And you wouldn't be angry at it,' he said, 'would you? You are too much of a gentleman. We didn't bring this on you. And suppose we sat down and cried. What good would that be? Let those cry who made the trouble,' he concluded, with energy. 'Time's money, you say. Well—*this* time *is* money. Oh! isn't it!'

"The commanding officer tried to keep under the feeling of immense disgust. He said to himself that it was unreasonable. Men were like that—moral cannibals feeding on each other's misfortunes. He said aloud:

" 'You have made it perfectly plain how it is that you are here. Your log-book confirms you very minutely. Of course, a log-book may be cooked. Nothing easier.'

"The Northman never moved a muscle. He was gazing at the floor; he seemed not to have heard. He raised his head after a while.

" 'But you can't suspect me of anything,' he muttered, negligently.

"The commanding officer thought: 'Why should he say this?'

"Immediately afterwards the man before him added: 'My cargo is for an English port.'

"His voice had turned husky for the moment. The commanding officer reflected: 'That's true. There can be nothing. I can't suspect him. Yet why was he lying with steam up in this fog—and then, hearing us come in, why didn't he give some sign of life? Why? Could it be anything else but a guilty conscience? He could tell by the leadsmen that this was a man-of-war.'

"Yes—why? The commanding officer went on thinking: 'Suppose I ask him and then watch his face. He will betray himself in some way. It's perfectly plain that the fellow *has* been drinking. Yes, he has been drinking; but he will have a lie ready all the same.' The commanding officer was one of those men who are made morally and almost physically uncomfortable by the mere thought of having to beat down a lie. He shrank from the act in scorn and disgust, which were invincible because more temperamental than moral.

"So he went out on deck instead and had the crew mustered formally for his inspection. He found them very much what the report of the boarding officer had led him to expect. And from their answers to his questions he could discover no flaw in the log-book story.

"He dismissed them. His impression of them was—a picked lot; have been promised a fistful of money each if this came off; all slightly anxious, but not frightened. Not a single one of them likely to give the show away. They don't feel in danger of their life. They know England and English ways too well!

"He felt alarmed at catching himself thinking as if his vaguest suspicions were turning into a certitude. For, indeed, there was no shadow of reason for his inferences. There was nothing to give away.

"He returned to the chart-room. The Northman had lingered behind there; and something subtly different in his bearing, more bold in his blue, glassy stare, induced the commanding officer to conclude that the fellow had snatched at the opportunity to take another swig at the bottle he must have had concealed somewhere.

"He noticed, too, that the Northman on meeting his eyes put on an elaborately surprised expression. At least, it seemed elaborated. Nothing could be trusted. And the Englishman felt himself with astonishing conviction faced by an enormous lie, solid like a wall, with no way round to get at the truth, whose ugly murderous face he seemed to see peeping over at him with a cynical grin.

" 'I dare say,' he began suddenly, 'you are wondering at my proceedings, though I am not detaining you, am I? You wouldn't dare to move in this fog?' "

" 'I don't know where I am,' the Northman ejaculated earnestly. 'I really don't.'

"He looked around as if the very chart-room fittings were strange to him. The commanding officer asked him whether he had not seen any unusual objects floating about while he was at sea.

" 'Objects! What objects? We were groping blind in the fog for days.'

" 'We had a few clear intervals,' said the commanding officer. 'And I'll tell you what we have seen and the conclusion I've come to about it.'

"He told him in a few words. He heard the sound of a sharp breath indrawn through closed teeth. The Northman with his hand on the table stood absolutely motionless and dumb. He stood as if thunderstruck. Then he produced a fatuous smile.

"Or at least so it appeared to the commanding officer. Was this significant, or of no meaning whatever? He didn't know, he couldn't tell. All the truth had departed out of the world as if drawn in, absorbed in this monstrous villainy this man was—or was not—guilty of.

" 'Shooting's too good for people that conceive neutrality in this pretty way,' remarked the commanding officer, after a silence.

" 'Yes, yes, yes,' the Northman assented, hurriedly—then added an unexpected and dreamy-voiced 'Perhaps.'

"Was he pretending to be drunk, or only trying to appear sober? His glance was straight, but it was somewhat glazed. His lips outlined themselves firmly under his yellow moustache. But they twitched. Did they twitch? And why was he drooping like this in his attitude?

" 'There's no perhaps about it,' pronounced the commanding officer sternly.

"The Northman had straightened himself. And unexpectedly he looked stern, too.

" 'No. But what about the tempters? Better kill that lot off. There's about four, five, six million of them,' he said, grimly; but in a moment changed into a whining key. 'But I had better hold my tongue. You have some suspicions.'

" 'No, I've no suspicions,' declared the commanding officer.

"He never faltered. At that moment he had the certitude. The air of the chart-room was thick with guilt and falsehood braving the discovery, defying simple right, common decency, all humanity of feeling, every scruple of conduct.

"The Northman drew a long breath. 'Well, we know that you English are gentlemen. But let us speak the truth. Why should we love you so very much? You haven't done anything to be loved. We don't love the other people, of course. They haven't done anything for that either. A fellow comes along with a bag of gold...I haven't been in Rotterdam my last voyage for nothing.'

" 'You may be able to tell something interesting, then, to our people when you come into port,' interjected the officer.

" 'I might. But you keep some people in your pay at Rotterdam. Let them report. I am a neutral—am I not?...Have you ever seen a poor man on one side and a bag of gold on the other? Of course, I couldn't be tempted. I haven't the nerve for it. Really I haven't. It's nothing to me. I am just talking openly for once.'

" 'Yes. And I am listening to you,' said the commanding officer, quietly.

"The Northman leaned forward over the table. 'Now that I know you have no suspicions, I talk. You don't know what a poor man is. I do. I am poor myself. This old ship, she isn't much, and she is mortgaged, too. Bare living, no more. Of course, I wouldn't have the nerve. But a man who has nerve! See. The stuff he takes aboard looks like any other cargo—packages, barrels, tins, copper tubes—what not. He doesn't see it work. It isn't real to him. But he sees the gold. That's real. Of course, nothing could induce me. I suffer from an internal disease. I would either go crazy from anxiety—or—or—take to drink or something. The risk is too great. Why—ruin!'

" 'It should be death.' The commanding officer got up, after this curt declaration, which the other received with a hard stare oddly combined with an uncertain smile. The officer's gorge rose at the atmosphere of murderous complicity which surrounded him, denser, more impenetrable, more acrid than the fog outside.

" 'It's nothing to me,' murmured the Northman, swaying visibly.

" 'Of course not,' assented the commanding officer, with a great effort to keep his voice calm and low. The certitude was strong with him. 'But I am going to clear all you fellows off this coast at once. And I will begin with you. You must leave in half an hour.'

"By that time the officer was walking along the deck with the Northman at his elbow.

" 'What! In this fog?' the latter cried out, huskily.

" 'Yes, you will have to go in this fog.'

" 'But I don't know where I am. I really don't.'

"The commanding officer turned round. A sort of fury possessed him. The eyes of the two men met. Those of the Northman expressed a profound amazement.

" 'Oh, you don't know how to get out.' The commanding officer spoke with composure, but his heart was beating with anger and dread. 'I will give you your course. Steer south-by-east-half-east for about four miles and then you will be clear to haul to the eastward for your port. The weather will clear up before very long.'

" 'Must I? What could induce me? I haven't the nerve.'

" 'And yet you must go. Unless you want to——'

" 'I don't want to,' panted the Northman. 'I've enough of it.'

"The commanding officer got over the side. The Northman remained still as if rooted to the deck. Before his boat reached his ship the commanding officer heard the steamer beginning to pick up her anchor. Then, shadowy in the fog, she steamed out on the given course.

" 'Yes,' he said to his officers, 'I let him go.' "

The narrator bent forward towards the couch, where no movement betrayed the presence of a living person.

"Listen," he said, forcibly. "That course would lead the Northman straight on a deadly ledge of rock. And the commanding officer gave it to him. He steamed out—ran on it—and went down. So he had spoken the truth. He did not know where he was. But it proves nothing. Nothing either way. It may have been the only truth in all his story. And yet . . . He seems to have been driven out by a menacing stare—nothing more."

He abandoned all pretence.

"Yes, I gave that course to him. It seemed to me a supreme test. I believe—no, I don't believe. I don't know. At the time I was certain. They all went down; and I don't know whether I have done stern retribution—or murder; whether I have added to the corpses that litter the bed of the unreadable sea the bodies of men completely innocent or basely guilty. I don't know. I shall never know."

He rose. The woman on the couch got up and threw her arms round his neck. Her eyes put two gleams in the deep shadow of the room. She knew his passion for truth, his horror of deceit, his humanity.

"Oh, my poor, poor——"

"I shall never know," he repeated sternly, disengaged himself, pressed her hands to his lips, and went out.

A GIRL FROM RED LION, P.A. *

BY H. L. MENCKEN

SOMEWHERE IN his lush, magenta prose Oscar Wilde speaks of the tendency of nature to imitate art—a phenomenon often observed by persons who keep their eyes open. I first became aware of it, not through the pages of Wilde, but at the hands of an old-time hack-driver named Peebles, who flourished in Baltimore in the days of this history. Peebles was a Scotsman of a generally unfriendly and retiring character, but

* from *The New Yorker* and *Newspaper Days*

nevertheless he was something of a public figure in the town.
Perhaps that was partly due to the fact that he had served
twelve years in the Maryland Penitentiary for killing his wife,
but I think he owed much more of his eminence to his adaman-
tine rectitude in money matters, so rare in his profession. The
very cops, indeed, regarded him as an honest man, and said so
freely. They knew about his blanket refusal to take more than
three or four times the legal fare from drunks, they knew how
many lost watches, wallets, stick-pins and walking-sticks he
turned in every year, and they admired as Christians, though
deploring as cops, his absolute refusal to work for them in the
capacity of stool-pigeon.

Moreover, he was industrious as well as honest, and it was
the common belief that he had money in five banks. He appeared on the hack-stand in front of the old Eutaw House every
evening at nine o'clock, and put in the next five or six hours
shuttling merrymakers and sociologists to and from the red-
light districts. When this trade began to languish he drove to
Union Station, and there kept watch until his two old horses fell
asleep. Most of the strangers who got off the early morning
trains wanted to go to the nearest hotel, which was only two
blocks away, so there was not a great deal of money in their patronage, but unlike the other hackers Peebles never resorted to
the device of driving them swiftly in the wrong direction and
then working back by a circuitous route.

A little after dawn one morning in the early Autumn of
1903, just as his off horse began to snore gently, a milk-train
got in from lower Pennsylvania, and out of it issued a rosy-
cheeked young woman carrying a pasteboard suitcase and a
pink parasol. Squired up from the train-level by a car-greaser
with an eye for country beauty, she emerged into the sunlight
shyly and ran her eye down the line of hacks. The other drivers
seemed to scare her, and no wonder, for they were all grasping
men whose evil propensities glowed from them like heat from
a stove. But when she saw Peebles her feminine intuition must
have told her that he could be trusted, for she shook off the car-
greaser without further ado, and came up to the Peebles hack
with a pretty show of confidence.

"Say, mister," she said, "how much will you charge to take me to a house of ill fame?"

In telling of it afterward Peebles probably exaggerated his astonishment a bit, but certainly he must have suffered something rationally describable as a shock. He laid great stress upon her air of blooming innocence, almost like that of a cavorting lamb. He said her two cheeks glowed like apples, and that she smelled like a load of hay. By his own account he stared at her for a full minute without answering her question, with a wild stream of confused surmises racing through his mind. What imaginable business could a creature so obviously guileless have in the sort of establishment she had mentioned? Could it be that her tongue had slipped—that she actually meant an employment office, the Y.W.C.A., or what not? Peebles, as he later elaborated the story, insisted that he had cross-examined her at length, and that she had not only reiterated her question in precise terms, but explained that she was fully determined to abandon herself to sin and looked forward confidently to dying in the gutter. But in his first version he reported simply that he had stared at her dumbly until his amazement began to wear off, and then motioned to her to climb into his back. After all, he was a common carrier, and obliged by law to haul all comers, regardless of their private projects and intentions. If he yielded anything to his Caledonian moral sense it took the form of choosing her destination with some prudence. He might have dumped her into one of the third-rate bagnios that crowded a street not three blocks from Union Station, and then gone on about his business. Instead, he drove half way across town to the high-toned studio of Miss Nellie d'Alembert, at that time one of the leaders of her profession in Baltimore, and a woman who, though she lacked the polish of Vassar, had sound sense, a pawky humor, and progressive ideas.

I had become, only a little while before, city editor of the *Herald,* and in that capacity received frequently confidential communications from her. She was, in fact, the source of a great many useful news tips. She knew everything about everyone that no one was supposed to know, and had accurate advance information, in particular, about Page 1 divorces, for nearly all the big law firms of the town used her facilities for the manufacture of evidence. There were no Walter Winchells in that era, and the city editors of the land had to depend on volunteers for inside stuff. Such volunteers were moved (a) by a sense of public duty gracefully performed, and (b) by an enlightened desire to keep on the good side of newspapers. Not infrequently they cashed in on this last. I well remember the night when two visiting Congressmen from Washington got into a debate in Miss Nellie's music-room, and one of them dented the skull of the other with a spittoon. At my suggestion the other city editors of Baltimore joined me in straining journalistic ethics far enough to remove the accident to Mt. Vernon place, the most respectable neighborhood in town, and to lay the fracture to a fall on the ice.

My chance leadership in this public work made Miss Nellie my partisan, and now and then she gave me a nice tip and forgot to include the other city editors. Thus I was alert when she called up during the early afternoon of Peebles' strange adventure, and told me that something swell was on ice. She explained that it was not really what you could call important news, but simply a sort of human-interest story, so I asked Percy Heath to go to see her, for though he was now my successor as Sunday editor, he still did an occasional news story, and I knew what kind he enjoyed especially. He called up in half an hour, and asked me to join him. "If you don't hear it yourself," he said, "you will say I am pulling a fake."

When I got to Miss Nellie's house I found her sitting with Percy in a basement room that she used as a sort of office, and at once she plunged into the story.

"I'll tell you first," she began, "before you see the poor thing herself. When Peebles yanked the bell this morning I was sound asleep, and so was all the girls, and Sadie the coon had gone home. I stuck my head out of the window, and there was Peebles on the front steps. I said: 'Get the hell away from here! What do you mean by bringing in a drunk at this time of the morning? Don't you know us poor working people gotta get some rest?' But he hollered back that he didn't have no drunk in his hack, but something he didn't know what to make of, and needed my help on, so I slipped on my kimono and went down to the door, and by that time he had the girl out of the hack, and before I could say 'scat' he had shoved her in the parlor, and she was unloading what she had to say.

"Well, to make a long story short, she said she come from somewheres near a burg they call Red Lion, P.A., and lived on a farm. She said her father was one of them old rubes with whiskers they call Dunkards, and very strict. She said she had a beau in York, P.A., of the name of Elmer, and whenever he could get away he would come out to the farm and set in the parlor with her, and they would do a little hugging and kissing. She said Elmer was educated and a great reader, and he would bring her books that he got from his brother, who was a train butcher on the Northern Central, and him and her would read them. She said the books was all about love, and that most of them was sad. Her and Elmer would talk about them while they set in the parlor, and the more they talked about them the sadder they would get, and sometimes she would have to cry.

"Well, to make a long story short, this went on once a week or so, and night before last Elmer come down from York with some more books, and they set in the parlor, and talked about love. Her old man usually stuck his nose in the door now and then, to see that there wasn't no foolishness, but night before last he had a bilious attack and went to bed early, so her and Elmer had it all to theirself in the parlor. So they quit talking about the books, and Elmer began to love her up, and in a little while they was hugging and kissing to beat the band. Well, to make a long story short, Elmer went too far, and when she come to herself and kicked him out she realized she had lost her honest name.

"She laid awake all night thinking about it, and the more she thought about it the more scared she got. In every one of the books her and Elmer read there was something on the subject, and all of the books said the same thing. When a girl lost her honest name there was nothing for her to do except to run away from home and lead a life of shame. No girl that she ever read about ever done anything else. They all rushed off to the nearest city, started this life of shame, and then took to booze and dope and died in the gutter. Their family never knew what had became of them. Maybe they landed finally in a medical college, or maybe the Salvation Army buried them, but their people never heard no more of them, and their name was rubbed out of the family Bible. Sometimes their beau tried to find them, but he never could do it, and in the end he usually married the judge's homely daughter, and moved into the big house when the judge died.

"Well, to make a long story short, this poor girl lay awake all night thinking of such sad things, and when she got up at four thirty A.M. and went out to milk the cows her eyes was so full of tears that she could hardly find their spigots. Her father, who was still bilious, give her hell, and told her she was getting her just punishment for setting up until ten and eleven o'clock at night, when all decent people ought to be in bed. So she began to suspect that he may have snuck down during the evening, and caught her, and was getting ready to turn her out of the house and wash his hands of her, and maybe even curse her. So she decided to have it over and done with as soon as possible, and last night, the minute he hit the hay again, she hoofed in to York, P.A., and caught the milk-train for Baltimore, and that is how Peebles found her at Union Station and brought her here. When I asked her what in hell she wanted all she had to say was 'Ain't this a house of ill fame?', and it took me an hour or two to pump her story out of her. So now I have got her upstairs under lock and key, and as soon as I can get word to Peebles I'll tell him to take her back to Union Station, and start her back for Red Lion, P.A. Can you beat it?"

Percy and I, of course, demanded to see the girl, and presently Miss Nellie fetched her in. She was by no means the bucolic Lillian Russell that Peebles' tall tales afterward made her out, but she was certainly far from unappetizing. Despite her loss of sleep, the dreadful gnawings of her conscience and the menace of an appalling retribution, her cheeks were still rosy, and there remained a considerable sparkle in her troubled blue eyes. I never heard her name, but it was plain that she was of four-square Pennsylvania Dutch stock, and as sturdy as the cows she serviced. She had on her Sunday clothes, and appeared to be somewhat uncomfortable in them, but Miss Nellie set her at ease, and soon she was retelling her story to two strange and, in her sight, probably highly dubious men. We listened without interrupting her, and when she finished Percy was the first to speak.

"My dear young lady," he said, "you have been grossly misinformed. I don't know what these works of fiction are that you and Elmer read, but they are as far out of date as Joe Miller's Jest-Book. The stuff that seems to be in them would make even a newspaper editorial writer cough and scratch himself. It may be true that, in the remote era when they appear to have been written, the penalty of a slight and venial slip was as drastic as you say, but I assure you that it is no longer the case. The world is much more humane than it used to be, and much more rational. Just as it no longer burns men for heresy or women for witchcraft, so it has ceased to condemn girls to lives of shame and death in the gutter for the trivial dereliction you acknowledge. If there were time I'd get you some of the more recent books, and point out passages showing how moral principles have changed. The only thing that is frowned on now seems to be getting caught. Otherwise, justice is virtually silent on the subject.

"Inasmuch as your story indicates that no one knows of your crime save your beau, who, if he has learned of your disappearance, is probably scared half to death, I advise you to go home, make some plausible excuse to your pa for lighting out, and resume your care of his cows. At the proper opportunity take your beau to the pastor, and join him in indissoluble love. It is the safe, respectable and hygienic course. Everyone agrees that it is moral, even moralists. Meanwhile, don't forget to thank Miss Nellie. She might have helped you down the primrose way; instead, she has restored you to virtue and happiness, no worse for an interesting experience."

The girl, of course, took in only a small part of this, for Percy's voluptuous style and vocabulary were beyond the grasp of a simple milkmaid. But Miss Nellie, who understood English much better than she spoke it, translated freely, and in a little while the troubled look departed from those blue eyes, and large tears of joy welled from them. Miss Nellie shed a couple herself, and so did all the ladies of the resident faculty, for they had drifted downstairs during the interview, sleepy but curious. The practical Miss Nellie inevitably thought of money, and it turned out that the trip down by milk-train and Peebles' lawful freight of $1 had about exhausted the poor girl's savings, and she had only some odd change left. Percy threw in a dollar and I threw in a dollar, and Miss Nellie not only threw in a third, but ordered one of the ladies to go to the kitchen and prepare a box-lunch for the return to Red Lion.

Sadie the coon had not yet come to work, but Peebles presently bobbed up without being sent for, and toward the end of the afternoon he started off for Union Station with his most amazing passenger, now as full of innocent jubilation as a martyr saved at the stake. As I have said, he embellished the story considerably during the days following, especially in the direction of touching up the girl's pulchritude. The cops, because of their general confidence in him, swallowed his exaggerations, and I heard more than one of them lament that they had missed the chance to handle the case professionally. Percy, in his later years, made two or three attempts to put it into a movie scenario, but the Hays office always vetoed it.

How the girl managed to account to her father for her mysterious flight and quick return I don't know, for she was never heard from afterward. She promised to send Miss Nellie a picture postcard of Red Lion, showing the new hall of the Knights of Pythias, but if it was ever actually mailed it must have been misaddressed, for it never arrived.

MAIN CURRENTS OF
AMERICAN THOUGHT[*]

BY IRWIN SHAW

F LACKER: ALL right now, Kid, now you'd better talk,"
Andrew dictated. "Business: Sound of the door closing,
the slow turning of the key in the lock. Buddy: You're never go-
ing to get me to talk, Flacker. Business: Sound of a slap.
Flacker: Maybe that'll make you think different, Kid. Where is
Jerry Carmichael? Buddy: (laughing) Wouldn't you like to
know, Flacker? Flacker: Yeah. (Slowly, with great threat in his
voice) And I'm going to find out. One way or another. See?
Business: Siren fades in, louder, fades out. Announcer: Will
Buddy talk? Will Flacker force him to disclose the where-
abouts of the rescued son of the railroad king? Will Dusty
Blades reach him in time? Tune in Monday at the same time, et
cetera, et cetera..."

Andrew dropped onto the couch and put his feet up. He
stretched and sighed as he watched Lenore finish scratching his
dictation down in the shorthand notebook. "Thirty bucks," he
said. "There's another thirty bucks. Is it the right length?"

"Uhuh," Lenore said. "Eleven and a half pages. This is a
very good one, Andy."

"Yeah," Andrew said, closing his eyes. "Put it next to Moby
Dick on your library shelf."

"It's very exciting," Lenore said, standing up. "I don't know
what they're complaining about."

"You're a lovely girl," Andrew put his hands over his eyes

* from *The New Yorker* and *Mixed Company*

and rubbed around and around. "I have wooden hinges on my eyelids. Do you sleep at night?"

"Don't do that to your eyes," Lenore started to put on her coat. "You only aggravate them."

"You're right." Andrew dug his fists into his eyes and rotated them slowly. "You don't know how right you are."

"Tomorrow. At ten o'clock?" Lenore asked.

"At ten o'clock. Dig me out of the arms of sleep. We shall leave Dusty Blades to his fate for this week and go on with the further adventures of Ronnie Cook and His Friends, forty dollars a script. I always enjoy writing Ronnie Cook much better than Dusty Blades. See what ten dollars does to a man." He opened his eyes and watched Lenore putting her hat on in front of the mirror. When he squinted, she was not so plain-looking. He felt very sorry for Lenore, plain as sand, with her flat-colored face, and her hair pulled down like rope, and never a man to her name. She was putting on a red hat with a kind of ladder arrangement going up one side. It looked very funny and sad on her. Andrew realized that it was a new hat. "That's a mighty fine hat," he said.

"I thought a long time before I bought this hat," Lenore said, flushing because he'd noticed it.

"Har-*riet!*" The governess next door screamed in the alley to the next-door neighbor's little girl. "Harriet, get away from there this minute!"

Andrew turned over on his stomach on the couch and put a pillow over his head. "Have you got any ideas for Ronnie Cook and His Friends for tomorrow?" he asked Lenore.

"No. Have you?"

"No." He pulled the pillow tight around his head.

"You'll get them by tomorrow," Lenore said. "You always do."

"Yeah," said Andrew.

"You need a vacation," Lenore said.

"Get out of here."

"Good-bye," Lenore started out. "Get a good night's sleep."

"Anything you say."

Andrew watched her with one eye as she went off the porch

on which he worked and through the living room and dining room, toward the stairs. She had nice legs. You were always surprised when a girl with a face like that had nice legs. But she had hair on her legs. She was not a lucky girl. "Oh, no," Andrew said as the door closed behind her, "you are not a lucky girl."

He closed his eyes and tried to sleep. The sun came in through the open windows and the curtains blew softly over his head and the sun was warm and comforting on his closed eyes. Across the street, on the public athletic field, four boys were shagging flies. There would be the neat pleasant crack of the bat and a long time later the smack of the ball in the fielder's glove. The tall trees outside, as old as Brooklyn, rustled a little from time to time as little spurts of wind swept across the base-ball field.

"Har*riet!*" the governess called. "Stop that or I will make you stand by yourself in the corner all afternoon! Harriet! I de-mand you stop it!" The governess was French. She had the only unpleasant French accent Andrew had ever heard.

The little girl started to cry, "Mamma! Mamma! Mamma, she's going to hit me!" The little girl hated the governess and the governess hated the little girl, and they continually reported each other to the little girl's mother. "Mamma!"

"You are a little liar," the governess screamed. "You will grow up, and you will be a liar all your life. There will be no hope for you."

"Mamma!" wailed the little girl.

They went inside the house and it was quiet again.

"Charlie," one of the boys on the baseball field yelled, "hit it to me, Charlie!"

The telephone rang, four times, and then Andrew heard his mother talking into it. She came onto the porch.

"It's a man from the bank," she said. "He wants to talk to you."

"You should've told him I wasn't home," Andrew said.

"But you are home," his mother said. "How was I to know that . . . ?"

"You're right." Andrew swung his legs over and sat up. "You're perfectly right."

He went into the dining room, to the telephone, and talked to the man at the bank.

"You're a hundred and eleven dollars overdrawn," said the man at the bank.

Andrew squinted at his mother, sitting across the room, on a straight chair, with her arms folded in her lap, her head turned just a little, so as not to miss anything.

"I thought I had about four hundred dollars in the bank," Andrew said into the phone.

"You are a hundred and eleven dollars overdrawn," said the man at the bank.

Andrew sighed. "I'll check it." He put the phone down.

"What's the matter?" his mother asked.

"I'm a hundred and eleven dollars overdrawn," he said.

"That's shameful," his mother said. "You ought to be more methodical."

"Yes." Andrew started back to the porch.

"You're awfully careless." His mother followed him. "You really ought to keep track of your money."

"Yes." Andrew sat down on the couch.

"Give me a kiss," his mother said.

"Why?"

"No particular reason." She laughed.

"O.K." He kissed her and she held him for a moment. He dropped down on the couch. She ran her finger under his eye.

"You've got rings under your eyes," she said.

"That's right."

She kissed him again and went to the rear of the house. He closed his eyes. From the rear of the house came the sound of the vacuum cleaner. Andrew felt his muscles getting stiff in protest against the vacuum cleaner. He got up and went to her bedroom, where she was running the machine back and forth under the bed. She was down on one knee and was bent over looking under the bed.

"Hey!" Andrew yelled. "Hey, Mom!"

She turned off the machine and looked up at him. "What's the matter?"

"I'm trying to sleep," he said.

"Well, why don't you sleep?"

"The vacuum cleaner. It's shaking the house."

His mother stood up, her face setting into stern lines. "I've got to clean the house, don't I?"

"Why do you have to clean the house while I'm trying to sleep?"

His mother bent down again. "I can't use it while you're working. I can't use it while you're reading. I can't use it until ten o'clock in the morning because you're sleeping." She started the machine. "When am I supposed to clean the house?" she called over the noise of the cleaner. "Why don't you sleep at night like everybody else?" And she put her head down low and vigorously ran the machine back and forth.

Andrew watched her for a moment. No arguments came to him. The sound of the cleaner so close to him made his nerves jump. He went out of the room, closing the door behind him.

The telephone was ringing and he picked it up and said, "Hello."

"Ahndrew?" his agent's voice asked. His agent was from Brooklyn, too, but he had a very broad A, with which he impressed actors and sponsors.

"Yes, this is Ahndrew." Andrew always made this straight-faced joke with his agent, but the agent never seemed to catch on. "You didn't have to call. The Dusty Blades scripts are all through. You'll get them tomorrow."

"I called about something else, Ahndrew," his agent said, his voice very smooth and influential on the phone. "The complaints're piling up on the Blades scripts. They're as slow as gum. Nothing ever happens. Ahndrew, you're not writing for the *Atlantic Monthly.*"

"I know I'm not writing for the *Atlantic Monthly.*"

"I think you've rather run out of material," his agent said lightly, soothingly. "I think perhaps you ought to take a little vacation from the Blades scripts."

"Go to hell, Herman," Andrew said, knowing that Herman had found somebody to do the scripts more cheaply for him.

"That's hardly the way to talk, Ahndrew," Herman said, his voice still smooth, but hurt. "After all, I have to stand in the studio and listen to the complaints."

"Sad, Herman," Andrew said. "That's a sad picture," and hung up.

He rubbed the back of his neck reflectively, feeling again the little lump behind his ear.

He went into his own room and sat at his desk looking blankly at the notes for his play that lay, neatly piled, growing older, on one side. He took out his check book and his last month's vouchers and arranged them in front of him.

"One hundred and eleven dollars," he murmured, as he checked back and added and subtracted, his eyes smarting from the strain, his hands shaking a little because the vacuum cleaner was still going in his mother's room. Out on the athletic field more boys had arrived and formed an infield and were throwing the ball around the bases and yelling at each other.

Dr. Chalmers, seventy-five dollars. That was for his mother and her stomach.

Eighty dollars rent. The roof over his head equaled two Ronnie Cook's and His Friends. Five thousand words for rent.

Buddy was in the hands of Flacker. Flacker could torture him for six pages. Then you could have Dusty Blades speeding to the rescue with Sam, by boat, and the boat could spring a leak because the driver was in Flacker's pay, and there could be a fight for the next six pages. The driver could have a gun. You could use it, but it wouldn't be liked, because you'd done at least four like it already.

Furniture, and a hundred and thirty-seven dollars. His mother had always wanted a good dining-room table. She didn't have a maid, she said, so he ought to get her a dining-room table. How many words for a dining-room table?

"Come on, Baby, make it two," the second baseman out on the field was yelling. "Double 'em up!"

Andrew felt like picking up his old glove and going out there and joining them. When he was still in college he used to go out on a Saturday at ten o'clock in the morning and shag flies and jump around the infield and run and run all day, playing in pickup games until it got too dark to see. He was always tired now and even when he played tennis he didn't move his feet right, because he was tired, and hit flatfooted and wild.

Spain, one hundred dollars. Oh, Lord.

A hundred and fifty to his father, to meet his father's payroll. His father had nine people on his payroll, making little tin gadgets that his father tried to sell to the dime stores, and at the end of every month Andrew had to meet the payroll. His father always gravely made out a note to him.

Flacker is about to kill Buddy out of anger and desperation. In bursts Dusty, alone. Sam is hurt. On the way to the hospital. Buddy is spirited away a moment before Dusty arrives. Flacker, very smooth and oily. Confrontation. "Where is Buddy, Flacker?" "You mean the little lad?" "I mean the little lad, Flacker!"

Fifty dollars to Dorothy's piano teacher. His sister. Another plain girl. She might as well learn how to play the piano. Then one day they'd come to him and say, "Dorothy is ready for her debut. All we're asking you to do is rent Town Hall for a Wednesday evening. Just advance the money." She'd never get married. She was too smart for the men who would want her and too plain for the men she'd want herself. She bought her dresses in Saks. He would have to support, for life, a sister who would only buy her dresses in Saks and paid her piano teacher fifty dollars a month every month. She was only twenty-four, she would have a normal life expectancy of at least forty years, twelve times forty, plus dresses at Saks and Town Hall from time to time ...

His father's teeth—ninety dollars. The money it cost to keep a man going in his losing fight against age.

The automobile. Nine hundred dollars. A nine-hundred-dollar check looked very austere and impressive, like a penal institution. He was going to go off in the automobile, find a place in the mountains, write a play. Only he could never get himself far enough ahead on Dusty Blades and Ronnie Cook and His Friends. Twenty thousand words a week, each week, recurring like Sunday on the calendar. How many words was Hamlet? Thirty, thirty-five thousand?

Twenty-three dollars to Best's. That was Martha's sweater for her birthday. "Either you say yes or no," Martha said Saturday night. "I want to get married and I've waited long enough." If you married you paid rent in two places, light, gas, telephone twice, and you bought stockings, dresses, toothpaste, medical attention, for your wife.

Flacker played with something in his pocket. Dusty's hand shoots out, grabs his wrist, pulls his hand out. Buddy's little penknife, which Dusty had given him for a birthday present, is in Flacker's hand. "Flacker, tell me where Buddy Jones is, or I'll kill you with my bare hands." A gong rings. Flacker has stepped on an alarm. Doors open and the room fills with his henchmen.

Twenty dollars to Macy's for books. Parrington, *Main Currents of American Thought*. How does Dusty Blades fit into the *Main Currents of American Thought*?

Ten dollars to Dr. Farber. "I don't sleep at night. Can you help me?"

"Do you drink coffee?"

"I drink one cup of coffee in the morning. That's all."

Pills, to be taken before retiring. Ten dollars. We ransom our lives from doctors' hands.

If you marry, you take an apartment downtown because it's silly to live in Brooklyn this way; and you buy furniture, four rooms full of furniture, beds, chairs, dishrags, relatives. Martha's family was poor and getting no younger and finally there would be three families, with rent and clothes and doctors and funerals.

Andrew got up and opened the closet door. In it, stacked in files, were the scripts he had written in the last four years. They stretched from one end of a wide closet across to another, bridge from one wall to another of a million words. Four years' work.

Next script. The henchmen close in on Dusty. He hears the sounds of Buddy screaming in the next room...

How many years more?

The vacuum cleaner roared.

Martha was Jewish. That meant you'd have to lie your way into some hotels, if you went at all, and you never could escape from one particular meanness of the world around you; and when the bad time came there you'd be, adrift on that dangerous sea.

He sat down at his desk. One hundred dollars again to Spain. Barcelona had fallen and the long dusty lines were beating their way to the French border with the planes over them, and out of a sense of guilt at not being on a dusty road, yourself, bloody-footed and in fear of death, you gave a hundred dollars, feeling at the same time that it was too much and nothing you ever gave could be enough. Three-and-a-third The Adventures of Dusty Blades to the dead and dying of Spain.

The world loads you day by day with new burdens that increase on your shoulders. Lift a pound and you find you're carrying a ton. "Marry me," she says, "marry me." Then what does Dusty do? What the hell can he do that he hasn't done before? For five afternoons a week now, for a year, Dusty has been in Flacker's hands, or the hands of somebody else who is Flacker but has another name, and each time he has escaped. How now?

The vacuum roared in the hallway outside his room.

"Mom!" he yelled. "Please turn that thing off!"

"What did you say?" his mother called.

"Nothing."

He added up the bank balances. His figures showed that he was four hundred and twelve dollars overdrawn instead of one hundred and eleven dollars, as the bank said. He didn't feel like adding the figures over. He put the vouchers and the bank's sheet into an envelope for his income-tax returns.

"Hit it out, Charlie!" a boy called on the field. "Make it a fast one!"

Andrew felt like going out and playing with them. He changed his clothes and put on a pair of old spikes that were lying in back of the closet. His old pants were tight on him. Fat.

If he ever let go, if anything happened and he couldn't exercise, he'd blow up like a house, if he got sick and had to lie in bed and convalesce.... Maybe Dusty has a knife in a holster up his sleeve.... How plant that? The rent, the food, the piano teacher, the people at Saks who sold his sister dresses, the nimble girls who painted the tin gadgets in his father's shop, the teeth in his father's mouth, the doctors, the doctors, all living on the words that would have to come out of his head. See here, Flacker, I know what you're up to. Business: Sound of a shot. A groan. Hurry, before the train gets to the crossing! Look! He's gaining on us! Hurry! Will he make it? Will Dusty Blades head off the desperate gang of counterfeiters and murderers in the race for the yacht? Will I be able to keep it up? The years, the years ahead ... You grow fat and the lines become permanent under your eyes and you drink too much and you pay more to the doctors because death is nearer and there is no stop, no vacation from life, in no year can you say, "I want to sit this one out, kindly excuse me."

His mother opened the door. "Martha's on the phone."

Andrew clattered out in his spiked shoes, holding the old, torn fielder's glove. He closed the door to the dining room to show his mother this was going to be a private conversation.

"Hello," he said. "Yes." He listened gravely. "No," he said. "I guess not. Good-bye. Good luck, Martha."

He stood looking at the phone. His mother came in and he raised his head and started down the steps.

"Andrew," she said, "I want to ask you something."

"What?"

"Could you spare fifty dollars, Andrew?"

"Oh, God!"

"It's important. You know I wouldn't ask you if it wasn't important. It's for Dorothy."

"What does she need it for?"

"She's going to a party, a very important party, a lot of very big people're going to be there and she's sure they'll ask her to play..."

"Do the invitations cost fifty dollars apiece?" Andrew

kicked the top step and a little piece of dried mud fell off the spiked shoes.

"No, Andrew." His mother was talking in her asking-for-money voice. "It's for a dress. She can't go without a new dress, she says. There's a man there she's after."

"She won't get him, dress or no dress," Andrew said. "Your daughter's a very plain girl."

"I know," his mother's hands waved a little, helpless and sad. "But it's better if she at least does the best she can. I feel so sorry for her, Andrew . . ."

"Everybody comes to me!" Andrew yelled, his voice suddenly high. "Nobody leaves me alone! Not for a minute!"

He was crying now and he turned to hide it from his mother. She looked at him, surprised, shaking her head. She put her arms around him. "Just do what you want to do, Andrew, that's all. Don't do anything you don't want to do."

"Yeah," Andrew said. "Yeah. I'm sorry. I'll give you the money. I'm sorry I yelled at you."

"Don't give it to me if you don't want to, Andrew." His mother was saying this honestly, believing it.

He laughed a little. "I want to, Mom, I want to."

He patted her shoulder and went down toward the baseball field, leaving her standing there puzzled at the top of the steps.

The sun and the breeze felt good on the baseball field, and he forgot for an hour, but he moved slowly. His arm hurt at the shoulder when he threw, and the boy playing second base called him Mister, which he wouldn't have done even last year, when Andrew was twenty-four.

THE GHOSTS*

BY LORD DUNSANY

THE ARGUMENT that I had with my brother in his great lonely house will scarcely interest my readers. Not those, at least, whom I hope may be attracted by the experiment that I undertook, and by the strange things that befell me in that hazardous region into which so lightly and so ignorantly I allowed my fancy to enter. It was at Oneleigh that I had visited him.

Now Oneleigh stands in a wide isolation, in the midst of a dark gathering of old whispering cedars. They nod their heads together when the North Wind comes, and nod again and agree, and furtively grow still again, and say no more awhile. The North Wind is to them like a nice problem among wise old men; they nod their heads over it, and mutter it all together. They know much, those cedars, they have been there so long. Their grandsires knew Lebanon, and the grandsires of these were the servants of the King of Tyre and came to Solomon's court. And amidst these black-haired children of grey-headed Time stood the old house of Oneleigh. I know not how many centuries had lashed against it their evanescent foam of years; but it was still unshattered, and all about it were the things of long ago, as cling strange growths to some sea-defying rock. Here, like the shells of long-dead limpets, was armour that men encased themselves in long ago; here, too, were tapestries of many colours, beautiful as seaweed; no modern flotsam ever drifted hither, no early Victorian furniture, no electric light. The great trade routes that littered the years with empty meat tins and cheap novels were far from here. Well, well, the cen-

* from *The Sword of Welleran*

turies will shatter it and drive its fragments on to distant shores. Meanwhile, while it yet stood, I went on a visit there to my brother, and we argued about ghosts. My brother's intelligence on this subject seemed to me to be in need of correction. He mistook things imagined for things having an actual existence; he argued that second-hand evidence of persons having seen ghosts proved ghosts to exist. I said that even if they had seen ghosts, this was no proof at all; nobody believes that there are red rats, though there is plenty of first-hand evidence of men having seen them in delirium. Finally, I said I would see ghosts myself, and continue to argue against their actual existence. So I collected a handful of cigars and drank several cups of very strong tea, and went without my dinner, and retired into a room where there was dark oak and all the chairs were covered with tapestry; and my brother went to bed bored with our argument and trying hard to dissuade me from making myself uncomfortable. All the way up the old stairs as I stood at the bottom of them, and as his candle went winding up and up, I heard him still trying to persuade me to have supper and go to bed.

It was a windy winter, and outside the cedars were muttering I know not what about; but I think that they were Tories of a school long dead, and were troubled about something new. Within, a great damp log upon the fireplace began to squeak and sing, and struck up a whining tune, and a tall flame stood up over it and beat time, and all the shadows crowded round and began to dance. In distant corners old masses of darkness sat still like chaperones and never moved. Over there, in the darkest part of the room, stood a door that was always locked. It led into the hall, but no one ever used it; near that door something had happened once of which the family are not proud. We do not speak of it. There in the firelight stood the venerable forms of the old chairs; the hands that had made their tapestries lay far beneath the soil, the needles with which they wrought were many separate flakes of rust. No one wove now in that old room—no one but the assiduous ancient spiders who, watching by the deathbed of the things of yore, worked shrouds to hold their dust. In shrouds about the cornices already lay the heart of the oak wainscot that the worm had eaten out.

Surely at such an hour, in such a room, a fancy already excited by hunger and strong tea might see the ghosts of former occupants. I expected nothing less. The fire flickered and the shadows danced, memories of strange historic things rose vividly in my mind; but midnight chimed solemnly from a seven-foot clock, and nothing happened. My imagination would not be hurried, and the chill that is with the small hours had come upon me, and I had nearly abandoned myself to sleep, when in the hall adjoining there arose the rustling of silk dresses that I had waited for and expected. Then there entered two by two the high-born ladies and their gallants of Jacobean times. They were little more than shadows—very dignified shadows, and almost indistinct; but you have all read ghost stories before, you have all seen in museums the dresses of those times—there is little need to describe them; they entered, several of them, and sat down on the old chairs, perhaps a little carelessly considering the value of the tapestries. Then the rustling of their dresses ceased.

Well—I had seen ghosts, and was neither frightened nor convinced that ghosts existed. I was about to get up out of my chair and go to bed, when there came a sound of pattering in the hall, a sound of bare feet coming over the polished floor, and every now and then a foot would slip and I heard claws scratching along the wood as some four-footed thing lost and regained its balance. I was not frightened, but uneasy. The pattering came straight towards the room that I was in, then I heard the sniffing of expectant nostrils; perhaps "uneasy" was not the most suitable word to describe my feelings then. Suddenly a herd of black creatures larger than blood-hounds came galloping in; they had large pendulous ears, their noses were to the ground sniffing, they went up to the lords and ladies of long ago and fawned about them disgustingly. Their eyes were horribly bright, and ran down to great depths. When I looked into them I knew suddenly what these creatures were, and I was afraid. They were the sins, the filthy, immortal sins of those courtly men and women.

How demure she was, the lady that sat near me on an old-world chair—how demure she was, and how fair, to have be-

side her with its jowl upon her lap a sin with such cavernous
red eyes, a clear case of murder. And you, yonder lady with the
golden hair, surely not you—and yet that fearful beast with the
yellow eyes slinks from you to yonder courtier there, and
whenever one drives it away it slinks back to the other. Over
there a lady tries to smile as she strokes the loathsome furry
head of another's sin, but one of her own is jealous and intrudes
itself under her hand. Here sits an old nobleman with his
grandson on his knee, and one of the great black sins of the
grandfather is licking the child's face and has made the child its
own. Sometimes a ghost would move and seek another chair,
but always his pack of sins would move behind him. Poor
ghosts, poor ghosts! how many flights they must have attempted for two hundred years from their hated sins, how many
excuses they must have given for their presence, and the sins
were with them still—and still unexplained. Suddenly one of
them seemed to scent my living blood, and bayed horribly, and
all the others left their ghosts at once and dashed up to the sin
that had given tongue. The brute had picked up my scent near
the door by which I had entered, and they moved slowly nearer
to me sniffing along the floor, and uttering every now and then
their fearful cry. I saw that the whole thing had gone too far.
But now they had seen me, now they were all about me, they
sprang up trying to reach my throat; and whenever their claws
touched me, horrible thoughts came into my mind and unutterable desires dominated my heart. I planned bestial things as
these creatures leaped around me, and planned them with a
masterly cunning. A great red-eyed murder was among the
foremost of those furry things from whom I feebly strove to de-
fend my throat. Suddenly it seemed to me good that I should
kill my brother. It seemed important to me that I should not risk
being punished. I knew where a revolver was kept; after I shot
him, I would dress the body up and put flour on the face like a
man that had been acting as a ghost. It would be very simple. I
would say that he had frightened me—and the servants had
heard us talking about ghosts. There were one or two trivialities
that would have to be arranged, but nothing escaped my mind.
Yes, it seemed to me very good that I should kill my brother as

I looked into the red depths of this creature's eyes. But one last effort as they dragged me down—"If two straight lines cut one another," I said, "the opposite angles are equal. Let AB, CD, cut one another at E, then the angles CEA, CEB equal two right angles (prop. xiii). Also CEA, AED equal two right angles."

I moved toward the door to get the revolver; a hideous exultation arose among the beasts. "But the angle CEA is common, therefore AED equals CEB. In the same way CEA equals DEB. *Q.E.D.*" It was proved. Logic and reason re-established themselves in my mind, there were no dark hounds of sin, the tapestried chairs were empty. It seemed to me an inconceivable thought that a man should murder his brother.

THE MINISTER'S BLACK VEIL—A PARABLE[1][*]

BY NATHANIEL HAWTHORNE

THE SEXTON stood in the porch of Milford meeting-house, pulling busily at the bell-rope. The old people of the village came stooping along the street. Children, with bright faces, tripped merrily beside their parents, or mimicked a graver gait, in the conscious dignity of their Sunday clothes. Spruce bachelors looked sidelong at the pretty maidens, and fancied that the Sabbath sunshine made them prettier than on week days. When the throng had mostly streamed into the porch, the sexton began to toll the bell, keeping his eye on the Reverend Mr. Hooper's door. The first glimpse of

---

[1] Another clergyman in New England, Mr. Joseph Moody, of York, Maine, who died about eighty years since, made himself remarkable by the same eccentricity that is here related of the Reverend Mr. Hooper. In his case, however, the symbol had a different import. In early life he had accidentally killed a beloved friend; and from that day till the hour of his own death, he hid his face from men.

[*] from *Twice-Told Tales*

the clergyman's figure was the signal for the bell to cease its summons.

"But what has good Parson Hooper got upon his face?" cried the sexton in astonishment.

All within hearing immediately turned about, and beheld the semblance of Mr. Hooper, pacing slowly his meditative way towards the meeting-house. With one accord they started, expressing more wonder than if some strange minister were coming to dust the cushions of Mr. Hooper's pulpit.

"Are you sure it is our parson?" inquired Goodman Gray of the sexton.

"Of a certainty it is good Mr. Hooper," replied the sexton. "He was to have exchanged pulpits with Parson Shute, of Westbury; but Parson Shute sent to excuse himself yesterday, being to preach a funeral sermon."

The cause of so much amazement may appear sufficiently slight. Mr. Hooper, a gentlemanly person, of about thirty, though still a bachelor, was dressed with due clerical neatness, as if a careful wife had starched his band, and brushed the weekly dust from his Sunday's garb. There was but one thing remarkable in his appearance. Swathed about his forehead, and hanging down over his face, so low as to be shaken by his breath, Mr. Hooper had on a black veil. On a nearer view it seemed to consist of two folds of crape, which entirely concealed his features, except the mouth and chin, but probably did not intercept his sight, further than to give a darkened aspect to all living and inanimate things. With this gloomy shade before him, good Mr. Hooper walked onward, at a slow and quiet pace, stooping somewhat, and looking on the ground, as is customary with abstracted men, yet nodding kindly to those of his parishioners who still waited on the meeting-house steps. But so wonder-struck were they that his greeting hardly met with a return.

"I can't really feel as if good Mr. Hooper's face was behind that piece of crape," said the sexton.

"I don't like it," muttered an old woman, as she hobbled into the meeting-house. "He has changed himself into something awful, only by hiding his face."

"Our parson has gone mad!" cried Goodman Gray, following him across the threshold.

A rumor of some unaccountable phenomenon had preceded Mr. Hooper into the meeting-house, and set all the congregation astir. Few could refrain from twisting their heads towards the door; many stood upright, and turned directly about; while several little boys clambered upon the seats, and came down again with a terrible racket. There was a general bustle, a rustling of the women's gowns and shuffling of the men's feet, greatly at variance with that hushed repose which should attend the entrance of the minister. But Mr. Hooper appeared not to notice the perturbation of his people. He entered with an almost noiseless step, bent his head mildly to the pews on each side, and bowed as he passed his oldest parishioner, a white-haired great-grandsire, who occupied an arm-chair in the centre of the aisle. It was strange to observe how slowly this venerable man became conscious of something singular in the appearance of his pastor. He seemed not fully to partake of the prevailing wonder, till Mr. Hooper had ascended the stairs, and showed himself in the pulpit, face to face with his congregation, except for the black veil. That mysterious emblem was never once withdrawn. It shook with his measured breath as he gave out the psalm; it threw its obscurity between him and the holy page, as he read the Scriptures; and while he prayed, the veil lay heavily on his uplifted countenance. Did he seek to hide it from the dread Being whom he was addressing?

Such was the effect of this simple piece of crape, that more than one woman of delicate nerves was forced to leave the meeting-house. Yet perhaps the pale-faced congregation was almost as fearful a sight to the minister, as his black veil to them.

Mr. Hooper had the reputation of a good preacher, but not an energetic one: he strove to win his people heavenward by mild, persuasive influences, rather than to drive them thither by the thunders of the Word. The sermon which he now delivered was marked by the same characteristics of style and manner as the general series of his pulpit oratory. But there was something, either in the sentiment of the discourse itself, or in the imagination of the auditors, which made it greatly the most powerful effort that they had ever heard from their pastor's lips. It was tinged, rather more darkly than usual, with the gentle gloom of Mr. Hooper's temperament. The subject had reference to secret sin, and those sad mysteries which we hide from our nearest and dearest, and would fain conceal from our own consciousness, even forgetting that the Omniscient can detect them. A subtle power was breathed into his words. Each member of the congregation, the most innocent girl, and the man of hardened breast, felt as if the preacher had crept upon them, behind his awful veil, and discovered their hoarded iniquity of deed or thought. Many spread their clasped hands on their bosoms. There was nothing terrible in what Mr. Hooper said, at least, no violence; and yet, with every tremor of his melancholy voice, the hearers quaked. An unsought pathos came hand in hand with awe. So sensible were the audience of some unwonted attribute in their minister, that they longed for a breath of wind to blow aside the veil, almost believing that a stranger's visage would be discovered, though the form, gesture, and voice were those of Mr. Hooper.

At the close of the services, the people hurried out with indecorous confusion, eager to communicate their pent-up amazement, and conscious of lighter spirits the moment they lost sight of the black veil. Some gathered in little circles, huddled closely together, with their mouths all whispering in the centre; some went homeward alone, wrapt in silent meditation; some talked loudly, and profaned the Sabbath-day with ostentatious laughter. A few shook their sagacious heads, intimating that they could penetrate the mystery; while one or two affirmed that there was no mystery at all, but only that Mr. Hooper's eyes were so weakened by the midnight lamp, as to require a shade. After a brief interval, forth came good Mr. Hooper also, in the rear of his flock. Turning his veiled face from one group to another, he paid due reverence to the hoary heads, saluted the middle aged, with kind dignity as their friend and spiritual guide, greeted the young with mingled authority and love, and laid his hands on the little children's heads to bless them. Such was always his custom on the Sabbath-day.

Strange and bewildered looks repaid him for his courtesy. None, as on former occasions, aspired to the honor of walking by their pastor's side. Old Squire Saunders, doubtless by an accidental lapse of memory, neglected to invite Mr. Hooper to his table, where the good clergyman had been wont to bless the food, almost every Sunday since his settlement. He returned, therefore, to the parsonage, and, at the moment of closing the door, was observed to look back upon the people, all of whom had their eyes fixed upon the minister. A sad smile gleamed faintly from beneath the black veil, and flickered about his mouth, glimmering as he disappeared.

"How strange," said a lady, "that a simple black veil, such as any woman might wear on her bonnet, should become such a terrible thing on Mr. Hooper's face!"

"Something must surely be amiss with Mr. Hooper's intellects," observed her husband, the physician of the village. "But the strangest part of the affair is the effect of this vagary, even on a sober-minded man like myself. The black veil, though it covers only our pastor's face, throws its influence over his whole person, and makes him ghostlike from head to foot. Do you not feel it so?"

"Truly do I," replied the lady; "and I would not be alone with him for the world. I wonder he is not afraid to be alone with himself!"

"Men sometimes are so," said her husband.

The afternoon service was attended with similar circumstances. At its conclusion, the bell tolled for the funeral of a young lady. The relatives and friends were assembled in the house, and the more distant acquaintances stood about the door, speaking of the good qualities of the deceased, when their talk was interrupted by the appearance of Mr. Hooper, still covered with his black veil. It was now an appropriate emblem. The clergyman stepped into the room where the corpse was laid, and bent over the coffin, to take a last farewell of his deceased parishioner. As he stooped, the veil hung straight from his forehead, so that, if her eyelids had not been closed forever, the dead maiden might have seen his face. Could Mr. Hooper be fearful of her glance, that he so hastily caught back the black veil? A person who watched the interview between the dead and living, scrupled not to affirm, that, at the instant when the clergyman's features were disclosed, the corpse had slightly shuddered, rustling the shroud and muslin cap, though the countenance retained the composure of death. A superstitious old woman was the only witness of this prodigy. From the coffin Mr. Hooper passed into the chamber of the mourners, and thence to the head of the staircase, to make the funeral prayer. It was a tender and heart-dissolving prayer, full of sorrow, yet so imbued with celestial hopes, that the music of a heavenly harp, swept by the fingers of the dead, seemed faintly to be heard among the saddest accents of the minister. The people trembled, though they but darkly understood him, when he prayed that they, and himself, and all of mortal race, might be ready, as he trusted this young maiden had been, for the dreadful hour that should snatch the veil from their faces. The bearers went heavily forth, and the mourners followed, saddening all the street, with the dead before them, and Mr. Hooper in his black veil behind.

"Why do you look back?" said one in the procession to his partner.

"I had a fancy," replied she, "that the minister and the maiden's spirit were walking hand in hand."

"And so had I, at the same moment," said the other.

That night, the handsomest couple in Milford village were to be joined in wedlock. Though reckoned a melancholy man, Mr. Hooper had a placid cheerfulness for such occasions, which often excited a sympathetic smile where livelier merriment would have been thrown away. There was no quality of his disposition which made him more beloved than this. The company at the wedding awaited his arrival with impatience, trusting that the strange awe, which had gathered over him throughout the day, would now be dispelled. But such was not the result. When Mr. Hooper came, the first thing that their eyes rested on was the same horrible black veil, which had added deeper gloom to the funeral, and could portend nothing but evil to the wedding. Such was its immediate effect on the guests that a cloud seemed to have rolled duskily from beneath the black crape, and dimmed the light of the candles. The bridal pair stood up before the minister. But the bride's cold fingers quivered in the tremulous hand of the bridegroom, and her deathlike paleness caused a whisper that the maiden who had been buried a few hours before was come from her grave to be married. If ever another wedding were so dismal, it was that famous one where they tolled the wedding knell. After performing the ceremony, Mr. Hooper raised a glass of wine to his lips, wishing happiness to the new-married couple in a strain of mild pleasantry that ought to have brightened the features of the guests, like a cheerful gleam from the heart. At that instant, catching a glimpse of his figure in the looking-glass, the black veil involved his own spirit in the horror with which it overwhelmed all others. His frame shuddered, his lips grew pale, he spilt the untasted wine upon the carpet, and rushed forth into the darkness. For the Earth, too, had on her Black Veil.

The next day, the whole village of Milford talked of little else than Parson Hooper's black veil. That, and the mystery concealed behind it, supplied a topic for discussion between acquaintances meeting in the street, and good women gossiping at their open windows. It was the first item of news that the tavern-keeper told to his guests. The children babbled of it on their way to school. One imitative little imp covered his face with an old black handkerchief, thereby so affrighting his playmates that the panic seized himself, and he wellnigh lost his wits by his own waggery.

It was remarkable that of all the busybodies and impertinent people in the parish, not one ventured to put the plain question to Mr. Hooper, wherefore he did this thing. Hitherto, whenever there appeared the slightest call for such interference, he had never lacked advisers, nor shown himself averse to be guided by their judgment. If he erred at all, it was by so painful a degree of self-distrust, that even the mildest censure would lead him to consider an indifferent action as a crime. Yet, though so well acquainted with this amiable weakness, no individual among his parishioners chose to make the black veil a subject of friendly remonstrance. There was a feeling of dread, neither plainly confessed nor carefully concealed, which caused each to shift the responsibility upon another, till at length it was found expedient to send a deputation of the church, in order to deal with Mr. Hooper about the mystery, before it should grow into a scandal. Never did an embassy so ill discharge its duties. The minister received them with friendly courtesy, but became silent, after they were seated, leaving to his visitors the whole burden of introducing their important business. The topic, it might be supposed, was obvious enough. There was the black veil swathed round Mr. Hooper's forehead, and concealing every feature above his placid mouth, on which, at times, they could perceive the glimmering of a melancholy smile. But that piece of crape, to their imagination, seemed to hang down before his heart, the symbol of a fearful secret between him and them. Were the veil but cast aside, they might speak freely of it, but not till then. Thus they sat a considerable time, speechless, confused, and shrinking uneasily from Mr. Hooper's eye, which they felt to be fixed upon them with an invisible glance. Finally, the deputies returned abashed to their constituents, pronouncing the matter too weighty to be handled, except by a council of the churches, if, indeed, it might not require a general synod.

But there was one person in the village unappalled by the awe with which the black veil had impressed all beside herself. When the deputies returned without an explanation, or even venturing to demand one, she, with the calm energy of her character, determined to chase away the strange cloud that appeared to be settling round Mr. Hooper, every moment more darkly than before. As his plighted wife, it should be her privilege to know what the black veil concealed. At the minister's first visit, therefore, she entered upon the subject, with a direct simplicity, which made the task easier both for him and her. After he had seated himself, she fixed her eyes steadfastly upon the veil, but could discern nothing of the dreadful gloom that had so overawed the multitude; it was but a double fold of crape, hanging down from his forehead to his mouth, and slightly stirring with his breath.

"No," said she aloud, and smiling, "there is nothing terrible in this piece of crape, except that it hides a face which I am always glad to look upon. Come, good sir, let the sun shine from behind the cloud. First lay aside your black veil: then tell me why you put it on."

Mr. Hooper's smile glimmered faintly.

"There is an hour to come," said he, "when all of us shall cast aside our veils. Take it not amiss, beloved friend, if I wear this piece of crape till then."

"Your words are a mystery, too," returned the young lady. "Take away the veil from them, at least."

"Elizabeth, I will," said he, "so far as my vow may suffer me. Know, then, this veil is a type and a symbol, and I am bound to wear it ever, both in light and darkness, in solitude and before the gaze of multitudes, and as with strangers, so with my familiar friends. No mortal eye will see it withdrawn. This dismal shade must separate me from the world: even you, Elizabeth, can never come behind it!"

"What grievous affliction hath befallen you," she earnestly inquired, "that you should thus darken your eyes forever?"

"If it be a sign of mourning," replied Mr. Hooper, "I perhaps, like most other mortals, have sorrows dark enough to be typified by a black veil."

"But what if the world will not believe that it is the type of an innocent sorrow?" urged Elizabeth. "Beloved and respected as you are, there may be whispers, that you hide your face under the consciousness of secret sin. For the sake of your holy office, do away this scandal!"

The color rose into her cheeks as she intimated the nature of the rumors that were already abroad in the village. But Mr. Hooper's mildness did not forsake him. He even smiled again—that same sad smile, which always appeared like a faint glimmering of light, proceeding from the obscurity beneath the veil.

"If I hide my face for sorrow, there is cause enough," he merely replied; "and if I cover it for secret sin, what mortal might not do the same?"

And with this gentle, but unconquerable obstinacy did he resist all her entreaties. At length Elizabeth sat silent. For a few moments she appeared lost in thought, considering, probably, what new methods might be tried to withdraw her lover from so dark a fantasy, which, if it had no other meaning, was perhaps a symptom of mental disease. Though of a firmer character than his own, the tears rolled down her cheeks. But, in an instant, as it were, a new feeling took the place of sorrow: her eyes were fixed insensibly on the black veil, when, like a sudden twilight in the air, its terrors fell around her. She arose, and stood trembling before him.

"And do you feel it then, at last?" said he mournfully.

She made no reply, but covered her eyes with her hand, and turned to leave the room. He rushed forward and caught her arm.

"Have patience with me, Elizabeth!" cried he, passionately. "Do not desert me, though this veil must be between us here on earth. Be mine, and hereafter there shall be no veil over my face, no darkness between our souls! It is but a mortal veil—it is not for eternity! O! you know not how lonely I am, and how frightened, to be alone behind my black veil. Do not leave me in this miserable obscurity forever!"

"Lift the veil but once, and look me in the face," said she.

"Never! It cannot be!" replied Mr. Hooper.

"Then farewell!" said Elizabeth.

She withdrew her arm from his grasp, and slowly departed, pausing at the door, to give one long, shuddering gaze, that seemed almost to penetrate the mystery of the black veil. But, even amid his grief, Mr. Hooper smiled to think that only a material emblem had separated him from happiness, though the horrors, which it shadowed forth, must be drawn darkly between the fondest of lovers.

From that time no attempts were made to remove Mr. Hooper's black veil, or, by a direct appeal, to discover the secret which it was supposed to hide. By persons who claimed a superiority to popular prejudice, *it* was reckoned merely an eccentric whim, such as often mingles with the sober actions of men otherwise rational, and tinges them all with its own semblance of insanity. But with the multitude good Mr. Hooper was irreparably a bugbear. He could not walk the street with any peace of mind, so conscious was he that the gentle and timid would turn aside to avoid him, and that others would make it a point of hardihood to throw themselves in his way. The impertinence of the latter class compelled him to give up his customary walk at sunset to the burial ground; for when he leaned pensively over the gate, there would always be faces behind the gravestones, peeping at this black veil. A fable went the rounds that the stare of the dead people drove him thence. It grieved him, to the very depth of his kind heart, to observe how the children fled from his approach, breaking up their merriest sports, while his melancholy figure was yet afar off. Their instinctive dread caused him to feel more strongly than aught else, that a preternatural horror was interwoven with the threads of the black crape. In truth, his own antipathy to the veil was known to be so great, that he never willingly passed before a mirror, nor stooped to drink at a still fountain, lest, in its peaceful bosom, he should be affrighted by himself. This was what gave plausibility to the whispers, that Mr. Hooper's conscience tortured him for some great crime too horrible to be entirely concealed, or otherwise than so obscurely intimated. Thus, from beneath the black veil, there rolled a cloud into the sunshine, an ambiguity of sin or sorrow, which enveloped the poor minister, so that love or sympathy could never reach him. It was said, that ghost and fiend consorted with him there. With self-shudderings and outward terrors, he walked continually in its shadow, groping darkly within his own soul, or gazing through a medium that saddened the whole world. Even the lawless wind, it was believed, respected his dreadful secret, and never blew aside the veil. But still good Mr. Hooper sadly smiled at the pale visages of the worldly throng as he passed by.

Among all its bad influences, the black veil had the one desirable effect, of making its wearer a very efficient clergyman. By the aid of his mysterious emblem—for there was no other apparent cause—he became a man of awful power, over souls that were in agony for sin. His converts always regarded him with a dread peculiar to themselves, affirming, though but figuratively, that, before he brought them to celestial light, they had been with him behind the black veil. Its gloom, indeed, enabled him to sympathize with all dark affections. Dying sinners cried aloud for Mr. Hooper, and would not yield their breath till he appeared; though ever, as he stooped to whisper consolation, they shuddered at the veiled face so near their own. Such were the terrors of the black veil, even when Death had bared his visage! Strangers came long distances to attend service at his church, with the mere idle purpose of gazing at his figure, because it was forbidden them to behold his face. But many were made to quake ere they departed! Once, during Governor Belcher's administration, Mr. Hooper was appointed to preach the election sermon. Covered with his black veil, he stood before the chief magistrate, the council, and the representatives, and wrought so deep an impression, that the legislative measures of that year were characterized by all the gloom and piety of our earliest ancestral sway.

In this manner Mr. Hooper spent a long life, irreproachable in outward act, yet shrouded in dismal suspicions; kind and loving, though unloved, and dimly feared; man apart from men, shunned in their health and joy, but ever summoned to their aid in mortal anguish. As years wore on, shedding their snows above his sable veil, he acquired a name throughout the New England churches, and they called him Father Hooper. Nearly all his parishioners, who were of mature age when he was settled, had been borne away by many a funeral: he had one congregation in the church, and a more crowded one in the churchyard; and having wrought so late into the evening, and done his work so well, it was now good Father Hooper's turn to rest.

Several persons were visible by the shaded candlelight, in the death chamber of the old clergyman. Natural connections he had none. But there was the decorously grave, though unmoved physician, seeking only to mitigate the last pangs of the patient whom he could not save. There were the deacons, and other eminently pious members of his church. There, also, was the Reverend Mr. Clark, of Westbury, a young and zealous divine, who had ridden in haste to pray by the bedside of the expiring minister. There was the nurse, no hired hand-maiden of death, but one whose calm affection had endured thus long in secrecy, in solitude, amid the chill of age, and would not perish, even at the dying hour. Who, but Elizabeth! And there lay the hoary head of good Father Hooper upon the death pillow, with the black veil still swathed about his brow, and reaching down over his face, so that each more difficult gasp of his faint breath caused it to stir. All through life that piece of crape had hung between him and the world; it had separated him from cheerful brotherhood and woman's love, and kept him in that saddest of all prisons, his own heart; and still it lay upon his face, as if to deepen the gloom of his darksome chamber, and shade him from the sunshine of eternity.

For some time previous, his mind had been confused, wavering doubtfully between the past and the present, and hovering forward, as it were, at intervals, into the indistinctness of the world to come. There had been feverish turns, which tossed him from side to side, and wore away what little strength he had. But in his most convulsive struggles, and in the wildest vagaries of his intellect, when no other thought retains its sober influence, he still showed an awful solicitude lest the black veil should slip aside. Even if his bewildered soul could have forgotten, there was a faithful woman at his pillow, who, with averted eyes, would have covered that aged face, which she had last beheld in the comeliness of manhood. At length the death-stricken old man lay quietly in the torpor of mental and bodily exhaustion, with an imperceptible pulse, and breath that grew fainter and fainter, except when a long, deep, and irregular inspiration seemed to prelude the flight of his spirit.

The minister of Westbury approached the bedside.

"Venerable Father Hooper," said he, "the moment of your release is at hand. Are you ready for the lifting of the veil that shuts in time from eternity?"

Father Hooper at first replied merely by a feeble motion of his head; then, apprehensive, perhaps, that his meaning might be doubtful, he exerted himself to speak.

"Yea," said he, in faint accents, "my soul hath a patient weariness until that veil be lifted."

"And is it fitting," resumed the Reverend Mr. Clark, "that a man so given to prayer, of such a blameless example, holy in deed and thought, so far as mortal judgment may pronounce; is it fitting that a father in the church should leave a shadow in his memory, that may seem to blacken a life so pure? I pray you, my venerable brother, let not this thing be! Suffer us to be gladdened by your triumphant aspect, as you go to your reward. Before the veil of eternity be lifted, let me cast aside this black veil from your face!"

And thus speaking, the Reverend Mr. Clark bent forward to reveal the mystery of so many years. But, exerting a sudden energy, that made all the beholders stand aghast, Father Hooper snatched both his hands from beneath the bedclothes, and pressed them strongly on the black veil, resolute to struggle, if the minister of Westbury would contend with a dying man.

"Never!" cried the veiled clergyman. "On earth, never!"

"Dark old man!" exclaimed the affrighted minister, "with what horrible crime upon your soul are you now passing to the judgment?"

Father Hooper's breath heaved; it rattled in his throat but, with a mighty effort, grasping forward with his hands, he caught hold of life, and held it back till he should speak. He even raised himself in bed; and there he sat, shivering with the arms of death around him, while the black veil hung down, awful, at that last moment, in the gathered terrors of a lifetime. And yet the faint, sad smile, so often there, now seemed to glimmer from its obscurity, and linger on Father Hooper's lips.

"Why do you tremble at me alone?" cried he, turning his veiled face round the circle of pale spectators. "Tremble also at each other! Have men avoided me, and women shown no pity, and children screamed and fled, only for my black veil? What, but the mystery which it obscurely typifies, has made this piece of crape so awful? When the friend shows his inmost heart to his friend; the lover to his best beloved; when man does not vainly shrink from the eye of his Creator, loathsomely treasuring up the secret of his sin; then deem me a monster; for the symbol beneath which I have lived, and die! I look around me, and, lo! on every visage a Black Veil!"

While his auditors shrank from one another, in mutual affright, Father Hooper fell back upon his pillow, a veiled corpse with a faint smile lingering on the lips. Still veiled, they laid him in his coffin, and a veiled corpse they bore him to the grave. The grass of many years has sprung up and withered on that grave, the burial stone is moss-grown, and good Mr. Hooper's face is dust; but awful is still the thought that it mouldered beneath the Black Veil!

A STRING OF BEADS[*]

BY W. SOMERSET MAUGHAM

WHAT A bit of luck that I'm placed next to you," said Laura, as we sat down to dinner.

"For me," I replied politely.

"That remains to be seen. I particularly wanted to have the chance of talking to you. I've got a story to tell you."

At this my heart sank a little.

"I'd sooner you talked about yourself," I answered. "Or even about me."

"Oh, but I must tell you the story. I think you'll be able to use it."

"If you must, you must. But let's look at the menu first."

"Don't you want me to?" she said, somewhat aggrieved. "I thought you'd be pleased."

"I am. You might have written a play and wanted to read me that."

"It happened to some friends of mine. It's perfectly true."

"That's no recommendation. A true story is never quite so true as an invented one."

"What does that mean?"

"Nothing very much," I admitted. "But I thought it sounded well."

"I wish you'd let me get on with it."

[*] from *Cosmopolitans*

"I'm all attention. I'm not going to eat the soup. It's fattening."

She gave me a pinched look and then glanced at the menu. She uttered a little sigh.

"Oh, well, if you're going to deny yourself I suppose I must too. Heaven knows, I can't afford to take liberties with my figure."

"And yet is there any soup more heavenly than the sort of soup in which you put a great dollop of cream?"

"Borscht," she sighed. "It's the only soup I really like."

"Never mind. Tell me your story and we'll forget about food till the fish comes."

"Well, I was actually there when it happened. I was dining with the Livingstones. Do you know the Livingstones?"

"No, I don't think I do."

"Well, you can ask them and they'll confirm every word I say. They'd asked their governess to come in to dinner because some woman had thrown them over at the last moment—you know how inconsiderate people are—and they would have been thirteen at table. Their governess was a Miss Robinson, quite a nice girl, young, you know, twenty or twenty-one, and rather pretty. Personally I would never engage a governess who was young and pretty. One never knows."

"But one hopes for the best."

Laura paid no attention to my remark.

"The chances are that she'll be thinking of young men instead of attending to her duties and then, just when she's got used to your ways, she'll want to go and get married. But Miss Robinson had excellent references, and I must allow that she was a very nice, respectable person. I believe in point of fact she was a clergyman's daughter.

"There was a man at dinner whom I don't suppose you've ever heard of, but who's quite a celebrity in his way. He's a Count Borselli and he knows more about precious stones than anyone in the world. He was sitting next to Mary Lyngate, who rather fancies herself on her pearls, and in the course of conversation she asked him what he thought of the string she was wearing. He said it was very pretty. She was rather piqued at this and told him it was valued at eight thousand pounds.

" 'Yes, it's worth that,' he said.

"Miss Robinson was sitting opposite to him. She was looking rather nice that evening. Of course I recognized her dress, it was one of Sophie's old ones; but if you hadn't known Miss Robinson was the governess you would never have suspected it.

" 'That's a very beautiful necklace that young lady has on,' said Borselli.

" 'Oh, but that's Mrs. Livingstone's governess,' said Mary Lyngate.

" 'I can't help that,' he said. 'She's wearing one of the finest strings of pearls for its size that I've ever seen in my life. It must be worth fifty thousand pounds.'

" 'Nonsense.'

" 'I give you my word it is.'

"Mary Lyngate leant over. She has rather a shrill voice.

" 'Miss Robinson, do you know what Count Borselli says?' she exclaimed. 'He says that string of pearls you're wearing is worth fifty thousand pounds.'

"Just at that moment there was a sort of pause in the conversation so that everybody heard. We all turned and looked at Miss Robinson. She flushed a little and laughed.

" 'Well, I made a very good bargain,' she said, 'because I paid fifteen shillings for it.'

" 'You certainly did.'

"We all laughed. It was of course absurd. We've all heard of wives palming off on their husbands as false a string of pearls that was real and expensive. That story is as old as the hills."

"Thank you," I said, thinking of a little narrative of my own.

"But it was too ridiculous to suppose that a governess would remain a governess if she owned a string of pearls worth fifty thousand pounds. It was obvious that the Count had made a bloomer. Then an extraordinary thing happened. The long arm of coincidence came in."

"It shouldn't," I retorted. "It's had too much exercise.

Haven't you seen that charming book called *A Dictionary of English Usage*?"

"I wish you wouldn't interrupt just when I'm really getting to the exciting point."

But I had to do so again, for just then a young grilled salmon was insinuated round my left elbow.

"Mrs. Livingstone is giving us a heavenly dinner," I said.

"Is salmon fattening?" asked Laura.

"Very," I answered as I took a large helping.

"Bunk," she said.

"Go on," I begged her. "The long arm of coincidence was about to make a gesture."

"Well, at that very moment the butler bent over Miss Robinson and whispered something in her ear. I thought she turned a trifle pale. It's such a mistake not to wear rouge; you never know what tricks nature will play on you. She certainly looked startled. She leant forwards.

"'Mrs. Livingstone, Dawson says there are two men in the hall who want to speak to me at once.'

"'Well, you'd better go,' said Sophie Livingstone.

"Miss Robinson got up and left the room. Of course the same thought flashed through all our minds, but I said it first.

"'I hope they haven't come to arrest her,' I said to Sophie. 'It would be too dreadful for you, my dear.'

"'Are you sure it was a real necklace, Borselli?' she asked.

"'Oh, quite.'

"'She could hardly have had the nerve to wear it tonight if it were stolen,' I said.

"Sophie Livingstone turned as pale as death under her makeup and I saw she was wondering if everything was all right in her jewel case. I only had on a little chain of diamonds, but instinctively I put my hand up to my neck to feel if it was still there.

"'Don't talk nonsense,' said Mr. Livingstone. 'How on earth would Miss Robinson have had the chance of sneaking a valuable string of pearls?'

"'She may be a receiver,' I said.

"'Oh, but she had such wonderful references,' said Sophie.

" 'They always do,' I said."

I was positively forced to interrupt Laura once more.

"You don't seem to have been determined to take a very bright view of the case," I remarked.

"Of course I knew nothing against Miss Robinson and I had every reason to think her a very nice girl, but it would have been rather thrilling to find out that she was a notorious thief and a well-known member of a gang of international crooks."

"Just like a film. I'm dreadfully afraid that it's only in films that exciting things like that happen."

"Well, we waited in breathless suspense. There was not a sound. I expected to hear a scuffle in the hall or at least a smothered shriek. I thought the silence very ominous. Then the door opened and Miss Robinson walked in. I noticed at once that the necklace was gone. I could see that she was pale and excited. She came back to the table, sat down and with a smile threw on it——"

"On what?"

"On the table, you fool. A string of pearls."

" 'There's my necklace,' she said.

"Count Borselli leant forwards.

" 'Oh, but those are false,' he said.

" 'I told you they were,' she laughed.

" 'That's not the same string you had on a few moments ago,' he said.

"She shook her head and smiled mysteriously. We were all intrigued. I don't know that Sophie Livingstone was so very much pleased at her governess making herself the centre of interest like that and I thought there was a suspicion of tartness in her manner when she suggested that Miss Robinson had better explain. Well, Miss Robinson said that when she went into the hall she found two men who said they'd come from Jarrot's Stores. She'd bought her string there, as she said, for fifteen shillings, and she's taken it back because the clasp was loose and had only fetched it that afternoon. The men said they had given her the wrong string. Someone had left a string of real pearls to be restrung and the assistant had made a mistake. Of course I can't understand how anyone could be so stupid as to

take a really valuable string to Jarrot's, they aren't used to dealing with that sort of thing, and they wouldn't know real pearls
from false; but you know what fools some women are. Anyhow
it was the string Miss Robinson was wearing and it was valued
at fifty thousand pounds. She naturally gave it back to them—
she couldn't do anything else, I suppose, though it must have
been a wrench—and they returned her own string to her; then
they said that although of course they were under no obligation—you know the silly, pompous way men talk when they're
trying to be businesslike—they were instructed, as a solatium
or whatever you call it, to offer her a cheque for three hundred
pounds. Miss Robinson actually showed it to us. She was as
pleased as Punch."

"Well, it was a piece of luck, wasn't it?"

"You'd have thought so. As it turned out it was the ruin of
her."

"Oh, how was that?"

"Well, when the time came for her to go on her holiday she
told Sophie Livingstone that she'd made up her mind to go to
Deauville for a month and blow the whole three hundred
pounds. Of course Sophie tried to dissuade her, and begged her
to put the money in the savings bank, but she wouldn't hear of
it. She said she'd never had such a chance before and would
never have it again and she meant for at least four weeks to live
like a duchess. Sophie couldn't really do anything and so she
gave way. She sold Miss Robinson a lot of clothes that she
didn't want; she'd been wearing them all through the season
and was sick to death of them; she says she gave them to her,
but I don't suppose she quite did that—I dare say she sold them
very cheap—and Miss Robinson started off, entirely alone, for
Deauville. What do you think happened then?"

"I haven't a notion," I replied. "I hope she had the time of
her life."

"Well, a week before she was due to come back she wrote to
Sophie and said that she'd changed her plans and had entered
another profession and hoped Mrs. Livingstone would forgive
her if she didn't return. Of course poor Sophie was furious.
What had actually happened was that Miss Robinson had

picked up a rich Argentine in Deauville and had gone off to Paris with him. She's been in Paris ever since. I've seen her myself at Florence's, with bracelets right up to her elbow and ropes of pearls round her neck. Of course I cut her dead. They say she has a house in the Bois de Boulogne and I know she has a Rolls. She threw over the Argentine in a few months and then got hold of a Greek; I don't know who she's with now, but the long and short of it is that she's far and away the smartest cocotte in Paris."

"When you say she was ruined you use the word in a purely technical sense, I conclude," said I.

"I don't know what you mean by that," said Laura. "But don't you think you could make a story out of it?"

"Unfortunately I've already written a story about a pearl necklace. One can't go on writing stories about pearl necklaces."

"I've got half a mind to write it myself. Only of course I should change the end."

"Oh, how would you end it?"

"Well, I should have had her engaged to a bank clerk who had been badly knocked about in the war, with only one leg, say, or half his face shot away: and they'd be dreadfully poor and there would be no prospect of their marriage for years, and he would be putting all his savings into buying a little house in the suburbs and they'd have arranged to marry when he had saved the last instalment. And then she takes him the three hundred pounds and they can hardly believe it, they're so happy, and he cries on her shoulder. He just cries like a child. And they get the little house in the suburbs and they marry, and they have his old mother to live with them, and he goes to the bank every day, and if she's careful not to have babies she can still go out as a daily governess, and he's often ill—with his wound, you know—and she nurses him, and it's all very pathetic and sweet and lovely."

"It sounds rather dull to me," I ventured.

"Yes, but moral," said Laura.

THE GOLDEN HONEYMOON*

BY RING LARDNER

MOTHER SAYS that when I start talking I never know when to stop. But I tell her the only time I get a chance is when she ain't around, so I have to make the most of it. I guess the fact is neither one of us would be welcome in a Quaker meeting, but as I tell Mother, what did God give us tongues for if He didn't want we should use them? Only she says He didn't give them to us to say the same thing over and over again, like I do, and repeat myself. But I say:

"Well, Mother," I say, "when people is like you and I and been married fifty years, do you expect everything I say will be something you ain't heard me say before? But it may be new to others, as they ain't nobody else lived with me as long as you have."

So she says:

"You can bet they ain't, as they couldn't nobody else stand you that long."

"Well," I tell her, "you look pretty healthy."

"Maybe I do," she will say, "but I looked even healthier before I married you."

You can't get ahead of Mother.

Yes, sir, we was married just fifty years ago the seventeenth day of last December and my daughter and son-in-law was over from Trenton to help us celebrate the Golden Wedding. My son-in-law is John H. Kramer, the real estate man. He made $12,000 one year and is pretty well thought of around Trenton; a good, steady, hard worker. The Rotarians was after him a long

* from How to Write Short Stories

time to join, but he kept telling them his home was his club. But Edie finally made him join. That's my daughter.

Well, anyway, they come over to help us celebrate the Golden Wedding and it was pretty crimpy weather and the furnace don't seem to heat up no more like it used to and Mother made the remark that she hoped this winter wouldn't be as cold as the last, referring to the winter previous. So Edie said if she was us, and nothing to keep us home, she certainly wouldn't spend no more winters up here and why didn't we just shut off the water and close up the house and go down to Tampa, Florida? You know we was there four winters ago and staid five weeks, but it cost us over three hundred and fifty dollars for hotel bill alone. So Mother said we wasn't going no place to be robbed. So my son-in-law spoke up and said that Tampa wasn't the only place in the South, and besides we didn't have to stop at no high price hotel but could rent us a couple rooms and board out somewheres, and he had heard that St. Petersburg, Florida, was *the* spot and if we said the word he would write down there and make inquiries.

Well, to make a long story short, we decided to do it and Edie said it would be our Golden Honeymoon and for a present my son-in-law paid the difference between a section and a compartment so as we could have a compartment and have more privacy. In a compartment you have an upper and lower berth just like the regular sleeper, but it is a shut in room by itself and got a wash bowl. The car we went in was all compartments and no regular berths at all. It was all compartments.

We went to Trenton the night before and staid at my daughter and son-in-law and we left Trenton the next afternoon at 3.23 P.M.

This was the twelfth day of January. Mother set facing the front of the train, as it makes her giddy to ride backwards. I set facing her, which does not affect me. We reached North Philadelphia at 4.03 P.M. and we reached West Philadelphia at 4.14, but did not go into Broad Street. We reached Baltimore at 6.30 and Washington, D.C., at 7.25. Our train laid over in Washington two hours till another train come along to pick us up and I got out and strolled up the platform and into the Union

Station. When I come back, our car had been switched on to another track, but I remembered the name of it, the La Belle, as I had once visited my aunt out in Oconomomoc, Wisconsin, where there was a lake of that name, so I had no difficulty in getting located. But Mother had nearly fretted herself sick for fear I would be left.

"Well," I said, "I would of followed you on the next train."

"You couldn't of," said Mother, and she pointed out that she had the money.

"Well," I said, "we are in Washington and I could of borrowed from the United States Treasury. I would of pretended I was an Englishman."

Mother caught the point and laughed heartily.

Our train pulled out of Washington at 9.40 P.M. and Mother and I turned in early, I taking the upper. During the night we passed through the green fields of old Virginia, though it was too dark to tell if they was green or what color. When we got up in the morning, we was at Fayetteville, North Carolina. We had breakfast in the dining car and after breakfast I got in conversation with the man in the next compartment to ours. He was from Lebanon, New Hampshire, and a man about eighty years of age. His wife was with him, and two unmarried daughters and I made the remark that I should think the four of them would be crowded in one compartment, but he said they had made the trip every winter for fifteen years and knowed how to keep out of each other's way. He said they was bound for Tarpon Springs.

We reached Charleston, South Carolina, at 12.50 P.M. and arrived at Savannah, Georgia, at 4.20. We reached Jacksonville, Florida, at 8.45 P.M. and had an hour and a quarter to lay over there, but Mother made a fuss about me getting off the train, so we had the darky make up our berths and retired before we left Jacksonville. I didn't sleep good as the train done a lot of hemming and hawing, and Mother never sleeps good on a train as she says she is always worrying that I will fall out. She says she would rather have the upper herself, as then she would not have to worry about me, but I tell her I can't take the risk of having it get out that I allowed my wife to sleep in an upper berth. It would make talk.

We was up in the morning in time to see our friends from New Hampshire get off at Tarpon Springs, which we reached at 6.53 A.M.

Several of our fellow passengers got off at Clearwater and some at Belleair, where the train backs right up to the door of the mammoth hotel. Belleair is the winter headquarters for the golf dudes and everybody that got off there had their bag of sticks, as many as ten and twelve in a bag. Women and all. When I was a young man we called it shinny and only needed one club to play with and about one game of it would of been a-plenty for some of these dudes, the way we played it.

The train pulled into St. Petersburg at 8.20 and when we got off the train you would think they was a riot, what with all the darkies barking for the different hotels.

I said to Mother, I said:

"It is a good thing we have got a place picked out to go to and don't have to choose a hotel, as it would be hard to choose amongst them if every one of them is the best."

She laughed.

We found a jitney and I give him the address of the room my son-in-law had got for us and soon we was there and introduced ourselves to the lady that owns the house, a young widow about forty-eight years of age. She showed us our room, which was light and airy with a comfortable bed and bureau and washstand. It was twelve dollars a week, but the location was good, only three blocks from Williams Park.

St. Pete is what folks calls the town, though they also call it the Sunshine City, as they claim they's no other place in the country where they's fewer days when Old Sol don't smile down on Mother Earth, and one of the newspapers gives away all their copies free every day when the sun don't shine. They claim to of only give them away some sixty-odd times in the last eleven years. Another nickname they have got for the town is "the Poor Man's Palm Beach," but I guess they's men that comes there that could borrow as much from the bank as some of the Willie boys over to the other Palm Beach.

During our stay we paid a visit to the Lewis Tent City, which is the headquarters for the Tin Can Tourists. But maybe you ain't heard about them. Well, they are an organization that takes their vacation trips by auto and carries everything with them. That is, they bring along their tents to sleep in and cook in and they don't patronize no hotels or cafeterias, but they have got to be bona fide auto campers or they can't belong to the organization.

They tell me they's over 200,000 members to it and they call themselves the Tin Canners on account of most of their food being put up in tin cans. One couple we seen in the Tent City was a couple from Brady, Texas, named Mr. and Mrs. Pence, which the old man is over eighty years of age and they had come in their auto all the way from home, a distance of 1,641 miles. They took five weeks for the trip, Mr. Pence driving the entire distance.

The Tin Canners hails from every State in the Union and in the summer time they visit places like New England and the Great Lakes region, but in the winter the most of them comes to Florida and scatters all over the State. While we was down there, they was a national convention of them at Gainesville, Florida, and they elected a Fredonia, New York, man as their president. His title is Royal Tin Can Opener of the World. They have got a song wrote up which everybody has got to learn it before they are a member:

> "The tin can forever! Hurrah, boys! Hurrah!
>   Up with the tin can! Down with the foe!
> We will rally round the campfire, we'll rally once again,
>   Shouting, 'We auto camp forever!'"

That is something like it. And the members has also got to have a tin can fastened on to the front of their machine.

I asked Mother how she would like to travel around that way and she said:

"Fine, but not with an old rattle brain like you driving."

"Well," I said, "I am eight years younger than this Mr. Pence who drove here from Texas."

"Yes," she said, "but he is old enough to not be skittish."

You can't get ahead of Mother.

Well, one of the first things we done in St. Petersburg was to go to the Chamber of Commerce and register our names and where we was from as they's great rivalry amongst the different States in regards to the number of their citizens visiting in town and of course our little State don't stand much of a show, but still every little bit helps, as the fella says. All and all, the man told us, they was eleven thousand names registered, Ohio leading with some fifteen hundred-odd and New York State next with twelve hundred. Then come Michigan, Pennsylvania and so on down, with one man each from Cuba and Nevada.

The first night we was there, they was a meeting of the New York-New Jersey Society at the Congregational Church and a man from Ogdensburg, New York State, made the talk. His subject was Rainbow Chasing. He is a Rotarian and a very convicting speaker, though I forget his name.

Our first business, of course, was to find a place to eat and after trying several places we run on to a cafeteria on Central Avenue that suited us up and down. We eat pretty near all our meals there and it averaged about two dollars per day for the two of us, but the food was well cooked and everything nice and clean. A man don't mind paying the price if things is clean and well cooked.

On the third day of February, which is Mother's birthday, we spread ourselves and eat supper at the Poinsettia Hotel and they charged us seventy-five cents for a sirloin steak that wasn't hardly big enough for one.

I said to Mother: "Well," I said, "I guess it's a good thing every day ain't your birthday or we would be in the poorhouse."

"No," says Mother, "because if every day was my birthday, I would be old enough by this time to of been in my grave long ago."

You can't get ahead of Mother.

In the hotel they had a card-room where they was several men and ladies playing five hundred and this new fangled whist bridge. We also seen a place where they was dancing, so I asked Mother would she like to trip the light fantastic toe and she said no, she was too old to squirm like you have got to do now days. We watched some of the young folks at it awhile till Mother got disgusted and said we would have to see a good movie to take the taste out of our mouth. Mother is a great movie heroyne and we go twice a week here at home.

But I want to tell you about the Park. The second day we was there we visited the Park, which is a good deal like the one in Tampa, only bigger, and they's more fun goes on here every day than you could shake a stick at. In the middle they's a big bandstand and chairs for the folks to set and listen to the concerts, which they give you music for all tastes, from Dixie up to classical pieces like Hearts and Flowers.

Then all around they's places marked off for different sports and games—chess and checkers and dominoes for folks that enjoys those kind of games, and roque and horseshoes for the nimbler ones. I used to pitch a pretty fair shoe myself, but ain't done much of it in the last twenty years.

Well, anyway, we bought a membership ticket in the club which costs one dollar for the season, and they tell me that up to a couple of years ago it was fifty cents, but they had to raise it to keep out the riffraff.

Well, Mother and I put in a great day watching the pitchers and she wanted I should get in the game, but I told her I was all out of practice and would make a fool of myself, though I seen several men pitching who I guess I could take their measure without no practice. However, they was some good pitchers, too, and one boy from Akron, Ohio, who could certainly throw a pretty shoe. They told me it looked like he would win the championship of the United States in the February tournament. We come away a few days before they held that and I never did hear if he win. I forget his name, but he was a clean cut young fella, and he has got a brother in Cleveland that's a Rotarian.

Well, we just stood around and watched the different games for two or three days and finally I set down in a checker game with a man named Weaver from Danville, Illinois. He was a pretty fair checker player, but he wasn't no match for me, and I hope that don't sound like bragging. But I always could hold my own on a checker-board and the folks around here will tell you the same thing. I played with this Weaver pretty near all morning for two or three mornings and he beat me one game and the only other time it looked like he had a chance, the noon whistle blowed and we had to quit and go to dinner.

While I was playing checkers, Mother would set and listen to the band, as she loves music, classical or no matter what kind, but anyway she was setting there one day and between selections the woman next to her opened up a conversation. She was a woman about Mother's own age, seventy or seventy-one, and finally she asked Mother's name and Mother told her her name and where she was from and Mother asked her the same question, and who do you think the woman was?

Well, sir, it was the wife of Frank M. Hartsell, the man who was engaged to Mother till I stepped in and cut him out, fifty-two years ago!

Yes, sir!

You can imagine Mother's surprise! And Mrs. Hartsell was surprised, too, when Mother told her she had once been friends with her husband, though Mother didn't say how close friends they had been, or that Mother and I was the cause of Hartsell going out West. But that's what we was. Hartsell left his town a month after the engagement was broke off and ain't never been back since. He had went out to Michigan and become a veterinary, and that is where he had settled down, in Hillsdale, Michigan, and finally married his wife.

Well, Mother screwed up her courage to ask if Frank was still living and Mrs. Hartsell took her over to where they was pitching horse-shoes and there was old Frank, waiting his turn. And he knowed Mother as soon as he seen her, though it was over fifty years. He said he knowed her by her eyes.

"Why, it's Lucy Frost!" he says, and he throwed down his shoes and quit the game.

Then they come over and hunted me up and I will confess I wouldn't of knowed him. Him and I is the same age to the month, but he seems to show it more, some way. He is balder for one thing. And his beard is all white, where mine has still got a streak of brown in it. The very first thing I said to him, I said:

"Well, Frank, that beard of yours makes me feel like I was back north. It looks like a regular blizzard."

"Well," he said, "I guess yourn would be just as white if you had it dry cleaned."

But Mother wouldn't stand that.

"Is that so!" she said to Frank. "Well, Charley ain't had no tobacco in his mouth for over ten years!"

And I ain't!

Well, I excused myself from the checker game and it was pretty close to noon, so we decided to all have dinner together and they was nothing for it only we must try their cafeteria on Third Avenue. It was a little more expensive than ours and not near as good, I thought. I and Mother had about the same dinner we had been having every day and our bill was $1.10. Frank's check was $1.20 for he and his wife. The same meal wouldn't of cost them more than a dollar at our place.

After dinner we made them come up to our house and we all set in the parlor, which the young woman had give us the use of to entertain company. We begun talking over old times and Mother said she was a-scared Mrs. Hartsell would find it tiresome listening to we three talk over old times, but as it turned out they wasn't much chance for nobody else to talk with Mrs. Hartsell in the company. I have heard lots of women that could go it, but Hartsell's wife takes the cake of all the women I ever seen. She told us the family history of everybody in the State of Michigan and bragged for a half hour about her son, who she said is in the drug business in Grand Rapids, and a Rotarian.

When I and Hartsell could get a word in edgeways we joked one another back and forth and I chafed him about being a horse doctor.

"Well, Frank," I said; "you look pretty prosperous, so I suppose they's been plenty of glanders around Hillsdale."

"Well," he said, "I've managed to make more than a fair living. But I've worked pretty hard."

"Yes," I said, "and I suppose you get called out all hours of the night to attend birth and so on."

Mother made me shut up.

Well, I thought they wouldn't never go home and I and

Mother was in misery trying to keep awake, as the both of us
generally always takes a nap after dinner. Finally they went, after we had made an engagement to meet them in the Park the
next morning, and Mrs. Hartsell also invited us to come to their
place the next night and play five hundred. But she had forgot
that they was a meeting of the Michigan Society that evening,
so it was not till two evenings later that we had our first card
game.

Hartsell and his wife lived in a house on Third Avenue
North and had a private setting room besides their bedroom.
Mrs. Hartsell couldn't quit talking about their private setting
room like it was something wonderful. We played cards with
them, with Mother and Hartsell partners against his wife and I.
Mrs. Hartsell is a miserable card player and we certainly got
the worst of it.

After the game she brought out a dish of oranges and we had
to pretend it was just what we wanted, though oranges down
there is like a young man's whiskers; you enjoy them at first,
but they get to be a pesky nuisance.

We played cards again the next night at our place with the
same partners and I and Mrs. Hartsell was beat again. Mother
and Hartsell was full of compliments for each other on what a
good team they made, but the both of them knowed well
enough where the secret of their success laid. I guess all and all
we must of played ten different evenings and they was only one
night when Mrs. Hartsell and I come out ahead. And that one
night wasn't no fault of hern.

When we had been down there about two weeks, we spent
one evening as their guest in the Congregational Church, at a
social give by the Michigan Society. A talk was made by a man
named Bitting of Detroit, Michigan, on How I was Cured of
Story Telling. He is a big man in the Rotarians and give a witty
talk.

A woman named Mrs. Oxford rendered some selections
which Mrs. Hartsell said was grand opera music, but whatever
they was my daughter Edie could of give her cards and spades
and not made such a hullaballoo about it neither.

Then they was a ventriloquist from Grand Rapids and a

young woman about forty-five years of age that mimicked different kinds of birds. I whispered to Mother that they all sounded like a chicken, but she nudged me to shut up.

After the show we stopped in a drug store and I set up the refreshments and it was pretty close to ten o'clock before we finally turned in. Mother and I would of preferred tending the movies, but Mother said we mustn't offend Mrs. Hartsell, though I asked her had we came to Florida to enjoy ourselves or to just not offend an old chatter-box from Michigan.

I felt sorry for Hartsell one morning. The women folks both had an engagement down to the chiropodist's and I run across Hartsell in the Park and he foolishly offered to play me checkers.

It was him that suggested it, not me, and I guess he repented it himself before we had played one game. But he was too stubborn to give up and set there while I beat him game after game and the worst part of it was that a crowd of folks had got in the habit of watching me play and there they all was, looking on, and finally they seen what a fool Frank was making of himself, and they began to chafe him and pass remarks. Like one of them said:

"Who ever told you you was a checker player!"

And:

"You might maybe be good for tiddle-de-winks, but not checkers!"

I almost felt like letting him beat me a couple games. But the crowd would of knowed it was a put up job.

Well, the women folks joined us in the Park and I wasn't going to mention our little game, but Hartsell told about it himself and admitted he wasn't no match for me.

"Well," said Mrs. Hartsell, "checkers ain't much of a game anyway, is it?" She said: "It's more of a children's game, ain't it? At least, I know my boy's children used to play it a good deal."

"Yes, ma'am," I said. "It's a children's game the way your husband plays it, too."

Mother wanted to smooth things over, so she said:

"Maybe they's other games where Frank can beat you."

"Yes," said Mrs. Hartsell, "and I bet he could beat you pitching horse-shoes."

"Well," I said. "I would give him a chance to try, only I ain't pitched a shoe in over sixteen years."

"Well," said Hartsell, "I ain't played checkers in twenty years."

"You ain't never played it," I said.

"Anyway," says Frank, "Lucy and I is your master at five hundred."

Well, I could of told him why that was, but had decency enough to hold my tongue.

It had got so now that he wanted to play cards every night and when I or Mother wanted to go to a movie, any one of us would have to pretend we had a headache and then trust to goodness that they wouldn't see us sneak into the theater. I don't mind playing cards when my partner keeps their mind on the game, but you take a woman like Hartsell's wife and how can they play cards when they have got to stop every couple seconds and brag about their son in Grand Rapids?

Well, the New York-New Jersey Society announced that they was going to give a social evening too and I said to Mother, I said:

"Well, that is one evening when we will have an excuse not to play five hundred."

"Yes," she said, "but we will have to ask Frank and his wife to go to the social with us as they asked us to go to the Michigan social."

"Well," I said, "I had rather stay home than drag that chatterbox everywheres we go."

So Mother said:

"You are getting too cranky. Maybe she does talk a little too much but she is good hearted. And Frank is always good company."

So I said:

"I suppose if he is such good company you wished you had of married him."

Mother laughed and said I sounded like I was jealous. Jealous of a cow doctor!

Anyway we had to drag them along to the social and I will say that we give them a much better entertainment than they had given us.

Judge Lane of Paterson made a fine talk on business conditions and a Mrs. Newell of Westfield imitated birds, only you could really tell what they was the way she done it. Two young women from Red Bank sung a choral selection and we clapped them back and they gave us Home to Our Mountains and Mother and Mrs. Hartsell both had tears in their eyes. And Hartsell, too.

Well, some way or another the chairman got wind that I was there and asked me to make a talk and I wasn't even going to get up, but Mother made me, so I got up and said:

"Ladies and gentlemen," I said. "I didn't expect to be called on for a speech on an occasion like this or no other occasion as I do not set myself up as a speech maker, so will have to do the best I can, which I often say is the best anybody can do."

Then I told them the story about Pat and the motorcycle, using the brogue, and it seemed to tickle them and I told them one or two other stories, but altogether I wasn't on my feet more than twenty or twenty-five minutes and you ought to of heard the clapping and hollering when I set down. Even Mrs. Hartsell admitted that I am quite a speechifier and said if I ever went to Grand Rapids, Michigan, her son would make me talk to the Rotarians.

When it was over, Hartsell wanted we should go to their house and play cards, but his wife reminded him that it was after 9:30 P.M., rather a late hour to start a card game, but he had went crazy on the subject of cards, probably because he didn't have to play partners with his wife. Anyway, we got rid of them and went home to bed.

It was the next morning, when we met over to the Park, that Mrs. Hartsell made the remark that she wasn't getting no exercise so I suggested that why didn't she take part in the roque game.

She said she had not played a game of roque in twenty years, but if Mother would play she would play. Well, at first Mother wouldn't hear of it, but finally consented, more to please Mrs. Hartsell than anything else.

Well, they had a game with a Mrs. Ryan from Eagle, Nebraska, and a young Mrs. Morse from Rutland, Vermont, who Mother had met down to the chiropodist's. Well, Mother couldn't hit a flea and they all laughed at her and I couldn't help from laughing at her myself and finally she quit and said her back was too lame to stoop over. So they got another lady and kept on playing and soon Mrs. Hartsell was the one everybody was laughing at, as she had a long shot to hit the black ball, and as she made the effort her teeth fell out on to the court. I never seen a woman so flustered in my life. And I never heard so much laughing, only Mrs. Hartsell didn't join in and she was madder than a hornet and wouldn't play no more, so the game broke up.

Mrs. Hartsell went home without speaking to nobody, but Hartsell stayed around and finally he said to me, he said:

"Well, I played you checkers the other day and you beat me bad and now what do you say if you and me play a game of horse-shoes?"

I told him I hadn't pitched a shoe in sixteen years, but Mother said:

"Go ahead and play. You used to be good at it and maybe it will come back to you."

Well, to make a long story short, I give in. I oughtn't to of never tried it, as I hadn't pitched a shoe in sixteen years, and I only done it to humor Hartsell.

Before we started, Mother patted me on the back and told me to do my best, so we started in and I seen right off that I was in for it, as I hadn't pitched a shoe in sixteen years and didn't have my distance. And besides, the plating had wore off the shoes so that they was points right where they stuck into my thumb and I hadn't throwed more than two or three times when my thumb was raw and it pretty near killed me to hang on to the shoe, let alone pitch it.

Well, Hartsell throws the awkwardest shoes I ever seen pitched and to see him pitch you wouldn't think he would ever come nowhere near, but he is also the luckiest pitcher I ever seen and he made some pitches where the shoe lit five and six feet short and then schoonered up and was a ringer. They's no use trying to beat that kind of luck.

They was a pretty fair size crowd watching us and four or five other ladies besides Mother, and it seems like, when Hartsell pitches, he has got to chew and it kept the ladies on the anxious seat as he don't seem to care which way he is facing when he leaves go.

You would think a man as old as him would of learnt more manners.

Well, to make a long story short, I was just beginning to get my distance when I had to give up on account of my thumb, which I showed it to Hartsell and he seen I couldn't go on, as it was raw and bleeding. Even if I could of stood it to go on my-self, Mother wouldn't of allowed it after she seen my thumb. So anyway I quit and Hartsell said the score was nineteen to six, but I don't know what it was. Or don't care, neither.

Well, Mother and I went home and I said I hoped we was through with the Hartsells as I was sick and tired of them, but it seemed like she had promised we would go over to their house that evening for another game of their everlasting cards.

Well, my thumb was giving me considerable pain and I felt kind of out of sorts and I guess maybe I forgot myself, but any-way, when we was about through playing Hartsell made the re-mark that he wouldn't never lose a game of cards if he could always have Mother for a partner.

So I said:

"Well, you had a chance fifty years ago to always have her for a partner, but you wasn't man enough to keep her."

I was sorry the minute I had said it and Hartsell didn't know what to say and for once his wife couldn't say nothing. Mother tried to smooth things over by making the remark that I must of had something stronger than tea or I wouldn't talk so silly. But Mrs. Hartsell had froze up like an iceberg and hardly said good night to us and I bet her and Frank put in a pleasant hour after we was gone.

As we were leaving, Mother said to him: "Never mind

Charley's nonsense, Frank. He is just mad because you beat him all hollow pitching horseshoes and playing cards."

She said that to make up for my slip, but at the same time she certainly riled me. I tried to keep ahold of myself, but as soon as we was out of the house she had to open up the subject and begun to scold me for the break I had made.

Well, I wasn't in no mood to be scolded. So I said:

"I guess he is such a wonderful pitcher and card player that you wished you had married him."

"Well," she said, "at least he ain't a baby to give up pitching because his thumb has got a few scratches."

"And how about you," I said, "making a fool of yourself on the roque court and then pretending your back is lame and you can't play no more!"

"Yes," she said, "but when you hurt your thumb I didn't laugh at you, and why did you laugh at me when I sprained my back?"

"Who could help from laughing?" I said.

"Well," she said, "Frank Hartsell didn't laugh."

"Well," I said, "why didn't you marry him?"

"Well," said Mother, "I almost wish I had!"

"And I wished so, too!" I said.

"I'll remember that!" said Mother, and that's the last word she said to me for two days.

We seen the Hartsells the next day in the Park and I was willing to apologize, but they just nodded to us. And a couple of days later we heard they had left for Orlando, where they have got relatives.

I wished they had went there in the first place.

Mother and I made it up setting on a bench.

"Listen, Charley," she said. "This is our Golden Honeymoon and we don't want the whole thing spoilt with a silly old quarrel."

"Well," I said, "did you mean that about wishing you had married Hartsell?"

"Of course not," she said, "that is, if you didn't mean that you wished I had, too."

So I said:

"I was just tired and all wrought up. I thank God you chose me instead of him as they's no other woman in the world who I could of lived with all these years."

"How about Mrs. Hartsell?" says Mother.

"Good gracious!" I said. "Imagine being married to a woman that plays five hundred like she does and drops her teeth on the roque court!"

"Well," said Mother, "it wouldn't be no worse than being married to a man that expectorates towards ladies and is such a fool in a checker game."

So I put my arm around her shoulder and she stroked my hand and I guess we got kind of spoony.

They was two days left of our stay in St. Petersburg and the next to the last day Mother introduced me to a Mrs. Kendall from Kingston, Rhode Island, who she had met at the chiropodist's.

Mrs. Kendall made us acquainted with her husband, who is in the grocery business. They have got two sons and five grandchildren and one great-grandchild. One of their sons lives in Providence and is way up in the Elks as well as a Rotarian.

We found them very congenial people and we played cards with them the last two nights we was there. They was both experts and I only wished we had met them sooner instead of running into the Hartsells. But the Kendalls will be there again next winter and we will see more of them, that is, if we decide to make the trip again.

We left the Sunshine City on the eleventh day of February, at 11 A.M. This give us a day trip through Florida and we seen all the country we had passed through at night on the way down.

We reached Jacksonville at 7 P.M. and pulled out of there at 8.10 P.M. We reached Fayetteville, North Carolina, at nine o'clock the following morning, and reached Washington, D. C., at 6.30 P.M., laying over there half an hour.

We reached Trenton at 11.01 P.M. and had wired ahead to my daughter and son-in-law and they met us at the train and we went to their house and they put us up for the night. John would

of made us stay up all night, telling about our trip, but Edie said
we must be tired and made us go to bed. That's my daughter.

The next day we took our train for home and arrived safe
and sound, having been gone just one month and a day.

Here comes Mother, so I guess I better shut up.

THE MAN WHO COULD WORK MIRACLES*
A PANTOUM IN PROSE

BY H. G. WELLS

I T IS doubtful whether the gift was innate. For my own part,
I think it came to him suddenly. Indeed, until he was thirty
he was a sceptic, and did not believe in miraculous powers.
And here, since it is the most convenient place, I must mention
that he was a little man, and had eyes of a hot brown, very erect
red hair, a moustache with ends that he twisted up, and freckles. His name was George McWhirter Fotheringay—not the
sort of name by any means to lead to any expectation of miracles—and he was a clerk at Gomshott's. He was greatly addicted to assertive argument. It was while he was asserting the
impossibility of miracles that he had his first intimation of his
extraordinary powers. This particular argument was being held
in the bar of the Long Dragon, and Toddy Beamish was conducting the opposition by a monotonous but effective "So *you*
say," that drove Mr. Fotheringay to the very limit of his patience.

There were present, besides these two, a very dusty cyclist,
landlord Cox, and Miss Maybridge, the perfectly respectable
and rather portly barmaid of the Dragon. Miss Maybridge was

---

* from *Tales of Space and Time*

standing with her back to Mr. Fotheringay, washing glasses; the others were watching him, more or less amused by the present ineffectiveness of the assertive method. Goaded by the Torres Vedras tactics of Mr. Beamish, Mr. Fotheringay determined to make an unusual rhetorical effort. "Looky here, Mr. Beamish," said Mr. Fotheringay. "Let us clearly understand what a miracle is. It's something contrariwise to the course of nature done by power or Will, something what couldn't happen without being specially willed."

"So *you* say," said Mr. Beamish, repulsing him.

Mr. Fotheringay appealed to the cyclist, who had hitherto been a silent auditor, and received his assent—given with a hesitating cough and a glance at Mr. Beamish. The landlord would express no opinion, and Mr. Fotheringay, returning to Mr. Beamish, received the unexpected concession of a qualified assent to his definition of a miracle.

"For instance," said Mr. Fotheringay, greatly encouraged. "Here would be a miracle. That lamp, in the natural course of nature, couldn't burn like that upsy-down, could it, Beamish?"

"*You* say it couldn't," said Beamish.

"And you?" said Fotheringay. "You don't mean to say—eh?"

"No," said Beamish reluctantly. "No, it couldn't."

"Very well," said Mr. Fotheringay. "Then here comes someone, as it might be me, along here, and stands as it might be here, and says to that lamp, as I might do, collecting all my will—'Turn upsy-down without breaking, and go on burning steady,' and——Hullo!"

It was enough to make anyone say "Hullo!" The impossible, the incredible, was visible to them all. The lamp hung inverted in the air, burning quietly with its flame pointing down. It was as solid, as indisputable as ever a lamp was, the prosaic common lamp of the Long Dragon bar.

Mr. Fotheringay stood with an extended forefinger and the knitted brows of one anticipating a catastrophic smash. The cyclist, who was sitting next the lamp, ducked and jumped across the bar. Everybody jumped, more or less. Miss Maybridge turned and screamed. For nearly three seconds the lamp remained still. A faint cry of mental distress came from Mr. Fotheringay. "I can't keep it up," he said, "any longer." He staggered back, and the inverted lamp suddenly flared, fell against the corner of the bar, bounced aside, smashed upon the floor, and went out.

It was lucky it had a metal receiver, or the whole place would have been in a blaze. Mr. Cox was the first to speak, and his remark, shorn of needless excrescences, was to the effect that Fotheringay was a fool. Fotheringay was beyond disputing even so fundamental a proposition as that! He was astonished beyond measure at the thing that had occurred. The subsequent conversation threw absolutely no light on the matter so far as Fotheringay was concerned; the general opinion not only followed Mr. Cox very closely but very vehemently. Everyone accused Fotheringay of a silly trick, and presented him to himself as a foolish destroyer of comfort and security. His mind was a tornado of perplexity, he was himself inclined to agree with them, and he made a remarkably ineffectual opposition to the proposal of his departure.

He went home flushed and heated, coat-collar crumpled, eyes smarting, and ears red. He watched each of the ten street lamps nervously as he passed it. It was only when he found himself alone in his little bedroom in Church Row that he was able to grapple seriously with his memories of the occurrence, and ask, "What on earth happened?"

He had removed his coat and boots, and was sitting on the bed with his hands in his pockets repeating the text of his defence for the seventeenth time, "*I* didn't want the confounded thing to upset," when it occurred to him that at the precise moment he had said the commanding words he had inadvertently willed the thing he said, and that when he had seen the lamp in the air he had felt that it depended on him to maintain it there without being clear how this was to be done. He had not a particularly complex mind, or he might have stuck for a time at that "inadvertently willed," embracing, as it does, the abstrusest problems of voluntary action; but as it was, the idea came to him with a quite acceptable haziness. And from that, following, as I must admit, no clear logical path, he came to the test of experiment.

He pointed resolutely to his candle and collected his mind, though he felt he did a foolish thing. "Be raised up," he said. But in a second that feeling vanished. The candle was raised, hung in the air one giddy moment, and as Mr. Fotheringay gasped, fell with a smash on his toilet-table, leaving him in darkness save for the expiring glow of its wick.

For a time Mr. Fotheringay sat in the darkness, perfectly still. "It did happen, after all," he said. "And 'ow I'm to explain it I *don't* know." He sighed heavily, and began feeling in his pockets for a match. He could find none, and he rose and groped about the toilet-table. "I wish I had a match," he said. He resorted to his coat, and there were none there, and then it dawned upon him that miracles were possible even with matches. He extended a hand and scowled at it in the dark. "Let there be a match in that hand," he said. He felt some light object fall across his palm, and his fingers closed upon a match.

After several ineffectual attempts to light this, he discovered it was a safety-match. He threw it down, and then it occurred to him that he might have willed it lit. He did, and perceived it burning in the midst of his toilet-table mat. He caught it up hastily, and it went out. His perception of possibilities enlarged, and he felt for and replaced the candle in its candlestick. "Here! *you* be lit," said Mr. Fotheringay, and forthwith the candle was flaring, and he saw a little black hole in the toilet-cover, with a wisp of smoke rising from it. For a time he stared from this to the little flame and back, and then looked up and met his own gaze in the looking-glass. By this help he communed with himself in silence for a time.

"How about miracles now?" said Mr. Fotheringay at last, addressing his reflection.

The subsequent meditations of Mr. Fotheringay were of a severe but confused description. So far as he could see, it was a case of pure willing with him. The nature of his first experiences disinclined him for any further experiments except of the most cautious type. But he lifted a sheet of paper, and turned a glass of water pink and then green, and he created a snail,

which he miraculously annihilated, and got himself a miraculous new toothbrush. Somewhen in the small hours he had
reached the fact that his will-power must be of a particularly
rare and pungent quality, a fact of which he had certainly had
inklings before, but no certain assurance. The scare and perplexity of his first discovery were now qualified by pride in this
evidence of singularity and by vague intimations of advantage.
He became aware that the church clock was striking one, and as
it did not occur to him that his daily duties at Gomshott's might
be miraculously dispensed with, he resumed undressing, in order to get to bed without further delay. As he struggled to get
his shirt over his head he was struck with a brilliant idea. "Let
me be in bed," he said, and found himself so. "Undressed," he
stipulated; and, finding the sheets cold, added hastily, "and in
my nightshirt—no, in a nice soft woollen nightshirt. Ah!" he
said with immense enjoyment. "And now let me be comfortably asleep..."

He awoke at his usual hour and was pensive all through
breakfast-time, wondering whether his overnight experience
might not be a particularly vivid dream. At length his mind
turned again to cautious experiments. For instance, he had
three eggs for breakfast; two his landlady had supplied, good,
but shoppy, and one was a delicious fresh goose-egg, laid,
cooked, and served by his extraordinary will. He hurried off to
Gomshott's in a state of profound but carefully concealed excitement, and only remembered the shell of the third egg when
his landlady spoke of it that night. All day he could do no work
because of this astonishing new self-knowledge, but this
caused him no inconvenience, because he made up for it miraculously in his last ten minutes.

As the day wore on his state of mind passed from wonder to
elation, albeit the circumstances of his dismissal from the Long
Dragon were still disagreeable to recall, and a garbled account
of the matter that had reached his colleagues led to some badi-
nage. It was evident he must be careful how he lifted frangible
articles, but in other ways his gift promised more and more as
he turned it over in his mind. He intended among other things
to increase his personal property by unostentatious acts of cre-

ation. He called into existence a pair of very splendid diamond studs, and hastily annihilated them again as young Gomshott came across the counting-house to his desk. He was afraid young Gomshott might wonder how he came by them. He saw quite clearly the gift required caution and watchfulness in its exercise, but so far as he could judge the difficulties attending its mastery would be no greater than those he had already faced in the study of cycling. It was that analogy, perhaps, quite as much as the feeling that he would be unwelcome in the Long Dragon, that drove him out after supper into the lane beyond the gas-works, to rehearse a few miracles in private.

There was possibly a certain want of originality in his attempts, for apart from his will-power Mr. Fotheringay was not a very exceptional man. The miracle of Moses' rod came to his mind, but the night was dark and unfavourable to the proper control of large miraculous snakes. Then he recollected the story of "Tannhäuser" that he had read on the back of the Philharmonic programme. That seemed to him singularly attractive and harmless. He stuck his walking-stick—a very nice Poona-Penang lawyer—into the turf that edged the footpath, and commanded the dry wood to blossom. The air was immediately full of the scent of roses, and by means of a match he saw for himself that this beautiful miracle was indeed accomplished. His satisfaction was ended by advancing footsteps. Afraid of a premature discovery of his powers, he addressed the blossoming stick hastily: "Go back." What he meant was "Change back"; but of course he was confused. The stick receded at a considerable velocity, and incontinently came a cry of anger and a bad word from the approaching person. "Who are you throwing brambles at, you fool?" cried a voice. "That got me on the shin."

"I'm sorry, old chap," said Mr. Fotheringay, and then, realising the awkward nature of the explanation, caught nervously at his moustache. He saw Winch, one of the three Immering constables, advancing.

"What d'yer mean by it?" asked the constable. "Hullo! It's you, is it? The gent that broke the lamp at the Long Dragon!"

"I don't mean anything by it," said Mr. Fotheringay. "Nothing at all."

"What d'yer do it for then?"

"Oh, bother!" said Mr. Fotheringay.

"Bother, indeed? D'yer know that stick hurt? What d'yer do it for, eh?"

For the moment Mr. Fotheringay could not think what he had done it for. His silence seemed to irritate Mr. Winch. "You've been assaulting the police, young man, this time. That's what *you* done!"

"Look here, Mr. Winch," said Mr. Fotheringay, annoyed and confused, "I've very sorry. The fact is——"

"Well!"

He could think of no way but the truth. "I was working a miracle." He tried to speak in an off-hand way, but try as he would he couldn't.

"Working a——! 'Ere, don't you talk rot. Working a miracle, indeed! Miracle! Well, that's downright funny! Why, you's the chap that don't believe in miracles.... Fact is, this is another of your silly conjuring tricks—that's what this is. Now, I tell you——"

But Mr. Fotheringay never heard what Mr. Winch was going to tell him. He realised he had given himself away, flung his valuable secret to all the winds of heaven. A violent gust of irritation swept him to action. He turned on the constable swiftly and fiercely. "Here," he said, "I've had enough of this, I have! I'll show you a silly conjuring trick, I will. Go to Hades! Go, now!"

He was alone!

Mr. Fotheringay performed no more miracles that night nor did he trouble to see what had become of his flowering stick. He returned to the town, scared and very quiet, and went to his bedroom. "Lord!" he said, "it's a powerful gift—an extremely powerful gift! I didn't hardly mean as much as that. Not really.... I wonder what Hades is like!"

He sat on the bed taking off his boots. Struck by a happy thought he transferred the constable to San Francisco, and without any more interference with normal causation went soberly to bed. In the night he dreamt of the anger of Winch.

The next day Mr. Fotheringay heard two interesting items of news. Someone had planted a most beautiful climbing rose against the elder Mr. Gomshott's private house in the Lullaborough Road, and the river as far as Rawling's Mill was to be dragged for Constable Winch.

Mr. Fotheringay was abstracted and thoughtful all that day, and performed no miracles except certain provisions for Winch, and the miracle of completing his day's work with punctual perfection in spite of all the bee-swarm of thoughts that hummed through his mind. And the extraordinary abstraction and meekness of his manner was remarked by several people, and made a matter for jesting. For the most part he was thinking of Winch.

On Sunday evening he went to chapel, and oddly enough, Mr. Maydig, who took a certain interest in occult matters, preached about "things that are not lawful." Mr. Fotheringay was not a regular chapel goer, but the system of assertive scepticism, to which I have already alluded, was now very much shaken. The tenor of the sermon threw an entirely new light on these novel gifts, and he suddenly decided to consult Mr. Maydig immediately after the service. So soon as that was determined, he found himself wondering why he had not done so before.

Mr. Maydig, a lean, excitable man with quite remarkably long wrists and neck, was gratified at a request for a private conversation from a young man whose carelessness in religious matters was a subject for general remark in the town. After a few necessary delays, he conducted him to the study of the Manse, which was contiguous to the chapel, seated him comfortably, and, standing in front of a cheerful fire—his legs threw a Rhodian arch of shadow on the opposite wall—requested Mr. Fotheringay to state his business.

At first Mr. Fotheringay was a little abashed, and found some difficulty in opening the matter. "You will scarcely believe me, Mr. Maydig, I am afraid"—and so forth for some time. He tried a question at last, and asked Mr. Maydig his opinion of miracles.

Mr. Maydig was still saying "Well" in an extremely judicial tone, when Mr. Fotheringay interrupted again: "You don't believe, I suppose, that some common sort of person—like myself, for instance—as it might be sitting here now, might have some sort of twist inside him that made him able to do things by his will."

"It's possible," said Mr. Maydig. "Something of the sort, perhaps, is possible."

"If I might make free with something here, I think I might show you a sort of experiment," said Mr. Fotheringay. "Now, take that tobacco-jar on the table, for instance. What I want to know is whether what I am going to do with it is a miracle or not. Just half a minute, Mr. Maydig, please."

He knitted his brows, pointed to the tobacco-jar and said: "Be a bowl of vi'lets."

The tobacco-jar did as it was ordered.

Mr. Maydig started violently at the change, and stood looking from the thaumaturgist to the bowl of flowers. He said nothing. Presently he ventured to lean over the table and smell the violets; they were fresh-picked and very fine ones. Then he stared at Mr. Fotheringay again.

"How did you do that?" he asked.

Mr. Fotheringay pulled his moustache. "Just told it—and there you are. Is that a miracle, or is it black art, or what is it? And what do you think's the matter with me? That's what I want to ask."

"It's a most extraordinary occurrence."

"And this day last week I knew no more that I could do things like that than you did. It came quite sudden. It's something odd about my will, I suppose, and that's as far as I can see."

"Is that—the only thing? Could you do other things besides that?"

"Lord, yes!" said Mr. Fotheringay. "Just anything." He thought, and suddenly recalled a conjuring entertainment he had seen. "Here!" He pointed. "Change into a bowl of fish—

no, not that—change into a glass bowl full of water with goldfish swimming in it. That's better! You see that, Mr. Maydig?"

"It's astonishing. It's incredible. You are either a most extraordinary . . . But no——"

"I could change it into anything," said Mr. Fotheringay. "Just anything. Here! be a pigeon, will you?"

In another moment a blue pigeon was fluttering round the room and making Mr. Maydig duck every time it came near him. "Stop there, will you," said Mr. Fotheringay; and the pigeon hung motionless in the air. "I could change it back to a bowl of flowers," he said, and after replacing the pigeon on the table worked that miracle. "I expect you will want your pipe in a bit," he said, and restored the tobacco-jar.

Mr. Maydig had followed all these later changes in a sort of ejaculatory silence. He stared at Mr. Fotheringay and, in a very gingerly manner, picked up the tobacco-jar, examined it, replaced it on the table, *"Well!"* was the only expression of his feelings.

"Now, after that it's easier to explain what I came about," said Mr. Fotheringay; and proceeded to a lengthy and involved narrative of his strange experiences, beginning with the affair of the lamp in the Long Dragon and complicated by persistent allusions to Winch. As he went on, the transient pride Mr. Maydig's consternation had caused passed away; he became the very ordinary Mr. Fotheringay of everyday intercourse again. Mr. Maydig listened intently, the tobacco-jar in his hand, and his bearing changed also with the course of the narrative. Presently, while Mr. Fotheringay was dealing with the miracle of the third egg, the minister interrupted with a fluttering extended hand—

"It is possible," he said. "It is credible. It is amazing, of course, but it reconciles a number of difficulties. The power to work miracles is a gift—a peculiar quality like genius or second sight—hitherto it has come very rarely and to exceptional people. But in this case . . . I have always wondered at the miracles of Mahomet, and at Yogi's miracles, and the miracles of Madame Blavatsky. But, of course! Yes, it is simply a gift! It carries out so beautifully the arguments of that great thinker"—Mr. Maydig's voice sank—"his Grace the Duke of Argyll. Here we plumb some profounder law—deeper than the ordinary laws of nature. Yes—yes. Go on. Go on!"

Mr. Fotheringay proceeded to tell of his misadventure with Winch, and Mr. Maydig, no longer overawed or scared, began to jerk his limbs about and interject astonishment. "It's this what troubled me most," proceeded Mr. Fotheringay; "it's this I'm most mijitly in want of advice for; of course he's at San Francisco—wherever San Francisco may be—but of course it's awkward for both of us, as you'll see, Mr. Maydig. I don't see how he can understand what has happened, and I dare say he's scared and exasperated something tremendous, and trying to get at me. I dare say he keeps on starting off to come here. I send him back, by a miracle every few hours, when I think of it. And of course, that's a thing he won't be able to understand, and it's bound to annoy him; and, of course, if he takes a ticket every time it will cost him a lot of money. I done the best I could for him, but of course it's difficult for him to put himself in my place. I thought afterwards that his clothes might have got scorched, you know—if Hades is all it's supposed to be— before I shifted him. In that case I suppose they'd have locked him up in San Francisco. Of course I willed him a new suit of clothes on him directly I thought of it. But, you see, I'm already in a deuce of a tangle——"

Mr. Maydig looked serious. "I see you are in a tangle. Yes, it's a difficult position. How you are to end it…" He became diffuse and inconclusive.

"However, we'll leave Winch for a little and discuss the larger question. I don't think this is a case of the black art or anything of the sort. I don't think there is any taint of criminality about it at all, Mr. Fotheringay—none whatever, unless you are suppressing material facts. No, it's miracles—pure miracles—miracles, if I may say so, of the very highest class."

He began to pace the hearthrug and gesticulate, while Mr. Fotheringay sat with his arm on the table and his head on his arm, looking worried. "I don't see how I'm to manage about Winch," he said.

"A gift of working miracles—apparently a very powerful

gift," said Mr. Maydig, "will find a way about Winch—never fear. My dear sir, you are a most important man—a man of the most astonishing possibilities. As evidence, for example! And in other ways, the things you may do. . . ."

"Yes, *I've* thought of a thing or two," said Mr. Fotheringay. "But—some of the things came a bit twisty. You saw that fish at first? Wrong sort of bowl and wrong sort of fish. And I thought I'd ask someone."

"A proper course," said Mr. Maydig, "a very proper course—altogether the proper course." He stopped and looked at Mr. Fotheringay. "It's practically an unlimited gift. Let us test your powers, for instance. If they really *are* . . . If they really are all they seem to be."

And so, incredible as it may seem, in the study of the little house behind the Congregational Chapel, on the evening of Sunday, Nov. 10, 1896, Mr. Fotheringay, egged on and inspired by Mr. Maydig, began to work miracles. The reader's attention is specially and definitely called to that date. He will object, probably has already objected, that certain points in this story are improbable, that if any things of the sort already described had indeed occurred, they would have been in all the papers a year ago. The details immediately following he will find particularly hard to accept, because among other things they involve the conclusion that he or she, the reader in question, must have been killed in a violent and unprecedented manner more than a year ago. Now a miracle is nothing if not improbable, and as a matter of fact the reader *was* killed in a violent and unprecedented manner a year ago. In the subsequent course of this story it will become perfectly clear and credible, as every right-minded and reasonable reader will admit. But this is not the place for the end of the story, being but little beyond the hither side of the middle. And at first the miracles worked by Mr. Fotheringay were timid little miracles—little things with the cups and parlour fitments, as feeble as the miracles of Theosophists, and, feeble as they were, they were received with awe by his collaborator. He would have preferred to settle the Winch business out of hand, but Mr. Maydig would not let him. But after they had worked a dozen of these domestic trivialities, their sense of power grew, their imagination began to show signs of stimulation, and their ambition enlarged. Their first larger enterprise was due to hunger and the negligence of Mrs. Minchin, Mr. Maydig's housekeeper. The meal to which the minister conducted Mr. Fotheringay was certainly ill-laid and uninviting as refreshment for two industrious miracle-workers; but they were seated, and Mr. Maydig was descanting in sorrow rather than in anger upon his housekeeper's short-comings, before it occurred to Mr. Fotheringay that an opportunity lay before him. "Don't you think, Mr. Maydig," he said, "if it isn't a liberty, I——"

"My dear Mr. Fotheringay! Of course! No—I didn't think."

Mr. Fotheringay waved his hand. "What shall we have?" he said, in a large, inclusive spirit, and, at Mr. Maydig's order, re-vised the supper very thoroughly. "As for me," he said, eyeing Mr. Maydig's selection, "I am always particularly fond of a tankard of stout and a nice Welsh rarebit, and I'll order that. I ain't much given to Burgundy," and forthwith stout and Welsh rarebit promptly appeared at his command. They sat long at their supper, talking like equals, as Mr. Fotheringay presently perceived with a glow of surprise and gratification, of all the miracles they would presently do. "And, by the bye, Mr. Maydig," said Mr. Fotheringay, "I might perhaps be able to help you—in a domestic way."

"Don't quite follow," said Mr. Maydig, pouring out a glass of miraculous old Burgundy.

Mr. Fotheringay helped himself to a second Welsh rarebit out of vacancy, and took a mouthful. "I was thinking," he said, "I might be able (*chum, chum*) to work (*chum, chum*) a miracle with Mrs. Minchin (*chum, chum*)—make her a better woman."

Mr. Maydig put down the glass and looked doubtful. "She's—— She strongly objects to interference, you know, Mr. Fotheringay. And—as a matter of fact—it's well past eleven and she's probably in bed and asleep. Do you think, on the whole——"

Mr. Fotheringay considered these objections. "I don't see that it shouldn't be done in her sleep."

For a time Mr. Maydig opposed the idea, and then he yielded.

Mr. Fotheringay issued his orders, and a little less at their ease, perhaps, the two gentlemen proceeded with their repast. Mr. Maydig was enlarging on the changes he might expect in his housekeeper next day, with an optimism that seemed even to Mr. Fotheringay's supper senses a little forced and hectic, when a series of confused noises from upstairs began. Their eyes exchanged interrogations, and Mr. Maydig left the room hastily. Mr. Fotheringay heard him calling up to his housekeeper and then his footsteps going softly up to her.

In a minute or so the minister returned, his step light, his face radiant. "Wonderful!" he said, "and touching! Most touching!"

He began pacing the hearthrug. "A repentance—a most touching repentance—through the crack of the door. Poor woman! A most wonderful change! She had got up. She must have got up at once. She had got up out of her sleep to smash a private bottle of brandy in her box. And to confess it, too! . . . But this gives us—it opens—a most amazing vista of possibilities. If we can work this miraculous change in *her* . . ."

"The thing's unlimited seemingly," said Mr. Fotheringay. "And about Mr. Winch——"

"Altogether unlimited." And from the hearthrug Mr. Maydig, waving the Winch difficulty aside, unfolded a series of wonderful proposals—proposals he invented as he went along.

Now what those proposals were does not concern the essentials of this story. Suffice it that they were designed in a spirit of infinite benevolence, the sort of benevolence that used to be called post-prandial. Suffice it, too, that the problem of Winch remained unsolved. Nor is it necessary to describe how far that series got to its fulfillment. There were astonishing changes. The small hours found Mr. Maydig and Mr. Fotheringay careering across the chilly market-square under the still moon, in a sort of ecstasy of thaumaturgy, Mr. Maydig all £ap and gesture, Mr. Fotheringay short and bristling, and no longer abashed at his greatness. They had reformed every drunkard in the Parliamentary division, changed all the beer and alcohol to water (Mr. Maydig had overruled Mr. Fotheringay on this point), they had, further, greatly improved the railway communication of the place, drained Flinder's swamp, improved the soil of One Tree

Hill, and cured the Vicar's wart. And they were going to see
what could be done with the injured pier at South Bridge. "The
place," gasped Mr. Maydig, "won't be the same place tomorrow. How surprised and thankful everyone will be!" And just at
that moment the church clock struck three.

"I say," said Mr. Fotheringay, "that's three o'clock! I must be
getting back. I've got to be at business by eight. And besides,
Mrs. Wimms——"

"We're only beginning," said Mr. Maydig, full of the sweetness of unlimited power. "We're only beginning. Think of all
the good we're doing. When people wake——"

"But——" said Mr. Fotheringay.

Mr. Maydig gripped his arm suddenly. His eyes were bright
and wild. "My dear chap," he said, "there's no hurry. Look"
Look"—he pointed to the moon at the zenith—"Joshua!"

"Joshua?" said Mr. Fotheringay.

"Joshua," said Mr. Maydig. "Why not? Stop it."

Mr. Fotheringay looked at the moon.

"That's a bit tall," he said after a pause.

"Why not?" said Mr. Maydig. "Of course it doesn't stop.
You stop the rotation of the earth, you know. Time stops. It isn't
as if we were doing harm."

"H'm!" said Mr. Fotheringay. "Well." He sighed. "I'll try.
Here——"

He buttoned up his jacket and addressed himself to the
habitable globe, with as good an assumption of confidence
as lay in his power. "Jest stop rotating, will you?" said Mr.
Fotheringay.

Incontinently he was flying head over heels through the air
at the rate of dozens of miles a minute. In spite of the innumerable circles he was describing per second, he thought; for
thought is wonderful—sometimes as sluggish as flowing pitch,
sometimes as instantaneous as light. He thought in a second,
and willed. "Let me come down safe and sound. Whatever else
happens, let me down safe and sound."

He willed it only just in time, for his clothes, heated by his
rapid flight through the air, were already beginning to singe. He
came down with a forcible but by no means injurious bump in

what appeared to be a mound of fresh-turned earth. A large mass of metal and masonry, extraordinarily like the clock-tower in the middle of the market-square, hit the earth near him, ricochetted over him, and flew into stonework, bricks, and masonry, like a bursting bomb. A hurtling cow hit one of the larger blocks and smashed like an egg. There was a crash that made all the most violent crashes of his past life seem like the sound of falling dust, and this was followed by a descending series of lesser crashes. A vast wind roared throughout earth and heaven, so that he could scarcely lift his head to look. For a while he was too breathless and astonished even to see where he was or what had happened. And his first movement was to feel his head and reassure himself that his streaming hair was still his own.

"Lord!" gasped Mr. Fotheringay, scarce able to speak for the gale. "I've had a squeak! What's gone wrong? Storms and thunder. And only a minute ago a fine night. It's Maydig set me on to this sort of thing. *What* a wind! If I go on fooling in this way I'm bound to have a thundering accident!

"Where's Maydig?

"What a confounded mess everything's in!"

He looked about him so far as his flapping jacket would per-mit. The appearance of things was really extremely strange. "The sky's all right anyhow," said Mr. Fotheringay. "And that's about all that is all right. And even there it looks like a terrific gale coming up. But there's the moon overhead. Just as it was just now. Bright as midday. But as for the rest—Where's the village? Where's—where's anything? And what on earth set this wind a-blowing? *I* didn't order no wind."

Mr. Fotheringay struggled to get to his feet in vain; and af-ter one failure, remained on all fours, holding on. He surveyed the moonlit world to leeward, with the tails of his jacket streaming over his head. "There's something seriously wrong," said Mr. Fotheringay. "And what it is—goodness knows."

Far and wide nothing was visible in the white glare through the haze of dust that drove before a screaming gale but tumbled masses of earth and heaps of inchoate ruins, no trees, no houses, no familiar shapes, only a wilderness of disorder vanishing at last into the darkness beneath the whirling columns and streamers, the lightnings and thunderings of a swiftly rising storm. Near him in the livid glare was something that might once have been an elm-tree, a smashed mass of splinters, shivered from boughs to base, and further a twisted mass of iron girders—only too evidently the viaduct—rose out of the piled confusion.

You see, when Mr. Fotheringay had arrested the rotation of the solid globe, he had made no stipulation concerning the trifling movables upon its surface. And the earth spins so fast that the surface at its equator is traveling at rather more than a thousand miles an hour, and in these latitudes at more than half that pace. So that the village, and Mr. Maydig, and Mr. Fotheringay, and everybody and everything had been jerked violently forward at about nine miles per second—that is to say, much more violently than if they had been fired out of a cannon. And every human being, every living creature, every house, and every tree—all the world as we know it—had been so jerked and smashed and utterly destroyed. That was all.

These things Mr. Fotheringay did not, of course, fully appreciate. But he perceived that his miracle had miscarried, and with that a great disgust of miracles came upon him. He was in darkness now, for the clouds had swept together and blotted out his momentary glimpse of the moon, and the air was full of fitful struggling tortured wraiths of hail. A great roaring of wind and waters filled earth and sky, and, peering under his hand through the dust and sleet to windward, he saw by the play of the lightnings a vast wall of water pouring towards him.

"Maydig!" screamed Mr. Fotheringay's feeble voice amid the elemental uproar. "Here!—Maydig!"

"Stop!" cried Mr. Fotheringay to the advancing water. "Oh, for goodness' sake, stop!

"Just a moment," said Mr. Fotheringay to the lightnings and thunder. "Stop jest a moment while I collect my thoughts . . . And now what shall I do?" he said. "What *shall* I do? Lord! I wish Maydig was about.

"I know," said Mr. Fotheringay. "And for goodness' sake let's have it right *this* time."

He remained on all fours, leaning against the wind, very intent to have everything right.

"Ah!" he said. "Let nothing what I'm going to order happen until I say 'Off!' ... Lord! I wish I'd thought of that before!"

He lifted his little voice against the whirlwind, shouting louder and louder in the vain desire to hear himself speak. "Now then!—here goes! Mind about that what I said just now. In the first place, when all I've got to say is done, let me lose my miraculous power, let my will become just like anybody else's will, and all these dangerous miracles be stopped. I don't like them. I'd rather I didn't work 'em. Ever so much. That's the first thing. And the second is—let me be back just before the miracles begin; let everything be just as it was before that blessed lamp turned up. It's a big job, but it's the last. Have you got it? No more miracles, everything as it was—me back in the Long Dragon just before I drank my half-pint. That's it! Yes."

He dug his fingers into the mould, closed his eyes, and said "Off!"

Everything became perfectly still. He perceived that he was standing erect.

"So *you* say," said a voice.

He opened his eyes. He was in the bar of the Long Dragon, arguing about miracles with Toddy Beamish. He had a vague sense of some great thing forgotten that instantaneously passed. You see, except for the loss of his miraculous power, everything was back as it had been; his mind and memory therefore were now just as they had been at the time when this story began. So that he knew absolutely nothing of all that is told here, knows nothing of all that is told here to this day. And among other things, of course, he still did not believe in miracles.

"I tell you that miracles, properly speaking, can't possibly happen," he said, "whatever you like to hold. And I'm prepared to prove it up to the hilt."

"That's what *you* think," said Toddy Beamish, and "Prove it if you can."

"Looky here, Mr. Beamish," said Mr. Fotheringay. "Let us clearly understand what a miracle is. It's something contrariwise to the course of nature done by power of Will...."

THE FOREIGNER[*]

BY FRANCIS STEEGMULLER

IF IT hadn't been raining as I came out of the cinema, I should have walked home: my apartment was nearby and the route anything but complicated—straight down the boulevard, crossing two streets and turning right on the third, the Rue de Grenelle, for about half a block. As it was, however, I hailed a taxi, and it was scarcely a moment before I realized that its driver, a ruddy-faced old man, was in the midst of an attack of perversity and nerves. "No! No!" I cried, as he started to turn up the *first* street, the Rue St. Dominique. "Two more blocks!" He muttered something, swung down the boulevard again, and then in a moment he was turning up the *second* street, the Rue Las Cases. "No! No!" I cried again. "The next one, please! The next street is mine! The Rue de Grenelle!" At this he turned around and gave me a baleful stare; then he spurted ahead, didn't turn up my street at all, and continued rapidly down the boulevard, as though forever. "But now you have passed it!" I cried. "You should have turned to the right, as I said! Please turn around, and drive up the Rue de Grenelle to Number 36."

To my horror, the old man made a noise like a snarl. Spinning his car around in a U turn on the slippery pavement, he speeded back, crossed the boulevard, and stopped at the corner of my street with a jerk. "Get out!" he almost screamed, his face crimson with rage. "Get out of my automobile at once! I refuse absolutely to drive you any further! Three times you

[*] from *The New Yorker* and *French and Other Follies*

have treated me like an idiot! Three times you have grossly insulted me! My automobile is not for foreigners, I tell you! Get out at once!"

"In this rain?" I cried, indignantly. "I shall do nothing of the kind. I did not insult you even once, Monsieur, let alone three times. You know quite well I did nothing but urge you, in vain, to drive me home. Now kindly do so. I shall give you a good *pourboire*," I added, more amiably, "and we shall take leave of each other in a friendly fashion."

He barely waited for me to finish. "Get out!" he cried. "Get out, I tell you! You have insulted me too often, and you will get out!"

I glanced at the rain. "Indeed I will not," I said.

His manner calmed ominously. "Either you will leave my taxi," he said in an even, hoarse tone, "or I shall drive you to the commissariat of police, where I shall demand the recompense due me for such insults as yours. Choose!"

"In such weather as this," I replied, "I have no choice. To the commissariat, by all means." And there we went.

The commissariat, only a few doors from mine, was not unfamiliar to me. I had been there several times before, on less quarrelsome matters, and as the driver and I entered the bare room side by side, the *commissaire,* sitting in lonely authority behind his desk, greeted me as an acquaintance. "Good afternoon, Monsieur," he said, calling me by name. "I can help you? What is it you wish?"

But the old man, to whom the *commissaire* had barely nodded, gave me no chance to speak. "It is I who wish!" he cried. "It is I who wish to complain against this foreigner! Three times he has treated me like an idiot, Monsieur! Three times he has insulted me grossly! I demand justice, Monsieur!"

The *commissaire* stared at him, his face expressionless; I felt that he, like me, was wondering in just what condition the old man was; then, turning to me, he asked me if I would have the kindness to make my deposition. He took up a pen, opened a large blank book, and as I spoke, took down my story in a flowing, plumy hand. The giving of my address to the driver, the two incorrect turns, the mutterings, the missing of my street, the rage, the ultimatum; all the *commissaire* inscribed imperishably in whatever the French call the Spencerian style; once or twice he interrupted me to reprimand the driver, who muttered beside me at various portions of my testimony. When I had finished, the *commissaire* continued to write for a moment, ended with a particularly fancy flourish, blotted his last line, and thanked me. Then he turned to the driver. "And now you," he said gruffly. "You depose, too, so that I may make up my mind on this perplexing question."

The old man, however, had no deposition to make. "Three times!" was still all he could say, in his thick, angry voice, gesticulating at the *commissaire* and glaring at me. "Three times, Monsieur! Three times treated like an idiot, and three times grossly insulted! By this foreigner! It is not to be borne, Monsieur!"

The *commissaire* looked up crossly from his notebook, where these accusations had been duly inscribed. "But the circumstances? Describe in detail what took place while you were with this gentleman. If the circumstances which he has related are not true," he said, casting me a glance of apology, "correct them."

But once again "Three times!" was all my accuser could say, and the *commissaire* laid down his pen rather briskly. "It is entirely clear," he said in a very definite voice, "that it is you, Monsieur, who are the injured party in this affair, and I shall be happy to indicate my decision by requiring this person to drive you to your door without charge. If Monsieur will now have the goodness to grant me the favor of a brief glance at his papers— a formality required by law in such cases as these—I shall dispose of the matter at once. Your *carte d'identité,* Monsieur, if you please."

Like a plummet, my heart sank. In my mind's eye I saw the desk in my study, and lying on it, forgotten, the identification card which foreign residents are required by French law to carry at all times. "Due to the penetrating rain, Monsieur," it hastily occurred to me as the only thing to say, "I have left my card at home, lest the moisture of the weather permeate it, and perhaps destroy it completely. In the morning I can easily bring it to you, Monsieur, and I hope that this will satisfy your requirements, which I realize are strict and necessary."

But I had done the unforgivable, and everything was changed and over with. "That will not satisfy the requirements," the *commissaire* said sternly, his face like stone. "It is true that you will bring your card here tomorrow morning, but in view of the present circumstance I am forced to alter my judgment in this affair. Due to the fact that it is raining, I shall request this gentleman to drive you to your door, but I shall require you to pay him not only for the entire journey from beginning to end but also for the time which he has lost by coming to this bureau. I assume, Monsieur," he said to the old man, "that you have left your meter running?"

The driver nodded, and the *commissaire* rose. "Then *au revoir,* Monsieurs," he said, unsmiling. "Monsieur will not forget tomorrow morning," and side by side, as we had entered, we left the commissariat. I had seen a gleam come into my accuser's eyes when the judgment had been reversed, but apart from that he had given no signs of triumph, and he continued to give none: he drove me home without a word. It was only when we arrived, and I handed him the exact fare, carefully counted out, that he spoke. "Monsieur has no doubt forgotten his promise of a good *pourboire,* that we might part in friendly fashion?" he said.

THRAWN JANET[*]

BY ROBERT LOUIS STEVENSON

THE REVEREND Murdock Soulis was long minister of the moorland parish of Balweary, in the vale of Dule. A severe, bleak-faced old man, dreadful to his hearers, he dwelt in the last years of his life, without relative or servant or any human company, in the small and lonely manse under the Hanging Shaw. In spite of the iron composure of his features, his eye was wild, scared, and uncertain; and when he dwelt, in private admonitions, on the future of the impenitent, it seemed as if his eye pierced through the storms of time to the terrors of eternity. Many young persons, coming to prepare themselves against the season of the Holy Communion, were dreadfully affected by his talk. He had a sermon on 1st Peter, v. and 8th, "The devil as a roaring lion," on the Sunday after every seventeenth of August, and he was accustomed to surpass himself upon that text both by the appalling nature of the matter and the terror of his bearing in the pulpit. The children were frightened into fits, and the old looked more than usually oracular, and were, all that day, full of those hints that Hamlet deprecated. The manse itself, where it stood by the water of Dule among some thick trees, with the Shaw overhanging it on the one side, and on the other many cold, moorish hill-tops rising towards the sky, had begun, at a very early period of Mr. Soulis's ministry, to be avoided in the dusk hours by all who valued themselves upon their prudence; and guidmen sitting at the clachan alehouse shook their heads together at the thought of passing late by that uncanny neighbourhood. There was one spot, to be

* from The Merry Men

more particular, which was regarded with especial awe. The manse stood between the high road and the water of Dule, with a gable to each; its back was toward the kirktown of Balweary, nearly half a mile away; in front of it, a bare garden, hedged with thorn, occupied the land between the river and the road. The house was two storeys high, with two large rooms on each. It opened not directly on the garden, but on a causewayed path, or passage, giving on the road on the one hand, and closed on the other by the tall willows and elders that bordered on the stream. And it was this strip of causeway that enjoyed among the young parishioners of Balweary so infamous a reputation. The minister walked there often after dark, sometimes groaning aloud in the instancy of his unspoken prayers; and when he was from home, and the manse door was locked, the more daring schoolboys ventured, with beating hearts, to "follow my leader" across that legendary spot.

This atmosphere of terror, surrounding, as it did, a man of God of spotless character and orthodoxy, was a common cause of wonder and subject of inquiry among the few strangers who were led by chance or business into that unknown, outlying country. But many even of the people of the parish were ignorant of the strange events which had marked the first year of Mr. Soulis's ministrations; and among those who were better informed, some were naturally reticent, and others shy of that particular topic. Now and again, only, one of the older folk would warm into courage over his third tumbler, and recount the cause of the minister's strange looks and solitary life.

Fifty years syne, when Mr. Soulis cam' first into Ba'weary, he was still a young man—a callant, the folk said—fu' o' book learnin' and grand at the exposition, but, as was natural in sae young a man, wi' nae leevin' experience in religion. The younger sort were greatly taken wi' his gifts and his gab; but auld, concerned, serious men and women were moved even to prayer for the young man, whom they took to be a self-deceiver, and the parish that was like to be sae ill-supplied. It was before the days o' the moderates—weary fa' them; but ill things are like guid—they baith come bit by bit, a pickle at a time; and there were folk even then that said the Lord had left the college professors to their ain devices, an' the lads that went to study wi' them wad hae done mair and better sittin' in a peat-bog, like their forebears of the persecution, wi' a Bible under their oxter and a speerit o' prayer in their heart. There was nae doubt, onyway, but that Mr. Soulis had been ower lang at the college. He was careful and troubled for mony things besides the ae thing needful. He had a feck o' books wi' him—mair than had ever been seen before in a' that presbytery; and a sair wark the carrier had wi' them, for they were a' like to have smoored in the Deil's Hag between this and Kilmackerlie. They were books o' divinity, to be sure, or so they ca'd them; but the serious were o' opinion there was little service for sae mony, when the hail o' God's Word would gang in the neuk of a plaid. Then he wad sit half the day and half the nicht forbye, which was scant decent—writin', nae less; and first, they were feared he wad read his sermons; and syne it proved he was writin' a book himsel', which was surely no fittin' for ane of his years and sma' experience.

Onway it behoved him to get an auld, decent wife to keep the manse for him an' see to his bit denners; and he was recommended to an auld limmer—Janet M'Clour, they ca'ed her—and sae far left to himsel' as to be ower persuaded. There was mony advised him to the contrar, for Janet was mair than suspeckit by the best folk in Ba'weary. Lang or that, she had had a wean to a dragoon; she hadnae come forrit* for maybe thretty year; and bairns had seen her mumblin' to hersel' up on Key's Loan in the gloamin', whilk was an unco time an' place for a God-fearin' woman. Howsoever, it was the laird himsel' that had first tauld the minister o' Janet; and in thae days he wad have gane a far gate to pleesure the laird. When folk tauld him that Janet was sib to the deil, it was a' superstition by his way of it; an' when they cast up the Bible to him an' the witch of Endor, he wad threep it doun their thrapples that thir days were a' gane by, and the deil was mercifully restrained.

---

* To come forrit—to offer oneself as a communicant.

Weel, when it got about the clachan that Janet M'Clour was to be servant at the manse, the folk were fair mad wi' her an' him thegether; and some o' the guidwives had nae better to dae than get round her door cheeks and chairge her wi' a' that was ken't again her, frae the sodger's bairn to John Tamson's twa kye. She was nae great speaker; folk usually let her gang her ain gate, an' she let them gang theirs, wi' neither Fair-guideen nor Fair-guidday; but when she buckled to, she had a tongue to deave the miller. Up she got, an' there wasnae an auld story in Ba'weary but she gart somebody lowp for it that day; they couldnae say ae thing but she could say twa to it; till, at the hinder end, the guidwives up and claucht haud of her, and clawed the coats aff her back, and pu'd her doun the clachan to the water o' Dule, to see if she were a witch or no, soum or droun. The carline skirled till ye could year her at the Hangin' Shaw, and she focht like ten; here was mony a guidwife bure the mark of her neist day an' mony a long day after; and just in the hettest o' the collieshangie, wha suld come up (for his sins) but the new minister.

"Women," said he (and he had a grand voice), "I charge you in the Lord's name to let her go."

Janet ran to him—she was fair wud wi' terror—an' clang to him, an' prayed him, for Christ's sake, save her frae the cummers; an' they, for their pairt, tauld him a' that was ken't, and maybe mair.

"Woman," says he to Janet, "is this true?"

"As the Lord sees me," says she, "as the Lord made me, no a word o't. Forbye the bairn," says she, "I've been a decent woman a' my days."

"Will you," says Mr. Soulis, "in the name of God, and before me, His unworthy minister, renounce the devil and his works?"

Weel, it wad appear that when he askit that, she gave a girn that fairly frichtit them that saw her, an' they could hear her teeth play dirl thegether in her chafts; but there was naething for it but the ae way or the ither; an' Janet lifted up her hand and renounced the deil before them a'.

"And now," says Mr. Soulis to the guidwives, "home with ye, one and all, and pray to God for His forgiveness."

And he gied Janet him arm, though she had little on her but a sark, and took her up the clachan to her ain door like a leddy of the land; an' her scrieghin' and laughin' as was a scandal to be heard.

There were mony grave folk lang ower their prayers that nicht; but when the morn cam' there was sic a fear fell upon a' Ba'weary that the bairns hid theirsels, and even the men folk stood and keekit frae their doors. For there was Janet comin' doun the clachan—her or her likeness, nane could tell—wi' her neck thrawn, and her heid on ae side, like a body that has been hangit, and a girn on her face like an unstreakit corp. By an' by they got used wi' it, and even speered at her to ken what was wrang; but frae that day forth she couldnae speak like a Christian woman, but slavered and played click wi' her teeth like apair o' shears; and frae that day forth the name o' God cam' never on her lips. Whiles she wad try to say it, but it michtnae be. Them that kenned best said least; but they never gied that Thing the name o' Janet M'Clour; for the auld Janet, by their way o't, was in muckle hell that day. But the minister was neither to haud nor to bind; he preached about naething but the folk's cruelty that had gi'en her a stroke of the palsy; he skelpt the bairns that meddled her; and he had her up to the manse that same nicht, and dwalled there a' his lane wi' her under the Hangin' Shaw.

Weel, time gaed by: and the idler sort commenced to think mair lichtly o' that black business. The minister was weel thocht o'; he was aye late at the writing, folk wad see his can'le doon by the Dule water after twal' at e'en; and he seemed pleased wi' himsel' and upsitten as at first, though a' body could see that he was dwining. As for Janet she cam' an' she gaed; if she didnae speak muckle afore, it was reason she should speak less then; she meddled naebody; but she was an eldritch thing to see, an' name wad hae mistrysted wi' her for Ba'weary glebe.

About the end o' July there cam' a spell o' weather, the like o't never was in that country-side; it was lown an' het an' heartless; the herds couldnae win up the Black Hill, the bairns were ower weariet to play; an' yet it was gousty too, wi' claps o' het

wund that rummled in the glens, and bits o' shouers that slock-
ened naething. We aye thocht it but to thun'er on the morn; but
the morn cam', an' the morn's morning, and it was aye the same
uncanny weather, sair on folks and bestial. Of a' that were the
waur, nane suffered like Mr. Soulis; he could neither sleep nor
eat, he tauld his elders; an' when he wasnae writin 'at his weary
book, he wad be stravaguin' ower a' the country-side like a man
possessed, when a' body was blythe to keep caller ben the
house.

Abune Hangin' Shaw, in the bield o' the Black Hill, there's
a bit enclosed grund wi' an iron yett; and it seems, in the auld
days, that was the kirkyaird a' Ba'weary, and consecrated by
the Papists before the blessed licht shone upon the kingdom. It
was a great howff, o' Mr. Soulis's onyway; there he would sit
an' consider his sermons; and indeed it's a bieldy bit. Weel, as
he cam' ower the wast end o' the Black Hill, ae day, he saw first
twa, an' syne fower, an' syne seeven corbie craws fleein' round
an' round abune the auld kirkyaird. They flew laigh and heavy,
an' squawked to ither as they gaed; and it was clear to Mr.
Soulis that something had put them frae their ordinar. He wasnae easy fleyed, an' gaed straucht up to the wa's; and what suld
he find there but a man, or the appearance of a man, sittin' in
the inside upon a grave. He was of a great stature, an' black as
hell, and his e'en were singular to see.* Mr. Soulis had heard
tell o' black men, mony's the time; but there was something
unco about this black man that daunted him. Het as he was, he
took a kind o' cauld grue in the marrow o' his banes; but up he
spak for a' that; an' says he: "My friend, are you a stranger in
this place?" The black man answered never a word; he got upon
his feet, an' begude to hirsle to the wa' on the far side; but he
aye lookit at the minister; an' the minister stood an' lookit
back; till a' in a meenute the black man was ower the wa' an'
rinnin' for the bield o' the trees. Mr. Soulis, he hardly kenned
why, ran after him; but he was sair forjaskit wi' his walk an' the

_____

* It was a common belief in Scotland that the devil appeared as a black man. This
appears in several witch trials and I think in Law's *Memorials*, that delightful
storehouse of the quaint and grisly.

het, unhalesome weather; and rin as he likit, he goe nae mair than a glisk o' the black man amang the birks, till he won doun to the foot o' the hillside, an' there he saw him ance mair, gaun, hap, step, an' lowp, ower Dule water to the manse.

Mr. Soulis wasnae weel pleased that this fearsome gangrel suld mak' sae free wi' Ba'weary manse; and he ran the harder, an' wet shoon, ower the burn, an' up the walk; but the deil a black man was there to see. He stepped out upon the road, but there was naebody there; he gaed a' ower the gairden, but na, nae black man. At the hinder end, and a bit feared as was but natural, he lifted the hasp and into the manse; and there was Janet M'Clour before his een, wi' her thrawn craig, and nane sae pleased to see him. And he aye minded sinsyne, when first he set his een upon her, he had the same cauld and deidly grue.

"Janet," says he, "have you seen a black man?"

"A black man!" quo' she. "Save us a'! Ye're no wise, minister. There's nae black man in a' Ba'weary."

But she didnae speak plain, ye maun understand; but yam-yammered, like a powny wi' the bit in its moo.

"Weel," says he, "Janet, if there was nae black man, I have spoken with the Accuser of the Brethren."

And he sat doun like ane wi' a fever, an' his teeth chittered in his heid.

"Hoots," says she, "think shame to yoursel', minister"; and gied him a drap brandy that she keepit aye by her.

Syne Mr. Soulis gaed into his study amang a' his books. It's a lang, laigh, mirk chalmer, perishin' cauld in winter, an' no very dry even in th' top o' the simmer, for the manse stands near the burn. Sae doun he sat, and thocht of a' that had come an' gane since he was in Ba'weary, an' his hame, an' the days when he was a bairn an' ran daffin' on the braes; and that black man aye ran in his heid like the owercomer of a sang. Aye the mair he thocht, the mair he thocht o' the black man. He tried the prayer, an' the words wouldnae come to him; an' he tried, they say, to write at his book, but he couldnae mak' nae mair o' that. There was whiles he thocht the black man was at his oxter, an' the swat stood upon him cauld as well-water; and there was other whiles, when he cam' to himsel' like a christened bairn and minded naething.

The upshot was that he gaed to the window an' stood glowrin' at Dule water. The trees are unco thick, an' water lies deep an' black under the manse; and there was Janet washin' the cla'es wi' her coats kilted. She had her back to the minister, an' he, for his pairt, hardly kenned what he was lookin' at. Syne she turned round, an' shawed her face; Mr. Soulis had the same cauld grue as twice that day afore, an' it was borne in upon him what folk said, that Janet was deid lang syne, an' this was a bogle in her clay-cauld flesh. He drew back a pickle and he scanned her narrowly. She was tramp-trampin' in the cla'es, croonin' to hersel'; and eh! Gude guide us, but it was a fear-some face. Whiles she sang louder, but there was nae man born o' woman that could tell the words o' her sang; an' whiles she lookit side-lang doun, but there was naething there for her to look at. There gaed a scunner through the flesh upon his banes; and that was Heeven's advertisement. But Mr. Soulis just blamed himsel', he said, to think sae ill of a puir, auld afflicted wife that hadnae a freend forbye himsel'; an' he put up a bit prayer for him an' her, an' drank a little caller water—for his heart rose again the meat—an' gaed up to his naked bed in the gloaming.

That was a nicht that has never been forgotten in Ba'weary, the nicht o' the seventeenth of August, seventeen hun'er' an twal'. It had been het afore, as I hae said, but that nicht it was hetter than ever. The sun gaed doun amang unco-lookin' clouds; it fell as mirk as the pit; no a star, no a breath o' wund; ye couldnae see your han' afore your face, and even the auld folk cuist the covers frae their beds and lay pechin' for their breath. Wi' a' that he had upon his mind, it was gey and un-likely Mr. Soulis wad get muckle sleep. He lay an' he tummled; the gude, caller bed that he got into brunt his very banes; whiles he slept, and whiles he waukened; whiles he heard the time o' nicht, and whiles a tyke yowlin' up the muir, as if some-body was deid; whiles he thocht he heard bogles claverin' in his lug, an' whiles he saw spunkies in the room. He behoved, he judged, to be sick; an' sick he was—little he jaloosed the sickness.

At the hinder end, he got a clearness in his mind, sat up in his sark on the bed-side, and fell thinkin' ance mair o' the black man an' Janet. He couldnae weel tell how—maybe it was the cauld to his feet—but it cam' in upon him wi' a spate that there was some connection between thir twa, an' that either or baith o' them were bogles. And just at that moment, in Janet's room, which was neist to his, there cam' a stramp o' feet as if men were wars'lin', an' then a loud bang; an' then a wund gaed reishling round the fower quarters of the house; an' then a' was ance mair as seelent as the grave.

Mr. Soulis was feared for neither man nor deevil. He got his tinder-box, an' lit a can'le, an' made three steps o't ower to Janet's door. It was on the hasp, an' he pushed it open, an' keeked bauldly in. It was a big room, as big as the minister's ain, an' plenished wi' grand, auld, solid gear, for he had nathing else. There was a fower-posted bed wi' auld tapestry; and a braw cabinet of aik, that was fu' o' the minister's divinity books, an' put there to be out o' the gate; an' a wheens duds o' Janet's lying here and there about the floor. But nae Janet could Mr. Soulis see; nor ony sign of a contention. In he gaed (an' there's few that wad ha'e followed him) an' lookit a' round, an' listened. But there was naethin' to be heard, neither inside the manse nor in a' Ba'weary parish, an' naethin' to be seen but the muckle shadows turnin' round the can'le. An' then, a' at ance, the minister's heart played dunt an' stood stock-still; an' a cauld wund blew among the hairs o' his heid. Whaten a weary sicht was that for the puir man's een! For there was Janet hangin' frae a nail beside the auld aik cabinet: her heid aye lay on her shouther, her een were steeked, the tongue projeckit frae her mouth, and her heels were twa feet clear abune the floor.

"God forgive us all!" thocht Mr. Soulis, "poor Janet's dead."

He cam' a step nearer to the corp; an' then his heart fair whammled in his inside. For by what cantrip it wad illbeseem a man to judge, she was hingin' frae a single nail an' by a single wursted thread for darnin' hose.

It's a awfu' thing to be your lane at nicht wi' siccan prodigies o' darkness; but Mr. Soulis was strong in the Lord. He turned an' gaed his ways oot o' that room, and lockit the door ahint him; and step by step, doon the stairs, as heavy as leed; and set doon the can'le on the table at the stairfoot. He couldnae pray, he couldnae think, he was dreepin' wi' caul' swat, an' naething could he hear but the dunt-dunt-duntin' o' his ain heart. He micht maybe have stood there an hour, or maybe twa, he minded sae little; when a' o' sudden, he heard a laigh, uncanny steer up-stairs; a foot gaed to an' fro in the chalmer whaur the corp was hingin'; syne the door was opened, though he minded weel that he had lockit it; an' syne there was a step upon the landin', an' it seemed to him as if the corp was lookin' ower the rail and doun upon him whaur he stood.

He took up the can'le again (for he couldnae want the licht), and as saftly as ever he could, gaed straucht out o' the manse an' to the far end o' the causeway. It was aye pit-mirk; the flame o' the can'le, when he set it on the grund, brunt steedy and clear as in a room; naething moved, but the Dule water seepin' and sabbin' doon the glen, an' yon unhaly footstep that cam' ploddin' doun the stairs inside the manse. He kenned the foot ower weel, for it was Janet's; and at ilka step that cam' a wee thing nearer, the cauld got deeper in his vitals. He commended his soul to Him that made an' keepit him; "and O Lord," said he, "give me strength this night to war against the powers of evil."

By this time the foot was comin' through the passage for the door; he could hear a hand skirt along the wa', as if the fear-some thing was feelin' for its way. The saughs tossed an' maned thegether, a long sigh cam' ower the hills, the flame o' the can'le was blawn aboot; an' there stood the corp of Thrawn Janet, wi' her grogram goun an' her black mutch, wi' the heid aye upon the shouther, an' the grin still upon the face o't—leevin', ye wad hae said—deid, as Mr. Soulis weel kenned—upon the threshold o' the manse.

It's a strange thing that the saul of man should be that thirled into his perishable body; but the minister saw that, an' his heart didnae break.

She didnae stand there lang; she began to move again an' cam' slowly towards Mr. Soulis whaur he stood under the saughs. A' the life o' his body, a' the strength o' his speerit, were glowerin' frae his een. It seemed she was gaun to speak, but wanted words, an' made a sign wi' the left hand. There cam' a clap o' wund, like a cat's fuff; oot gaed the can'le, the saughs skreighed like folk; an' Mr. Soulis kenned that, live or die, this was the end o't.

"Witch, beldame, devil!" he cried, "I charge you, by the power of God, begone—if you be dead, to the grave—if you be damned, to hell."

An' at that moment the Lord's ain hand out o' the Heevens struck the Horror whaur it stood; the auld, deid, desecrated corp o' the witch-wife, sae lang keepit frae the grave and hirsled round by deils, lowed up like a brunstane spunk and fell in ashes to the grund; the thunder followed, peal on dirling peal, the rairing rain upon the back o' that; and Mr. Soulis lowped through the garden hedge, and ran, wi' skelloch upon skelloch, for the clachan.

That same mornin', John Christie saw the Black Man pass the Muckle Cairn as it was chappin' six; before eicht he gaed by the change-house at Knockdow; an' no lang after, Sandy M'Lellan saw him gaun linkin' doun the braes frae Kilmackerlie. There's little doubt but it was him that dwalled sae lang in Janet's body; but he was awa' at last; and sinsyne the deil has never fashed us in Ba'weary.

But it was a sair dispensation for the minister; lang, lang he lay ravin' in his bed; and frae that hour to this, he was the man ye ken the day.

THE CHASER*

BY JOHN COLLIER

ALAN AUSTEN, as nervous as a kitten, went up certain dark and creaky stairs in the neighborhood of Pell Street; and peered about for a long time on the dim landing before he found the name he wanted written obscurely on one of the doors.

He pushed open this door, as he had been told to do, and found himself in a tiny room, which contained no furniture but a plain kitchen table, a rocking-chair, and an ordinary chair. On one of the dirty buff-colored walls were a couple of shelves, containing in all perhaps a dozen bottles and jars.

An old man sat in the rocking-chair, reading a newspaper. Alan, without a word, handed him the card he had been given. "Sit down, Mr. Austen," said the old man very politely. "I am glad to make your acquaintance."

"Is it true," asked Alan, "that you have a certain mixture that has—er—quite extraordinary effects?"

"My dear sir," replied the old man, "my stock in trade is not very large—I don't deal in laxatives and teething mixtures—but such as it is, it is varied. I think nothing I sell has effects which could be precisely described as ordinary."

"Well, the fact is—" began Alan.

"Here, for example," interrupted the old man, reaching for a bottle from the shelf. "Here is a liquid as colorless as water, almost tasteless, quite imperceptible in coffee, milk, wine, or any other beverage. It is also quite imperceptible to any known method of autopsy."

* from The New Yorker

"Do you mean it is a poison?" cried Alan, very much horrified.

"Call it a glove-cleaner if you like," said the old man indifferently. "Maybe it will clean gloves. I have never tried. One might call it a life-cleaner. Lives need cleaning sometimes."

"I want nothing of that sort," said Alan.

"Probably it is just as well," said the old man. "Do you know the price of this? For one teaspoonful, which is sufficient, I ask five thousand dollars. Never less. Not a penny less."

"I hope all your mixtures are not as expensive," said Alan apprehensively.

"Oh dear, no," said the old man. "It would be no good charging that sort of price for a love potion, for example. Young people who need a love potion very seldom have five thousand dollars. Otherwise they would not need a love potion."

"I am glad to hear that," said Alan.

"I look at it like this," said the old man. "Please a customer with one article, and he will come back when he needs another. Even if it *is* more costly. He will save up for it, if necessary."

"So," said Alan, "you really do sell love potions?"

"If I did not sell love potions," said the old man, reaching for another bottle, "I should not have mentioned the other matter to you. It is only when one is in a position to oblige that one can afford to be so confidential."

"And these potions," said Alan. "They are not just—just—er——"

"Oh, no," said the old man. "Their effects are permanent, and extend far beyond casual impulse. But they include it. Bountifully, insistently. Everlastingly."

"Dear me!" said Alan, attempting a look of scientific detachment. "How very interesting!"

"But consider the spiritual side," said the old man.

"I do, indeed," said Alan.

"For indifference," said the old man, "they substitute devotion. For scorn, adoration. Give one tiny measure of this to the young lady—its flavor is imperceptible in orange juice, soup, or cocktails—and however gay and giddy she is, she will change altogether. She will want nothing but solitude, and you."

"I can hardly believe it," said Alan. "She is so fond of parties."

"She will not like them any more," said the old man. "She will be afraid of the pretty girls you may meet."

"She will actually be jealous?" cried Alan in a rapture. "Of me?"

"Yes, she will want to be everything to you."

"She is, already. Only she doesn't care about it."

"She will, when she has taken this. She will care intensely. You will be her sole interest in life."

"Wonderful!" cried Alan.

"She will want to know all you do," said the old man. "All that has happened to you during the day. Every word of it. She will want to know what you are thinking about, why you smile suddenly, why you are looking sad."

"That is love!" cried Alan.

"Yes," said the old man. "How carefully she will look after you! She will never allow you to be tired, to sit in a draught, to neglect your food. If you are an hour late, she will be terrified. She will think you are killed, or that some siren has caught you."

"I can hardly imagine Diana like that!" cried Alan, overwhelmed with joy.

"You will not have to use your imagination," said the old man. "And, by the way, since there are always sirens, if by any chance you *should*, later on, slip a little, you need not worry. She will forgive you, in the end. She will be terribly hurt, of course, but she will forgive you—in the end."

"That will not happen," said Alan fervently.

"Of course not," said the old man. "But, if it did, you need not worry. She would never divorce you. Oh, no! And, of course, she herself will never give you the least, the very least, grounds for—uneasiness."

"And how much," said Alan, "is this wonderful mixture?"

"It is not as dear," said the old man, "as the glove-cleaner, or life-cleaner, as I sometimes call it. No. That is five thousand dollars, never a penny less. One has to be older than you are, to indulge in that sort of thing. One has to save up for it."

"But the love potion?" said Alan.

"Oh, that," said the old man, opening the drawer in the kitchen table, and taking out a tiny, rather dirty-looking phial. "That is just a dollar."

"I can't tell you how grateful I am," said Alan, watching him fill it.

"I like to oblige," said the old man. "Then customers come back, later in life, when they are rather better off, and want more expensive things. Here you are. You will find it very effective."

"Thank you again," said Alan. "Good-by."

"*Au revoir*," said the old man.

TITLE INDEX

AUTHOR INDEX

Including biographical notes and a selected list of the author's
principal works.

SEE YOUR BOOKSELLER FOR THESE
BANTAM CLASSICS

SELECTED ESSAYS, LECTURES, AND POEMS, Ralph Waldo Emerson, 0-553-21388-1

TEN PLAYS BY EURIPIDES, Euripides, 0-553-21363-6

APRIL MORNING, Howard Fast, 0-553-27322-1

MADAME BOVARY, Gustave Flaubert, 0-553-21341-5

HOWARDS END, E. M. Forster, 0-553-21208-7

A ROOM WITH A VIEW, E. M. Forster, 0-553-21323-7

THE DIARY OF A YOUNG GIRL, Anne Frank, 0-553-57712-3

ANNE FRANK'S TALES FROM THE SECRET ANNEX, Anne Frank, 0-553-58638-6

THE AUTOBIOGRAPHY AND OTHER WRITINGS, Benjamin Franklin, 0-553-21075-0

THE YELLOW WALLPAPER AND OTHER WRITINGS, Charlotte Perkins Gilman, 0-553-21375-X

FAUST: FIRST PART, Johann Wolfgang von Goethe, 0-553-21348-2

THE WIND IN THE WILLOWS, Kenneth Grahame, 0-553-21368-7

THE COMPLETE FAIRY TALES OF THE BROTHERS GRIMM, The Brothers Grimm, 0-553-38216-0

ROOTS, Alex Haley, 0-440-17464-3

FAR FROM THE MADDING CROWD, Thomas Hardy, 0-553-21331-8

JUDE THE OBSCURE, Thomas Hardy, 0-553-21191-9

THE MAYOR OF CASTERBRIDGE, Thomas Hardy, 0-553-21024-6

THE RETURN OF THE NATIVE, Thomas Hardy, 0-553-21269-9

TESS OF THE D'URBERVILLES, Thomas Hardy, 0-553-21168-4

THE HOUSE OF THE SEVEN GABLES, Nathaniel Hawthorne, 0-553-21270-2

THE SCARLET LETTER, Nathaniel Hawthorne, 0-553-21009-2

THE FAIRY TALES OF HERMANN HESSE, Hermann Hesse, 0-553-37776-0

SIDDHARTHA, Hermann Hesse, 0-553-20884-5

THE ODYSSEY OF HOMER, Homer, 0-553-21399-7

THE HUNCHBACK OF NOTRE DAME, Victor Hugo, 0-553-21370-9

FOUR GREAT PLAYS: A DOLL'S HOUSE, GHOSTS, AN ENEMY OF THE PEOPLE, and THE WILD DUCK, Henrik Ibsen, 0-553-21280-X

THE PORTRAIT OF A LADY, Henry James, 0-553-21127-7

THE TURN OF THE SCREW AND OTHER SHORT FICTION, Henry James, 0-553-21059-9

A COUNTRY DOCTOR, Sarah Orne Jewett, 0-553-21498-5

DUBLINERS, James Joyce, 0-553-21380-6

A PORTRAIT OF THE ARTIST AS A YOUNG MAN, James Joyce, 0-553-21404-7

THE METAMORPHOSIS, Franz Kafka, 0-553-21369-5

THE STORY OF MY LIFE, Helen Keller, 0-553-21387-3

CAPTAINS COURAGEOUS, Rudyard Kipling, 0-553-21190-0

THE SWISS FAMILY ROBINSON, Johann David Wyss, 0-553-21403-9
EARLY AFRICAN-AMERICAN CLASSICS, 0-553-21379-2
FIFTY GREAT SHORT STORIES, 0-553-27745-6
FIFTY GREAT AMERICAN SHORT STORIES, 0-553-27294-2
SHORT SHORTS, 0-553-27440-6